Colin de Silva was born in Ceylon (now Sri Lanka) and grew up there. During the Second World War he served as a commissioned officer in the British Army. From 1946 to 1956 he was a member of the Ceylon Civil Service, and in 1962 he emigrated to Hawaii, where he now lives.

His first novel, *The Winds of Sinhala*, was published in 1982 and quickly became an international bestseller.

By the same author

The Winds of Sinhala

COLIN DE SILVA

The Founts of Sinhala

PANTHER
Granada Publishing

Panther Books
Granada Publishing Ltd
8 Grafton Street, London W1X 3LA

Special overseas edition 1985

First published in Great Britain by
Granada Publishing 1984

Copyright © Colin de Silva 1984

ISBN 0-586-06245-9

Printed and bound in Great Britain by
Collins, Glasgow

Set in Baskerville

To my mother
Rose Mary Weerasinha de Silva
of the princess breed

Acknowledgements

The faith of Mark Barty-King caused Granada Publishing to acquire rights in my first novel, *The Winds of Sinhala*, for the United Kingdom, the Commonwealth countries and other areas outside the United States. His drive, supported by a most professional staff, helped that novel to become an international bestseller, still available on the shelves of booksellers. I would like to think that it is his confidence in me as an author which influenced the selection of *The Founts of Sinhala* for publication. For this I thank him and his staff.

My two editors at my American publishers, Doubleday & Company, Inc., were successively Miss Blair Brown and Mr Reid Boates, who in the two-year process of editing *The Winds of Sinhala* taught me more about the craft of writing than I had learned in the twenty years preceding. I thank them both.

Mrs Marcia Krueger, my secretary, and Miss Heidi Helm acted diligently as readers and made useful suggestions; Mrs Krueger's patience and dedication in typing the many drafts were exemplary. I thank them.

While generally based on reference and history books, such as William Geiger's translation of the *Maha Vamsa* and various treatises, all of which I acknowledge with thanks, *The Founts of Sinhala* has of necessity to be a work of historical fiction. The moral conflicts created by the historical characters are those I have assumed from their recorded acts, highlighted through some fictitious characters.

Prologue

As in a misted dream, I heard the scrape and creak of the
opening door and sensed the approach of the guards and the
man who sought to destroy me. Though I had done him no
wrong, he had accused me of treason, of conspiring to kill the
king, and of heresy. Heresy? What more is heresy than truth
discovered that threatens the secure paradise of the foolish?
As for conspiring to kill anyone, least of all a man I loved,
the very truth I had discovered, now termed heresy, made
this accusation absurd.

They had strapped me by the wrists to the sides of the
great teakwood cross, my arms stretched to their fullest, my
dangling feet tied firmly at the ankles to the upright with a
mere wedge of support for the soles. Before long a slow fire had
started at my shoulders, spread to my back and finally
wracked my entire body.

I did not know how long they would keep me thus, but
had desperately resolved not to hope for release, because
that was a gateway to weakness. Nor would I permit myself
to consider showing my captors my mettle, which would
have been but a product of pride, not of strength. Whatever
they did to me, I would try to remain myself, Lala Sinha-
Bahu, a prince by birth, by choice a follower of Gautama
Buddha who died but forty years ago, and yet by instinct a
believer in the One God.

They had nailed the cross to the far wall of the windowless
room, lit by a single yellow flare stuck into a bronze holder
on the entrance wall. Its flame hissed in an endeavour to
penetrate the corners of the long narrow room, but it only
wavered and petered out around the cross, leaving a thin
film of resinous grey smoke pungent in my nostrils, grating
inside my throat. The heat was intense, the air close.

The burning within my body became excruciating agony,

pulling, twisting, churning bone and muscle. My weight seemed likely to tear my arms from their sockets. I itched, powerless to scratch myself.

For hours I used my yoga training to keep the torture segregated from my feeling self, to see this pitiful body as a distinct entity from the mind that received its anguished messages. With unrelenting determination, my *atman* clung to its one hope of salvation, love for the man who had unjustly imprisoned me and now so cruelly tortured me.

Finally, my eyes closed, I suddenly found myself released from my body. I saw it sagging on the cross, the spinning head slumped, the breathing slow and laboured.

The illusion lasted but a few moments, for I was soon back in torment. I tried to focus on my enemies, but I could not see them through the red-black haze of my drooped lids. Now I became numb, conscious only of a singing in my ears that turned to a rushing roar, the prelude to a blackness that was about to engulf me.

'A prince indeed! A worthy descendant of the lion!' My enemy was sneering, his voice harsh to my ears as a crow's croak. 'You would not have needed to test your mettle if you had taken the truth drug. But you still refuse?' He laughed low, without mirth. 'Well, a little gentle coaxing perhaps, Prince Lala Sinha-Bahu . . .'

He must have signalled the guards, for one of them grabbed me by my long hair and yanked my head back so roughly that my neck nearly snapped. While another forced my jaws open, a third stuck a funnel into my mouth.

Some instinct made me hold my breath before a sticky liquid nearly choked me. I could neither taste nor smell it but knew it must be *youma*, the drug that causes hallucinations. It felt warm inside my chest and when it reached my stomach. Somewhere inside me I can still feel sensation, I thought . . . and gagged. Too weak to retch, I began to choke, the liquid drooling from my mouth, the funnel hard inside it, searing my palate and tongue.

8

They stopped pouring, awaited my agonized recovery . . . then poured again . . . and again . . . and again . . .

My will to resist slowly eroded. My last conscious thought was a frantic clinging to my love for my torturers.

A cold evening lies weary on a bare hill. A wooden cross is etched stark against a stormy sky. In the red-black light of a single torch held by their leader, grim-faced guards in gleaming armour, carrying swords, shields and spears, push back a surging crowd. Men scream and shake their fists at the cross, metal strikes metal, but all I hear is silence, an ear-singeing, roaring silence, as of the approach of tempest winds, all I smell is blood and all I taste is a warm, sticky liquid.

Whom do they revile? The figure of a man suddeny materializes on the cross. He is in agony, his body broken, but all I sense is numbness.

Through the roar of the stillness, I hear his voice: I love you, I forgive you.

Can this be me?

A distant blackness wells up from within me, bearing some knowledge I cannot grasp. It mounts up to reach my mind: That is not you, but God in you, made manifest five centuries from now, unto eternity.

Unto eternity! This dying man will rule the world? What do *I* have to give it?

A voice whispers, Whatever brought you to this moment.

I maintained the record, I tell myself, wrote it in the formal Arya fashion; but I have also included in it all that was human, the hope and despair, loyalty and anguish, each man dangling on the slow-twisting rope of his destiny, *kharma/vipaka*, cause and effect.

From the darkness that envelops me, a tiny spark of light emerges like a glint of daybreak in a black tunnel. As this light starts to spin, I hear its music, a thrumming as of a thousand sithars continuously striking the same note. The grand melody of space, of the entire universe.

Great golden spheres fall before me, bursting to give forth scents of attar, frankincense, odours of Edom. As my spirit breathes them with joy divine, the music grows louder, the spinning light becomes brighter.

Finally, when there is only radiance, not even a vestige of darkness, rainbow colours begin sparkling from on high. Everywhere is love, love. The force that binds a man's body beneath his skin, the magnetism that holds the world and the planets together. Love. The elements, Fire, Air, Earth, Water, all embodied in this boundless infinity of God.

I know I am reaching God at last.

I no longer have a body. My *atman*, freed of its shackles, is growing to gigantic size, unclouded by a shadow, unrestricted by human dimensions. It begins taking great strides, bouncing high to the beat of the music, ecstasy in each step until it soars like a bird.

Those wondrous colours enrapture me, clothe me, but with the purity of morning dew. I am being bathed, cleansed, before being taken to God.

I am immortal. I am the light, the great giver. I shall bestow immortality on humanity. I shall immortalize an entire race, the Sinhala People, by revealing its early history, its founts.

PART I
The Exiles

Chapter 1

Two days of continuous battering by the raging storm on the great ocean and each of prince Vijaya's seven hundred comrades came to the conclusion that they had not only been exiled for their crimes by their fellow men but were also being punished by their gods. They swore that they would lead better lives in the future, if the gods would spare them. My twin brother, Prince Vijaya alone, fearing no man and believing in no god, merely found himself witnessing what he had brought to those he led and vowed to himself that from now on he would give them enlightened leadership.

Three ships tossed, plummeted and sagged on mountainous waves, the sails torn to ribbons, masts snapped by howling winds, cockleshells completely at the mercy of the elements. With our steersmen strapped to their helms, our drenched oarsmen half-dead at their rowlocks, it was a wonder that we lost only four men on our ship, swept overboard by the killer surf. The miracle was that the ships were not separated.

The storm hit not long after we were driven away from the port of Sopara on the eastern seaboard of the continent by the Great King's army soon after we had landed there. For my brother's reputation had preceded him. The townsfolk knew that he and his seven hundred followers had been completely lawless in our native land and had finally been banished, heads half-shaved as a mark of shame, when Prince Vijaya plotted to seize the throne from our father, the King of Sinha-Pura.

I was the only volunteer on board. I had led a life as blameless as my twin brother's had been criminal, and had asked to be allowed to accompany him into exile because I could not bear to be separated from him. I was also unique in that, of all on board, I alone prayed, particularly to my One God, for deliverance from my own foolish choice!

13

On the third night the winds abated, the dark clouds scattered and we crowded the decks in relief. In the light of a blood-red moon, I saw the wall of foaming white ahead. For a moment, I could not comprehend what it was, only knew sudden fear in my belly. Then I recognized it.

'Reef!' I cried.

The seas were still running high. We would be dashed against the treacherous rocks. A great swell seized our three ships simultaneously, bobbed them up and sent them surging madly forward. By yet another miracle, we were swept through an opening and thrust into a maelstrom of warring breakers. Our ship bucked, reared, tilted and careened like a great horse gone mad, then surfed forward on a long white wave.

Standing on the bows, clinging frantically to the rail, I was blinded by stinging sea-spray. When my vision cleared, I glimpsed the pale outline of a sandy beach fringed by dark trees.

From then on it was easy. We beached our ships, set no guards, merely sank upon the wet sand, utterly exhausted, like a few hundred grounded whales. We might have been murdered as we slept, but did not care so long as our bodies could rest on firm soil instead of raging water.

Lying back, I found I was so tired I could not fall asleep. I said a prayer of thankfulness to Lord Krishna, the Compassionate, and to my new-found One God, then gazed up at the moon. It was silver now, the blue heights of the sky pricked with sparse stars and scarred by white clouds. My tired eyes were irresistibly drawn to the red planet that causes storms. It glowered in anger, then became a bloodshot eye, mocking me. I shuddered. My priestly training told me this star would bring evil, wherever its radiant beam fell.

I looked down at myself. Silver moonlight clothed my half-naked body. I glanced sideways at my twin brother. His magnificent frame gleamed with a reddish glow, from the broad muscular shoulders, along the sharp-etched muscles of his stomach and the narrow waist to the legs, solid as treetrunks. The contrast with my fair, lean, long frame was so great that I raised my head to look more closely. The glow had vanished. I laid my head back wondering whether it had come from his own ruddy skin, body hair, beard and half-shaven locks, or through some trick of the light, assisted by my fevered imagination.

'Can't you sleep, Prince Lala Sinha-Bahu?' Prince Vijaya demanded in quiet tones so that the men would not overhear.

'No,' I responded. 'My mind feels ice-bright.'

'Me too, but only because I have so much to think about.'

'Such as?'

'For one thing, I know *Amma*, our mother, was desperately worried about us. I took her so much for granted. During the storm, I realized what I had done to her and I want no more of it.' He paused and I could sense his embarrassment. 'I . . . er . . . I want her to be proud of me. Also . . . I love these men.' His voice was softer. He seemed to be speaking to himself. 'I never had to put on a front with *Amma* and she was always there to comfort me. She took our exile hard.'

'She loved you most of all,' I commented in a dry, matter-of-fact voice. 'You and her father, Sinha the lion. She told me that you are the living image of Sinha, a handsome, red-haired giant, with leonine features and tawny eyes.'

'I am the reincarnation of our grandfather,' he declared, equally matter-of-fact.

'Right down to the wild independence, the refusal to submit to authority!'

But I knew that it was not stubborn strength of mind and body alone that had interested my brother. His fascination with growing things had begun with wonder at the appearance of a tiny green shoot in the black soil of a small flower bed in which he had been permitted to plant an onion and had culminated in an absorbing interest in crops and

15

their attendant reservoirs, dams, anicuts and irrigation channels, which our father, the King, had created in the kingdom he had established. My brother had studied agriculture, therefore, with as great an interest as he had followed the exploits of the great Arya Emperors Kyroos and Dharroos.

'I realize that there was always a congenital conflict between *Appa* and me,' he declared, glancing sideways at a sharp snore that had escaped one of the men lying not far from us. 'But all that is over. I had the strangest feeling the moment I lay down just now. The earth seemed to say to my body, you are home at last – all other soil, including that of your birthland, is foreign to you.' He paused, raised his head and cocked an ear landward. 'Do you hear that?'

I sat up. 'No. What did you hear?'

'The tap of a single drum, the tinkle of a cymbal.' He listened again. 'It's not a sound though, just a pulse beat from the body of the earth, drumming and twinkling a message of welcome to me. Ah, now it has merged into the beating of my heart.'

I was amazed. My brother never spoke like this, being as practical as I am imaginative. Was he possessed? Had the dangers of the voyage unhinged his mind?

'I owe something to *Amma* and our men, and I have finished running,' I heard him say. 'We shall make this land our home, whether we walk its earth as conquerors or lie in it as corpses, and whatever our faiths, we will be worthy men in the future. All of us.'

Perhaps it was the tremendous relief at his words that caused my tiredness suddenly to catch up with me. My eyelids felt heavy as iron. I sank back to the earth. 'Go to sleep now,' I bade him wearily. 'Pleasant dreaming tonight. You can be anything you want tomorrow.'

The storm had come, as always at this time of the year, from the direction of the setting sun and the four stars of the night sky. It had lashed the island for days, flattening great trees and destroying huts. Though its fury had abated earlier in the day, an impenetrable pall still lay over the great ocean and the roar of pounding waves in the distance proclaimed that its menace had merely passed elsewhere.

Sounds of the night's revelry from the village city, Sirisa Watta, had finally died down. The Princess Kuveni knew that her people would all be in a drunken stupor, following the celebrations which should have begun six days ago, except that this had been the first night without rain for a week. They should have consulted her before fixing the *nakath*, the auspicious day, for her sister's wedding. Her prophecy would have been more reliable than the findings of the astrologers. And she could have been the bride, had she so chosen, instead of being exiled from the palace.

The stillness of the night immediately around her was disturbed by the hoot of an owl. It resounded through crystal-clear air beneath a sky now lofty in parts, the blue heights pricked with sparse stars, the depths bedded by low grey clouds. Only an occasional drip from an overhanging branch spoke of the torrent that had passed.

She searched for her *tharuwa*, her star, and found it: the red one, glowing in anger because she had not offered him her worship during the days of the storm.

Take pity on me, Lord, she silently begged, and be not incensed. I have rare offerings for you tonight, enough to appease you.

Flare in one hand, gleaming knife in the other, she stepped out of the house. The black earth was damp to her bare feet. Beneath her dark, uncovered breasts, her heart was beating with excitement. She threaded her way slowly between green manioc shoots and jagged treestumps to the shrine at the far end of the *chena*, where the dense jungle began. It was dedicated to Reeri Yakseya, the most cruel and powerful of all the demon gods. Presently, she discerned his monkey face in the flickering flame, within the little

17

wooden hut set on a single post. His body was that of a man, the skin a fiery red. He rode a red bull proudly, as if he would burst through the votive offerings of nine kinds of flowers, of sandalwood, lizard entrails and the grinning white skull from the *sohana*, the graveyard. Not even the demon of storm had been able to destroy him or his possessions.

The fat cockerel tied to a stake close by the shrine clucked nervously and flapped its wings.

She halted before the shrine and looked up at her *tharuwa* again. It glowed between bats hanging like little black sacks from a stark, dead branch. Though they were sleeping, she could feel their awareness of her.

'Red planet god above, red demon god upon a red bull below. You are both one.

'Your priestess worships you in the light of darkness, the glow of her flare one with you in redness as her red lips give you praise in this second watch before midnight, the time you have set aside for her offerings.'

She flung her knife on the ground. Its point embedded in the soft soil. The handle quivered as if with life. Good.

She placed her flare in the socket behind the shrine. A breath of wind from the womb of the dark jungle made the red flame waver. Its grey smoke, lightly wafted towards her, bore the smell of resin.

A chant rose from the hut, a haunting echo of the dark accompanied by the tap of a single drum. The voices, sparkling like silver ornaments on the dark breast of night, were those of her two female attendants. From the fold of her white loincloth, she produced the *kanya-nool*, thread woven by a virgin, that she had spun from local cotton and placed it before the god. Only a virgin could satisfy him. Only a virgin could be his priestess. Her virgin womanhood began to pulsate.

'O demon god, I am Kuveni, a virgin, not yet sixteen and a princess. Never before have you known a princess. I

18

deserted my betrothed, the young and virile Prince Tikka, defying my father, King Kalu Sena, in order to come to you. He exiled me from Sirisa Watta, village city of our Yakka tribe, for having thus broken the laws of our clan.

'I have no regret. I am dedicated to you. I will give you my life, my death if need be.'

The chant wove into her senses, suddenly freeing her slender body. She bowed her head, the palms of her hands moving up beneath her generous breasts, cupping them, offering them to the god. Her hands moved outward to him, head up, giving her breasts to him, then back again, head down . . . outward to him, giving again . . .

'Come, suck my virgin breasts. As we mortals suck the earth, mother of us all, so shall you suck me . . .'

Her slim hips began swaying seductively from side to side, her movements sinuous as those of a snake, feet beating time with the drum. Her arms spread sideways, palms downwards. She wove them, fingertips, wrists, elbows, shoulders coiling, moving like a snake.

'Of a snake was the earth born . . . For you I become a snake, offering you the earth . . .'

Chanting and drumming, she danced a whole watch, giving herself in physical union with her god in the night's solitude, for no mortal dared witness it. Suddenly, a bell rang from the hut, a single peal, clanging above the chant, stilling it on the instant, in the middle of a note, like an anguished cry stifled by death's clamour. Her womanhood throbbed and spurted. Her screams from the orgasm of her union with her gods rent the night. They ended in shuddering involuntary noises. Her attendants came up behind her to stand still as twin statues. Panting, she sank to her knees, hands poised in worship above her black hair. Only the resonance of the bell, now silent, brought her back to reality.

Again she felt her wetness and lifted her head.

Are you pleased with my virgin body, my *prana*?

19

The red god grinned at her like an echo of the grinning white skull. She raised dark eyes to the heavens. The red *tharuwa* grinned back.

She rose to her feet and walked swiftly to the cockerel. She stooped and seized it by the red wings, held it squawking and screeching towards the god.

'Vouchsafe me sight, my great *tharuwa*, ruler of my *lagna*. Reveal your bidding to me!'

The cockerel struggling vainly in her hands, she stared at the red flame of the flare. It hissed at her. Long moments passed. She barely heard the swish of skirts or saw the two women coming up on either side of her. They seized the screaming cockerel, baring its pale yellow breast before her.

'Vouchsafe me sight, my great demon god. Reveal your bidding to me!'

The flame grew larger. Her eyes widened at seeing the colours of the heavens reversed. Above her, the blue of the sky contained the red planet. Before her, the red fire contained a blue centre that became larger and larger. It was the time of omens. A man's body appeared, tall, muscular, hairy, shimmering red-gold. The red of the flame matched his hair, which was soaking wet. His face was leonine. A crown appeared above him. Why not upon his head? Ah, he is but a prince . . . what holds up that crown then? A pair of hands with strong, stubby fingers. The hands of one born under the lion *lagna* . . . her own hands. The fierce, tawny eyes of the prince became twin points of fire . . . They faded away.

The vision died. Only the flame remained, sputtering now. And the sharp-etched face of a red prince in her mind.

Puzzled, she gazed first at the red god then up at the red planet.

'Having had me, do you reject me now because I am no longer virgin in your eyes?'

A hollow silence, hideous in its intensity, was the only response.

'Speak to me,' she begged, spreading her arms wide. Tears broke loose from her smarting eyes, coursing down her cheeks.

'Speak to me,' she implored again, her voice resounding into the jungle. 'Do you not want me any longer?'

A peacock's shrill screams crashed through the night. 'No..! No..! No..!' The cockerel's querulous grumble echoed more quietly. 'No..! No...! No..!' The skull grinned mockingly at her.

Abruptly, the Princess Kuveni stooped and snatched up her knife. In one swift movement, she rose, blade upraised, then plunged it into the breast of the cockerel. A shrill death screech slashed through the air, ending in a rattle and a sigh. Feathers twitching, the body struggled even after life had left it.

Chapter 2

I must have had a bad dream after the first deep sleep was over, for I woke stifling a groan and sat up with a start, breathing deeply. The morning air was cool in my nostrils, my groan trailed into the mewing of seagulls flying low over a pearly ocean.

Prince Vijaya and our comrades were still asleep. Lying on the strangely copper sand, they were indeed sea creatures of different colours, in black loincloths, thrown ashore by the storm. The loose pink lips of fat Rama, lying close to me, were pursed to permit snores to slurp through them. He reminded me of that potbellied fish with the round-shaped mouth perpetually framed in an 'o' of surprise.

I felt a moment of urgency. We should look to our safety. Then reason asserted itself. If this region was inhabited, we would surely have been confronted by now. Besides, action is my brother's prerogative, another reason why I had elected to go into exile with him, for Prince Vijaya will be a figure in history when all of us are forgotten. I am as certain of this as of my own role as the recorder of his life. Among the few possessions I brought with me therefore on this dreadful voyage were stylus and papyri.

I drew up my knees and hugged them with my hands, giving silent thanks to God for our deliverance from the ocean and praying for His power in this alien land. He was still new to me, as One God, so I also softly thanked Lord Krishna and prayed for protection from Great Brahma, the Creator.

Now I found myself enjoying the moments of quiet before the others awakened. In the distance, a pink canopy of dawn was beginning to colour the western sky above a shining silver sheet of ocean. Wavelets lazily ambling towards the shore were white-laced with foam, their ceaseless splash and hiss upon the beach a caress. But I was not deceived. The vast life-force hidden in these waters had been revealed to me in its most dreadful form.

My eyes sought the silhouettes of the ships, dark against the rosy sky, a grim reminder of our banishment from the land of our birth, sanctuaries in that raging storm. Seagulls mewed and creaked, soaring around the broken masts, searching for food. We had been wise to find some remnant of strength and draw the ships higher on the beach after we disembarked, for who knows, we may need them to flee once more, in spite of Prince Vijaya's decision to remain.

My attention was attracted by a sudden movement. I glanced sideways. My brother had awoken and sat up. Palms on the sand, he levered himself to his feet in one swift motion, lithe as the lion from whom we are descended. He gazed around him alertly. Seeming satisfied, he walked a few steps towards the lapping water. I looked at him in admiration, for he seemed like a young, golden-skinned god, with proud, leonine features, though the unshaven half of his auburn locks hung in disarray down to his brawny shoulders. He looked down at the palms of his hands, staring at them as if fascinated. Finally, he smacked them together, dusting the sand off, wiping them on his black loincloth. Hands on hips, he gazed at the horizon. He looked exactly like the descriptions of our grandfather, Sinha, the bandit king of the Lala jungle, a legend of his time.

I rose to my feet and took but a single step towards my brother, but he swung round on the instant, his knees bent, his long knife already drawn from his waist, gleaming in the ready position. The sun caught his wide eyes. They were tawny as a lion's, with piercing black pupils and a cat-like intensity. The whites, red-veined from salt water, had the shiny glaze of ferocity. Seeing me, he came erect and relaxed, the snarl softening into a smile. He tucked his knife back into his loincloth.

'Ha! It's you, Prince Lala. You are stealthy as a lion from

23

the Lala country of our grandfather that gave you your name.' His voice was deep, with the resonance of one accustomed to addressing large contingents of men.

'It is you that looks like a lion,' I replied, angrily, 'with your great mane of reddish hair.'

'Spare me your wit so early in the morning and tell me where we are.'

I turned to survey the empty jungle. 'How would I know?'

'You're our *guru*, the only learned one among us.'

'I'm not a sea captain.'

'But you have visions.'

'Visionaries see into the future. I can only tell you where we will be, not where we are.'

'All right then, where will we be?' A hint of anxiety entered the tawny eyes.

'When?'

'One year from now?'

'Ruling this land.'

'H'mm . . .' His face brightened. 'Good.'

'From my observation of the direction of the winds that drove our ships, a fleeting southern star during a lull in the storm last night and your shadow now, I guess that we have travelled a long way south.'

His eyes, narrowing, scanned the treeline. I turned round, following his gaze. 'Not a sign of human life . . .' He paused abruptly. 'See there, however . . .' He nodded towards a slight break in the green foliage. 'Let's go over and take a look.'

He started threading his way through the sleeping bodies with me behind. About two hundred cubits farther south, we came upon a passage, meandering through the trees.

'This could not have been created by elephants or other animals. Look at those wagon tracks.' He made to follow them, then paused. 'Let us send a patrol out to see where this path leads.'

We returned to the nearest of the sleeping men. He shook

two of them. 'Kahola! . . . Ajit! . . . Wake up!'

'Wha . . ? Where are we?' They sat up, drowsy and groggy, scratching hairy chests sleepily, hardly alert marauders.

'That's what you're going to find out! Up now, get your weapons.'

The two men leapt to their feet, Kahola lean and tall, Ajit squat. Others beside them jerked at the disturbance, raising their heads, questions breaking through drowsy voices.

'Look there!' Prince Vijaya pointed. 'Check where the track leads. If you are not back by the time my shadow has reached this far, I shall send after you.' He had given the men the space of half a watch. It would enable them to go about a mile inland, moving cautiously, and return.

'Up now, all of you, and assemble in your companies!' The familiar authority had returned to Prince Vijaya's voice and his whole being exuded energy. 'Commanders to me by my ship.'

As Kahola and Ajit moved off, the men rose to their feet, assembling in the seven companies, each of one hundred, created two years earlier by their leader. Prince Vijaya and I cut down to the water's edge, then directly across, moving towards the ships. The water felt chill to my bare feet, its white froth tickling the toes lightly. I found boyish delight in squelching through the wet sand.

By the time Prince Vijaya and I climbed the ladder of the first ship to stand on its deck, the seven commanders had assembled on the beach below us, their companies spread in columns behind them, swords at the side, spears glittering at the ready. In spite of our collapse last night through sheer exhaustion, our little army was fine-honed as a warrior's sword.

Prince Vijaya surveyed the men from the tall prow and a glint of satisfaction briefly lit his face. Squaring his shoulders, he issued his orders.

'Ujjeni's company shall form a box around the three ships for their immediate defence. Vijit, your men shall filter into the jungle to set up warning outposts and delay any attack. Position twenty of them on either side of that track over there. Anu, your men shall beach the ships higher and unload them. Sumitta's company, collect driftwood for fires and prepare a meal for us. The wet flour is but dough for our cakes, already salted! See whether you can get some of those coconuts.'

He nodded in the direction of the palms, now swaying before a sudden wind. I sensed the men's growing eagerness.

'Uraw, your company shall set up earthworks at arrow's distance from the ships, so they can be defended. Use this task for some shooting practice. Some of Pandu's company shall repair the masts and hoist new sails, with the rest in reserve. Upa's men shall make up the first bath detail and then relieve Ujjeni's company to start a rotation for bath and food.'

He raised both hands aloft. 'We lost seven of our comrades to the storm, men whom we loved. Let that be our final sacrifice to the gods, by whose will we encountered death and came through alive. I know full well that there is not one among you who did not swear to mend your ways if you were spared. So be it. This is how I shall lead you in future, but first we must have a home, a kingdom of our own. I declare that it shall be on this land. Let us now swear another oath, that we will establish a kingdom here . . .' he paused, lowered his hands and stared at his palms, 'which we shall call Thamba-Panni, because of its copper beach-sands, or die in the attempt.' He raised clenched fists. 'What say you, men?'

The cheers that reached for the heavens gave him his answer.

Standing on the prow of the ship, I watched the men at their appointed tasks. I could not help but think back on all that had transpired, the causes of our present situation. Our grandmother, the Princess Suppa Devi, who favoured me,

26

had told me the whole story, which started almost fifty years ago.

She was the daughter of the King of Vanga, in the north central region of the continent, by his queen consort, Mayavati, a princess of Kalinga, the adjoining kingdom that sprawled to the eastern seaboard. When she was born, a court astrologer had foretold that she would flee the palace and mate with a lion, becoming a source of anguish to her parents. Her father therefore had her imprisoned in a seven-storey tower specially constructed in the centre of his palace fortress. When she was fifteen, she contrived to escape. She shaved her head, disguised herself as a boy and joined the great caravan that proceeded west to Harappa and Mohenjo Daro. When the caravan entered the forest lands in the Lala country, it was attacked by a gang whose leader was a notorious brigand chieftain of royal Pahlava blood, named Sinha, or lion, in the Sanskrit language. Some said that Sinha had the name bestowed on him because he had the strength, courage and ferocity of a lion and was therefore king of the Lala jungle. Others maintained that he was named after his royal origins from the foremost of the Pahlava clans, known as lions. He was certainly a magnificent specimen of manhood and of leonine appearance.

Sinha somehow pierced the veil of the Princess Suppa Devi's identity that day and carried her off to his jungle hideout. They fell in love and lived happily together there.

Within a year, the couple had twin children. By now, the princess was so deeply in love with Sinha that she named the boy Sinha-Bahu, son of Sinha and the girl, Sinha-Seevali, daughter of Sinha.

My grandmother told me that for as long as she could remember she had been moved by a compulsive sense of destiny. Confined in her tower as a child, she knew that she would escape some day. The very day she was abducted by Sinha, she discovered that he had a tender heart, for when he attempted to ravish her she showed herself gentle and giving, so that he had responded from some hidden depths of himself and had even placed a four-petalled jungle jasmine on her pubis before taking her virginity.

I looked up and noticed that three of our commanders, Ujjeni, Anu and Uraw, were standing close to one another, obviously deep in private conversation while their men toiled around them. Ujjeni and Anu had always been close friends, but I had noticed them trying to draw Uraw into their alliance during the voyage. Why should I feel this tremor of disquiet merely because three commanders huddled together?

Having started his company off on their task of building the earthworks, Uraw strolled over to Anu, who had supervised the beaching of the ships and now stood chatting with Ujjeni whose men were guarding the vessels. Anu's squat body seemed more tightly muscled than ever from the hardships of the past days, while Ujjeni's looked positively skeletal. They were both staring at the cooking fires, the grey smoke from which curled into the green jungle beyond. Ujjeni in particular seemed fascinated by the yellow flames, roaring and sputtering from damp wood.

Anu nodded a greeting. His hooked nose, dipping like the beak of a bird above the brown moustache, was strangely out of place in that broad face. 'It's good that we will make a stand at last,' he remarked. 'I'm tired of running. Also, I'm sick of the ocean. Give me a warm fire any day.'

Ujjeni gave his deep hee . . . hee . . . hee belly-laugh, but it was mirthless. The prominent yellow teeth, emerging beneath purple lips that could never quite close over them, were bared in a smile that did not reach the deep, sunken eyes. 'Fire cleanses,' he asserted. There was something fanatical about the way he said the words. He paused and continued. 'Somehow, I am confident that together we shall carve out a kingdom of our own here, but the three of us

28

must unite to ensure that we are not displaced as our leader's advisers.'

Uraw knew Ujjeni to be a man well pleased by his own intelligence. At thirty-two, he was the second-in-command of the little bandit army, and he alone, of all the senior men of this group of seven hundred, could understand the leader's moods. The past weeks had revealed that Prince Lala was also attuned to their leader, but more through the instinct of a twin. Undoubtedly Prince Vijaya would be grateful that Prince Lala had joined their exile voluntarily. He must consider that gesture an act of brotherly love and that was how Uraw too had seen Prince Lala's growing influence, until Ujjeni had argued that it was merely ambition, spurred by the knowledge that the exiles would some day, somehow, make good.

'These are days when men carve out kingdoms for themselves,' Ujjeni added, dropping his voice beneath the sounds of spade and shovel so that the men milling around them might not hear. 'All our years of loyalty to Prince Vijaya can finally earn us our true reward if we are wise and trust no one. Where was Prince Lala when we were imprisoned and brought to trial? I don't want to lose my birthright again to a leader's brother.' The dark, sunken eyes glowed fiercely as he stared into the fire.

'Does that fire remind you of the night we escaped the Great King's men?' Anu enquired softly.

Uraw was surprised to hear Anu referring to a boyhood experience that the men had, as if by tacit consent, never discussed during the past years.

Now the words broke forth savagely from Ujjeni, though his voice remained low, like the waters of an underground stream. 'I do indeed remember.' He turned towards Uraw and paused, then seemed to make up his mind. 'You might as well know the facts. I was a frightened fourteen-year-old boy in the fertile Magadha countryside, where my noble father was lord of the Sala district and Anu's father was the neighbouring overlord. King Bimbisara's brother, Puri, was governor of our district. He levelled false charges of treason against both our fathers. They were not even given a chance to defend themselves before Puri's soldiers arrived to burn down our mansions. Our parents were killed. Anu was only twelve at the time. Only he and I, of our entire families, escaped the slaughter. We met by chance that night in a copse of *ashoka* trees that grew between our two properties. Together, we watched the distant flames destroying all we had in life. We then made common cause, journeying to the home of a friendly uncle of Anu's in the adjoining kingdom of Lala, where we grew up.' He glanced at Anu. 'I know why this moment reminds *me* of that terrible night. What makes you remember it?'

Anu hesitated, scratched the back of his head. 'It's hard to explain,' he finally volunteered. 'But looking at those fires I suddenly had the feeling that all the intervening years were simply a bridge between the two events.'

Uraw jerked to attention and noticed Ujjeni stiffening. They looked at one another. Anu was neither fanciful nor intuitive. The harsh screech of parakeets from the adjoining jungle rose above the sound of digging. One of the men broke into a ribald song.

'How strange!' Ujjeni remarked. 'I felt the same.' He nodded towards the wet, wooden sides of the ships towering over them. 'Perhaps we should set fire to the ships, now that they have served their purpose. Two fires to connect two severed pasts. Hee . . . hee . . . hee!' He grew thoughtful. 'Fire is our offering to god Agni. Only sacrificial fire will cause the end of our misfortunes.' The words seemed to escape him without thought, but his expression told that they came from the fiercest, most bitter part of him. Does he hate fire because it once consumed his past, Uraw wondered. Or does he love it because it portends something for his future? An answer nagged Uraw but he could not grasp it.

'I wonder what became of Puri,' Anu reminisced. He

glanced at Uraw and explained. 'Puri was the half-brother and closest adviser of the Great King Bimbisara. He misled the Great King, produced false evidence and personally conducted the attack on our parents and the two family mansions. Afterwards he seized our vast lands and wealth.'

'Puri!' Ujjeni hissed. 'He proved that one must never allow the flesh and blood of kings to have too much influence with them. It produces a deadly combination of emotional appeal; there is an influence from within, and the king's tolerance gives the adviser power without accountability and makes him dangerous.' He glanced fiercely at Uraw. 'This is why Anu and I are disturbed by Prince Lala's increasing influence over our leader. Why would someone wish to leave security and position, accept uncertainty and peril, except for some deep underlying hope of eventual personal gain? Anu and I built up our position with Prince Vijaya through years of danger and sacrifice. I don't mind admitting that I cherish my position as the second-in-command of our magnificent little army.' His voice grew fierce. 'I'm not going to have a Puri done on me again.'

'You're a bitter man,' Uraw interjected. The words escaped him before he could hold them back.

Ujjeni turned on him slowly. His eyes were so deadly that Uraw felt a shiver go up his spine.

'Yes, I'm a bitter man,' Ujjeni said flatly. 'And you'd better believe it. What else d'you think has sustained me through the years?' He paused. 'Let me tell you something. I was the oldest in our family and should have been my father's heir. But I had a handsome younger brother, Raja. He was very like Prince Lala in appearance, the same slim build, wide shoulders, narrow waist, the same regular features, well chiselled, a deep cleft on the chin. Only his eyes were different in colour, brown instead of Prince Lala's greeny-brown. Handsome men, bah! I hate them. You can never trust them.' He paused. 'Well, one day, when Raja was eleven and I was twelve, my father told him, "We named you well, *baba*, for you look a prince. You shall be my heir." Then he turned to me and his lip curled in scorn. So that was why he had named me Ujjeni, I realized. Ujjeni! What kind of a name is that? One that you would give a dwarf, a clown? I remember going to a looking-glass there and then. I stared at the reflection and saw myself for the first time. Yes, I saw a skeleton, with a death's head face, the lean body of a lizard and the beginning of a hunched back. Something cold and hard entered me. Sure, it was the product of bitterness. I resolved that I would never change my name. I'd rise above it. I'd give it dignity and meaning. I'd use my brains to captivate men. I'd make them fear me, respect me, since I could not make them love me. From then on, I hated Raja. I felt every insult, sensed every feeling of pity for my appearance and began noting the revulsion of men. I had worshipped my father, but my handsome brother had stood in the way of my union with him. I did what I had to do. Now, for all my horror of that night when my father and mother, my three younger brothers and sisters, my numerous cousins and family retainers were massacred, a part of me rejoices that Raja, the prince, was also destroyed.'

Save in your own mind, Uraw reflected sadly. Ujjeni's story had stirred the depths of compassion within him. Aloud he muttered. 'I'm sorry. It must have been hell for you. But please be assured that I for one care about you as a person.'

Ujjeni seemed not to have heard. 'As for Puri,' he grinned devilishly. 'I arranged for Puri to disappear.'

'You?' The incredulity in Anu's rather high-pitched voice was matched by the expression in his brown eyes. 'How in the name of the devas did you manage that? And why didn't you tell me all these years.'

The hee . . . hee . . . hee belly-laugh escaped Ujjeni almost without thought. 'And risk being accused of murder some day? No, no, that's not my style. I can tell you now though. My share of the spoils from our first raid with Prince Vijaya went to disposing of Puri. I personally journeyed to Sala and lured Puri to the home of a magnificent woman he desired. One can always draw a man out if one knows his weaknesses. *Thuggee* awaited Puri with the open arms he expected from this woman.' His voice went deadly cold, expressionless. 'I assure you that Puri paid the full price for his betrayal. His death was long, lingering and excruciatingly painful.' He seemed to savour the recollection. 'I was present and enjoyed every moment of it.' He paused. 'I finally burnt him slowly to death. I cleansed him with fire.'

Uraw and Anu gazed at Ujjeni in astonishment. He sensed their thoughts. 'You both think I'm mad, don't you?' He enquired.

Anu reached out and briefly laid a hand on Ujjeni's knee. 'No, old comrade. You've never been mad, only different, always. You're deep and thoughtful. It was you who persuaded me to leave my uncle's place when I was only twenty-one and journey to Sinha-Pura, the new kingdom, to seek our fortunes in a land of opportunity. It was you who finally managed to bring us to the notice of Prince Vijaya and devised the means to join him. It was your manoeuvring that enabled us to get rich quickly, to become Prince Vijaya's closest comrades and finally his commanders. Now you are virtually his second-in-command, but we have lost our fortunes. We look to your brains to restore them.'

'And I shall!' Ujjeni promised. 'We are on the threshold of great events. Stick with me – you too, Uraw – and you will know your rewards.' He turned abruptly and clumped away.

Anu gazed after Ujjeni with respect in his eyes. 'Now there's a remarkable man!' he exclaimed. 'He has a reason for everything he does. It makes me wonder why he revealed his story to you today, Uraw. He must trust you and need your support.' He pondered awhile and seemed to make up his mind. 'I might as well tell you something else if we are going to be united. But first give me your sacred Arya oath that you will not divulge what I'm going to tell you.'

Uraw suddenly felt himself caught up in a gigantic wave of events. Without volition, he replied. 'I swear it.'

'Not even to Ujjeni?'

'Not even to Ujjeni.'

'All right then. I happen to know that when Ujjeni was fourteen, he discovered that my father was plotting against the Great King Bimbisara. How he did so, I'll never know, except that he was remarkable even then. He also learned that Puri had wind of the plot and had obtained the Great King's approval to arrest my father. Ujjeni thereupon warned my father, who laughed at him. After all, how could a fourteen-year-old boy know what was planned in the royal palace? Ujjeni then went to Puri and falsely implicated his own father in the plot in exchange for Puri's promise that he would inherit the family title and possessions when his father was arrested. Well, you know the rest of the story. Puri betrayed Ujjeni, murdered our families, seized everything and tried to kill us both. We escaped and now I find that Ujjeni's vengeance reached out over the years and across hundreds of miles.'

Chapter 3

After we had broken our fast, Prince Vijaya and I paced the copper sands, awaiting the return of Kahola and Ajit from their scouting mission. Around us, the men were busy with their allotted tasks and the sound of shovels on sand, the scrape of stores being dragged up the beach and the grunts of those labouring under heavy loads marked their diligence. It was obvious that everyone was glad to be on land again with the sun warming his body and drying the earth and our ships.

'I propose using you like the sounding board of a drum in fulfilling my new life's purpose,' my brother suddenly stated. 'Your position will henceforth be that of my second-in-command.'

I felt a surge of joy at his words. My brother had always been so secret and uncommunicative that I had sometimes wondered whether he trusted anyone. Then the thought that I would be displacing Ujjeni intruded and a shiver of apprehension ran through me. Yet why should I be afraid? As I was the leader's brother, my new status should not offend Ujjeni or any of the other commanders. Besides, I would always be self-effacing, I knew, and would never make them feel inferior.

'You are too cunning to ask me questions,' I heard Prince Vijaya observe. 'I believe I am going to need that good kind of cunning, which comes from maturity.'

Being indeed too cunning to respond, I contented myself with an enigmatic grin, hoping to convey the impression of wisdom and maturity.

'As I told the men just now, we have stopped running,' my brother continued. 'I asked myself this morning, who am I? The answer was simple and it fed the reply to another question, what do I want to make of my life? I am our grandfather, Sinha, reborn – not merely a reincarnation but truly the same man reborn. That is why our mother came to love me so devotedly. Like our grandfather, I want a kingdom. I don't want it bestowed on me, I want to carve it out with my bare hands, so that all men may respect me. Unlike our father, I do not care about love. All I require is respect and fear. This can only be achieved through power, absolute power within the framework of whatever I command, so I shall work ruthlessly for absolute power, over territories and over those who live in them.'

A brave speech for a man who did not own even one grain of soil.

He stopped in his tracks and turned to look at me, searching for my reaction. I stopped as well, avoiding his gaze, staring reflectively at the gleaming sands. I was hard put to it to keep my expression blank, for his words had reached me. Within me, relief that he was going to stop running at last – for I considered all his actions up to now a flight from something, someone, perhaps even himself – struggled with a barely definable fear of his aims. I had no experience of leading people, but I knew well enough the need for respect. Yet there seemed to be a fallacy here. 'I cannot deny that you have complete control over our comrades because they respect you,' I began, fumbling for the words. 'Yet power . . . absolute power . . . respect without love . . . I don't know . . . I simply don't know.'

He grunted, eyeing me intently. 'It's all right so long as you say you don't know, and never oppose me. I would crush any opposition.'

I looked him squarely in the eye. 'I'd never oppose you. I think you know that.'

He smiled, eyes crinkling, projecting the warmth of his affection into me. 'That's the one thing I'm sure of – your absolute obedience. It's essential for a leader to have that.

'I have all the advantages of birth and training,' he

36

continued. He resumed his walk and I fell into step again beside him. 'First and foremost, I am a true Arya. Not a half-baked Arya, part Dasa by birth and choice, but a true scion of the original Arya invaders who set power and conquest above all else and finally took over the entire continent.' An unwonted note of enthusiasm, tingling with excitement, had crept into his voice. 'The Aryas are the noble ones, a master race. I want a kingdom that can be expanded, and I want absolute power over it so that I can give all my subjects the benefits of Arya discipline and culture.' He quickened his pace as his excitement grew and he seemed to be talking to himself. 'That is the destiny that blindly drives me on.'

How little I had known of my brother's innermost thoughts these past twenty-two years. I felt that a new man, a stranger almost, was talking to me.

Then I realized with a shock that, though he had come to roost at last, my brother was still the victim of his old restlessness. And somewhere inside me fear stirred, because there are limits to the territory a man can acquire, limits to power. When my brother reached these limits, in which directions would his restlessness turn?

He noted my contemplation, for he frowned, then glanced up at the sun and down at his shadow. 'Time's up,' he stated. 'And Ajit and Kahola have not returned.'

His shadow on the copper sand, now glinting in sunlight, and the sun which had cleared the treeline told me that the time was indeed up.

'What do you propose?' I enquired.

'I'm ordering Rohan to take his section inland and find out.'

The patrol, spears in hand, bows slung, quivers at the shoulder, swords at the side, was soon striding briskly in single file towards the wagon track. The ten men were led by a *kshashtriya*, Rohan, a lean, swordblade of a man with dark hair coiled into a top-knot above tanned skin.

That was a long, anxious watch. It went by without

37

Rohan and his men returning.

The sun was well risen now, glaring at us from above the treeline as if angry at having been shut out by the days of rainstorm. Prince Vijaya summoned the commanders. Standing beside our ship, he outlined the alternatives.

'We can send out a stronger contingent, or march inland with our entire force to search for our comrades,' he declared. 'Whatever course we follow, our first priority is to rescue them. That we must do at any cost.'

'What if they are dead?' Ujjeni enquired gloomily, a nervous leer on his death-mask face.

'They are not dead!' Prince Vijaya turned on him fiercely. 'And we shall rescue them.'

'How?' Ujjeni demanded.

Prince Vijaya was thoughtful a moment, then his tawny eyes flashed and the great jaw tightened. 'Prince Lala and I shall go alone to investigate. It may require stealth to unravel this mystery. Besides, there's no point in risking too many men.'

I welcomed the prospect of facing this danger with my brother, though I doubted my capacity for stealth, in which respect Ujjeni would probably have been a better choice.

Arrow on bowstring, sword loosened in the scabbard for ease of draw, I accompanied my brother along the beach. We walked along the fringe of the jungle, our bare feet crunching on the still-damp beach sand. Reaching the track, we found ourselves in the jungle and moved quietly in the shadow of tall trees, past gleaming wet bushes and green vegetation, avoiding the black mud puddles. The track soon led through a choking welter of scrub and skeletal branches. We had barely gone one hundred paces inside the jungle when I was struck by the eerie silence, as if the shrill cries of mynah birds and the creak of parakeets we had earlier heard were hushed on the order of a jungle god so that he could listen for the vibration of our coming.

We had agreed to take it in turns to lead. My brother

scouted ahead first with drawn sword, bow slung on his shoulder, trying to penetrate the foliage with his sharp eyes. It was impossible to probe more than a few cubits inside such dense jungle. Whatever had taken our men might have leapt out at them unexpectedly. I followed, giving him cover, long arrow on taut bowstring, willpower on tense nerves.

The track curved to the right. Our shadows, mingling with prickles of light and shade, were soon moving towards the west, standing upright wherever the sun lay on the bushes. The air was close, the smell of dank, drying leaves stifling.

When I saw the fork in the track, a thrill of excitement branched through me. It must be man-made, for animals do not create forks. So we could expect a village close by. I had to steady my breathing as we walked slowly and silently forward, heel first, then ball of the foot, in the approved manner for hunters in this sort of terrain. My brother seemed to be enjoying the danger, but I must confess to feeling more the hunted!

We paused at the fork. A narrower path to our left went straight for about fifty paces, then veered back towards the shore. The wider road on the right curved to disappear eastwards round a deep bend.

'Which way?' I enquired softly.

Before Prince Vijaya could reply, a vicious bark ripped through the air, shattering the stillness like a tree before an axe. My heart thudded almost to a stop.

We jerked towards the direction of the sound. A black dog had appeared along the bend of the wider track. Its white teeth were bared in a snarl.

Sword in hand, Prince Vijaya sprang towards the dog. It turned tail and fled, its black tail stiff and high in the air. It is a bitch, I thought. Could it have come on the orders of a priestess?

We followed the bitch and soon broke through the jungle into a clearing bathed by noonday sunlight encased by tall trees, some of them stark from the storm's havoc. The bitch had vanished. Instead, the silver waters of a pond on which green lotus leaves and pink blossoms were floating glittered before us. The smell of wet animal fur hung heavy on limp air. A sudden breeze sprang up, wafting the odour of raw human excrement, herald of evil spirits but drying my sweat, easing the prickles on my skin.

Prince Vijaya and I paused, then looked as one in the direction of a humming noise. I identified the sound even before my eyes found its source. It was a spinning wheel.

We both saw her at the same time, beneath the spreading green branches of a tall *mara* tree on the bund at the far end of the pond, a dusky, black-haired maiden sitting on a low stool, spinning. Her hands spun cotton yarn, her spirit, quietude and storm, nobility and evil.

Prince Vijaya tightened his grip on his sword and started forward impulsively towards the maiden.

She gave no sign of having observed our arrival and merely continued her work, the sound of the wheel like the angry hum of bees in the silvery noon air.

I hastened behind my brother. 'Wait!' I urgently cautioned him, laying a hand on his shoulder.

He paused in his stride. 'Why?' He flung back over his shoulder at me. 'That woman must know where our comrades are.'

'Surely, Prince. But what if they are imprisoned?'

'Then we shall release them by force.'

'Accomplish what ten men failed to do?'

'Yes.' He turned to face me now, the tawny eyes fierce, though paler in the bright sunshine.

'She pretends not to notice us. She may be a demon.'

'I don't believe in demons.'

'What of the . . ?' I was about to mention the black hound but decided against it. If this young maiden was a demon priestess, she could have changed herself into a bitch, appearing in that form to entice us to death or imprisonment, but this was not the moment to speak of it to my brother.

'What of the what?' he demanded impatiently.

'Don't you think it would be better for us to proceed with wisdom?' I glanced along the track, observing the imprints of the dog's claws on the soft sand above a clutter of men's footmarks. 'Look over there, for instance.' I pointed towards the track. 'That is obviously the direction in which our comrades went. Let us first see where their footprints lead.'

He faced the pond again. 'You are right.'

I followed him once more, finding a strange comfort in his massive frame, hair glinting red, the easy stride, his fearless outlook. He paused, inspecting the footprints more closely now. Those of the dog veered right along the black mud bordering the pond.

Prince Vijaya stopped at the water's edge. 'The men's footprints go into the pond but do not come out,' he observed soberly. 'They may have gone in to bathe and drowned, or been sucked into soft mud.'

'Could they not have swum and got on to that bund?' I nodded across the pond to where the maiden continued to spin. The hum of her wheel now had the undercurrent of a hard reeling sound.

'Impossible. The bund wall is too high and the water is obviously too deep there. Besides, they were all fully armed, so where are their weapons? They could not have swum across carrying all their weapons.'

'You're right. There's a mystery here. Just in case that is a demon, let us proceed with care. I believe I can handle her.'

It went against his grain but he was practical enough to nod agreement. I cannot say I was not afraid. Actually, the thought of facing a demon terrified me.

Two white lake birds flew in from the treeline, angling low to skim over the water. One of them dived with a splash, to reappear dripping but empty-beaked, leaving only ripples behind. The fish had got away. Would we?

I blinked against the sun's glare on the mirror surface of the pond. The heat was making me sweat. It could have been partly my fear. Yet I drew strength from the source of heat, Great Agni, god of the sun, who would protect us, for in his fire, Prince Vijaya's sword had been tempered. It could slay any demon. I touched my *yantara*, an even better weapon, and fresh courage flowed into my being, new strength to my weak knees.

Then I remembered God, my One God, and a great calm came over me. It was a wondrous experience. For the first time in my life, in a moment of stress, I saw gods and demons as a part of God's body, a knowledge of them and charms part of his plan to overcome them. Dimly too I perceived that some of the fear was simply in my mind.

I walked along the water's edge towards the bund, black mud squelching again beneath my bare feet. My brother followed me silently. I could, however, sense his total watchfulness.

We skirted the western edge of the pond and turned, alert for danger from every side but our eyes still on the maiden. A pale white cloud momentarily shadowed the sunlight. With its passing, something had changed. It took me a moment to realize what it was. The spinning had stopped, the echo of its hum still hanging over the lake, soft as the after-glow of a beacon. The maiden had risen to her feet and was staring in our direction.

A fragment of sunshine fell through the branches and lit up her face. She was very dark, with red lips slightly parted showing a flash of white teeth beneath a flat nose on a round face. She was dressed only in a white cloth, secured tightly around a narrow waist. Her naked breasts were large, full but pointing, held up without a sag by some miracle of youth and race. Her figure was lithe, yet she looked stocky because she was less than three and a half cubits, five foot three inches tall. It was her eyes that held my attention even from that distance away. Large and dark, they were clearly hypnotic.

Before I could resume walking, her voice came floating across the water. Its notes, clear as a silver-gold bell, confirmed my belief that, if human, she must be a priestess.

'Welcome, sirs. You seem to have travelled far. And I have awaited your coming.' She spoke a rough dialect, but we could understand it.

'Madam, we are searching for twelve men we have lost,' my brother shouted, his voice harsh. 'Where are they?'

'How would I know?'

I had a moment's inspiration. 'Where are we?' I demanded. 'What country is this?'

'You are in Lanka-dwipaya, the island of Lanka, the resplendent land.'

My brother and I exchanged glances.

We knew a great deal about this country from our reading of history. Lanka has three races. The Nagas, a cultured, civilized people who may have been Arya originally, but were mixed with that other race, the Dasa. These were the Chola, Pandya and Chera of the continent's southern kingdoms, who had crossed the 'seas to settle on Lanka's northern shores. The third race of Lanka are the Yakka, so named because they are half-civilized, worship demons and live primitive lives, hunting or producing only for their own needs. From her appearance, this lady must be one of them.

Lanka is also said to have a sprinkling of Arya who came originally to trade but remained to colonize the south-eastern part of the island. There is said to be a temple for the god E-Ra on the southernmost part of the coast in a town called Devun Dara, which has a roof of gold that serves as a beacon for the trading ships that have gone there for centuries to attend a great annual trade fair.

'Now that you have found me, why do you need your men?' I heard the woman enquire.

'She knows where our men are,' Prince Vijaya muttered.

By unspoken consent, we broke into a run. In seconds we

stood before her. I unslung my bow, my gaze taut on her. Swift as a swooping bird, my bow-string was around her neck, pulling her towards the prince. Her face broke up in fear.

Prince Vijaya's hand shot out like a striking lion's paw to grip her long black hair. He raised his sword to plunge it into her bare chest.

'Wait!' She gasped, her dark eyes piteously pleading.

'Wait!' I echoed.

Prince Vijaya paused, his sword almost between the twin dark mounds of her breasts. 'You know what happened to our men,' he grated. 'Their tracks go into the pond but do not come out. Give us back our comrades or you shall perish this instant.'

Writhing in my brother's grasp, she turned her tormented gaze on him. 'Spare my life and you shall have more than your comrades,' she begged.

Prince Vijaya looked at me. I nodded. He withdrew his sword and released her hair. I removed my bowstring from around her neck. 'All right, lead us to them,' he directed shortly.

She stood beside her stool and spinning wheel breathing deeply. She had begun sweating with fear, so that rays of sunlight shredded by the leaves overhead made her black body gleam like polished ebony. As if a spell had been broken, the air suddenly resounded with the shrill cries and whistling of birds. A wind riffled through the leaves bringing the odour of hot, dry soil and cooling our bodies.

'Tell me, how did you capture the men?' Prince Vijaya demanded.

She smiled a secret-knowledge smile. 'By the oldest weakness of men. Women. The first two saw my female attendants bathing naked in the pond. They flung away their weapons and waded in, little knowing that there was soft mud in between. When they were stuck, we noosed them from the bank like stuck animals, brought them out our captives and picked up their weapons. You were clever to notice their footprints going into the water but not coming out.'

'So they are alive?' the prince demanded.

'Certainly. They are prisoners in my village.'

'Is that how you got the other ten men as well?'

'Yes.'

'You speak of naked women,' my brother interrupted. 'You yourself seem to be a person of some authority. Why do you not cover your bosom as other civilized women do?'

'This is *our* civilization,' she retorted proudly. 'In our society, only women of high rank are permitted to bare their breasts. Lesser people and slaves may not expose their lowly persons to the public gaze.'

I was tempted to remark that the only test of see-worthiness should be the beauty of a woman's breasts but refrained. This was no time for levity, or philosophy.

'What rank are you?' Prince Vijaya enquired.

'I am a princess.'

'Your name?'

'Kuveni. I am the daughter of Kalu Sena, the black one, who is *gamani*, king of this region.'

Before my brother could reply, I sensed danger and glanced towards its source.

A crowd of men and women had emerged silently from the trees surrounding the pond and fringing the bund. The men were bare-bodied, wearing only dark span cloths around their loins. They all had beards and moustaches, even the younger ones sporting a fuzzy growth. The women were dressed in coloured waistcloths, the sleeveless bodices cut square around the neck to reveal the first bulge and cleavage of their breasts. They were dark, without exception, some of them almost black, stocky of build with out-thrust chests and pushed-back buttocks. They had long black hair, mostly matted, framing the same broad, flat features as their princess. Though uncivilized in appearance they were clean and their dark eyes shone with intelligence. They all carried weapons, some the short-bow others swords and knives, axes and even digging tools.

The Princess Kuveni smiled at our surprise. 'You see, we can overcome you both easily, by sheer force of numbers.'

'Not easily, madam,' Prince Vijaya replied grimly. His grip tightened on his sword. 'Just try.'

She took in his giant figure, towering over her retainers, who had now formed a circle around us, still silent, their eyes on their mistress. Her gaze ran over the great gleaming muscles, the latent power of him, and her admiration showed. 'Let me lead you to your men,' she said gently. She turned eastward. 'Make way there. These two are the leaders. They and their comrades shall be our honoured guests.'

'What of their ships?' The high-pitched voice belonged to an older man. He was diminutive, almost a dwarf, with kinky grey hair shot with black, his skin wrinkled except where it stretched tight across a well-rounded belly, large and shiny as that of a woman advanced in pregnancy. He must be the revered village elder, for he stood confident and firm on his spindly legs.

'What of them, Pina?'

'Are your gods to be denied the toll they extract from the great sea in storm?'

'I conferred with my god last night. As you well know, he is more powerful than all other gods. The toll shall be his alone, as he shall demand it, through me.'

Her words sounded so prophetic that I felt a thrill of foreboding.

Pina seemed about to protest, but a granite glance from Kuveni, surprising from one so young, silenced him. He slung his bow across his chest and stood aside. Like an army troop changing direction, the other Yakka made way.

'Podi, bring my spinning things and stool,' the princess commanded. She looked at us. 'Follow me,' she said.

Chapter 4

Prince Vijaya held his sword at the ready, every sense alert for danger as he followed Princess Kuveni along a worn sandy track still damp from the rain and rutted by wagonwheels. Yet he was strangely attracted to the young woman and realized with amazement that even when he had his sword at her breast, ready to kill her, some magnetism of the princess, something familiar in her expression, had touched him. Now, despite his wariness, he felt an unwonted tenderness towards her and it reminded him of what his mother had once told him. 'You have sensitivity hidden within you, *baba*, and I hope it does not bring you pain.' Had that been only six months ago?

The Princess Kuveni certainly had a seductive walk, the pushy buttocks swaying seductively beneath her narrow waist. Not all the possible dangers of his situation prevented the beginning of an erection. He told himself that he was walking behind her to run her through with his sword at the slightest sign of treachery, not to penetrate her with his manhood. Security before sex. He grinned to himself at the thought.

Relieved when they finally emerged into open land, he relaxed his sword arm and increased his pace to walk beside the princess. On either side of the track was evidence of the Yakkas' livelihood. Trees had been felled in patches of jungle, then fired, burning out branches and undergrowth which were then cleared. The blackened soil was planted between the charred remains of tree-stumps with manioc for its roots and leaves, yellow maize, a pittance of hard-wrung green paddy and some vegetables. Much of this cultivation had been flattened by the rains, probably the only water source of these people other than the pond.

'Is this your normal method of livelihood?' he enquired of the princess.

'No, our hunters are a different, prouder breed,' she responded, somewhat tartly. 'They come out of the jungle periodically to barter pork and venison for the maize and rice of our villagers. We Yakka are an ancient people.'

'I'm sorry, I meant no offence,' he declared.

She glanced up at him sharply and he knew that she had appreciated the apology.

They soon came to the first hut, a crude, small affair of bamboo wattle and grey mud daub with a roof of dried coconut branches, not even thatched, and a dung floor. A lean-to at the back contained burnt clay pots on a wooden stand. Beside the hut, a gnome of a woman with gaunt cheeks, toothless gums and stringy grey hair industriously wielded a winnowing fan containing rice paddy. She barely glanced in their direction. There were no visible sanitary facilities; the residents probably performed in the jungle, or perhaps in the *chena* in order to add their manure to Nature's endowment.

Accustomed as he was to flowing green wheat and barley fields, the neat peasant cottages of Lala and Sinha-Pura, the whole scene seemed pitiful to the prince. Even the chickens chip-chipping in a small stockade were scrawny. What an opportunity this land presented to someone with knowledge and leadership, a lump of gold or uncut stones ready for the jeweller's craft. He glanced sideways again at the princess. This time she returned his look boldly and he felt their impact on each other like a single drum-roll vibrating through two bodies. A strange vulnerability entered her eyes, then she looked away quickly.

The track widened. Unaccustomed to the tremendous heat and humidity, he was grateful for the shade of the green coconut palms that now lined it. The compounds became larger and better planted, the huts slightly more spacious. Dark women, some with stumpy little children, bulbousstomached, or babies in crude bassinets, bent over patches of onion and chilli beds. The children must have the worm disease, he concluded. The women came erect briefly and made obeisance to the Princess Kuveni, murmuring a greeting as they knelt and touched foreheads to the ground.

A larger building, of sturdier wattle and white-coated daub, its roof of a rough red tile, appeared to the right. It was guarded by a dozen men, who stood with drawn swords or spears resting on the ground.

The princess halted. 'Your comrades are safe and well in that building,' she declared. 'You may visit them now. My people will serve you the noon meal. You shall sup with me tonight, Prince . . ?' Her look was a question.

'. . . Vijaya! I am Prince Vijaya Sinha-Bahu of Sinha-Pura.' He inclined his head backwards. 'This is my twin brother, Prince Lala Sinha-Bahu.'

'So you are of Pahlava origin, descended of lions. I might have known. We have no lions here, but I have heard tell of them.'

'What of my men on the beach? There are almost seven hundred.'

'They may assemble in this village. Our barns hold more than enough rice and foodstuffs, washed ashore from ships wrecked on our reefs, to feed them for a number of days. After that . . .' An inscrutable expression crossed her face. 'With so many well-armed men, fearless, of big frame and strong sinew, men of resolution and daring, who knows, Prince Vijaya Sinha-Bahu, scion of lions? Anything is possible.'

After talking privately to Prince Vijaya, the Princess Kuveni retired to her cottage while the prince and his men were reunited, word being sent to their comrades on the beach. The cottage set within a compound of tall trees, was constructed of wattle and brown daub, with a tile roof. It was built around a small centre courtyard. When her loom had been set up on the inside verandah that circled the courtyard, now bathed in pre-noon sunlight, the princess sat on one of the wooden settles scattered around the verandah to await Rupa, her attendant. As she listened to the buzzing of bees and smelt the *kapuru* flowers wilting in the heat, she realized that she had taken a decisive step. She didn't know where it would lead her, but was certain that it was her destiny.

Rupa, a lean woman of thirty-five with a gaunt face, came up from the rear of the cottage, tying her black hair in a knot. She saluted her mistress with the palms together greeting. 'You sent for me, my lady?'

'Yes, Rupa. I have welcomed the white strangers to our village. They must be protected from my father and my sister's bridegroom Prince Tikka. I have told their Arya leader my whole story and I can see that he is for me.'

'Why have you done this, my lady?'

'My gods led me to it. The whites will be my instrument of vengeance.' She paused, smiling reflectively. 'Also, I'm taken with this handsome prince, named Vijaya. He captivated me even while he held his sword at my breast. Do you know, after I got over my first terror, I saw that swordblade as a symbol of penetration by the prince and shivered with desire for him in the noonday sun.'

'Is this wise, my lady?'

'What do I have to lose, Rupa? I have been banished from the capital by my father, rejected by my family and the nobility and therefore discarded by all our people, except those in this village who perform menial services in the fort. Any why? Because I objected to women being treated as chattels and refused to abandon my duties as a priestess of Reeri Yakseya. It was not right, so I intend to be the god's instrument to destroy those who rejected me.'

'Right and wrong do not exist as such for our people, my lady. We have tribal customs based on whatever our leaders find to be good or bad for themselves. We obey because they are the strongest among us. We also have rituals dictated by the gods, after the priests decide what the gods demand. You should follow these customs if you want to be happy. And in particular you should not go against your father.'

'Why not, Rupa?' The princess demanded fiercely. 'I have tried to remember one single act of kindness from my father, Kalu Sena, either towards me or to my dead mother, the gentle Princess Polamitta. All he ever afforded us were the bare bones of a home, food and clothing, flung at us, like bones to pi-dogs. What customs do we really have? The strongest warrior or hunter always takes over the tribe and retains his hold on it by fear even after his physical strength has gone.' Her voice rose in anger. 'The Nagas, the Dasa and the Arya are different. They regard their kings as gods, so that people of royal blood are sacred and their word becomes truly the word of the gods. As a Yakka princess, I merely had my household tasks in the so-called palace. If I did not do these duties adequately, I was screamed at, or beaten.' She paused for breath, gazing wide-eyed at Rupa.

'You are working yourself up in order to justify what you plan to do,' Rupa remarked dryly. 'Please calm yourself.'

'Why should I?' The princess demanded passionately. 'Why should I, Rupa? Do you know what would have happened to me if I had remained in the palace? My father would have forcibly taken me. Already he was beginning to give me the finger signs. Our people mate like the animals of the jungle. Our women accept their lot. I alone am different. I will not be treated like an animal. I am a human being and I want to be treated as the women of other races are treated. I see this stranger, Prince Vijaya, as knowing how to treat a woman. Why, he even apologized to me just now. Can you believe that? A man apologizing to a woman?'

After our captive men had been released Prince Vijaya drew me aside. 'From all that the Princess Kuveni told me, this Yakka kingdom is ripe for a takeover,' he declared, his tawny eyes gleaming with suppressed excitement. 'King Vijaya of Thamba-Panni! How does that sound to you?'

I could see that the mischief in his voice cloaked the beginning of a more serious ambition. 'Excellent, Sire,' I responded, half-joking. 'But I should prefer you to be a *maha raja*, Great King.'

He grinned boyishly. 'All right then, subject and slave, send messengers to the beach directing the commanders to organize relays and transport the flour, rice, spices, food-stuffs and baggage from the three great ships to that large barn. 'When that's done, tell them to join us here for the noon meal.'

By the time the task was ended, the Yakkas had prepared our food. This consisted of small balls of paste they called *kurakkan*, made from a root pounded with a mortar and pestle into a powder, then cooked in water and eaten with a touch of ground chilli on the tongue.

We ate seated together at a rough trestle table, grateful for the shade of the spreading tamarind tree under which it had been placed. The noonday glare was unbearable and the heat was appalling to us, from a cooler clime, but the Yakka did not seem to mind it.

The *kurakkan* balls sat like lumps of rock in the stomach. Great food for the poor, because the feeling of fullness would last over a long period, but we Arya merely felt distended after the first mouthfuls.

'These damned things are like sling-shots,' Prince Vijaya whispered to me. 'They won't even leave room for wind in the stomach. We shall give the princess a real repast tonight. Show her what it means to be civilized!'

I glanced sharply at him, drawn by the current of an idea. He had told me of his urge to create a kingdom only that morning. Could it be that he also had a hidden need to teach, to uplift people, something he had never been able to do in our native Sinha-Pura?'

He must have caught the drift of my thoughts for he

smiled happily behind the twig toothpick he was wielding between his large yellow teeth. 'Finding such a primitive people could be a rare opportunity,' he declared, then relapsed into his own thoughts.

Before the first shades of evening began to fall we were installed in seven empty barns in the compound of the princess. Hardly luxury in comparison with palace life, but a veritable heaven after our days and nights crowded into those stinking ships, soaked to the skin, almost living in our own vomit and excretions because of the ceaseless buffeting of the storm. Ajit, Kahola and the ten imprisoned men came in for many rude jokes from their comrades.

'To a fool, the orifice is golden!'

'Behold the men who favoured the naked and were nearly dead!'

'Did you inherit your organs to make water or make waves?'

The princess ordered her men to erect a tent for Prince Vijaya beneath a spreading tamarind tree in the clearing beside the house. It was furnished with Pahlava carpets of red, green and blue to cover the bare earth and a great bed on which were large cushions of gold and silver cloth. All this had to come from a wrecked Arabi trading ship, for any Yakka luxuries had to come from vessels grounded on the reef by storms.

Meanwhile, our best cooks began to prepare an Arya evening meal at which the princess and the village elder Pina would be our guests. I could not escape the conclusion that this dinner would be momentous.

Chapter 5

As he followed the Yakka Prince Tikka from their quarters in the Priti fort, heading towards King Kalu Sena's palace, Hamy, the prince's aide, looked at the straight back of Prince Tikka, who walked ahead of him along the avenue of tall slender *na* trees, some of the leaves pink, white blossoms on the ground, noting how lithe and alert his leader was, slim and very tall for a Yakka but with the power of a coiled python within him. The waist was slim, the skin of the bare torso dark as ebony, the muscular limbs taut against tight blue pantaloons, the long, black hair, gleaming with scented oil, hanging carelessly down to his shoulders. Hamy was suddenly touched with pride at being the aide of such a man, a fearless prince, a doughty fighter, a daring hunter. Yet those other qualities . . . he sighed.

'What's the sigh for?' Kira, his portly companion, enquired softly. Kira was Prince Tikka's other aide.

Hamy shrugged. 'I don't know,' he replied. 'Perhaps it's because I'm uneasy about the arrival of the Arya.'

'Have no fear,' Kira bade him. He nodded towards Prince Tikka. 'Our prince will give King Kalu Sena a swift kick on his buttocks and force him to destroy the Arya.'

'He tried this morning and Kalu Sena merely put it off until his daughter's nuptials with our prince are ended. That's six days to go. Meanwhile, the Princess Kuveni has given them food and shelter.'

'Kuveni has no power. We'll kill the Arya and none of her followers will dare interfere.'

'Kill seven hundred well-armed men when we have no men of our own down here?'

'Certainly. Our prince has a plan. He'll use King Kalu Sena's men, take the enemy by surprise at night.'

'The Yakka are experts at that kind of action, but I still have a feeling of disquiet.'

'We'll know soon enough,' Kira said. 'King Kalu Sena will just have to cooperate, seeing that we have only our wedding party available to fight. But I'm glad, aren't you, that Kuveni declined to marry our lord. She's a strange one. Who wants a Yakka priestess for a queen? But the younger sister, she's a tasty morsel!' He smacked his thin lips and ran a red tongue over his black moustache. 'Oh, here we are.'

They had arrived at the wooden entrance doors of the palace, which was built of *kabook* earth, and roofed with white tiles. Prince Tikka's nuptial celebrations had commenced the previous day and would continue for another six, so the doors were hospitably open.

Guards standing at ease bowed low, palms together, as they passed through the hallway on to the verandah that ran around the four sides of the centre courtyard. Yellow *kapuru* flowerbeds, a small pond beside which brown and black ducks waddled and a mixture of green *anodha* bushes, temple flowers and jak trees adorned it. The rich sharp scent of ripe guava clung to golden air that was rent by the screech of mynah birds.

King Kalu Sena received them in his hall at the front end of the verandah. Though he held court, received petitions and administered justice in this room, it also served as a common dining room for the king, the princes and noblemen. It reeked of stale *ra* toddy, lemon and chilli, onion and garlic.

Kalu Sena, a dark, bearded man, barrel-chested and built like a gorilla, was seated on a settle at the head of the long, ebony dining table. He smiled a greeting, revealing teeth discoloured from chewing betel nut and the *ada thoda* leaf, then forced bloodshot eyes to focus on Prince Tikka. 'Ah *bana*, son-in-law,' he cried. 'How good to see you again. I thought you would be sleeping off the effects of this afternoon's drinking bout.' He scratched the black hairs of his bare chest with strong, stubby fingers and hiccuped. 'You *uda rata* folk can't put it away like we do.' He hiccuped again. 'But since you are up and about, come, have another goblet of our *ra.*'

Prince Tikka perched on a settle opposite the King, and seized a clay goblet full of the sour-smelling liquid with a touch of white foam on top. Head back, he raised it to his lips and drained it. He bottom-ended the goblet to show it was dry, then slammed it down on the table. 'There, that will show you how the *uda rata* people drink, lord,' he declared. He wiped his mouth with the back of his hand. 'Now to important business.'

King Kalu Sena came suddenly, unexpectedly alert. 'I know, I know,' he responded. 'You want us to destroy the Arya. Well, as I always say, first things first. This is our country. The Arya are strangers. We must treat them with courtesy. What will my people think if I interrupt the nuptial celebrations to go after the first pack of foreigners to land on our shores, eh? Tell me, tell me.' He jerked inwards with dark fingers, demanding a quick reply.

'That you were prudent,' Prince Tikka replied.

King Kalu Sena stared at him in disbelief. 'Prudent?' He demanded. 'And you think that's all right.' He began to laugh. 'The prudent King Kalu Sena, who is so scared of a bunch of white faces that he forgets hospitality, forgets custom and murders them. Faugh! That is not my image, Prince.' A cunning gleam entered his eyes. 'And remember, they have three ships, probably laden with good things. We don't want to scare them away, do we?'

'It's not my image either and well you know it.' The prince controlled himself with an effort. 'Perhaps prudent is not the right word.'

'Bold and daring!' Kira interposed and Hamy trembled for him. Prince Tikka did not brook interference, but this time he merely nodded agreement.

The king's eyes focused on Kira. 'Those are better words,'

he granted. His eyes sought Prince Tikka again. 'But you, *bana*, why are you so bloodthirsty?' He grinned.

'We are outraged that these Arya dared land on our shores without your permission,' Prince Tikka responded. 'And now we are even more outraged to learn that your renegade daughter has given them shelter.'

King Kalu Sena fixed an alert gaze on Prince Tikka. 'What would you have me do?' He demanded.

'Indeed, you must not interrupt the celebrations, Lord,' Prince Tikka stated smoothly. 'But we can start tomorrow's revelries later than usual. Give me five hundred men – you can summon them from the villages by tomorrow night – and I'll make ready a plan to steal into the village and kill every one of the Arya before we dine tomorrow.' He licked his lips. 'As well as those who have given them shelter.'

Hamy shivered. He knew that Prince Tikka would like nothing better than the destruction of Princess Kuveni for her rejection of his suit. His leader was one of the most vengeful men in a clan dedicated to revenge. As a man of compassion, not given to violence, Hamy knew himself to be unusual.

King Kalu Sena nodded emphatically. 'That's a good idea,' he declared. He raised his goblet, drained its contents and banged the goblet on the table so hard that it shattered. He flung the broken remnant still clutched in his hand over his shoulder. It clattered against the wall and fell to the floor. 'We eat, we drink, we fornicate, we sleep tonight. Tomorrow we make a surprise attack on the white pigs and massacre them.' He studied Prince Tikka awhile, with beady black eyes. 'You're smart,' he finally declared. 'I should be careful of you.' He nodded to himself as if he had just learned something important, then shot a suspicious glance at Prince Tikka. 'If you lead my men, they will accept you as their leader. Are you planning to displace me and rule the two kingdoms before I die?'

'I respect you too much for that. The thought never even

entered my mind,' Prince Tikka declared. But Hamy knew that he lied. His prince had even greater ambition, for he dreamed of conquering and ruling the whole island of Lanka, all four kingdoms.

'Kolla!' King Kalu Sena shouted for his chief attendant.

A slim man with wrinkled black skin, his white hair tied in a knot at the nape of his scrawny neck, soon knelt before the king.

'Summon my chiefs immediately,' the king commanded. 'Rouse them from their drunken slumber if necessary. Tell them we are about to plan a great attack, with over a thousand men. Also have my spies, Gona and Suramba, attend me. I want a complete report on all that's going on in the village.'

The attendant rose and backed out of the hall.

King Kalu Sena directed his gaze at Prince Tikka. 'There now, you need worry no more. We'll kill the wretches before the moon sets tomorrow.' He reached for a fresh goblet of *ra*. 'Now drink up.'

As night began to fall, fires glowed in the *chena*. Our men had lightly fried chicken spiced with salt, onions, black pepper and lime and were now simmering it in rice with a touch of saffron. There was also a dish of the pulse we call dhal, onion pickles, white curds and a red hot mixture of dry fish ground with grated coconut and red peppers. The aromas were delicious, bringing memories of the Sinha-Pura palace. This would be our first good meal since we left our native land over a week ago.

After we had bathed in the pond and changed into fresh clothes, I assembled all our men in long rows in the compound. As dusk laid its soft mantle upon them, they seemed to have become imbued with its inevitable solemnity, their voices hushed. A jackal howled from the jungle. The entire village, clad in their brightest clothes, thronged the roadway outside.

Prince Vijaya stood beside me, facing a wooden altar I had hastily erected beside the tent. On this altar I had placed a red clay bowl of cooked rice, a small white cup of water and a garland of wild yellow *kapuru* flowers. Beside them, incense glowed in a metal brazier from the ship, wafting its heady scent into the cooling air.

The Princess Kuveni watched, dark-eyed, mysterious, at her doorstep, some distance away. She could not participate in our worship but seemed intensely interested in it.

I was dressed for my role in white *dhoti* and *kurtha* overshirt. Raising the cup of clear water high in the air, for all our men and their gods to witness, I lifted my eyes to the heavens and chanted:

'O great Brahma, creator of the universe, of storm and calm, of men and all things, we give thee thanks for our deliverance from exile and the ocean. We pray that we may have found sanctuary at last. We offer thee our first drink in token of our submission.'

I poured the water on to the dark earth, which drank it, slobbering greedily.

'O great Krishna, who vanquished all demons, we thank thee for our deliverance from gods, demons and men this day. We offer thee our first food in token of our submission.'

I grasped the rice bowl and flung the rice in the air, so that its grains were scattered upon the dark earth.

I reached for the garland of flowers.

'O dread Kali, goddess of death, goddess of many forms, we thank thee for our deliverance from death. We offer thee our bright garland of coloured flowers in token of our submission in this life.'

I placed the garland on one of the altar posts. It seemed to look back mockingly at me, as if saying: You speak of life. Death will follow, for some very soon, for each one of you inevitably, because you were born of my womb and will finally be received into it.

I shivered in the cool, dusky air.

'To thee, great Agni, god of fire, we offer this burning incense. To thee, O Purusa, god of breath and the wild winds, we offer thee our breathing.

'May the gods and their devas guard and protect us now and always.'

Eyes closed, but with mind and spirit open, I then said my prayers to my God. They had to be unspoken, unknown to these men if they were not to turn and rend me.

I opened my eyes to find the cadaverous Ujjeni's glittering gaze upon me. His look was strange. Had he penetrated my private prayers? In that uncertain light, his face was more like a skull than ever, yet his eyes burned into mine like those of an inquisitor confronting a heretic.

As I trembled with an unaccountable dread, a lizard chirped its ill omen.

As soon as the ritual was over Prince Vijaya drew me aside. 'I need to talk to you,' he said.

We strolled away from the compound, watched by the Princess Kuveni. Turning right at the entrance, we instinctively moved away from the direction of the ocean. Grey smoke coils from our cooking fires drifted above the roadway. The villagers gazed curiously at us, murmuring softly to one another in the strange sing-song inflections of their language. I was hungry and hoped that we would not be away too long, for the spicy odours of the food made my stomach growl.

Before long we left the glow cast on the track by the cooking fires. It was now so dark beneath the overhanging branches that I stumbled on a root. Recovering, I adjusted my sword, paused, shut my eyes for several seconds to heighten the darkness, then opened them again, regaining my night-sight. As we strolled silently along, the voices of our men gradually faded away. An occasional cackle of laughter became an intrusion upon the silence of creaking crickets.

A large patch of darkness loomed before us with the shadowy outline of a stile before it. The track veered to the left. A sudden clash of music from reed pipes and the wild beating of drums arose. Prince Vijaya cocked his head in its direction. 'What's that?' he demanded.

'The Princess Kuveni mentioned something about revelry in Sirisa Watta to celebrate her sister's wedding. This is the second night. It will go on five nights more. Imagine seven straight nights of carousing!'

My brother grunted. 'They must have hard heads and tough stomachs to take all that liquor.'

'If they can eat their beastly *kurakkan* they should be able to stand anything.'

By tacit consent, we removed the upper bars of the stile to hop over it. The dark patch was revealed as a kind of a bund, with steps cut into it.

Before we reached the top of the bund, I saw the dark sheen of waters quietly rippling before a breeze. This was a larger pond than that we had seen earlier in the day. I guessed it was meant for another village, perhaps one that served the capital directly.

'These ponds are the basis of their village life,' Prince Vijaya observed soberly. 'Their soil seems very fertile, yet they have only small ponds, small villages, and they water crops by rain or by hand. I should like to teach them modern methods of irrigation and agriculture.'

'How will you do that?' I demanded. 'You have neither the right nor the power. The Yakkas may drive us away tomorrow.'

His eyes gleamed in the half light. 'You know better than that,' he asserted. 'We're going to establish a kingdom here. I feel it in my bones. It's time I changed my ways. I'm twenty-two years old. What have I achieved so far?'

'You tell me.'

'I committed every crime except murder.'

He sounded surprisingly bitter at himself and I could not

help an echo of it in my own heart. 'You were good at it all. Is that not the measure of success?' I enquired.

'I am asking for your help not your cynicism.'

'I can only help you within the ambit of your ideals and standards.'

'Having had none, I would like to develop some.'

'That is certainly a first step, but only a beginning. All you have been, all you have done, has entered your consciousness, your very *atman*. Like a trained animal responding, it will make you do as you have taught it, often emerging when you least expect, sometimes even without your being aware of it. You now feel a compulsion to change your entire lifestyle. It will not be easy.'

'I would like to make a beginning.' He sounded almost humble.

I had never known him like this before; he had always been proud, arrogant, overbearing.

'How can I help you?' I enquired gently.

'First, by telling me of your own ideals and aspirations and those of the great Arya monarchs, such as Kyroos and Dharroos, whose administrations you studied while I was more interested in their military achievements . . . and of course their economic systems. Second, by assisting me to shape my ideals and advising me how best to govern . . . myself and others. Finally, by being my spiritual watchdog.'

I faced him in utter amazement. He looked down at his bare feet, avoiding my glance.

'Am I hearing right?' I demanded.

'Yes.' He looked fiercely up at me and the words came out harsh as a scrubbing stone. 'It is good for every man to have his moment of abasement once in a while. Otherwise he will forget where he comes from, whither he is going, and will stumble upon the rocks of foolish pride and conceit. This is my moment, but make no mistake. I do not abase myself before you, but only before my ignorance. I seek your knowledge. And that knowledge is not you, nor does it belong to you. The me that stands abased links somewhere inside with a spark of decency and the flame of self-preservation.' His voice softened. A faraway look entered his eyes. 'I have a feeling that we shall make history tonight.'

A silence suddenly fell upon the earth, as if all beings were hushed at his words. I knew a moment's awe as I gazed upon him. Then a jackal howled from the jungle across the pond as if in derision, and the moment was gone. The wail and beat of distant music flowed back towards us, some shouting from the celebrations in the city and raucous laughter.

I looked away from my brother, up at the sky, seeking a portent. A distant yellow star plummeted down in blue space. I silently said a prayer for my brother's *atman*. May his former life end like that star.

'Will you support me in achieving it?' he asked.

'I did not have to come into exile with you,' I gently reminded him.

'I know.' Through the half light, I could see his eyes misting. 'You alone of them all.'

'We have not talked about it before, but you should also realize that I came because I felt you had a date with destiny and that it was part of my own destiny to help you and to witness your keeping of it. All you have just said merely confirms my intuition.'

'Is that all?'

I knew what he was seeking, but also understood him too well to give him a direct answer, to tell him I had been moved by my love for him. 'No that is not all.'

He nodded, bright faced, and clapping a brawny hand on my shoulder, he turned me back in the direction of the compound, so that I saw them before he did. The two dark figures had followed us so stealthily that even the normally alert Prince Vijaya had not perceived them. The upraised knife of the first assassin gleamed. A few seconds more and it would have been in my brother's back.

My sword flashed out even as I shouted my warning. I

leapt to the left, my blade slashing sideways in the same smooth movement as my draw. It whizzed past Prince Vijaya and sank into the bearded cheek of the attacker. He screamed and dropped sideways, his knife missing my brother by inches, clattering to the ground as the man clutched his face. I drew back my sword and lunged downwards, getting him in the side of his stomach. He fell to the ground now holding back his entrails.

Prince Vijaya had already sprung aside. In an instant, he stood massive beside me, sword drawn.

The remaining man came rushing up, long knife upraised, yelling. Like two dancers in a ballet, my brother and I thrust together. Each sword went neatly through the chest. The man was dead before we withdrew them.

We searched the darkness beneath the bund with urgent eyes, ears and senses. Satisfied that there were no others, we turned our attention to the first assailant. He was groaning and gasping now, near death. Prince Vijaya stepped forward, stooped, grabbed him by the hair and yanked him up as if he were a hound. The man screeched with pain. He was dark and squat, obviously a Yakka. My sword had opened his face from ear to mouth. Blood poured out of the gash, dark in the half light.

'Who are you?' My brother demanded fiercely. 'What's your name?'

'The king's men.' The sound was a painful croak through the extension of his mouth so that I could barely distinguish the words. 'Name . . . gug . . . Gona.' He was still holding back his entrails with both hands.

'Any more of you?'

'No . . .' He stiffened, his breath rattled, then he went limp, his hands flopping sideways.

Prince Vijaya let him go. The body collapsed untidily.

My brother turned towards me slowly. Eyes shining, he saluted me with his bloody sword. 'You saved my life,' he stated simply. 'I'll not forget.'

Indeed I had saved his life, but I had also killed my first man and helped kill my second, reacting naturally against the threat to our safety. Would I have reacted in the same way if only my own life had been involved? With horror, I realized that I would. My training in the palace had instilled in me the attitude of a killer. What had it done to my *atman*? What would this dreadful event make of me? A priest or a killer? Was it right to kill in a just cause? The questions would haunt me, I knew. Prickles broke out over my entire body. I started to shiver and tremble. My body was soon bathed in sweat. I hoped that my brother would not notice.

For a while Prince Vijaya scanned the track intently. 'The fellow spoke the truth,' he finally observed. 'We would have been attacked by now if there were more of them.' He stooped to wipe his sword on the grass and I followed suit. 'They were probably spies. We can expect trouble soon, unless we dish it out first. Let's get back to our meal.'

Chapter 6

We decided that we would not tell the Princess Kuveni or our men of our near escape from death. It would be a poor reward for our hostess and could drive our men to fury and reprisals. It would be best for us not to be implicated in the killing of any local people when the bodies of the assassins were discovered the next day.

By the time we threaded our way through the throng of still-curious onlookers at the entrance to the compound, the Princess Kuveni had vanished, probably into her house, and our men had laid out the trestle table in front of the tent with twelve stools around it. On the table were twelve platters of burnt clay and twelve goblets.

The squat Kahola came up to Prince Vijaya grinning. He was dressed in a blue *dhoti*, but bare-chested. His mass of black body-hair must surely save him from the evening's coolness. In his hands, Kahola held a large earthenware jug. 'The Yakka people offer us their wine,' he explained, pouring a whitish liquid into the first goblet. He was obviously drunk.

Prince Vijaya shot Kahola a sharp glance. 'What kind of wine is it?'

Kahola laughed, pouring the liquid into the next goblet. 'A heady one, I am assured. They make it from the juice of a coconut tree's heart, which they gather in potsh overnight.' He raised the jug aloft. 'They call it *ra* because it ish liquid sunshine . . . hic!'

Prince Vijaya must have seen his opportunity. He banged the table with a furious fist so that the platters rattled and some of the wine from an over-full goblet spilled white on the table. 'Who gave you permission to drink?' he roared.

Kahola straightened, miraculously sober before the leader's

anger.

'Lord . . . we have always . . .'

'You were in trouble once today attempting to womanize. Now you have been drinking and could create worse for us all.' Prince Vijaya's anger was feeding on his words. 'Summon the men!' He shouted. 'Have them assemble before me in their ranks immediately.'

The trembling Kahola turned and made to leave.

'Leave that jug behind!' Prince Vijaya directed, more quietly.

Kahola placed the jug on the table and fled in the direction of the cooking fires around which most of our men had gathered, a mass of moving shadows against the yellow-gold flames, laughing, shouting, some even dancing. A few of them had turned at their leader's bellow and were looking curiously in our direction.

The seven companies were soon assembled before us.

Prince Vijaya drew himself to his full height, hands clasped behind his back. Head slightly bent, he looked broodingly up at the men without speaking, deliberately eyeing every single rank, using silence to disconcert them. Sure enough, some of them began to fidget nervously. Only Ujjeni and Vijit remained calm and imperturbable.

The silence became louder, penetrated only by the crackle of the fires, as the murmuring voices of the villagers to the rear died down.

'Do you men know why we are here today?' Prince Vijaya brought the question growling out of his chest in his deep tones, startling as the first rumble of thunder.

Fat Rama, ever jolly, essayed an answer. 'Because you saved us from the storm and the Yakkas, Lord.'

Someone let out a titter. Prince Vijaya's head shot in its direction. 'Let any man who thinks this is a comedy step forward,' he finally grated. 'As for you, Rama, I only saved you from your lust.'

No one moved. The prince surveyed them once more,

deliberately letting them be consumed by silence. 'I will tell you why we are here,' he finally shouted and had the full attention of all the men. 'Because we have been drunkards, drug-addicts, rapists and some even murderers.'

A collective gasp arose. The leader had never spoken thus to them before.

'All this is over. I failed you when I led you into it. I shall not fail you here. We have been running a long time, you and I, my comrades. As I told you this morning, here we stop.' He pointed a finger at the ground.

Silence again. And still no response. Even the drunks were sober now. Prince Vijaya was handling his men as he alone knew how, this time for a purpose totally different from any in the past five years. I suddenly felt that those years had been directed towards this one supreme moment.

I looked up at the heavens, seeking my One God.

Inscrutable are Thy ways, O God. I thank thee for them.

Your first prayer of a new kind, body of my body. That is good, but why do you always look for me in my heavens, as you have searched for your many gods, your demons, in the past? Why do you search with your eyes and your silent voice at all? Why not with your nose, or your ears, or better still, why do you not merely know me, bear me witness?

Before I could even think of the answers, my brother had begun speaking again.

'We have reached for pleasure in liquor, drugs, sex, but it has not brought us true joy or peace, only banishment and the abhorrence of all decent human beings,' Prince Vijaya continued. 'So we shall remain in this land and alter our lives. I offer you no other choice.'

He surveyed the men for any sign of opposition. Finding none, he resumed, his voice rising. 'Hear then, the first edicts I give you as your commander in the country I have named *Thamba-Panni*:

'You are forbidden liquor and drugs for one month.

'You may conquer, but not steal.

'You may not rape or molest women, only take them as

wives or concubines.

'You will follow the laws of Sinha-Pura in this territory until I give you new laws.

'We are the Arya, the noble ones. We shall prove ourselves noble. We shall bring civilization to this land as our ancestors once brought it from their own lands north of the sixteen kingdoms to an entire continent.

'Hear me and obey. Anyone among you who does not so wish may leave now, never to return.'

As he swept the gathering with fierce eyes, I knew that he had all the weapons. Not only did he tower head and shoulders above them all, a direct descendant of Sinha, King of the jungle, their acknowledged leader, but they had nowhere to go! Not one of them moved.

The Princess Kuveni had never sat at a formal feast before, nor had she ever been treated with so much honour and respect. The feasts in her father's palace were rough, bawdy affairs at which everyone slobbered over dishes of chicken and venison, combined with great draughts of *ra*, and which somehow repelled her as gross. The women did not participate in these events, merely cooked the meals, no more than the chattels in which the food was cooked, then ate the left-overs. She resented that. Also, accustomed as she was to the rough diet of her own people, the food she was now eating tasted like that of the gods.

She glanced at Prince Vijaya seated beside her. She had told him more than she had learned from him. His speech to his men had made him seem almost a god, because of his colour, one of the good gods. He would make a good ruler of her kingdom, uplifting the people from the darkness in which they lived and giving its women their due place.

No sooner had the meal ended than the usual hush that emanates from well-filled bellies fell on the compound. The shrill, nasal wail of the *naga salaam* trumpets, the underlying deep drums throbbing to a wild beat from the city, began to intrude. She was being choked by it. The noise growing louder and louder in her head until it seemed to claw at her flesh, rend her bones. She clapped her hands to her ears but the sounds would not go away. They were already inside her, seeded before she was born. Desperately her eyes sought her *tharuwa*. It winked, glowed and blazed outwards. Destroy that which you cannot contain, it commanded.

Suddenly, she made up her mind and became very calm. She placed her hands on the edge of the table and straightened up. Strangely the sound died down. She laid a hand on Prince Vijaya's forearm, noting how her blackness contrasted with his ruddy skin and the fine red gold hairs. The dark priestess and the red demon god, the right combination.

'My lord, since you have obviously decided to stay in our land,' she declared. 'I shall deliver you a kingdom, provided you are man enough to take it, with me for your spouse.'

For a few moments, Prince Vijaya looked at her in astonishment, but he quickly nodded his agreement. 'Madam, I accept your offer and your condition.'

Historic words. Somewhere within me, I heard a drum roll announce a new destiny.

While the remains of the dinner were being cleared, Prince Vijaya directed that flares be brought up to a sandy area beside his tent. He then had our seven commanders gather around the sand so that the princess could draw us the fort's location and layout. It was sited on a hill, at the first bend of a broad river that ran from east to west along its north base. The river then veered due south before resuming its westward journey to the ocean, not far north of where we had landed.

'The river provides a natural defence on two sides of the hill,' the princess explained. 'My father's father had wide ditches constructed along each of the two remaining sides, which are the east and south boundaries of the hill. He

70

planted the ditches heavily with stakes and thorn bushes. I shall guide you along a secret trail that leads through the eastern ditch. The main access to the city is here . . .' She pointed with a dark stubby finger. 'A single bridge runs across that ditch to large wooden entrance gates ribbed with iron beneath a granite archway joining the earthwork ramparts.'

I was about to ask why the sides of the ditches had not been razed, to permit the river water in, thereby creating a moat, but quickly realized that these people had not yet advanced to a stage where they could harness nature to that extent. Apart from the ditches, they had only an earthwork rampart all round the base of the hill to augment its defences.

'All the royal Yakka families will be in the citadel for the wedding celebrations,' the Princess Kuveni finally assured us, after she had completed diagrams. 'From what I know of our people, they will all be drunk on *ra* and the vigilance of the guards will be non-existent. If you don't act tonight, my father may send his men after you tomorrow.'

My brother gave me a grim look in acknowledgement. He stood up and began issuing his orders.

Lowering grey clouds soon piled up from the south-west to obscure the sky and darken the earth as the Princess Kuveni led us unerringly to within a few metres of the river. Here the village lay to our right, the city to our left. All sounds from the fort had died down. I was relieved to see the rafts, which the princess told us had brought wedding guests downstream.

My brother and I crawled alone through light undergrowth, beneath the cover of dark, spreading branches that hid the sky, until we reached the edge of the bank. It dropped sharply down a few feet into the turgid, relatively calm waters of a sort of cove, with the swift-flowing mainstream beyond. As the princess had told us, a single canoe and twenty long bamboo rafts, each capable of carrying forty or so men, were moored at this natural landing area. Two blobs of shadow to our right, seated on the ground and leaning back against posts must be the sentries. Keen-eyed, I moved my gaze slowly from right to left, then back again, but could detect no more men. The only sound and movement were those of the creaking rafts and the rushing waters.

My brother jabbed a silent finger, pointing down the bank. It was slippery and smelt of wet mud. I started wiggling down head first. A sudden sound brought me up short. My breath caught. My heart started to thud. It took me only a few seconds to realize that the sentries were sleeping and had began to snore loudly, in unison.

Then we were side by side on level ground, flat on our bellies, literally heading for our respective targets. The soil was more sandy here, with jagged fragments of pebble that scraped my bare chest. The snoring became louder. I could see the outline of my sleeping sentry clearly now. He had his back against the post, his head, lolling sideways, jerking each time a snore escaped him.

I rose silently to my feet, as one with Prince Vijaya towering beside me. His teeth shone white briefly through the darkness. I removed the garotte from around my waist. Holding it with both hands, I tiptoed till I was just behind the post, leaned forward and dropped the rope to the level of the sentry's throat. An instant when I saw that he was shaggy-haired, bearded and bare-chested, then I drew the rope back in one swift motion, crossing my hands behind the post. He jerked convulsively, the croak that nearly escaped him turned into a tortured gasp. He was wide awake now. Eyes popping, his hands clawed frantically at the rope in a futile effort to free himself. His waist and hips moved upwards reflexively, then sagged. He started to jerk up and down spasmodically as if in the throes of an orgasm, then suddenly stiffened and went limp. I did not let go my grip, just drew the rope even tighter, with a silent prayer for his *atman* and mine.

When I was certain that he was dead, I relaxed the rope and allowed the body to sink sideways to the ground. It lay slumped and still, except for a slight twitching of the limbs.

I glanced to my right and saw that my brother had killed his man too. The twin defenders of the evening had become twin assassins in the night.

Two companies of our men, under Vijit, filed up, boarded the rafts and slipped downstream in the darkness. They would attack the fort on its northern flank. Pandu's company assembled close to the southern ditch. They would be led through it by the village elder, Pina, who had thrown in his lot with us. Uraw's men were already lining the path leading to the village to prevent any rescue from that source. The other three companies, under Ujjeni, were to make a frontal assault once the gates were opened. The signal for the combined assault was to be the cry of a peacock.

At our headquarters in a copse fronting the fort, Prince Vijaya slung a coil of rope over his arm. The princess, standing before him, looked at him across the darkness. Her large dark eyes were luminous and tear-filled. I understood her feelings. Within minutes she would have betrayed her people, taking a step as irreversible as death. We had trusted her, a total stranger, and she had placed her life in the hands of strangers.

The princess reached out both hands and grasped my brother's right hand. She bent on one knee, raised his hand to her forehead and placed it there in a gesture symbolizing total submission to him. I could have wept.

She rose, released his hand, turned round and headed resolutely for the fort. We hastened after her along the dark trail until we reached the edge of the trees bordering the cleared area in front of the ditch. A fragment of song reached us and an inebriated laugh. A woman's voice, shrill with anger, snapped through the air. A dog barked. The horrid smell of *pada* fruit, reminiscent of the odour of passing wind, hung faint on the air. The earthworks loomed ahead, about six cubits, nine feet, tall. The bridge and entrance to the citadel were to our right.

Side by side we broke through the cover of the trees and, crouching low, threaded our way across the cleared ground over tufted grass, dodging round an occasional bush. Finally we stood at the edge of the long dark mass that was the ditch. It must have had to be about fifteen cubits wide, possibly ten feet deep.

The princess made her way slowly south, keeping to the edge of the ditch. She paused and bent low to grasp a root with both hands. She tested it, turned and scrambled downwards quietly to the bottom of the ditch. Prince Vijaya followed with me close behind. We stood beside one another in total blackness. A horrible stench of human excrement and rotting carcasses smote me, so violent that I gagged. The fort's inmates must use the ditch as a refuse dump.

The princess reached out a hand and took my brother's. He in turn grasped one of mine. Forming a short human chain, we angled inside the ditch, led by the princess.

The brief walk was a nightmare. It was pitch black here, warm and close. We had to bend to avoid overhanging branches. We twisted and wound our way slowly between stakes and tall undergrowth, soon bathed in sweat. Suddenly, ugh! I trod on soft, slippery night-soil. I barely adjusted to it when my feet went through flesh and bone with a crunch-squish that spoke of some small, dead animal. I began sweating even more profusely with repulsion. Thorns seemed to reach out for me with a diabolical life of their own, piercing, scraping. I dared not let go my brother's hand, so had only one with which to hold aside branches that seemed determined to claw at me. I worried about my eyes and suddenly felt sorry for the prince, who had both hands full. At that moment, a jagged branch took me in the forehead and I saw stars. Half-blinded, I turned my head aside only to tread on a sharp stake. I nearly cried out loud with the pain.

What a wretched place in which to die, I thought, then realized that it really would not matter. My body, dead, would be no better than these grisly remains.

We finally broke through. Oh, the blessed feel of the side of that ditch! Even the smells accumulated along the way no longer mattered.

The rest was easy. We soon climbed to the base of the earthworks. It was almost bright here after the darkness of the ditch.

My brother reached out and laid a gentle hand on the Princess Kuveni's cheek. He stood there briefly, communicating his thanks to her, then turned and handed me the coil of rope. He then squatted, hands half raised. I grasped them, stepped off his knee to climb on to his shoulders and as he stood up was hefted to the level of the earthworks, which were topped by blocks of stone masonry. I flashed a smile at the princess and she turned round to return to Ujjeni's company and the frontal assault.

I felt for a firm enough hole in the stone masonry, slipped the rope from my arm and dug the hook into the crevice, then pulled, testing for hold. The rest of the coil snaked to the ground. I clung to the rope to make certain it was secure, topped the rampart and lay down flat. Prince Vijaya came up the rope with practised ease.

Flares burned along the main avenue leading from the entrance gates to the palace, actually no more than a large residence. In the centre of its dark roofline a square glow revealed the courtyard. Here and there, patches of light flamed on side streets or poured out of buildings but most of the citadel was in darkness.

The reedy wail of a pipe suddenly pierced the stillness. A nasal male voice broke into a chant, slurring the words. I tried to locate its direction, but a loud laugh suddenly distracted me. The palace door had opened, releasing an oblong flow of light. Three men tottered through it, dark figures weaving their way along the front street.

Soon I could distinguish the men in the flare-light. They were all dark and bearded, dressed in light coloured tunics and short pantaloons. The one on the left was short and fat, the one on the right, slim and slight. The man in the centre was tall for a Yakka. He cursed his two companions, then suddenly pushed the slim one roughly. The light of a flare fell on a lean face. I could imagine dark, gleaming eyes beneath the high forehead. He carried himself with arrogance, even in his drunken swagger, and his two companions treated him with deference.

The truth struck me more by instinct than by judgement. This must be the bridegroom, Prince Tikka, formerly betrothed to the Princess Kuveni. If so, what was he doing outside the palace instead of on his nuptial bed?

The three men turned into a side street and vanished into its darkness. Prince Vijaya tapped me on the arm and nodded towards the entrance gates.

Two sentries stood guard on either side. They wore dark tunics and loin cloths, carried swords at their sides and held spears in the easy position, hafts on the ground. Behind each was a small guard house.

The sentry closest to me was my target. My brother started squirming away along the rampart, slow, silent and rhythmic, like a giant reptile. His body became a shadow, then vanished behind the archway.

My timing must be perfect. I inched forward to about six cubits from my sentry and paused. I did not look directly at either sentry or even focus my mind on them, for there is no surer way to attract attention than by giving it.

When I judged that my brother had gained his position, I reached for my waist with my right hand and gently slid my knife from its sheath, my sword still strapped to my side. The bone knife handle felt good to the touch, sent a surge of security through me.

I grasped the cold metal tip of the blade firmly, never taking my eyes off that dark figure, then stood up suddenly and, in one swift motion, raised my arm and flung the knife. Without pausing to see its effect, I bent low and leapt the nine feet down, just in time to prevent the clatter of the sentry's spear on the ground. The stricken sentry slumped forward on his knees, groaned twice, then tumbled flat on his face.

I stood poised, spear ready for the throw. But it was unnecessary. My brother too had got his man and was erect, spear in hand. We drew our bloody knives from the corpses, wiped them on our loin cloths and sheathed them. Twins in a death ballet, I thought.

We rushed to the gates, quietly eased out the two heavy bars of solid wood and placed them to the side. Praying that the gates would not creak and that our men would be just outside, I undid the latch and slid the iron bolts. I grasped one of the great handles. Slowly, ever so slowly, the gate swung inwards. Leaping outside, I gave the peacock scream.

In less than a minute, Ujjeni and his men, the Princess Kuveni with them, had broken across the open ground to pour over the bridge in two single files. They sped on tiptoe into the two guardhouses. The Princess Kuveni joined us, her dark eyes shining with excitement, then ran ahead to guide our frontal assault force to the houses of the leading families by uttering the cry of a night-bird in front of each.

A series of thumps, some groans, a shout, a scream, curses came from the two guardhouses. Our men began emerging through the doorways, wiping bloody knife blades before sheathing them.

Prince Vijaya and I silently sped towards the palace. Shadowy figures leaping down from the distant earthworks announced that all our companies had reached their objectives. As we reached the palace doors, we heard the night-bird cries.

The palace, well-lit by flares, was silent as a graveyard. We knew the rooms in which the king and his chief supporters would be sleeping. Faint screams and curses told me our men had begun their bloody work. I wished I could feel even a spark of pride in it.

Prince Vijaya faced the Yakka *gamani*, Kalu Sena, in the centre courtyard of the palace. We formed a ring to witness the single combat.

Kalu Sena was a dark, bearded man, rotund but strong, built like a gorilla. Though bleary-eyed from his drinking bout, he was very alert and aware, armed with a battle-axe in one hand, a short sword in the other. My brother, a red giant, with flare-light golden on his muscular body, held his sword in one hand, knife in the other.

Kalu Sena moved first, battle-axe swinging. My brother leapt back in time. The axe flashed past him, but swung right back and up again, swift as a striking snake, slashing across his chest. My heart sank. A great, long weal of red furrowed the red-gold hairs. The blood-drops appeared. My brother staggered back. The sword dropped from his hand with a clatter. The stagger saved him from the axe as it slashed down again on the instant, missing him by an inch.

Kalu Sena was swung sideways by the very force of his blow. Recovering with speed, my brother turned round and sidekicked Kalu Sena on the chest with his left foot. The *gamani* gasped, swayed backwards. My brother was on him, springing inside his guard like a lion. The knife drove straight home into Kalu Sena's waist. He gasped and twisted with pain. My brother leapt behind him to his left and got him by the neck. Body pressed to Kalu Sena's back, massive left forearm across the black throat, he squeezed. The smaller man struggled vainly to release himself. His battle-axe and sword clattered to the granite floor. He flailed desperately to and fro, trying to escape the deadly grip.

As Prince Vijaya stuck his knife again and again into Kalu

Sena the king's struggles weakened. His eyes began to bulge, as the knowledge of death entered them. Suddenly he went limp and collapsed. Blood drooled from his nostrils, and with the blood from his wounds stained the white flagstones. My brother let him go, stood over him, panting.

I sprang forward to check the prince's wound. He merely grinned as he stayed me with an upraised palm.

'Spread word of the king's death,' he commanded. 'We must end the slaughter.'

The Princess Kuveni broke past us. She stared down at her dead father a few moments, then knelt beside him. She covered her face with her hands as her body began shaking with sobs. We stole away to permit her the dignity of guilt in private.

It was only when I hit the front street that I remembered Prince Tikka. Instinct told me that he could be a dangerous enemy. Had our men got him?

Pandu came racing by. 'We must find Prince Tikka,' I shouted after him. 'Has he escaped?'

'I'm searching for him too,' he shouted back. 'I'm told he slipped through the gates.'

Drawing my sword, I soon caught up with Pandu. 'He would head for the canoes,' I cried. 'Let's make for the landing area.'

Side by side we plunged over the bridge into the darkness, sprinted across the open ground and hit the trees. We reached the river bank in record time and stood there, panting.

Too late. A tall figure, a smaller one and a fat one were dark blobs on a canoe that had cleared the cove and entered the mainstream. There was no catching them. I cried out in frustration and was answered by a frenzied bellow. 'Murderers! Assassins!' A shrill voice cried out of the darkness. 'The curses of the demons be upon you. I shall return.'

The first shock at what was taking place in the fort had

79

penetrated Prince Tikka's brain through the foggy cloud created by liquor and repeated sexual intercourse with the starkness of forked lightning out of a stormy sky. Impelled by a strong instinct for survival he had fled with his companions to the boats on the river bank. His scream of defiance had been instinctive, the product of a fury he could afford because he had escaped. Now, as he was swept downstream, still panting, sweating, his lungs pumping, his heart thudding, he felt relief and exultation sweep through him. The cold night air began to clear his mind and to dry the sweat on his body.

'How did this happen?' he asked Hamy. 'That mother-fornicating Kalu Sena. Why in the name of hell didn't he listen to me? He is probably dead now. I advised the son-of-a-bitch to massacre the Arya immediately, while they slept on the beach. But no. He was so full of wind and *ra* and shit, he wanted to take them on at leisure. Relax, my son-to-be, I shall show you the power of our Yakka kingdom, which you shall inherit one day, now that you are marrying our younger daughter. And do you know what else he said?' Prince Tikka was talking more to himself than to his comrades. 'He told me I had made the right choice, that his older girl was a devil and an uncooperative bitch, quite frigid. He then made the forefinger in the hole gesture and assured me that my bride was far more of a woman. Now how would he have known that unless his cock had been sure? I thought to myself, well you mother-fucker, if you have fucked your daughter too, I hope you taught her how to do it good. Ha! She was good, but not good enough for the finest cocksman of Lanka. All I ask of a woman is that she service me well. I'm a lusty bugger. Do you know I once counted seven orgasms in a single night, from three women in succession? They simply can't stand my ferocity. I grind away inside them, like a pestle-wielder inside a mortar, until even the frigid ones finally scream in ecstasy.'

Your virility is also caused by your lack of imagination,

Hamy thought, for it is imagination that makes a man's mind soar, taking away his staying-power on its wings. Why do you have to brag at a time like this? Could it be to compensate for having to flee like a frightened hare?

'Foreplay is for the weak,' Prince Tikka continued. 'It is the act, the thrust, the sheer movement that counts.'

'You are rightly called *pie-karaya*, cocksman,' Kira mumbled.

'It certainly saved my life tonight,' Prince Tikka rejoined. 'For I left my exhausted bride to find another woman.'

Steering the boat across the speeding waters, Prince Tikka seemed to be in an unusually talkative mood, as if the defeat of this night somehow compelled him to prove himself in other ways.

'We'd all have been dead if I had remained, but I've been highly sexed since boyhood, when I first found delight in my cock through masturbation,' he asserted. 'As I grew older, I had my fill of women, but their only use was to service me sexually. Love, romance? Pah, I leave those to the weak. The only romance in life comes from power, the power of life and death, the power to rule, the power of a lusty man. I forced my way into that woman's home tonight, after my bride became so exhausted that she lay on the bed like a lump of turd. When I seized the other woman in her home, she pretended outrage, but I could tell from the way she finally lay back and spread her legs that she lusted for me. And when I dropped my pantaloons and entered her. Ah! What delight from a smooth, but firm, wet cunt that knew how to clutch. She actually knew the trick. She was approaching orgasm when you fellows came into the room to warn that devil's work was afoot. I couldn't don my pantaloons fast enough.' He paused, reflecting. 'The calls of the night-bird, did you hear them?'

'Yes, lord,' Kira assented. 'They seemed to come from the homes of our princes, noblemen and chiefs.'

'H'mm . . . a signal of some sort.' Prince Tikka scanned the dark outlines of the approaching river bank, then tightened his hold on the rudder. Water began to splash over the sides as he eased the craft towards the bank.

Prince Tikka's eyes sought the starry skies, seeking his planet, that of the scorpion. 'Hear me, god of my planet!' He cried. 'Hearken to me all ye gods of the Yakka people. Grant me vengeance against the murderous Arya who are aliens in this land and have no faith in you. Now that Kalu Sena is dead, give me his kingdom, give me all the kingdoms of Lanka so that I can bend them to your will and mine. I know this to be my destiny.'

He pounded his thigh with a clenched fist in sheer frustration. 'Why? Why? Why?' he cried into the darkness, then calmed as he answered his own question.

'I know why,' he declared quietly. 'My father, King Gonda of the *uda rata* kingdom, is old and dying. King Kalu Sena had no male progeny but his three nephews, the Princes Loku Sena, Mitta Sena and Podi Sena, would have been in the line of succession. All of them died tonight to open the way for me. I had planned to succeed to the throne by marriage; now destiny has shortened the chain.' He struck his breast with a clenched fist; his voice echoed across the water to the Arya on the farther river bank: 'The gods have chosen me, Prince Tikka, to be the first ever Great King of Lanka,' he cried. 'Any why not? I passed the Yakka survival test at the age of twelve. I learned how to handle weapons from the finest spearmen, sword and knife fighters. I learned jungle-lore from the keenest most daring Yakka hunters. I can stalk a deer, pin a running hare with an arrow, shoot with certainty at a sound, thrust a spear at a charging boar, battle a leopard at close quarters. I am the best and greatest Yakka. And I am alive tonight!'

Chapter 7

As I stared at the dark, rushing river, Prince Tikka's words seemed to echo and re-echo through the night air. We were indeed assassins and murderers. Was it hereditary in my case? Ignoring Pandu's return to the fort, I stared sightlessly into the darkness, recalling the tales my grandmother had told.

As her twin children grew older, the Princess Suppa Devi began entreating her husband Sinha to return to civilization for their sakes, so that they could enjoy their royal heritage. He had persistently refused, not only because he was, after all, a much-wanted bandit, but also because he enjoyed his freedom and the natural state of the jungle life he led.

So our grandmother fled the jungle hideout, taking the twins with her, sixteen years after Sinha had abducted her, leaving Sinha broken-hearted with his faithful companion Uday.

Uday had joined Sinha's bandit army when he was fourteen. He had liked his giant leader, respected him for his courage, strength and powers of leadership, and he had fallen in love with Sinha-Seevali the girl twin, the moment he set eyes on her. When she left, he began to brood, to think, to wonder whether he should take his life. Finally he decided to learn about the Buddha's doctrine. To his delight, he heard one day two years after Sinha's family had deserted him, that the Buddha was to preach at a nearby fortress.

The white sandalwood paste on his face an effective disguise, clad only in a *verti*, the single orange cloth of a *sadhu*, long, matted hair streaking untidily over his shoulders, Uday mingled with the crowd outside one of the Lala king's fortresses. In the past two years Sinha had extended his forays into the Lala kingdom like a maddened giant, as if he could allay the pain of his heart only through sheer ferocity and brutality. His principal targets had become the king's men, symbols of the door that had closed in on his happiness. Uday knew that the people, especially the nobles and the rich *vaishyas*, were demanding action, but the King of Lala was old and dying, lacking both energy and motive to rid the kingdom of this scourge. Uday had lived with Sinha during those years and had grown to love the giant. How much of this was compassion, how much admiration, he did not know. Whatever it was came from within him and had brought him today to listen to Gautama – called the Buddha, or Enlightened One by many, known as the Compassionate One by all.

Since he was disguised as a *sadhu*, Uday was permitted that morning to make his way to the front of the crowd pressing around the base of a *pipul* tree. Under its spreading branches, the Buddha sat cross-legged in the lotus pose. He was just over fifty, dressed in a single yellow robe covering one shoulder. His pale skin, tanned dark by exposure to the sun, bore not a single wrinkle. A radiant aura, a magnetic yet loving force, emanated from him. Beneath a completely shaven head, his face was broad, round and flat, with the Cathay cast of the Sakya clan of Nepali. Uday's attention was drawn irresistibly to eyes that were dark and penetrating, eyes that, while observing his very *atman*, were gentle as a doe's, peaceful as forest pools in the twilight.

'. . . I then sought the way of the mendicant, even that of the Jina created by our brother, Vardhamana,' the Buddha was saying in a mellow voice. He spoke each word evenly, without any accent at all, so that his speech sounded like the trickle of a small stream in which the kindness and compassion of his eyes were reflected like filtered sunlight. 'I sought the way of the river crossers. I reached the fifty-two levels of consciousness, the fifth stage of the yogi, and comprehended the eighty-four thousand rebirths of the pious

Gosala. Not in any of these, nor in the reaching for purity of my brother, Maha Vira, the Great Hero, nor in the gods of the Dasa and the Arya, nor in the Wise Lord, the one God, Ahura Mazda, of the prophet Zarathustra, did I find enlightenment.

'Finally, one full moon night, as I sat beneath a *pipul* tree in Saranath, meditating, having conquered all desire and craving, I perceived the four Noble Truths and the Noble Eightfold Path and was immediately wafted into the ultimate level of consciousness which is non-consciousness and enlightenment. Thus, having become a Buddha, did I escape from the chain of causation which is birth, life and death. Today, I am, because I am a Buddha, though I am not, because I no longer am.

'My dear ones, all living things are equal. King and beggar, *brahman, kshastriya* and *harijan*, man and woman, human and animal, insect, tree and rock are all equal links in the chain of causation.

'Birth makes no Brahman, nor non-Brahman makes
'Tis life and doing that mould the Brahman true
Their lives mould farmers, tradesmen, merchants, serfs;
Their lives mould robbers, soldiers, chaplains, kings.

'By birth is not one an outcast.
By birth is not one a Brahman,
By deeds is one an outcast
By deeds is one a Brahman.

'The lowliest among you can become a Buddha by understanding the four Noble Truths and following the Noble Eightfold Path. Thus alone will your *kharma*, causes, produce that volition at your final death moment that will have the *vipaka*, effect, of a better rebirth; and through successive such acts of volition you will finally be projected into enlightenment, either at death or during your lifetime. Buddhahood is open to each of you, my dear ones, so are you all equal.

'Remember all things are governed by *kharma/vipaka*, cause and effect. You will observe this immutable law every moment of your lives. The wind blows, the leaves fall. Seed is scattered on the ground, it grows if the causes are there, but it can only be the plant, the tree of its cause, the seed. Just as there will be no tree if you eliminate the seed, so if you eliminate the cause, desire, you will eliminate the effect, suffering. For desire causes the effect, craving, craving causes the effect, clinging and clinging the effect, suffering . . .'

Uday's fascination with the Buddha's words was interrupted by an intangible cross-fire that drew his gaze. His eyes met those of a hulk of a man, most of whose face was covered by a shawl. He knew those eyes. He would know them anywhere. They belonged to Jawum, an informer.

Suddenly he heard a commotion behind him. Murmurs arose from the crowd. Someone shouted, 'Make way there in the king's name.' The crowd began to part like earth before a plough.

The Buddha paused. Yet his eyes did not change direction or expression.

A group of soldiers clad in red pantaloons and white *shulwas*, led by a tall, haughty looking young captain with a fierce black moustache and square beard, broke into the open space between the front row of spectators and the Buddha.

'Pray forgive this intrusion, Lord,' the young captain requested in a commanding voice that sought no excuse for his conduct. 'But we have an important edict of our king and this gathering is an opportune time to reach many of his subjects. With your permission . . .'

The captain nodded peremptorily to a fat man clad in a white *dhoti* who sweated beside him and who now produced a scroll from his waist with an air of self-importance, opened it, cleared his throat and began reading in the high-pitched voice of a eunuch.

'For years now, our country has been ravaged by the bandit known as Sinha, the lion. He has grown stronger each day and in the last two years has become the scourge of Lala.

'We can destroy this man and his comrades by force of arms, but such is not the way of *manta yuddhaya*, the diplomatic war that enlightened Arya monarchs practise.

'In the golden years of our wisdom, we have come to realize that the stream must be dammed at its source, the spring. The bandit, Sinha, whom we have already proscribed, is that spring. So, to any *kshastriya* of noble birth who will bring us proof of the death of the bandit, Sinha, in the form of his head on a pole, we shall confer the highest honour of our realm. We are old and without any male progeny. Such a doughty warrior shall become our heir and shall receive in addition . . .'

Uday did not hear the recital of concubines, land, cattle and treasure that followed, for his eyes had become drawn to those of the Buddha. It seemed to him, for the first time that morning, that a direct, personal connection was established between the two of them, the non-man with a doctrine and the bandit with a search.

Suddenly Uday felt that this Buddha knew who he was and had love, compassion and a message for him. It brought him a moment of peace, tranquillity, upliftment such as he had never experienced before, as if he was soaring like a bird through a peaceful sky into a distant land.

Then the need for survival intruded. He tore himself from the Buddha's gaze, seeking Jawum. The man had vanished.

Uday edged away through the crowd, knowing that the perception of The Compassionate One followed him.

One day soon afterwards, seated on the ledge in front of the cave, Sinha told Uday a story he had carried locked in the recesses of his mind for years. It was a common one in those times. His father had been of royal blood, the *raja* of one of the kingdoms of Lala, descended from the lion clan of the original Arya. A usurper, named Palia, had led an armed group to seize the kingdom. Sinha had been only six years old when he saw his father tortured and butchered before his eyes, his mother raped and murdered, the palace, his home, gutted. He had escaped and run away. One last look at the blazing palace and he had sworn vengeance on the real enemies, the rich royalty who had done this foul deed. Then he sought refuge in the forest, where he had grown up, surviving as the animals did.

He started his campaign of vengeance when he was only fourteen, making a foray alone into Palia's territory. As he grew older and more successful, he attracted others from his old royal family to him, because the sub-kingdoms were frequently the victims of oppression. And so Sinha's group grew through the years into a little army of well-born men, all bound by a common bond, the desire for vengeance against oppressors and the *vaishya* who supported them.

The story left Uday with a sense of gloom that carried over to the next morning, although when Sinha rolled back the entrance slab of the cave Uday could see the promise of a beautiful sunny day outside. Sinha went for his usual plunge in the stream and Uday busied himself making *chupatti* for their morning meal. The feeling of gloom persisted, changing to an acute depression that cast a pall even over the bright cooking fire that sputtered between the three flat stones holding the cooking pot. The venison in the pot, a tough meat, had been simmering overnight, so that the odours of bay leaves, cloves, coriander and oregano clung fragrant to the air.

Uday placed the *chupatti* on one of the hot stones and walked to the entrance of the cave. The heat of the fire had flushed his face and was making him sweat. Sounds of daybreak, the crowing of jungle-cocks, rose above the twitter and chirp of birds. The sky above the treeline was a pale blue-rose colour, herald of a clear, bright day.

Why was he so depressed, he asked himself. Was it because Sinha's story had brought back memories of his own boyhood tragedy? Was it that Sinha's hidden grief over the loss of his new family had reminded him of his own loss, Sinha-Seevali? Was he sighing, like all men, for what he could not have?

'When we are strong enough to attack the Lala palace, then we shall continue the search for our loved ones,' Sinha said quietly, 'and bring them back home.' Two years later and the giant still longed for his family.

Uday returned to the fireplace and stirred the cooking pot. The ladle remained stationary in his hand when a voice reached him faintly through the cave's entrance.

'*Appa!*'

He stood still, as if turned to marble. For a moment his heart too was as cold, then gladness suddenly seized him. He knew that voice. And only Sinha-Bahu would call Sinha father.

Uday's heart began to beat with excitement. Perhaps the whole family had returned, Sinha-Seevali too. He shook his hands clean and wiped them thoroughly with a wet cloth, then turned and ran for the entrance, shot through the cleft in the rock and stood still. He should not intrude on the reunion between a man, a lonely, proud man, and his family. He stepped soundlessly along the ledge until he could pause at its edge, with a side view of the glade well below eye-level.

Such a beautiful drama. At the sound of his son's voice, Sinha had climbed down the cliff and stood stark naked at its edge. The sun, having just cleared the treetops, cast slanting rays on his magnificent body, turning it to ruddy granite, the fine red-gold hairs on the chest gleaming. A sudden ray trapped in the auburn locks made them flame. His shaggy beard and superb muscles, his arms outflung to greet his long-lost son, made Sinha seem a creation of the Lord Agni, the sun god.

Sinha-Bahu had emerged from the darkness of the jungle, but still stood in the dappled shadow of the spreading green branches of a tall *neem*. He had become a replica of his father, tall, big-boned, with the same splendid muscles. Only his hair was dark and his face a blur. Indeed, Sinha-Bahu is not whole, he is not real, Uday thought, merely his father's shadow, save that he is dressed in dark pantaloons and *shulwa*, a long sword at his side dangling from a broad leather belt, a bow in hand and an arrow at its string.

Father and son faced each other across the clearing, the leonine giant bathed in sunlight, glowing with delight, his son, a great tiger in the shadow, his body obscured, both indefinably linked by white-gold sunlight, the blue heavens above them, the green spread of branches bathing in the sun's rays, the haunting shadows of the jungle beyond. A light breeze swept through the gorge, bringing the scent of wild jasmine. Even the earth laughs at this meeting, Uday thought. Like an echo of his own delight, Sinha's joyous laughter rang through the air. 'My *beta*, boy, you have returned!' he shouted.

The bowstring twanged its own music. The arrow hissed. Uday glanced sharply in its direction, heard Sinha's laugh break off into a gurgle. Head jerked back, Sinha swayed on his feet, bewilderment on his face, an arrow at his throat. He made no attempt to pull it out.

The bowstring twanged again. A second arrow sped to its mark, this time in Sinha's chest. Once again, the giant merely jerked backwards at the impact, but he still made no attempt to advance or escape, his love-force for his son tangible as the sunshine.

The string twanged a third time. Uday came out of his stupor. He started running towards the path leading down the cliff but stopped on one of the rough steps, marvelling at the scene below.

Sinha had sprung sideways in a mighty leap, landing on his feet several yards away. With a swift gesture, he tore out the arrows that pierced his head and chest. Red blood gushed forth to stain the sunlight. His roar of rage stifled by his own blood, Sinha bounded across the clearing like a racing lion.

The bowstring twanged again. The arrow hissed and struck Sinha square in the chest. He wrenched it aside impatiently. His speed undiminished, he made for his son.

Sinha-Bahu cast aside his bow. His long sword gleamed and flashed as he stepped forward into the sunlight, feet well-spaced, weapon at the ready.

Sinha was almost on him now. Ten paces, five, arms reaching out, the fingers like claws, the great body driven by an indomitable force.

He is invincible, Uday thought. He will take his son with him.

Sinha staggered and paused, then forced himself upright, like a weight-lifter raising a huge rock. His legs seemed unable to support him. He took one more step forward, the powerful arms still reaching out. He trembled at the knees, his arms slowly dropped without volition. He stood a few moments, wobbling now like a drunken man, his son's sword only a hand span away from his heart.

Like a great tree crashing before the final blow of the woodsman's axe, Sinha fell at his son's feet.

It was several moments before Uday recovered from the shock of seeing Sinha-Bahu kill his own father in so cowardly a manner. Parricide was the most deadly sin of the Arya code, hideous, unforgivable.

When he finally recovered, a red haze of fury such as he had never known before blinded him. He shook with the urge to kill this despicable young parricide. Instinctively aware that he should only fight with a cool head, however, his grip on the step above him tightened while he paused to clear his brain, willing the mists of rage to dissipate.

Finally, he was ready to resume his descent. He glanced down at the glade. Sinha-Bahu was standing to a side of the dead body, his upraised sword held firmly in both hands. Uday started in horror as the great sword flashed through the sunlight. A dreadful thwack-crunch sounded across the clearing. Sinha's head jerked to life as it was severed from the body, only to fall back lifeless, grotesque as a separate entity.

The Lala king's edict flashed through Uday's brain. Sinha-Bahu would take the dead man's head back as proof that he had earned the reward. He watched the young man kneel and wipe his bloody weapon on the turf, imagining that he could see the bloodstains smearing the green grass. You kneel now to cleanse your sword, he thought, not to worship your great father, but how will you ever wipe the stain from your heart?

Secretly Uday followed the parricide son back to Lala. The people had never been told of Sinha-Bahu's relationship with the dead Sinha, and now they hailed the young man as a hero. A sackful of Sinha's hoarded treasures and another containing the severed head helped Sinha-Bahu claim the promised rewards, for the old king had just died and Sinha-Bahu was consecrated King of Lala. Meanwhile he was already married to his twin-sister, Sinha-Seevali, Uday's love.

When Uday finally managed to obtain an interview with the princess, he felt obliged to tell her the truth, that her husband had not killed her father in fair combat as he had claimed. Only then did Uday realize the hatred she had for her mother and her husband. She told him that she had been forced into the marriage by the Princess Suppa Devi, though it had been explained to the world that the union had been effected, as was customary whenever necessary, to keep the bloodline pure. In Uday's presence, the princess swore eternal vengeance on her husband.

Appalled at what he had done, guilt-ridden at having innocently unleashed evil, Uday journeyed to Bana-raj to become a disciple of the Buddha.

* * *

By the time I returned to the entrance gates of the fort the fighting had ended and relative calm reigned. Our men were pouring into the palace courtyard, sweat-strewn, bloodied, wounded. Swords in hand, the fires of battle still burned in their eyes, but they all seemed strangely subdued.

An occasional bellow of rage, a shouted command, followed by a scream of pain, told of some Yakka, braver than the rest, who had continued resistance only to be cut down. The aftermath of battle, however, remained, its anger, its heat. The unmistakable odour of new death suffocated the darkness, stifling the whimper of the brown pi-dog sniffing the face of a grizzled corpse, perhaps its former master. Strangely, the distant village slept on, ignorant of the momentous change that had taken place this night.

Prince Tikka's last defiant words kept ringing in my ears, causing my heart to tremble. Yes, we were indeed assassins and murderers who had stolen upon our victims at dead of night and executed them while they slept. Now that the danger and excitement were over, reaction was setting in and I became filled with a sense of loathing and revulsion. *Some* heroes, *some* princes, I thought savagely. I could not help feeling unclean as I walked between the hissing flares of the dark avenue towards the palace. Would even fire purge me of the evil of the night, or time ease its dishonour?

The shouting had almost completely died down, so the woman's shriek from a small cottage on the side street reached me loud and clear. 'No! No! I beg you, don't! Please spare her. She's a virgin.' The words were spoken in a dialect with which I was familiar.

I stopped abruptly, turned right and ran towards the cottage, burst in through the open doorway and paused. The small front room, sparsely furnished with settles, was lit by two tapers on sconces set in the whitewashed walls. It was empty.

A great thwack was followed by an agonized shriek, quickly cut into a strangulated gurgle. There came the thud of a body collapsing and a death rattle.

A deep, grainy voice, unmistakably Ujjeni's, exclaimed, 'Good, you've killed the bitch!'

A soft moan of grief filtered through the half-open door of the bedroom.

Drawing my sword, I plunged inside the room, but was brought up short, sickened by what I beheld. In the yellow taper-light, flickering at my entrance, a tall, bearded Arya, I could not place his name, was wiping his bloody sword on the cushion of a pallet bed at the far side of the room. A plump, grey-haired woman lay untidily, face upwards, on the dark, dung floor in front of the bed. Her white robe was red with blood from a great sword slash, gaping like an obscene mouth across her neck. The larynx showed white tendons, pulsed with the reflex of death. Her head was askew, the sightless eyes staring. A young girl, dressed in blue, knelt beside her corpse, reaching slender hands, trembling with horror, towards it. Ujjeni stood to one side, his lustful gaze intent on the girl. I could tell that his blood was up from the violence and killing. All three people held their positions in a gruesome tableau at my entrance.

The girl looked at me with fresh terror in her large, dark eyes. I noticed her face, poised on a long, slender, swan-like neck, with the strangest sense of shock. Framed by long, wavy black hair, it was a perfect oval, the skin wondrously fair but lightly tinctured beneath with a hint of pink frangipani petal. The eyes were almond-shaped and of such a dark brown that they were almost black. Her bones were small and delicate, the dilated nostrils thin and fine, the mouth a perfect bow, red as the pomegranate. I knew this face, whether it was the product of my dreams of beauty or some memory of a past birth. My heart started to pound and the blood rushed to my ears. At that moment, I knew that I, the celibate priest, had fallen in love.

She must have sensed my interest and mistaken its intent. A soft cry escaped her slender white throat, tearing at my heartstrings. But I had no time for introspection, for both men had turned at the interruption. Anger and hatred flamed in Ujjeni's sunken eyes when he recognized me, to be met by a rage such as I had never felt before. 'Is this one of the enemy houses Princess Kuveni showed you?' I demanded hotly.

'N . . . no!' The Arya replied, hesitant, glancing at his chief. Ujjeni merely continued to glare at me.

'Then what are you doing here?' I demanded. 'I heard this poor woman cry for mercy and now you have killed her.' I pointed at the corpse with my sword.

'She stood in the way.' Ujjeni replied, his hand tightening on his drawn sword. 'But we owe you no explanations, Prince.'

I prepared for his attack, but, thinking swiftly, decided to keep him talking instead. 'In the way of what?'

'The spoils!' Ujjeni retorted, jerking his head towards the girl. 'To the victors belong the spoils . . . that's an old Arya saying, a *warrior's* saying.' His implication was obvious, that a priest would not know.

'All those sayings vanished tonight before the decree of my brother, Prince Vijaya,' I declared. 'Henceforth, women are inviolate in this kingdom.'

'You'll have to enforce it,' Ujjeni grated. His swordpoint came up, circling. I took a quick glance at his comrade. The man was hanging back, intimidated as I had intended by my reminder that our leader was my brother.

Focussing my attention on Ujjeni, I came on guard. 'So be it, but remember you are accountable.'

Ujjeni drew a deep breath. Some of the madness left his gaze but his eyes held mine. 'We are Prince Vijaya's loyal, devoted servants,' he ground out.

'Then obey his edicts.' I chose that last word deliberately and bared my teeth in a smile that I could not force into my eyes. 'You have just committed murder.'

The swordpoint wavered slightly. 'Not so,' Ujjeni retorted

firmly. He was obviously thinking now. 'The Yakka bitch was executed by Puri for refusing to give us information as to where Prince Tikka is hiding.'

The girl sprang to her feet. 'That's a filthy lie,' she cried, her pleading eyes on mine. She seemed to have developed some confidence in me. 'They never asked where the prince was. They simply smashed into the house then came for me. Loki tried to stop them and they killed her, the foul fiends.' She looked defiantly at Ujjeni.

He started towards her. 'Filthy Yakka bitch, how dare you contradict me . . .'

She stood her ground, unafraid. 'It's the truth that contradicts you.' She straightened to her full height, slim, tall, filled with the courage of desperation. 'Go on, kill me! Prove you are indeed murderers.'

Ujjeni paused. 'Filthy Yakka bitch!' he repeated, but this time the words were a substitute for action.

'I'm no Yakka. I'm a Dasa Chola and proud of it.'

Her desperate courage had a calming effect on us. Ujjeni was clearly confounded and I decided to divert his attention. 'What is a Dasa maiden doing in a Yakka fortress?' I enquired, dropping my swordpoint.

'My father is a goldsmith. We live not far from here. Loki and Ranna helped sell his wares. Loki has been like a mother to me since my own *amma* died five years ago, so my father sent me here to comfort Loki when Ranna died of the chest disease last week.'

'Filthy low-caste Dasa whore!' Ujjeni hissed, wanting to wound with words now.

'Not by birth is the Brahman made, but by words and deeds.' I was quoting the Buddha and Ujjeni knew it.

'Blasphemy!' he yelled at me. 'The gods dictate caste and perpetuate it.'

'Not so,' I rejoined swiftly. 'The gods may dictate our births, but they expect nobility in our lives, especially from the Arya, the noble ones.' I noticed the girl's eyes straying to

Loki's corpse, the grief suddenly returning to her, heart-rending. 'How ignoble of us to discuss philosophy when this lady needs to be alone with her dead and her grief.'

I was rewarded by a grateful glance. 'You need not be afraid any longer,' I reassured her. 'Prince Tikka escaped down the river in a raft.' I jerked my head at Ujjeni and Puri. 'Prince Vijaya will need his commanders to assemble outside the palace. What's done here can't be undone. I shall report the incident to the prince as being caused by a misunderstanding. Why don't you both leave now, I shall join you as soon as I have made suitable arrangements for this young lady's safety.' I was suddenly consumed with an urgency to be alone with her.

Ujjeni hesitated for a moment but I felt that this was only a show of independence. 'If our leader needs me, I shall go to him.' He sheathed his sword and looked the girl straight in the eye. 'I'll see you again, low-caste bitch,' he promised softly. He turned to fasten me with a deadly gaze. I did not need words to receive the silent promise of revenge. The light caught the sheath guard of his sword with the sharpness of a single, muted thunder-clap. He stalked out of the room, gaunt, hump-backed, followed by Puri with his fresh-blooded sword.

'You have made a bad enemy,' the girl said gently, fixing me with large dark eyes which had turned softer now. 'You rescued me from death, Prince, or from a fate far worse . . . I thank you.' Tears straying down her fair cheeks, she made deep obeisance to me, rose, seized my hand and kissed it.

My breath caught and my throat started to ache. 'My name is Sundari,' she continued. 'I'm indeed of lowly caste and never thought that I would be saved one day by a high-born prince. You are of the Arya, the noble ones? I'm not surprised.'

Conscience smote me. 'I'm Prince Lala Sinha-Bahu, from Sinha-Pura on the continent,' I responded. 'My brother and I with several hundred comrades were washed ashore by the storm last night. We are conquerors of your kingdom tonight, but I'm afraid we did not do so with nobility. Nevertheless the fighting is over now. I shall go and find someone to look after you.'

I bowed, turned on my heel and left. I had barely entered the front room when I heard Sundari's heart-rending cry. 'Oh, Loki, Loki, my *amma*,' followed by uncontrollable sobbing.

Tears stung my eyes as I left the cottage. In the semi-darkness outside, I paused to touch the wetness of my hand, which Sundari's own tears seemed to have cleansed of the blood of those Yakkas whose only crime had been that they stood in the way. I paused alone there, under the stars, for many minutes, thinking about what had happened to me, feeling a fierce urge to protect Sundari. The figures of our men moving about the avenue, their calls to one another, the barking of a dog, the smell of stale garbage wafting from the moat, faded into the background. I did not know whether to be elated or worried about what had happened to me. It was an impossible love. Nothing could come of it. Sundari was grateful but had shown no response. I shrugged and moved towards the palace.

By good fortune, in the main avenue I came across Bala, a silver-haired widower not given to molesting women. He was an aide to Vijit, the only one of the seven commanders whom I really trusted. I explained the situation to him and he readily agreed to escort Sundari to the village and guard her with his life, if need be, so long as I set his absence right with his chief.

Bala and I returned immediately to the cottage. I called aloud to Sundari before we entered. She came into the front room, tall, almost stately, in her blue skirt, the blouse stained with Loki's blood. To my surprise, she carried a bag in her hand. She looked remarkably composed, as if she had made up her mind to accept her loss, her eyes alone speaking of grief under control. A tremendous surge of respect and admiration for her character swept through me.

She paused in front of me, greeted Bala with a swift appraisal from beneath lowered lids and smiled wanly. 'You see how completely I trust you,' she stated simply.

'My comrade, Bala, is completely trustworthy,' I assured her. 'He will conduct you to the house of the Princess Kuveni in the village. It will be safer for you than remaining alone in the fort. I'm sure the princess will agree to your spending the rest of the night there. I shall see you returned safely to your father with an escort tomorrow. In the morning, Loki will be buried by Yakka ritual with the other Yakka dead. You have my word on it.'

She reflected a moment, then seemed to make up her mind. 'We heard of your arrival shortly after you landed. Loki told me that King Kalu Sena had planned to massacre you all in good time, so don't feel bad about your actions.' She paused, eyes still lowered. 'I pray you will forgive a commoner for talking thus to a prince.'

'On the contrary, I am honoured by your concern. Yet the ignoble intentions of others do not justify similar action on our part, so our guilt must remain. It is for us to make the future right and just for all who dwell in this kingdom for the very reason that the new rule was born of betrayal, stealth and murder.'

I felt Bala tense at my words, but Sundari's eyes grew luminous and I sensed feeling for me, but only for an instant and I could have been mistaken, for her gaze was immediately downcast, lowly, proper. 'You'll not see Loki again.' I softly advised her. 'But remember that what bound you to each other was love and that love will always be with you.' I could have added that my own love too would be with her, but it seemed inappropriate.

'We must leave,' I directed and, turning to the door, led the way to the avenue. Vijit emerged from the opposite side street, leading a host of his bloody, sweat-streaked men. I explained the situation to him, taking care not to expose Ujjeni's guilt, wondering whether this omission might not be a mistake. A decent man, Vijit readily agreed to releasing Bala for the night.

Returning the salutes of the men we passed, but ignoring their curious glances, I escorted Sundari and Bala to the fortress gates and bid Sundari farewell with the hands together greeting. She made obeisance again, never once looking at me. I watched the two disappear into the night, hoping that Sundari would give me even a single backward glance. In vain. Her figure was soon enveloped in the gloom.

As I turned away from the fortress gates, I saw my brother's massive figure emerge through the open doors of the palace followed by a group of men and hastened towards him. He paused when I reached him. His leonine face was set and tight, but the tawny eyes sparkled. The wound on his chest was a dark crescent of congealed blood in the flare-light.

'I'm afraid Prince Tikka got away,' I advised him.

His smile was grim. 'He and I will meet again some day,' was his response. I wondered at it because my brother was not given to intuition or prediction. 'But you, Prince Lala, what is this I hear about your giving aid and comfort to the enemy?'

For an instant, I was perplexed, then the truth dawned on me. Ujjeni had obviously given him a false report about the incident involving Loki and Sundari. A pity I could not have got to my brother first. 'What have you heard?' I enquired.

'That you prevented Ujjeni from obtaining information as to Prince Tikka's whereabouts from a Yakka woman.'

I knew then that I had a ruthless enemy in Ujjeni, one who would not hesitate to lie for his own ends, but I was not disposed to tattle on him. 'Ujjeni was mistaken,' I responded. 'If the Yakka woman did have information, which I doubt, it was Ujjeni's comrade who with a hasty swordthrust prevented us from obtaining it. He had already killed the woman by the time I got to the scene.'

'I see.' He paused. 'That is not exactly as I understood it, but no matter. What is one more death tonight? Law and order will commence tomorrow. And what about the low-caste Dasa girl whom you snatched from Ujjeni? I thought you were a priest by profession and a celibate by choice.'

He was being flippant, happy in victory, but I could not believe my ears. 'Snatched from Ujjeni, Prince?' I enquired incredulously. 'She is not a chattel to be snatched. By your own decree tonight, you gave women a safe place in this kingdom. She is therefore on her way, under escort, to where she will spend the night.'

'Oh!' His shaggy eyebrows lifted in surprise. 'Where have you sent her?'

'To the village with Vijit's aide, Bala, to spend the night in safety until I can have her escorted back to her father tomorrow. As for the dead woman, Loki, I expect to give her a decent burial tomorrow with the other Yakka dead.'

'Yes, that's important.' Some of the battle tension was now leaving his face. 'Having conquered the kingdom by violence, we must ensure the continuance of its subjects' customs and traditions until . . .' He stopped abruptly.

'Wisely spoken,' I stated, remembering our conversation earlier that evening. Had it been such a short while ago?

'We now have a kingdom,' my brother observed softly. 'A few hours ago, we were homeless vagrants cast on a foreign shore by a storm. Tonight, we have found a haven.' His voice changed abruptly. 'See that it remains so, Prince,' he directed me. 'I am your twin and can sometimes perceive your thoughts, though it is you who is usually the more sensitive. There's something different in you at this moment. What it is, I cannot say. You are a priest and should not take a woman. If ever you do, let it be by marriage to an Arya princess or some princess of royal blood, to strengthen this kingdom of Thamba-Panni.' He paused, knowing my thoughts. 'Follow my example. I plighted my troth to the

Princess Kuveni because she is of royal estate and could deliver me a kingdom. That is right and proper. You had best cast aside your desires, lustful or proper!'

'I want to be frank with you, Prince,' I replied. 'I believe that all races, all people, are equal. Nations or individuals may conquer and rule, but all pass away. A few hours ago, you asked me to be the voice of your idealism and your principles. Permit me to make my first suggestion. Please cast aside prejudice and any ideas about the superiority of any individual or master race. In your kingdom of Thamba-Panni, let life and our actions throw up true leadership. You have it in you, because you are a born leader, destined to rule. You need no crutches of race, rank or caste any more than our grandfather, Sinha, did when he made himself lord of the Lala jungles.'

He eyed me thoughtfully for a few moments, then seemed to make up his mind. 'I'll consider that,' he said. 'Meanwhile, don't even think of taking this alien woman as a concubine. If she belongs to anyone, it should be to Ujjeni.'

'No, Prince,' I retorted. 'She belongs to no one but to God.' I took his sudden anger at my reference to the One God with calm eyes, but was secure in the power of my God within me. 'I shall never even consider taking any woman who does not desire me.' Then prudence intervened, so I did not add the words that welled up within my mind, that I loved Sundari and would never forget her. However, some measure of courage made me add, very quietly, 'Let me assure you, though, that she will never belong to anyone against her will while I'm around.'

Only when I saw pain flicker across his tawny eyes did I realize that, having felt the total force of my love for him all these years, he must know, as my twin, when some part of that love-force was diverted elsewhere. And it hurt him. Abruptly he side-stepped me and moved towards a group of men approaching. I turned to see the commanders. They lined up around him, awaiting orders.

'Let there be an end to the killing,' Prince Vijaya directed. 'Ujjeni, your company shall man the walls, secure the fort against counter-attack and take over the village. Pandu, have your company mop up inside the fort. Uraw, your men shall tend the wounded and move the dead in wagons to the clearing, where we shall have them all cremated or buried according to their rites tomorrow. By the way, you will find two more dead on the bund of the pond we passed on the way here tonight. Vijit, your company shall camp in the compound of the princess, to guard it tonight and get some rest. The remaining three companies shall sleep in the fort for one watch then relieve the other three. Prince Lala and I shall spend what's left of the night in the compound, where we can be reached by runner.'

In moments, the commanders were barking their orders to their men. Prince Vijaya surveyed the commencement of the operation and awaited the assembly of Vijit's men. He then strode towards the entrance, beckoning me to follow. I hastened to catch up with him.

'Why aren't we sleeping in the fort?' I enquired.

His smile was whimsical. 'The Princess Kuveni has prepared a splendid tent for me at her residence. It would be churlish of me not to use it.' The tawny eyes twinkled.

While my brother proceeded to his splendid tent, I sought my mat and cushion in the nearby barn that was to serve as a temporary barracks. Tired though I was, my mind was white and bright, so many thoughts racing through it. Pity and horror at the slaughter, home so far away, all that lay ahead, but mostly the longing to see Sundari again. I simply could not believe that I, who had never loved a girl before, could feel so strongly for one in an instant. Linked with wonder at the working of destiny was concern, even apprehension at its hopelessness. Sundari and I were far removed from each other by birth, rank, race, caste, religion. And yet, my feelings were so strong that I believed none of this would matter if love bridged the two spirits.

103

Here began my real problem. Sundari had treated me only with gratitude and respect. I tried hard to read something into the glance she had given me during that instant on an instant, to find something in her voice, the feel of her, but I knew that I was merely projecting my wishes. Why, she might even be betrothed to someone else, though she could not be married if she was a virgin.

After a while, the temptation to see her at once grew strong, imperative. She was just a few yards away in the house. I thought of a dozen excuses, but I knew I would not get closer to where she slept than the entrance to her house. Finally, I gave up speculation and basked in the state of being in love. My imagination soared as I conceived a dozen sweet situations in which we declared our love for each other. Then I fell into sleep and had beautiful dreams of her.

Chapter 8

A bitter grin streaked across Prince Tikka's face in the darkness. 'You see, Hamy, it pays to stray from the nuptial bed!' He exclaimed. 'I hope you're glad now that I buffeted you for trying to prevent it.'

Hamy made no comment. What was there to say? Prince Tikka's statement was the truth. As frequently happened, however, the prince had drawn from that truth a general conclusion that suited himself. No one cared about the truth and honesty that Hamy had learned of during a visit to the Buddha temple at Kalyani-ja. In the Yakka world, there was neither reward nor praise for honesty. You were honest only if it were possible, or necessary for survival. There were the gods and there was self. Even the gods were those needed for self: the gods of trees and animals, the river, the wind, the sun and the rain, the planets and stars, the demon gods, or *yakseyas*, who dominated the lives of the tribes. Survival was a balancing act, like a man on a toddy-tapper's rope between two palm trees, placating the good gods, appeasing the demon gods, setting off one against the other.

Making no comment, Hamy busied himself with using the oar to brake the boat as it approached the pale, running scar of the bank beneath the treeline. Safe at last. The wash of water was music to his ears. His relief found expression in a loud belch. It brought back the sick taste of the *ra*, palm liquor, combined with wild pig-meat and bee's honey. He hawked and spat into the sand against which the boat now scraped, rocked and came to a standstill. Hamy leapt ashore, grabbed the side of the vessel and held it fast for Prince Tikka to disembark. The Prince placed a swift kick on Kira's pudgy rear, nearly catapulting the man into the river, then jumped on to the narrow beach, agile as a deer. With a groan, Kira clambered ashore.

Hamy glanced up at Prince Tikka. The young man stood erect, tall, lean and supple in the dark, seemingly completely recovered. 'What shall we do with the boat?' Hamy enquired.

'We have no further need of it. Let it go.'

Boats were as valuable as wagons. Such waste went against Hamy's grain, but he knew better than to argue, or disobey orders. He let go his hold. The boat seemed to waver, as if undecided. Then it began slowly drifting away. Where would it end? In the ocean? On the reefs? Our lives will be drifting too from now on, Hamy reflected sadly; only the darkness of uncertainty, the unknown river of life and the ocean of death lie ahead.

As if to confirm his conclusions, Prince Tikka's voice slashed through the semi-darkness. 'These white invaders number only seven hundred. Yet they are trained soldiers and we will not overcome them by direct assault, but by hunting them piecemeal, unless Yakka and Naga, Dasa and even our local Arya join in exterminating them. The gods saved the three of us from the massacre so that we can wreak vengeance and become the saviours of our people.'

Hamy thought: You say 'the three of us' and 'we', but you only mean yourself. You regard this as an opportunity to achieve your ambitions sooner.

Torn by conflicting emotions, the Princess Kuveni paced her small, windowless bedroom, staring at the smoky flame from *kekuna* nut kernels on a sconced skewer. She had readily agreed to give Sundari, whom she knew, refuge in her house.

Up to this point, all her decisions and actions had seemed quite clear, flowing naturally. She had told herself that she was merely the instrument of the demon-god's vengeance and his command that she offer the prince a crown. Her feelings for the prince were obviously part of the god's

106

dictates. By carrying out these orders faithfully, she had also wreaked her own vengeance on her father, her family and her peers and had hopes of becoming the prince's consort.

Why then was she now troubled? Why were unfamiliar feelings of guilt, remorse and doubt floating through the certainty she had known before, like the vague dark clouds of a forgotten dream? Such feelings were foreign to her. She needed help to justify them, or overcome them.

The three things she knew with certainty at this moment were that she did not regard her father's death as any great tragedy, that it opened a great future for her, and that she lusted for prince Vijaya. What a magnificent body he had, towering over even the men of his own race, what glorious colouring, how exciting that mass of red hair! As for those tawny eyes with the black points that seemed to penetrate her being . . . penetrate . . . she felt her pubis quiver at the thought of his man thing entering her.

Abruptly, she opened her wooden box, picked up a pale blue silken shawl that had come from a ship destroyed in a storm the previous year, its entire crew killed. She drew the shawl round her shoulders, the material cool against her skin. Strange, she thought, for my body is fevered and I am covering my breasts to go to a man for whom I shall presently be removing all my clothes.

The men in the compound and her attendants were all fast asleep when she stole out of her abode. Only the dark shapes of sentries at the gate and patrolling the boundaries of her property spoke of men awake. The air was almost cold outside and the night lay pale below brilliant starlight. She started at the squeak of a mouse. She did not fear jungle animals, but she feared mice! She could smell its musty odour above the fragrance of the sandalwood scent she wore, the finest, from Kasi, one of the sixteen kingdoms of the continent.

Her heart thudding against her ribs, her breathing expectant with desire, she stole down the pathway and cut

107

across the sandy garden, between the wild jasmine shrubs, towards the glow beneath the spreading tamarind tree that was the entrance to the tent. She moved so quietly, she was not observed; this pleased her for after all she was the product of generations of superb jungle hunters.

The prince had not extinguished the taper inside his tent and she wondered at that as she paused awhile in the darkness outside. When she entered she saw him standing at its far end, a gigantic figure completely stripped except for his black loincloth. He showed no surprise at seeing her, merely stood still, looking. She paused, her gaze drawn irresistibly to him, her breath catching at the naked desire in his eyes. He exuded a magnetism, a sheer lust, that drew a body response from her as if she was a jungle animal in heat.

Moments passed while they stood looking at each other. Her breath began to catch, her nostrils distending, her body clamouring for the feel of him. Her heart thudded when he moved, coming slowly towards her, his feet soundless on the Pahlava rugs. She took in the tremendous muscles of his chest, the flat stomach, the bulging biceps, the massive thighs, before her gaze fixed itself at the centre of his loincloth. His maleness thrust hard against it in a great erection.

Then he was by her, holding her so close to him that she could barely breathe. Swept by the intensity of his desire, she pressed her pubis against him, circling with her hips to madden him. A groan escaped him. He began kissing her face, her neck. Suddenly, unable to contain himself, he tore aside her shawl and flung it to the ground. He reached a great hand for her cloth and almost ripped it off her waist. He lifted her off the ground and flung her on the gold velvet cushions of the great bed. He grabbed his loincloth, but she placed a soft hand on his. He looked at her, surprised. She gently undid the cloth. His maleness, released from its confines, was a thing of wonder, for she had never seen anything of that colour or size before.

She had no time even to think, however, for he was upon her in a trice. The weight of him flattened her breasts, crushed her body gloriously. All the pent-up desires of weeks must have found their outlet, for he raised his buttocks to make immediate entry. And she was eager to receive him, in spite of the pain that awaited her.

Suddenly he paused. The blazing desire left his eyes, to be replaced by pain, some unspoken pain. He rose abruptly from the bed and stood looking down at her, the tawny eyes roaming from her face to her generous, pouting breasts, the black nipples hard with desire, to the slim waist, the full buttocks and plump legs. His eyes finally rested on the short, downy black hair of her pubis. He remained, looking. The expression on his face changed. Abruptly he turned and left the tent.

She could have screamed with disappointment. What manner of man was this? Did not Arya know how to make love? A sniff escaped her and tears welled up in her eyes. Glancing sideways, she saw him re-enter the tent. He walked slowly to her, hands behind his back, his expression luminous. He gazed at her awhile, seeming to drink in her beauty, then slowly brought his right hand forward. It held a jasmine flower, incongruous in those large fingers. A small, scented white jasmin, its petals half-open. She did not know what he intended with it, but was caught up in some magic of his feelings.

Slowly, he laid the flower above her cleft. She had never known that such things existed. When a Yakka desired to couple with a woman who was not his, he would make the sign, the thumb and forefinger of his left hand forming a circle, the forefinger of his right hand poking in and out of it. She herself was somehow revolted by the gesture, but a woman would not mind if she desired it too, for she would then rise and make her way into the jungle as if she intended to relieve herself. The man would join her by another route and find her lying on her back in a little cave of vegetation with leaves for a bed. The woman would raise her cloth, then her legs and the man would grasp her breasts as if they were the ears of a mule, plunge inside her and ride away until his juices ran out, the closest to tenderness being kisses of indrawn breaths rained on the woman's cheeks. She knew all this from gossiping with her attendants. Now this Prince had placed a wild flower on the object of his desiring. Strange emotions that she could not identify rose within her, brought tears to her eyes, for people offered flowers only at their shrines.

Prince Vijaya responded by lying down beside her. The hardness of his body now filled her with dazed ecstasy. He began adoring her with his fingers, his mouth. She had never dreamed of such love-making. Her being was soon afire, pulsing, throbbing, trembling. She desired all he gave, but soon it was all too much. She could feel herself vibrating towards the familiar climax, only this time it would come from deep within her, unlike anything she had known before. Surely he could see that she was dazed, could bear his caresses no more. He entered her with a wondrous tenderness and she gladly gave him the virginity she had once thought to hold exclusively for her planet and her god.

I was asleep on the rough mat in the barn closest to the tent when I was shaken awake.

My first conscious thought, perhaps from my dreaming, was of Sundari. I opened my eyes, foolishly expecting to see her. Instead, I saw my brother's leonine face, the red beard combed. He had obviously bathed too, smelt of sandalwood and looked surprisingly fresh. Yet he was a reminder of last night and brought me the sick taste of killing.

I wish I could say that I was alert and leapt to my feet on the instant. On the contrary, I looked at him crossly, with bleary eyes, for he had interrupted my dream. Besides his spruce appearance was a distinct affront to lesser mortals who need their sleep. 'What do you want?' I enquired grumpily. Few things can convey resentment more than a sleep-coated voice and I'd be hanged before I gave him a civil greeting.

'Arya traditions in our court,' was his astonishing reply. His smile, through the groomed beard, belied any hint of levity. 'My spouse has returned to her cottage and I'm ready for work. There's much to be done.'

I knew he was referring to the schedule of Arya kings which demands waking with the birds but decided to evade the issue.

'What court?'

'My court. The court of the kingdom of Thamba-Panni.'

'You're mad.' I turned on my side and tried to make myself more comfortable, a difficult process on a hard dung floor and a rough mat and I in no mood to practise mind-control.

I felt a sharp prick on my neck and jerked my head sideways, my eyes popping open. The steel blade of a drawn sword met my astonished gaze. My eyes shifted to my brother's face.

'I told you last night that this kingdom could do with some law, order and discipline,' he declared pleasantly. 'It's going to start at the top. First, there's me. Then, there's you. We're all going to practise the schedules of the Arya courts with immediate effect. Since I took over the kingdom last night, immediate effect means this morning.'

'I took over the kingdom,' he had said. I could have told him that he could not have done so without some slight outside help, but this did not seem an opportune moment for such niceties. I therefore started scrambling to my feet, whereupon he withdrew his sword and sheathed it. I knew he would have used it if I had disobeyed him.

'If you were in such a hurry, why didn't you start immediately after our . . . er . . . victory last night?' I demanded, still surly.

'I did. I organized our immediate territory against any

111

counter-attack, rendered excellent service to the princess who opened the kingdom to us, thereby commencing to fulfil my pledge to her. I stayed awake and worked hard in the interests of my sleeping followers.' He grinned. 'A noble example that would have rendered a lesser mortal immobile. But then . . .' he paused and gave that false sigh I knew so well, 'kings are not mortals really, but gods who have entered the earth.'

'You certainly seem to have made a triumphant entry last night,' I grunted. But I did not feel as flippant as my words implied, because his own had sent a chill of dread through me. It had taken but two assaults, one on a sleeping people, the other on a recumbent princess, to give birth to the god king idea in my brother's mind. He and I were so different from each other in this respect. And yet, were we? For we were one in the intensity of our beliefs, a dangerous state, I recognized, if ever there was cause for conflict between us.

'Have the commanders rouse the men to assemble in the courtyard of the fort within the hour,' Prince Vijaya threw over his shoulder as he strode out of the building. 'They can eat after receiving their orders.' He paused in his stride. 'You can take time off and some of the men to have that young woman escorted back to her home in one of the wagons we now own.'

I bathed quickly at the well behind the Princess Kuveni's house, hoping for even a glimpse of Sundari. She did not appear. I rather suspected that the women of the house were up and about much before dawn and cursed myself for not waking earlier.

By the time the seven commanders assembled in the palace courtyard, dawn had just broken and lay grey upon air of the limpid coolness that heralds a warm day. To my surprise, Ujjeni greeted me with the friendliest of grins.

The fort had been cleared of the dead. They were laid out in grisly piles in the open space opposite the fortress gates, circled by cawing black crows. Only red bloodstains on the

112

flagstones and the lingering stench of death told of their past existence. Our men were going about their duties, or patrolling the walls, or performing their ablutions by the river, as if they had been here all their lives.

Prince Vijaya stated his object clearly and succinctly: to hold the kingdom he had seized. The means were simple: to consolidate and strengthen the defence of the fort, to establish control over the Yakka people of the entire kingdom. It was when he came to the method of achieving his object that I discovered how deeply he had been thinking. 'We shall enlist the entire Yakka population of the region,' he declared. 'Firstly, to ensure our security and secondly in order to promote agriculture. The Yakka people of the villages surrounding the fort will be organized immediately into labour details. The first detail will divert the waters of the river into the barrier ditches of the fort, creating a moat to give the fort water defences on all sides. The second will build parapets and sentry towers on the walls, converting them into ramparts. The third will gather and store food in the fort, against siege. The fourth will perform cooking, hauling and other tasks for our men.

'All available horses in the region will be commandeered to form the first Arya cavalry and chariot units in Lanka, under Vijit, our cavalry expert. Although all our men are *kshastriyas* of noble birth, with no desire perhaps to perform the duties of lowly castes, they will supervise all this work, using the knowledge they have gained from observing these operations in our homeland, combined with their brains and imaginations.

'As our Arya ancestors used cavalry and chariots to seize and subdue an entire continent, so shall we use them, on a much more modest scale, to control this island,' Prince Vijaya concluded.

I must confess to being amazed at my brother's vision, not the least because I had never dreamed that he had been thinking on these lines. I had observed his powers of leadership in wrongdoing. He was now demonstrating these powers more positively for good, so why should I be surprised? Elated though I was, one sickening question disquieted me. The Yakka people were being harnessed into labour. Would they end our slaves?

Chapter 9

Was my own love life to be as futile as Uday's had been?

Hungry though I was, I decided to do without breakfast in order to use the time to visit Sundari and arrange to have her safely returned to her father without delay, not the least because I feared Ujjeni's intentions. I therefore drew Vijit aside and obtained his permission to use Bala once more for the assignment. Vijit's whimsical smile told me that he knew I had more than a casual interest in this girl and sympathized with me. I also commissioned a small wagon belonging to the palace with a white-haired Yakka driver to be at the Princess Kuveni's house shortly.

The track leading to the village was alive with our Arya, mostly tall, bearded men, bare-chested, with muscular bodies and sharp eyes, smiling as they saluted me, returning from the lake bund where they had performed their ablutions. In the dappled morning sunshine beneath the tall trees, they looked rested and more relaxed than I had ever seen them. If they felt any remorse at last night's massacre, they certainly did not show it.

As I came to the stile, two clean-shaven Arya section leaders emerged, leading a detail that carried a large, improvised stretcher covered with brown blankets. 'We found the two dead Yakka on the bund, Prince,' one of the commanders explained. 'As Prince Vijaya commanded, I'm taking them to the fort to be buried with the rest of the Yakka dead.'

'Good,' I replied and hurried on, trying not to think.

The scent of baking *chupatti* and frying boar flesh from the field kitchens we had set up the previous afternoon assailed my nostrils and caused the pangs of hunger to sharpen within me even before I reached the entrance to the Princess Kuveni's compound, moved by the pangs of love! Some of our men had already started filing past the ovens where the cook detail were serving them breakfast on green banana leaves. Others were gathered round the clay pitchers that had been placed at intervals, ladling fresh water into their goblets. We would not be dependent on the Princess Kuveni for food any longer, because we had discovered large quantities in King Kalu Sena's warehouses, some of it stored for the hundreds of wedding guests at the nuptial celebrations. I had already ordered an inventory to be taken and had sent out hunting and foraging parties with instructions to take details of food and materials commandeered from the local population, so that compensation could be paid. There was to be no plundering, nor any appropriation that would leave the owner depleted. These were necessary measures until we could establish a proper system of government, tithes, taxes and the feudal duties of subjects to their ruler and the ruler to his subjects.

A couple of the Arya who were standing close by looked curiously at me as I entered the compound. To my surprise, one of them was the bearded Puri. What was he doing here, I wondered as I returned the men's greeting and passed on. I knocked on the wooden entrance door and, while waiting for a reply, turned casually to look in their direction again. Some of the men had begun walking away, but Puri remained watching. A cold thrill of apprehension ran through me. He had obviously been detailed by Ujjeni to keep an eye on Sundari. Why?

Before I could even begin to think of an answer, the front door opened, letting out a whiff of warm, closed up air. A thin, gaunt woman of middle age and serious countenance, clad in a dark blue skirt and bodice stood before me.

'I'm Prince Lala Sinha Bahu, brother of Prince Vijaya,' I introduced myself.

The woman made obeisance, then stood erect. 'My name

is Rupa,' she declared softly. 'I'm the Princess Kuveni's hand-maiden. What can I do for you, Prince?'

'With the permission of your mistress, I'd like to talk to the young lady, Sundari. I'm making arrangements to send her back to her father.'

'My mistress is still sleeping, but Sundari is ready and waiting for you.' The smile that crossed Rupa's face was swift as sunlight on a cloudy day. 'You are kind indeed to be concerned about the lowly. Please follow me.'

Sundari is not lowly, I thought, she is a princess in her own right. Then, with a flash of determination, which illuminated my spirit, else I will make her one.

I followed Rupa to the small ante-room. 'Please sit down and wait here,' Rupa said. 'I'll be a moment, because Sundari is at the back of the house and she will need to say her farewells.'

It struck me only then that Sundari would have been assigned a mat and pillow in some small, airless room in the servants' section at the rear of the house. The real impact of the Yakka system in which women were treated as chattels by men and of the Arya and Dasa social orders based on caste, which is no more than the nature of a man's work, hit me for the first time and my spirit cried out in anger against them. The farmer had been given eminence in the caste system because he produced food, the substance of life, more important to man than clothing or platters, goblets and wagon-wheels. In like manner, the Arya had decreed the cow to be sacred, the white cow, symbol of the triumph of light over darkness, most sacred of all. The caste system was therefore no more than a sacred Arya cow! I determined to move heaven, earth and my brother to right these iniquities in our new kingdom of Thamba-Panni regardless of the consequences, if for no other reason than to prevent a prison comprising the two attitudes of Yakka and Arya which would make life unbearable for a woman of low caste. I sat on one of the four ebony settles in the room, my brain working furiously on ways in which I could achieve this change as I waited eagerly for Sundari to appear. I thought of the first moment when our glances would meet. Surely there would be instant recognition this time, her eyes luminous on mine, each of us knowing the truth and confessing it to the other without a single word being spoken. My mouth loosened and my eyes crinkled in joyous anticipation.

I heard the rustle of her skirt, the soft sound of her bare feet on the flagstone floors, breathed a sharp scent of some incense perfume and stood up to greet her. She stood slender and tall before me, dressed in green skirt and bodice, a chunky gold necklace at her slender white throat, heavy gold bracelets around her slim wrists. Her fair face seemed ghostly in the semi-darkness. She placed her bag on the floor, made obeisance to me, came erect again. All the while, her eyes remained downcast and my soaring heart returned to my throat, to be gulped down, sinking to the depths of me. Moments of silence passed while I simply stared at her, unable to speak. Never once did she raise her eyes, or move from her posture of humble submission and I could sense some unutterable sadness in her spirit. She was somehow different from the fiery-spirited maiden of last night and I realized that the change had occurred when the reality of events that must have seemed like a dream finally hit her. What a stunning impression that reality must have brought, a near escape from rape, witnessing horrible violence for the first time in her life in the murder of the woman who had taken her dead mother's place and even perhaps the realization of her place in society.

Finally, I could not stand her embarrassment any longer. I cleared the husk from my throat. 'I've made arrangements for you to return to your father immediately,' I said in formal tones. 'You will have the use of one of King Kalu Sena's wagons. Bala, the man who escorted you here last night will accompany you. I presume you can show them the way?'

'Yes, Prince.' The words were tonelessly spoken, as if she were in a state of shock. I longed to take her in my arms and comfort her, but that was an impossible dream, besides she was encased in the marble of her withdrawal. Was it from me, or the world? 'You are indeed noble to look after a helpless woman of such low caste,' she suddenly added.

Until that moment, I had never realized how down-trodden people of the lower castes must feel. My heart rose with words gushing forth, but my mind replaced them with banalities, which alone seemed right for the occasion. 'Madam,' I began, 'we conquered this kingdom, which my brother has renamed Thamba-Panni, last night. We intend bringing law and order here, which includes safety for women and I hope, equality for all, regardless of race or sex.' Wanting to impress her, I must have sounded boastful and pompous. 'We may have made an inauspicious beginning, but it is the end that matters.'

'Forgive me for saying so, Prince, but since I am a person of low caste, you should not address me as "madam".'

'But that is exactly what I'm trying to tell you,' I cried. 'Women are the equals of men, even their superior in many respects. And it is not a person's caste that should dictate his station but nobility in all aspects of his life. This is the order I want to try and establish in this kingdom.'

She came close to displaying emotion for the first time. 'Pardon me, Prince, but my father, though but a goldsmith, is a learned man and a student.' Her voice was soft and mellow, as I remembered it. 'He has studied the Upanishads, the Bhagavad Gita and most available writings. He has tried to teach me all he knows. From this knowledge, I would humbly suggest that it would be impossible for one man, however noble, to alter a system or to change the wickedness in the hearts of some men, evidence of which we both had last night.'

At least we were talking to each other. 'No, no,' I assured

her, wanting to maintain the communion. 'Has your father not told you of what Gautama, who is called the Buddha, or Enlightened One, achieved on the continent to bring equality to women and reduce the differences between castes?'

'My father has studied the teachings of the Buddha too and so have I. Both of us are taken with the Doctrine. We might even be converted some day. While the teachings are righteous, however, they are in conflict with the religions of the Arya and the Dasa people. It takes many years for people to change their habits and their religion. As for the truly wicked . . .' She sighed. 'No system will change them.'

I was elated to find that, young as she was, Sundari was a thinking person, one with whom a man of intellect could commune, though this was no less than I had sensed in her from the beginning. She was a rare treasure and it made me even more desirous of breaking through to her. 'Equality, religion, wickedness, are all human attributes,' I stated. 'They are nothing before the eternal, infinite works of God.'

She raised her eyes to me for the first time. They were so large, dark, translucent. 'You believe in God then, Prince?'

'Yes,' I responded. 'I believe in One God.'

She searched my soul with those deep eyes for the truth of my beliefs, not for my feelings, I realized sadly. 'That is good,' she finally declared, lowering her eyes. She paused and the words came out of hers as if she had not willed them. 'But I'm afraid you will suffer for Him.'

I suddenly felt terror sizzle through me, for her words seemed prophetic. I stared at her, smitten dumb.

'You have been more than kind,' she said softly. 'Now, I hope I can leave and go home.' She seemed like a child then, the transition incredible.

'Certainly,' I said. 'If you will remain here a few minutes, I'll have the wagon brought up and call for your escort.'

'I'm unused to such fine treatment,' she began.

'Then please accept it with joy,' I begged her. 'It is what I

120

would always like to give you.'

She shook her head. 'For a woman such as me, this can only happen once in a lifetime,' she declared firmly.

The sound of ribald laughter intruded from the compound, as if to echo her sentiment. Inside the ante-room was a strange silence. I broke it. 'Where do you live?' I enquired.

'In a coastal township called Mada Kalapuwa, Mud Lagoon.'

'Is it far from here?'

'About twenty miles away.'

'Is your father well known there? I mean, are there other goldsmiths in the town?'

'There are none, so he is well known in the region.'

'Good. I hope to visit you soon.'

'That would not be advisable,' she stated, firmly and decisively. 'But I shall never forget you.' There was finality in the words.

Feeling completely despondent, flattened, I led the way to the sunshine outside. The open bullock wagon had arrived and was waiting at the entrance, facing the direction of the shore from which we had arrived yesterday. It struck me that the route to Mada Kalapuwa would be straight along the track, past the fork at which we had turned right. Bala, bare-chested and fully armed with sword, shield and spear was talking to the wagoner. Puri still loitered at the entrance.

I helped Sundari into the back of the wagon. The wagoner placed her bag inside. Bala clambered in and sat opposite Sundari. The wagoner took his seat.

'Farewell, Sundari,' I said. 'May God guard you. Send for me if you ever need me.'

'Farewell, Prince,' she responded, her eyes downcast.

The wagoner clicked his tongue and nudged the black bull's rear with his toe. The wagon started forward with a creak. 'Guard her with your life, Bala,' I bade, in despair.

'Yes, Prince,' he responded, surprised.

The wagon rattled over a bump. One of its wheels had a squeak. A trace of incense perfume hung in the air.

The hot sun beat down merrily on me, but my heart beat sadly.

Three nights later, and Princess Kuveni lay back on the gold cushions of her nuptial bed in the tent she had prepared for Prince Vijaya. She had been waiting impatiently many hours for him to come to her. At first, it had been with desire stirring in her womb and lightly prickling her womanhood, the urge to be touched, for penetration and movement. Now it was almost midnight and unreasoning fear had replaced all else.

On the night that he seized the Priti fort, her husband had hastened back to his tent. Since then, he had been very late every single night. Why? When he had left for the fort that morning, he had warned her he might be late. But this late, every night? As the hours dragged by, the princess had begun to worry, because she had no standard by which to compare an Arya ruler with a Yakka.

When a man conquered a territory in her region, he made others work for him, seizing whatever he desired, ruling by brute force not by brainpower. Therefore her Yakka father had, as the king, dispensed justice for a brief while each morning, then generally spent the rest of the day enjoying himself, practising with weapons, hunting, or feasting, invariably devoting his evenings to drinking and carousing, his nights to lying with women. The idea of a work routine was therefore foreign to the princess as it was to the men of her tribe, who worked only as the need arose.

Could the prince be with some other woman? She shuddered violently at the question. Men, especially the young and lusty ones, were hardly ever faithful to their women, yet she could not bear the thought of sharing the body of her prince with anyone else. The possibility that his magnificent loins might, at this very moment, be locked with those of some other woman, perhaps even her younger sister, that his superb member might be moving stiff and hard within different moist female flesh, was unbearable. With an effort, she shook herself free of the images she had conjured.

Could the prince have abandoned her? The question flashed through her mind suddenly, searing it, leaving her truly terrified. After all, he now had what he needed, the kingdom. What other use could he have for her? And she was well accustomed to abandonment in Yakka society.

As her fears expanded, the cricket chirpings from outside the tent grew louder and louder, weaving into her senses, heightening her anxiety. She stared beyond the dim golden light from two flickering oil-lamps on a little table at the far corner of the tent, towards the patch of darkness that marked the entrance through which the prince would arrive. How many times had she glanced sideways in this direction, until her neck had begun to hurt? Suddenly feeling stifled, she found the pungent scent of incense overpowering. Her eyes drifted to the brazier on which coals glowed faintly red, emitting tiny curls of grey smoke. That first night, the scent of incense had been so exciting, tonight it was smothering her. The Yakka, being a hardy, jungle people, never used anything to repel insects.

A mosquito whined past her face. Lost in her thoughts, she ignored it until it settled on her bare chest and punctured the skin. She waited until the insect was glutted, then swiftly slapped it. She looked down casually at the tiny bloodied corpse on her palm before flicking it away with a finger, then wiped the hint of blood on her palm against the silken bedsheet. Realizing that her Arya husband, with his insistence on cleanliness and form, would not approve, she sat up to examine the red smudge on the sheet. It was so faint in the dim light that she shrugged and flopped back on the bed, feeling hot and tired.

An owl hooted from the nearby jungle. She could imagine

it poised on some dark branch, only its large, bright eyes visible, staring fixedly, starkly through the gloom. Her mind drifted to bats hanging from stark branches, connected with a jerk to the tree above Reeri Yakseya's shrine.

This was the fourth night that she had not worshipped her demon god. She needed his help to keep Prince Vijaya true to her.

Suddenly, from the distance Reeri Yakseya's face came spinning towards her, grinding to an abrupt halt between her eyes, just a blank red monkey face convulsed with rage, the sharp eyes glaring. Behind the face, the red planet gleamed, a moon-halo, half-hidden by a transparent, grey cloud.

She shrank back on the cushions, closing her eyes to shut off the vision, thankful for the resulting black-red of closed lids.

What was the meaning of the demon god's visitation? Was it a reminder of her duties, or had he come to inform her that he and the planet were keeping the prince away from her as punishment for her neglect of them? Demon gods sometimes turned on their human masters and servants and destroyed them. Whatever the causes, she must placate her god. The night was beginning to stifle her.

Frantic, she leapt out of the bed and tightened her waistcloth. What if the prince returned before she did? She would cross that *edanda*, footbridge, when she came to it.

Drawing her blue shawl close around trembling shoulders, she sneaked out of the tent into the pale night that now seemed to receive her dusky body like a silken mantle. She ran lightfooted to her house. Within minutes, she had woken her two female attendants. Flinging aside her shawl, she soon moved through the cooler air at the back of the house towards the flickering glow of the tiny lamps on the shrine. The steady tap of a drum and the finger cymbal accompanied her. Goose pimples sprang crisp on her dark, pouting breasts. Her bare feet slipped occasionally on a clump of grass, an exposed treeroot. She no longer cared whether the prince's men saw her or not.

She paused before the shrine. The red cockerel, tied to the post beside it, awoke to grumble querulously.

Her gaze moved to the figure of the red god riding his red bull atop the wooden shrine.

Puzzlement creased her brows. She looked more closely, staring hard through the gloom. A stab of fear forked through her entrails at what she was not seeing, its aftermath rising in her chest to halt her breathing. She gazed piteously upwards. The stark branches were dead, devoid of life, the sleeping bats that once adorned them were gone. She gulped, then scanned the clear, blue sky, brilliant with stars, searching for the red planet. When her eyes finally locked on to it, she found it to be small, glowing faintly red, just another star behind a thin, grey veil of a cloud.

Her frantic gaze fell back on the demon god. He remained just a painted statue.

Her stomach seemed to drop to her feet, driving her breath upwards again to smother her with fear. Her demon god and her planet no longer had life in them. Why? Why had the life-force left them? To punish her? What for? Because she had neglected them night after night for the pleasures of her body? She would cast all else aside and return to her gods, if only they forgave her, afforded her another chance.

Had the gods abandoned her because she was no longer a virgin? In that case, might not her prince abandon her too? The hideous questions, with their unshakeable, unchangeable basis, gripped her, left her shaking. A dark hand flew to her throat to ease its choking. The sweat broke out all over her body in that cool, night air.

Now she felt desolate, bereft, abandoned by men and gods.

'O demon god! O Reeri Yakseya, do not leave me, I beg you.' The words came bubbling through her parched lips, like pitch trickling before an intense fire. 'Do not desert me, do not punish me. I only did as you bade me.'

The owl hooted, in derision, from somewhere in the jungle. Wildly, she looked up again at the red planet. Wildly, her mind sought for the means of appeasing it, of bringing it back to life.

Anything, anything you desire, so long as I have your power and protection once more.

A broad grin cracked through the grey cloud-veil, to reveal a dark, cavernous mouth above which a single, red eye appeared on the face of the planet, to wink at her.

Hope fluttered tremulously in the breast of the princess. You have come to life again, my planet god. I thank you.

Power began to seep through her trembling limbs, the sweat dried swiftly on her body. She came alive, the fire, the old magnetism pulsing through her. Wide-eyed, ecstatic, she continued to stare at the planet-god.

The planet winked its red eye at her again. Its laughter echoed through the heavens, ending in a sudden, cold gust of wind that raged through crackling branches.

Now she looked at her demon-god, eagerly searching. The drum-beat and the cymbal-chink were bringing the statue throbbing into reality: A *billa* toll . . . a *billa*, toll, went the drum. A *billa*, toll, a *billa*, toll, chinked the higher note of the cymbal. What toll would they take? She did not care.

A faint glow lit the red monkey face of the god. Not knowing that the wind had swayed overhanging branches to cast starlight on the shrine, the princess gazed spell-bound. Her heart beat wildly against her ribs as the god's face slowly came to life. The statue grew larger, a frog's croak merged into the bull's grunt, she even heard the clip-clop of its hooves, The red god began trotting his red bull once more, rising and falling proudly above the votive offerings of white jasmine flowers and the light from the two clay *pana*, lamps.

Relief, such as she had never known before, flooded the princess. Without conscious thought, her hands moved up her head, palms together in worship. Then a sudden shiver streaked through her body. The gods were demanding their *billa*, toll. Until a few nights ago, she could offer them her virginity. What would they now expect from her? What did she have to give them? No longer reasoning, she began her dance.

Chapter 10

When Prince Vijaya finally returned to the tent, after a long, hard day, he expected to find the princess bathed, perfumed and asleep, as he had instructed her. Instead, she was lying back on the gold cushions of the bed, wide awake, staring blankly up at the roof of the tent. The smell of her sweat, mixed with a strange, disgusting odour, smote him when he paused at the entrance. Her body ws covered with a blue, silken shawl, against which her large breasts thrust upwards in resistance. She took no notice of him.

'Why aren't you sleeping, *larla*, beloved?' he enquired.

She sat up slowly, still in the trance-like state that had seized her at the shrine and still the victim of jealousy. 'Why should you care? You obviously have no time for me.'

She knew he stiffened, though imperceptibly. His tawny eyes flashed, but he kept calm. 'As you can see, wife, I do have time for you. Why else would I be here?'

'After you have done all else.'

'What else?' His deep voice was puzzled.

He is pretending, she thought. 'You tell me,' she said aloud.

'Only my duties as the ruler of Thamba-Panni.' He was struggling to be patient.

It irritated her, made her want to push him to the limits of explanation. 'Like what?' she demanded peremptorily.

'I have official work to do, before which all personal desires must give way. The kingdom had no proper government, so I am trying to introduce the Arya system.'

'Oh! So now we have it. The Arya are a god-race, while we Yakka are less than dogs at their beck and call.'

'You said it, not I.' His voice was still gentle, loving.

'People are whatever they make of themselves. The Yakka can either be dogs or gods.'

She was nonplussed. Her mind was fogged. The demons that attacked her could give her carping, harsh words but not arguments in a debate. She changed her line of attack. 'Do you come to a dog then, or a goddess.'

'You can be what I made you the first night, a goddess, or a . . . bitch.'

Remembrance of that night flashed through her with the force of a brilliant sunlight, clearing the mists. 'You were late in coming to me the first night too, lord,' she said, her voice more gentle.

A mocking smile crossed his leonine features. 'As I recall it, I did not come to you, but you to me, Princess, and we were both late for our conjugal pleasure, because we had duties to perform.'

She could not avoid the laugh that rose to her lips, driving away the last of that horrible mist. It made her feel herself again, free, the Princess Kuveni who adored this prince she had known but a few days. 'You may not have come to me, lord, but you did indeed wait for me.'

'Certainly. And you kept me waiting. Tonight it's my turn.' He paused, the giant frame half stooping, eyes searching her face. 'But what caused you to be different tonight?'

Inexplicably she hardened, wanting to hurt him because she had been hurt. Words came which she had no desire to speak. 'That which I had before you came into my life.'

He sensed her changed attitude and froze. The tawny eyes flashed. 'How dare you address me in this manner?' He strode towards the bed.

She flung aside the shawl to reveal the dark smudges on her breasts. He paused in his stride. 'What on earth are those?' he demanded. Then comprehension dawned. 'Blood! Why, that's dried blood.' Anxiety gentled his face. He stooped to kneel beside the bed, his deep voice full of solicitude. 'Are you wounded? Did anyone hurt you?'

Such tender concern gave her a feeling of power over him, a kind of dominance that brought with it the desire to hit back, to wound him. 'No one hurt me. This blood is a gift.'

'From whom.'

'Not from whom . . . to whom. To my gods.'

'What gods?'

'My demon-god, Reeri Yakseya, and my planet god.'

Comprehension dawned in his eyes even as they sought her lips and found confirmation in the bloodstains around her mouth. 'That horrible smell,' he whispered to himself. 'Cockerel blood!' He jerked upright, towered above her, disgust on his face. 'Prince Lala told me you were a demon priestess,' he noted, his voice deadly quiet, its deep tone chill. 'That one of your rites involves the sacrifice of a cockerel to your gods and the drinking of its blood. Is that what you did tonight?'

'Yes!' The word came out defiantly, but she searched his expression for some sign of softness, a hint of love. She found none. Instead, the proud face was set in grim lines, the whole of him so majestic that she quailed. 'Yes,' she repeated, but in a half-whisper, like a child telling the truth in order to be excused some wrongdoing. 'When you didn't come, I was so scared. I thought you had abandoned me. I had no one . . . so . . . so I went to seek my gods . . .'

A deep, red flush suffused his cheeks. His expression grew even more grim. 'Madam!' he growled. 'You and I made a bargain one night, you to deliver me a kingdom and I to take you for my spouse. Implicit in this bargain, as far as I am concerned, were that I would rule the kingdom wisely and that you would be a worthy spouse. You kept your promise and delivered me a kingdom. I took you for my spouse. Now it's up to you to fulfil the real purpose of your own promise. I expect you to be a worthy wife.'

On two separate nights, she had made two successive bargains, one with a prince, the other with demon-gods. Caught in the vice of her own making, she looked

130

imploringly through her tears at the prince, not knowing how to beg his forgiveness.

'Tonight, I am the ruler of this kingdom that I have named Thamba-Panni,' he proceeded. 'You are my subject, as well as my consort and will henceforth obey my laws and the rules of my household.'

All else fled from her before his majesty. Humbly, she nodded her acquiescence.

'Everyone in this kingdom will be permitted to worship their gods.' The tone of his voice had changed. He seemed to be delivering an edict. Each word was succinct, crystal clear, strangely dropping into her brain like the beat of a new drum, a more compelling cymbal through cool, night air.

She felt confused. I am afraid for my life, afraid of what my gods might inflict on me, she thought, and yet I must dance to the tune of this prince's words, because he is strong, because he is physically present, because he dominates me. Mostly because I love and need him.

'My rules do not permit a spouse who leads alien rituals, or rituals of any kind,' the prince continued. 'You may therefore worship any gods you please, but you will be my spouse, not a priestess, in this court. Do . . . you . . . understand?' Each word of the question came out separately, with dramatic intensity.

Her entrails turned to curd within her. A gust of wind broke through the entrance of the tent. The flames from the oil lamps danced, cast wavering shadows around her, driving a chill dread into her being. A hyena howled from the jungle, a lizard chirped. The smell of incense gripped her by the throat. 'Yes,' she whispered, suddenly tired, deathly afraid.

'Go then and wash that disgusting blood and sweat from your body. Perfume yourself and return as my queen.'

I was up at the cock's crow the following morning, after another restless night, full of dreams whenever I did fall asleep which I could not recall when I awoke, except that many were, as always these nights, of Sundari.

I had begun brushing my teeth with the chewed end of a *kanda* stick at the well behind the Princess Kuveni's house when my brother joined me. Even the pale grey light of dawn could not hide the dark rings around his eyes and the strange look on his face. My heart went out to him, because this was the first time that I had ever seen him troubled. Not even when he and his followers were arrested by our father, King Sinha-Bahu or when they were all finally banished from Sinha-Pura had he shown any emotion. He even carried the half-shaven head, intended as a mark of shame, proudly. 'I shall cut the other half only when the shaven half grows sufficiently long,' he had told me. 'By then I might also have something to be proud of.'

He reached for a clay jug, stooped over the open well and dipped the jug in the cold water. It filled with great bubbling sounds. He came erect, raised the jug and poured water over himself.

'Br . . . r . . . r . . .' He gasped and shook himself.

'Feel good?' I enquired.

'I needed that. Anything for cleanliness this morning.'

I held myself back from asking the inevitable question that leapt to my mind. Instead, I seized a jug myself, filled it and poured it over my own head, opening my mouth to receive some of the cool water. It tasted good. I rinsed my mouth, gargled and spat out the water in a stream I directed on to the nearby turf.

Prince Vijaya stood beside me, his golden skin gleaming droplets, like dew on his red hair and beard. 'You're a cunning devil,' he stated, a half-grin on his face.

'Merely your twin,' I grunted.

His tawny eyes went soft for a moment. He shook his head. 'You're really something. I like you, twin-devil.'

'You merely love your own image.'

He stared at me, puzzled, for a few seconds, trying to

132

comprehend my meaning. When it finally dawned on him, he gave a great guffaw that rang through the air and sent two grey doves winging swiftly out of their nests in the green branches of a banyan tree beside the well. 'You are a devil,' he repeated, sputtering.

'You said that before.'

He took stock of me, suddenly serious. He could change moods in an instant, I knew. 'Finish your washing,' he commanded abruptly. 'I have something to tell you. We can talk as we stroll down to the fort for *chupatti*.'

We changed into white *dhotis* and were being saluted by the guard as we strolled through the compound entrance when Ujjeni hastened up to us. In that grey light, Ujjeni's face was more a death-mask than ever, but there was something else in his eyes now, some half-hidden triumph that alarmed me.

'May I join you in your walk, lord?' Ujjeni enquired.

My brother looked at me before replying. 'Certainly.'

Ujjeni caught that look. For a moment, I saw something akin to hatred in his glance at me, but it was gone so swiftly that it could have been my imagining. He fell into stride on Prince Vijaya's left and we began walking slowly down the track towards the fort. The mud from the rains had dried, so the brown sand crunched beneath our bare feet.

'Lord, the reason why I desired to talk to you was because I have a report of serious import to make. I would prefer to make the report to you privately. No offence to Prince Lala of course.' He smiled apologetically at me, revealing prominent yellow teeth between black-red gums in a jaw shaped like two circular combs.

'Prince Lala is my personal aide, my deputy and my brother,' Prince Vijaya observed shortly. 'There's nothing you cannot tell me in his presence.'

My heart leapt at his words, but again I caught that brief look of hatred on Ujjeni's face. It came and went before his jawline closed on his unctuous smile, so that for one split second he looked like some yellow-toothed demon smiling with his mouth but not with his eyes. 'Lord, one of my guards reported an unusual occurrence in the compound last night,' he stated as we continued walking beneath dark branches. He looked at my brother's face, but found nothing save a mask there. Whatever Prince Vijaya knew, he was not talking about. 'I hesitate even to mention it, because it is an event involving the Princess Kuveni, but I deem my duty to you above all else, so I crave your permission to speak.'

'You may speak freely.' Prince Vijaya nodded, his face still expressionless.

'My aide, Puri, who was on duty at the east side of the compound, witnessed an unfortunate event last night. He observed the Princess Kuveni dancing to her demon-god before her shrine and witnessed the sacrifice and disembowelling of a red cockerel and the drinking of blood.' He went on to give details of the rite. 'Human sacrifice, animal sacrifice, blood sacrifices of any kind are abhorrent to us Arya.'

Vijaya stopped at the stile leading to the bund of the pond and faced Ujjeni. 'You did well to report this to me,' he declared. 'I know it must have been hard for you.' He reached out and clapped a hand briefly on Ujjeni's bony shoulder. 'What you have said is no more than the truth. The Princess Kuveni is a priestess of the ancient Yakka religion. She is entitled to follow any code of religious conduct she desires, so long as it does not conflict with my edicts as the ruler of this kingdom.'

Ujjeni looked at my brother squarely for once. 'Lord, I must humbly request you, when you consider such edicts, to remember that our men will be fearful if their own gods and precious customs are offended.'

'A point well taken, Ujjeni. But equally well must we ensure the right of the indigenous people to worship their own gods, especially at a time when we are moving to a period of intense change in the manner of their lives.' He smiled briefly. 'Surely the vast pantheon of our gods will permit the inclusion of some foreign gods.'

'My lord, forgive me, but our men will not take kindly to demon worship and blood sacrifice.'

My brother clicked his tongue impatiently. 'They have no choice for the present,' he retorted. 'We cannot move into a country and change it overnight. Change must be planned and must take place gradually. Our first priorities must be security, the consolidation of our victory and the expansion of our military domination over the entire Yakka kingdom. We must bring law and order, good government, to the lives of the Yakka people. When prosperity has them in thrall, we shall organize their religious lives and customs to the dictates of civilization and seal their subjugation. Tell the men that our gods will approve such a plan.'

Ujjeni's face lit up, making even the cadaverous cheeks seem fuller. 'Praise be to the devas!' He exclaimed. His eyes glowed with open fanaticism. 'We will convert this heathen, this barbaric race in due time. It was meant to be.'

'Have a care,' I interjected. 'The spouse of our leader is a member of that same race.'

Ujjeni glared at me, then turned his gaze to Prince Vijaya. 'You are our leader and we will follow you to the gates of hell,' he declared with sudden unwonted passion. 'We will obey your every dictate to the letter and the spirit. But I beg you to consider this humble submission before it is too late. Take this princess for your spouse, your consort. But when you select a queen, let it be an Arya lady of royal birth.'

'Why?'

'Do you ask me why, lord? Do you not know it in your own heart and mind? Do you not feel it in your *atman*? You are the instrument of destiny.' Ujjeni's voice rang out through the now-silver sunshine like that of a prophet. 'We were all no more than criminals. We have changed overnight, not merely for our own good, but because we are

135

destined to found a new Arya nation. Nothing, no one, shall stand in the way.'

My brother was caught up in Ujjeni's spell. Or perhaps it was the spell of his own making which Ujjeni's words had merely touched, like the fingers of a *veena* player on the strings, of the *tabla* master on his drum. His tawny eyes flashed, his face became set. 'In this too you have spoken wisely,' he responded. Then his natural sense of honour intervened. 'But any thought of a queen for me, any discussion about my personal life or of any lady in it, I shall not permit.'

Ujjeni knew better than to push Prince Vijaya farther. His deep-set eyes relaxed and he injected a hint of warmth into them. 'Of course, it shall be entirely your personal concern, lord, as to whom you marry, whom you cohabit with, whether it be an Arya princess who can give us an Arya succession, or a demon priestess who will integrate the two races.' Oh! He was devilishly cunning, this Ujjeni. 'May I ask a question on behalf of my men?'

'Certainly.'

'Will you be permitting demon rites to continue.'

'The Yakka people may have any religious rites they choose and we will not interfere.' Then came the moment of truth. 'The Princess Kuveni will, however, cease to lead or participate in any abhorrent ritual from now on. We cannot mix religion and the State.'

Ujjeni glanced triumphantly at me. He knew my views. I coughed lightly to attract my brother's attention. 'Where does that leave me, Prince? Am I no longer to be the priest of our men.'

Prince Vijaya looked at me as if I were a traitor. 'You do not practise barbaric rituals,' he grated.

'Barbarism is a relative term,' I protested mildly. 'What is at issue is the principle of conflict between religion and the State.'

'It has always been so,' Ujjeni put in shrewdly. 'The

priesthood has always sought to use its hold on men's spirits, even their superstitions, to dominate the State and to rule kings.'

I had a glimpse then of what could be, but only a glimpse, too fleeting for me to heed its warning. 'Well, you certainly need have no fear on that account from me,' I assured my brother.

He smiled, knowing me. His expression was so warm it must have cut Ujjeni to the quick. 'You, I trust implicitly, Prince.' He turned to Ujjeni. 'There is one reservation I have regarding alien beliefs. I will not permit any godless religion in this kingdom.'

Ujjeni grinned his triumph at me, saluted my brother and headed back towards the village.

'Let us walk up to the bund,' my brother suggested. 'There are things I wish to tell you.'

We walked up the steps leading to the bund, where he and I had so lately killed our first men together. The sun was beginning to cast its first rays over the treetops, turning the grey waters of the pond to silver. We sat on the grass and he told me of his experience with the Princess Kuveni the previous nights, without omitting a single detail. 'I thought I had it all,' he concluded, 'I wanted to shower my love on her, give her everything that has been bottled up within me for years. But,' he shrugged his shoulders so helplessly that my heart went out to him, 'anything that sullies an idealistic love, whether it be blood, dirt, a crude gesture or vulgar words, can kill it. How different it was the first night. I felt for Kuveni as a virgin, as the epitome of female beauty, so that it was a sacred mating. Last night, the memory of the cockerel's blood, its sickly smell, the knowledge of her barbarism, remained even after she had bathed.' He shuddered slightly. 'Our mating was an expression of my passion to forget, to ease the horror. It was rough and wild, a combination of love and hatred, attraction and repulsion. Can a few moments make such a difference in two human lives?'

What could I say in the face of a situation fraught with tragedy for which no one was to blame and which seemed without remedy? 'Since you do have love for the princess in your heart, why not give her understanding as well,' I urged. 'Teach her to be all you want. You can start immediately by moving her to the fort, away from the influence of that shrine in her compound. Also, return early to her tonight. Give her a chance.'

His eyes clouded. 'I want to,' he assured me. 'I shall certainly try. But how does one overcome repulsion?'

'Repulsion is a reaction. Accept what there is with the conviction that you can change it and you will not know the pain of repulsion.'

He stared at me, contemplating my words. 'You're right,' he finally said. 'And wise beyond your years. I shall certainly try, but what about my need for someone I can idealize?'

'Create your ideal from the material you have. The princess adores you.'

We talked on and somehow the conversation drifted back to his remarks regarding godless religions. I may have subconsciously led it in this direction, because I was deeply concerned.

'When you spoke of godless religions just now, did you mean those that are ungodly, or those that have no belief in gods?' I finally enquired, inspired by my fascination with the Buddha's doctrine.

'I meant any religion that does not believe in gods.'

'Why?' I cried.

'It requires a combination of the thinking man and true strength to abandon belief in gods, which in its essence is the expression of a man's need for health, well-being and prosperity. Is that not how the pantheon of gods became built, one for every need of man? Ten thousand gods! Just one man, who has no belief in gods, can be bad enough, especially if he is a leader. A combination of them can be a serious threat to every king's rule. Remember what happened to King Bimbisara on the continent?'

'But he embraced the Buddha's doctrine, which merely declares that gods are unnecessary for man in this life.'

'So the doctrine became a source of danger to King Bimbisara. It emasculated him and created a group of people, led by his son, who seized power.'

'His son, Ajatha Sastri, was a parricide and therefore no true Buddhist.'

'Nor a true Arya either, for parricide is the most abhorrent of sins in the Arya code. Remember our own father?'

Chapter 11

That same afternoon I returned in a wagon to the compound to organize the transportation of some goods to the fort. The pressure of work had taken my mind off most else save underthoughts of Sundari, but each time I remembered my conversation with my brother I was disturbed by some of the policies he had stressed. Of especial concern to me was the likely effect of my interest in the Buddha's doctrine on him. Yet, when the wagon trundled past the stile and the bund, recollection of the hurt, no less, that his idealistic feelings towards the Princess Kuveni had provoked made me sorry for him. Being a romantic myself at heart, I could well understand how crudeness could affect such a love.

I was not surprised when the handmaiden, Rupa, came to the barn and told me that her mistress would like private conversation with me. When I followed Rupa into the bright heat of the afternoon, the glaring sun was directly overhead so that every scrap of shade was a mercy. Headaches, fevers and prostration can be caused when the sun's rays fall directly on the soft top of the head, or the nape of the neck. The heat was more unbearable than during the Sinha-Pura summers, because the air was thicker, more humid. I could not blame the men carrying stores for the occasional impatient note in their voices when someone dropped a package or did not move out of the way quickly enough.

The Princess Kuveni awaited me, seated on a rough couch, on the verandah that ran round the small *meda midulla*, centre courtyard of her house. This had a flagstone floor opening into the garden and was supported by whole coconut trunks, the cross-beams of which were coconut rafters holding up the yellow-white tile roof. I noticed that these upright coconut trunks, placed at the overhang of the roof, had been hollowed and that long side gutters of hollowed wood led to them, so that rainwater could escape into the garden, watering the beds of yellow *kapuru* flowers and pink and white jewel-weed plants, a rather ingenious architectural device in what was after all a semi-primitive culture.

The princess was wearing a waistcloth of dark blue, apparently her favourite colour. Her large pouting breasts, shaped like a certain variety of papaya, only very dark, were as usual bare. She rose to greet me, her black, gleaming head barely reaching to my shoulders. 'I am glad you were able to come,' she said, her golden-bell voice low. She turned to the attendant in dismissal. 'Go now, Rupa, I wish to be alone with the prince.'

'I was hoping you and I could talk,' I began, as soon as Rupa was out of earshot. I noticed that the princess was standing. During my short time in Lanka, I had discovered that according to Yakka custom, a woman would not sit while an older man remained erect. I indicated the couch. 'Why don't you sit there, while I use this stool.' I dragged a three-legged stool close enough to her couch for us to speak without raising our voices.

For several minutes, in accordance with the manners of our region, the princess talked pleasantries, the *chena* crops following the seasonal rains, Rupa's family, a Yakka hunt that was being organized to bring in hare, venison and wild boar flesh. She asked me for details of my past, our family, the life of the Sinha-Pura Court.

Then, out of the blue, she fired her first real question at me. 'Is your brother interested in my younger sister, Janaki? Has he cohabited with her?'

I was so stunned that for a few seconds I merely gaped at her with dropped jaw. I wish I had shown greater composure, but I was very young.

Noting my amazement, the princess went on to explain.

'Janaki is a very attractive girl. She is only a year younger than me and of fairer skin. Prince Tikka inspected both of us and wanted her, but decided at first to marry me because I was older and the heir.'

I had recovered by now. 'How did you know that?'

'Janaki told me.'

'Why do you suspect my brother of infidelity?'

'My sister is lusty, your brother is virile.'

'Why should it bother you?'

'Fidelity is important.'

'Is that a Yakka custom.'

'No, but it's what I want. I'd die if he lay with any other woman.'

'No, you won't,' I replied gently. 'By the way, in what month were you born?'

'I am of the scorpion *lagna*.'

'Ah! Then you have to watch your jealousy, so please listen carefully to me. You have a very responsible position. You are the spouse of the new ruler of your kingdom. Suddenly, in the space of a day, you have become elevated from the role of an exiled priestess to one of power and responsibility. You are bound to fulfil the duties of this new estate, foremost among which is to make Prince Vijaya happy, regardless of the cost to you, not because he deserves happiness more than you, but because the kingdom depends on the wellbeing of its ruler.'

She pondered this awhile, her eyes downcast. A bird twittered irritably from a tall pomegranate bush in the courtyard.

'That's good advice,' she finally said. 'That sort of thing is not in our Yakka way of life.' She went on to give me her version of last night's incident.

'The role of Yakka women has not been important up to now,' I responded, when she had finished. 'Women play a significant part in the Arya courts so there is much we shall be introducing here that will be completely new.' I paused and held her with a gentle gaze. 'Also, my brother needs to revere you, as he once revered our mother.'

'True.' She stared into space. 'He even worshipped at my shrine.'

I pretended not to know what she meant. 'Keep it that way by being a good goddess to him, always clean, always beautiful, always of fragrant scent, always gentle and well-mannered. If you destroy that image, what is left to worship?'

'Nothing, nothing,' she wailed. Her eyes went red and the tears burst forth. 'I simply could not handle him, because I was two people last night, one me, the other possessed.'

'By your need for your demon god . . . I understand,' I assured her gently. 'But remember everything I have asked you to do is within your control.'

She gazed piteously at me, the teardrops falling like tiny crystals down her dusky cheeks. She wiped them with the back of her hand.

'Lesson number one,' I said, smiling to ease her tension. I proffered her my cloth-square. 'Never wipe yourself with the back of your hand. Always carry a piece of cloth and use it!'

She sniffed, smiled back ruefully at me and accepted the cloth. 'I'm afraid I have driven my prince away from me for ever.'

'You can always get him back, so long as you become once more the earth-goddess he first worshipped.'

'Can I? Can I?' Her voice was eager.

'Definitely. I know him as I know myself.'

'I'll really try.'

'Let me also assure you that the Arya gods will protect you against your own. Your god, Reeri-Yakseya, for instance, is the most savage of demons, subject in power only to the King of Demons, Wessa Monny, whose subjects abound in every part of the sky. Wessa Monny's laws are cruel, ruthless. His punishment is generally death, his lesser penalties are burning, boiling, roasting, broiling, impaling, flaying alive, pouring molten metal down the throat, driving sharp nails into the crown of the head, thirty-two such in all. He has viceroys, ministers and officers to administer his government. He has delegated unlimited powers to Reeri Yakseya, who has had over one hundred different incarnations and can therefore manifest himself as eighteen *avatars*.' I had to pretend that I believed all this superstition myself.

Her eyes became round as plates again. 'How do you know all this?'

'I studied it in Sinha-Pura.'

'Then you must also know that on every third day of the week the chiefs attend a Yaksa Sabhawa, where they have to give an account of their activity to Wessa Monny. How will Reeri Yakseya explain my desertion of him?'

'There are gods more powerful than demons,' I responded. 'I shall invoke their might to help you conquer these demons. You had evidence of that in my *yantara* and the consecrated swords.'

She smiled then, a smile of secret knowledge. 'And I was told of your brother's coming and had it confirmed even as I felt the vibrance of his sword at my heart.'

'Well, the first thing we must do is to get you away from this house. I'll ask my brother to permit you to move to the fort today. Would you mind being there so soon after . . ?'

'After my father's death? No. I'd rather face the spirits of the dead than those of any demon-gods.'

'By the way, whose is that black bitch my brother and I saw that led us to you that first day?

This time her smile was of mischievous, open knowledge. She was a child really, in many ways. 'You are so clever, don't you know already?'

'I did not need to know in order to overcome the demon-bitch, Princess.'

'I shall be eternally grateful to you, Prince.' She was changing the subject. 'But what I want most of all is to keep my man.'

'That is in your hands.'

There was not much more to say, so I bade her farewell and left her seated on the couch. 'I'll see myself to the door,' I said.

Only when I stepped into the bright glare of the front garden did I realize that I might have made a mistake in not having the attendant woman usher me. Ujjeni was at the gate, staring at the entrance door as if awaiting my exit. He gave me an odd look.

Rupa, the Princess Kuveni's handmaiden, gasped as the two men moved unexpectedly towards her from the evening shadows on either side of the track below the bund of the small village lake. She had left her residence that morning, to spend the day with her parents and younger brother and sister in the village surrounding her mistress's compound. Having dallied at home too long, she had been hurrying back to the palace in order not to be late in serving the princess her night meal.

She stopped short, her heart beating faster, clutching her green shawl more closely around her as if for protection. She was relieved when she recognized the two commanders, but only for a moment, for when she noticed that one of them was the lean humpback named Ujjeni her heart started thudding against her ribs. She instinctively feared this man, with his skeletal frame and his death-mask face. Her sensitive spirit warned her he was evil, though he had never so much as glanced at her. She looked swiftly at the other man. It was the squat and broad-shouldered commander, with a square face and a long hooked nose, the one they called Anu. He at least had always seemed normal.

'You have nothing to be afraid of,' Ujjeni reassured her. The very fact that he was gentling his grainy voice, giving her a wide, insincere smile with those prominent yellow teeth beneath dark purple gums made her uneasy. 'My colleague and I merely wish to talk to you in private.'

Without ever once touching her, the two men placed themselves on either side of her, directing her over the stile and up the steps of the bund. Once they reached the top, she saw the sheet of grey-black water spread before her, shrouded by the dark trees fringing its banks beneath a heavy overcast sky. There was not a breath of wind to move the clouds and the smell of stagnant mud from the lake was overpowering. Or was it fear that stifled her breathing? An eerie howl rent the air, echoing through into her brain and finding its outlet in a shiver before she identified the sound as a hyena's cry.

What did these men intend with her? If they only wanted to talk in private, why escort her to the lake? They must mean her some harm. With her lean frame and gaunt cheeks, she did not attract men, so they could not want to molest her sexually. She broke into a sweat and began to tremble with fear.

'The Yakka exude a strong musty odour, especially when they sweat,' Anu observed in obvious disgust. 'Why don't we just drown this cat in the lake?'

If there was one thing Rupa feared, it was water. She could not swim and water even in a bucket somehow terrified her. Staring at the lake, terror of its dark, foreboding depths smote her entrails.

'No! No!' Ujjeni demurred. 'She has done us no harm. We should merely question her. That's what you agreed to.'

'Yes, but I've changed my mind, because this creature is really no more than a vicious witch, with her demon worship and her charms. We should drown her now, like any other witch, when we have the chance.'

Speechless, Rupa began to tremble and shake, her teeth chattering, her large dark eyes going from one man to the other. Why were they doing this to her? Should she beg, plead for her life? A sob escaped her. 'I'll do anything you say, lords, but please don't throw me into the water. If you must kill me, do it some other way.' She glanced down at Anu's sword, gibbering with fear now. 'P . . . please . . . please . . . I beg you, lord, cut off my head, but don't throw me into the water.'

Anu flung back his black-bearded face and laughed through white teeth. 'Ah! So you are afraid of water. You must indeed be a witch.'

'No!' Rupa wailed. 'I'm not a witch . . . Just afraid of . . . of . . .' She broke off, as Anu stepped in front of her. He reached out with his left hand, grabbed her by the hair, jerked downwards to lift her face towards his. He stared fixedly at her. For a moment she held his gaze, then the dark brown pebbles of his eyes, strangely separated by the great nose, seemed to take on individual lives of their own, lives of fire, searing her with their implacable purpose. She let loose a great cry, hysterical screams welling in her throat.

A sharp, stinging pain on her right cheek brought her abruptly back to sanity. Anu had slapped her. She fell silent and closed her eyes. Her body now jerking with silent sobs, she was conscious only of Anu's heavy breathing.

'Now, Anu, there's no need for violence.'

She heard the words but could not believe that Ujjeni of all people was intervening on her behalf. Had she misjudged the man after all? Her cheek was smarting, her head aching, her entrails were watering, ready to let go. She opened her eyes and rolled them imploringly towards the death-mask face. To her surprise, Ujjeni's expression was actually kindly. He was her one hope. 'Save me, lord,' she implored him.

Ujjeni laid a restraining hand on Anu's shoulder. 'Look, friend, we're in this together, you know. The fact that this woman has taken part in barbaric rituals to demon gods and fears water does not mean she's a witch. Why you'll soon be accusing our own Prince Lala of being the lover of that low-caste Dasa bitch, Sundari.'

'Well, isn't he?'

'How would I know? Why don't you ask the woman? If you spare her life, perhaps she might confess. Anyway, what good would she be dead, either to us, or to the king?'

Anu gave Rupa's hair a vicious tug and she felt her bowels move, soiling her cloth and trickling down between her legs. She knew the men were wrinkling their noses at the sudden odour, but she could not smell it herself, so transfixed was she by terror.

'Will you tell us all in exchange for your life?' Anu demanded.

'Yes! Yes! I'll tell you all, lord. I'll do anything you bid me.'

'See, it's as I said,' Ujjeni insisted. 'This poor woman is but a tool of her mistress and our Prince Lala.' He thrust his face towards her, his leer now evil. 'Aren't I right?'

'Yes, lord. Yes, lord. Yes, lord. I'm but a poor woman of the village. I do as I'm told.'

'You see, Anu,' Ujjeni declared triumphantly. 'She is a poor, ignorant woman, misled. How dreadful it must be for her. Like tonight. One moment she is walking peacefully from her parents' home to the security of the palace and the protection of her mistress. The next, she is in fear of her life, of death by drowning. By drowning, of all things. Drowning in these dark, dreadful waters, with no protection from anyone. Have you no pity?'

'Pity! For a Yakka witch?' Anu paused. 'Well . . .' He dragged out the word his hard eyes intent on Rupa. 'Pity? No! . . . Mercy! . . . Perhaps, but on certain conditions.'

In a daze, Rupa heard Ujjeni's questions and gave him the untruthful answers she knew he required. Somewhere dimly within her were recollections of her duty to her mistress, but they were as obscured by the mingling clouds of her terror and relief as the stars in the evening sky above her. She gave Ujjeni the promises he sought, aware that she had become his spy.

* * *

Walking away from the bund, Ujjeni looked triumphantly at Anu. 'You see, it worked,' he stated quietly, pausing at the top of the steps.

'By the devas, you are the cleverest man I have ever known,' Anu declared, the admiration in his voice reflected in the warmth of the hand he clapped briefly on Ujjeni's bony shoulder.

Ujjeni expanded under his friend's praise, the words and the gesture sweet to him. Few men and no woman thought to reach out and touch him physically, because he was so unattractive. 'It was a classical ploy,' he volunteered. 'The person whom the victim fears unexpectedly acts as the sympathetic friend, while the normally easy-going type plays the tough role. They toss the victim from one to the other, high and low, low and high, on a see-saw of terror.' His mirthless hee . . . hee . . . hee . . . laugh rose from deep within his belly, but quietly this time. 'Some research is, however, a prerequisite. You find out all you can about the victim, all the weaknesses, the areas of terror, so that the tough one can smite at those while the other exudes compassion.'

'You were smart to check in such a casual fashion with the other female attendants in the palace and to have your aide bribe the parents to talk . . . oh so unknowingly about their daughter and her dreadful fear of water.'

'I will do anything to set Prince Vijaya free,' Ujjeni cut in fiercely. 'He must be freed from any influence that Kuveni or Prince Lala may exert over him. Our leader agreed to paying Kuveni too big a price for the betrayal. Cha! Imagine us Arya having a barbarian queen. And Prince Lala and she are obviously plotting something. I saw Prince Lala emerge from a secret meeting with her this very afternoon. It will take time, perhaps even years, but you and I can save our leader if we stick together as in the past. I think of Prince Vijaya as a father or a brother.' He suddenly

149

felt emotional and tears pricked his eyes. Prince Lala stood in the way of his being Prince Vijaya's deputy and closest confidant. So had his own brother, Raja, once stood between him and their father.

Chapter 12

True to his word, Prince Vijaya not only had the Princess Kuveni moved to the palace that same afternoon but also completed an early dinner with his commanders in the palace hall so that he might not keep the princess waiting for that one night at least. This left the seven commanders to their own devices while the night was still young. They had each been allocated a cottage within the fortress and Uraw was thankfully leaving the palace for his new home when Ujjeni accosted him at the front door. 'Let's stroll down to the river,' Ujjeni suggested. He half turned to show that Anu was with him, a squat, broad-shouldered figure framed in the taper-light of the ante-room. 'I have a project on which I'm going to need your help.'

Uraw hesitated. 'I'm really quite tired,' he protested. 'Can't it wait for tomorrow?'

Ujjeni's lips curved to reveal the yellow teeth and purple gums in a mirthless smile. He looked ghoulish in the light of the hissing flares that lit the main avenue. 'This won't take long,' he insisted. 'King Vijaya has agreed that Anu and I should inspect a couple of the adjoining coastal towns where traders live who might be taxed. We've found some good horses and wagons. We expect to leave early tomorrow and return by nightfall.'

In spite of his tiredness, Uraw felt a spurt of interest. 'That sounds like fun, but why do we need to stroll down to the river? Let's discuss it here.'

Ujjeni glanced around conspiratorially. 'This is something we should not share with anyone else. It's my very own idea.' He winked and leaned towards Uraw. A gust of bad breath emerged as he whispered hoarsely. 'I'd like us to get the credit for bringing in the first taxes in our new kingdom of Thamba-Panni.'

'Oh!' Uraw looked about him too. There was no one close by. The other commanders and Prince Lala were still inside the palace, but soldiers, section leaders and captains were walking along the main avenue and side streets or were gathered in little knots, chatting before retiring for the night. The sky above was bright blue, littered with thousands of sparkling stars, the rush of the river provided a musical background to the murmur of voices that lay peacefully on the resinous pungency of the air. 'Well, it's a pleasant enough night,' Uraw declared. 'Let's go.'

They strolled past the saluting guards at the entrance to the fortress. 'We'll be back shortly,' Ujjeni advised their commander.

It was cool on the river bank. Uraw recalled the tension within him just four nights before, when he had held his company in readiness, not far away, to prevent help from the village reaching the fort. He kicked a stone into the water rushing below and listened for its splash. His tiredness began to dissipate. 'It's so quiet here,' he observed. 'Most enjoyable. I'm feeling better already.'

'We won't have much opportunity for this sort of enjoyment in the immediate future,' Anu advised. He adjusted his belt and burped. 'That was a good dinner. The food's improving. What a change from the weevils on board ship.'

Ujjeni gave his hee . . . hee . . . hee belly laugh. 'Makes a man's mind wander to other things,' he said. 'When you are satisfied with a full stomach and an empty bed, you have grown old.'

Uraw knew what Ujjeni meant, but it surprised him, because Ujjeni never seemed to need anyone or anything, merely responded to situations in the efficient, ruthless manner that had propelled him into leadership. 'Strange words, coming from you, comrade Ujjeni,' he stated.

That mirthless belly laugh escaped Ujjeni once more. 'I need nothing as a general rule, but there's something I very much desire now and would like Anu's help and yours to obtain.' His gaze became intense. 'I'll return the favour some day.'

'What is it?'

'I saw this young woman the night we took the fort and I can't get her out of my mind.'

'The Dasa girl? I heard about her, but I didn't know . . .' Uraw shot a questioning glance at Ujjeni, then at Anu.

'Comrade Ujjeni is never one to wear his heart or his desires on his sleeve,' Anu interposed in his high voice. He scratched his black beard reflectively.

Ujjeni nodded. 'Besides, there was some competition that night from our prince-priest, who would have liked to taste the offering himself.'

'Oh, no! Prince Lala is not like that,' Uraw protested.

'What d'you know about Prince Lala?' Ujjeni demanded fiercely. 'Surely you must see that he's out to wield power from behind the scenes, perhaps to seize it some day after all of us have prepared the way.'

'Huh-uh. I'm afraid I can't agree.'

'Tell him!' Ujjeni bade Anu.

'Ujjeni found the young woman. She's a low-caste Dasa and should have been his by right of discovery. Prince Lala saved her, supposedly from attempted rape – can you imagine that? – Ujjeni to be guilty of *attempted* rape when he could have consummated it?' Anu's laugh rang out, somewhat brittle. 'Anyhow, Prince Lala sent her back to her father, but not until after a private visit to her in Kuveni's cottage that night.'

'I don't believe it.'

'Ask Puri and that woman, Rupa, who is Kuveni's servant,' Ujjeni interjected. 'I had Puri keep watch that night because I suspected what was going to happen. Prince Lala slept in the adjoining warehouse. While Kuveni was with our leader in the tent, Prince Lala sneaked out after the men fell asleep. The bitch quietly let him into the house. Rupa confirmed all this to Anu and me this very evening. When Prince Lala had Sundari dispatched back home, he made sure that only Bala and the wagoner knew where she was going.' His eyes glowed. 'Do you think it right for Prince Lala to have taken what was mine? Is that loyalty to one's comrades?' His voice grew fierce, intense. 'I tell you, Uraw, I fell for that girl. I want her. I need her. I'm going to have her by fair means or foul.'

Uraw struggled against disbelief. Ujjeni seemed genuinely taken by the girl. Why would Ujjeni lie, or Anu, or Puri? Perhaps he had been mistaken about Prince Lala. 'Why don't you appeal to Prince Vijaya?' he enquired.

'For one thing, he is inclined to side with his brother at present.' Ujjeni stared into space, his sunken eyes brooding in the semi-gloom. 'That will change with time, but for now I'm also reluctant to burden the king. He has problems enough already, establishing our rule and dealing with that demon bitch, his spouse. Ha! Spouse indeed! Listen to what she did last night.' He told Uraw. 'There's need for change if we are to make this a worthy kingdom. And our king needs help desperately from loyal aides. He should have been content to take the woman Kuveni for a concubine. We are the Arya, the noble ones. We must have an Arya queen and Arya succession.'

'But you say this young woman, Sundari, is a Dasa.'

'What the hell do you think I want her for? Ujjeni burst forth. 'The Dasa women are supposed to know all the tricks of the trade. This woman is young, fair as an Arya, beautiful. I'd be hard put to it to find someone like her in this island. I want her for my own until I find an Arya bride some day.'

Uraw was genuinely puzzled, also concerned that he might become involved in conflict between Ujjeni and Prince Lala. 'How can I be of help?'

'By coming with Anu and me tomorrow to the town where

154

Sundari lives. If I go alone, or if only Anu accompanies me, it would seem as if the journey was undertaken specially for the purpose of seeking out the girl. Everyone knows how close Anu and I are, but no one realizes that you are one of us now. Your presence will give greater credence to our story that we are only going to collect our first taxes from the Dasa traders.'

Uraw certainly did not want to be 'one of us' but he could summon no resistance. Ujjeni was both plausible and compelling. 'Aren't we only going to collect taxes?' he asked, timorous.

'Yes. And you alone shall receive the credit for it and shall present the first gathering to our prince, which means a share for you and advancement in his esteem.'

'How d'you know people will pay taxes? After all, we're new here. And on what basis will you assess them?' Uraw paused, helpless.

Ujjeni's grin was evil. 'We'll take whatever we can get. If they refuse, we'll take it by force.'

'But that's what we've always done, plundering people. And we were punished for it. I thought we'd got away from all that.' Uraw had indeed longed to change his way of life and had therefore heartily endorsed his leader's first edict that night in the Princess Kuveni's compound.

Ujjeni sniffed. 'What more is taxation than legalized plundering? In the final analysis, it is the ability to enforce demands that determines the phrase used. So we'll rob more discriminately in the future, an entire people instead of merely the rich and call it taxation. Grow up, friend.'

Uraw knew that he did not have it in him to achieve certain things on his own, yet he hungered for them. Wealth would certainly bring him much that he wanted, including women and comfort. 'But how d'you know where to go?' he demanded feebly. He suddenly felt an urge to extricate himself from the situation despite the tempting inducements. 'You said just now that Prince Lala . . .'

Ujjeni interrupted him. 'Ah! That's what Prince Lala *tried* to do, but he didn't succeed. I had Puri secretly follow the wagon which took the woman and Bala away. She lives with her father, a goldsmith, in a coastal town about twenty miles from here, called Mada Kalapuwa, inhabited principally by Dasa and Arabi immigrants. They are all rich, mostly traders. We can bring in a goodly haul of gold, silver, jewellery, spices, cloth and imported goods for our king's treasury. You'll be rich and famous almost overnight.'

Uraw warmed to the temptation. 'But why give all this to me?' He enquired warily 'You can have the girl, the money and the glory yourself.'

That hee ... hee ... hee belly laugh rose above the gurgle and flow of the river, to become a part of the darkness. Uraw shuddered.

'I'm a leader, as you said a while ago.' Ujjeni's grainy voice was gentle but firm. 'I can make my own way, so I can afford to be generous, to share with my close partners. There's enough wealth here for all of us, but not everyone can find glory. You need me, Uraw. For the present, all I want is the girl.' His voice turned low and intense. 'My loins ache for her, my lower belly lusts for her. I hunger to penetrate her, to impregnate her with my seed, as never before. Also, my spirit clamours for justice. It demands that I teach Prince Lala a lesson.'

'And what about Anu?' Uraw turned to face the squat, hook-nosed commander. 'What's there in it for him?'

Anu merely smiled back enigmatically, then glanced sideways at Ujjeni for reply.

'Anu has something priceless already, for which he will help me without stint,' Ujjeni stated.

'And what is that thing beyond price?'

'Tell him, Anu.'

'Ujjeni's friendship.' Anu was suddenly in deadly earnest. 'You'll find him a better friend than enemy, Uraw.'

They left in the semi-dark hour before dawn the next day.

Ujjeni rode a bay Scindhi, Anu a chestnut and Uraw a grey Arabi mare. They were all armed to the teeth and led by a small wagon to which they had harnessed a tough cross-breed horse of indeterminate origin, dappled grey and black in colour. Since Puri knew the way, they made good speed past the sleeping village. Ujjeni had taken care to post some of his trusted men as sentries at the entrance to the fort and in the compound of the princess, so that the direction in which they went would remain a secret. Even King Vijaya did not know any more than that they were going to scour the countryside for a few miles around the fort to obtain first-hand information as to the nature of the land, its residents and the prospects for tax-gathering.

King Vijaya and I breakfasted together the next morning in the room he had taken over for his study in the Priti palace. This was a small room with flagstone floors, fronting the centre courtyard verandah and furnished with a long, yellow jak wood desk and settles. It was cool and shady in here and from the right side of the desk, where I was sitting, I faced early morning sunlight, white gold on the dark green leaves of an *anodha* bush, and could hear the cheep of mynahs.

We were still on our standard fare of *chupattis*, but now these were served with fried pork and boiled eggs, with fresh milk, papaya and banana on the side.

The king had a very pleasant night with the Princess Kuveni, he told me and was obviously rested and relaxed. 'I was downhearted yesterday, but a marriage is like everything else, I guess. It requires hard work and understanding. A regular schedule, with time off for one's family is indeed important.'

'We must certainly save you from exhaustion, Sire,' I responded, light-heartedly. 'You have a tendency to over-exert yourself in whatever chamber!'

He grinned. 'Over-work is a relative term. Your celibacy must make the bedchamber seem like hard labour, but you should try it some time.' He paused. 'By the way, what happens to the shrine and its demon god now that the princess has moved to the palace?'

'I hope they will remain and rot.'

'You know, all this business of demon worship is new to me. You have studied it, so tell me what it's all about.'

'There are three forms of Demonology. First, demonism, which is the worship of demons or evil spirits.'

'Is that what the princess practises?'

'Yes. Then we have Capuism, which is the worship of gods, demi-gods and deified heroes.'

'The Arya and Hindu practice.'

'Right. Finally, we have Grahaism, which is the worship of planets and stars, a form which the princess has integrated with her beliefs. The *Capuas* and *Cattadiyas* are priests who intervene to prevent, avert or minimize the malign influences of demons and planets. Man is for ever creating his own demons then finding remedies against them!'

'Do you believe in gods and demons?'

'They are in people's minds, are they not?'

'That evades my question.'

'I am very much in the formative stage of new beliefs, inclining towards the one God.'

'Ahura Mazda?'

'No. Closer to Jahweh, the God of the Wandering Tribe of the desert lands.'

'So long as you don't stop believing in a god or gods, I don't really care.' Typically, he shot off at a tangent to a more important subject. 'Are you in love with the girl, Sundari?'

'I'm not sure . . .' I was not ready to tell him the truth.

'Do you desire her?'

'Not physically or sexually.'

'What is it you feel?'

I lied again. 'I don't know.'

'Forget about her then. You have important work to do

158

and a position to maintain.

'I'll try,' I responded dismally. Suddenly, for the first time in my life, I could not talk to him.

Prince Vijaya went on to give me his list of the departments to be headed by each of the seven commanders who would form his Council of Ministers:

Finance and Internal Security: Ujjeni
Armed Forces: Vijit
Agriculture and Lands: Anu
Commerce and Industries: Uraw
Justice and Local Government: Upa
Health and Education: Pandu
Roads and Transportation: Sumitta

Ujjeni in two key posts. It was certainly not a good morning for me!

Heading north and west, Uraw, Ujjeni and Anu rode behind the rattling wagon, maintaining an even pace until the track finally hit the seashore and became a gravelled road veering directly northwards beside the copper-sand beach fringed with green groundcover. The dark silhouettes of their three ships, masts repaired, appeared a mile or so to the south and they increased their pace. They ate cold *chupatti* and fried pork while they travelled. 'It's important for us to complete our mission and return by nightfall,' Ujjeni had urged.

The ocean stretched pale grey towards the western horizon. By the time daylight cleared the dark shadows beneath the branches overhanging the track, the sun was dancing silver on slow waves heading from a pink horizon towards the shore. Gulls, searching for food, mewed above the sough of a gentle surf ending each journey scattered on the sand. A steady breeze brought dank odours of seaweed and, once, the stench of rotting fish.

Uraw would normally have found peace in these

159

surroundings, but the feeling that he had allowed himself to be sucked into a situation that was not really to his liking kept surfacing. He had to acknowledge that greed and ambition had not been his only motivations, he had been afraid to refuse Ujjeni.

They met no one along the road other than the occasional fisherman, swirling his net in the shallows. After two hours of riding, the coconut trees bordering the beach were replaced by the circular fan-like leaves of the palmyra palm, the soil became more sandy and jungle gave way to scrub and swampy flats. The first indications of their destination were a shimmering lagoon and salt pans in the distance. Then long rows of houses appeared, straggling along a wide spit of land separating ocean and lagoon. Fishing boats were drawn up high on the coppery beach. The track became cobbled. 'That is Mada Kalapuwa,' Puri called over his shoulder.

'Let's ride ahead of the wagon now,' Ujjeni directed. 'It will look more impressive. Puri, you show us the goldsmith's house after we've spoken to the people.' He spurred his horse forward with a clippity-clippity-clop of hooves.

Uraw and Anu followed him, cantering side by side, the wagon rattling behind them. Ujjeni urged his horse to a faster pace. They passed dark-skinned men, bare chested, clad in white verti-cloths, who gazed curiously at the strangers. Once they hit the township, more men appeared, hurrying about their business or simply standing in front of their homes, which were set behind an unending line of *cadjan*, plaited coconut leaf fencing. There was no sign of women. 'This must be the Arabi sector,' Ujjeni commented. 'They keep their women hidden.'

Indeed, the first women they saw in the centre of the township were obviously of the sweeper class, for they walked gracefully, carrying long brooms at the shoulder. They all wore bright coloured saris, loosely wrapped, with neither jacket nor bodice, providing glimpses of swinging breasts.

160

When they reached a sandy, treeless square in front of a Hindu temple in the centre of the town, Ujjeni raised his hand, signalling them to stop. The temple was a small but ornate yellow and red brick building, rectangular in shape, with doors on each side and no windows. A few meanly clad beggars squatted outside staring sadly into space. Uraw noticed that one of them was blind and another was seated with a stump of brown leg showing. They all came to life and rattled platters, clamouring for alms when the visitors halted. Devotees and passers-by stopped and turned to look.

Ujjeni rose in his stirrups. Silence suddenly filled the square. 'Hear me, all you people of Mada Kalapuwa,' he shouted. 'We are the Arya, the noble ones. Our army arrived here from the continent four days ago and conquered your kingdom, which we have renamed Thamba-Panni. Our leader is Prince Vijaya Sinha Bahu of Sinha-Pura. He is now the king of Thamba-Panni. My name is Ujjeni. I am King Vijaya's chief deputy and a commander of one of his seven companies. My two companions are likewise his deputies and commanders. On my right is Anu, on my left Uraw. We come here in peace, on a mission for our king. Have your *panchyat*, village council, your elders and leading artisans and traders attend us here without delay.'

Uraw expected that people would scurry to do Ujjeni's bidding, but to his surprise nobody moved. The people merely continued gazing curiously at Ujjeni as if they had not understood. 'Maybe they don't know your dialect,' Uraw volunteered.

'They know it,' Ujjeni stated grimly. 'They are being defiant. Passive resistance they call it.' He straightened up on his bay, his bare, bony chest gleaming with sweat, and seized the lance at his pommel. He couched it and clip-clopped his horse slowly, deliberately towards a lean tall man clad in a yellow robe beneath long white hair and flowing beard, who stood in the sunlight, close to the front door of the temple. He reined in his horse when the lance point was at the man's throat. The man merely looked up at him without flinching, dark eyes calm, serene.

Ujjeni turned sideways in the saddle to face one of the groups of men. 'If you do not carry out my command immediately, this holy elder will pay the price,' he said pleasantly. 'Each time you fail to obey, one of your people will die.'

The men he had addressed looked at one another questioningly. A small rotund man with a shiny bald head and plump cheeks, dressed in a creamy silken verti and with caste marks on his forehead, moved forward. 'No need for violence at the temple,' he declared. 'We shall summon those you desire.'

'Who are you?' Ujjeni demanded.

'I am Pillai, lord, head of the *panchyat*.'

'What is your profession?'

'I'm a trader.'

'In what?'

'Imported goods mostly.'

'You seem to be a civilized, well-organized group. Tell me how is it that you have been kept in subjugation by the near-barbaric Yakka.'

'They were here before us, lord. We are settlers who came over individually for trade, as other Dasa have done in the northern areas for farming. None of us is of the warrior caste, so we accept our lot as we find it. All we want is to be left in peace to pursue our trade, practise our religion and enjoy our families. We are no threat to any ruler, but rather an asset, because we promote industry, so we are left alone.'

'Excellent!' Ujjeni withdrew his lance and replaced it in the saddle socket. 'Do as you're commanded and we shall get along famously.' He gave a diabolical grin. 'Hurry now, for we have other towns to visit.'

'There are no other towns on the seaboard. The closest is Mantota to the north and that is many miles away.' Pillai turned on his heel and hurried away.

Uraw felt a stab of misgiving. Had Ujjeni come here to collect taxes or a concubine?

Within minutes, men started hurrying into the square, singly, in twos and threes, talking to one another in undertones, obviously apprehensive about what was in store for them. They kept glancing at Ujjeni, who remained motionless, impassive, then at the wagon. Uraw noticed that they were all well-dressed, mostly bare-chested. Some wore loose over-shirts, others, obviously the Arabi, had on tight pantaloons and turbans. One of the Dasa, clad in blue silk, was a magnificent specimen of manhood, tall, dark, wide of shoulder, lean of hip, his regal bearing accented by a hawklike face, hooked nose and proud eyes. Uraw was, however, more struck by an older, elegant looking man, who seemed to be making himself as inconspicuous as possible. He was lean and tall, slightly hunched, with silver grey hair and regular, aristocratic features. The caste marks on his high forehead nonetheless showed him to be of a lowly caste. He was dressed only in a simple white home-spun verti cloth but a closer look revealed scholarly depths to his dark eyes.

Ujjeni had quietly directed them not to dismount, so they sat their horses silently in the sunlight. An occasional cow wandered through the square. Flies buzzed around and Uraw's chestnut kept jittering its skin. The scent of jasmine and temple flowers mingled with the sharp odours of incense and dung. A typical Indian township, Uraw reflected.

When about thirty men had assembled around them, though at a respectable distance away, Pillai reappeared. 'We're all here now,' he announced. 'As many as could be rounded up immediately.'

Ujjeni surveyed the gathering in silence. A crow's harsh caw intruded, a cow mooed, a bell clanked in the distance. Ujjeni continued a brooding silence, as if binding those present in a spell. When he finally spoke, it was like the

163

unlocking of a door. 'You are the leaders of this township,' he declared. 'You should feel honoured that yours is the first to receive feudal notice from our king. Under the Arya system, this is a contract of mutual obligation. The king gives you protection, roads, schools, hospitals, good government. You render him physical services in exchange and pay him tithes and taxes. In order to commence the operation of this contract, we are calling on you today to pay taxes, which we have come to collect. Since this is our first call, we intend leaving it to your discretion as to how much you will contribute to enable us to start the government. Make no mistake, however, for we will soon prepare a list of householders with their trades, professions and occupations. Taxes based on wealth and productivity will thereafter be imposed by the king's edict from time to time and collected regularly at source by his officials. Records will be maintained so that every household shall pay its fair share. Go now and return with your gifts to the new king. If you don't wish to be generous, I advise you to be fair, for those who are not will be taxed at double the normal rate after we are in a position to make accurate assessments of wealth.'

A murmuring arose among the assembled men as they consulted one another. Ujjeni leaned back in his saddle and stretched. His bay moved a step back and pawed the ground. Uraw waited almost breathlessly. This was the sort of mission that should have been undertaken by a heavily armed group of men. Could three strange Arya convince fifty Arabi and Dasa men of standing that they should give up some of their wealth on demand? Uraw could not help admiring Ujjeni for his seeming unconcern. He appeared to accept submission from those present as a foregone conclusion and it was this perhaps that turned the event in his favour.

Pillai stepped forward. 'We, the residents of Mada Kalapuwa, welcome our new king and offer him allegiance,' he declared in firm tones. 'We are especially glad that we will henceforth be ruled by a civilized race. We will gladly contribute to the royal treasury, without question or condition, for we have been heartened by your statement that King Vijaya intends fulfilling his part of the feudal contract. Such has not been the case in the past. The road along which you travelled, law and order in this township and all its amenities have been established by our *panchyat*. We therefore humbly request a visit from our new king, or an audience with him in the near future, after the urgent duties that must face him have been fulfilled.' He glanced away and Uraw noted that a strange look passed between him and the scholarly man. 'We also humbly request that the rights and institutions, customs and traditions of the Dasa and Arabi people who make up most of our township be recognized and permitted to continue and that the sanctity of person and property be assured.'

Uraw could not help the feeling that the last remarks were pointed. Pillai knew who Ujjeni was. If Ujjeni had the same impression, he gave no indication of it. 'We are the conquerors,' he countered flatly. 'Let there be no mistake about that. You can be assured that our king will fulfil his obligations as he deems necessary and that the rights of your people will be safeguarded subject to the greater demands of the realm. You may disperse now and return within the hour.'

Nothing could be more general than that, Uraw thought in disgust. Uncomfortable in his role, he began sweating more profusely. As the assembled men began to leave, Puri dismounted from his wagon, hastened up to Ujjeni and whispered to him.

Ujjeni nodded. 'I thought so,' he said. He rose in his stirrups and pointed. 'You there!' he called. The men turned round, then glanced in the direction of the pointing finger. The scholarly man had stopped without looking back.

'I mean you, with your back to me,' Ujjeni said. The man slowly turned round. His eyes met Ujjeni's 'Come up here.'

Ujjeni gestured with long, skeletal fingers. 'The rest of you may leave.' He sat back in the saddle.

The scholarly man walked slowly up, while the others left the square with backward glances.

'What's your name?' Ujjeni demanded.

'Rasiah.' The man had a curiously rich voice.

'Your profession?'

'I'm a goldsmith, lord.'

'Good. Are there any other goldsmiths in this township?'

'No sir.'

'You have a daughter named Sundari?'

'Yes sir.'

'Your wife?'

'She's dead.'

'Any other children?'

'I have a younger son.'

'His name?'

'Ramiah.'

'He is apprenticed to you?'

'Yes sir.'

Uraw had thought that the commander would bludgeon his way to getting what he wanted, but to his relief, Ujjeni's natural cunning now came to the fore.

'You know, Rasiah, my king is going to need a goldsmith in his court,' Ujjeni said. 'It will be a very important appointment and it strikes me that you might be just the man for the job.'

Rasiah made no reply, merely waited, his dark eyes expressionless, for Ujjeni to proceed.

'The job would carry a very fine salary for doing the king's work, plus whatever you could make from other customers, which would of course be very high since the king's goldsmith could charge premium prices. Also, the appointment would be free of tax, so you would not have to contribute anything, from this very moment onwards.'

Ujjeni, you are indeed crafty, Uraw thought. You know

166

what bait to offer human fish. Yet I somehow feel that it is the wrong bait for this particular goldsmith. As if to echo the sentiment, two crows who were pecking at a ripe yellow banana trampled on the soil of the square flew away with squawks of alarm at the approach of one of the beggars. 'What have I to do in order to receive such honour and prosperity?' He heard Rasiah enquire gently.

Ujjeni stared at the man, obviously nonplussed. 'Well,' he began, then cleared his throat. He stared at Rasiah, trying to penetrate the man's *atman*. 'I'll be honest with you,' he finally stated, the grainy voice hushed and so respectful that Uraw wondered whether the man was playing a part. 'I wish to do honour to your daughter Sundari as well. I have seen her and she has won my heart.'

'You say you wish to do her honour, Sir?'

'Yes.'

'Are you asking for her hand in marriage?'

The look of incredulity on Ujjeni's face was almost comical. Then his anger burst forth. 'Marriage? *Me*, an Arya of noble birth, marry a low-caste Dasa bitch? You must be out of your mind, goldsmith. You must have mud for brains.' He paused, spittle on the sides of his mouth, trying to control his fury. 'Now listen to me, goldsmith.' His voice had become deadly quiet. 'I'm going to give you seven days in which to appear at the Thamba-Panni court with your daughter. I shall take her to my house and she shall become my concubine. Nothing more. How I shall treat her and what comes out of it for you and your family will be determined by the manner in which she fulfils her duties to me.' He paused. 'Go now. Bring your taxes. Your arrogance has lost you a golden opportunity.'

Rasiah drew himself to his full height. 'My lord, I do not need seven days, seven hours or seven seconds in order to follow the dictates of pride and honour,' he responded. 'I am a man of lowly station in life, a not-very-rich goldsmith, so all I have is within me. I beg of you to leave me and my family alone, for what you ask can never be.'

Hatred flamed in Ujjeni's sunken eyes. Uraw sensed that it was not because he was being crossed but because he could not penetrate Rasiah's dignity. He suddenly felt unclean, wished he were miles away.

'You heard my command, goldsmith,' Ujjeni said softly. 'Execute it, or you and your family shall be destroyed.'

The mission seemed successful, for Ujjeni, Anu and Uraw returned to the palace with a full wagonload of gold, silver and jewels, ornaments and artifacts, silks, linen and leather goods, fish and produce, but as they rode back, Uraw wondered how much he had lost by being a part of the expedition.

Chapter 13

While I was aware that Ujjeni, Uraw and Anu had departed on an experimental mission to collect taxes, I never suspected where they had been. So I was just as delighted as the king when they returned that evening with their wagonload of wealth and we had the goods stored in a small warehouse within the fort.

'Uraw must get the credit for collecting most of this,' Ujjeni said generously. Uraw flushed and looked down.

'You shall all receive your share,' my brother declared. 'And you, Uraw, shall receive the best part of it.'

Meanwhile, our plans for the defence and administration of the kingdom were proceeding apace.

My brother intended more than the conversion of those ditches outside the Priti palace into moats. He was using the exercise for an experiment in irrigation control, which, if successful would be the beginning of a new phase in the agricultural economy of Lanka. Commencing the very day after we captured the fort, it took one week to excavate the soil and to build the twin sluice gates adjoining the river bank outside the fort. When the soil was dug away and the outer gates were removed, the waters of the river would flow into the two ditches that served the fort. Marvelling at how much my brother had observed of the methods of constructing irrigation works in Sinha-Pura in the midst of his life of crime, I was even more impressed by the ingenuity and inventiveness he displayed in those areas in which he had acquired no knowledge.

The open area opposite the fort had been cleared of the corpses that had once strewn it. Our dead comrades had been cremated, the dozens of Yakka dead had been dumped into great pits and buried with flowers sprinkled over the graves, as was their custom.

When we pressed the Yakka labour, we had not disclosed our intention to them. Now, their task done, they and their fellow villagers seemed apprehensive as they began to assemble on the river bank that sunny morning. It suddenly dawned on me that they probably feared that they had been summoned for a mass execution, since they were surrounded by our men, heavily armed.

Having no concept of orderliness when in a crowd, they stood wherever they could, about two hundred men, women and children, in a semi-circle we made them form. The men were dressed mostly in animal skin loincloths or in homespun cotton, their dark, hairy chests uncovered, the long black hair shiny with oil; the women wore shabby waistcloths of red or green cotton, with shawls covering their breasts. The silver-haired Pina strutted about, trying to allay fears and inspire confidence, especially in the women who seemed fearful indeed. Only the Princess Kuveni, standing behind King Vijaya and me at the entrance to the fort, was at ease. Breasts bare, clad in a tight, blue silken waistcloth, flowers in her hair, she wore her normal jasmine scent, while the rest of the Yakka had their characteristic odour of musty skin, unwashed clothes and animal fur.

I suddenly thought of Sundari as one with the Yakka and a great white flame of compassion for them filled me. From the well-springs of this compassion, I felt deeply for their helplessness. Up to this moment, I had been reacting to these people as a voluntary exile from my own native Sinha-Pura, joined inextricably with my brother and his comrades in a desperate attempt to find or create a resting place. My first experience of the Yakka had been of a hostile people, the day we arrived, a people whom we had to be wary of as possible adversaries or even assassins. The passing days had somewhat allayed my fears, but the mistrust had remained, a natural symptom of the instinct to survive. Thamba-Panni was a place, a territory, that afforded me some hope of a permanent refuge, its Yakka inhabitants somehow shadow figures. Not even the palace attendants, nor the labour force, had registered with me as individual human beings, with thoughts and desires, feelings and aspirations. They had to make room for us, or be displaced. They were no more than a herd to be moved, jungle to be cut down to provide us with a habitation and a home, odd cows to be milked, the tree that might afford shelter. The Princess Kuveni had been the only exception. The knowledge that I could have been so heartless now shocked me. I realized for the first time that here were a people, too many of them with the same pathetic look of hopelessness and despair in their large, dark eyes.

I instinctively walked towards a woman who was suckling a baby at her breast. She was dressed in a faded waistcloth. She could not have been more than thirty, but her wrinkled skin, gaunt features and lean frame made her seem over fifty years old. Her baby was black and ugly, but she looked at it with her large eyes as if it were her greatest treasure. My shadow fell on her and she looked up with a start. Terror shot through her face when she saw me standing in front of her and she grasped her baby protectively.

'Do not be afraid,' I assured her gently. I reached out and stroked the baby's head lightly. Her breath caught in fear. 'I am Prince Lala, brother of the king, whom you see standing there. Please tell your people that you are here this morning as our guests. We love you all and want to be a part of your country. We hope to prove to you today that we can be good for you.' I looked round at the Yakka, smiling at them. They hesitated, noticed my hand caressing the baby's head and began to return my smile, tentatively at first, then openly. That one gesture of mine had spoken to them more than any words.

A boy of about eight sidled up to me. His unwashed face was gaunt and dark, his ribs pushed against his skin above a stained half-sarong. It was his expression of dumb misery that smote me. When he found his voice is sounded rusty somehow. 'Are you really a prince?' he enquired.

'Yes, indeed,' I turned to look down at him.

'They told me you are all *goni-billas*, demons, who will eat us some day.'

I was astounded. 'Well, you can see that we don't eat human beings, least of all children.' I squatted before him. 'What is your name?'

Some of the misery left his face. He stuck a shy forefinger in his mouth. 'Silindu.'

'That's a lovely name. Do you know what it means?'

'No.'

'It means "graceful". And I think you are graceful. Do you live in the village?'

'Yes.' He was grinning his shy delight now.

'What is your father's name? Is he here?'

'I have no father or mother. I live with my grandmother. Her name is Achchi. We are very poor.' He reached out and touched my white silken tunic with grubby fingers. 'You look like a deva.'

I felt my eyes prickle with tears. 'I am no deva,' I responded. 'Just a human being, like you. I am going to arrange for you and your grandmother to receive food from the palace every day, so you will grow big and strong.'

His eyes shone. 'And become a hunter?'

'A mighty hunter.' I patted his cheek and stood erect. I could feel the warmth of the crowd of Yakkas.

'Can I see you again, Prince?' His voice choked on the question and I choked inside with the realization that seeing me again was more important to him than food. I resolved then and there that the Yakka children, with their bulbous stomachs and grubby faces, would have some hope in life. As I returned to take my place beside my brother, I noticed Ujjeni standing behind me. His look was one of contempt for me. His eyes swept towards the Yakka. They could have been rotten meat in the market. He despised them. He

172

would exploit them ruthlessly.

I would have to protect the Yakka from Ujjeni and his like. They lived uncomplicated lives, tilling, sowing, reaping or hunting for food as and when they needed it, or starving whenever their skills, their diligence or their gods failed them. I simply could not let them exchange one bondage for another, though they seemed willing enough to remain compliant subjects of their new masters in the life of perpetual subjection they did not even think to question.

Prince Vijaya and I were dressed alike for the occasion in white *dhotis* and *kurthas* rescued from our ships. The Princess Kuveni stood dark and beautiful to one side of us, in that silken cloth of shining blue, a shade too dark for her dusty skin. Her black hair, washed and oiled, gleamed down to below her waist, her eyes were lustrous. She looked young, eager, intense. My brother had told me that she was trying to be a good wife to him. I wondered what it would be like to have Sundari for my wife.

On the green turf of the riverbank, a table draped with white cloth had been placed, containing the offerings to our men's gods, flowers, water, incense and perfumed oil. An occasional arrow hissed through the air as one of our archers fired at a crow that swooped down, cawing, to investigate the altar.

I acted as priest for the occasion. In a loud chant, I invoked Brahma, Agni and Purusa, then Parvati, whose sister is the Great Ganga and who therefore commands the river-force. Silently I prayed to my One God for his blessing. I was getting closer to Him each day. As my comprehension of Him increased, I had found myself better able to make a compartment, within my comprehension of His reality, for the gods of other men.

When I had finished my chant, Prince Vijaya held up his hands for silence. His red locks gleaming in the bright sunshine, he looked as magnificent as a god. He now surveyed the crowd without speaking, until he had their total attention. Soon, you could hear nothing, except for the cry of a child, quickly hushed, and the cough of a man with a bad cold. When the prince finally spoke, his voice was deep, resonant, the tones measured.

'You are about to witness one of the miracles that can be wrought when gods and men unite. While labour on this project represents the joint endeavours of Arya and Yakka, nothing would have been accomplished without the favour of the gods. Great Agni brought us sunshine to end the floods of the rainy season. Great Parvati, sister of our river goddess, gradually reduced the flow of her waters so that we could build our sluice gates without fear. Great Purusa gentled his winds, Great Brahma smiled upon us all . . .'

I was amazed. My brother believed in no gods, yet here he was, setting aside his views for the needs of the people. The man was a politician too, able to use other men's beliefs, even when they were not his own, to achieve his goals.

'We have taken your princess for our consort,' my brother continued, gesturing to where the Princess Kuveni stood. She smiled shyly, her gaze fixed on him in frank adoration. 'She is under our protection, so no man may cross her, still less do her harm. More importantly, however, she is under your protection, for she is the symbol of the Yakka people in our combined rule. Together, we shall build a new kingdom.' The prince's eyes began to gleam and he raised a clenched fist aloft. 'A land in which there is food and clothing for all, a land in which men, women and children may walk without fear, a land of endeavour and the sharing of the fruits of that endeavour, a just kingdom, a *dharma dwipaya.*'

He surveyed the Yakkas, commanding their attention, then looked up at the cloudless blue skies as if for divine inspiration. He turned towards the men at the sluice gates. 'Let our gods show us their will,' he shouted. 'Dig away the dirt, men, raise the sluices, hack away the outer gates!'

My heart started to beat faster. This was the moment of

truth. If we failed, we would be set back more than the week of labour it had taken to prepare for the event. If we succeeded, we would inspire the Yakka to awe of our gods, perhaps even converting some to the beliefs of our men. I held my breath. What if we did fail? Would we look foolish and thus lose some of the hold we had begun to acquire over these people?

Our men bent to the wheels that would slowly raise the great gates to allow the river waters into the moat.

Would the wheels turn? Would the men be strong enough to get those wheels to lift the upper gate? If the gate did rise, would the force of the water smash through, destroying the entire sluice and our hopes? This event on a sunny morning, beneath a cloudless blue sky would either set us back, or herald the beiginning of a new era for Lanka.

That same morning, over a hundred miles away, Hamy accompanied by Kira attended Prince Tikka, who awaited audience with King Ra-hula, ruler of the *pata rata*, the low-country kingdom, in the audience chamber of his palace in the city of Kalyani. All three were dressed in clothes provided at the palace, white dhotis, the back flap pulled high, *Naga* fashion, to reveal some of the thigh at the rear, with white *kurthas*, overshirts. They were bathed, combed and, unusually for them, scented with a sandalwood paste.

Although cool breezes rustled through the giant green *mara* and flame trees scattering the palace gardens, Hamy found it warm and close in the audience chamber, a long narrow room served by an entrance foyer. Only the high roof, about twenty cubits tall, supported by enormous columns of brown teakwood, kept the chamber from being like an oven, for it was ventilated only by high, grilled windows, the front entrance doors and those leading from its rear to the royal dining chamber, beyond which Hamy caught glimpses of the centre courtyard.

King Ra-hula's throne was placed on a wooden platform

before the far wall of the chamber, the king seated on it in the lotus pose, his crossed feet and ankles resting on his thighs. Hamy concluded this must be the famous golden throne, once the cause of a dispute between King Ra-hula and his neighbour, Ra-dha, King of Sita Eli-ja in the *udarata*, the up-country kingdom. Gautama, who had once been a prince of the Sakya clan, which ruled the northern kingdom or the great continent and who claimed to be a Buddha, had come over to settle the dispute. Some folk said that Gautama had flown over in an air chariot, as Hamy's ancestor, Ra-vanna, had done when he abducted the beautiful Sita, wife of Ra-ma. The Buddhist converts of Lanka claimed that the Buddha had simply materialized from Isipatana, in the north of the great continent, by using *iddhi* powers.

After the Buddha had judged that King Ra-hula was entitled to the throne, it was a short cry to the latter's conversion to the doctrine, Hamy reflected cynically. The king obviously decided that a man of such sound judgement as the Buddha must be speaking the truth. So the passing of this priceless material object to him had made him accept the treasure of a doctrine that preached the valuelessness of material things!

Hamy had made it a point to listen to the wandering Buddhist ascetics from Kalyani, who went about the Yakka kingdom with shaven heads and yellow robes, carrying the black begging bowls and *indikola* palm-leaf parasols. These men lived without possessions, begging for food, finding shelter wherever it was available. Gonda, the king of the *uda rata*, Prince Tikka's father, regarded them with good-natured tolerance, but he might have tortured them or even put them to death for sacrilege had they not been the subjects of the powerful Kalyani ruler.

Now here was the Kalyani ruler, also wearing yellow robes and a shaven head, granting audience from the golden throne. Hamy found it incongruous, yet he was impressed by the King's appearance. King Ra-hula was a tall, very dark-skinned man of great dignity. There was not a single wrinkle or layer of fat on his body, though Hamy knew him to be over sixty years old. He had a large, flat face, cast in the Dasa mould, with wide, heavy cheekbones, flaring nostrils and a square jaw. His teeth, between thin lips, were white as mother-of-pearl. It was his eyes, however, beneath the broad forehead steeply sloping up to the gleaming head, that commanded attention. They were large and dark, with no visible pupils, peaceful yet possessed of a strange magnetic, perceptive quality such as Hamy had only observed in some of the Buddha's disciples. Certainly no Yakka ever looked like this Naga king, for the more cultivated Yakka generally had hot eyes that could bow in subjugation, or thrust deep, in hatred, but were continually searching, shifting.

The three of them advanced to the dais, made obeisance to the king and stood erect, awaiting his command. When he spoke, the king's voice was pitched high, soft and gentle. 'We are sorry to have kept you two days before seeing you,' he stated. 'As you have probably been told, our venerated leader, Lord Buddha, passed away on the night of the last full moon, twenty-one days ago, in the *sala* of the hall of the Holy Grove, the Upa wata, in Kusi Nara, within the realms of the late High King Bimbisara's territory.'

The king mopped his brow with a large yellow handkerchief and looked, for some reason, at Hamy. It was a searching gaze, Hamy noted before dropping his eyes, as was the custom when a king looks at one directly.

'It is nonetheless a dire calamity,' the king continued. 'Fortified though we are by the true doctrine of our Lord – for that is our refuge, the legacy he left to us and to posterity for ever – we had thought that the Buddhas do not die.' A tiny line of puzzlement appeared between the king's shaven brows. 'But we believe that death is the true, the final entryway to the eternity of the Enlightenment he obtained in this life. One has to die in order not to be reborn.' He paused, reflecting, and his brow cleared.

'Though we have already received information as to the facts, pray give us details, cousin, of all that transpired in King Kalu Sena's fort.'

Hamy noted the 'cousin' with surprise. The king was a Naga, in no way related to the Yakka Prince Tikka. He must feel a kinship with us now that we have a common intruder on our soil, Hamy guessed.

Prince Tikka's voice had a sharp edge to it as he recounted the events of the massacre. The king listened without comment.

'Once we got to the opposite bank of the river,' Prince Tikka ended. 'We confined our travel to the early hours of dawn and night, in order to avoid detection. We could not know to what extent the accursed Arya had penetrated beyond the fort. We holed up in scrub or jungle during the bright hours of daylight and slept wherever we could at night. Not having weapons to hunt with, we . . . er . . . seized food whenever we could lay our hands upon it. We kept heading for your kingdom. What a blessed relief when we finally heard the speeding waters of the Kalyani river nine days later and smelled the mud of its flats . . .'

You are crafty as well as arrogant, Prince, Hamy thought. You are displaying respect, offering subtle flattery and even speaking like a *kavi*-master, a poet. Also, though you are accustomed to a court where the king is merely the greatest thug, you adjust your attitudes to the rules of this one. There is more in you than I thought.

'After almost three days of wandering on the other side of the river, it took us but a day to get to your court,' Prince Tikka concluded. 'Since we were unknown in this kingdom, we dared not act otherwise than as wandering beggars. I thank my demon god that we were not mistaken for *ahikuntakayas*, gypsies, because of our matted locks and ragged appearance. Your city walls were unmanned, its gates open, so we soon reached the palace and contacted your chief attendant, whom I knew from my last visit to you.

He recognized me, provided us with quarters and arranged for this audience with you. I request that he be commended for his hospitality.'

'We shall reward him suitably, but his acts are his own reward to himself. We trust that you are comfortably lodged and well looked after?'

'Without a doubt, lord.'

'That is well and you and your companions may stay with us as long as you desire. We are certain, however, that your visit has a purpose, else you would not have chosen to come here instead of returning directly to your own kingdom.'

'You are indeed wise, lord.' Prince Tikka looked down at the paved floor a moment, then directly up at the king. His dark eyes flashed with a fire so intense that they seemed to shoot red flames. The calm look was gone. His body shook. His voice was hard as a fire-kiln. 'Our people, all our kinsmen, have been massacred by these seven hundred Arya invaders. King Kalu Sena should have annihilated them first, on the very night they landed, while they slept exhausted on the beach. I begged him to do so, but he preferred to wait until his daughter's . . . er . . . my betrothal ceremonies, were concluded. Perhaps his judgement was clouded by the *ra* we had all been consuming during the whole day, while waiting for the rains to abate. Whatever the cause, the king paid the price of over-confidence in himself and of underestimating the enemy. This is always the price of the hunt, lord, when we do not sufficiently credit the cunning of the leopard and bear or the unpredictability of the elephant in *musth*.'

Prince Tikka paused to test the king's reaction. He found none. The expressionless eyes remained enigmatic.

'I don't wish to make the same mistake.' Prince Tikka's sharp voice was suddenly hoarse. 'My desire to avenge my fellow kinsmen, the seizure of my soil, the deadly insult offered to me at my betrothal and the enslavement of my people, will be controlled by my very hatred of these murderers, by my desire to exterminate them all, after . . . I repeat, *after* I have made them suffer. There is no leader of any consequence left in our kingdom, save the king, my father, who was too weakened by the fever-disease even to attend the betrothal. It would take me too long to rally the few remaining chiefs and their followers to this cause. By then, the invader might have entered our territory. So I have come to you for help in driving him away, before it is too late.'

The clatter of a bowl from the dining room disturbed the stillness of the chamber. The odour of *brinjal* cooked in coriander spice and lime juice intruded. Hamy knew that the king, like Buddhist *bhikkus*, ate only one meal a day, vegetarian at that, before the noon hour. Prince Tikka should curtail this audience.

'Hmmm. We see . . .' King Ra-hula's eyes drifted from the Prince's face to those of his two companions. He seemed so unperturbed, serene, in the face of a possible threat to his kingdom, that Hamy felt a tinge of admiration. 'What would you have us do?' This king was obviously not about to act like a fish and take the bait. 'But before you answer, tell us, have you heard of *maitriya* and *ahimsa*?'

'No, Sire.'

'Please proceed then to tell us what you request.'

'You will undoubtedly be alarmed, lord, at the news that King Kalu Sena died in single combat with this Prince Vijaya, that the victors have been improving the defences of the Priti fort and are now commandeering all available horses in our kingdom. All this is information we gathered from gossip that had reached the few people we talked to on our way here. I seek your help in attacking the enemy immediately, before he has time to improve his defences and invade our kingdoms.'

'You still have not told us what you expect us to do, Prince.' The king's voice was gentler than ever, yet it held a chiding note to it.

'Send your army out to attack the Arya, or at least to harry them, delay them, until I can raise the Yakka people, perhaps the Arya of the south as well, and we can make a combined assault.'

'But we no longer have any army in the *pata rata* kingdom.'

Prince Tikka's jaw dropped. He started forward, his small eyes nearly popping out of his head like dark buttons pushed through a buttonhole. 'What?' He recovered himself and stopped. 'I mean . . . I don't understand, Lord.'

'I'm sure you will not, Prince, but let me explain.' A benign, tolerant smile crossed the king's dark features, like sunlight emerging through a cloud. 'As you may not know, our Lord Buddha's doctrine teaches us to eliminate desire, because desire causes craving, craving causes clinging, clinging causes suffering. Once desire ceases, we reach *arahat*-ship, sainthood. When we are striving for the cessation of desire within us, even the desire to cease all desire, how can we join you in these desires that have seized you, nay that appear to be consuming you, for vengeance, for torturing, killing, seizing territory?' The king's glance held a hint of shrewdness. 'All these *akusala kharma*, evil actions, would act to our detriment, though they might help you achieve your own aims, whatever they may be.'

The king paused to allow his words to sink in. The tinge of admiration Hamy first felt had become a gushing flow.

'Not knowing things as they truly are makes one accumulate *kharma*, action and *vipaka*, its fruit, frequently bitter,' the king continued. 'Thus said the Enlightened One. If a mango seed is *kharma*, the fruit is its *vipaka*, consequence. The bark, the leaves, the flowers of the tree are all inevitable consequences arising from the first seed, which could produce nothing else. So it is with man and his actions. Man has no continuing stream of consciousness, nor does he go to the blue skies, to the dark waters or to the belly of the earth, when he dies. He is reborn from the effects of the life he leads in this birth to a state that is the consequence of the *kharma* he accumulated. We of the Doctrine do not even believe, as your people do, in man's rebirth as the bird, animal, or tree they represent in this life. Thus with us humans, as with all living things, no *kharma* is accumulated when one has completely eradicated craving and understands things as they really are.'

The king paused, his dark eyes searching Prince Tikka's face. He gave no evidence of what he saw there, but proceeded in his gentle sing-song voice. 'Your present form, Prince, is merely a manifestation of the kharmic force. So is mine. You think of yourself as a being. All you are is a combination of matter that has thrown forth a mind, as that mango seed brought forth a delicious fruit. So in our lives, there is no actor, merely the action. What you make of this composition of mind and matter that is you and yet not you will determine its every state, including that which will be when your body reaches death, as you call it. People and things die from one of four causes. Would you like me to tell you what they are?'

Prince Tikka nodded. 'Yes, Sire.' Hamy could sense his thoughts. No harm humouring this old fool so long as he helps drive out the Arya.

'When we are born,' King Ra-hula explained. 'We are the product of the force of reproductive *kharma*, which in turn resulted from the last thought moment of our previous birth. Once the energy of that reproductive *kharma* is spent, the activities of our material form, in which the life force was embodied, cease even before old age. Without energy, that life form collapses. Do we make our meaning clear?'

Hamy knew Prince Tikka to be a fighter and a hunter, never a philosopher. While the prince could comprehend King Ra-hula's words, he would be impatient with them. Hamy could not help but feel relief at hearing the prince reply steadily. 'Indeed, I do, Sire. Your words make sense.'

'Not our words, Prince, but those of our Enlightened One,' the king responded. 'Now to the four causes of death as Lord Buddha explained them. The first is the exhaustion of the force of reproductive *kharma* that gave rise to the birth. The second is the end of the life term of that force, which results in natural death, such as through old age. The third is the simultaneous exhaustion of the reproductive *kharmic* energy and the life term. The last is the exhaustion of the force of reproductive *kharma* before the end of its life-term. The first three of these we call timely death, the last untimely death. To quote you an example, an oil-lamp may be extinguished due to exhaustion of the wick, exhaustion of the oil, simultaneous exhaustion of both wick and oil, or some extraneous cause, like a gust of wind. It is therefore essential for us, in this life, to prepare for our next birth. Instead of generating hatred and fury, please therefore start guiding your thought processes now, while you are still young, so that your last thought, when your life ends, will lead your mind and matter to a higher state in your next life-process.'

Hamy glanced again at Prince Tikka. The average Yakka could not begin to comprehend what King Ra-hula had just said. Prince Tikka probably did, but was now bewildered as to the reason for this flow of words. He had asked for help from this king, and received a priestly sermon. The king is so wise, Hamy thought. Does he not know that you do not wish to grasp what he offers? Then the truth dawned on him. Being wise, King Ra-hula was merely gentling his refusal of Prince Tikka's request through a discourse he knew would confuse. And yet in his very gentleness was unbelievable strength. Hamy looked up at the king. The large, dark eyes were suddenly fixed on him. This king, who has the power of physical motionlessness, can project his inner force with incredible intensity, he realized. He knows that I alone of the three visitors appreciate what he is saying. His look is a challenge, a command, to what I know not as yet, though I shall contemplate it in the days ahead.

'B-but, lord . . .' Prince Tikka stammered. 'All I'm asking for is the help of your army of five thousand fighting men.'

King Ra-hula's smile was bland. 'When we had word of the death of our Lord Buddha, we wondered what we could do as a tribute to him and as evidence to him in Sansara that we are his dedicated followers. We finally decided to order our soldiers to become an army for the doctrine, seeking Enlightenment, fighting to overcome only the enemy, desire. So our army was disbanded as a military unit seven days ago. The instruments of death have become givers of life.'

Chapter 14

As they strained at the wheels that would raise the sluice gates, the muscles of the men began to gleam with sweat. I held my breath, listening to the men grunting with intensified effort. Then I heard a squeak of protest and thought I saw a tiny, ever so tiny movement.

I released my breath, sucking the warm air gratefully into my lungs. Almost imperceptibly, the upper part of the gate began to rise. The green waters around it rippled, then were drawn through the opening below with a great, slurping sound. Soon the waters began pouring into the ditch in a streaming flood.

A gasp arose from the Yakka, a great cheer from our men rent the air and sought the skies.

The workers now stopped turning the wheels and merely clung to the handles, allowing the waters to keep rushing in at an even rate, splashing louder than the river, sparkling like a reflection of the gladness within me.

My brother raised his brawny arms high again for silence. The cheering stopped abruptly. An uncanny stillness reigned, as if the earth was hushed to hear his words.

'Behold, the miracle!' The prince exulted. 'And I promise you more.' He paused at a sudden, unexpected muttering in the Yakka ranks. One arm dropped to his side, the other extending to the source of the sound, the broad finger pointing. 'You! Come forward and say what you desire aloud.' His eyes glittered dangerously.

It was old Pina who stepped hesitantly through the line of guards to stand alone upon the green sward. He looked diminutive beside our men, his dark, wrinkled skin gleaming in the sunshine, the white hair fluttering before a breeze that sprang from across the river. Yet he possessed a strange dignity, which I recognized as coming from this land that had belonged to him and his ancestors from time immemorial, the dignity of a people linked with their native soil, their trees and sunshine, their birds and beasts, their rivers.

'We delivered you a kingdom, prince, in the hope that you would better our lot.' Pina's high-pitched voice was surprisingly decisive and firm, his gaze on Prince Vijaya intense and unafraid. 'You have already started improving our lives in many areas. Yet I, as a village elder, have seen a way of life slipping from our grasp and it frightens me. Today, you and your Arya comrades have tampered with the river goddess, for whatever purpose. We are all amazed, for we have never before witnessed such a miracle. Yet you have dared to harness our goddess to your needs and I, for one, am terribly afraid, lest the gods destroy us all for this act of sacrilege.' He half turned and looked at his people, most of whom nodded vigorously or murmured in assent, 'Ahey! Ahey!'

I had expected my brother to erupt in anger. Instead, he surveyed Pina thoughtfully. Finally, the words came out quietly, as if uttered by some force other than himself. 'We, King Vijaya Sinha-Bahu, son of kings, are an instrument of the gods,' he declared. It was the first time he had called himself king. 'We alone are responsible for what you term an act of sacrilege. So it is only us and us alone the goddess must destroy.'

Suddenly, Prince Vijaya spun round and faced the river. Slowly, solemnly, he took off his *kurtha* and dropped it on the grass. His *dhoti* followed and he stood naked, save for the white loincloth around his magnificent limbs. 'If you are against us, Parvati, river goddess, if you deem our act to be one of sacrilege, destroy us now,' he cried in a loud voice. 'If you love us, however, receive us into your

186

embrace and deliver us back safely to our people.'

He took six running steps towards the river, raised his hands together over his head and dived gracefully into the waters. He clove them expertly, tips of fingers, hands and head first, leaving barely a ripple. Smoothly, he disappeared into the river. Seconds went by, during which the Yakkas rushed forward to crowd the bank. 'He's dead!' . . . 'The river goddess has destroyed him!' . . . 'Didn't I tell you?' . . .

More seconds sped by. A sigh arose from the Yakka ranks. A child began to cry.

Suddenly, a head, now dark with the water, reappeared about a hundred yards from the bank.

'Look! There he is!' It was Pina, pointing a shaking finger.

The dark head vanished. The Yakkas gasped, this time in apprehension. The river goddess had released the irreverent prince only to torture him before sucking him into her maw again.

To my crafty brother, who had swum the waters of the Ganga, the great river of the Indhoos, this Lanka river was but a stream. He had obviously noted that the Yakkas were hunters, not swimmers. Those who did take to the water jumped in feet first, with a great bang, then dog-paddled, splashed, blowing and grunting. They knew nothing about the arts of swimming.

So my brother swam under water to impress the Yakka and also to avoid the main thrust of the current, bobbing up only fleetingly for air. He finally reappeared on the opposite bank, almost directly opposite the fort, clambered up it and turned to face the Yakkas, his arms extended to the skies, a godly figure proclaiming his triumph.

By the time he swam back, climbed the sluice gate and sprang to the dry soil of our bank, he was more than a hero to the simple Yakka. He was a person who had been received into the deepest embrace of the river goddess and been returned safely. Therefore he was a god.

Prince Tikka left his audience with King Ra-hula in Kalyani, capital of the *pata rata*, the low-country kingdom, with seeming good grace, many compliments as to the king's spirituality and great protestations of friendship. Hamy knew, however, that the young prince was carefully restraining his anger. It exploded when the three Yakka men reached the prince's quarters.

'The accursed son of a whore, what does he think he is doing?' Prince Tikka roared. He began pacing the small bedchamber like a caged black panther, seeking a way out of some captivity imposed on him by the king's action in changing his fighting force to a missionary one. 'Is he mad? How does he think he will rule his kingdom without an army?'

'Perhaps he is counting on this non-violent religion to change people's lives so that an army will not be necessary,' Kira suggested tactlessly.

Prince Tikka paused in his stride and turned on Kira with such fury that the fat man blanched. 'You stupid *haraka*, bull, can you stop crime through religion?'

'Religious people generally avoid crime, Lord,' Kira persisted, still trying to be helpful.

Prince Tikka lashed out with the back of his hand. The sound of the stinging slap across Kira's pudgy cheek cracked through the room. Kira rocked sideways, stifling an exclamation of pain. His hand went to his cheek, which had turned white with the blow then became suffused with colour. 'I'm sorry, Prince,' he muttered.

'That will teach you not to fart through your mouth.' Prince Tikka swung towards Hamy. 'Do *you* have any windy comments?'

Hamy shrugged and spread his palms out. 'Who, me? I'm too foolish to have any comment and too wise to utter it, Lord. And I would exchange neither my wisdom nor my folly for a blow.'

The prince glared at him, the brown eyes flashing fire. 'You'll be too smart for your own good one of these days.' He spat into a brass spittoon in the corner of the room, turned on his heel and walked up to the grilled window, where he paused, staring outside.

Once again, Hamy wondered at his loyalty to this prince, a loyalty that had survived many tests, especially that of the absence of deep love. It had started when he was a boy, six years older than the nine-year-old prince. He was bathing in the Sita Eli-ja lake when he slipped into a hole and got stuck in the mud. Prince Tikka, who happened to be passing by, had observed his plight. At the risk of his own life, the Prince leapt into the water and saved him. Full of admiration and gratitude, Hamy's father had pledged his life to the prince. He sought an audience with King Gonda, Prince Tikka's father, and upon Prince Tikka's urging Hamy was appointed a tutor and aide of the prince. A man without any family, after his father died, he had lived in the home of an uncle, a *veda rala*, physician who had brought him up and then used him as a helper in his profession. The new appointment gave Hamy his freedom, but made him the prince's liege man for ever.

'You must look to the long-term good, in this situation, Prince,' Hamy now advised. 'When a king gives up his army, he surrenders his kingdom.'

'To whom?' Prince Tikka seemed to be addressing the limpid air outside.

Children's shouts arose from the palace gardens. Is that the answer, Hamy wondered. Has King Ra-hula then given up his kingdom to its children? Aloud, he said, 'To whomever is powerful enough to seize it.'

'You mean someone from our *uda rala* up-country kingdom?'

'No. That could still involve war and take too much time. What I mean is that every king has an enemy within.'

189

'Such as?'

'Who am I to say, Lord? After all, we are guests of King Ra-hula here. All I know is that the Kalyani kingdom goes by Naga laws of succession to the ruler's heirs, but King Ra-hula has no children and military commanders sometimes wrest leadership in defiance of such laws.'

'How would that help us?'

'A military leader strong enough to seize this kingdom would also be ambitious enough to invade the adjoining one.'

Prince Tikka swung round, his white teeth flashing in a smile. He smote palm on fist. 'That's it! No wonder I keep you around. In spite of your stupid, bumbling ways and your love of religions, you have flashes of genius. It would indeed be easier to arrange a military takeover of Kalyani from within than to invade the kingdom. That would be our quickest means of wreaking vengeance on the accursed Arya.'

Hamy realized that he might have extended a double-edged sword to his prince. A strong, new king in Kalyani, ambitious enough to take arms against the Arya, might become a source of danger to the *uda rata* kingdom as well. But campaigning in the hills had always deterred aggressors, and this was not the time to produce counter-arguments either so Hamy held his peace.

'I know the very man who can do it,' Prince Tikka stated triumphantly.

The passing days had not dimmed my thoughts of Sundari; indeed they only increased my desire to see her. The feeling I developed for the Yakkas that morning had opened some sluice gates in my mind as well. During the rest of that day, I found myself regarding the differences of race, religion and caste between Sundari and me as nothing, especially if we loved each other. I would take her for my wife, regardless of these differences and any opposition from my brother, the king, if she loved me and would have me. With the impetuosity of youth, I decided that I would ride to Mada Kalapuwa the very next morning and find out.

I obtained leave from my brother on the pretext of taking the day off to explore the countryside for irrigation projects, which I fully intended doing, and obtained Vijit's approval to take Bala with me. I can't say that I was proud of my deceit, but I saw no purpose in arousing my brother's anger and opposition if Sundari was to deny my suit.

Bala and I rode out together at dawn the next day, I on an Arabi grey I liked, Bala mounted on a Scindhi bay. When we passed the pond at which the first encounter with the Princess Kuveni had taken place, as a sop to my avowed mission I checked to see how we could construct a channel that would irrigate many acres of land.

Pushing west to the ocean and then north, we came across a small lake that could bring several more hundred acres under cultivation. We then pushed on hard for Mada Kalapuwa.

It was past noon by the time we reached our destination. The sun shone fiercely down from a burnt blue sky on palmyra and scrub. The air was clear and dry, but I was sweating profusely beneath my white *kurtha*, overshirt. Not surprisingly, the township was deserted except for beggars dozing in the temple square. This was the hottest time of the day, when people stayed indoors to avoid the heat, some people, that is, I reflected sardonically, not fools in love! Even the mangy pi-dogs, heads between paws, stretched on the warm sand in the limited shade of scrubby palmyras, barely opened their eyes at our passing.

We trotted through the single street of the township until we came to a fork, passing only three people, a bare-bodied fisherman with a net, a limping beggar and a washer-woman. Bala indicated the right-hand fork and we turned to find ourselves beneath giant tamarind trees. We rode between the brown *cadjan* fences of an avenue until we saw the silver waters of the lagoon ahead of us, then stopped at the last entry way in the *cadjan* wall on the left. 'That is it!' Bala exclaimed.

'You wait outside,' I bade him. 'Would you please mind my horse?'

'Certainly, Prince.'

I dismounted, handed Bala the reins and paused outside the tall gates, also of *cadjan* but reinforced by a wood frame. So this was where Sundari was born and had grown up. She must have known a great deal of security in such a township surrounded by her own people, all living a civilized existence, visiting her Yakka friends, until a few nights ago, when the noble ones arrived and shattered that security.

I opened the gate, walked inside the garden, then closed the gate behind me. I proceeded through the compound. The house was built of local bricks, plastered white, surmounted by a roof of yellow, half-round tiles and shaded by a tall tree, in the green branches of which mynahs twittered. It had a verandah in front, with a half wall on which green plants in red clay pots had been placed; below a row of wild jasmine bushes scented the air. A coral-strewn walkway, bordered by beds of yellow *kapuru*, led to the front entrance. The rest of the garden consisted of carefully cultivated beds of green onions and red chilli, the grey sand in between swept clean. At the back were a well and an outhouse, separated by a watermelon creeper on a *massa*. The whole place was rural, peaceful, embodying the life-style of the Dasa, who are an ancient civilized race; but it also had some special aura which had to come from the spirits of the people who dwelt here.

I walked up to the verandah, noticing black ebony settles placed along the wall behind tables across which Sundari's father obviously transacted his business. The traditions of his caste forbade him to work with any metal except gold and made it a sin to adulterate the gold. His gold would be kept in a strong room inside the house, which seemed to consist of a living room in front and an open courtyard in the centre, with bedrooms opening on to it. I wondered what precautions would be taken to safeguard the gold and decided that people would bring their own gold to Sundari's father and he would only accept whatever he was working on at any one time. For the rest, the community was probably mutually supportive in regard to security.

Before I could take further stock of the interior, a black and white dog came racing out of the house, barking furiously, skidded to a halt in front of me and remained there, snarling, as if daring me to take one step farther. Not being disposed to test his disposition, I merely stood my ground, smiling at him.

'Quiet, dog, . . . be quiet,' I heard a deep voice say.

A tall, dark man, slightly stooped, clad only in a white verti-cloth, emerged through the shade of the living room. His face was lean and ascetic. As the light from the verandah threw it into relief, I noted the scholarly look and the dignity of the eyes. This must be Sundari's father. 'Go,' he commanded the dog quietly and it slunk away reluctantly towards the rear of the house.

He must have recognized me for an Arya, because the enquiring look in his eyes changed to an icy calm. 'What can I do for you?' he asked.

'I'm Prince Lala Sinha-Bahu, brother of the new king of Lanka. You must be the father of Sundari.'

His expression relaxed somewhat.

'Yes, my name is Rasiah. My daughter told me about you, Prince. You were kind to save her from the forces you let loose in our kingdom.'

For a moment, I was taken aback, but I quickly realized the truth of what Rasiah had said. 'You are right,' I gently agreed. 'We did indeed let loose these forces, but now we hope to maintain law, order and decency.'

'I'm sorry, Prince, but we have no evidence of such

aims.'

'What d'you mean.'

'Don't you know?'

'Know what?'

'That your officials have already visited us and appropriated our possessions, claiming that these were taxes.'

I was bewildered. 'What officials,' I began. Then the truth struck me. 'You mean three men, one of them lean, gaunt . . .'

'Yes.' The word came out most emphatic, as hostile as a normally gentle person could make it.

I was tempted to tell him the truth, that neither King Vijaya nor I had known where the wagonload of goods had come from, but I could not weaken the administration we had commenced by showing that we were divided. Then a question started hammering in my brain. Why had Ujjeni come to this particular township? How had he known how to get here? Puri! That was it. Puri had followed Sundari's wagon on Ujjeni's instructions. The situation was far more dangerous than I had imagined. A sudden anxiety gnawed at me. 'Did the tax collectors visit your homes?' I enquired.

'No, Prince. They made their announcements and collections in the square of our Hindu temple.'

I was so relieved that I made the mistake of deciding to change the conversation to less controversial channels, hoping to establish personal communication with this man, who had not even asked me to sit down. 'Your daughter told me you were interested in the Buddha's doctrine, though you are a Hindu. I too am a student of it.'

He smiled faintly then, revealing very white teeth. 'Yes, I'm more than interested. My daughter and I are almost converts.'

'That's a great step for a Hindu.'

'Millions of Hindus have already taken that step on the

194

continent.'

I reached for a straw. 'I hope we can get together and discuss the Doctrine some time,' I volunteered.

He froze on the instant. 'That's hardly likely,' he stated flatly. 'We are separated by more than distance. I'm but a lowly goldsmith and you are a prince.'

'Not by birth is the Brahman made,' I quoted, smiling.

He would not relent. 'Why have you come to my house, Prince?' he demanded. 'If you have official business, please state it, otherwise please excuse me for I have work to do.'

I was stunned by his apparent ingratitude. The least he could have done for a man who saved his daughter from rape and sent her back safely to him was to offer him a seat and some refreshment. My reaction must have shown in my face, for he continued. 'Please don't think me inhospitable, Prince, or ungrateful, but my first duty is to safeguard my family. Your personal actions hitherto have been noble, but others of you . . !' He paused and shrugged. 'Why do you not leave us in peace?'

There was something here I could not fathom and I could see no way of penetrating this man's mask, so I decided to be bold. 'I want you to know that I have fallen in love with your daughter,' I said quietly, holding his gaze with all the sincerity I could command. 'I came here in the hope of seeing her.' I raised a hand as a look of alarm crossed his face. 'No,' I assured him. 'You must not be afraid. She is as safe with me as she would be with you. My intentions towards her are honourable. I wish to get to know her better, with a view to asking you for her hand in marriage.'

He was stunned. His normal composure left him. 'Marriage?' he enquired. 'You mean . . .'

'Yes, I want to marry her. I'm an Arya priest as well as a prince. Yes, I know that our caste system should prevent a prince from being a priest, but I don't believe in the dividing lines of caste. A man must march to the drumbeats of his spirit, which is why I can consider marrying your daughter. I've never loved a woman before, or had anything to do with one. The moment I set eyes on your daughter I felt she was destined for me from past births.'

Tears filled his dark eyes. 'You do us great honour, Prince and your words do you even greater honour.' He shook his head sadly, seemed about to say something but held back.

'Will you give me permission to pay court to your daughter?' I enquired humbly.

'I wish that I could . . . I really wish I could.' His voice broke. He paused, uncertain. 'It is a matter of my honour and my word,' he finally said. 'My daughter is already betrothed to Pattakanu, the son of a goldsmith living in the township of Nuge-gama, south of here in the Kalyani kingdom, and they are to be married in three days. The marriage was arranged through matchmakers, but we have known the family for years and Sundari grew up almost as a sister of this worthy young man. The union will create a stronger unit for us within our caste structure. He will be arriving here this evening and will stay in our house; my daughter will move out with friends until her wedding.'

My heart cried out, oh no, oh no, you can't do this. Cancel all your plans. Send word immediately to this suitor to stay away. Sundari can't marry anyone but me. She is mine.

Ironically, my own honour forbade the outcry. I could not possibly be less than anyone else in honour, especially the father of the woman I loved. 'I wish Sundari and her future husband every happiness.' I felt the words jerking out of me in a croak, but this was only an illusion from my shattered emotions. 'I'm sorry. I would not have come if I had known. Please convey my good wishes to your daughter. And . . . and . . .' I gulped to steady myself. 'Let me know if I can be of any service to her. Farewell.'

As I turned to leave, I thought I heard a sob from the

interior of the house, but it must have come from my own heart. I believe Rasiah exclaimed, 'Farewell, Prince,' before I walked away. I stumbled against the closed entrance gates, blind, for the light had gone out of the sun.

The following evening, Uraw, who had been ordered by the king to oversee the cleaning of the ships' hulks, returned to the fort to find a message from Ujjeni awaiting him at the guardhouse. He was to wait there for Ujjeni and Anu, whom the guard commander would summon immediately. Feeling some qualms at the urgency of the message, Uraw informed the guard commander that he would await Ujjeni on the river bank. He strolled across the bridge, turned left and made for the place where Ujjeni, Anu and he had had their earlier discussion, avoiding the groups of Arya who were playing *marsok* on the open ground. He paused at the water's edge, gazing westwards to look at the setting sun. The sky was ablaze with red and gold beneath grey mushrooms of clouds lined with silver. A land breeze brought the scent of cinnamon from a raft being poled downstream. The shouts of the men were fainter here, so that the flow-sound of the river soothed him, yet he was dissatisfied with himself. The king's praise and his share of the taxes had been pleasing to him, but he knew he had not earned them and he wondered what he had allowed himself to become enmeshed in. He felt committed to whatever course of action Ujjeni decided upon and he simply did not want to be so involved. He had always been keen to study religions, especially the Buddha's doctrine, and to maintain a historical chronicle. Now, looking to the west, where the continent lay and the ships were beached, he suddenly decided that he would start maintaining a record of all that had transpired since they were cast on Lanka's shores. It made him feel better. As for his involvement with Ujjeni, he would continue it until his conscience, or life itself, finally forbade it.

No sooner had he made the decision than he heard Ujjeni's voice almost at his elbow. 'Ah! There you are, comrade!'

The two men had come upon him silently. Uraw turned. 'I thought it best that we meet here,' he explained. 'Because I'm sure what you wish to discuss is private. But I have some important work to finish tonight, because the ships need . . .'

'. . . material for caulking,' Ujjeni interrupted, a smile stretching over the purple gums and yellow teeth. 'I have already found it for you. However, I too have some urgent business to complete tonight, because of the change of plan I'm proposing. We must ride to Mada Kalapuwa first thing in the morning.'

'But I thought you gave Rasiah seven days. That's the day after tomorrow.'

'Events have necessitated a change of plan. Do you know where Prince Lala was yesterday?'

'No.'

'At Mada Kalapuwa.'

'Really? How d'you know?'

Ujjeni grinned. 'I make it a point to know everything that's going on.' He paused, fixing Uraw with a compelling look. 'You realize this creates the need for urgency?'

'How so?'

'Firstly, he may have laid a claim to my girl with her father. Secondly, he may have discovered the facts about our tax levy on the people there.'

'We did nothing wrong.'

'Oh yes, we did. We extracted the taxes and then . . . of course . . .' Ujjeni coughed, his smile deprecating. 'We gave the king a wrong impression as to who really collected the taxes.'

Uraw realized he had been trapped. 'What do you propose?' he enquired.

'Cutting short the seven days' notice I gave Rasiah and

riding to Mada Kalapuwa at crack of dawn tomorrow to demand surrender of the girl. Oh, and by the way, my spies tell me there's a fabulous Arabi woman, well versed in the sexual arts, available in the township. You can look her over and bring her back, if you like her, to keep house for you.'

Uraw had not slept with a woman in weeks. His scrotum sparkled at Ujjeni's suggestion.

Chapter 15

This time, Ujjeni, Anu, Puri and Uraw were all on horseback. With no wagon to slow them down, they made the journey to Mada Kalapuwa in under three hours, reaching its environs in the forenoon. They clattered through the township at a fast trot, followed by the curious glances of gaily dressed crowds, including women today in bright coloured saris, who thronged the streets. It was the day of the weekly fair and the temple square was lined with *cadjan* booths that had sprung up overnight. Pillai, the leader of the *panchyat*, came to view, walking towards the temple. He looked sharply at them, seemed surprised, hesitated and walked on.

Uraw felt a sudden qualm. 'Did you see him?' he enquired.

'Yes,' Ujjeni replied. 'He could cause trouble.'

'He wouldn't dare,' Anu stated. 'The people of Mada Kalapuwa are said to be peaceful and compliant.'

'Never underestimate an opponent and always remember that most people have a line beyond which they can't be pushed.' Ujjeni squared his bony shoulders.

They rode on in silence. Puri, now leading, veered right at the fork into the sun-dappled avenue. The people they passed studiously avoided looking at them.

'They all live on this avenue and yet are afraid of eye contact.' Anu observed.

'Because it could invite trouble,' Ujjeni explained. 'Also, it betokens their lowly caste. They regard us as people of consequence, since only princes, noblemen, the warrior castes, ride horseback. This is the street of the artisans.'

Yet the avenue was clean, and the houses seen above the

200

brown *cadjan* fences seemed well constructed. The waters of the lagoon soon shone ahead of them, so peaceful in contrast with their mission that Uraw asked himself, are we the purveyors of conflict, even of doom, bringing confusion wherever we go? What am I doing to my *atman*? These thoughts saddened him so much that he felt a compelling urge to turn and gallop away. But would that be enough? Surely his real responsibility was to prevent evil. He looked sideways at Ujjeni, riding beside him. One sharp glance from the sunken eyes and Uraw knew he would never dare openly cross the man. Since he did not have the courage to remonstrate, the least he could do was to avoid doing anything wrong himself, to remain a silent spectator. That way no blame could attach to him either. He ignored the still small voice within him that whispered, you allowed yourself to be a silent spectator five days ago and the result is that today you are heading towards becoming an active participant. Men take but a step at a time into the quagmire of evil, conscious only of each step they take until they suddenly find themselves totally submerged. But I am merely in this for wealth and the good life, his mind responded, surely then there is no evil in me. Ah yes, the voice retorted, you are making a vocation of material things and these desires will cause you to be vulnerable, especially before a man who might manipulate your desires to gain his own ends. What he intends would then be your real quagmire.

What shameful thoughts, Uraw's desires clamoured back. How can you think thus of a friend and comrade who is merely pursuing his own desires! How dare you stand in moral judgement over him?

Puri stopped at the closed cadjan gates of the last house on the left of the avenue.

'Open them!' Ujjeni commanded, jerking his head towards the gates.

Puri urged his horse until it was alongside the gates,

undid the latch and pushed the gates open.

'The three of you wait outside,' Ujjeni directed. He slowly clip-clopped his horse into the compound, drew rein, facing the front verandah, seeming to menace the house. 'Anyone here?' he shouted.

Rasiah, the goldsmith, clad in a white *verti*, slowly emerged from the dark interior. He blinked at the sunlight, recognized the rider and bowed to salute him, palms together lowly fashion, then came erect and waited, eyes downcast.

'You remember me?' Ujjeni demanded.

'Yes, Lord.' The words were quietly spoken.

'I've come to collect the girl.'

'She is not here.'

'I told you to have her here in seven days.' Ujjeni's menace impregnated his voice.

'Indeed, Lord, but today is the sixth day.'

'You dare to quibble with me, you low-caste *pariah*?'

'I merely speak the truth, Lord. Pray forgive me if it sounds like quibbling.'

'Well, where is the girl?'

'She is not at home.'

'Have her brought here then. Immediately, I command you.'

'The girl is not for you.' The voice was youthful, stern, angry. A young man of middle height had materialized on the verandah. As he stepped into the sunlight, Uraw saw that he was strong and muscular, his skin golden, the hair black and shining. His broad features were floridly handsome in the typical Dasa mode. 'Sundari is betrothed to me and we are to be married tomorrow.'

Rasiah gazed despairingly at the young man, but Ujjeni tensed with anger. 'And who the devil are you?' There was a dangerous edge to Ujjeni's voice.

'My name is Pattakanu.'

'And my name is Ramiah. I'm Sundari's brother.' The

202

boy who spoke had emerged round the side of the house to stand beside Pattakanu. He was dark-skinned, slim and tall, but he could not have been more than twelve. Uraw felt a surge of admiration for the pluck of these two young people, remembered Ujjeni's admonition regarding the limits to which people could be pushed.

'Oh, it is the young cockerels who are strutting now,' Ujjeni observed calmly. Uraw could sense the conflict within him, pride, anger, frustration against wisdom, cunning.

'Hee . . . hee . . . hee.' The deep belly laugh suddenly escaped Ujjeni and Uraw could not restrain a shudder. 'Well, goldsmith, it seems as if my mission has been foiled,' Ujjeni finally declared. 'I never knew your daughter was betrothed.' His hot eyes travelled to Pattakanu's face. 'And to such a handsome young man.' He paused. 'Pray forgive our intrusion. It only remains for me to wish the bride and bridegroom every happiness . . . er . . . once they are married.' He turned his horse and the sunlight caught his face. The smile showing yellow teeth and purple gums was belied by the evil expression in his eyes. He clip-clopped slowly towards the gate, halted and threw back over his shoulder, 'Is it part of your custom to have the bridegroom live with the bride before marriage?'

Young Pattakanu flushed before the contempt in Ujjeni's voice. 'No, Lord,' he retorted angrily. 'My bride stays with friends of the family, because I'm here for certain religious rites tonight.'

'Just you three males, isn't that unusual? Besides, you must have many valuables here, gifts from friends and relations. Is it safe?'

'My family will be here tomorrow for the ceremony.' A proud note entered Pattakanu's voice. 'And we are well armed and able to look after what is ours.'

'Well, that explains it.' Ujjeni hesitated, and Uraw, sensing the struggle within the man, felt pity for him. It must be hard for Ujjeni to discover that the handsome, young, virile Dasa, the very opposite of him in appearance, would be coupling with the object of his desire tomorrow night.

'You are wise to preserve your bride's chastity and reputation before your marriage,' Ujjeni commented. 'You are an estimable young man. I'm only sorry that your bride-to-be had not been as mindful of her virtue while she was away from home. Ask the goldsmith whether his daughter is still a virgin.'

Dear devas, what an evil thing to do, Uraw thought, near sick with disgust. The three stricken Dasa stood immobile, posed like statues before the house. Ujjeni eased his seat, signalling his bay forward. Uraw turned his mount and followed in a daze. He heard the drone of angry voices ahead. To his surprise, a crowd of men, brandishing staves and knives, led by Pillai, were rushing down the avenue.

Ujjeni spurred his horse ahead of his companions. For one moment Uraw thought he was going to ride through the crowd, trampling anyone who did not get out of his way beneath relentless hooves. But at the last moment he drew in the animal sharply, causing it to rear in front of Pillai. The crowd paused. Ujjeni righted the horse and the hee . . . hee . . . hee . . . belly laugh escaped him once more. 'As you can see, Pillai, we are returning after paying our respects to the bride's family and bridegroom,' he shouted. 'Are you the wedding party?'

Pillai looked bewildered. 'We . . . er . . .' he recovered himself. 'Yes, we are the wedding party,' he said, then turned and shouted to the men behind him. 'Make way there for the Arya lords. They are leaving and will not return.' There was a wealth of meaning in his voice.

The man moved aside. Ujjeni looked at each of those who were close to him quietly, silently, then his gaze drifted to Pillai. 'You are wise to make way for the Arya,' he said softly. 'Never forget.' He dug his heels into the horse's flanks, the men parting to his rush like grass before a scythe.

The allocation of revenues to the various branches of government always creates conflicts. In my case it proved to be worse because I was attempting to introduce a sophisticated financial system to a country that had hitherto been governed by the simple rule that the king grabbed whatever he pleased from his subjects and gave them only what he desired. There is an old saying, let the rice boil before you attempt to share it, which I knew that the new ministers, except possibly Vijit, would probably ignore, because they were all fired with enthusiasm for their work and responsibilities. Where they were concerned – and indeed all the Arya comrades – the scale had certainly tipped in the opposite direction. From being a bunch of careless, carefree bandits, they had begun to attack their goals with new life and vigour, each anxious to make his mark. My basic problem was to find the funds of men and material they all needed to accomplish these goals.

Our first conference on my five-year plan was held in King Vijaya's study early in the morning ten days after we took over the kingdom. I had prepared for it by sending out men to make a rapid assessment of the country's resources.

The entire council of commanders sat around the yellow jakwood table with my brother at its head. Each of them had his own plans, so they had to be eager to hear what I had to offer. Of them all, only Ujjeni, seated on my brother's left, while I was at his right, seemed not only tense and watchful, but tired and sleepy, with black smudges showing even on his dark complexion beneath the sunken eyes.

At the king's request, I commenced the proceedings. 'My plan for raising revenues is simple,' I stated. 'While gold, including any coin we may introduce into the kingdom, silver, gems and such materials are important as media of

205

exchange, I believe that the real wealth of a country lies in its raw materials and its labour, both of which we have an abundance of in Thamba-Panni. What we require is time to harness them in order to generate such income to our Treasury as will enable us to embark on a five-year programme of development.'

'How much time?' The king enquired sharply.

'As much time as it will take to produce crops in the sort of abundance that will fill the government barns and granaries we shall build.'

'You want us to wait that long?' Ujjeni enquired incredulously.

I knew a stab of disquiet. Here I was with a carefully worked out plan and the questions were pouring in before I even began to unfold it. 'Why don't I proceed with what I have to say first and the questions can follow?' I suggested, directing my gaze to the king. 'Since we are going to meet regularly in Council, that might be a good policy to follow at all times.'

'Seems good to us,' King Vijaya nodded. 'Please proceed, Prince.'

'A quick survey of the resources of Thamba-Panni reveals that this kingdom lags far behind the other three kingdoms in productivity. People here till, sow, fish or hunt merely to satisfy their immediate needs, which include laying staple foods by for emergencies such as times of flood and drought. The king's granaries are, however, full from levies he made on his people and from cargoes of ships sunk on the reef. The one heavily cultivated region is, strangely enough, that which has the least rain and is almost barren, up north, due to the industry of its immigrant population.' I carefully avoided calling them the Dasa! 'An advantage that accrues from this situation is that the Yakka people will work for their keep. This will give us the labour needed for the major irrigation works I propose for jungle areas, which we must clear and bring under cultivation.' I turned towards Ujjeni. 'That aspect of my plan should please you, Minister.'

My brother was eyeing me expressionlessly. 'It will all depend on your plan, Prince,' he responded.

'You are right, Sire. To continue, my immediate task is to provide you all with the labour and material necessary for your work. This means food, shelter and implements in all cases.' I looked at Vijit. 'In the case of the armed forces, it also involves uniforms, weapons, armaments, horses, chariots and wagons. As I mentioned earlier, our kingdom is rich in raw materials. While we cannot use valuable commodities such as gold, silver and gems to buy services locally, they are a fine source of barter with the neighbouring kingdoms and the continent.'

Knowing I finally had the rapt attention of everyone present, I deliberately thumbed through my *olas*, feeling a little self-important, I must confess. 'What I am about to say is an extension of the plan by which the king had the defence works of the fort and its moats constructed,' I continued. 'I shall start with agriculture and industry, for those are productive enterprises which can generate the wherewithal for the future. Our primary goal should be to bring thousands of acres of land under cultivation. To do this more easily, I have earmarked certain areas which have lakes that can readily be converted into reservoirs that by the construction of dams with sluice gates will serve irrigation channels taking water to the cleared areas, which will then be the king's lands. These can be cultivated with rice, vegetables and spices. We can make cultivators of those who labour on each project and each family will be permitted to be a tenant of a two-acre plot and build a home on it to our specifications, provided he performs *raja-kariya*, feudal duties and gives a portion of his crops to the king. These families can use the timber from the felled jungle, wattle, mud-daub and thatch to build their houses. We will also give each of them a cow and poultry.'

My brother's eyes were gleaming with excitement. 'Ah! Thousands of acres of rice-fields, homes set in groves of coconut, jak-fruit, mangoes and bananas,' he declared, a tremor of excitement in his voice.

'Prince Lala but anticipates my own plan, 'Ujjeni put in somewhat petulantly. 'His task was only to provide the wherewithal and he has made no mention of that.'

The king, however, did not appear to hear him. 'Pray proceed, Prince,' he commanded. 'We shall try not to interrupt you again.'

'Since the Yakka people do not set much store by gold, silver and gems, except for ornaments, I propose that you issue a decree to the effect that only the government can mine and that whatever products lie beneath the earth's surface belong to you. These commodities would of course be extremely valuable for barter purposes, so we would have a three-pronged drive to assemble what we need in order to launch our five-year plan. First, we will assemble whatever produce and products are available into the king's barns and granaries to supplement what we already have. Second, we will make an all-out effort to produce the precious metals needed for barter with neighbouring kingdoms. Third, we will launch our irrigation and land development programmes.' I paused. 'Perhaps you might like to discuss these proposals before I proceed with further details.'

'Does anyone have any comment to make?' King Vijaya's tawny eyes swept the men around the table.

I had been so engrossed in my presentation that I had mind for little else. Now for the first time, I felt some trepidation as to how my proposals would be received and it made me aware of the increasing heat of the morning, a trickle of sweat down my back, beneath my white tunic, the sough of a hot wind outside and the scent of my own sandalwood paste.

'No comment, Sire,' or a shake of the head was the

general response, though I had a feeling that Anu and Uraw looked at Ujjeni before responding.

'I don't think the prince's plan goes far enough,' Ujjeni said when the king's gaze finally rested on him. 'He is being soft with the Yakka. They have their stores and their reserves. Some of them, especially the nobles, are rich. I say we take over whatever they have.'

'We have already taken over the barns and granaries of the dead princes and nobles,' the king responded.

'But there is much more we can accumulate, Sire. For instance, why should we seek to purchase horses, cattle, poultry, looms, wagons, bullocks to draw them, when we can seize these things?'

'By what moral right would we do that?' Vijit demanded, his chiselled face set.

'By the right of the victor to seize the spoils,' Ujjeni retorted fiercely.

'You call that a moral right?' Vijit sounded as if he could not believe his ears.

'Yes.' Ujjeni had become relaxed again. He gave his hee . . . hee . . . hee belly laugh. 'You misunderstand my statement, Minister. Remember that the victor also has duties and responsibilities when he is an Arya. In our case, we are already preparing plans for the development of this kingdom, to which we'll bring peace and prosperity. The Yakka will be making a contribution towards their own progress if we take over their property.' He turned on his settle to face the king, his sunken eyes glowing, no longer tired. 'Besides, we have served our ruler by delivering him a kingdom. Everything,' his voice dropped, 'I repeat, everything in this kingdom belongs to him.'

'In theory, yes,' my brother responded drily. 'In practice, we hold it all in trust for the people.' His tawny eyes flickered to mine and I nodded approval. 'Does Prince Lala have any comment to make on that thesis? After all, he is our political philosopher.'

I was filled with a great gladness that my brother was seeking me as the source of his ideals. 'I certainly do, Sire,' I replied warmly. 'First, let me state that I heartily concur with your argument. Then, let me explain how I think it can be made to work in practice.' I looked at him questioningly.

'Go on,' he affirmed.

'Everything in a kingdom does belong to the ruler in theory, because he has the right to take it back at any time. Yet a ruler must also respect the time-honoured traditions of his people. This *charlithraya* has the force of law in our Arya kingdoms, unless specifically changed by decree of the king, which is the highest form of the law. Yet the king's decrees must also be governed by *dharma*, righteousness and *nyaya*, justice, if there is to be that constancy which is so important in government. Constancy can also help create a contented nation, which is the ultimate aim of government. We must therefore respect the customs and traditions of the Yakka people.'

Noticing Ujjeni flash a knowing glance at Anu and Uraw confirmed in my mind my feeling that they were in league with one another. 'Do you propose that we permit these primitive people to continue with their barbaric customs?' There was a sneer in Ujjeni's grainy voice.

'The customs of the Yakka fall into two broad categories,' I asserted. 'Their daily lives and their religion.' I looked squarely at King Vijaya. 'I do not think you would want to interfere with their religion by decree, Sire. Surely any change must be made by the power of influence, not the influence of power?' I smiled. 'After all, theirs is not a godless religion, nor one that would make them rebel fanatically.'

'Agreed,' the king responded tersely.

'Then, as far as their daily lives are concerned, we also have two broad areas. The first, their traditional observances, the second, their system. It is their system

210

alone that we must change, but I suggest that these changes should be gradual.'

'What do you propose?' the king demanded. 'We sense you have something as fundamental as the rest of your proposals in mind.'

'Yes, Sire. I suggest that you proclaim throughout the kingdom that all land, including forests, all minerals, all livestock, all goods and products in this kingdom belong to you by the right of conquest. Through your royal benevolence, however, you further decree that every person who has any rights to own, or occupy, or use all such, through grants or custom, shall continue to enjoy such rights. All other land, goods and products shall vest in you, to be held for the use and benefit of the people. Everyone, regardless of rank, shall pay taxes or tithes. I shall set up the fiscal machinery for this purpose, using the village headman under government supervisors. In order to permit people to pay taxes instead of tithes, should they so desire, I propose that we mint a new gold coin of the realm, from King Kalu Sena's hoard, which will have a definite value instead of the worthless coinage now prevailing. This will encourage those who have gold to bring it to our treasury, so that we can use it in exchange for goods and services from abroad.' I turned to the king, my whole being a-tremble with enthusiasm. 'I pray that you approve these measures, Sire.'

King Vijaya did not need the tapping of approval around the table from all except Ujjeni and Anu to reveal his endorsement of my plan. As his twin, I could sense it in every fibre of his being.

Something made me look towards the door. Across the open verandah, two bare-bodied Yakka gardeners stood beside a flower-bed of yellow *kapuru*. One was short and pot-bellied, the other lean and stringy. They had obviously overheard every word of what had been discussed for they were grinning their approval at me. I made a mental note to ensure privacy and secrecy for our future Council meetings. Yet I could not help but be glad that these common Yakka liked my ideas. I glanced at Ujjeni and was met by a stony stare from the sunken eyes in the death's head face and the vibration of envy and hatred from his being. In a flash, I knew that I would always fight for the Yakka, champion their rights against Ujjeni and men of his kind.

The meeting proceeded to the plans of each of the ministers. The direction of Ujjeni's land development programme came first and we then went on to the building of roads and forts, the establishment of schools and the system of justice, the creation of village and the king's courts, setting up cottage industries and the means of export and import, a customs agency, the possibility of using the three vessels on which we had arrived as the nucleus for a merchant fleet and the inauguration of various government departments.

Our meals were served while we worked and it was almost midnight before we finished. The king's presence and his wisdom, no less, prevented points of disagreement from expanding to major areas of dissension. There were many problems ahead of us, but what a golden opportunity the Arya bandits had been given.

Chapter 16

I remained in the study to talk briefly with my brother after the ministers departed, glowing when he praised me for my endeavours. 'Together we shall build a mighty kingdom,' he ended, 'and shall expand it until all four kingdoms of the island become one, under our suzerainty.'

'Then you will be a Great King.' I laughed good-humouredly. 'It will be more than our father or grandfather achieved.' Yet I felt disquiet at the knowledge that his expansionist ambitions might have to be achieved by force.

He regarded me seriously. 'That has always been one of our aims,' he declared, much to my surprise. 'To achieve what no one else in our family, including our grandfather Sinha, has achieved.' He paused. '*Amma*, mother, will be proud.'

I was surprised at this desire to receive our mother's admiration, but it had been a long, exhausting day and I bade him goodnight and walked down the darkened verandah towards my room. The torches had been extinguished, except for one at the far end of the verandah, which was now lit mainly by a late moon setting behind the dark outline of treetops to the west. A lizard chirped. I paused and stretched, gazing upwards at the blue sky laced with fleecy clouds for some revival of energy. I took a deep breath. The scent of queen-of-the-night hung on the air, mingling with some other smell which I could not quite place. I heard the door to my brother's bedroom slam as he closed it behind him. The verandah was now deserted. Or was it? I started as a shadow came towards me from behind a bush in the centre courtyard. I reached for my sword and a voice said softly in the Dasa dialect. 'Do not be alarmed, Lord. I'm but a messenger from Mada Kalapuwa. My name is Pillai.'

My heart leapt. The man's mission was obviously secret, he must have come from Rasiah, or perhaps even from Sundari. My quick glance swept around the entire courtyard. It was deserted. 'Come into my bedroom,' I bade the man, pointing with my drawn sword.

I could make him out now, a slim, dark youth, so ordinary-looking as to be nondescript. I gestured to him to walk ahead of me, in case he was an assassin. Following him, I identified the strange smell as sesame seed oil, which the Dasa use.

I left the door of my room open for safety. In the yellow light of the tapers, I noticed that despite his youth, Pillai's bearing was dignified, but he looked so grim and drawn that he could not be the bearer of good news.

'Who are you?' I demanded.

'My name is Pillai, Lord,' he repeated quietly. 'My father, whose name I bear, is head of the Mada Kalapuwa *panchyat.*'

'How did you get in?'

He smiled faintly. 'My father has close Yakka friends who work in the palace. I entered the fort before dusk, stayed at their home and was smuggled in here after everyone had retired for the night. I did not realize that your conference would take so long, Lord, but my orders were to deliver the message to you tonight.'

I knew a flash of anger that a stranger should have been thus permitted entry into the palace and resolved to tighten security measures, but my eagerness for his message swept all this aside. 'What is your news?' I sheathed my sword.

A sigh that was almost a groan escaped him. 'Such tragic events!' He exclaimed and my heart started to pound. 'Last night . . . last night,' he faltered, unable to go on.

Alarm suddenly seized me. I took two steps forward,

gripped him by the shoulders and shook him. 'Speak up, man,' I commanded.

He recovered with a tremendous effort, cleared his throat. 'Rasiah, the goldsmith, Ramiah his son and Pattakanu, his intended son-in-law, were murdered in their house late last night. We think it must have been the work of bandits who wanted to steal the gold and ornaments sent as wedding presents.'

I froze in horror, yet my guts felt weak. 'Dear god, how were they killed. Was the girl, Sundari, killed too?'

'No, she was not. Thanks be to the gods at least she was spared, though for what?'

'Who did it?'

'We don't quite know.' He began to sob; soon the tears were streaming down his dark cheeks. 'The house was on fire and by the time we neighbours became aware of the blaze, it was too late to do anything.'

'You spoke of murder just now, could it not have been an accident? I mean a fallen lamp, something like that?'

He wiped away his tears. 'How could three adults have been burned to death while they slept, Lord? Besides, there was no trace of Rasiah's gold in the ruins and we found a stab wound on Rasiah's charred chest. And then . . . and then . . .' he took a deep breath and steadied himself. 'Pattakanu's face, which had miraculously been left intact by the fire, showed marks of horrible mutilation, probably caused by a knife . . . and . . . and . . . ugh . . . his genitals were missing. It was so horrible, it looked like a grudge slaying. But who could have had a grudge against such decent people?'

I shook myself free of the numbing sense of horror. 'I want you to tell me the whole story exactly as it happened,' I directed him. 'But first, where is Sundari?'

'She was with my father when I left, but she will be on her way to a safe place soon.'

'Where?'

'I don't know. My father would not divulge it even to me. He bade me give you this message.' Pillai cleared his throat. '"The gods will avenge this foul deed some day. Strange that it happened just before the seventh day, when the man Ujjeni said he would come to take Sundari for his concubine."'

This was news to me and I stared at Pillai in amazement. He trembled, then squared his shoulders and went on resolutely. '"The Arya have been murderers and rapists of the Dasa since they first invaded our continent thousands of years ago. They may not be guilty of slaying Rasiah, Ramiah and Pattakanu, but they have, at the least, been the harbingers of evil. If Prince Lala truly loves Sundari, let him prove his love by ending all Arya pursuit of her, including his own, and leaving her in the peace we are now seeking for her."' Pillai stopped, his eyes downcast. 'That is the message, Lord.' My father requests your princely oath on it.'

The world of yellow taper-light seemed to spin before me. When it came back into focus, I stared at Pillai aghast. A hint of pity showed on his face, somehow shaming me, I swallowed, found my aching throat dry. My hand accidentally touched my sword hilt. Its coldness reminded me that I had to act like a prince. There was so much I did not know. 'Tell me all,' I commanded.

I learned the truth from Pillai with dawning anger and horror. Ujjeni's first visit, his ultimatum, his second visit, his rage at being foiled, the way he looked today, with dark shadows under his eyes, the horrible mutilation of young Pattakanu . . . all of it convinced me that Ujjeni had ridden through the night to carry out this terrible mission. Why had Sundari's father not told me all? My frantic mind searched through my conversation with Rasiah, something nagged and finally lay exposed. If I had not tried to impress Rasiah by changing the conversation to the Buddha's doctrine because I was so relieved to imagine that Ujjeni

216

had only visited the town to collect taxes, Rasiah would have told me all and the three men might still be alive. Dear God, why? why? why? I wanted to beat my brains against the wall.

Instead, I looked Pillai in the eye, with a steadiness I did not feel. 'Before I give my oath, I want you to answer some questions.'

I questioned him in detail, trying to find some evidence, some lead that would point the finger of guilt. When I finally ran out of questions however, I was none the wiser, except for a deepening of my suspicions.

Noting my frustration, Pillai said, 'It's too late to do anything for the dead people, but I for one hope that our new king will investigate these murders and establish law and order in this kingdom. I believe it is for this reason and also to have you ensure that this man Ujjeni does not attempt to abduct Sundari that my father sent me to you. He must trust you.'

'I'm glad to hear that, but how can we catch the murderers when we have no evidence? Tell me again, is there nothing unusual, nothing you have discovered that might point to anyone?'

'No, Lord. Bandits ride into our town about once a year and we protect ourselves as best we can. We don't know where they reside, only that it is in the forest to the east of our township.' He paused, thinking, then his eyes lit up. 'Oh, just one fragment of news omitted. A woman who lives down our street went to her outhouse shortly after midnight and heard the galloping of fierce hooves. She was afraid even to look but saw a solitary horseman sweep past before returning to her bed.'

'Horseman! Did you say a solitary horseman?'

'Yes, Lord.'

I knew then that it was indeed Ujjeni who had done the deed. Now I had only to uncover evidence of his absence from the fort last night. Even as the thought entered my mind, I somehow knew it was in vain. Ujjeni lived alone and he would literally have covered his tracks. Neither Anu nor Uraw, nor Puri would volunteer any evidence, not the least because they could become implicated in the murders. Also, should I tell my brother of my suspicions? There was no way in which he could launch an official investigation – establishment of our system of justice had not even begun and he was too totally committed to our new plans to be able to divert men or resources to solve a murder mystery in an outlying township. Besides, how could he start his rule over a new kingdom with allegations that one of his commanders, now a minister, was a brutal murderer?

I made up my mind. 'Listen,' I bade Pillai. 'You may take my oath to your father. I shall keep away from Sundari for the present. I shall also ensure through my brother, the king, that Ujjeni does not leave the palace for the next two days at least, so that your father can get Sundari away, and that there are no reprisals against your father or your town.' Brave words, since I did not quite know how to give them effect. 'If you uncover any further evidence,' I added, 'let me know. You may leave now, the way you came, for you had best not be seen with me.'

He rose to his feet, made lowly salutation and walked out through the door, leaving me with the smell of his sesame oil and the pain of his tragic tale.

Prince Tikka had allowed two days to elapse before contacting Prince Jaya, a nephew of King Ra-hula and commander of the Kalyani army, on the pretext that he wished to pay his respects and renew the acquaintance. Prince Jaya sent word back that he would be available the following morning, at the end of the audience watch, and invited Prince Tikka to have the noon meal with him.

Prince Tikka decided that Kira, who was prone to speaking out of turn, should not go on this mission. Why me, Hamy thought, but nonetheless made appropriate noises of gratitude when Prince Tikka bade him attend. Dressed in blue pantaloons and white tunics, they walked down the street to Prince Jaya's mansion, which adjoined the palace. A *thirikkaley*, two-seater buggy, drawn by two white Scindhi bulls went smartly by, the clip-clop of the bulls' hooves on the grey cobbles beating out a rhythm for the jingling bells around the beasts' necks. It found a response in the quicker beat of Hamy's heart. If Prince Jaya was a loyal, devoted subject of the Kalyani king, he could have them both imprisoned and executed. Tension made Hamy more aware of physical discomforts. Being from the cool of the hill-country, he was unaccustomed to the heat and could feel a trickle of sweat coursing down his back and moisture gathering between his toes. His sandals did not fit him and his corns had started to ache. A red-curtained palanquin went by, carried on the brawny shoulders of four bare-chested retainers. Hamy caught a glimpse of a dwarf seated within, probably the court jester, a wise man riding in style, while they had elected to walk.

The white-tiled roof of Prince Jaya's red-brick mansion appeared to their left between green branches of purple blossomed shower trees that bordered a high masonry wall. They stopped at the brown teakwood gates and Hamy rapped on them with his knuckles, while Prince Tikka struck a pose, staff on the ground, the arm holding it extended in *thalasthani*, worthy fashion. A small aperture in the gate was opened, through which a sentry peered.

'Prince Tikka is calling on Prince Jaya by appointment,' Hamy announced.

'You are expected and welcome, Prince.' The sentry hastily opened the gates. He wore a red *dhoti*, Dasa fashion. His chest was bare, his short sword hung at his side. He saluted with his spear. If he wondered why a prince was walking over from the palace, with a single attendant, he did not show it.

Another sentry approached from a small guardhouse

beside the gate to lead the way to the mansion. They passed through a pleasant garden, with green lawns and large beds of flowering yellow *kapuru* interspersed with short red temple-flower trees. Grey doves cooed, brown mynahs grumbled and black *kondayas* twittered in the branches of tall jak trees. A cool breeze sprang from the broad Kalyani river behind the house and rustled through the leaves, bringing the sweet scent of ripe mangoes.

The sentry handed them to a covey of servants, in red *dhotis* and white sashes, gathered at the entrance foyer, which led to a large room into which Prince Tikka and Hamy were ushered. Sunlight from the courtyard beyond revealed ebony settles placed against the walls and a high-backed chair of carved black ebony at the far end. This had to be some sort of audience chamber.

But Hamy was not prepared for the man sitting on the chair. Prince Jaya was enormously fat. His fair-skinned face, shiny with sweat, was large, round and pudgy, with slits for eyes astride a large nose. His black moustaches bristled above full red lips and a clean-shaven chin. The pectorals of his bare chest hung like a woman's. He wheezed as he rose, cleared his throat and gave the *namaskaram* greeting, palms together, loosely held at chest level. '*Ayubowan*, greetings, Prince!' he exclaimed, his voice surprisingly high-pitched, almost like a eunuch's. Hamy wondered at the man to whom they were about to entrust their fortunes, possibly their lives.

They returned Prince Jaya's salutations. The slits of the prince's eyelids opened briefly when he surveyed Hamy, revealing black, glittering eyes. Hamy immediately understood why this portly prince had been given command of King Ra-hula's army. He was strong, ruthless, clever and full of inner energy.

Prince Jaya bade them be seated while he resumed his chair. They discussed the weather, crops, mutual friends, in the approved fashion. Prince Jaya made jokes and his high-pitched giggle unfailingly accompanied them, each time revealing pearly white teeth beneath the black moustaches. Finally, they meandered to the events in the Yakka kingdom. As with King Ra-hula, Prince Tikka told his tale fully, his anger, bitterness and hatred pouring forth unbridled this time.

Prince Jaya listened without comment, until Prince Tikka finally introduced the subject on his mind. 'I hear the Kalyani army has been converted into a religious force,' he observed boldly. 'Does it not weaken your kingdom?'

The dark slits of eyes opened briefly. 'Spiritual force is stronger than any other force,' Prince Jaya responded without conviction. 'By the way, we are trying to plant a new variety of mango in my orchard. Would you like to see it?'

Prince Tikka was taken aback. He stared at his host. 'Certainly,' he finally stated, obviously bewildered by the abrupt change of topic.

Prince Jaya heaved himself up from his chair with a grunt. 'This way.' He led his companions through the verandah into the centre courtyard, walking slowly, tap-tapping with his silver-mounted ebony staff. As they moved along a white-sand walkway towards a square pool on which dark green lotus leaves and pink lotus flowers floated, Hamy could not help noting the elegance of his surroundings.

Prince Jaya veered to the right and paused before a plant with the usual long green leaves of the mango, only thinner. He pointed with his staff. 'It is dangerous to talk inside a house nowadays, even one's own,' he stated pleasantly. 'What the kingdom lacks in force to maintain internal security, it makes up for in guile. *Tchikay!* It is not very nice, but it's the best we have.' He turned to resume his walk. 'They are not the king's spies, but those of others of ambition.'

'I came to see you because I believe there should be an end to this silly state of affairs,' Prince Tikka announced to the broad back.

Prince Jaya paused in his stride. 'How should it be ended?' he quietly threw over his shoulder.

A crow's caw disturbed the stillness. It seemed to echo the question. 'How? . . . how? . . . how?'

'By restoring your army to its former power,' Prince Tikka retorted fiercely.

'The army is divided.'

'Then those who want to restore the old order must receive outside support.'

Prince Jaya resumed his walk. 'Where would such support come from? I cannot command it, being but the son of the king's sister, not even his heir.'

'The *uda rata*.'

'And you would ensure it?'

'Yes,' Prince Tikka hissed.

'Who would lead in Kalyani?'

'You.'

Prince Jaya turned round with surprising speed. 'You realize your words are treason?' The question came out cold as frost, in the high mountains.

Hamy was stunned, his stomach turned to jelly. Prince Jaya nodded slowly and deliberately. This is it, Hamy thought, he will send for his retainers and have us arrested.

'I find a little bit of treason most enjoyable, don't you?' Prince Jaya continued urbanely. The slits opened slightly to show twinkling eyes. 'You must, however, first demonstrate the fighting capability of your kingdom and your leadership of it. Also, what is there in this for me?'

'It will take several months for me to get our kingdom organized,' Prince Tikka protested. 'Meanwhile . . .'

'Meanwhile, I don't propose hooking your fish for you,' Prince Jaya responded, smiling pleasantly.

Hamy could not help but admire Prince Jaya's poise.

These Kalyani people were cultured, showed class, not only in their city and its buildings but in their personal attitudes.

Prince Tikka's black eyes glittered with anger. He was about to say something but held himself back. He pondered a few moments. 'Remember, if you take a risk you might become king of the three kingdoms and make a bid for the fourth.'

'What about you?'

'Being much younger than you, I would be your prince regent and of course your heir.'

'Thank you for the fish-bait, but it strikes me that all the risk is mine. Instead of these glorious things you offer, *aney*, I might end up being the sacrifice. A fat man like me hardly looks his best at the end of a stake or wedged into a cauldron of oil. It could even be uncomfortable and, as you see, I adore my comfort. No, cousin, my analysis of the situation here indicates that we will need more than brave words, promises or naked ambition to establish unity within our army and to restore the old order. Either we must be invaded immediately by the Arya, or my militant group must have outside help. Just let me know when you're ready to demonstrate that you can provide it.'

'Don't you recognize the urgency of the situation? Can't you use the presence of the Arya to unite the army? After all, these men are foreigners, with strange new gods.'

'I've put out feelers and failed. Remember we are now a *dharmista*, righteous state. We believe in non-violence and in charity towards our enemies. You can't fight that. As for new gods, the Buddha's doctrine has no gods, so how can gods, old or new, affect our people?'

Prince Tikka stiffened and drew himself to his full height. His earnestness made him look almost regal. 'My people and I have always permitted the Buddha's doctrine,' he declared. 'I have no fear of men who do not believe in gods. Without the power of the gods, they are weak,

223

dependent only on their frail bodies and minds.'

Prince Jaya's eyes crinkled in a tolerant fashion. 'Is that not all we have in this life?' He enquired. 'Frail bodies and minds. And is it not the bodies and minds of other men that always oppose us?'

'They are of no use without the strength of gods to make them super-human,' Prince Tikka countered fiercely. 'I myself believe in our gods, though I don't worship them. It is only people with new gods that cause me alarm, for they could make men stronger than our own could.' He paused, then his eyes shone with sudden resolve. 'Let us end this part of our conversation now, cousin, because I think we understand each other.' His smile was white, but the tight brown cheeks suddenly looked pinched, the eyes grim. 'I shall, in the months ahead, demonstrate my power to you and then I shall be back with what you need to give you the strength to make your people unite against our common foe.'

Chapter 17

Tired though I was, I lay on a sleepless bed after young Pillai left, many thoughts and feelings whirling through my brain. The desire to ride through the night to Sundari regardless of all else, including the word of honour I had so impetuously given from my state of shock, sometimes became so intense that I was hard put to restrain it. The night was cool, yet the darkness oppressed me and my body so fevered that I found myself sweating. Some compulsion to stave off near-madness made me rise and go to the verandah outside.

The moon had set, but the bright stars seemed to mock me, the scent of queen-of-the-night was sickening and the cricket chirpings became an irritation. Finding no peace here, I went back to bed and resumed my restless tossing. I had lost control of my mind. I constructed a dozen ways in which the murders took place, reliving what each of the dead must have experienced when awoken by the silent assassin. That fine, scholarly man, Rasiah, who had impressed me so much, was so quiet and dignified. Why did his life have to end in violence? I was glad I had not met his son, Ramiah, or young Pattakanu, especially young Pattakanu. Pity, horror, love, need, guilt, wondering where Sundari was and what her state of mind must be, conjecture, indecision were my companions that night, the worst that I have ever known.

Towards dawn, I turned to God for help and came to decisions as to what I should do. First and foremost, I had to honour my princely word and avoid making any contact with Sundari or the township. Strangely, it was not merely pride and upbringing that threw up this decision, but the conviction that my absence from the scene could spell greater security for Sundari. From this, it was an easy step to the next decision, that I must use that absence to keep Ujjeni too away. I had been immature in my attitude so far. I loved Sundari and wanted her happiness more than my own, yet I could not overlook the needs of the kingdom we had taken over. I must proceed with caution and restraint, matching Ujjeni's cunning with my own. Besides, the man might not even be guilty. I should therefore set aside thoughts of retribution and vengeance and concentrate on obtaining whatever I could acquire discreetly.

I drowsed off towards dawn and woke up feeling grainy. When I had finished my ablutions at the well in the centre courtyard, my looking-glass showed red veins framing the green eyes and the chiselled features somewhat drawn.

My brother and I had commenced the practice of breaking our fast together before the duties of the day began, so I found him in his study as usual. Having made obeisance, I sat down next to him, noticing that he looked none too happy.

'You don't look so good this morning, Sire,' I remarked. 'Did you have a bad night?'

'Yes.'

'What happened?'

'Oh, the usual. Our wife expects us to maintain a peasant's schedule and service her bed early each night.'

'I thought she has accepted the demands on a king's time.'

'She has indeed, but this was one of those nights. We suppose it's difficult for a young woman like her to have a husband who turns up late night after night, frequently too preoccupied with servicing the nation to service a wife!'

'I'm glad you are able to understand, Sire.'

'We understand the cause but cannot stand its effect. H'mm. What's for breakfast?'

'Nothing new. *Chupatti*, roast pork, milk and fruit.' The

odours of breakfast intruded. 'Here it comes.'

The attendants entered with the serving bowls and our platters, served us and left, so that the king and I could talk in private.

My brother broke off a piece of *chupatti* and started chewing. 'Go . . . ood!' he exclaimed. 'Better than anything we had on board ship. Everything is relative.' He glanced sharply at me. 'But you . . . you don't seem to have slept well either. Why not?'

I swallowed the bite of pork I had taken, set down the remains of the slice on my platter and looked him squarely in the face. 'Something terrible has happened.'

He looked calm but instinctively reached out to place his hand briefly on mine, then withdrew it and waited for me to speak.

I told him the whole story, as I had decided to do, of my visit to Mada Kalapuwa, of Ujjeni's two visits, omitting only my offer of marriage to Sundari and my suspicions.

He listened without comment, or any display of emotion except that he passed a hand across his brow when I told him about the murders. Long minutes of silence passed.

'What would you like us to do?' He finally enquired. 'It's obvious that we cannot set aside pressing affairs of state that affect the lives of hundreds of thousands of people to investigate these murders, however tragic. In due time, when we have our administration established, the prevention of crime and its punishment will be foremost on our list.'

'You are right, Sire,' I responded steadily. 'That's the conclusion I reached last night. But there are some things you can do to give the people of Mada Kalapuwa a feeling of security. Send a message to the older Pillai, who is head of the *panchyat*, that you have taken official note of the murders, which have been reported to you. State that you are aware of the visits paid by Ujjeni and me to the township and our declared purpose. Make it clear that you believe neither of us was involved in the tragic events but have nonetheless decreed that none of your ministers shall visit Mada Kalapuwa, except by official invitation of the *panchyat*, for at least one year, or until your administration has been firmly established there.'

'You want us to issue such an order to our ministers? What will the reactions of Ujjeni, Anu and Uraw be? Won't that amount to a reprimand?'

'You never feared issuing reprimands when they were needed, Sire.'

He half-smiled. 'You're right.'

'Besides, you can take the sting out of your directive by first obtaining a promise from the ministers on the grounds that you consider it to be necessary for the welfare of the state. You can further soften the blow by telling them that I have already given you my promise.'

'Good. Peace with honour, we think. We are glad that you, see the need for all of us to work together, Prince. We will surely have differences of opinion, sometimes even violent, but we must avoid feuds at all costs and pull together for the welfare of the kingdom. Ujjeni in particular is going to be extremely useful, even essential, for our purposes. He is by far the ablest of the ministers.' He paused. 'Almost as able as you.' Then he laughed softly, his tawny eyes, holding mine, softened. 'But how tragic all this has been for you.' He reached out to place his hand on mine again and my own eyes misted. 'Little brother, we are both suffering in our personal lives at the same time, twins indeed.'

We had converted the large, common dining room of the Yakka palace within the fort into a formal audience hall. The floors were of square red-brick tiles, the mud walls were plastered white. The king and I adjourned to this room when we had finished breakfast.

The ministers were already seated on settles around the long, narrow conference table of black ebony when we entered the hall. They rose and made obeisance, a practice we had started on our own since my brother became king. He acknowledged the greeting and took his place at the head of the table, while I sat at the vacant seat on his right.

True to his word, as soon as everyone was seated, King Vijaya informed them of the murders, the possibility of suspicion falling on me or any of the commanders who had visited Mada Kalapuwa, my oath not to visit the township and his opinion that it would be best if all those present should accept a similar restriction. I could feel Ujjeni flash an occasional glance at me while the king spoke and sensed the undercurrent of concern in him, but I avoided his gaze, listening with downcast eyes. When the king had finished speaking, he asked for the views of each of the commanders in turn, shrewdly commencing with Vijit, who happened to be sitting next to me and who readily agreed, ending with Ujjeni, who sat as usual on the king's left.

Though Ujjeni too readily acquiesced, I could not escape the realization that he attributed the king's action to me and detested me the more for it.

The king nodded his pleasure. 'May all our problems be solved with the same unanimity,' he said. 'Now to the most important business of the day. 'We consider that our first priority should be to expand our army. We expect Prince Tikka to strike against us in the near future, so we shall assemble a force of four thousand men, with supporting services, under arms within the next three months.'

Vijit's eyes widened. 'We are a little less than seven hundred, Sire. Do you mean to invite mercenaries from the continent then?'

'No! That would be dangerous. Mercenaries often turn against their own masters to seize power. We mean to integrate the Yakka into our army.'

'Would that not be even more dangerous?' Ujjeni enquired.

'Not if it is properly organized.' The king paused. His

wide fingers beat a tattoo on the table. 'We shall use the Yakka only as bowmen and infantry, heavily supervised by our own men. We shall have thirty infantry companies, each made up of ten of our men and ninety Yakka. These companies shall consist of archers, spearmen and in-fighters with sword, battle-axe and knife. It will be easy for the Yakka who are expert with the short bow to learn to shoot our long bow. During the period of training, every infantry soldier shall also help in the production of weapons, chariots, wagons, catapults and war materials. We shall have four companies of cavalry, each consisting of fifty of our men as riders and fifty Yakka as fighting grooms. Finally, we shall have four companies of chariots, similarly organized, and two hundred Yakka to help us man the catapults and flame-ball throwers.'

'A superb plan, but what about the defence of the fort, Sire?' It was Anu speaking.

'Good question,' the king replied. 'The fort must be totally secure at all times, so the Arya elements of the infantry companies shall guard it in turn. The Yakka will not participate.'

'Won't the Yakka be upset at such lack of trust?' The question broke loose from me before I could think.

'Too bad if they are,' my brother responded. 'They must first prove themselves loyal.'

'What about roads, Sire?' Vijit, the cavalryman asked. 'How will our cavalry and chariots reach trouble centres rapidly without roads?'

'That is an integral part of our plan. We shall start building roads immediately, bridging rivers and streams, to the north, east and south-west boundaries of the kingdom. This was how the King of Kings, Dharroos, maintained control over his vast empire. His system of roads ensured swift reporting and prompt execution of his justice.'

'That's a brilliant idea, Sire!' I exclaimed admiringly. 'Papyrus and clay tablet records show that the Emperor not only established roads over which his armies could move swiftly but also a courier service so efficient that news could travel the distance of over one hundred *yojana* from distant Sardhees to his capital Soo-sa in seven days, whereas caravans took almost one hundred days to complete the journey. No courier had to ride for longer than a day to reach the next post, where food, water, shelter and the next courier, with a fresh horse, awaited him. Our own task is relatively easy. We have neither the distances nor the hot, dry lands to traverse.'

'True. And since you know so much about the methods of the King of Kings, Prince, you shall be the one to plan our road system and help our minister establish it. We shall personally command the army, though Vijit is minister of the Armed Forces. One of the cavalry companies, when established, shall become our palace guard.'

'The Ten Thousand Immortals,' I murmured.

'What's that?'

'Nothing of importance,' I stated. The Immortals had been the personal bodyguard of Dharroos, his assurance against rebellion and assassination.

'We hereby appoint you, Prince Lala, our regent, to establish the administration of this sub-kingdom,' the king continued. 'In this capacity, you shall head the Treasury and administration. You shall be responsible for the appointment of administrators at the palace and in every district and village. Your officials shall maintain accurate records of all work done in the villages, all produce taken, all revenues collected respectively for the ruler, for the government and for our men. Incidentally, we also expect you to establish a palace ceremonial, protocol and our daily schedule, to ensure that our time is not wasted but is put to the best use for the people.'

'A formidable list of duties, but I am honoured, Sire,' I stated. 'I swear my fealty to you, my enthusiasm and devotion to my duties.'

'Finally, Uraw as minister of Commerce must use our three ships. There is much we can produce here for the kings and traders of the continent. We in turn require their materials, horses, iron, silk, clothing and their expertise. Since the Yakka kingdom has no real artisans, rather than importing them from the other three sub-kingdoms we shall encourage members of the twenty-eight craftsmen's guilds of the continent to make their homes here, but only if they are Arya.'

'The devas be praised, a new Arya invasion!' Ujjeni exclaimed fiercely. 'The cavalry and chariots to conquer, the industry to remain as conquerors.'

'Perhaps,' King Vijaya responded drily. 'But first the vision to become immortal.'

The same night, after another long day of planning and discussion, Ujjeni, Uraw and Anu walked out of the palace together. The sky was cloudy and overcast, threatening rain. Even the flares lighting the main street seemed to be listless, feebly trying to penetrate the dense blackness of the night, the smell of resin thick and heady. Somewhere a dog whined. A storm is brewing, Uraw thought, as he turned at the intersection of streets to proceed to his own quarters. He felt a restraining arm on his shoulder and turned to find Ujjeni beside him, Anu a little way behind. In the uncertain light, Uraw suddenly had the impression that Ujjeni's face was merely a skull with blazing eyes staring out of black sockets.

Noting Ujjeni's suppressed fury, Uraw felt a cold chill going down his spine. 'You seem upset,' he ventured tactfully.

'Of course I'm upset,' Ujjeni ground out. 'That upstart, Prince Lala got to his brother and manipulated him to obtain our promises. You see, that's the danger I've warned you about.' He paused, thinking, and suddenly calmed down. 'No matter. I'll get him some day. He'll find that I meet fire with fire.' He laughed shortly at some secret joke. 'As for the Dasa bitch, by the gods, I desired her. She could have quenched the fire in my loins.'

'She's gone for good now,' Anu suggested, soothing. 'You'll never see her again, so put her out of your mind.'

'You're right,' Ujjeni agreed. 'No woman is worth that much. From now on, it's celibacy for me, so I can accomplish my greater goals.'

It dawned on Uraw that neither Ujjeni nor Anu had expressed any regret at the murders, or sympathy for the girl in her bereavement. Suddenly seized by a thought, he looked deep into Ujjeni's eyes. 'Did you organize the murders?' he enquired.

Ujjeni's face registered astonishment, but only for a moment. 'That's a good question,' he responded. 'The only answers I can give you are . . . you'll never know and I'll never tell!' His hee . . . hee . . . hee . . . hee belly laugh issued from the depths of him, quietly echoing through the night.

Uraw knew in that instant that though he was in Ujjeni's grip at present, some day, somewhere, somehow, his own instincts of decency would enable him to break loose.

'Enough of that,' Ujjeni said softly. 'Now that we know Prince Lala's position in the new kingdom, it is essential that those of us who feel alike should talk. Let us go to my house now.'

'Talk about what?' Uraw demanded.

'About how best to serve our ruler, the Great King,' Ujjeni responded quietly.

'Why should the three of us talk about it alone? Why not the entire Cabinet?'

'Discuss such a matter in open meeting with Prince Lala present?' Ujjeni wrinkled his eyebrows. 'You must be out of your mind. Remember that not all the ministers think as we do.'

It made sense, but Uraw nonetheless felt a great

reluctance. 'I just don't like the idea of talking behind peoples' backs,' he muttered. He shot a glance at Anu, but found no support.

'Hear me out before you make up your mind,' Ujjeni requested earnestly. 'You, Anu and I, more than any of our comrades, believe in the Arya tradition.' Ujjeni cleared his throat and spat into the darkness. 'Am I right?'

'I suppose so.'

'Then we must unite to influence our king in the right direction. Don't we owe it to him?'

'Certainly,' Uraw readily agreed. 'We're the king's advisers, that's what he needs us for, but the entire Cabinet should pull together.'

'Right. But did you notice how Prince Lala took up for the Yakka when the question of guarding the fort came up? I mean, that's incredible. He expects us to trust these barbarians with our lives. The three of us need to speak with one voice in such a vital matter and on others too, such as our gods, our religion and our race. It will benefit our king, for not all his advisers think as we do.'

'You are right,' Uraw admitted grudgingly.

'We're fighters, not administrators,' Ujjeni continued. 'We're all fumbling in a sphere in which we have neither training nor experience, but Anu and I feel that there is nothing magical about the tasks ahead, so long as we use our heads and are guided by our principles.'

'I'll go along with that.'

'The first object of those of us who believe in Arya supremacy must be to ensure that nothing is done to weaken it. We have an Arya ruler, who unfortunately has contracted to marry a Yakka.' Ujjeni paused then added hastily, 'We must always remember that he did it for our good and give him every backing in his goals, including that of an Arya succession.'

'An Arya succession, one of the king's goals?' Uraw remonstrated. 'How can that be when the offspring of his marriage will be part Yakka and the heirs to the kingdom?'

Ujjeni's eyes suddenly blazed in anger. 'Would *you* want to be ruled by a part-Yakka?'

Uraw felt his guts turn weak before that terrible look and the thrust of the question. The idea of being the subject or even a minister of a part-Yakka ruler was obnoxious to him. 'Of course not,' he blurted out. 'Nor would most of our men.' He realized that he could have been disloyal to his leader and hastened to make amends. 'But we must give unquestioned loyalty to our ruler. The decision as to who shall succeed him must be his alone to make.'

Ujjeni calmed down. 'Of course. But don't you see that is one area in which we three can guide our leader, especially against the influence of one who treats the Yakka as our equals?'

'More than any of us, Prince Lala has the ear of his brother,' Anu chimed in.

'And why not?' Uraw questioned. 'Being the king's twin, he could end up the heir.'

'We have a strange phenomenon here of the like minds of twins with different outlooks,' Ujjeni retorted. 'I have observed it closely for weeks now. Our Great King is an Arya conservative at heart, like us all, but Prince Lala is an out-and-out liberal. The danger is that our ruler could so identify himself with Prince Lala's like mind that he might allow it to direct his judgement, cloud his outlook and affect his actions.'

Ujjeni allowed his statement to sink in, then drove home. 'We had direct evidence of Prince Lala's affinity with the Yakka on the day we opened the sluice gates. He even sends food to that little boy's family every day. Also, he is a close friend of the Yakka princess.' Ujjeni was keeping his voice down, but his tone was as intense as a licking flame.

'What was he doing in Kuveni's house that afternoon. I mean, what can they possibly have in common. Plotting, no doubt, in order to obtain more power? Are we then to serve two masters? Whom would that affect? Not the prince but us . . . us . . . us . . .' He gestured inwards with long, talon-like fingers to give the words emphasis. 'And what of his interference with my rights to that girl? I mean, he saved her from me only to have a go at her himself. Why did he go to Mada Kalapuwa? Tell me, tell me. And don't you see how he has manipulated the king to prevent us from going there too? He has cut directly into one of our sources of personal wealth – Anu's, yours and mine – and how can I now deliver to you the Arabi woman I promised without visiting the place?'

Uraw was so full of the seeming logic of Ujjeni's words that he barely heard the lizard's warning chirp.

PART II
The Master Race

Chapter 18

One year went by, during which the pain of not even knowing where Sundari was and grief at all that had transpired slowly eased. Yet I knew that Sundari was the only woman I would ever love and it took a lot of effort not to start enquiries as to her whereabouts. Vijit's kindness had helped, though its results created the emptiness that hurt. Shortly after the day we made our oaths Vijit dispatched Bala to Mada Kalapuwa. Bala came back with the news that Sundari had been sent away by the elder Pillai to safety. No one knew her whereabouts and Pillai was not talking. The local people conjectured that Sundari had been sent to the care of relatives in one of the Dasa towns of the continent. As far as Ujjeni and I were concerned, she could have been on another planet.

Enquiries I made immediately after the murders, revealed no evidence whatever as to who could have committed them, so I gave up, hoping that, if Ujjeni was indeed the guilty party, his inner anger had been assuaged by the death of those innocents and the symbolic mutilation of the young man who dared to be a rival. Life would find Ujjeni out.

We made enormous progress with our plans that year. We completed the three highways to our borders, north, east and south-west, which not only facilitated military movement but also helped with the transport of produce, for we built twelve reservoirs in areas close to the highways which brought several thousand acres of land under cultivation. Since each reservoir meant new villages, King Vijaya's dream of a countryside dotted with peaceful homes was being fulfilled.

We established the Great King's barns in which the king's one-fifth share of all produce was stored and governmental barns for the one-fifth share that was to be used for improvements to the kingdom which also contained buffer stocks for emergencies. Our men were happy to receive a one-fifth share for their own supervisory work and the Yakka cultivators found new riches in their remaining two-fifths.

Our army had increased to four thousand men, fully trained, complete with long-bowmen, cavalry, chariots and artillery in the form of catapults, flameball-throwers and battering rams. It helped in the administration of the Great King's justice, maintained through the village courts and the government magistrates. We had opened trade with the Kalyani kingdom and the Ruhunu kingdom to our south, as well as with some of the southern kingdoms of the continent, ignoring only Prince Tikka's *uda rata* kingdom, since it was entirely Yakka.

In short, through sheer hard work, tenacity and careful planning, we had wrought miracles in the land of our adoption. To me, however, the greatest of these miracles was that the Yakka people had slowly adapted to the new system, now appreciated their place in our society and were not only becoming prosperous and contented, but were beginning to show initiative, enterprise and independence.

When the attendant summoned me to my brother's presence that morning in the cool month of Vesakka following the rains, I was working on the returns of productivity for the end of our first year of rule of Thamba-Panni. As I rose to follow Suramba, the lean, silver-haired Yakka attendant, dressed in a white *dhoti* and red sash, the palace uniform I had introduced, I could not help noticing that he held himself erect and walked with a pride that had been absent one year earlier, for King Kalu-Sena had treated his retainers like dogs.

I entered the king's study and made obeisance. My brother was seated alone at his yellow jakwood desk. His hair had been cut to an even length and shone red to his shoulders. His beard and moustache gave added character to his leonine features. He was bare-chested, the muscles huge, without any trace of fat.

'Bad news,' he announced without ceremony. 'Please sit down.'

I perched myself on my usual settle and waited for him to speak.

'Prince Tikka has finally struck. Two nights ago he led a raiding party of about two hundred guerillas against our south-western settlement, Mihiri Gama, killed a dozen Yakka soldiers, looted our barns and set fire to them, destroyed our sluice gates and retired to the hills.'

A spurt of fear flashed though me. 'A successful raid, Sire. Why did we not have some warning from our spies in the *uda rata* kingdom?'

'The raid was probably so carefully planned that not even the participants knew what was intended until the event.'

'What do you propose doing, my lord?'

'Nothing.' The king's chair scraped on the paved floor as he pushed it back, stretching his legs and steepling his fingers on his chin. 'We can offer reprisals, raid the *uda rata* villages, kill more people, do more damage than Tikka has done, but that would only be a show of strength. We would merely be dispersing our energy and resources to teach Tikka a lesson he will not learn. He is a mortal enemy who will keep seeking to destroy us.'

'What's wrong with reprisals, Sire?' I demanded, though the thought of hurting innocent people sickened me. 'They would at least deter those in the border villages from giving Prince Tikka support and it would certainly aid the morale of our own villagers. Besides, our men will be furious at the news and will expect action from you.'

'There will be a time for action. Blind deeds can do no good. We must first find out what this is all about. What is Prince Tikka's 'ultimate object? What are his present objectives? What strength does he command?'

The past year had been full of surprises for me in regard to my brother's foresight and intelligence. Now I was discovering a new facet of his character, restraint; but my blood was beginning to boil at the outrage and the setback to our endeavours. 'How can we protect ourselves from future raids?' I demanded. 'Prince Tikka has obviously planned his course of action for a whole year. Now that he had made his first strike, he will surely strike again and again. We cannot remain idle while he systematically destroys what we have worked so hard to achieve.'

'How to prevent him is the question. He has the initiative. We can't spread our entire army throughout the kingdom to protect every village.'

I could not help the thought that we were facing retribution for the raids my brother and his men had carried out in Sinha-Pura.

'Why did Tikka select Mihiri Gama for his first raid?' The king's tone was contemplative. 'It is very far south of his own borders, closer to Kalyani.'

'How can that have any significance? He probably . . .' I hesitated, thinking more deeply.

Moments of silence trickled away in the sand-clock on his desk. Suddenly, I began to see the light. 'The Kalyani king converted his army to a body of devotees of the Buddha's doctrine upon learning of the Buddha's death,' I began. The king nodded his encouragement.

'There must be an element in that army, especially its leaders, who oppose this move. It proved to be a good one for us, because it has given us time to consolidate and develop our own kingdom.' The thoughts were now falling into place in my brain like the spokes of a wheel into its sockets. 'The Kalyani army was the only one in Lanka that could have effectively opposed us. The *uda rata* kingdom merely has several hundred men under arms and the scattered village life of its people makes the build-up of a regular army well-nigh impossible except with time and the kind of resources a Yakka kingdom does not possess. Prince Tikka wants to act fast, not only because of his bitter hatred, but because he can see us getting stronger by the day. His best source of assistance therefore is the Kalyani army. The dissidents in it are probably not strong enough to act on their own and are looking for some support from the *uda rata*. This raid is a signal of strength to them.'

My brother grinned and jerked his head back admiringly. 'See how clever you can be when you use your brains, even though you are black-haired and not red-haired.'

'What has hair colour got to do with it?'

'Well, obviously people with red hair have the most brains.'

'I never doubted that since we were little and you showed how clever you were during our studies.'

'What do you mean *during* our studies?'

'You were clever enough not to do them.'

He threw back his great head and guffawed, revealing those large, white teeth. We were so close, I did not have to make good jokes to cause him to laugh. 'One of these days we must appoint a court jester,' he observed. 'It is essential that every court has some light-heartedness, especially during moments of gravity, so that we do not make over-solemn decisions or develop over-earnest characters. Any man, especially a king, must be able to laugh at himself. Until we make such an appointment, you will suffice!' He paused. 'Do you think the kingdom of Thamba-Panni is now well set-up and well governed?' He shot the question suddenly at me, as he frequently did, his agile mind flitting from subject to subject. 'It's especially important for us to make the assessment in the light of this ill news.'

'Let me recapitulate some of what we have done, my

lord,' I replied. 'In the months that followed our seizure of the kingdom, we advanced steadily northwards and westwards, taking irrigation to the Yakka villages, compelling the people to abandon their *chena* method of cultivation. Apart from our twelve major reservoir projects, we made them tie their cattle for manure in their own fallow lands, then asweddumize the enriched land with controlled waters from their lakes and ponds, sowing and tilling, reaping the produce in abundance. We had them plant rice and vegetable crops in these new lands, growing only home produce of onion, chilli and spices, besides their own crops of *kurakkan* and manioc, in the harsher *chena* plots. We insisted on poultry and dairy farming in accordance with Arya methods. We introduced Arya respect for the cow, giver of life, but stopped short of decreeing veneration for it. At first, the Yakka resisted, though not physically, so our goals had to be accomplished under the watchful eyes of our soldiers. As our cavalry force under Vijit expanded, we were able gradually to extend our sphere of operations, so that by the end of this first year, when the rains started again, we were as far south as the Kalyani river and east about four *yojana* up to the foothills. As for the northern lands, after we pushed about one *yojana* from our capital, we discovered that these lands were already well cultivated.' I paused for breath.

'How is the *raja-kariya* system we introduced working?'

'Very well. The Yakka have come to see that it is a two-way system. They are now happy to give one-fifth of their produce to you, one-fifth to our men who supervise them and one-fifth for the government. They have seen how this last share has been used for improvements, the creation of roads and for emergencies such as drought and flood. Their own two-fifths share has given them riches beyond their dreaming. Most importantly, they have seen that labour brings rewards and they have come to trust the government not to exploit them. As I said, they resisted at first, but things became easier after you had the headman of Badda Gama executed for not cooperating. Certainly it helped us get the Yakka's military and manual labour services more readily.'

'Can they see that we are in turn performing our own feudal duties and responsibilities?'

'Of course. Surely you have observed that, Sire?'

'A king is somehow removed from the people. He observes less, wants to believe more. He generally depends on reports, which are not always reliable.'

'You will be pleased to know too that the Yakka are responding well to self-government. Our *panchyat* system, which they call *gan-sabhawas*, a play on the *yakse-sabhawa* of their demons I believe, enables them to regulate their daily lives and needs. Their headmen are beginning to administer our Arya laws. Our magistrates are dispensing justice fairly and firmly in each sub-district. You have indeed created a stable kingdom, Sire.'

'Are the people happy?'

I was taken aback. This had been one of my own concerns, but I had never expressed it to anyone. 'Any time you change a people's way of life, they become confused, Sire, and you cannot expect happiness overnight. Yet I believe they are now content.'

'Only our wife is discontented,' he responded. 'The demons of suspicion, jealousy, possessiveness often drive her insane.'

'Suspicion and jealousy spring from insecurity, Sire. Perhaps she will change when she takes your seed and conceives.'

He shook his head gloomily. 'Not likely. Her feelings of insecurity are too deeply rooted. Besides, she is not well-bred, has no real class. We are not sure that a part-Yakka heir . . .' He stopped abruptly, but I felt a stab of apprehension at what he had been about to say.

'Against this background, we shall continue giving the people cause to support us and they will be our first bastion against Prince Tikka's attacks. We shall try creating while he destroys.' The king shot off again at a seeming tangent. 'In that belief, we have an important mission for you, Prince. You shall represent us as a one-man embassy to the Kalyani kingdom to establish relations with it and to discover who Prince Tikka's allies might be. You shall try to negotiate a non-aggression pact with King Ra-hula, which will give us much needed time to fulfil our objectives in Thamba-Panni, and will certainly consolidate the people's support.'

It took two weeks for the messengers we sent to Kalyani seeking King Ra-hula's royal approval for our visit to return with his assent, two more weeks for our preparations for the mission to be completed. Three days later, I arrived in the Kalyani palace, where I was quartered, my retinue being accommodated elsewhere. I was impressed with the palace and its elegant appointments, which spoke of a cultured society.

King Ra-hula received me in his audience hall the morning after my arrival. It was one of those strange days when sunshine alternated with thin, hissing drizzles, making the earth a mosaic of light and shadow, the air a mixture of haze and brightness that causes animals to droop, birds to twitter irritably and the humidity to become overpowering. The palace attendant assigned to me had observed in rhyme:

> Au-vai, vas-sai
> Nariya-ge', magul-ai.
> The sun and the rain
> It's the jackal's wedding.

– in other words, a foxy sort of day!

The presents I had brought the king included a beautiful red, green and blue patterned Pahlava rug, gold cups and platters, an exquisite alabaster statue of an unknown Naga

246

warrior, all prizes seized from ships wrecked off the coast and stored in the Yakka treasury. Only the fine Scindhi bay was one of our own imports from the continent.

I had not expected to find a king wearing the yellow robe of the Buddha's disciples seated in the lotus pose on a gem-encrusted throne more magnificent than that of my father in Sinha-Pura. Yet why not? Had not the High King Bimbisara of our region worn the yellow robe after he embraced the Buddha's doctrine?

Dressed in white silken tunic and pantaloons, gold belt and gold sandalled shoes myself, I found the audience hall warm and reflected that the king must be cooler in his loose yellow robe. In spite of his Buddhist detachment, there was a hint of approval in King Ra-hula's appraising glance at me when I paused before the dais on which his throne was placed to make obeisance. I had thought I was alone with the king, but I now became conscious of the two silent, yellow-robed figures seated, also in the lotus pose, behind the throne. Their eyes were downcast, the shaven heads gleaming like glazed mirrors of pale blue. They appeared to be lost in meditation, but I had the uncanny sensation of being watched by inner eyes.

'You have come a long way to bring us your king's greetings, Prince Lala Sinha-Bahu.' The gentle, sing-song voice seemed to come from somewhere outside the broad, dark visage of the ruler. 'We thank your king for the beautiful gifts he has sent us and we thank you for bringing them. They shall be used for our people. You shall take back with you some of our own most precious gifts, of a different kind. We hope you had a pleasant journey and are comfortably lodged.'

'I bring you greetings, Sire, from our King, Vijaya Sinha-Bahu, ruler of the kingdom he had named Thamba-Panni,' I declared. 'I thank you for your solicitude on my behalf. I had a very pleasant journey. Your kind arrangements were so perfect that we were only three days

247

and two nights on the road. Yet it was a long time, since my goal was to reach your royal presence. By your graciousness too, our ferry-crossing over the great river was smooth. And again thanks to your generosity, Sire, I am very comfortably lodged. The journey back will indeed seem longer.' I thought the king's eyes twinkled for a moment at the compliments, but the broad, heavy features were relaxed and remained immobile.

'As you have doubtless observed, we now lead the simple existence of our revered Lord Buddha's disciples, but we try not to forget the needs of our lay brethren, especially our guests.' Surprisingly, the king then came directly to the point. 'We understand the object of your mission is to establish diplomatic relations between our two kingdoms, a very civilized and laudable purpose.'

'My sovereign will be gratified to know that you approve of his purpose, Sire.'

'We did not say we approve, Prince.' A mischievous glint sparkled briefly in the dark eyes. 'Merely that we thought the idea civilized and laudable.'

I knew then that I had to keep my wits sharp in dealing with this king, to listen carefully to his every word, to appraise each one of mine. 'Forgive me, my lord, for not making my own response clear. I have been at fault through my foolish inability to express myself in terms worthy of your royal comprehension. I did not mean to imply that you had given your royal consent to the establishment of diplomatic relations between our two kingdoms. I merely wished to express my king's undoubted gratification that you had graciously approved his purpose.'

He blinked once then. Realizing that I had in truth expressed myself correctly the first time, a grudging admiration skimmed across his eyes. 'You are a child after our own heart, Prince Lala,' he finally conceded. 'Perhaps we should keep you in our court to become one of us, or perhaps you should remain in it as the representative of your king. You may even find some merit in our attempts to abandon all desire, including the desire to end desire, to cultivate the mind, which in this life is our focal point of *kharma*, cause, and *vipaka*, effect. Right Understanding, Right Thinking, Right Meditation, Right Livelihood, Right Conduct, these are part of the Noble Eightfold Path which we follow. We also try to practise *ahimsa*, forbearance even towards our enemies and *maitriya*, loving kindness. What does your king practise?'

For a moment I was taken aback. How could I tell this king that my brother was an atheist and an agnostic, though I had a shrewd suspicion that he already knew. 'Forgive me, Sire, but I do not know what lies in the depths of any man's mind, frequently not even in mine.' I smiled to rob the words of any offence. 'Actions alone do not necessarily reveal what lies beneath.'

This time he seemed to have expected some such answer, for there was no change in his expression. 'We thought your king must practise *ahimsa* because he made no move to punish the *uda rata* people who destroyed your beautiful new village, Mihiri Gama, so close to our north-eastern border, about one month ago.'

He was really alert and tough, this king. No wonder he had remained on his throne even after he rendered his army ineffective. What did he want now? What was the thrust of his questioning? 'The truly strong, like you, Sire, do not need to resort to brute force, or physical violence,' I stated. 'Since my king too is truly strong and confident in his strength, he has held back from any reprisal. But I would add, very respectfully, that he will resist any armed invasion with like force.' I believed that I ought to demonstrate some strength and was rewarded once again by that single blink of the king's eyelids.

'We hear you have a very well-trained, fast-moving army, including new vehicles called chariots that look like low *thirikkalayas*, buggy-carts, but are drawn by horses, with

249

which your ancestors conquered the continent thousands of years ago.' His mellow voice became even more gentle. 'Our own philosophy is to disarm the enemy with generosity, to soothe him with all our material possessions if need be. This will not be difficult for us, because we have already renounced our possessions and own merely those of the *bhikku*, a yellow robe, a black begging bowl, a palm-leaf umbrella, an *indikola* fan, a pair of sandals, like our revered Master, Lord Buddha, the Enlightened One. He ruled most of your continent with his doctrine, why can we not, we humbler ones, regulate our small kingdom with it? We have discovered the mastery of our own senses to be more important than dominating the bodies of men. When we have indeed mastered all our own senses, desire is eliminated. When desire is eliminated, craving is eliminated, clinging is eliminated, suffering ceases. The desire to rule no longer exists.'

How then and why do you rule your kingdom, I wondered, but contented myself with saying, 'My king has no desire to expand his territory, Sire. He merely wishes to govern it well. If we are invaded, however, we will not only repel the attack, but will launch a counter-offensive against any such enemy and undoubtedly conquer his kingdom.'

He caught the implication of my words and smiled. 'Who are our enemies but ourselves, dear child?'

I looked him squarely in the face. 'My humble submission, Sire, is that until a person renounces all other responsibility except to himself and his *kharma*, he has the potential of being an enemy to himself and therefore to others and he will correspondingly have the enemies of his station.'

'Well put, as always, Prince Lala Sinha-Bahu. You are indeed a precocious child, ready for the supreme gift we expect to bestow on you. Before we do, pray tell us, what are your king's immediate desires.'

I could not miss the ironic emphasis he placed on the

word 'desires'. Realizing that it would only be a waste of time to go through the usual parleying that could take days in this sort of exercise, I decided to be direct. 'My king anticipates trouble from the *uda rata*. He therefore desires to secure our southern frontier with you by a non-aggression treaty. He does not believe that the forces behind the destruction of Mihiri Gama intended that move merely as the beginning of a series of guerilla acts against our kingdom or as the precursor to an invasion. We are too strong for the *uda rata* army. My king perceives the destruction of Mihiri Gama, so close to your own borders, to be a signal of strength to elements within your kingdom, which would then seize power from you, re-activate your army and finally invade Thamba-Panni.'

I paused to survey the effect of my words. Finding not the slightest response of any kind. I plunged on. I had nothing to lose and everything to gain. 'Frankly, Sire, if we can be certain of comparative peace for at least one year longer, my king believes we will be strong enough to resist attack from any source and to consolidate all the economic gains and the wellbeing we have brought to our people.'

'So you want us to cooperate in making you strong, in order that, like the young bull-elephant in the herd, you may one day turn round and rule us?'

'Yes.' The word came hissing out of me through a force I could not control and I felt my stomach blanch with fear after I uttered it.

I expected an outburst, dismissal from his presence. Instead, he gave me the sweetest of smiles. 'Those of us who have the blessed gift of the inner sight perceive these things, so you have done well to answer us truthfully, Prince.'

I marvelled at the gentleness of his voice and somewhere within me there stirred the desire to be like him.

'We are able to perceive much concerning the future of our kingdom and yours,' the king continued. 'As well as things about your personal life, dear child, that even you, with your extraordinary powers of mind and heart, would marvel at. We are impressed by all you Arya have done since you began ruling the Yakka. We do not approve of violence but we recognize that it has to exist, because of the forces of *kharma/vipaka*. Not all men are born to be Buddhas, or even *arahats*. As long as the average man has to be governed other than by the need to attain Enlightenment, it might as well be through strong, enlightened rulers.' His eyes flashed with some sort of divine fervour and his tones rang out. 'But make no mistake about it, in time to come, the sacred city of Kalyani, its sacred temple, another sacred city which your own king shall establish which even he will not realize the significance of, this blessed island of Lanka, united, will be the centre of Lord Buddha's doctrine.' He gave me a direct look of compassion beyond my wildest imagining. 'And you, Prince and child, will play your own role in this sacred achievement.'

As if from some miracle of King Ra-hula's creation, I felt the heat of flames, heard their crackle and roar and smelt their pungent smoke. My skin became fevered, but a chill wind blew from within me so that I shivered. Then a great exaltation seized me and it was as if my body had ceased to exist, my mind with it, while my *atman* soared free as the sky, free as all space and the Universe. I am finding God, I thought. Since this king has rejected God, it is the one thing about me that he cannot comprehend, my discovery of God; therefore though he can send my spirit out of my body, as he has now done with his strange powers, he cannot control its direction.

The king's voice broke into my vision and I returned to the warmth and humidity of the audience hall. I tried to shake off the tremor of some fear which had entered me.

'You shall have your treaty,' the king declared. My heart leapt and my fear was immediately forgotten. 'Meanwhile, we have an even more precious gift for you.' He reached for a little bell on a golden stool beside his throne and rang it.

'Its messenger is a visitor who came to us a few days ago.'

I knew instinctively at which of the two sets of double doors behind the dais I should look. As they opened silently a yellow-robed figure stood framed in the doorway. I could not distinguish the face, which was in dark shadow, but the whole exuded an aura of undefinable peace.

As the figure advanced slowly into the room, a shaft of light, I do not know from where, illuminated the face. The skin was fair, drawn tightly over bones cast nobly in the Arya mould. The shaven head was beautifully shaped. The eyes though downcast, were obviously fine and dark.

The figure paused. The eyes lifted to mine. My heart leapt and my lips formed his name silently, for I could not give him greeting without the king's leave. 'Uday!'

Chapter 19

The last time I had seen Uday was in Sinha-Pura, which he had visited the year before my brother and his comrades were exiled. When he left the Lala palace after his final meeting with the Princess Sinha-Seevali, he had headed for Bana-raj where he sat at the Buddha's feet and learned the doctrine. It was inevitable that in a few years he should don the yellow robe of the *bhikku*. He then changed his name to Sri Ravindra. Having visited many cities of the continent as a missionary, he finally returned to Sinha-Pura and was cordially received.

Uday fascinated me and I came to love him. He taught me the doctrine, but the time before I went into exile had been too short for me to become a convert and my slowly emerging belief in God had created a barrier. It was at this time that Uday and I drew sufficiently close to each other, however, for him to tell me the story of his life, including his time with Sinha and his love for my mother.

Recovering from the shock of seeing him, I greeted Uday as befitted his station as a *bhikku*, bowing low with my palms together before my eyes. He acknowledged the greeting with a slow inclination of his head, his eyes still downcast. Though over fifty years old, his chiselled features were firm and his skin smooth as a boy's, evidence that the Doctrine was as good for a man's physical well being as for mental peace and spiritual attainment.

'We need not introduce you to each other,' King Rahula observed. 'The Venerable Ravindra and you will have much to speak of, so we have requested that *dana*, the one meal that we who observe *dasa-sila*, the ten precepts, partake of before noon each day, be served to you together in the courtyard. There, you can talk in private.' His smile was kindly. 'Within a palace words may fall upon alien ears. Outside, only the birds will share your communion.' He tossed the edge of his yellow robe over his shoulder in a smooth gesture, moved his limbs gracefully from the lotus pose and stood erect, palmyrah leaf fan in hand. With an echoing rustle of their robes, the two attendants rose silently in unison behind him, like dancers backgrounding their lead.

As I made obeisance to the king, I could not escape the feeling that I was part of a play which this wise man had written around some drama in his life. 'We have also arranged for you to meet some of the principal figures in our court,' he concluded. 'These include the commander of our missionary army, our nephew, Prince Jaya.' He paused and cleared his throat. 'You should find him specially interesting.'

Though the sun was now almost directly overhead, it was cooler in the courtyard. That hissing rain had ceased, the splash of water came now from an ornamental cascade, the deep blue of the sky was scattered with humps of pluming white clouds like thick cotton. Fragrant scents of boiled rice, overlaid with the tang of vegetables cooked in spices and lime, reached my nostrils from two black begging bowls containing our meal, placed on two yellow mats facing each other on the green grass beneath the shade of a spreading banyan tree. Beside each bowl was a matching mug, containing a drink I could see was *nannar*, *sarsparilla* syrup with *cassa-cassa* seeds in it, another mug of fresh drinking-water, bowls for washing the hands before and after the meal and white napkins. Mynahs screeched and love-birds whistled all around us.

Only after he sat in the lotus pose and I had taken my place cross-legged on the mat facing him did Uday raise his eyes to mine. They were even darker, more luminous, deeper than I remembered them to be, but their peace remained the ultimate as before. 'We find joy in your presence,' he stated softly.

'And I in yours, venerable sir.'

'That is as it is,' he observed. 'As you can see, you will share our simple meal of vegetables and rice.'

'My joy in being with you would make any food pleasing.'

'You have not changed in spite of all that has transpired within you since we last met.'

I knew instantly that he was referring to the evil he believed me to have inflicted on my *kharma* through my actions. He knew I had killed men. He could see it all as if I carried a painting of my deeds wrapped round my body. I had conveniently excused these actions by transferring them to the *dharma* focus of my mind, which called for that obedience to the duty of my station that we Arya and even the Hindu Dasa believe to be a necessary extension of the true self. Uday's gentle gaze had brought back the prickings of conscience, the recurring moments of horror and strangely, even some concern about my One God's reaction.

'We can talk about the things that concern you later,' Uday suggested with a smile. 'For the present, let us eat, but first we would like you to take *pan-sila*, the five precepts, that all who believe in good may take, regardless of their station or faith. As you may recall, *ata-sila* is a higher state of eight precepts and *dasa-sila* are the ten precepts, which anyone can observe for periods of time, but to which we *bhikkus* dedicate every moment of our mortal lives.'

'I would be privileged to take *pan-sila* with you,' I stated.

'Please forgive me, child. Not with me, but with yourself.' His smile robbed the correction of any offence. 'Let us commence.' He lowered his head.

'*Namo thassa bagavatho, sama san Buddhassa . . .*' He began chanting the words in quiet, deep tones.

My own head lowered, eyes closed, palms placed instinctively together, above the forehead this time, in the position of worship, I allowed the music of his voice and the meaning of the words to penetrate my *prana*, my life-force. It was a strange, beautiful sound in that garden and I soon found myself wafted outside my body, my spirit soaring on the chant to merge into the throb of the universe. I was a part of all things, a conscious, exalted part of the eternal, infinite, boundless body of God.

The chanting ended. On its last faint echoes, my spirit was drawn swiftly back to my body. It was such sweet ecstasy before and now such pain, my first mind-thought was that my eyes were wet with tears through which I found myself staring at Uday. We gazed at each other awhile, he with complete knowledge of me and some compassion, the source of which I could not place.

We ate slowly and in silence, using our fingers delicately so that the food did not reach above the first joints. The simple food was, however, deliciously cooked and I enjoyed every peaceful moment of the meal. When we were done, bare-chested palace attendants, dressed in white *verti* with blue sashes, appeared as if from nowhere. They helped us wash our hands then served us creamy curd with the dark brown honey of Lanka that I knew was tapped from the heart of the *kitul-palm*.

When we had done, the attendants vanished, taking our empty dishes with them.

Uday broke the silence. 'You will continue to add to your own development because you continually seek knowledge to fulfil your destiny. When we were your age, we too went through the process of robbing, wounding, maiming, killing, acquiring *akusala kharma*, evil causes, yet it was these very acts that finally caused us to choose the road to salvation. Your life will follow this same pattern.'

'How can you know, venerable sir?'

He smiled, his gentle smile again. 'There is no magic to

it. Like things have a like response to similar stimuli.'

A sudden awareness of the inevitability of cause and effect struck me. 'In other words, the things we do to others are impelled by our desires for ourselves, making us, in turn, creatures of those desires, indeed the victims of them. It has been so amply demonstrated in the lives of my grandfather and grandmother, my parents, my brother, even in my own life. If such terrible consequences can flow from acts during our lifetime – the killing of an insect possibly giving birth to the murderer – how much more significant must they be in their impact on our continuing consciousness?'

'We of the doctrine do not believe in a continuing stream of consciousness,' Uday countered. 'Human beings, indeed all life-forms, merely *are*. Where we go in each successive manifestation of life, which we call re-birth, is decided by our last thought moment, which in turn is conditioned by all that we think, say, do, each act of consciousness in this life. Yet each life form is a separate *kharmic* manifestation fraught with suffering – birth is suffering, life is suffering, death is suffering. Since you have not eliminated the clinging that causes suffering from your life, Prince, we fear the news we bring will cause you grief.'

A light breeze rustling through the banyan leaves, whispered apprehension. My stomach began its familiar churning. What could his news be?

He held my eyes with a steady gaze. 'Both your parents and your grandmother died recently. One of our reasons for responding to the invitation of the venerable Sri Rahula to come to Kalyani immediately was to bring you the news personally and be of some comfort to you. Oh yes, we knew you were here. Your achievements in Lanka are even the subject of the songs of minstrels on the continent. Having got to Kalyani, we learned of your proposed visit to the palace and decided to await your arrival.'

I had given up any thought of ever seeing my family

again, but that all three were dead? Did death really go in threes? The full impact of the news had not hit me. I had heard the words merely as words and it seemed to be someone else's voice that enquired, 'How did they die?'

'Soon after your brother was exiled, your father, stricken by guilt and remorse at all the evil he had wittingly and unwittingly wrought in his life, abdicated the throne in favour of your brother, Sumitta, and retired to Sinha's cave in the Lala jungle to live the life of a hermit, doubtless to expiate his misdeeds. His death came about in a tragic manner. In the very glade where he had committed his most heinous crime, he was pierced in the throat by the arrow of an expert hunter who had mistaken your father's deep cough for that of a tiger and loosed a shaft at the source of the sudden sound. Your mother, hearing the news, journeyed to the forest, collected her husband's remains and immolated herself on the pyre.'

A gasp escaped me. Pictures of the events began to form in my mind and I vividly re-lived the anguish that my father and mother must have known. Oh, the pity of it. I had never been close to my parents – my brother would be crushed to learn of *Amma*'s death – but for the first time, I saw these two people as human beings, capable of suffering, knew their long, countless hours of grief, of hatred, finally of remorse. I suddenly felt that Uday had to be mistaken. 'But *suttee* is Hindu custom,' I protested feebly, still unable to face up to the truth. 'We are Arya. Besides, didn't my mother accept the Buddha's doctrine through your teachings? And how did my grandmother die?'

'Embracing the doctrine alone cannot release us from the forces of *kharma/vipaka*,' he replied gravely. 'Your mother's action was the inevitable consequence of past births and her life in this birth.' A sigh escaped him, unusual for a *bhikku*. 'We first journeyed to Sinha-Pura to give your mother the gift of the doctrine because we felt we owed it to her for having told her the truth of her brother's crime, which embittered her whole life and caused such havoc in the lives of so many others.' He sighed again, more heavily this time. 'As you know, she was aware of your brother's plot to seize power but did nothing about it. When the attempt failed, its hideous consequences made her embrace the doctrine not long after your ships departed Sinha-Pura leaving her a broken woman. We can only hope that she and your father will have better rebirths. In contrast, your grandmother died suddenly in her sleep the night she received the news of your parents' death.'

'So she died peacefully?'

'Who knows? Your parents at least must have been at peace when they died, but your grandmother?' He shrugged. 'She once believed herself to be a vehicle of history, but she only lived to see the futility of her actions. Her first husband murdered, her two children dead in the very forest from which she thought she had liberated them, her oldest grandchildren banished and living in some strange land. No, being the kind of person she was, the person she had made of herself, she must have been frustrated, bitter, confused. A quick death is no pointer to peace of mind. Only what lay hidden beneath the silence of pride in your grandmother's indomitable mind is what would have wafted her to her next birth.'

'What then was the purpose of it all?' I cried in despair.

'There is cause and there is effect. Purpose is only a concept of the human mind. It has no place in *sansara*.'

'But my grandmother had dreams of history. Were they merely the product of her foolish imagining then, her blind ambition?' I was suddenly filled with a great sense of hopelessness. 'Surely there is no meaning to life if we abandon purpose? What good is any of it?'

Uday fixed me with a strange look, which combined tranquillity with intense willpower. 'Do not despair. Though your grandmother did not witness it in her lifetime, the history of which she was the womb is indeed being fulfilled in your lives. Why even the two of us are making history at this very moment.'

His words brought me as a person into the conversation. Then the full impact of his news hit me. I was filled with a great emptiness. I would never see my parents or my beloved grandmother again. Tears sprang to my eyes.

Disasters came by the dozen. In the distant capital of our kingdom, Thamba-Panni, King Vijaya received news by fast messenger of the destruction of another of his model villages, Veyan Gama, also close to the Kalyani border. Greatly disturbed, he summoned his ministers to dinner with him in the great hall. The conversation was general, while they ate their *chupatti* and roast chicken. Only when the attendants had cleared the table and closed the hall doors did the king announce the ill news. The ministers listened in silence. When he had finished, questions flashed across the table, the conflicting answers as gusty as the rain squalling on the roof. What were the options? Should they retaliate? If so, how? What opposition could they expect? What form should the response take – a deputation to the *uda rata* king, mild action, severe reprisals, an outright invasion? In the latter event, what would be the impact on the remaining two kingdoms, *Ruhunu rata* in the far south and Kalyani? How would it affect the non-aggression treaty Prince Lala was attempting to negotiate?

The multitude of factors unfolded, the available options took shape and the hours rolled slowly by without agreement. King Vijaya finally wearied of the interminable discussion. 'We will take no decision until Prince Lala returns from Kalyani,' he declared firmly. 'We need whatever new facts the prince may bring before evolving any plan. Besides, the wisdom and counsel of the prince will be invaluable.'

He looked at Ujjeni. Had he seen a spark of anger in the minister's eyes?

While the discussion was going on, the Princess Kuveni had been lying in bed, awaiting the king, unable to fall asleep. The royal bedchamber adjoined her own room, both fronting the centre courtyard of the palace. The canopied bed, complete with golden silk sheets and cushions, that she had originally set up for Prince Vijaya in the tent she had erected for him on the night of his arrival in Lanka, had been placed at the far wall of the room, beneath the high grilled window, upon a large green and red Pahlava rug. For the first time in over a year, the princess was finding the bed uncomfortable. The flames of tapers in sconces placed on a table by the bed threw a fitful, eerie light within the room. Her eyes drifted from the open door to the couches of seasoned brown tamarind wood, with a grain resembling red flames running up them, that had been placed against the walls. Should she try to sleep on one of them instead? She felt unaccountably afraid to leave the bed.

Unaware of the reason for the king's delay, the princess found herself experiencing the familiar tension. As it slowly gripped her mind, the old restlessness, the fears that had never really died, emerged from within her.

The past year had been comparatively peaceful, except when she could not control her suspicions. She and King Vijaya had fallen into an easy routine, despite their quarrels, which she recognized were caused by her demands. As he brought the kingdom under control and gave it prosperity, she began to admire him even more. If he had believed in gods, she might have thought them more powerful for good than her own demon gods, which were really the devil in her, stirring whenever she was upset or felt insecure.

Tonight, her husband was late again, when she had such important news to give him and Prince Lala was away in distant Kalyani. She felt emotional, distraught, the familiar feeling of rejection rising within her like chill mists on a black night.

She lay back fighting the dread sensation, listening to the rain pummelling the roof as if trying to crash through and swamp her, watching the taper-flames dance, their wisps of smoke curling and billowing in the breezes released by rain gusts. The heavy scent of incense began to stifle her . . . a familiar sensation . . . resin, the demon smell. Suddenly she found herself fighting a mad impulse to dash naked through the deluge to the abandoned shrine of her demon gods.

Groaning aloud, she started tossing and turning, unable to get comfortable on cushions that had become too warm. Unidentifiable sounds began buzzing in her head and merged into the hissing of the rain. She tossed her head from side to side in an effort to shake off the noise. Her black hair, sweeping her face, irritated her. Impatiently, she swept it behind her ears with her hands.

Prince Vijaya found her wide-eyed, staring blankly at the silken canopy of the bed, when he finally came to the bedchamber jagged from all the thinking and debating, the need to make decisions, sorrow and anger at the deaths of the settlers. One look at his wife's taut body, her fixed gaze and he knew something was wrong. 'You're not yet asleep, *larla*,' he observed standing beside the bed and looking down at her. 'What's wrong?'

Only her dark eyes shot sideways towards him. Observing the anxiety in his expression, the old desire to wound seized her. 'You ask me what's wrong?' Her voice was flat, toneless, as if she were repeating a lesson. 'What was wrong that kept you when I needed you? I have waited for hours. Where have you been?'

'In council with my ministers.' He hesitated, wondering whether to give her the bad news.

She mistook his hesitation for guilt. 'You have no need to invent lies.' She closed her eyes. 'If there is one thing I can't stand it's lies. It is a way of life with the Yakka. I had thought you Arya were different.'

'And so we are.' The king's voice was still gentle, the leonine features soft. 'Please tell me what's bothering you.'

'I needed you tonight and you were not here. It's as simple as that. Only my gods are constantly with me.'

'My thoughts are constantly with you.'

'When I need your physical presence, what good are your thoughts?'

He stiffened. 'Madam,' he began.

'Don't call me "madam",' she directed impatiently. 'You always do that when you want to talk to me like a child.'

'We have the right to talk to you any way we please.' That low growl had entered his voice, the lion's warning. 'We are the king.'

She sat up in bed. 'Oh, so you are here as the king, not as my spouse? Give me leave to spring from this bed and make obeisance to you, Lord.'

'Have a care,' he warned.

'I should. Yes, I should indeed have a care. And do you know why?'

He suddenly went taut, his gaze became stern.

'I'm with child,' she screamed. 'That's why I wanted you with me tonight. I'm bearing your child. Do you hear? One single night when I wanted you so desperately, and where were you? Whoring, no doubt.' She was almost snarling now, hating herself for it but unable to control herself. 'You say you were in council with your ministers. Good for you. I hope your mating with them tonight will give each one of them your child.'

King Vijaya stared at her aghast.

I had another bad night, haunted by the lives and deaths of my parents and my grandmother, which took me back to that night over a year ago when I had received news of the murders of Rasiah, Ramiah and Pattakanu. Great waves of longing for Sundari seized me. Where was she? Perhaps she was dead. Gloom and depression filled me. There was no meaning to life when it was so full of suffering.

Yet I was up early the next morning to prepare for my call on Prince Jaya. Although he lived close to the palace, in the seclusion of his brick mansion with the broad Kalyani River flowing lazily behind it, I went by palanquin, accompanied by six of my attendants. I was ushered into the audience room and greeted my host with the traditional '*Ayubowan!*' of Lanka.

I must confess to surprise at discovering that he was so enormously fat. Literally filling the high-backed chair on which he was sitting, with those great, loose pectorals on his bare chest, a fair skin and high-strung voice, he could have been mistaken for a palace eunuch on our continent.

He bade me be seated on an ebony couch with red cushions placed beside his chair. Like all obese men, he breathed deeply, the nostrils flaring with each inhalation. 'We hope you didn't get wet, Prince.' He was referring to last night's showers. 'These unseasonal rains can cause irritating colds. You should take plenty of *kottha-malli*, coriander tea, on your return to the palace. And tell your attendants to put ginger and garlic in it. They have a nasty habit of forgetting. Lazy devils. You must inhale the smoke first. It clears the breathing passages. Then you drink the tea to help with the cold or fever and eat the garlic to strengthen your chest.' He beamed at me, went into a bout of coughing, brought up phlegm and spat expertly into a brass spittoon. 'Tchickay! I seem to be getting the accursed thing myself.' The slits of eyes opened revealing the penetrating, black dart of his gaze. 'One has to be careful, no? Specially when one is as big as I am. The bigger the fellow, the bigger the cold, I say.'

I felt horrible repulsion at imagining the dimensions of Prince Jaya's colds, but responded politely. 'Men of stature always pay a price for it.' I wanted to test his reactions.

'Ah! What a nice thing to say, no?' he replied. His pudgy face creased into a smile, the teeth pearly white beneath bristling, black moustaches. 'You are indeed a courtier, Prince.'

He was giving flattery back for flattery. A clever man, there was no use fencing with him. 'Your king desired me to be the first to inform you that he and my own king have concluded a non-aggression pact between our two kingdoms.'

Only a tiny quiver of his cheeks and a single tick beneath the right eye betrayed that I had struck home. You don't like that, I thought. Why?

The prince recovered in an instant. 'How nice,' he observed. 'Very timely too, no?' He paused. 'Let me also be the first to give you some news. Unfortunately, it is not as good as your own. You know the village our people call Veyan Gama?' I nodded. It was one of our twelve new villages. 'Aney, our people are so bad. They call it Veyan, because that is their name for white ants and you white people built it. This village was destroyed by brigands last night. Tchikay! Nowadays no one is safe from these terrible people, no?'

Coming as it did on the heels of the destruction of Mihiri Gama, I was shocked by the news but covered up swiftly. 'I had not heard the news, Prince and I thank you for giving it to me.' I said smoothly, without a trace of the tremors I was experiencing. 'As you say, these brigands are indeed getting rather tiresome.'

'Will your king tire of it soon? What do you think he will do?' A humorous crease appeared in Prince Jaya's fat cheeks, making him look like a great mischievous child.

I recognized that the burning of this second village was yet another signal, but to whom? To Prince Jaya? Why else was he so concerned to discover my brother's likely response? If that were true, Prince Jaya must be the chief conspirator in Kalyani. Did King Ra-hula even suspect him? Why had he sent me personally to give the news of our non-aggression treaty to the Prince?

The answer hit me with a thud like that of a hammer. King Ra-hula knew or at least suspected the truth. In his wisdom, he was using me, very appropriately, as a message-bearer to his suspected opponent. How then should I react now? If Prince Tikka and Prince Jaya joined forces, we would have to face a showdown with them, but our kingdom, Thamba-Panni, needed time to become strong enough to face such a coalition. I leaned forward confidentially, 'I hope you will not betray my trust, Prince, but I must tell you that the reason we sought this non-aggression pact is because we were too weak to go to war, or even to undertake reprisals for the destruction of our village, Mihiri Gama. Now you say Veyan Gama, too, has been attacked, but we are still not ready to retaliate. We need more time and we hope you will do everything in your power to obtain it for us. My king and I look to you for personal support, to prevent any disturbance of the present balance of power between Thamba-Panni and the *uda rata* kingdom. Some day we shall show you our gratitude.'

He nodded his head solemnly. 'I will certainly keep what you say in the strictest confidence,' he assured me. 'And you shall have my fullest support.' He smiled sweetly at me with a crinkling of the eyes. 'I must also give you another titbit of news that came my way this morning,' he finally volunteered. 'Aney! I don't know why people bring these things to me. They must think a fat man is a fitting receptacle for gossip.' He let out a high-pitched giggle and his whole body shook, the pectorals shimmering like curd, at what he obviously thought was his own wit. 'The *uda rata* king, Gonda, suffered a sudden, mysterious death. The new ruler of that kingdom is his son, Prince Tikka.'

When I returned to the palace, my first thought was to send a messenger to King Vijaya with the news, but I decided that he would have had it already. To my delight, I was informed by the chief attendant that my noon meal was to be served in the palace courtyard and that once again I was to partake of it with Uday. Although he would be prudent enough not to refer to the deaths in my family, the presence of a man connected with them, with my native Sinha-Pura and with my boyhood was my one solace.

We sat on mats opposite each other, Uday very relaxed in the lotus pose. I was grateful for the shade of the banyan tree that protected me from the sun that glared down out of a cloudless blue sky.

Two bare-chested attendants served rice and curry into our black begging bowls and withdrew.

A dog barked in the distance, children's voices arose faintly, reciting a *kavi*, poem, all somehow part of the unruffled peace of the Kalyani palace.

We had been eating in silence. 'What do you think causes the tangible feeling of peace in this palace, venerable sir?' I asked Uday.

'The doctrine embraced by the king and most of his people,' he responded.

'Is everybody really happy, or is this peace something negative, the stagnant waters of a hidden forest pool that never knew a stream?'

'How poetic! What do you think?'

'I have always believed that to know ecstasy one must be willing to submit to anguish, to feel hope one has to be ready for despair.'

'The atmosphere of the palace comes from people who have traded happiness for contentment. They have accepted a levelling of emotions, a relinquishing of the peaks and valleys. The rains can come, tempest winds blow, but not all the sound and fury can disturb the inner core of peace here, which emanates through our having discovered the truth about life, our freedom from its inner storms.'

'What if your discovery too is an illusion?' I demanded.

'Does it matter, so long as what we think we know is

sufficient to act as the immovable anchor of our lives? Would you not be satisfied with such a life?'

'I don't know. Certainly, my brother would not be.' I knew that the words were the outlet to a need within me for discussion of the differences I had noted between my brother and myself. 'As his twin, I can't be very different, can I?'

Uday continued chewing a mouthful of food. 'Your brother and you are alike in that you both seek far-reaching goals, beyond those of other people, and pursue those goals relentlessly,' he finally stated. 'It's how you get there that makes the difference.'

I finally asked him the question that had been bothering me increasingly this past year. 'Supposing one day they clash? Supposing our very goals are different?'

'It is not your goals that are different,' he finally repeated, his voice gentle. 'You both want a peaceful, prosperous country and a contented people. Your differences lie in your motivations, values and ideals. Your brother is concerned with things, you with human beings. Yet you are both selfish in pursuing what you desire. You are the two arcs of a perfect circle, spreading away from a common point. When you have reached the widest point of separation, you will converge again to become joined once more.'

His words frightened me. My brother had been the anchor of my life, but during the past year I had found myself chafing at its restraints.

Sensing my reaction, Uday continued calmly, 'People of different views and ideals have frequently united to achieve a common objective, only to discover, when they reach it, that the differences between them remained far greater than those they had to overcome in getting there. You have been united with your brother these many years, subjugating your own ideals for that unity which had no set or defined purpose. Now that you are both on a new threshold of life, you must face it as the grown-up individuals you are, no longer as twin children.'

We finished our meal in silence. When the attendants had finished clearing their dishes, Uday broke that silence. 'You are ready, we believe, to hear the Paticca Samupāda of the Buddha,' he declared. 'The words literally mean Dependent Origination, but they reveal the manner in which the cycle of birth and re-birth operates. Please understand that this sermon of our Lord Buddha relates only to Samsāra, the process of birth and death. It is not a discourse on the evolution of the world from primordial matter. It deals with the cause of rebirth and suffering. It does not attempt to show the absolute origin of life.' He paused. 'Avijjā, or Ignorance of the Four Noble Truths, is the first cause of the wheel of life, or Samsāra, wandering again and again, that unbroken process of the Aggregates, Elements and Sense-organs. Ignorance clouds right understanding. Arising from Ignorance are Volitional Activities, all of which, whether moral or immoral, prolong our wandering in Samsāra. Yet good actions can help end our wandering. Arising from Volitional Activities is Vinnāna, Re-linking Consciousness, which links past and present. Simultaneously with the appearance of re-linking consciousness, Nāma, Mind and Rūpa, Matter, come into being. Salāyatana, or the Six Senses, are the inevitable adjuncts of Mind and Matter. Is that clear so far?' He lifted his eyes to mine.

I smiled. 'I hear your words and comprehend them, Venerable Sir, but the meaning is so deep, I shall need time for a fuller understanding.'

'That is good.' He looked down again. 'Because of the Six Senses, Phassa, Contact, is inevitable. Contact leads to Vedanā, Sensations, from which Tanhā, Craving arises. Craving produces, Upādāna, attachment, which conditions the Khamma (Bhava), which in turn determine Jāti or the nature of future birth. Old age, or Decay and Death, Jarā-Marana, are the inevitable consequences of birth. The only way out of this is to cease all Cause, for without Cause there is no Effect. Only the complete cessation of Ignorance can reveal the Cause and lead to the cessation of birth and death, which are suffering and the causes of suffering.'

As Uday described to me the modes of birth and death, the planes of existence, how rebirth takes place, what is re-born and the doctrine of *Anatta*, no-soul, I knew I must somehow consider what he was saying separately from all my past knowledge and beliefs, including those of *atman*, of the continuing stream of consciousness, of the Hindu theory of reincarnation and of *Ahura-mazda* and the Light-source religion of the Farsi. I had to measure his words as something totally new, as if I had no previous philosophical knowledge, nor even any insight of my own, if I was to understand the Buddha's new views of birth and re-birth, cause and effect.

It required such enormous powers of concentration and comprehension to follow what Uday was saying that I was exhausted, my mind raw with the effort, by the time he finished. Yet I must say that my attention had not wavered, even for a single moment, and I was fascinated by the logic of the sermon, save for two questions that I did not wish to voice: Where did it all begin? Where, when and how did the first cause arise?

He lifted his eyes to me and smiled gently, perhaps in recognition of the efforts I had been making, of which I knew he had been uncannily aware even while he spoke.

'May I ask you one question,' I said when he had finished. 'Why specially for me?'

His look became enigmatic. 'Perhaps because the blessed gift of the inner sight tells us that you are fertile soil on which to sow the seed of the doctrine. Soil which will reproduce in abundance.'

As I held his glance, my stomach started unaccountably to churn and my eyes widened, for I recognized that its cause was some knowledge Uday had. He lowered his gaze and the moment passed. 'Will you please observe *dasa-sila* tonight? Meanwhile study this chart.'

'It would give me great joy.' I studied the scroll.

'In that event, you must not take any more food or drink today. Just moisten your lips with water if you become thirsty. Keep your thoughts pure. Try and abandon all desire, even that to eliminate desire. You can then live the life of the *bhikku* for this short period and emerge from it with your mind cleansed, your being at peace.'

'What does the observance of *sila* entail?'

'The First Watch of the night extends from sundown for four hours. During this period, you will hear the doctrine from us, meditate and, when necessary, discourse with us to clear your doubts, questioning us on any intricacies of the doctrine.'

'That would be most helpful.'

'The Middle Watch extends thereafter to two hours after midnight. During this Watch, you will become aware of questions in your own mind as to the doctrine. Our Lord Buddha even had celestial beings question him during this period, so such questions will slowly arise in your own mind.'

I had barely been aware of the light breeze that had riffled through the leaves. I'm already improving my powers of total concentration, I thought delightedly. I shall resume my practice of yoga as soon as I return to Thamba-Panni and increase my powers to the fullest.

'The Last Watch extends from two hours after midnight to sun-up,' Uday concluded. 'This Watch is divided into four parts. The first is devoted to walking up and down, for mild physical exercise. The second is for mindfully sleeping on the right side. The third is for attaining the cessation of desire, or *arahat*-ship. Our Lord Buddha himself enjoyed the bliss of Nibbhana at this time. The last hour is spent in attaining the Ecstasy of Great Compassion. At this hour, you radiate thoughts of loving-kindness towards all beings, surveying the world to see where your knowledge can be of service, going wherever you discern the need.

'This was the life Lord Buddha led?'

'From the day he attained enlightenment, he occupied himself only with religious activities. He slept for only four hours a day, one hour at night, one hour at dawn and two hours at noon. He sought his own food, inconveniencing no one. He led a life of voluntary poverty, a man born a prince of the noble Sayka clan in the northernmost kingdom of the continent, begging for food from door to door, wandering from place to place for eight months each year. He died in his eightieth year.'

'I doubt that I will ever reach such a stage.'

'You will not.' His reply was calm and certain. 'Yet you will reach your own heights.'

'Don't we all?'

He smiled gently, more to himself than to me. 'You were ever the philosopher.'

I glanced at the blue skies again, through the green banyan leaves trembling before a breeze. A yellow leaf broke loose and fluttered to the ground. There it would decay and promote new life. I saw the strength and structure of the tree, of Uday seated before me in the lotus pose. I heard the sound of those children's voices, lightly streaked by the chirp of a bird. I smelled the drying grass, the faintly hot breath of the wind. Cause and effect. All as logical as the chart I held in my sweaty fingers.

Only a great Creator could have produced such perfect logic of cause and effect. He had to be the origin.

Chapter 20

Late the next evening, the yellow-robed Uday and I took our final walk in the Kalyani palace courtyard before my departure for Thamba-Panni. The earth, preparing for its night's rest, had laid a mantle of peace upon the palace, beneath a canopy of pale blue sky, bordered in the west by deep hues of roseate gold. Doves cooed their bedtime tales in the green branches of flame-covered poinciana trees and even the normally harsh cawing of crows was muted. The yellow-green blossoms of a queen-of-the-night bush cast their perfume on the balmy air and I breathed its scent deeply, knowing delight in the beauty of the earth as we paced the flagstone walkway.

Reading my thoughts, Uday looked at me and smiled. 'Finding joy in whatever is around us, even people, does not have to be a subjective experience,' he remarked, in his deep, gentle voice. 'So long as there is detachment and craving is avoided, our delight becomes more eclectic, more refined, more exquisite. We appreciate the beauty for itself, separate from other responses that can only destroy the purity of what we find, like plucking the flower for its fragrance.'

We reached the end of the path and turned right, walking towards the women's quarters. I saw her on the upstairs verandah, where the light was uncertain. My first impression was of a small, delicate face, wondrously fair, perfectly oval, with masses of wavy black hair around it. From the height of her above the verandah rail, she was slender and tall. She was a ghost from the past, so like my beloved Sundari that I must be hallucinating. Then her eyes locked with mine and the same startled expression entered them as I knew had shown in my heart. Dear God, it was Sundari, my Sundari, and no other. What could she be doing here?

A delicate hand, with long, tapering fingers, flew to her slender throat. I could almost see the quiver of her nostrils. Like a deer jerking away from a hypnotic flame, she swung her eyes towards Uday, then turned and fled, leaving behind a hollow where she had once stood and the empty thudding of my heart.

I had paused in my stride without knowing it. Now I turned to face Uday, amazed to find that his look was one of total understanding. 'That . . . that was Sundari, was it not? Sundari from Mada Kalapuwa?'

'Yes.' His smile was indulgent.

'How did she come to be here?' I was completely bewildered now, but all sorts of wild thoughts and even hot rays of white hope were flashing through me. 'I was told that she was somewhere on the continent with relations.'

'She is very much here, as you can see.'

'Do you know her whole story?'

'Yes, King Ra-hula told me all.'

I felt a spasm of anger. 'Then why did you not inform me before, so that I could meet her, talk to her?'

'Such is not the way of this court, where we prefer to allow cause and effect to operate.'

Damn your philosophy, I wanted to say, surprised at the unfamiliar expletive in my mind, but my training held. Instead, my eyes wandered back to the upper-storey verandah. It was empty, yet I had the absurd feeling that Sundari was watching me, so I drew myself to my full height.

'By chance, if you wish to call it so, or by the operation of *kharmic* forces, as we believe, the girl and you have now met again quite naturally,' Uday continued gently. 'It is better so than any attempt at matchmaking.' A look of deep conviction on his face, he gathered his yellow robes more closely around him. 'You are young,' he added softly. 'You have a long road ahead of you. These events are part of your *kharma* and that of Sundari's, undoubtedly from your previous births, so understand them.'

'What is she doing in the palace?' I demanded.

'Her dead father was very interested in the doctrine, a great student of it in fact, though he was a Hindu by birth and a goldsmith by profession. He had an invitation from King Ra-hula, whom he had already met several times in the palace, to come and live here. Sad to say, he had arranged to do so as soon as his daughter was married. After his death, the trader, Pillai, who is also known to the king, begged permission to send Sundari instead, for safety. Our gracious king did more. Since she too is a student of the doctrine, he made her a ward of this court. She has lived here for one year now, and the king, who has no children, treats her as his daughter. She is such a good, gentle person that she has even won my heart in the few days I have known her. Her present desire is to become a *bikkshuni*, a female monk.'

My heart sank. 'Is she firm in her decision. I mean . . .' I hesitated, looking appealingly at him.

'You mean you once wanted to marry her and you still do? It speaks well for you.' A note of surprising hardness entered his voice. 'Some of your comrades have behaved ignobly and their conduct does not reflect well on your brother's rule. As a matter of fact, the only reason why your brother, King Vijaya, obtained the non-aggression treaty he sought was because you were the messenger.' He paused, gentling. 'But the blessed gift of inner sight, and all you have achieved in Thamba-Panni since you conquered it, have assured our King that you will do well by all the people of Lanka eventually.'

'Didn't the king care about race, caste, upbringing?'

'The doctrine teaches us that all men and women are equal. As for Sundari, she is more equal than most!'

'That's wonderful. It's how I feel, too, and I want to establish the equality of everyone in Thamba-Panni.' My need to talk to Sundari then burst forth. 'I want to meet Sundari, right now.'

He shook his head. 'She must make up her mind as to what she wants to do,' he advised. 'We must not attempt to alter her *kharma* by influencing her decisions.'

'But she might end up following the course she has set her mind on, though her heart may tell her otherwise,' I cried desperately.

'So be it then,' he replied with total firmness. 'Let *kharma/vipaka* take its course. If you do not see her again on this visit, you will surely be back.'

My heart cried out. How long must I wait? And what if I never return?

In that instant, I knew that *kharma/vipaka* was God's will. My seeing Sundari again, her being in the Kalyani palace when she could have been far away on the continent, her presence on the balcony at that particular moment, Uday's visit here from such a great distance, which alone made me walk in the garden this evening, none of it was mere coincidence but indeed the will of the Creator of whose body we are all a part.

That night the knowledge that Sundari and I were under the same roof fired me with intense longing just to see her. It was wonderful to know that she was safe and so close, but frustrating that I might have been at the other end of the earth for all the good it did me. I ended up deciding that *kharma/vipaka* was an excellent philosophy, but that I would give the *kharma* some slight kick in the pantaloons to obtain the *vipaka* effects I desired.

Unexpectedly, King Ra-hula, made no reference to Sundari or to the destruction of our border village, Veyan Gama, during my final audience with him the next morning. He even mentioned the succession of Prince Tikka to the *uda rata* throne only in passing. For my part, I had determined that the new treaty would give me some opportunity for future visits to Kalyani to see Sundari again.

Since he had renounced all material possessions, King Ra-hula did not send presents back to King Vijaya. 'This treaty of non-aggression and free trade is our gift to your king and to the people of Thamba-Panni,' he declared, handing me the scroll of *ola*. 'It is a precious gift of our faith and trust. Remember, however, that all things, including treaties, monarchs and their kingdoms, are transient.' Had sadness tinged his voice? 'Only the doctrine will endure for ever.' He paused and drew from the folds of his yellow robe a square package wrapped in red silk which bore his seal. 'You have here yet another gift for your king, which you may accept only on your solemn oath, on behalf of your king, that it will not be opened unless there is strife in Kalyani.'

I gave the king my oath, and he handed over the package with a gentle smile.

We left for Thamba-Panni immediately after the audience. Only young Viswan, one of my trusted aides, stayed behind in the palace, as a clerk to record trade between the two kingdoms, but also vested with certain other duties I assigned him. I wished that I could be the one to stay.

Three mornings later, I was back in our own capital.

King Vijaya greeted me in his study with open arms. We had not been separated for so long since our early teens, when I had been sent to our grandmother, in the Lala palace, for my studies. Any differences between us suddenly seemed to melt. As he held me to him, I felt his life-force merge with mine and sensed some pain.

He released me and sat at his yellow jakwood desk. I eased myself on to my usual settle at his right, but gingerly, from saddle-soreness.

'Tell us how you fared,' the king directed.

278

'We have our treaty, Sire,' I replied. Standing up, I proffered him the *ola*, right hand outstretched, left hand at right elbow. He took it, skimmed through its contents and placed it on the table.

'Splendid!' he exclaimed. 'You have done a great job.'

I resumed my seat, elated. 'It is what we wanted, Sire,' I declared. 'But only the future will tell what it is worth. Here is something else, however, which King Ra-hula commanded me to hand you personally.' I presented him with the red silk package. 'I took the liberty of giving him your sacred oath, which he demanded, that you will only open the package if there is strife in the Kalyani kingdom.'

He turned the package, examined the seal. 'I wonder what it could be.'

'I, too, have wondered, Sire, but I haven't any idea.'

He placed the package on his desk, his tawny eyes still curious on it. 'What do you have to report?'

I recounted everything that had transpired in Kalyani, including details of my conversation with Prince Jaya, my suspicions and the actions I had taken. He listened attentively, the tawny eyes keen, their black pupils intent. I then gave him news of my meeting with Uday and of the deaths of our parents and our grandmother, omitting only Sundari's presence in the palace. He took it all without visible reaction.

'We are now orphans,' he declared, with an attempt at light-heartedness, when I had finished. He paused, reflecting. 'So our brother, Sumitta, is king! He will make a good ruler.' His eyes went moist. 'And *Amma* is dead!' He shook his head. 'It's hard to believe. She seemed immortal. What a way to die.' The significance of our mother's final union with our father must have hit him, for he suddenly smashed the table with a clenched fist. 'Why did she have to throw herself on his pyre?' he cried. 'She hated him.'

Only then did it dawn on me that part of my brother's hatred for our father was caused by jealousy. It appalled me and yet explained everything.

As if conscious that he had said too much, my brother recovered his poise with a great effort. 'We have no time for official mourning,' he began, then paused, thinking. 'Life is funny,' he finally exclaimed. 'When some depart, others enter.'

'What do you mean?' I enquired.

He looked at me strangely, then responded abruptly. 'Kuveni is pregnant.' His tone was so flat that I gazed at him in surprise. He stared grimly at me for a few moments and I noticed that the whites of his eyes had red veins to them from lack of sleep. He placed his elbows on the table, then told me of all the events of his latest encounter with the Princess Kuveni.

Finally it came. 'Kuveni has forced us to a decision. If the child looks like a Yakka, we shall disown it. Only an Arya, or one who looks Arya, shall succeed us in Thamba-Panni.'

I was stunned. 'But the Arya law of succession, Sire? What of the law?'

'We are the king.' He was uncompromising. 'We make the law. If we deem our Yakka children unfit, you, Prince, as our younger brother, shall succeed us.'

'I, Sire?' I was aghast.

'Come to think of it, you would make a good king. Have you no ambition in that direction? The people love you.'

'None whatsoever. I only desire to serve. Remember I am your twin. When you die, I shall die too.'

He stared at me suspiciously for a few moments then looked away, but only to shoot a quick glance back at me as if he had hoped to catch me off guard. I was seeing a new man. What had got into him? I helplessly felt that his arc of the circle had moved away from mine. 'We trust you,' he said simply. 'But our decision is final. We were brought here by destiny to establish true Arya culture in this island. The Yakka are savages, barbarians.' He spat out the words, angrily venting the disappointment of his love life.

'Sire, do not have contempt for your subjects,' I pleaded.

He leaned forward, glaring at me, then suddenly relaxed. His moods had become like sunshine and shadow when clouds move rapidly across the sky. 'You are right. We must not allow our distaste for Kuveni to colour our judgement of her entire race.'

'Please don't pass judgement on the Princess Kuveni either until I have had an opportunity to speak to her.'

'You may speak to her, but . . .' His expression became wistful. 'We had hopes of a great love.' He stared sadly into the distance and began drumming on the desk with his fingers. 'Now it has ended.' He abruptly pushed away from the table. '*Amma* is gone.' He stifled a groan. 'Now there is nothing left.'

Perhaps he was right.

The Princess Kuveni received me in her room just before noon, bidding me sit beside her on an ebony couch. She was obviously withdrawn into some world of her own.

I told her how pleased I was to hear that she was going to have a baby.

'Your brother is not pleased,' she retorted.

'He would be if you gave him a chance,' I countered, then urged her to remember her responsibilities and the need to be attractive to her husband. She listened listlessly. 'You have a child in your womb now,' I ended. 'Why don't you tell me why you behave as you do? It is important for the king and your unborn baby.'

'It's not the king's baby.'

'What?' I was flabbergasted.

She smiled then. 'It's not what you think. I have been true to your brother, but his rejection of my baby proves him an unworthy father. My own father rejected me, so I know what it means.' She patted her stomach, almost dreamily. 'This child must have been fathered by my demon gods.'

A love that had commenced with the fanfare of trumpets and the drumbeats of passion had ended with the whimper of an unborn child. I stumbled out of the room, shocked beyond belief.

Vijit was leaving the king's study when I returned to it. He greeted me in the friendliest manner, and we paused on the sunlit verandah to chat awhile. I had always liked him, not the least because his chiselled features, fine dark eyes and trim moustache made him look like a young Uday.

'I've just presented my report and recommendations on the expansion of our cavalry and chariot forces to the king,' he explained, with that crinkle-eyed smile I found so engaging. 'I hope you'll support them, but we are in great shape already.'

'Splendid. And I think I have bought us some more time, because I have just concluded that treaty with King Ra-hula.'

Buoyed by his congratulations, I gave him a brief rundown of what had transpired during my visit.

'How can a king rule without an army?' Vijit enquired when I ended.

'This one does. He believes in moral force.'

'Can that stop crime? Some people are attracted to crime the way a bee is to honey.' He nodded towards the courtyard, where a bee was buzzing above a yellow flower.

'Apparently crime has decreased in the Kalyani kingdom since its people have become so involved in their new religion.'

'But crime does not stem from lack of morality alone. Why should you ascribe the decrease to religion?'

'Apart from deeds of passion, crime has two basic causes,' I replied. 'Want, need, on the one hand and covetousness on the other. It would appear that King Ra-hula has helped eliminate need by bestowing the royal lands to the Buddhist *vihares*, temples, mandating them to pass the benefits to the people under supervision of the royal administration. What remains by and large therefore is covetousness, a quality that can indeed be attacked and even destroyed by the moral force of a religion that advocates the elimination of desire. Having received the king's beneficence, the people of Kalyani are charged with a personal duty to the realm, to be good, and to ensure good, unsupervised. They seem to be responding. Of course there will always be the exceptions, including the clever ones who will try to exploit the situation.'

'Sounds rather naïve to me. If what you say is true, how long can it last? I can't see people refraining from robbing, assaulting, raping, looting, just because their bellies are full, their bodies clothed, a roof has been placed over their heads and their minds are absorbed by Four Noble Truths. Isn't that what this Buddha claims to have discovered?'

'Yes, in answer to your question. As for your thesis . . .' I grinned. 'Do you consider what happened to a certain Prince Vijaya and his several hundred comrades either naïve or transitory?'

He looked at me puzzled a few moments, then broke into a roar of laughter, his shoulders shaking, his eyes twinkling merrily. 'Well put, Prince. I certainly invited that sword-thrust, didn't I?' He sobered. 'How long can King Rahula's influence on Kalyani last though?'

'Only as long as evil, ambitious forces are held back by the first penetration of the king's new order and the reflexes of obedience to his old order.'

'When d'you think the turning point will arrive in Kalyani?'

'That's what I shall be watching closely.'

The gods had favoured them with a dark night, but they walked cautiously beneath tall trees, up the winding path leading through thick bushes to the top of the hill. The sky was obscured by a heavy pall of grey clouds and one of the men behind them stumbled occasionally on a stone or a root. 'Some hunters!' King Tikka grunted sarcastically. 'They can only fart in the dark!'

Hamy could not deny King Tikka the right to regard those who stumbled with scorn, because the king was proving himself once again as sure-footed as a cat. Though the air was cool, not a breath of wind stirred and Hamy found himself sweating with the exertion and suspense. They had pushed hard since dawn to reach their destination and he could smell his own high odour. An owl hooted from the dense jungle above them and he shivered.

When they reached the crest of the hill, King Tikka laid a restraining hand on Hamy's arm. The ground on the other side sloped sharply down into inky blackness, relieved only by a great square of lights pricked out about a half-mile away.

'There's the fort,' Kira muttered.

'Somebody must have told you,' King Tikka responded sarcastically. 'What else would it be, you stupid bull? Some night monster's lit-up arse?'

Accession to the throne has not altered his disposition, Hamy thought. Well, what can one expect of a *polonga*, viper?

Construction of the fort, located two days' journey from the Thamba-Panni palace at the eastern border of the kingdom with the *uda rata*, had been completed two days earlier. King Tikka had been well briefed by his spies as to its layout and the surrounding land. It housed the garrison of fifty Arya and three hundred Yakka, intended to provide protection for the settlements that had been established in a region of several square miles of cultivable land served by a reservoir created from a natural lake in a neighbouring range of hills. Completion of the fort had been timed by the Arya to coincide with the reaping of the first harvests of paddy and grain, so the king's barn and granaries within it were heavily stocked with produce.

The Yakka settlers retained their aversion to the cold humours of night, but not King Tikka and his *uda rata* guerillas for whom night and day made no difference to their implacable purpose. For all his own normal apathy, Hamy could not help being fired by the success of the past months. His leader had raised an army of two thousand men, including five hundred cavalry, and had trained them to near perfection in the use of weapons and in guerilla tactics. The well-planned and successful raids on Mihiri Gama and Veyan Gama had proved the Yakka army's mettle and boosted its morale. It was with excitement therefore that Hamy followed King Tikka along the narrow cattle track that led downhill, admiring his leader's erect figure, dressed in black. There was no vegetation in the rock escarpment, so they could see the track, but the entire attack force was alert for danger. A dog barked across the plain, the lonely sound ripping like a knife through the blanket of night. King Tikka stiffened and stopped, holding out his hand in warning. Only after the lapse of a few minutes, when the noise had died down completely, did he start advancing once more. The track led round a rock outcrop, then sloped even more steeply down so that they leaned well back as they walked. Hamy sighed with relief when they finally reached an open meadow at the bottom of the hill. He turned to see how the portly Kira was faring and found him sweating profusely, but grinning through the darkness. King Tikka looked as fresh as a prowling leopard.

Hamy started counting the men, all dressed in black, as they filed past to assemble at the glade. He nodded to Ratana, Loki and Suramba, the lean, tough leaders of the three detachments, each marching ahead of one hundred. All the men were armed with knives, swords and spears, bows strung on the shoulders, quivers at the back. He smiled at those he knew, eyes in the semi-gloom, noticing how well-knit the bodies even of the stouter ones were. When the last man had passed him, he walked up to where King Tikka stood apart. 'All three hundred men present, lord,' he reported quietly.

'Good. Follow me.' King Tikka strode forward through the semi-gloom to lead the raid, as always obviously enjoying the danger and the thrill of battle ahead.

Hamy followed. His heart began to beat faster. This was the most critical part of the operation. Soon, it would only require a pi-dog's bark, or a dropped weapon to alert the enemy. If they missed this opportunity, it might never arise again. Having just completed building the fort, the Arya would not be expecting an attack. Also, they would be tired and would not have settled into a proper guard routine.

They wound round black clumps of bushes until they hit the highway, which led straight as an arrow to the dark mass of the fort about a half-mile away, the yellow blobs of light from the sentry towers like topaz on a gigantic black headdress. As they wraithed silently on to the highway, the men formed three lines behind their commanders. Never one to find delight in battle, Hamy's palm felt clammy on the haft of his spear.

As they marched steadily on, with more certainty now, King Tikka looked back at Hamy. 'Pray to your special god that our friends have done their work,' he said quietly. Yet he was breathing easily, lithe, very relaxed.

Hamy took stock of his surrounding. What had obviously been scrub and jungle had been cleared and paddy-fields lined the highway, with the faint glimmer of water indicating an irrigation channel. The fields would stretch into the distance, Hamy knew. The Arya certainly understood how to develop land. Wagon ruts on the dirt road meant that they had also organized the collection and distribution of produce. Hamy trod on soft dung and cursed under his breath.

Rows of peasant huts, shuttered against the night, now appeared on either side of the road. They had entered the little township beneath the fort. No lights showed.

A single shout shattered the stillness. King Tikka froze. Hamy stopped abruptly, his stomach knotting. He could feel all three files of men stiffen. A Yakka chant followed, the notes and words drunkenly slurred. King Tikka relaxed. Some idiot, drinking in the dark. Ranna *deviyo*, please do not let any of the pi-dogs awaken, Hamy prayed and had his response in a low, warning growl from one of the huts. The dog appeared silently, a slow-pacing shadow. No one moved. The dog reached Hamy and sniffed at him, cold snout on bare calf. Hamy held his breath, though his heart was pounding. The dog wagged its tail, stretched against its fore-paws, yawned and lazily turned to limp back to its home, leaving behind a smell of mangy fur. Hamy breathed easily again.

Still as statues, they allowed long minutes to pass. Finally, King Tikka raised his arm and pointed ahead with his spear. Silently, they resumed their march.

A conch shell sounded its slow wail, signalling the commencement of the midnight watch. They had timed their arrival to perfection. Alert, watchful, they strode across the bridge spanning an irrigation channel that served as a moat to the entrance. The great gates swung slowly open as if by magic, with only the tiniest squeak. 'All is well, lord,' a hoarse voice whispered.

King Tikka, Kira and Hamy stood aside while the men filed inside, making for their allotted positions as they had planned and practised. When the last man had entered, the gate slowly swung back. Dark figures shot the bolts and replaced the massive bars.

Hamy surveyed the scene. The road, lit by hissing flares, continued on to a building which he knew to be the commander's quarters, then fanned out on both sides of the structure, behind which would be the king's barns, the granaries and the stables. The low buildings along the rampart walls would be the soldiers' barracks, those fronting them, residences. In the open square, chariots and catapults were massed in orderly rows.

'All the sentries in the towers have been killed, lord, save for those who are with us.' The hoarse voice belonged to a tall figure in the uniform of a Yakka officer of the Arya army.

'Good, Jora,' King Tikka responded, his teeth white in a fierce grin. 'You shall be rewarded.'

King Tikka waited until he was certain that each of his men was in place, a company of one hundred to massacre the sleeping soldiers on each side of the fort and the third company to surround the buildings in the centre and deal with the officers and the commander who were housed in them.

'Remember Priti.' King Tikka's expression was so terrible to behold that Hamy blanched before the eyes that were fiendish with glee, the face as dreadful as an *avatar*'s.

King Tikka raised his spear aloft and moved silently forward. All the Yakka in sight seemed to stiffen involuntarily before advancing to their given objectives.

Hamy followed as King Tikka loped purposefully along the main street, making for the commander's house. A shout arose from one of the barracks, followed by a scream, then another and another, breaking into a hellish din from the buildings all around them. Startled curses, shrieks of agony, the ringing of metal on metal rent the air. The doors of the officers' quarters burst open and a group of Arya emerged, swords in hand, shields held aloft.

Someone shouted a command. A great twanging was followed by a series of hisses as arrows arched against the sky and found their mark. Several of the Arya fell, an arrow sticking from the throat of one like a single great quill from a porcupine.

The Arya leader barked an order. His men massed

together swiftly, their shields held over their heads so that they looked like a single, huge tortoise.

King Tikka flung his spear, straight and true at the leader, who took it in the chest, faltered in his stride and fell. Hamy and Kira followed wildly with their own spears, but they glanced off the shields of their opponents. Sword flashing aloft, King Tikka uttered a blood-curdling cry and hurtled forward. Dear Ranna *deviyo*, this is a madman. Nothing, no one can stop him, Hamy thought, and leapt after his leader, brandishing his sword. As they closed in, for an instant Hamy could make out faces, mostly dark-eyed, fair-complexioned and bearded. He hacked wildly at a young, curly-haired boy. The youth parried the blow, reversed his own sword and slashed back. Hamy flung himself sideways in the nick of time. The blade cut the air across his face. Hamy straightened his sword and the youth ran into it. As the point sank into the soft flesh of the stomach, red blood appeared around it and Hamy felt the old fear and revulsion at killing churn his guts into water. Fearful lest he betray himself and become an object of ridicule, with a tremendous effect he controlled himself. Then, as the mass of the Arya closed in around him, Hamy became enveloped by a blinding red haze that was somehow darkness. With a frenzied bellow, he went mad. cutting, thrusting, chopping with no art, as if he were clearing jungle. Beside him, King Tikka's demented laugh was a herald of death.

Chapter 21

Disasters, like death, come in threes. I duly reported my discussion with the Princess Kuveni to my brother during the mid-day meal, which we shared in his study. He listened grim-faced, especially to my pleas that he show some compassion towards the princess, make some attempt to be reconciled with her and have some faith in the Yakka people. His eyes went cold and hard when I reminded him that the child Kuveni bore in the womb was his future heir. When I had done, he pondered awhile, then drew a deep breath, but before he could speak, the figure of Suramba, the silver-haired chief attendant, his blue and gold uniform hanging on a bony frame, stood at the open door. The old man made obeisance and begged leave to enter.

'What is it?' the king demanded impatiently.

'My lord, a messenger from Upa Gama has just arrived with urgent news. He craves immediate audience.'

My brother's eyes flickered to mine. We both undoubtedly had the same thought. Upa Gama was our newly-established fort in the foothills at our northern border with the *uda rata* kingdom. It had been built to protect the settlements created under the supervision of our commander, Upa, who had reported back to the palace two days earlier since his mission had but a few days to completion.

'Bid him enter immediately,' the king commanded.

I recognized the man who bustled in as Nanda, one of Upa's young Arya captains, but only from his uniform, the white *dhoti* and red tunic, and his short, burly figure. The face of the soldier kneeling before the king was barely recognizable through the layer of dust caked by sweat and the clotted blood from a sword-slash extending from the temple to the fierce black moustache and his unshaven chin. He rose at the king's bidding, breathing deeply, the droplets of perspiration large as water sapphires on his skin.

'My lord,' he stated. 'I wish I were the bearer of happier tidings.'

'You are wounded,' the king remarked anxiously. 'We should have our physician look to you first.' He rose to his feet and I with him. He nodded at me. 'Prince . . .'

I turned to leave the room, but Nanda interrupted, contrary to established form. 'Forgive me, lord,' he begged of my brother. 'But I did not seek immediate audience with you for medical attention. My report must come first.'

King Vijaya hesitated, then sat down while I remained standing. 'You are a true soldier. Proceed, with your report, Captain.'

'My lord, the *uda rata* Yakka did to us exactly what we did to them here in this very fort a year ago, on our first day in Lanka. Just as they were betrayed then, we too were betrayed. We had completed building the Upa Gama fort two days earlier and were proud of it, for it was well-defended by earthworks, wooden palisades, sentry towers and cat-walks. Three nights ago, at the commencement of the midnight watch, some of our Yakka soldiers secretly killed the loyal sentries in the towers and opened the gates to King Tikka and about three hundred of his men. Caught in our sleep, we fought back desperately for over an hour. Only fourteen of our fifty Arya and twenty-three of those Yakka who had remained loyal to us were able to escape, by massing together, hacking their way to the gates and slipping out into the darkness. I was alone and fought my way towards them but was finally surrounded by a crowd led by King Tikka himself. It was only when the king smote me down with his sword that I lost consciousness and was taken prisoner.' Nanda reached up and gingerly touched the terrible slash on his cheek. 'The whole enemy operation was perfectly planned, and I must say, King Tikka proved himself to be a fearsome warrior.'

'Your wound is an honourable one,' the king observed soberly. 'But pray continue.'

'There is not much else to say that you cannot conjecture, lord. After the battle, Upa Gama was Mihiri Gama and Veyan Gama repeated. When I came to again, it was daylight. King Tikka and his men had occupied the fort. The king told me that he had spared my life so that I could act as his messenger.' Nanda paused, reflecting. A fierce note entered his voice. 'I felt that his choice of me, one of your commanders, was intended to rub salt in your wound, so I considered inviting him to kill me instead, for they even had my sword. But on reflection, I decided that it was more important for you, my king, to have first-hand information.'

The king was visibly moved, as I was. 'We are above such insults, Nanda, and your life is more valuable to us than any gesture.' His massive jaw tightened. 'Besides, you have lived to avenge this deed.'

'Thank you, lord. To continue, before I was allowed to leave the next day, I was compelled to witness the Yakka destroy our entire village . . .' His voice broke. 'Homes were burned down and the colonists driven away like cattle. Then, the victors breached our dams, blocked our irrigation channels and stole our produce from the barns and granaries.' He paused and tears filled his eyes. 'I never knew how horrible it would be to witness the death of an entire community.' He drew a shuddering breath, then cried out. 'A boon, lord. I beg a boon. Grant us vengeance, vengeance on these traitorous Yakka.'

The king looked squarely at me. 'We have held back too long,' he growled, then turned to Upa. 'Your boon shall be granted.' His voice was deathly quiet. 'We shall indeed exact vengeance.'

Nanda calmed. 'Thank you, lord. Thank you. Forgive me for raising my voice, but I have endured the tortures of the defeated.' He hesitated. 'Oh, I nearly forgot. King Tikka sent you this message. He reached inside his tunic, produced an *ola*, knelt and proffered it to the king, left hand to right elbow, in the approved fashion. He rose as the king unrolled the *ola* and began to read aloud.

'To the assassin, Vijaya.

'This letter and your commander, our captive, will bring you evidence of the Yakkas' mettle.

'You now have proof that we shall meet fire with fire, blood with blood, death with death. Also, by the will of our demon gods, we, Tikka, king of the *uda rata*, will eat your black liver some day.

'We command you to withdraw immediately from our sacred Yakka soil. Board your ships and begone whence you came, else you will all be slowly destroyed. First Mihiri Gama, then Veyan Gama, now Upa Gama. Where will we strike next? You do not know, but you will live in fear of the event.

'If you remain in Lanka, you will face our wrath and that of the free Yakka people, for you accursed Arya will never have a place in this country. Fort by fort, village by village, we shall recover our lost territory. We have already slain over fifty of your seven hundred comrades and over two hundred disloyal Yakka. Foul murderer, your turn too will soon come.

'Should you have any claim to courage, you who call yourselves the lion race, cease skulking in your lairs. Come forth to Upa Gama - your Upa Gama that is now ours - and fight.

'Otherwise, be for ever branded as cowards and bullies, the pi-dogs of the world.

'King Tikka of Lanka.'

As if this terrible, boastful message was not enough to cut into my heart, my brother, the king, looked across at me after reading it and said very quietly: 'You see, Prince, how dangerous it is to give the Yakkas trust and compassion.'

It was the cold, bleak look in his tawny eyes, revealing a

subtle separation from me because of the tragedy that had struck us all, that hurt me most, for it was almost as if, for those moments, he had aligned me with those who had betrayed him.

Sparks of anger flashing in his tawny eyes, the king stared into space awhile, then looked at me. 'We march for Upa Gama in two days. Have the commanders assemble here immediately so that we can draw up our plans for the move. Meanwhile, we shall also deal with the enemy in our midst.' His voice grew soft in terrible contrast with his bottled-up rage. His gaze jerked towards Nanda. 'Do you know which of the Yakka soldiers betrayed us?'

'Pretty much, Sire.'

'You have their names and the villages from which they came?'

'Yes. Some of them are even from the village here.'

'Have your commanders seize their immediate families wherever they are and hang them publicly.'

'Sire,' I broke in, the horror I felt reflected in my voice. 'You will be punishing innocent people.'

'Certainly. It will deter others who are innocent today from becoming guilty tomorrow.' There was a grim finality in the king's expression and that warning rumble in his voice. 'Since you do not appear to have any stomach for this work, Prince, have Minister Ujjeni execute it.'

'But, Sire, the rule of law . . .'

'*We* are the law.'

Our plans were quickly formulated and the commanders left to get men and mounts, chariots, artillery, supplies and wagon trains ready. A feeling of excitement had seized the fortress. The Arya were all thirsting for vengeance and ready for battle after a whole year in training.

Moving a large force of men to the attack is easier commanded than accomplished. Since I was responsible for the logistics of the action, it was late by the time I went to bed. I had intended sleeping in a little, so I was not pleased to be awakened at the crack of dawn by my wrinkled, old attendant.

'What is it?' I enquired irritably.

'Forgive me, lord,' he responded, still kneeling. 'But terrible events have occurred in the village.'

Thinking it was another Yakka attack, I swung out of bed in an instant and reached for my sword. 'Stand up, man and tell me what's wrong,' I commanded.

The attendant rose to his feet, trembling. 'You will not need your sword, lord,' he quavered, rising to his feet. 'Only your tears. Pray forgive me, I cannot speak of it, so please follow me to the village.'

I donned pantaloons and a tunic and hastened after him in the semi-gloom, barely hearing the crowing of cocks and the first piping of birds. We hurried along the deserted palace corridors, past sleepy-eyed night guards awaiting their reliefs. It was almost light by the time we sped across the green *maidan* fronting the fort and hastened beneath dense branches along the path in the jungle that separated the *maidan* from the village. By the time we reached the small glade at its edge it was lighter and to my surprise I saw a group of about a hundred Yakka men, women and children silently huddling together, mutely staring across the glade. My guide pointed a shaking finger in the direction of their gaze.

At first, my mind refused to accept what my eyes were beholding. This must be part of a dream or a play. Then it came into focus. Dangling from the high branches of trees was a collection of still bodies, dressed only in span-cloths, the necks grotesquely to one side. In horror, I counted twelve. My mind would not function for anything less mechanical. As I stared at them, a sharp wind sprang up, causing the bodies to twist on their ropes. Twelve Yakka from our own village hanged for crimes committed by others in a fort two days' march away.

I heard a groan and the sound of weeping. My attendant had broken down. His voice was the signal for a single moan from the Yakka crowd, followed by the heart-rending cries of women. 'Aney! . . . Apoi! . . . What will my poor, orphan children do?'

Ujjeni had done his work swiftly, efficiently, ruthlessly. A man after the king's new heart, I thought bitterly.

Like a sleep-walker, I crossed to inspect each body. I have seen paintings of men who have been hanged. They seem peaceful enough, though the whole impression of broken necks and lifeless bodies is pathetic. There is nothing peaceful about a man who has actually been hanged. He strangles to death. His goggling eyes are staring, his face is blackened with pain, the jaw hangs loose, the tongue protrudes. One by one, I identified each tortured face. These were men I had known . . . Rattha, the red-faced, Gona, the bull, the hunch-back Suramba, his hairy limbs loose and disjointed. Disgust, rage, compassion began to fill my being. The weeping and wailing of the crowd, who did not even dare to recover the dead bodies of their men, reached inside me, connecting with the clamour for release that had been pounding at me.

Then I came to the last body and stared at it, aghast. My body felt fevered, my skin chill.

No, it couldn't be. Why would he be involved? He had no relations. As the grim reality smashed through my defences, I knew I could not evade this grisly knowledge, or the challenge it extended. The slim, slight body slow-twisting in the wind was that of my little ten-year-old friend Silindu, the graceful one . . . graceful even in death.

I will not speak of my grief. Silindu had paid the price for being dear to me. Ujjeni had wreaked vengeance on him and on me. I stood there in the cold dawn staring at the boy's wracked face. What had his thoughts been when he was roughly seized and herded together with those selected for death? Had he wanted to appeal to me to save him? Dear God, did he think I was in some way responsible for his fate? Did he suffer much when the rope tightened against his scrawny throat? My eyes burned. Tears of horror and frustration welled up from within them. Then outrage burst forth in a great roar as if signalling my freedom from some bondage, I knew not what. I turned to the crowd of Yakka. 'Before my God and your gods, this must never happen again!' I shouted. I stretched my arm in the direction of the fort. 'We shall demand justice from our Great King.' I walked slowly, slowly up to the crowd, paused before them and surveyed each tearstained eye. 'Follow me, all of you,' I quietly commanded. 'Your loved ones must not have died in vain. We shall go to the palace and we shall, in this kingdom of Thamba-Panni, forge today a new method of ensuring justice for all men. Remember, no violence. Follow me in single file.'

As I turned towards the fort, I knew they were fearful and suspicious, not merely of the Great King, but even of me and my intentions. What right did I have to expect trust from them in the face of this greatest betrayal of all?

It was old Pina who gave them the lead. 'I trust Prince Lala,' he cried. 'Even our kings did not do this to us. Let us follow his lead to death if need be. Otherwise what would we have to live for?'

As I marched steadily towards the fort, I knew that the Yakka had begun to follow me in twos and threes. They were all behind me by the time I crossed the *maidan* and approached the entrance to the fort.

'You can let all these people in, on my authority,' I commanded the astonished sentries at the gates. They must have known of the tragic event and were fearful of a riot.

One of them summoned the guard captain, but I simply waved him away and strode forward, followed by the Yakka.

Ignoring everyone we met, not even acknowledging their salutations, I strode to the audience chamber, followed by the Yakka. I felt tight, inflexible, unyielding. And there was something in me that must have showed in my face, my eyes, my expression, that permitted no man to dare cross me. I knew then that this too was part of my personal destiny.

Once in the audience hall, I assembled the Yakka in orderly rows. For the first time, I noticed hope in the staring eyes of some of the men. Buoyed, I sent word through my ancient attendant to the king, begging immediate audience. He must already have been informed of the strange event, for he came promptly, dressed in black pantaloons and white tunic. Obviously enraged, he gave me a withering look as he sat facing us on his ornamental chair, placed on a dais to serve as a throne. I made my obeisance. I did not quail when I rose from it, but defiantly held his gaze until the anger slowly faded from his tawny eyes.

He came straight to the point. 'What is the meaning of your extraordinary conduct, Prince? And what is this rabble you have brought with you?'

'Sire, this is no rabble. Each one of these people is your subject and we are all here to beseech your justice.'

'We?' The shaggy red eye-brows arched. 'Did you say "we", Prince? Is that the royal plural, or do you include yourself in the category of those you say are beseeching our justice?'

'I have no claim to the royal plural, as you well know, Sire. I am here with these people as an aggrieved subject.'

'How?' He barked the question sharply at me.

'First because my desire to see the king's laws followed

298

will make me a supplicant whenever they are broken, whoever the sufferer may be.'

'A rabble-rousing concept.'

'No, Sire. A concept that can only come from a deeper devotion to the king and his laws than hitherto conceived.'

He pondered that in silence then waved an impatient hand at me. 'Go on.'

'I am also affronted because the Arya law that forbids reprisals against children, unless they have been proven guilty of a crime, has been broken. I am deeply and personally aggrieved.' With a tremendous effort, I fought down the sob that rose within me. 'I repeat, I am deeply and personally aggrieved because my young friend and protégé, Silindu, a boy of no more than ten, has been most foully, cruelly and unjustly murdered.'

He came erect and alert then. 'Did you say this boy, whom we know, has been murdered? How?'

'He was hanged along with eleven men of the village, as part of the reprisals against the Yakka soldiers who betrayed us at Upa Gama.'

'Why the boy? Did he have relatives among the Yakka soldiers at the fort?'

'I assure you, he did not. If he did, I would surely have known, Sire.'

He fingered his beard thoughtfully. 'We see ... H'mmm.' He made up his mind. 'Your complaint shall be investigated.' His gaze swept the Yakkas. 'Meanwhile, see to it that these ... er ... our subjects disperse without delay.' He began rising to leave.

I knew his technique. Appear to concede on what seem to be the most important issues, then break up the opposition. He did not know that the most important issues to me were liberty, fair-play, justice. 'I beg your pardon, Sire, but these your subjects are my witnesses to the cowardly crime that has been committed. You have frequently said that justice may not sleep even for a moment, lest it die. Your justice has always been swift and all men feel safe with you in consequence. I beg you to grant me that swift justice and the presence of my witnesses during your investigation, which must be here and now since we ride for Upa Gama tomorrow.'

Anger flamed in his eyes for a moment, then a hint of admiration which extinguished it. He knew I had neatly pre-empted him. What he still did not know was the anger that seethed within me, held in check by what had caused it, that I would never be his man again in the sense that I had been before, that I would be a rebel, as he had once been, whenever there was a cause.

'Very well,' the Great King responded. 'You have stated your case. Now call your witnesses.'

'I humbly request that you also summon Minister Ujjeni, since the crimes were committed by those under his command.'

I saw hesitation reflected in his tawny eyes and held his glance squarely, challenging. A strange expression flitted across his face and his cheek twitched once, just below the right eye. The battle raged within him a few moments. Finally, loyalty won, but I would never know whether it was loyalty to me, to justice, or to his own self-interest. What I did realize, with a pang, was that I had played into Ujjeni's hands by impetuously demanding his presence. He could now listen to all the evidence and frame his defence.

Ujjeni arrived almost immediately. I had a shrewd suspicion that his spies had told him what was happening and he had been awaiting the summons. He was calm and unctuous as usual, his yellow toothcombs showing in smiles, the purple lips vainly trying to cover them as he made obeisance to the king. One single glance of malevolent hatred he shot at me and one quick look of withering scorn at the Yakka, before he took his place in front of the

300

throne, the perfect, devoted subject.

He listened silently while King Vijaya explained the reason for his summons and stated my grievances, nodding sympathetically at the right times, making out to the king that he too was on the side of justice.

'What do you say, Minister?' the king finally enquired.

'Am I on trial, Sire?' The question was blandly put. The king was taken aback. 'Certainly not, Minister.'

'As your loyal, devoted subject and one of your Ministers, I must agree with Prince Lala that a foul crime has been committed,' Ujjeni stated, his grainy voice modulated. 'As you know, Sire, you entrusted me with the solemn duty of extracting reprisals from the Yakka people by executing the families of those who had betrayed us at Upa Gama. Having the list from Nanda, who brought us the terrible news, I caused my staff to track down the families immediately. On my instructions, small groups of my men have fanned out through the kingdom to carry out your royal command. They obviously commenced closest to home, which I for one deem wise because it will be a deterrent to further betrayal when we march tomorrow.' His tone hardened and the dark, sunken eyes now had a bleak stare to them. 'I therefore fail to see what Prince Lala's charges are.'

'That a ten-year-old boy has been most cruelly and foully murdered,' I burst forth. 'Did the Great King's command include such a grisly deed?'

Ujjeni turned towards the king. 'Sire, I fear that Prince Lala is a trifle intemperate this morning.' His glance swept across the hall. 'I am told that he stormed into the fort, leading a mob. Now he forgets the rules of decorum in your royal presence.' His sigh of great understanding merely infuriated me. 'The prince has been under a great strain and you should graciously forgive him.'

I was suddenly the accused. Knowing I had to use

301

ingenuity to survive, I addressed the king calmly. 'Sire, I humbly crave your pardon if I have breached the rules of courtly conduct, but I can offer no apology for desiring passionately – yes, passionately – to have your justice vindicated. You did indeed command reprisals. Now, what you must determine is whether these were effected as *you* would have had them done. Has there been brutality, excess, in the execution of your commands?' I pointed an accusing finger at Ujjeni. 'Your minister here must answer that.'

'The king has already stated that I am not on trial,' Ujjeni began, his tone haughty.

'We will not have you bickering in our presence,' the king interrupted sternly, the warning growl in his voice. 'Least of all with the public present. There are two matters requiring our judgement. The first of them is whether there was excess in the hanging of eleven men from the neighbouring village. You, Prince, will give us the names of the men who were executed. We will check it against the list of those who betrayed us at Upa Gama. If they are not close relations, the men who caused the executions will be punished with death. A life, for a life illegally taken, is our law. As to the other matter . . .' He leaned forward in his chair and looked so directly at Ujjeni that I knew he realized the truth. 'By whose orders was the boy, Silindu, hanged?'

Ujjeni spread his hands and shrugged. 'I'm afraid it's too late to extract justice from him, Sire.'

'What do you mean?' The king's voice was sharp and dangerous.

'The mission was accomplished under the direct command of one of my captains. You know him, Sire.'

'His name?'

'Asoka.'

'Have him brought here.'

'I'm afraid that is impossible, Sire, unless you want his body.' Ujjeni was a model of concern.

'What on earth do you mean?'

'Asoka was killed by an unknown assassin shortly after he returned from his mission this morning, stabbed in the back while entering his home.'

'Ye gods.' The king stared into space, speechless.

Ujjeni flashed me a glance of malignant triumph, then the mask of concern immediately swept over his face again, but not before I got his message. Unknown to anyone else, he must have given Asoka the order to hang Silindu, then had Asoka killed to silence him.

'It must have been a Yakka reprisal.'

I heard Ujjeni's words through a red mist of anger. 'Never!' I cried, glaring at him. 'I am witness to the fact that the entire Yakka population remained in the village, terrified.'

'Can you vouch for them all, Prince?' My brother's voice was gentle but sarcastic. 'We doubt it.' He pondered awhile. 'This is a sad turn of events,' he finally stated. 'You will undoubtedly bend every effort, Minister, to discover who murdered your captain. Meanwhile, we have some serious blood-letting ahead of us and enough is enough. Send messengers immediately to call back those men you have sent to other villages to extract reprisals. The example of the Priti village will do.' He directed his gaze at me, a hint of sympathy in his eyes. 'Nothing can bring the dead to life, Prince. We sympathize with you in the loss of your young friend. Yet a single life is little enough to sacrifice for the good of the kingdom. Your little Silindu has not died in vain.' He raised his voice so that all the Yakka in the room could hear him. 'As you can see, the boy, Silindu, has just saved many lives. Also we now decree that future reprisals, which we hope will never again be necessary, shall not be by execution unless prior warning has been given.'

303

We have scored a victory for liberty and justice this morning, I thought, deriving some measure of comfort from it in my sorrowing heart. Why then do I have this dread feeling of defeat? Had more than Silindu died upon that tree?

The next evening I called on the Princess Kuveni to bid her farewell. She received me in her chamber adjoining the verandah. Though the sunlight was late golden in the courtyard, the room was in shadow and the dark face of the princess had a mystic quality to it when I entered and made salutation. She was seated on an ebony couch with red cushions on it. At her bidding, I sat on a settle to one side of the couch. It was only then that I realized that the face of the princess had softened and that the black eyes had a luminous, almost tender quality to them.

She came straight to the point. 'Prince Lala, I wish your brother had one fragment of your compassion,' she declared impulsively, her rich voice vibrant.

'Princess, I don't know what you mean. My brother, the king, is a man of great compassion.'

She held my gaze steadily. 'Can you swear to that?' she demanded.

I reflected a few moments, then dropped my gaze. 'I am here to bid you farewell,' I responded, deliberately evading the subject. 'We ride for Upa Gama early tomorrow.'

'You are kind to call on me. It's wonderful to realize that there is at least one person in my life who cares.'

'Princess, you have many people who care for you, including my brother if you would only give him the chance. Remember what you promised me on more than one occasion? Why do you not trust him? Why can you not give him love instead of bitterness?'

'Prince Lala, when I had the greatest offering of my love to give your brother, news of the conception of his seed within me, he was not here to receive it. And when he did come, he spurned it.'

'How can you say that?' I cried, desperate.

'I can and I do. You know the kind of man he is. Do you think he was not responsible for the death of your friend, that poor little boy. *Aney*, who will pay for what the destitute child suffered? Will a man who caused such a death have compassion even for a wife and child?'

Tears stung my eyes at her reference to Silindu, but I rose to my feet and eyed her sternly. 'Madam, I will not hear ill spoken of my brother the king.'

She had risen with me. She barely reached my shoulder. 'And I say that you are a noble fool to give him such uncompromising loyalty.' She paused as if a sudden thought had struck her. 'And yet, when you faced the injustice done to my people, your loyalty was to the principle.' She gazed at me with affection. 'Yes, that's it. You are first a man of the people. No wonder they have started to love and respect you, to regard you as the champion of their rights.' She nodded, smiling now, but sadly, through pearly white teeth. 'I betrayed only the royalty and noblemen who exploited my people and me. I certainly did so because my heart desired your brother, because my spirit hungered for vengeance, because my ambition soared. But I tell you this, Price Lala. I also hoped for a life of equality for my people because of the words your brother addressed your comrades on your first night in our village. My present bitterness is therefore not for myself alone but for what is being done to the Yakka by the racist Arya.'

I stared at her in silence, smitten dumb by her honesty and truth.

'You shall remember this day well, Prince Lala,' she commanded, prophecy in her voice, the priestess speaking now. 'You were born naked yesterday from the dead body of the boy you loved and his companions in death. You have been clothed by the truth of my people's love for you. You will never be the same again, for you have changed from being your brother's shadow into a flesh and blood person. Henceforth, you shall be the champion of all people who are poor and oppressed, wherever they may be.'

Chapter 22

My brother was cool towards me after our confrontation but I sensed in him a new respect for me. The attitudes of the Arya were as expected, those, like Vijit, who believed in honourable conduct, congratulating me, others, who bore the brand of Arya superiority, remaining cold and aloof, with most not appearing to care one way or another. Though my resolution remained a hard knot inside me, the night was as bad as that on which I had the news of the murder of Sundari's family, only worse in a way, because of grief at Silindu's death. I could have killed Ujjeni with my bare hands. Indeed, I wondered at times whether that would not be a fitting execution, to rid the world of such a fiend.

The morning after my talk with Kuveni our attack force swept out of the Priti fort, the long column extending for almost a mile through the cool, grey dawn. As I trotted beside my brother, the pounding of hooves and the creak of leather were as irritating as the grains of fine sand that seemed to scratch my eyelids from lack of sleep. I had had Silindu and the other dead Yakka given a decent burial, but the knowledge that I would never see that perky little face again, nor hear the gentle voice, kept stabbing at me, adding to the grievous sense of loss that had enveloped my being.

The terrible words Ujjeni uttered after the Yakka had left the audience hall, delivered with a strange ferocity in his high, grainy voice, haunted me. 'Pardon me, Sire, but it is time we faced the facts. We conquered Thamba-Panni because Yakka betrayed Yakka, offspring turned against parents. Why would they not betray us? They are an accursed race, doomed to become extinct because they prey on one another and even on their benefactors. I am sorry that an innocent boy has been killed, but his death is no more than a link in the process of the Yakka's self-inflicted genocide.'

And what of my grim-faced brother, towering in the saddle beside me? Despite my own sorrow, my deepest beliefs and convictions, to my utter amazement, new feelings began touching me, the desire to act as one with my brother and my comrades, pride in our band of soldiers, a clamour to avenge the deaths of our men and the destruction of our endeavours. Such is the nature of man.

We rode at the head of the column, preceded only by our advance guard, a company of cavalry, one hundred strong, under Vijit, pennants fluttering in the breeze. The main body, immediately behind us, consisted of two companies of chariots and bullock-drawn wagons which contained two companies of bowmen, three hundred foot-soldiers and a small group of men for the catapults that followed in the rear with our baggage train. Two more companies of cavalry formed our rearguard, making a total of one thousand fighting men.

My brother had somehow sensed my feelings, for he suddenly turned in his saddle and smiled at me. 'You see, Prince, there's more to life than philosophy,' he observed quietly. 'There is survival. Survival of the strong. Our grandfather, Sinha, was strong. Do you know what caused his destruction? He allowed those intangibles, emotion, love for his son, faith in the boy, to sway his judgement, his natural caution. He was weak and vulnerable before them. A ruler must beware of love, the enemy within.'

Such an attitude could only have emerged from deep-rooted pain. I felt unutterably sad for my brother.

We headed directly east that first day, the highway we had built running straight through stretches of green paddy undulating before every wind, the silver streaks of our irrigation channels slashing through them, the glistening waters of an occasional reservoir in the distance. Flights of paddy birds skimmed rapidly through the air in their darting, nervous twitter-flight, brown and black cattle grazed in stockades, a proud red cockerel led its brood of hens across our path, the smell of dung manure was frequently wafted to us by a breeze.

We had our noon meal of *chupatti* and chicken on the green banks of a muddy river, now swollen with rain in the hills, then pushed on along its banks towards the green hills that loomed shadowy in the distance. King Vijaya had been thoughtful for some time. 'We created these roads so that the king's justice here in Lanka could be as swift as that of the Emperor Dharroos in the desert regions,' he suddenly observed. 'We shall get to Upa Gama in much faster time than Tikka would ever dream and take him by surprise.'

We pressed on for many hours before we finally halted for the night, selecting a tree-covered hill beside the river for our headquarters. Soon the red-gold campfires of our troops spread around us like tiny scattered forest fires observed from a mountain-top.

After we had eaten, my brother and I lay side by side on our blankets, with our saddles for pillows, beneath a clear, deep blue sky brilliant with stars. A stray breeze wafted the smell of wood-smoke from the fires, tinged with an increasing odour of our men's night soil. Only the deep murmur of voices and an occasional laugh intruded the presence of our men upon the flowing-sound of the river, the constant creak of crickets and the croaking of bullfrogs from the swampy ground immediately north.

I tried to reach for God, but my mind and my searching spirit were enmeshed by a sort of physical fog through which I could not penetrate to the reality of Him. It left me feeling dismayed that I might not have His protection, His loving concern, when I faced danger tomorrow. I found it difficult to fall asleep and envied my brother, soon snoring beside me, his relaxed approach to whatever we faced.

We awoke to the cries of game-cocks at the false dawn, performed our ablutions in the river and moved on. With daylight, a mountain range loomed purple-blue in the distance. The highway veered south and I felt the sun gentle on my left cheek.

'It's going to be a warm day,' my brother observed as he slow-trotted beside me. 'We have just evolved a new plan. Rather than formally investing the fort, our cavalry and chariots will race ahead to force an entry while the enemy is off-guard. We will not be expected till tomorrow night, you know.'

'You mean to split our forces?'

He nodded. 'The element of surprise will more than offset the risk.' He raised his hand to stop the column and sent for the commanders. When they arrived, he outlined his plan. He and I, with Vijit leading two companies of our cavalry and Upa commanding one company of chariots, would gallop ahead to Upa Gama. 'Tikka reportedly has three hundred men, so will we,' the king reasoned. 'If we fail to break in, we shall surround the fort and await the main body.'

The commanders returned to their units and within minutes our attack group was cantering towards Upa Gama. The king, Vijit and I now rode at the head of our column, side by side, our flagbearer immediately in front, with six mounted scouts well ahead.

We rode for over two hours before reaching the foothills of the mountain range. We hit a brown river, swollen with rains in the mountain country, its banks bordered by tall trees sloping towards the fast-moving waters, took a long, looping bend dappled by sunlight and shadow and saw six riderless horses trotting towards us. As one, we reared to a stop. My heart contracted with fear.

'By the devas!' Vijit exclaimed. 'They have got our scouts.' He made to spur his horse forward.

King Vijaya reached out swiftly and gripped his arm. 'No, Vijit!' He directed fiercely. 'This is a trap.'

Before he could issue a command, we heard the crash of axes against wood, the splitting of trunks and the crumbling roar of trees to our front and rear. As one, my brother, Vijit and I swung our mounts right, signalled the men behind us to follow and headed towards the river. The horses neighed shrilly, bucking and rearing, but we controlled them and plunged into the water. In moments, the river was a medley of men on horseback, crying to their mounts, urging them downstream, King Vijaya and I leading. Wild screams, the clash of metal, the grinding of wheels and the neighing of horses told us that the rest of our men were being attacked. We must go to their rescue, I thought, but there was no way. The sick feel of defeat churned my stomach, raised bitter bile in my throat.

A horde of Yakka, screaming, cursing, shouting obscenities, began pouring down the hillside to the highway. A hail of arrows and stones began whizzing around us. A young Arya cavalryman shrieked with pain. As I looked back, he teetered off his horse, clutching at an arrow sticking grotesquely from his neck. He splashed into the water while his steed swam on, unhurt. The man must be dead, for his body disappeared, leaving red stains on the river. Other men around us screamed and fell, but the rushing waters were too swift for us to go to their aid. I heard my brother cursing softly.

The Yakka were now running along the highway, keeping pace with us, holding their fire because of the screen of trees. We could see fierce faces, mostly bearded, and stocky bodies clad in loincloths. How stupid we had been to underestimate them.

The river swung from the highway. My brother pointed to a gap in the trees. 'See what they did,' he panted. 'They hacked the tallest trees above the highway to where only a stroke or two of an axe would topple them. As soon as we entered the area, they chopped the trees down, neatly separating us from our chariots, which they then attacked. We were saved only because we took to the river.'

We were carried past the scene of the action. 'Get all the survivors to follow us downstream!' King Vijaya roared.

With shouts and beckoning hands, I urged the men scattered along the bank to head for the river. More riders began arcing into it. A few were struck by Yakka arrows and fell into the water. A hail of stones blasted us. A rock exploded on the side of my head. Stars spangled before my eyes. I began blacking out and knew I was slipping from my saddle. I leaned forward, released the reins and clutched my horse's neck. My legs tightened instinctively.

'You all right?' In a daze, I heard my brother's voice. Its concern inspired me to an enormous effort of will. I shook my head, reached with one hand for some water and splashed it on my face. The mists began to clear. I gripped my reins and came erect. 'I'm all right now,' I said, summoning a smile for him through lips that felt numb and tight.

Hamy looked at King Tikka with increased respect. The tall figure, lean and supple, clad in dark blue pantaloons and white tunic, had acquired a lift to his dark head, a new dignity, almost a majesty. He now sat astride a captured Arya chestnut at the fringe of the grove of trees bordering the clearing, looking very much the conquering warrior. His tight, cleanshaven features were aglow, the nostrils distended, the black eyes shining.

'We did it!' King Tikka exulted. 'We took the Arya on in battle, worse armed and equipped than them, with less men . . . and sucked the marrow from their bones.' He bellowed with laughter, pointing down the slope. 'Look at them run!'

Hamy reined back his captured steed, a bay, to glance at the fleeing Arya forces. 'I feel so proud!' he exclaimed.

'Proud to be a Yakka, Lord. You have indeed given us back our pride. You and you alone.' He turned in his saddle to take a good look at his fellow countrymen who had achieved such a stunning victory. They were all clad in black, men of varying ages, most with dark, hairy bodies. Many had long black hair and moustaches, only a few wore sandals. Unshod feet, the horny soles immune from thorns and spikes, gave them the silence of jungle animals. They all carried short bows and spears, long knives at the waist, some bore axes or hatchets dangling from their shoulders, handles to the front.

'You may well look at our comrades,' King Tikka remarked soberly. 'They are the old breed of seasoned hunters, spawned by the harsh jungles in which they survive, whom we have developed into a new breed of warriors.' His voice became charged with emotion. 'We are all linked by common bonds, the urge to live as our forefathers have done, to share our villages only with *palachiya*, leopard, *bolakanda*, elephant, *kalumeniya*, bear and *bochchediga*, wild boar. We will not be herded into collective farms. We will only accept what Nature yields, in *chenas* or open ground. We will not destroy tree and jungle to harness our gods to our will. We hate alien gods. We have united as one race to achieve victory.'

Hamy observed his comrades more closely. Their curses and jeers, their derisive hoots, showed a lack of sobriety and discipline. He knew a moment of dismay. Would they ever be warriors enough to take on the well-trained Arya in open battle, or were they condemned to conduct guerilla warfare for the rest of their lives?

Kira raced up on foot. 'Lord, let us pursue and destroy them,' he urged.

The king's eyes smouldered with the impulse to kill his hated enemies, but he shook his head. 'No! Not today. Let them go, for they will soon reach their own ground. They are superior in numbers, and we would only invite defeat. One day soon, we shall defeat them in open battle.'

313

We headed our horses to the river bank and breasted its slope. A defeated, discouraged band, we trotted away from the scene of the ambush, the clippety-clop . . . a . . . clop . . . clippety of our horses hooves a sad drum-beat to the dirge of ignominy chanting within our spirits. I glanced at the king, riding grim-faced beside me. 'Do we rejoin our main column and return to the attack, Sire?' I enquired.

He shook his head gloomily. 'The timing is not right,' he said, almost to himself. 'We had best return to Priti, so order the men to re-group. Trying to fight Tikka on his own terms, on ground of his own choosing without adequate intelligence, was a horrible mistake. It has cost lives. We must await our opportunity to strike back some day. Meanwhile, no new settlements close to the *uda rata* border. The invincible Arya have been defeated by over-confidence.'

I sensed torment within him, but it was something he had to bear alone. How would he face his Arya comrades, the army, the administration, the palace servants, the people, even the Princess Kuveni? Most of all, how would he live with his own guilt, especially when we collected our dead and wounded?

He echoed my thoughts in the strangest manner. 'How could this happen to a god-king?' I heard him utter.

The months went by without any open clash between Ujjeni and me. We maintained a studied neutrality under King Vijaya's watchful eyes, for he had warned us that he expected his ministers to maintain peace with one another.

Meanwhile, the Yakka army was increasing at a rate that alarmed us, while support for us had begun to dwindle. During this period, some instinct prevented me from ever mentioning Sundari to my brother, or to anyone else for that matter. Yet she was always in my mind and I vainly searched for some excuse to return to Kalyani. Meanwhile, despite the setback, King Vijaya maintained an appearance of calm.

Seven months later, a passing storm hit Thamba-Panni, causing some damage to the king's barns. Inspecting the damage took me longer than I had anticipated so I was late for the weekly dinner meeting of the King's Council. Rain was gusting in through the *meda midula* of the palace as I hastened to the great hall, sheeting so fiercely across the open verandah that I shrank against the far wall to avoid getting really soaked instead of merely wet. An early moon battled vainly against dark, obscuring clouds. The flares hissed and smoked with every gust of wind so that the smell of resin overlaid the stench of damp mud and rotting vegetation. I gratefully ducked into the relative quiet of the hall, where golden flares flamed against the walls and yellow tapers on the long teakwood dining table fluttered with every gust of wind.

'Miserable night!' I exclaimed, as a sudden gust slammed the door I was closing behind me. I made obeisance to the king, and rose to my feet. 'Forgive me for being late, Sire, but I have been on the king's business. I trust you received my message.'

'Yes, Prince. Pray be seated. What damage has the rain caused to our barns?'

'The winds took the roof off five of them, so the paddy and spices have been soaked. I organized relays of men to remove the produce to empty barns and much of the paddy was saved, but the spice crop has been destroyed.'

'An ill omen!' Ujjeni observed gloomily. Uraw and Anu, seated on either side of their friend, vigorously nodded their agreement. Upa, Sumitta and Vanga were noncommittal, while the dashing Vijit smiled contemptuously at the superstitious remark.

I took my seat beside my brother. 'Why an ill omen?' I enquired challenging.

Ujjeni looked towards the king, who nodded a stony-faced assent. 'The Princess Kuveni started her labour just as the storm commenced,' Ujjeni stated flatly. Then a grim note

315

entered his voice. 'We shall soon know where the future of the kingdom may lie.'

I was more than amazed, I was aghast. That Ujjeni was ruthless in pursuing his objectives, fanatical in his belief in Arya superiority, I knew. But that he should use an unborn child, callously condemning it as unlucky in order to shatter its future, filled me with contempt. I turned towards the king for support, but his face was impassive. Pity and horror seized me, for here was a man about to inherit his firstborn child and it was only an embarrassment to him, not a source of joy.

King Vijaya sensed my reactions. 'The princess will be safe; I have directed the midwives to attend her,' he said as if that were concession enough to his duties as a husband and a father-to-be.

'What a night on which to arrive on this earth,' Anu thrust in shrewdly.

'What a night to conjure up for the earth as a companion of birth!' Ujjeni countered.

The king shrugged off the subject. 'Gentlemen, to business again. Pray continue your report, Minister Ujjeni.'

'Sire, the troops, the real troops, our Arya comrades, who have shared fair weather and storm, a homeland and exile with you, have approached their captains to demand that . . .'

The king's shaggy, red eyebrows lifted. 'Demand?'

'Not of you, Sire,' Ujjeni explained, smoothly avoiding the trap of his own making. 'They have demanded that their captains plead with you to take some firm action that will restore morale. You know the shame they feel at the reverses we have suffered for over a year. They are longing to invade the *uda rata*.'

The king's anger subsided. 'Not yet, Minister,' he responded. 'Have the captains tell the men that we await the opportune moment. But promise them this from us, on our sacred oath. We shall indeed invade the *uda rata* some day.

They can then avenge their comrades, erase the insults we have endured and take their fill of blood and prosperity from the fertile *uda rata* kingdom.'

Ujjeni knew better than to push, but I had no doubt that he had exercised subtle pressures before I ever arrived at the meeting. I wondered whether this sudden demand for fulfilment and self-respect came from the men or from Ujjeni himself and whether it had some connection with the birth of a non-Arya heir.

'For your own ears and within the four walls of this room alone, gentlemen,' the king proceeded, 'we have been awaiting the one fatal mistake King Tikka is bound to make. Let us continue to be patient.' He smiled.

It was midnight by the time the meeting of the council ended. The storm had abated and the rain had eased somewhat, but the sky remained overcast, with the sheen that betokens more rain, confirmed by the distant growl of thunder and swiftly bared and shuttered flashes of lightning-glow.

The Princess Kuveni had been moved to the most private area of the women's quarters for the delivery of her baby. I walked from the meeting to the passageway that led from the verandah to her room and knocked on the closed door of the women's quarters. As it opened, I heard the groans of the princess in one of her spasms, ending in a wild scream. Pity for her and for the poor creature she would produce, whose future was so uncertain, gushed forth within me, leaving a great hopelessness at the awful circumstances that some people must battle from birth upwards. My thoughts were interrupted by the gaunt-faced Rupa, her skinny figure clothed in the inevitab'e blue cloth and blouse, responding to my knock.

'How is your mistress?' I enquired.

'The pains are coming more frequently, Lord, so it should not be long now. But this is one of the worst I've known.

She's so big, the baby must be very large and heavy, and she's really suffering.' A series of screams from within confirmed her statement.

'You have received my instructions to have the princess sponged and prepared for the king's visit?'

'Yes, Lord.'

'Have my attendant wake me when the baby is born and everything is ready for our visit. If it is before the dawn watch, I shall summon the king so that we can call on the princess immediately.'

'Very well, Lord.'

I walked back to my room along the deserted corridor, in the light of flares that suddenly seemed lonely. The screams of the Princess Kuveni kept ringing in my ears. I felt unutterably sad that two people such as my brother and the princess could know the attraction that caused them to mate and produce a single fruit, and yet become more separate than plants remote from each other in the period of nine months. Surely of all living things, mobile and immobile, only man is remote from man. Being capable of the most complete union with Nature and with his own self, through the ability to send his mind into all things, he will always be as lonely as my brother must be tonight. How sad for him that I had to arrange his visit to his wife and child after the delivery, when he would have known such excitement, such vibrance, if love and concern had generated pride and spontaneity in the event. How sad for both of us that I could not tell him about Sundari.

Pondering destiny, I paused at my door, turned round and walked across the verandah to look at the sky. The rain had ceased and there was that sizzling hiss in the air that follows heavy rain on parched earth.

What of my own destiny? Did it lie to the south, where Sundari slept at this moment? I conjured a vision of her sensitive face, the black masses of curly hair framing exquisite bones, the delicate fair skin, and longed for her. There was nothing specific that I could associate that longing with, because I did not know her, yet I simply longed for her.

Suddenly I felt very depressed. I lifted my eyes to the heavens, then back within me, seeking God. I suddenly connected with the reality of Him, the consciousness of the Eternal, Infinite God of Whom I was a part. How unimportant and insignificant the affairs of men seemed before countless years and the unending spread of space that were all part of God. Then I knew that my special communion with God had only begun. God has a place for me, I thought. Instead of bemoaning our fate when seeming adversity strikes, we should comprehend that He may simply be pointing us in a different direction, which may well stretch even beyond death. The faint echo of a scream from the women's quarters reached me. The struggle to be born, taking place in the palace at that very moment, told me that birth and death are kin.

The princess was in labour the entire night and it was dawn when Rupa sent me word through my attendant that her mistress awaited her husband and me. The king was already up and about, having awakened, in accordance with the Arya schedule, to the first birdsong. He received my news without any trace of emotion, but promptly accompanied me to the women's quarters, followed by his aide and our attendants. Though the verandah flares had been extinguished, a faint tinge of resin hung upon the grey half-light. The courtyard was strewn with fallen leaves, some scattered on the yet unswept verandah.

Was the baby a boy or a girl? My attendant had not been told and my brother did not even enquire. What would it look like? Its future would depend on whether it looked Arya or Yakka. What a sad gamble for it.

319

I knocked on the door of the women's quarters and Rupa opened it, her eyes red-rimmed from lack of sleep. She made obeisance and stood aside for us to pass. A dark, narrow corridor led to a small room in which pale daylight, filtering through high, grilled windows and, augmented by the light of tapers on the bare walls, revealed the princess lying on the white linen cushions of a high bed at the far end. The room was devoid of any furniture save an ebony chest on a table littered with clay pots.

The princess greeted us with a wan smile. Her sensuous face, though scrubbed, was drawn and tired. She had grown older in a single night. As we approached the bed, the scent of her sandalwood reached my nostrils.

My eyes sought the baby she was holding. At first, I did not comprehend what I saw, then the truth struck me with the force of a thunderbolt. She was holding two bundles.

The king too was obviously puzzled. 'Are you wet-nursing . . .' he began, then went rigid.

'My Lord,' the princess said, all gentle sweetness. 'I have delivered you twins, both beautiful. A boy and a girl.' There was pride in her dark eyes.

My brother remained briefly in shock before leaning forward to see the babies, a dispassionate inspection, devoid of emotion. My eyes followed his gaze. One look at those tiny, wizened faces and my heart sank. They were like two little black monkeys – monkey monkeys, not the human monkeys that most babies look like.

'We are glad you came safely through your ordeal,' the king said formally.

The large dark eyes of the princess sought his face. She was hoping that the gift of the babies would somehow change her situation. What a forlorn hope, I thought. An event that had ceased to be blessed and sanctified by love could never produce communion.

'I wish you a speedy recovery, madam,' King Vijaya said.

'Please let Prince Lala know if you require anything.'

The princess closed her eyes wearily. A teardrop sparkling like a water-sapphire escaped through the black lashes and rolled down her dark cheek.

Chapter 23

Two weeks later, three *yojana* away from our fortress and two *yojana* from the Kalyani capital, Hamy stood in the cool night air in the upper reaches of the great river, watching the Yakka troops threading their way down the blackness of the steep river bank to the rafts moored below. Clad only in deerskin loincloths, with light linen cloaks to ward off the chill, their shadowy lines emerged endlessly from the dark groves of coconut, mango and breadfruit trees. Hamy saw the vague silhouettes of short bows, quivers of arrows at the shoulder, the odd spear gleaming dully and heard the occasional clank of axe or sword. He felt a surge of pride at the disciplined army of Yakka King Tikka had fashioned out of wild hunters by sheer will, ferocity and ruthlessness. He looked up at the sky, checking for the possibility of rain. Not a cloud darkened the broad swathe of the countless stars spangled like fireflies on a *kohamba* tree. A whisper of wind rustled the bamboos along the grassy bank and rippled gently above the flow-sound of the dark, gleaming river waters. Glancing down, Hamy could distinguish the first rafts, already heading towards the black smudge of the opposite bank about fifty yards away, topped by a contoured skyline. Only when the splash of quiet poling reached his ears did he feel the full impact of tonight's operation. The *uda rata* Yakka were actually invading another kingdom, on a scale hitherto unknown in history. Thrilling to the knowledge, he glanced sideways at his leader, King Tikka, standing immobile on his left. Clad only in the familiar deep blue pantaloons he had begun to affect since his visit to the Kalyani palace a year ago, the tall, supple King Tikka seemed very relaxed, yet there was an inner vibrance to him,

322

as of a leopard on the prowl. The pudgy Kira on the king's left, dull, unimaginative, was unconcerned as usual.

'Lord, here we are again, the three of us, standing once more on a river bank,' Kira said quietly. 'The last time we did so, we gave the Arya a bellyful of their own brand of betrayal.'

'Twice before, however, we were fugitives on river banks,' King Tikka responded dryly. 'This time we are truly the avengers.'

Hamy's thoughts wandered back over the past months of intense activity, characterized by the indomitable will, the implacable purpose, the unflagging drive of a single man with a desire for vengeance and a blazing need for conquest. Hamy knew his king to be a parricide, who had poisoned his own father in order to inherit the *uda rata* kingdom, but he had no great feelings about it. There is life, there is death, he reflected, which are but words for changes that only man regards as drastic.

During the past months, Hamy had, however, found himself torn occasionally between the relative tranquillity of the Yakka life of the past and the material progress gained under the Arya. Which was better, to be a docile subject of the first rank under the authoritarian rule of Yakka chiefs, or second-class subjects under the more progressive Arya? He was glad he did not have to make a choice for anyone, especially himself. He was glad too that his thoughts were free, because King Tikka would scoop his brains out if he knew!

The cry of a nightbird echoing across the river disturbed Hamy's reflections. 'Our entire force has made the crossing unobserved,' King Tikka exulted. 'This time the nightbird's call works for *us*.'

'Did you ever discover the truth about the calls we kept hearing during that night in Sirissa Watta, lord?' Kira enquired.

King Tikka's eyes gleamed like twin coals of fire in the

dark. 'Did we not tell you?'

'No, Lord.'

'It was Kuveni, that demon's bitch. May she roast in King Wessa Mony's hell.' The king sobered. 'Spies reported to us that she moved from house to house of the important men in the fort, her own flesh and blood, mark you, uttering those cries, so that the Arya could find the inmates in the dark and destroy them.' The quiet venom in the king's voice was more deadly than any raging.

You revile the princess for destroying what you call her flesh and blood, yet you poisoned your own father, Hamy thought cynically. Everything depends on who speaks the word, who does the deed. Equality is merely the right to criticize others for what we ourselves are invariably guilty of.

'Traitorous whore!' Kira interjected.

'She shall pay for her treachery,' King Tikka promised pleasantly. 'That is part of our plan.'

'She gave you tonight's opportunity, lord,' Hamy reminded the king.

King Tikka snorted. 'Ever the philosopher, Hamy. It is because she gave it to us that we shall have the power to punish her.' He laughed shortly, then cocked an ear at a creaking sound from the river. 'Ah! Here comes our boat.'

'You were so wise to select this place for the crossing, Lord.' Kira was fawning again and Hamy hated it. 'The ford is on the border of the *uda rata* with the upper reaches of the Kalyani kingdom, where the great river runs from north to south, so we were able to send the rafts downstream openly, carrying timber, and to unload them here for our army at its assembly point. Only your wisdom had our troops come here by sections so that there would be no evidence of our plans.'

'Now the rafts will go downstream and be available for the second corps, also of a thousand men, to cross closer to the Kalyani capital before daybreak,' King Tikka observed with satisfaction. 'We ourselves will march through the night, link with them and surround the city before noon tomorrow.'

'Are you going to get to King Ra-hula before he has his only meal for the day, lord?' Kira gave that high-pitched giggle which Hamy always found annoying. 'Some forbearance, I beg you.'

'We are going to show that superior bastard the error of his ways,' King Tikka promised softly.

The palace guards lining the foyer were dressed, as during their last visit to Kalyani, in white *dhotis* and blue sashes. The flaps of the *dhotis* were tight-drawn between the legs, Dasa fashion, revealing the rear of the knees and the lower thighs. They bowed, touching palms to chest, as King Tikka and Prince Jaya, Hamy and Kira at their heels, burst towards the audience hall. They were all dressed in dark blue pantaloons and gold tunics, the uniform King Tikka had decreed for his immediate guard. King Tikka alone carried a naked sword. No one made a move to stop them. Hamy marvelled at the speed a man as huge and bulky as Prince Jaya could generate, his massive upper body erect, his fat legs swinging madly from his hips, while the portly Kira could only manage a sort of running waddle.

'Sons of bitches,' Prince Jaya puffed pleasantly, inclining his head towards the attendants. 'As always, they can only manage to get their hands up to their noses for me. They never raise their hands up to their heads.'

'Don't worry,' King Tikka assured him. 'They shall soon raise their hands, palms together, to their heads and give you proper obeisance, or have neither hands nor heads.'

They paused at the open doors of the audience hall. The room was in shadow, except where pre-noon sunlight streamed through the high windows between the grilles of yellow and red stripes of lacquer. A faint scent of incense clung to the air. Hamy peered between the soaring teakwood columns that held up the ceiling and roof, past his two leaders, towards the platform at the far end of the hall.

Two tall, ten-tiered brass oil-lamps, their lighted multi-wicks erect like a series of yellow-gold fangs, threw up occasional wisps of smoke and lit the gleaming throne. On it, the yellow-robed King Ra-hula sat cross-legged in the lotus pose. The inevitable two attendants, also in yellow robes, eyes downcast, squatted in the lotus pose on either side. Standing to the left of the platform was a tall, lean figure, also yellow-robed, with the extremely fair skin of the Arya.

'It's a trap!' King Tikka muttered, his eyes darting to the darkest corners of the hall. 'An ambush!'

'*Apoi*, no, cousin,' Prince Jaya reassured him. 'This is the way they always behave. Tchk! What is the use of that sword. Put it away.'

'No!' King Tikka ground out. He advanced down the aisle towards the throne, followed by Prince Jaya, Hamy, Kira and the soldiers crowding behind. He came to a stop at the platform and looked up at the throne. King Ra-hula simply ignored him, continued in his meditative pose, back of the palms on the thighs, eyes closed.

'We have seized control of your kingdom,' King Tikka shouted. 'We have a combined army of two thousand men from our *uda rata* kingdom and three thousand from the army you emasculated over a year ago, whose manhood we have restored. Prince Jaya will hereafter function as King of Kalyani. If you wish to retain your position in name, you may do so, but you shall direct the remainder of your missionary forces to take up arms immediately and unite with us in destroying the Arya invader. As for the golden throne on which you sit, it is now ours. We shall have it returned to the *uda rata* where it belongs.'

King Ra-hula, seeming not to hear him, gave no reply.

King Tikka lost his temper. 'Answer us when we speak, *para balla*, filthy dog,' he screamed. 'We are your master now.'

'He cannot answer you while he is in meditation.' The words, uttered in calm, deep tones, came from the tall Arya, who now moved up to stand beside the throne.

King Tikka turned fiercely on him. 'Who the devil are you?' He demanded.

'That is the Venerable Sri Ra-vindra, missionary of the Buddha's doctrine from the continent,' Prince Jaya advised.

'Ah! Another of those accursed Arya,' King Tikka was trying to calm himself.

'Accursed only by the evil of our *akusala kharma*,' the *bhikku* replied calmly. 'If being born an Arya is accursed too, it could only be the *vipaka*, effect, of a previous manifestation of our birth.'

'Confound you, what rubbish are you spouting?' King Tikka roared. He raced up the steps of the platform, naked sword gleaming in his hand, and stood towering above the seated figure of King Ra-hula. Prince Jaya made no attempt to follow, merely watched steadily through slitted eyes.

Hamy looked back at the throne. At that moment, King Ra-hula opened his eyes. He did so quite naturally, the lids slowly lifting, the gaze gradually returning to its outside focus, but still deep and expressionless. Here is a man facing another who has a drawn sword, Hamy thought, and he is as relaxed as before a cool breeze. At that moment, a light breeze did indeed sweep through the open door, making the flames from the lamps dance to cast highlights on the king's dark, broad face so that it shone like polished ebony.

'Welcome to Kalyani, nephew.' King Ra-hula said.

Hamy heard a hiss of indrawn breath. His eyes went swiftly to its source. King Tikka's face had assumed an expression of such demoniac fury as he had never witnessed before. He remembered the King's many expressions of hatred at King Ra-hula's superior ways, advanced intellect and unmatchable spirituality. King Ra-hula, you are playing with the fire of a man's inferiority, Hamy reflected. I beg you, don't, please don't. It's a madman who stands before you.

'We have seized your power in this kingdom,' King Tikka

grated.

'How could you, nephew?' King Ra-hula's sing-song voice was very gentle. 'The kind of power we have exercised over this kingdom for more than a year has not been something we possessed or that another man can seize. The only power in our blessed Kalyani is the moral force of its people.'

'You keep the moral force. We'll take your army and all your possessions.'

'You were welcome to take them at any time without the need for this violent intrusion.' The calm, dark eyes drifted down to Prince Jaya's face. 'Even our other nephew here could have taken all such things if he so desired, without having to plot as he has done these many months.'

Prince Jaya's eyes widened momentarily, then narrowed to the merest slits again.

'Prince Jaya could have had it all for the asking without having to share it with you, nephew,' King Ra-hula advised.

This time a tiny escape of breath told of Prince Jaya's reaction.

'You were both safe enough until you embarked on this foolish, dangerous enterprise,' King Ra-hula continued. A slow, sad smile lit his face. 'Now you have to reckon with each other, do you not?'

'Don't listen to him, cousin,' Prince Jaya urged. A strident note had entered his normally high-pitched voice. 'He is a very clever man. He tries to drive a wedge between us.'

King Tikka began trembling with uncontrollable fury. In this state, he was capable of crazy actions. Hamy wished he had the courage to intervene, to say something.

King Ra-hula's gaze drifted to King Tikka's face. 'Our nephew's words remind us, we must not allow you to drive a wedge between us and our religious routine,' he said blandly. 'It is almost time for our single meal of the day, which must finish before noon. With your leave, we shall now take *dasa-sila*, the ten precepts.' Elbows apart, he placed his palms together, and raised them to his forehead.

328

'Namo thassa bagavatho arahatho samma-sambuddhasa,' he chanted.

'Homage to the blessed one, the exalted one, the fully Enlightened one.'

The two attendants behind the king and the Arya *bhikku* placed their palms together before their closed eyes and joined in. The group was in a play again, this time not a mime but with words.

There was something haunting, ethereal, about the chant, the drama of the high tones of the Naga and the deeper ones of the Arya blending in perfect unison, a melodious union of voices. Hamy was fascinated.

'Buddham saranam gacchāmi
Dhammam saranam gacchāmi
Sangham saranam gacchāmi
Sangham saranam gacchāmi'.
I go to the Doctrine as my refuge
I go to the Sangha, the Noble Order of Monks, as my refuge.

The four men repeated the chant three times.

What happened next was like an extension of that drama. 'Damn you to hell! Go then to your refuge!' King Tikka cried hoarsely. Spittle appeared at the side of his mouth. He drew back his sword and plunged it between King Ra-hula's elbows, right through the yellow robe, into the stomach.

King Ra-hula's body moved back with the impact. That was all. No grunt, no gasp, no groan. As the red blood started to well around the sword inches inside his guts and began staining the robe, he calmly went on with his chant.

'Duti-yam' pi Buddham saranam gacchāmi
Duti-yam' pi Dhammam saranam gacchāmi
Duti-yam' pi Sangham saranam gacchāmi'
For the second time I go to the Buddha as my refuge
For the second time I go to the Doctrine as my refuge
For the second time I go to the Sangha as my refuge

King Tikka stared wide-eyed, incredulous, at the wounded man before him, his hand frozen around his sword hilt.

King Ra-hula's voice continued gentle but firm:

'Tati-yam' pi Buddham saranam gacchāmi
Tati-yam' pi Dhammam saranam gacchāmi
Tati-yam' pi Sangham saranam gacchāmi'
For the third time, I go to the Buddha.

King Tikka screamed aloud like a wounded animal, his voice resounding in the high-ceilinged hall. Though petrified with disbelief, Hamy noticed Prince Jaya's eyes wide open for once, filled with horror. The entire hall became hushed, save only for the echoes of the scream.

The scream changed to a roar. 'Curse you! Curse you! Curse you! Why don't you die?' King Tikka drew his sword out of King Ra-hula's body, thrust again and withdrew the sword. Blood spouted dark red from the gaping wound, soaking the yellow robe. White ligaments and pale pink intestines spilled out. The king coughed once. His eyes went blank. Never abandoning his form of worship, he slumped back against the chair, then slowly collapsed sideways, locked into the lotus pose. The sword inside him sustained his life until it was withdrawn, Hamy thought dully.

Prince Jaya broke the silence. 'Tckikay, that was not a nice thing to do, no!' He exclaimed, but very soberly. 'We had not planned to kill the . . .' Hamy knew that Prince Jaya was going to use the word "man", but he changed it to . . . '*Maharaja*, Great King.'

King Tikka looked wildly around. He raised his bloodied sword aloft. 'We now have the kingdom!' He dashed madly down the steps. The waiting soldiers cleared a path for him, then turned to race after him, Kira waddling behind.

Hamy remained rooted to the spot. Prince Jaya did not move either.

'Panatipata veramani-sikkapadam samadiyāmi.'
I undertake to observe the Precept to abstain from destroying the life of beings.

The three men remaining on the platform were calmly proceeding with the ten precepts. The irony of their words plunged like a pointed stake into Hamy's heart.

A great sob escaped Prince Jaya. He stared a while at the tableau on the platform. 'It was indeed a trap . . . a moral ambush,' he muttered, then turned abruptly and walked slowly away.

A great calm seized Hamy. The full force of the tragic event would smite him only later. He knew the precepts and was suddenly determined to stay to the end of their observance, regardless of the cost.

'I undertake to abstain from taking things not given.
I undertake to abstain from all unchastity.
I undertake to abstain from sexual misconduct.
I undertake to abstain from false speech.
I undertake to abstain from spiritous drinks, malt liquors and wines, all of which are foundations for heedlessness.
I undertake to abstain from taking food at unreasonable times.
I undertake to abstain from dancing, singing, music and unseemly shows; from the use of garlands, perfumes and unguents; and from things that tend to beautify and adorn the person.
I undertake to abstain from high and luxurious seats.
Jatarupa-rajata-patiggahana veramani sikkhapadam samadi yāmi.
I undertake to abstain from accepting gold and silver.'

As the taking of the tenth precept ended, Hamy suddenly felt chill, bereft, alone. It was as if only the chanting that had just been withdrawn from his body had sustained him. Now, like King Ra-hula once King Tikka's sword was withdrawn, some part of him died.

Turning on the instant, Hamy fled the audience hall. All four of those men on the platform had known exactly what would happen. They had not lifted a finger to prevent it. What kind of men, what kind of gods were these?

He ran through the shadows of the building to its entrance and paused before the glare of the noonday sunlight. Tears were streaming down his cheeks. He did not know for what he wept, unless it was for shadows that no sunlight could ever disperse.

The ending of the *dasa-sila* poured faintly out of the building.

Sadhu . . . Saa . . . dhu . . . Saaa . . . dhu . . . Saa . . . a . . . a!
Holiness . . . holiness . . . holiness . . . indeed!

Hamy clapped his hands to his ears to shut out the sound, then fled blindly through the sunshine.

King Vijaya and I were on the *maidan* the following morning, watching our men practising with weapons, when we heard the sound of galloping hooves above the gasps and grunts of the men. Soon the rider brought his lathered mount to a rearing stop before us. It was Viswan, his face bathed in sweat, droplets even hanging from his dark beard. He slid off the saddle stiffly and clung to it a moment, torso heaving, to catch his breath. He ran towards us and sank into obeisance, then raised his small, well-shaped head, his thin nostrils dilating, and clambered to his feet.

'You have ridden all the way from Kalyani,' King Vijaya noted abruptly. 'Why didn't you use the messenger relay?'

'Lord, I have been riding without pause since noon yesterday.' Viswan's voice was hoarse. He cleared his throat. 'My news had to be delivered to you at first-hand.'

The king's bushy eyebrows shot up. 'And your news?'

'King Tikka invaded the Kalyani kingdom with two thousand men last morning. They came in two columns, one from the north, the other from the eastern boundary, and surrounded the capital. They were immediately joined by Prince Jaya with three thousand men of the former Kalyani army, who threw aside their robes to take up arms again.

The Kalyani capital is in their hands, therefore the entire kingdom, without any resistance.'

'What of the king?' I broke in. 'King Ra-hula.'

'King Tikka ran him through with his sword while he sat on his throne in the lotus pose.'

'Dead?' King Vijaya enquired.

'Very, my Lord.'

Thoughts went whirling through my brain like dancing dervishes, while my whole being cried out in anguish. I should not properly question Viswan until the king had finished with him, but I could not hold back what was closest to my heart. 'Was anyone else killed?'

'Only a few soldiers of the king's former bodyguard, who took up arms against the intruders. The new order seemed disposed to maintain a good profile in the palace and with the people.'

'There was a monk, a follower of the Buddha's doctrine from abroad, named Ra-vindra, in the Kalyani palace. What of him?' Viswan's words had convinced me of Sundari's safety.

'The venerable monk was safe when I left, Prince.'

Above the horror, my heart thudded once with joy. Thank my God, Uday was safe. I only prayed that Tikka would not try to take Sundari. My one hope was that he would, at this stage, wish the Nagas to think him civilized. But King Ra-hula, that wise, gentle, spiritual man, why would anyone want to kill him? 'Only a beast could have murdered such a king,' I heard myself say aloud.

The king turned back to Viswan. 'You are tired and need rest,' he stated. 'Your zeal and dedication to duty are commendable and shall be suitably rewarded.'

Viswan glowed visibly, some of the tiredness shedding off him as if it had merely been a mantle. 'I thank you, Sire.' He bowed, the palms of his hands together.

'So now, have some food, drink and rest,' King Vijaya commanded. He exuded purpose, even seemed pleased at

333

the tragic turn of events. 'We shall need to question you fully in a few hours. Meanwhile, we have much to do.'

'One final question, with your permission, Lord?' I intervened. The king inclined his head in assent. 'Did you manage to get away without any trouble?' I enquired of Viswan.

'The arrangements you had made for my getaway were perfect, Prince.'

'We shall call on you for a full report at the end of the noon watch,' King Vijaya advised Viswan. 'Meanwhile, Prince Lala here will see you have a room in the fort for your rest.' He turned his gaze to me. 'Have the commanders order their forces into instant readiness by the end of the noon watch, Prince, then present yourself in the audience chamber with their parade states.'

Chapter 24

When Viswan gave my brother and me details of King Ra-hula's death, my heart was filled with pity and enormous reverence for the dead king. Two human beings whom I had come to love, the little boy, Silindu and the gentle King Sri Ra-hula, both foully murdered. Sundari's father, brother and husband-to-be murdered. Where was God? If only I could withdraw from His cruel world of human beings and find refuge in a monastery, away from the violence which seemed to swirl around my brother. I suddenly remembered that the violence of creation had been around me all the time – storms, wars, murder, desertion – and yet, I had come to find God. Surely He could not be less real merely because the violence became more real to me.

I arranged with the chief palace attendant for Viswan to have food, a bath and a room, then hastened to join King Vijaya in his audience chamber. He was seated at his yellow jakwood desk, on which lay a red package which I immediately recognized as the one I had carried from King Ra-hula on my return from Kalyani. The king held it up. 'Since there is strife in the Kalyani kingdom, we may now open this,' he declared, breaking the seals of the package, undoing the string and removing the red cloth covering. A small sheaf of yellow *ola* parchments was exposed, with a letter on the top. The king commenced leafing through the parchments. When he spread them out on the desk, I was puzzled to note that they were maps and plans. Gazing curiously at them, the king's tawny eyes suddenly widened, his interest quickened. He picked up the letter and began to read aloud.

'To Vijaya Sinha-Bahu, King of Thamba-Panni, Ra-hula, King of Kalyani, sends greetings.

'By the time you read this letter, our present being will be seeking its new birth in *Samsara*, the wheel of rebirth. What we now send you will then be of no consequence to us, but you will have use for it.

'We are convinced that we will acquire much good *kharma*, much merit, by giving you these maps and plans of Kalyani, for the gift of which we expect that you will bring to our people and to the whole of Lanka such benefits as those who seek to overthrow our *dharmista*, just and religious, rule can never provide. Though the *akusala kharma*, evil cause, of bloodshed is inevitable from their actions, should you prevail, the ultimate effects of bloodshed can be joyous for our people and for the doctrine.

'You, King Vijaya Sinha-Bahu, may not be the direct instrument of the noblest and greatest that our island has yet to achieve, but you can be the fount and the origin of a new era and of many mighty works the like of which man has never witnessed. In years to come the name of our island, Lanka, shall resound through the world as the home of the true doctrine. It shall shine across the seas, from the radiance of a giant crystal that will one day top a pinnacle rising from the tallest *stupa*, temple, of its times, built in a unique city, created by one yet to come.

'Use the information we send you wisely. If you succeed in your military endeavours, rule our land for the betterment of all its peoples, regardless of race, caste and religion, so that you can have a better rebirth – even though you may not believe in it.

'Be especially kind to those who follow the true doctrine, we beseech you, for it is greater than you and you will never extinguish it.

'We remain yours in this present life, though not in our future death,

Sri Ra-hula, King of Kalyani.'

My eyes prickled with tears as I heard the words. I pictured the wise king in his yellow robes, seated in the lotus pose on the golden throne he obtained through the judgement of Lord Buddha. I heard the gentle voice repeat the words of his letter in its sing-song fashion. I wondered whether his reference to caste was in any way connected with Sundari and me.

336

'He was indeed a remarkable man,' I heard my brother say. 'Yet his death shows us that in the final analysis only physical force triumphs.'

'No, no Sire!' I demurred. 'Surely the manner of his dying reveals the power of mind over body and is a triumph of goodness over violence.'

The king smiled cynically. 'It depends on where you're looking from,' he observed. 'It is a ruler's duty to be strong in every way.' He resumed his study of the letter. 'If he did have what you have often referred to as the blessed gift of inner sight, why does he not predict the outcome of the struggle he knew would ensue, which incidentally did not require divine inspiration to anticipate?'

I looked at him curiously, in an almost detached fashion. The black pinpoints of his eyes blank, he was now staring at the letter, obviously provoked by something in it. 'Your friend was wrong in his assessment,' he remarked, somewhat petulantly now. 'We are not merely an instrument of the future. We are all of it. We are history and no doctrine can be greater than the king.' He tapped the letter. 'King Rahula's downfall was caused when he allowed the doctrine to usurp the throne.' His eyes lifted to mine and I was stunned to find his glance was coldly appraising, the massive jaw tight.

He blinked once and seemed to cast aside his mood, then began studying the charts. 'Ah!' He exclaimed delightedly, holding up a detailed map for my inspection. 'Perfect, just perfect!'

The conference of commanders lasted until evening. It was not one of decision-making, for King Vijaya had already made his decision and initiated the proceedings by detailing his plan and giving orders for the march.

Uraw left the conference elated by the king's decision but with mixed emotions. He had not been feeling well the whole day. His bones were chilled, his muscles ached, his skin was sore and his body was frequently shaken by cold shivers. He wished that the march could be postponed until he had had at least one good night's sleep in the arms of the plump Arabi mistress Ujjeni had found for him, as promised.

'Uraw!'

Think of the devil . . . Ujjeni's voice made Uraw turn around.

The gaunt man materialized through the gloom between two lighted flares. One of them hissed, emitted a gust of grey smoke, flung the sharp odour of resin into the heavy air, from which it appeared that Ujjeni had in fact emanated. Ujjeni smiled at him. At that very moment, a cat screeched and another m . . . m . . . mawed, deep, low and angry, in the feline's eternal sex duel. The sounds could have emerged from Ujjeni's open mouth.

Uraw shivered, not with the fever this time. 'Our time has arrived,' Ujjeni declared quietly. 'We shall win the battle ahead and the Yakka lover will become a Naga lover.'

'I don't want to talk about it tonight,' Uraw protested.

'Hasn't everything I warned you of come true?' Ujjeni demanded fiercely. 'Soon there will be an added threat to Arya supremacy, for we shall be heavily outnumbered by the combination of Yakkas and Nagas.'

'Does it matter?'

'Does it matter?' Ujjeni demanded incredulous, raising long, skeletal hands in the air. 'Listen. The gods decree birth and station by *kharma*. A person only has the rights of his station. To extend more to people of lower estate is a violation of a law more fundamental than any established by a king, since *dharma* requires us to fulfil all the duties and responsibilities of our stations ruthlessly, unflinchingly. Those of us Ministers who have seen the light agree that Prince Lala can be a dangerous influence on the king. The time has come now for us to wrench this evil connection asunder, like a dead foetus from its mother's womb, lest Prince Lala infects the entire kingdom.'

Up to now, Uraw had merely acknowledged Ujjeni's cleverness. Now he began to feel a hint of disquiet. 'Are you trying to manipulate me, my friend,' he burst out. 'If so, to what end? What are your deepest motives? Are you merely trying to protect the king and ensure the wellbeing of the Arya state, or do you have personal ambitions?'

Ujjeni shook his head as if in disbelief. 'Am I really hearing this from you? Can this be my friend, Uraw speaking, whom I have trusted and helped so much? I have brought you wealth, position, even a woman. Oh, ingratitude!'

'I don't want to hurt or disappoint you,' Uraw protested. 'But I must say that, though I disagree with Prince Lala's liberal notions, I like the young man. I have always found him to be the soul of honour. Perhaps he is too honest to survive in a cold-blooded, cynical world, too unrealistic, too idealistic for the welfare of our new kingdom.'

'Pah! You are wrong in your assessment. Prince Lala is a liberal who, like all liberals, uses the concept for his own ambition. But even if he were only an idealist, you know that such people are dangerous and should never be placed in positions of power.'

'But surely the combination of Prince Lala's idealism with the stern realism of our king can provide a necessary balance and thus a source of moral security for the state. Also, don't people like me need the Prince Lala's around as a voice of conscience?' Weariness suddenly consumed Uraw. He was in no condition to argue. 'Listen, my friend, I'm sick,' he stated. 'I'd like to get a couple of hours' rest before we leave. The king openly declared his position today. Henceforth neither Yakka nor Naga, but only Arya, are to be trusted, as the superior race. All that you, Anu and I have discussed these past months has been vindicated.'

'Why don't you come over to my place now for just a short while,' Ujjeni urged. 'Others beside Anu will be present.'

'Will Vijit be there?'

'Vijit is a loner. He'll never join us. Who needs him anyhow? It is critical for the rest of us to meet before we leave tonight. The seeds I have planted in our king's mind have borne fruit at last, thanks to the devas and to our Lord Indra the Destroyer. We must plan immediately for the future.'

'You're a genius.' Uraw hoped to escape through flattery.

'No! Merely a loyal subject of King Vijaya and a humble instrument in the creation of an Arya super-race on this island.'

'But why do you need me tonight? I'm exhausted by the shivering fever. My bones are chill, my skin feels dry and my muscles ache.'

'And your nose is beginning to run. The evil humours in your body will dissipate in a couple of days if you take a *cassaya* mixture I shall give you. Tonight, more than ever, we need to plan how we can press home our advantage during this campaign. Also, supposing something were to happen to the king in battle?'

Comprehension dawned on Uraw. 'I see. You fear that Prince Lala could become our ruler.'

'What else? And then we shall have to live in a liberal Yakka/Naga-loving state.'

'I have it.' Yet Uraw was feeling confused. His head had begun throbbing and all he still wanted was to crawl into bed.

Ujjeni lowered his voice even more. 'We must plan to protect ourselves and all we have worked so hard for these many moons. Prince Lala must never succeed to the throne. If he does, we are finished as Arya and our place in history will end. It is we, the Council of Ministers, who must rule in any interregnum until we can organize a pure Arya succession.'

'How will we do that? Our king has a Yakka queen and two children by her.' Uraw paused. 'Surely you don't mean to have them all killed?'

Ujjeni leaned close. 'That too if need be,' he hissed,

spraying Uraw with wet breath. 'The king is unhappy with his queen and does not want those heirs of mixed blood who look like monkeys. It is up to us, his Ministers, to arrange suitable alternatives, though with discretion.'

It was all too much for Uraw in his condition. Total physical weariness suddenly swept over him. He felt dizzy. I shall collapse if I don't go home and rest, he thought. Anything to be able to go home. 'Listen,' he said. 'You know I'm with you all the way. Make the decisions and I'll stand behind them so long as all six of us are agreed.'

'You promise.'

'Yes, yes, I do.'

'On your sacred Arya honour, the honour of a nobleman of the highest caste.'

Uraw hesitated, then was smitten by another gust of weariness. He simply had to get rid of Ujjeni. Besides, didn't he agree with what all the man stood for? 'On my sacred Arya honour,' he vowed.

The night after King Vijaya left on his Kalyani campaign, the Princess Kuveni lay alone on her bed in the room within the women's quarters which she now occupied permanently. The two babies were fast asleep in their *kenaf* bassinets beside the bed. She had sunk into a state of hopelessness since that day when the king had visited the babies for the first time and treated her so formally. When he and her friend, Prince Lala went to war, her despair had slowly begun to be replaced by feelings of humiliation, anger, bitterness and the desire for vengeance. She felt deeper anger against her husband than she had ever felt towards her father. She associated King Vijaya with her betrayal of her people. Now he had shamed her and it was gnawing at her mind like a hungry jackal attacking bones.

She glanced at Rupa, standing over the bassinets, her gaunt face gleaming in the taper-light, occasionally waving a yellow *indikola* fan to drive away the whining mosquitoes the end of the rains always brought. Rupa was so staunch, her only trusted friend, yet she was also a constant reminder of her act of betrayal, which had begun to haunt her since she lost the love of the king. 'Rupa, I have nothing left,' she suddenly exclaimed. 'Not even hope, for I had thought that these babies would unite my husband and me. What a *musala*, miserable wretch I am to be left only with shame.' Tears flooded her eyes and rolled down her cheeks.

'Why do you say that, my lady? Rupa quietly enquired. 'Even if the king does not sleep with you any more, he can't ignore his heirs. Surely your children will reunite you both some day. It will be for the good of the kingdom. Is there anything special that ails you tonight, my lady?' Rupa's voice was low, mellow and soothing.

The princess looked deeply at Rupa. The warm yellow glow of the taper lights now threw the attendant's cheek-bones and tight brown skin into relief. I have known Rupa since childhood and I can trust her, she thought. 'Not specially . . . er . . . No, that's wrong. *Aney*, I don't know, Rupa. Sometimes I feel like a lost soul, stricken by *tanicama*, total loneliness, which demons inflict on human beings. Silly as it may sound, I have felt a new loneliness since the king departed. While he was here, beneath my despair there was always hope that he might come to me.' She broke off, waves of self-pity gushing through her.

'Perhaps the king would have responded to trust, to some other approach than your attacking him unjustly,' Rupa suggested tactfully, well aware of what had transpired.

'What other approach when he neglected me, when he was not there at the time I needed him most. What should come first, a kingdom or a human being, his wife?' A gust of anger at her helplessness swept the princess. 'Are we human beings, we Yakka women, or chattels?'

'Chattels, my lady. The pots men use for their cooking.'

'Not me, Rupa. No man will ever treat me as a chattel. If I were so inclined, I could have remained in my father's palace, married Prince Tikka and . . .' Her voice trailed off as she remembered how Prince Tikka treated his women.

'How about being gentle and loving with the king?'

'I can't.'

'Why not? I know you have it in you.'

'I do, but he must bring it out. Besides, it's probably too late already.'

Rupa sighed. 'Someone must break the deadlock. Otherwise, the more withdrawn you get with a man, the more he drifts away.'

'How would you know?'

'I had a lover once.'

'You never told me.'

'There was nothing to say. He was a hunter. I lost him by being young and foolish like you – I was only thirteen at the time. We are the physically weaker sex, my lady. We can only rule our men if we let them treat us like chattels, but become as necessary for their sustenance as the cooking pot. I realized this too late, for I was taken into the service of the palace and . . .'

'Your life ended.'

'That life ended. A new one began. One can always start a new life.'

'I don't want a new life, I want the old one, that life I was promised, for which I gave up everything, my people, my kin, my father. Besides, we women should not have to use cunning to possess the same rights as men.'

Rupa shrugged. 'I for one am too small and weak to fight for anything. I take whatever life gives me.'

'Well, I want to fight, Rupa. Will you help me?'

Rupa stared at her awhile, then comprehended her meaning. 'I am bound to help you in your duties as a priestess,' she responded.

'I knew I could depend on you. Let me think about it.' The princess watched a moth flutter around the yellow flame of one of the wall-tapers. I'm like that moth she thought. Suddenly, its flutter sounds seem so tiny that they only heighten the silence of the world. She felt herself drawn into that silence and it did not take her long to doze off.

When she awoke again, Rupa was lying on her mat on the floor and the entire palace had to be asleep, for the sand-clock on the table showed that it was past the midnight hour. Indeed, the whole world *was* asleep . . . and she alone in it. She began to cry, silently at first, then racked by sobs, tasting the salt tears as they ran into her mouth.

Rupa was awake on the instant, concern on her face. 'What is it, my lady? You sound like a lost child.'

'I feel like one. Where can I turn for comfort?'

'Turn to yourself my lady.' The mellow voice was soothing. 'That is the only source.'

'Noo . . . o!' The princess drummed her heels on the bed in sheer frustration. She looked through the window grille at the sky outside.

On the instant, she heard the flap of wings, saw a streak of black between two grilles and sat up, startled, her eyes searching. She knew what it was even before she identified the tiny bat, now hanging from a brown rafter, looking at her with its piercing dark eyes. She recalled those other bats hanging on stark branches in the jungle. An owl hooted in the distance. The smell of resin from the incense burners intruded into her consciousness.

She broke into a cold sweat, yet her body was suddenly fevered. Her gods had sent their messsengers. She had known true happiness, true security, even sexual release, only when she worshipped her demon gods and cohabited with them. She had deserted them, for what?

Fear mounted within her and her breathing became laboured, her heart thudding against her ribs. 'Rupa, I gave my virginity to a mortal, pretending it was the god's command,' she whispered. 'In truth, I did so because I desired the man. My one hope is to go back whence I came. I must become a priestess of my gods again. I must cease cohabiting with a mortal, swear never more to co-habit with men or to bear any more children. I must dedicate my babies to my gods. As for King Vijaya . . .' Her laugh was bitter. 'I shall ensure that he has no other progeny, so that my children shall rule the kingdom when he dies.' She glanced at the bassinets, feeling fiercely protective of the two little mites that lay in them. Flesh of her flesh, blood of her blood, bone of her bone, the products of her body and her sustenance, her milk-filled breasts stirred with intense tenderness for them, a surging desire to be suckled so that she could give them life through the stuff of her body.

She realized that Rupa had made no comment. 'You and I are returning alone to our house tomorrow.' she declared. 'Bindu can look after the babies. You can move about more freely than I. You know the things you must gather for me from the jungle. Two evenings hence, you shall help with the ritual.'

Two days later, they walked through the shadows of evening towards the ancient graveyard in the heart of the jungle which contained the fresh grave necessary for the ritual, not knowing that Prince Vijaya was on the eve of battle. When she told the fortress commander that she felt lonely in the palace with the king gone, the commander agreed to her moving back to her house for the time being. She carried a clay image of King Vijaya in a small bag slung over her shoulder. She had personally sculpted it, incorporating in the clay a few red-gold hairs from the king's head, some of his nail clippings, two threads of a *dhoti* worn by him and a small handful of sand he had once walked on. His full name was written on the base of the image.

Rupa carried the rest of the materials, nails specially made of a composition of gold, silver, copper, iron and lead, a *mal bulath thattuwa* on which to place a flower offering, a few *rath mal*, *idda mal* and jasmine flowers, each kind packed in a separate, large *goda-pora* leaf. She also had in her sack a human bone, some popped-rice, a cobra's fang, each wrapped in separate leaves, some human blood in a clay container, also a young king-coconut cut down at one end so that it could be easily pierced, a *kanya nool*, a virgin thread, a small fire-pot and some resin.

Having eluded the guard at the rear of the house, the two women now threaded their way along a narrow dirt path. The sunlight barely squeezed through the dense branches of *sal* and wood-apple pressing overhead. Thorn bushes blocked both sides of the path, making it hardly visible. Parakeets chattered in the tree-tops, an occasional oriole whistled, a strange bird went 'berp . . . berp, berp, berp . . .' and skimmed through the branches, startling the princess. She glanced at Rupa, noting her unhappiness about the whole adventure; but nothing could soften the cold, hard knot of determination in her own mind. She had to perform this ceremony for her survival and for that of her twin children.

The path curved into a small sunlit clearing. A herd of deer stopped grazing, heads lifted at the intrusion, then bounded away leaving the smell of stale fur.

They went through the clearing and entered the relative darkness of the jungle again, walking in silence. Now the princess felt only anticipation at what she was about to do, a sense of finality.

The next clearing was fringed by dark jungle trees. It contained rows of low, black-earth mounds, scattered with yellow *kapuru-mal*, white and red temple flowers and white jasmine, the Yakka burial ground. Some of the petals were fresh, from recent burials, others were fading, or had died and decayed. The clearing was strangely still, as if deserted by man, animal, bird and even insect.

The princess opened her bag, Rupa her sack. They laid their materials on the black soil at the edge of the clearing. They made two *pidayni thattuwas* by placing upon each *thattuwa* the human bone, popped rice, human blood and a cobra's fang. They placed both *thattuwas* and the king coconut on the most recent grave. The princess stepped on to

346

the grave while Rupa traced the white *kanya-nool* around it. The princess lay on the grave with her head to the north. The earth felt vibrant beneath her bare back. Her naked breasts tingled in response. She reached out, took one of the *thattuwas* and placed it at her right, the other on her left. Rupa deposited the fire-pot and resin near her right foot.

When Rupa withdrew to the edge of the clearing, the first veils of darkness began to spread over the golden sunlight. Placing the image of King Vijaya between her dark breasts, the princess began chanting her *angam*, charm, to the soft accompaniment of Rupa's *geta bere*, drum.

'Oh Brahma, Vishnu and Siva, may you be adored. O demon of red blood, of heart's blood, of rotting flesh, of graves and corpses, receive these my offerings. Look at them with your thousand eyes. Oh Brahma, Vishnu and Siva, may you be adored.

'Stop ye, Pilliran and Nilliran, for Wessa-Mony's power is great. There is not a demon who does not feel his power.

'Stop you, Kaluga Pillai, for Vishnu is great. His authority prevails over all demons.

'Stop thou, Elendri Deva!

'Stop, all ye demons! I make this sacrifice to you. I dedicate this human being to you. Blood of a delicious taste is my offering, heart, lungs, liver and marrow, all delicious, are yours. I deliver the human being upon my breasts to you. Take charge of him.

'Thou, Reeri Yaksanee, look upon him instantly, look upon his limbs and sinews, his virility. Lust thou to make him thine alone, so that he will spawn no more children save through thee, until after he has lain in death upon a similar grave. Remove the seed from his fruit, so that if his tree rise and grow, it shall never procreate.

'O Brahma, Vishnu and Siva, adoration be to you. The powers that originated from Queen Yasadora and the powers belonging to Vishnu, as they now prevail at the temple of the cannibal demons who once destroyed the

Prince Wisamatoma – by their powers I deliver this being to your charge.

'O Siddhi Maha Sohan *dewatawa*, thou son of Gajacumbacari, I deliver this being to thy charge.

'By these powers I command thee to deliver this human charge to Reeri Yaksanee, who will so lust for him that she will remove him from all other women and eat up all future seed from his twin fruit, so that if his tree reaches for the sun it shall be barren.

'Take this being for thine own, Reeri Yaksanee. I deliver him to thee. Hold him for thine own, so that all other beings who love him save thy priestess, who shall safeguard him for thee, shall ever drop away from him like shells from dried seed.

'Take charge of this being, Maha Sona *dewatawa*!

'Take charge of this being, Billay *dewatawa*!

'Take charge of this being, Dalla Sena, chief of demons. Take him.

'Thou, Siddhi Maha Sohan *deatawa*, look at him and take him.'

She held up the image of King Vijaya with both hands. 'All ye gods and demons, take charge of this being. Deliver this being to Reeri Yakseya, who will hand him over as a gift to his spouse, Reeri Yaksanee.

'Let this be so.'

She repeated the charm to the soft beat of Rupa's drum, over and over again, 108 times. Night had long fallen by the time she finally ended. Now she was ready for the *jeewum* that must accompany all charms.

She sat up. The drumming stopped. Rupa glided up and handed her the sandalwood paste in a little silver container. Holding the lid open, she pronounced the charm over the contents three times, then closed the lid with her right hand while holding the container on the back of the left hand.

She placed the container to the left side, opened it again and rubbed sandalwood paste on the image of King Vijaya, to make of him a scented offering. She closed the lid of the container again.

Rupa produced flint and tinder. The flame sparked and took. She applied it to the resin, which soon glowed red in the darkness, emitting grey smoke curls.

As soon as the smell of the resin smote her nostrils, the princess began her chant again.

'O restless spirits of the dead that wander without home, bear this human being upon the wings of incense, upon the grey smoke from the black resin. Suck his red blood, eat his lungs, eat his liver, eat his white marrow, eat out his heart for your sustenance, consume his seed as your reward for bearing him to Reeri Yakseya, who will bequeath him as a gift to his spouse, Reeri Yaksanee.'

It was ended. She was bathed in sweat. Childbearing had sapped some of her vitality. She felt utterly exhausted by the strain of concentration, the force, the will, the intensity she had brought to bear upon the ceremony. Yet a feeling of calm had taken root within her. She had created a storm, been ravaged by it and finally been left in peace.

She became conscious of that perpetual night sound, the creaking of crickets. The scream of a peacock burst through the branches, sounding like the wail of a lost soul. The air had turned cold. She shivered.

As she rose to her feet, she remembered that her charm would mean separation for King Vijaya even from his twin brother, Prince Lala, whom she respected and admired. Her heart blanched.

Then the full force of this, her own irrevocable sexual separation from King Vijaya, swept over her, turning her entrails to water. She was indeed the lost soul. Not even the thought of going back to her demon gods as their penitent priestess, their new matron, could comfort her. The tears started. She would never become whole with her spouse again.

She screamed aloud and ran sobbing though the jungle.

Rupa followed, sick at the thought of having to report the event to the hated Ujjeni.

Chapter 25

We lay beneath the stars, listening to the distant sounds of revelry from the enemy encampment, waiting for the dawn which would bring death to some of us, glory to others. Though the palace was far away, I was in the Kalyani kingdom again, which I had hoped to revisit under different circumstances. I wondered what Sundari was doing and whether I would ever see her again, since we were in foreign territory, heavily outnumbered, two thousand to the enemy's five thousand. Yet this was the opportunity for which King Vijaya had been waiting, when King Tikka would become over-confident and risk open battle with us because he had the manpower. King Ra-hula's maps had helped my brother select the site for battle, about one *yojana* east of the Kalyani capital. 'We shall move here and await the enemy,' he had stated.

Our army had swept out of the fortress as planned on the very night that Viswan brought us news of the seizure of power in Kalyani and we managed to reach the river in relative secrecy, knowing that the crossing would expose our move to the enemy. Our force, which included two companies of cavalry and two of chariots, each of one hundred men, had effected the crossing on rafts we commandeered.

We had had two full days in which to reconnoitre the area thoroughly. Our artillery and long-bowmen had tested the actual battle site for range, our front-line elements were ensconced behind earthworks and all our men were fully rested. The enemy had responded immediately to the challenge. Our spies and patrols reported their entire force moving against us in mass formation, leaving Kalyani unguarded. Now, the sounds of laughter and song from their distant campfire, around which a great deal of local *ra* was obviously being consumed, drifted across the lonely plains above the chirp of crickets.

King Vijaya had selected a superb site for the action. We were positioned on two wooded hill features, with a valley between fronting a long grassy plain. The river was to our right and a swamp to our left. This meant that our bowmen could fire their volleys from under cover and we ran no risk of attacks on our flanks or rear. There would also be other advantages, if the king's plan worked.

I found myself unable to sleep, my mind white, bright, alert even when I closed my eyes. The hard ground, with my saddle for a pillow, my brown leather armour, my knife, sword, shield and spear beside me, were grim reminders of where I might be tomorrow. Though I knew that my *atman* was not ready for death, I was not really afraid to die. My strongest fears were of being maimed, blinded, incapacitated for life, unable to see Sundari again, or to woo her.

And there was God, gazing directly, almost accusingly, at me from the starlit blue skies, with never a cloud to veil His gaze. He seemed so clean, so pure up there, while I lay breathing the stench of the night soil from our field latrines. Not all my clinging to *dharma*, the duty of my station, enabled me to reconcile my contemplated actions with the love of God, so that the moral conflict kept turning and twisting within me.

I shivered at the chill of the night and glanced towards my brother, a dark outline covered by his cloak. He was fast asleep. Even as I watched, those familiar snore sounds began to escape him. How different we are in this respect, I thought, and yet, are we not really alike, since each of us is an extreme of a different sort, my brother in his totally relaxed state and I in my introspective condition? Realizing this unloosed terror. I fought the feeling desperately, trying to identify my fears, telling myself that ignorance alone causes fear, but in vain. I began to tremble and shiver, the sweat running cold down my spine. My feet were exposed and cold, one way in which fear can enter a man. I drew my cloak over my legs.

I looked up at the blue heavens, the myriad winking stars echoed by the blinking of fireflies on the dusky treetops, seeking God again in my need. And I connected with Him.

Do not be afraid, God said clearly in His voiceless message. *Those you face are just as afraid as you are. Those who must die, will die, but what more is the end of life than a change, no different from the ageing of your body moment by moment, only accelerated by your heightened perception of its single moment? What is death, but the sloughing off of the body, as a river casts off the silt it carries, a snake its skin or a man his clothes? I do not recognize your life and death as separate identities. All is* kharma/vipaka, *cause and effect, within my own body as I ordain, so you will remain a part of it whatever your state. Have no terror either of death, or the morrow, for before you die you may have to endure more than untimely death.*

The first warning of the approach of that grim dawn was the cry of jungle cockerels, to which I had awoken, my limbs stiff with the cold. Silly birds, I thought crossly, you always crow at the false dawn, not knowing that it is but the first brash attempt of the sun to light up the earth, only to slide off before succeeding the next time by a slow, sneak attack. Will you cockerels never learn?

Silly men, I imagined I could now hear those cockerels replying. You fight, you kill, you never learn, until death lays you low. I shivered, threw off my cloak and stretched. I rubbed the sleep from my eyes and rose to my feet, noticing that my brother's resting place was vacant.

Our entire camp was stirring, but men were as yet only dim figures in the gloom, folding their blankets or testing their arms with the chink or clank of metal. A breeze stirred hopelessly in the dark branches and revived the foul smell of night soil. What an ill omen, I thought dismally, such a smell with which to start the day. I went to find a vacancy in our field latrines on the river side of our hill, returning the 'Greetings, Prince!' coming from the slumber-coated voices of men I passed with a cheerfulness I did not feel.

By the time the eastern sky behind us began to glow with the first rose-gold of the morning sun, like a tassel beneath a vast umbrella of pale blue sky, we were all in position, I sitting my grey Arabi at our headquarters on a tree-shaded promontory half-way up the hill overlooking the valley. Branch and bush to our side and in front of us had been cleared by our men, so that we could not only see the entire battlefield and our bowmen, foot-soldiers and pike-men immediately below us, but also into the flat land behind us, east of the valley, where our cavalry, chariots and catapults had been massed. Our formations seemed so solid that I could not help a glance of admiration at the great bulk of King Vijaya, firmly astride his black mount, Indra, beside me.

As we waited for the enemy to make their move I became aware of the flow-sound of the river, gleaming gold in the dawn-light, the whistle of birds in the trees, even the drip of diamond dewdrops hanging from dark branches and the leather-sweat odour of our mounts. The ko-ha-a . . . a . . . of the köel bird resounding through the air was like a call to arms, till I realized that, unlike us, foolish human beings, Nature was certainly not waiting breathlessly for the battle to be joined.

Our men were strangely quiet and I wondered what they were thinking. I could feel their auras, a strange mixture of dread, tension, courage, unconcern. Someone, doubtless moved by bravado, must have made a joke, for the sound of laughter came up the hill, a little strained, a little forced, not the hearty bellow of men feasting round a camp-fire during exercises.

At that moment the sun cleared the distant hills and my eyes swept across the plain. How green it looked, until some trick of the cloud-wounded sun turned parts of it into great splotches of blood-red, beyond which, to my dismay, I saw the great host of the enemy line silently drawn up about a thousand yards away, row upon row of fighting men in close formation, sunlight glinting occasionally on a weapon, serried spears thrusting though the air like spikes from some vast moat.

I heard the creak of my brother's saddle. He had risen in his stirrups to stare intently across the plain. 'How did they do it?' he demanded almost to himself. 'Our patrols reported none.'

'Do what?' I enquired.

'See there!'

My eyes followed his pointing finger. My heart missed a beat when I identified what I had seen. 'Elephants!' I exclaimed, and counted. 'Twenty of them. Obviously protected by leather, with fortified howdahs on their backs.' I pondered awhile. 'They must have been brought up during the night. That makes twenty to one against us. What do we do now?'

Before he could reply, a commotion arose from the valley below us. Someone was scrambling fast up the hillside from our left flank.

Ujjeni broke through the trees, panting and sweating in spite of the coolness of the morning, his chest heaving, the comb-shaped jaws wide with the effort of catching his breath. We wheeled our horses to face him. There was open fury in the sunken sockets of his eyes. He paused and made obeisance to the king.

'What's wrong, commander?' King Vijaya's voice was authoritative and surprisingly calm.

'Evil news, Sire.' Ujjeni panted. 'Some Yakka in one of Upa's companies, in reserve, sabotaged most of our chariots last night and have disappeared.'

'What have they done?'

'Removed the sharp-bladed scythes from the wheels. Now

we can only use the chariots to transport our men behind the enemy lines, not as attack vehicles.'

'Any solution?'

'Yes, Lord. Thank the devas, Vijit brought along spares. But it will take us at least an hour more before we can repair the damage. I hope my Lord's timing will not be upset.'

'Could you shorten the time span with assistance from up front?'

'No. Only so many can work on the wheels at one time.'

'Have it done as quickly as possible then. Meanwhile, we shall proceed as planned, except that the chariots will attack only when every single one of them is in perfect offensive operation. Go now and look to it personally.'

Ujjeni could not resist a thrust. 'You can see, Lord, why it is that your other loyal commanders and I advised against trusting these Yakkas.' He glared at me malevolently. 'It should be a good lesson to all Yakka-lovers.'

He listened to King Vijaya's further orders and smiled appreciatively, then made obeisance, turned abruptly and ran down the hillside.

I glanced at my brother, furious at Ujjeni's unjust generalization, but unwilling to debate any issue at this critical moment. The king undoubtedly sensed my mood, for he looked at me grimly. 'There's much truth in what our loyal Ujjeni says,' he asserted bluntly. He paused, reflecting. 'With trouble up front and in our rear, a river at one flank and a swamp on the other – by our own choice to prevent attacks – we seem to be surrounded by troubles.' Yet he did not appear to be unduly disturbed. While I greatly admired his fortitude, however, I was hurt by his obvious displeasure with me, especially at such a moment, when we were about to join desperate battle with a ruthless foe.

Suddenly I became filled with that strange sense of bleak isolation I had experienced briefly the day I saw Silindu's corpse dangling from the tree. This time, however, it created a sudden cold fury within me, followed by a determination, hard as frost on the high mountains, to be my own person in the future. Then gladness came for I realized that I was now totally free to pursue my love for Sundari.

As we awaited the start of the battle, King Vijaya pondered this fresh example of Yakka treachery aloud. 'We have been so good to the Yakka, especially those in the army,' he declared harshly. 'We have uplifted them from their miserable condition and dealt with them all justly.' His face twisted. 'This is it. We thought that we should not judge the entire race because of a few traitors, that we must not blame Yakka for siding with Yakka, that we as the king must rise above our subjects in wisdom and understanding. But there comes a time when even a king has to recognize that there are good and bad subjects, loyalists and traitors. Yakka, Naga, they are all alike, treacherous, never to be trusted.'

Ujjeni could not have succeeded more in his aims if he had quietly engineered the sabotage himself.

Chapter 26

King Vijaya mince-gaited his black Scindhi horse to the edge of the promontory, where most of our men could see him, and paused, surveying our troops. He had not yet donned his leather helmet, so his red hair glistened in the sunlight. The commanders had already been warned to look to this point for signals and they began calling to their men for attention. In a few minutes, our forces were hushed into silence, all eyes turned intently upon the magnificent figure in brown leather cuirass firmly astride his great steed.

The king rose, stood on his stirrups and raised his right hand. 'Listen to us, men,' he cried in that deep voice he could pitch into the distance. 'We are opposed by a force almost three times our own in number. Our enemy have even brought twenty armoured elephants to the front during the night. At our rear, their spies have sabotaged our chariots. So what do we do?' He brought his hand down, then looked to his left down the valley and slowly turned his massive head to the right at our front. No sound emerged in the stillness, so engrossed were we with our king, so totally absorbed by his presence. Long moments passed while all gazed at him, almost with a single pair of eyes.

Suddenly, his great laugh bellowed forth from him, shocking us. It rolled down the valley and along the hills. It spread across the plain. He pointed sideways, his right arm outstretched towards the enemy lines. 'We laugh them to scorn!' he roared. 'Laugh now, men. Laugh at this pitiful enemy! Here is the moment we have waited for to avenge the insults, the pillaging of our villages, the murder of our comrades. We are superior to this rabble force in courage, in training, in discipline, in determination, in the will to triumph.' He paused. 'Laugh now!' he roared again. 'Laugh with us. Send back your answer to those who will rot on the battlefield today.'

The laughter broke from our ranks, hesitant at first, then gathering in volume and momentum until it became an enormous flood of sound rolling through the valley and across the plain, many of the men pointing at the enemy. From being a response to a command, our laughter soon became part of our bodies, minds and spirits.

I could sense a tremour going through the enemy line even at that distance. Those men out there could not know what to make of this unexpected development. Even as I stopped laughing, trying to discern the enemies' reaction, the king's hand slashed down, demanding silence. The laughter died away sooner than it had commenced, but the very air vibrated with the new heart and spirit of our men.

'We have planned our response to those elephants,' the king shouted through the silence. 'You shall soon witness it. This day shall be a historic one for our new nation, for it will end with our possession of two kingdoms instead of one. Swear now before the gods you cherish most that you shall win or die on this battlefield. Only blood, blood, blood, red enemy blood can quench our thirst for vengeance, redeem the blood of our dead comrades. We command you now. Give us back our Sinhala battle-cry.' His voice rose to an enormous roar. 'Kill! Kill! Kill!'

He paused, tawny eyes blazing, magnificent.

'Kill! Kill! Kill! . . . Kill, Kill, Kill!' The answer reverberated across the plain and to the heavens. I found myself screaming it involuntarily. Kill! Kill! Kill! My entire being swaying beyond the limits of madness.

The King raised his hand for silence. 'Now give us your sacred oath!' he bellowed. 'Victory or death!'

'I swear . . . I swear . . . I swear . . .' The sounds arose deafeningly from two thousand throats. This king was a god and we were his to command.

As the great noise died down an answering roar rolled back from across the plain, the defiant screams of the enemy. Their trumpets began to wail, their drums to throb. Their champions broke through the wall of soldiers, dancing in front of their troops, hurling insults, boosting the morale of their men, working them up to blood-lust. The battlefield became a welter of sound, above which the trumpeting of the enemy elephants rose.

Early that same morning, Uday, the Venerable Sri Ravindra, sat in meditation in his cell in the Kalyani palace. Clad in the yellow robe of the *bhikku*, cross-legged on his mat in the lotus pose, he was so absorbed, having just completed the observance of the *Dasa-sila*, the ten precepts, that he made no response when the attendant opened the door and entered, unbidden. The small Naga, half-bent with age, the wrinkled black skin pouching on his body, long white hair hanging over his shoulders, was dressed in the white *dhoti* and sash of the *upasakaya*. He knelt before the monk. 'Forgive my intrusion, venerable Sir, but I have the news that you desired me to bring to you regardless.'

Uday flickered out of his meditation. 'You did right,' he assured the man. 'Give us your news.'

'The trading ships arrived in our harbour last night, venerable Sir. The traders landed immediately. They are now well on their way.'

'Trade that benefits the people of this realm is as our saintly fellow *bhikku*, the venerable Sri Ra-hula, desired,' Uday responded. 'All is well.'

The twenty enemy champions were all huge men, clad in leather corselets, with helmets and thigh guards, their great swords drawn, shields at the arm. They led the dense array of their slow-marching troops, leaping in the air, pointing towards our lines, shrieking, hurling insults and imprecations at us, cavorting, stiffening the morale of their men.

360

Behind them, the grey figures of the plodding elephants soon became more definitive. They were followed by the flag man of each company carrying its gaudy banner. Then came the foot soldiers, marching to the 'the-ra! the-ruppa-ra . . ! the-ra! . . . the-ruppa-ra!' of the drums, which kindled the body while the wailing of trumpets blazed it to a frenzy. I patted my nervous horse's neck to calm it.

In contrast, our own ranks had fallen silent. All our companies displayed only one flag, the gold Sinha, lion, rampant, sword in upraised right paw against a blood-red field, and we had neither pipes, trumpets nor drums to stiffen us.

As the enemy drew closer, faces came to view in the sunlight. One of the champions was a veteran with long silver hair and a dark, hatchet face. A leading infantry commander had heavy, saturnine features topping a tall, gaunt body. One of the pike-men was so fat and round-faced that his snarling teeth sat strangely upon features that should have been jolly. To his right was a serious-faced youth, no more than a boy in his mid-teens, marching with intensity in his slender face, uttering no sound. This was not a mass, but people, individuals, human beings. Suddenly, I was glad I could not see their eyes, lest I know compassion, or see the hatred, the anger, the determination to kill me and experience fear.

The king silently sat his black steed, intent upon the approach of the enemy, controlling the backward movements of the horse, permitting each toss of its fiery head with gentle hands. Suddenly, he raised his right hand and brought it slashing down. A faint, sizzling sound arose. Seconds passed while the enemy advanced, shouting, cursing.

I did not count the number of flashes until the flame-balls from the catapults beneath us were in the air. Twenty of them rocketed across the pale blue sky like shooting stars, trailing smoke. They fell just short of the advancing elephants, which squealed above the din. The enemy front ranks hesitated.

The screaming enemy champions brandished their weapons, urging their men forward. The smell of pitch from the flame-balls clawed its way into my nostrils.

The next twenty flame-balls sailed across the air. Two of them struck an elephant, spreading fiery pitch over its armour. One scored a direct hit on a howdah. As it blazed, men dived from it, their clothes smouldering. The giant beasts began stampeding, trunks upraised, trumpeting madly. The battlefield became a nightmare of sound as they turned and charged back, scattering men like soil before giant grey ploughs. The enemy ranks broke.

Then I saw him.

Sitting firmly astride a grey horse, the Yakka King Tikka, clad in leather armour, appeared at the front of his troops, almost a lone rider. Using his whip, supported by one of his champions, he literally lashed his men back into line. Soon they were joined by the enormous Prince Jaya, a brave figure on a great charger.

The enemy regrouped and resumed their advance, led by those two inexorable figures on horseback.

'Prepare to fire! . . . Fire!' I heard the commands above the din, then a single great twang, and the hiss of arrows. The volley arched into the air, threw speeding shadows on the green grass below. Enemy shields were lifted in defence, but men fell screaming before the accuracy of the volley.

'Prepare to fire! . . . Fire!'

The second volley was even more deadly. It was followed by a third, a fourth, a fifth, a sixth. The enemy were falling like flies, screaming, cursing, shrieking in pain. But still they kept advancing. A thrill of admiration shot through me, followed by a throb of fear at having to face such determined men in close combat.

King Vijaya signalled with his hand again. Our cavalry surged forward in column, lances upright, pennants fluttering, led by the dashing Vijit. The pounding of horses' hooves drumming above the clamour of battle, they broke through the valley, fanned out and halted.

Vijit barked an order. The lances were levelled in a single movement, staves pointing at the heart of the enemy. A single trumpet sounded. The cavalrymen charged, yelling out their battle cries. They gathered speed, hit the advancing enemy with the force of a thunderbolt and burst through, cutting huge swathes through the great body mass. As men fell, the enemy line gave. Horses squealed and reared. A few of our riders disappeared beneath the seething mass of humanity. I saw King Tikka and Prince Jaya valiantly fighting off four of our cavalrymen.

Just before their momentum ended, the cavalry broke engagement, wheeled to make a full circle and galloped back, Vijit still at their head, lances gone, slashing through the mass of enemy with long swords. They regrouped at the entrance to the valley. Grooms gave them spare lances and they charged again, yelling fiercely, but they were too close to the enemy to develop a full gallop. Running into a solid wall of resistance, they wheeled round and galloped back. The enemy bowmen at their rear started firing volleys. Arrows came like bees at us, swarming through the air. Some of our men fell, screaming, others clawed at arrows in their bodies.

The enemy were now close to our earthworks. The hail of our javelins sent men reeling. King Tikka and Prince Jaya spurred their horses ahead, leading their men inexorably forward. I could see them now, tough, sweating men with blood-lust in their eyes.

Our sharp pikes halted them at the earthworks, thrusting, bloodied, withdrawing only to thrust again. The enemy hurled a great mass of spears, but to no avail. Thrust, withdraw, thrust. Our pikes were being used with telling effect from behind the earthworks, but as one enemy fell he was instantly replaced by another. There was no stopping them. Led by King Tikka and Prince Jaya, they would swamp us by sheer weight of numbers. My stomach vibrated with fear.

It happened suddenly. In the distance, a great shuddering at the enemy's rear, like a stream disturbed by the flood waters of a burst dam, the enemy ranks parting as if a giant scythe had slashed through them.

'They made it!' King Vijaya cried, rising in the saddle.

And indeed they had. Our cavalry and chariot squadrons that King Vijaya had sent across the ocean from Thamba-Panni in our three ships and other boats he had comman-deered, had landed at the Kalyani harbour and raced eastwards to take the enemy in the rear exactly as the king had planned from King Ra-hula's maps. They were now cutting our stunned foes into ribbons.

At that very moment, with a thunder of wheels, our reserve chariots, their repairs completed, burst from the valley to crash through the enemy's front. .

Hit in the front and the rear, hemmed in by the river and the swamp, even the bravest of the enemy became confused. They broke ranks and turned, not knowing which way to go. Some men leapt into the water. Others dashed into the swamp. King Tikka and Prince Jaya began spurring their way through the jostling mass of men, heading for the river.

'King Tikka is mine, leave him to me!' King Vijaya screamed, forgetting the royal plural. He drew his sword, yelling out his battle-cry, 'A Lion to the kill! A Lion to the kill!' and set his horse down the hillside.

I pointed my sword and followed him screaming, demented, the blood-lust raging within me, throbbing with joy at the release of fear.

In the wake of our chariots, we cut through the enemy, trampling those in our way beneath our horses' hooves. The animals neighed and whinnied, but kept charging on urged by our spurs. I parried a sword-thrust at my right leg, circled my sword and ran my opponent through the throat. First blood, I exulted as I saw it red upon my sword blade.

From then on, it was a massacre. I lost count of the number of men I killed, slithering over the fallen amid the din and chaos of that battlefield. The cries of the wounded mingled with screams for mercy as men fell and were trodden underfoot. Soon it was impossible to distinguish friend from foe, but I followed the commanding figure of King Vijaya, towering over everyone else as he fought his way towards the river. He took a spear thrust on the side of his chest beneath his arm and jerked sideways, nearly falling off his saddle. I spurred my horse, transferred my sword to my left hand and hacked his opponent down.

Blood began trickling from the king's wounds, but he only laughed. He nodded his thanks to me and urged his horse forward. As I changed my sword arm again, I felt a searing stab on my right shoulder. The pain was so vivid, stars shot behind my eyes. I nearly blacked out. With a tremendous effort of will, I swung my horse round and charged my opponent just as he drew back his spear for a second thrust.

I would have been too late, but King Vijaya burst in, his sword swinging. I saw terror in the enemy's eyes as he went down before the weight of the king's horse. I shouted my thanks to the king.

That was a mistake. One should never be diverted even for a moment in close fighting. A spear thrust upwards at me. In panic, I tried to wheel away. A sword shot forth. The spear was deflected. The king had saved my life again. 'That's twice,' he shouted, without looking at me. 'We are even now!'

Through the mass of savage, bearded faces, the glinting weapons, the clash of metal, the screams and groans, I remembered having saved my brother's life twice, once on the bund in the Yakka village and again today. He had wiped out the score.

With a wild cry, the king spurred his horse into the teeth of the fighting.

My brain cleared. I was bleeding from my wound but did not care.

Through a gap in the wild mêlée, I saw King Tikka ride furiously to the water's edge. I made after him. Too late. Horse and man vanished over the bank, accompanied by great numbers of the enemy who were leaping madly into the river. Prince Jaya attempted to follow but his horse shied at the last moment. The great, fat body slithered off the horse's back. Then the gap between the men closed and I was fighting for my life again.

As King Tikka's horse hit the water, he slid off its back to ease the weight, then reins in hand swam alongside the animal. He directed the horse downstream for he had to make the best speed and place the greatest distance between himself and the battlefield. He fought back tears of rage. Hamy appeared swimming beside him. 'May the gods damn them all,' King Tikka screamed. 'Five thousand men and twenty elephants against two thousand and we were beaten by cunning. Oh demon gods, why do you not flay King Vijaya alive, then burn him in hell?'

You do not want to admit that you have been out-generalled, then overwhelmed by superior tactics and training, Hamy thought sadly as he dog-paddled towards the opposite bank. Our men fought valiantly against these odds. It was your vanity that demanded victory in open battle. Now over a year of effort has ended. Discreetly, he remained silent.

'It was the accursed Nagas who first broke under the enemy assaults,' King Tikka cried between breaths. 'Our two 'housand Yakka stood firm. I'll kill that fat Prince Jaya if I ever lay hands on him.'

The river was full of men. A few, who could not swim, cried aloud for help, flailed madly and sank in great gurgles of sound. The water was cold. Hamy looked over his left shoulder. A familiar face grinned at him. Kira, with his habitual grin.

King Tikka must have noticed Kira too. 'What the hell is there to smile about when all is lost?' he demanded. 'Wipe that grin off your face, or I'll bury it in this water.'

Kira looked around him, puzzled, searching for someone who might be grinning. He composed his features into a scowl, then spat water. 'What happened to that pig, Prince Jaya?' he demanded.

'Fell off his horse on the river bank.' Hamy gasped the reply between dog-paddles.

'Lucky for him,' King Tikka shouted. 'Else, I'd have his liver. Now shut up and keep on swimming. We must escape to fight the accursed Arya another day.'

Still gripping his horse's reins, King Tikka ducked as a hail of enemy arrows splashed into the water just ahead of them. Hamy followed suit. He swallowed water and came up spluttering. He heard men's shrieks and saw three of them sink, arrows sticking out of them like great pins. Patches of red appeared on the water but were quickly swept away.

How they got safely to the other side, Hamy never knew, but once they clambered up the slippery bank and stood dripping beneath the shelter of trees, King Tikka took command as naturally as if he had never lost it. He assembled all those who had escaped, even the wounded, and lined them up. A head count showed two hundred and thirty-one, all Yakka. Each group fled to its own security, Hamy thought idly, the Naga to the swamp, the Yakka across the river. A few of the men looked disheartened, but most of them were angry, ashamed, eager for battle again. Stragglers kept joining them, attracted as brave men are to the rallying point. Knowing the fierce pride of the Yakka hunters, Hamy could not help glowing even in defeat.

King Tikka surveyed the assembled men, all of them wet, most of them bedraggled and without weapons.

'We do not have much time, men,' he declared. 'For we

are now greatly outnumbered and the enemy will soon be here. But your presence tells us that this is not the end, merely a new beginning. We have discovered the measure and strength of the Arya in open battle. Henceforth, we shall only attack his weakness.'

Chapter 27

Prince Jaya sat on the trampled green grass of the river bank
bathed in sweat, his fat legs spread out before him, holding
his right thigh with both hands.

Firmly astride his black charger, King Vijaya towered
over the fallen prince and stared down at him grimly. The
prince essayed a weak smile, then his great body stiffened
and his plump features crumpled in a grimace of pain, the
slits of the eyes almost disappearing.

The battle was over. Its pandemonium had died down to
a strange stillness heightened by the occasional groan of a
wounded man. Crows circled overhead, small black boats
sailing on a cloudless blue sky. A pitiless noontime sun beat
down, its heat sharpening the smell of raw blood. Our men
crowded behind us, watching their king.

Prince Jaya lifted his head again, the slits opened and the
dark eyes peeped from behind them. '*Aney!* I fell from my
horse, no?' he said, as if that explained everything.

A surprised expression flitted across the king's face. He
was panting lightly, his nostrils flaring. 'So we observe,' he
commented drily. His tawny eyes gleamed with anger, the
black pinpoints sharp, but he said no more.

Moments passed. Still the king made no comment but
merely continued to look down at Prince Jaya. The men
behind us shifted uncomfortably. Someone cleared his
throat.

Prince Jaya smiled again. 'I think I have broken my leg,
Sire. Otherwise I would have greeted you as befits a king,
with obeisance.'

'Your greeting did indeed befit a king. Three thousand of
your own men offering us obeisance, not to mention two

thousand of your ally's subjects. Over four thousand of them
are now making a permanent obeisance to someone or
something. Not to us. To your ambition perhaps? Or could
they be worshipping that wise King Ra-hula whom you so
foully murdered?'

'*Tchikay*, why do you say that? It was that rascal Tikka
who murdered our king. I was stunned. It really made me
sick, you know. So I asked myself, how to join a murderer?
But after all, the deed was done and Kalyani needed me,
because otherwise Tikka would have seized the throne.'

'H'mm. Interesting. So you are a patriot after all.'

The plump face lifted with a curious pride, the fat body
stiffening in dignity. 'Not even in victory can you accuse me,
Sire, of not being a patriot. Each of us had his own way of
demonstrating love for country. I showed mine by organizing the overthrow of a king who emasculated our people.
Kalyani has been unconquered for centuries. The substitution
of moral force for physical made us weak and vulnerable.
Your very presence here with such a superbly trained body
of fighting men demonstrates your faith in military power.
Why then do you fault me for a similar belief? After all, is
that not what we are talking about?'

The king's leonine face grew thoughtful. 'So you say that
it is common belief in military power that creates adversaries. We . . . ll that sounds simple, but you may be right.
You did indeed become our adversary. Now we have won
and you have lost. So you must pay the price.' The king
began to turn away.

'Take him . . .' he began. And I knew he was going to say
'and hang him if you can find a stout enough rope, otherwise
behead him.'

'*Tchikay!*' The Prince observed calmly. 'We lost, no?'
Something in his voice made the king turn back to stare at
him. The black eyes now gleamed mischievously. 'King Ra-
hula was a dangerous man because he did not believe in
gods. That is the weakness of Buddha's religion, such non-

belief also makes a man dangerous, no?'

I glanced sharply at the king and knew that, by some chance in a million, Prince Jaya had struck the right chord. The Prince must have noted it too, because he went on quietly. 'Now, I for one am a man who believes in gods, so I pose no personal threat to you, Sire. The fact that I opposed you on the battlefield merely indicates that I made an error of judgement. When you seized the kingdom you now call Thamba-Panni, you subjugated the Yakka people. Kalyani is a more civilized, sophisticated kingdom. Its people will not readily give you subjection. You may have me killed, but I believe you too wise for that.' A bold smile crossed his face. 'Otherwise, why did you talk to me when you could have ordered my summary execution. You know you can use me, alive, whereas you may find me a greater enemy dead.'

The conquering king and the fallen prince stared at each other in the glaring sunlight. Can you conquer yourself, my brother, I wondered, and be wise in victory?

Long moments passed while my brother, frowning, struggled against pride, the desire for vengeance and whatever else tormented him, wisdom even. Finally, his brow cleared. 'You are right, Prince,' he declared. 'Your life shall be spared if you give us your solemn word of honour to be loyal and true to us, never to oppose us.'

'I do not know what honour I have left, Sire,' Prince Jaya observed with great dignity. 'For I no longer understand what honour is.' His eyes twinkled. 'Do you?' He pondered, seeming to gather his thoughts. 'I do not really value my life beyond my pride,' he finally proceeded. 'After all, what is life if there is no pride in it? Yet I'm not certain whether my unshaken pride means I have any honour left. So, having nothing on which to swear, I shall simply give you my word. I shall be your loyal, devoted subject while you rule my people wisely. If this is enough for you, spare me and use me. Otherwise . . .' The impish smile reappeared. He drew a finger sharply across his neck and made a clicking noise. 'Slit my throat, for you will be hard put to find a rope strong enough with which to hang me!'

While you rule my people wisely . . . I remembered the words in King Ra-hula's letter. Reflecting on what the word 'wisely' meant to the dead king, on my brother's disenchantment with his Yakka and Naga subjects and his increasing belief in Arya supremacy, I wondered what the value of Prince Jaya's offer could be. Would it prove to be only as good as the conqueror permitted? Yet, Prince Jaya had put the king in a position where refusal to accept the promise would have been a public rejection of the plea to rule wisely. With that, all Prince Jaya's actions and words during the brief conversation fell into place. With grudging admiration, I acknowledged his cunning.

'You are hereby appointed Prince Regent of Kalyani, under suitable supervision.' I heard my brother's decree almost with consternation. 'We shall expect you to travel throughout the kingdom and enlist the support of the people to our rule. Many of your kinsmen have been killed in battle today, so your family status and your personal influence will count even more. We shall not demean ourselves or you with threats, but you well know the consequences of treason, or even disloyalty.' King Vijaya turned his mount. 'Summon the commanders to our headquarters,' he directed me and rode back towards the hill.

The men began to disperse to their pre-appointed assembly areas. 'A wise and merciful king,' one of the Arya observed quietly.

'I don't know, *machan*, brother,' his companion replied. 'The fat one seems as cunning as a jackal to me.'

King Vijaya, having dismounted and removed his leather cuirass, awaited us on the promontory. Hot and sweaty from battle, the blood clotting on my clothes, my shoulder wound throbbing and stiffening, I was grateful for the shade of that banyan tree.

The commanders arrived in relays, Vijit first, his dare-devil smile white beneath the black moustache. Sweaty and bloodstained, he seemed very pleased with life and had a right to be for he had acquitted himself with distinction. Ujjeni came next, his face more like a death's head than ever with strain, his features grim and drawn. He and his reserves, being fresh, had been flung into the forefront of the battle as soon as our cavalry and chariots from the ships had smashed through the enemy's rear. They had literally massacred the broken groups of the enemy, a task after Ujjeni's heart, I told myself grimly. Pandu and Upa, the chariot commanders, came next, followed by Uraw, Sum-itta and Anu together.

When he finally faced us, the king stood tall, his hands clasped behind him in his usual pose. 'So King Tikka escaped!' He stated in disgust.

'But, Lord, I saw him plunge into the river,' Sumitta demurred. 'Surely . . .'

'Men saw him and his horse clamber safely to the other side,' the king interrupted. 'No matter. We shall pursue him without delay.'

'Let me take a troop of cavalry after him immediately, Lord,' Vijit begged.

King Vijaya regarded him thoughtfully, then shook his head. 'No, we feel that the final settlement of this contest will be between us two kings alone,' he declared. 'We estimate that three to four hundred of his men made it safely across the river. They will fade into the countryside and head for home, then resort to their former tactics. We cannot afford to let that happen. Our body count reveals one hundred and twelve of our troops, including eighty-eight Yakkas, killed, with thirty-three seriously wounded. We have killed at least three thousand of the enemy and taken seven hundred prisoners, including their own wounded. With three hundred Yakka across the river, we can assume that the remaining survivors are Naga, who escaped through the swamp.'

'Begging your pardon, Sire.' It was Ujjeni intervening, his yellow tooth-comb smile smug. 'But we no longer have any seriously wounded enemy.'

'How so?'

'The only safe enemy is a dead enemy, Lord. Besides, we don't have facilities to care for so many wounded. I had them put out of their misery.'

I recoiled with horror, then heard the king say, in astonishment, 'You mean you had them murdered?'

'Exterminated would be a better word, Sire.' Ujjeni shot me a venomous glance as if daring me to intervene. 'Most of them were Yakka vermin who brought about this battle, who organized the sabotage of our chariots, whose king is your implacable foe, who destroyed our villages and threaten your life. They were not murdered, therefore, but as I said before, merely exterminated.' He held the king's gaze boldly. 'This is a war, Sire. We cannot afford the men to guard prisoners. And it will be a telling lesson to others.'

King Vijaya eyed Ujjeni grimly, then nodded slowly, accepting the challenge to his own ruthlessness. 'Very well,' he conceded. 'Make arrangements for the burial of the Yakkas, with their usual ritual, including flowers on the grave, and for the cremation of the Nagas and of our men with appropriate rites. Upa, two of your companies shall see to it, after which we have another task for you. Meanwhile, Uraw, start having fires built and get out the cooking pots so that our men can have a hot meal within the hour. Pandu, you shall gather any remaining prisoners together for we propose using them in the future, especially the Kalyani Nagas.'

Among the commanders only Vijit seemed to share my revulsion at Ujjeni's ghastly deed and he had acknowledged it with a single, swift glance towards me. We have entered a grim phase of our life, I reflected. We are conquerors of yet another kingdom, this time taken in open battle instead of through a single night's massacre, but what's the difference?

I directed my attention to the king's battle orders.

'Our intentions are first to take the capital city of Kalyani and secure the Kalyani kingdom. To this end, Upa shall head battle group one, consisting of two companies of cavalry under Vijit's deputy commander, Rohan, one company of chariots under Pandu, three companies of foot soldiers and one of bowmen. Battle group one will speed to Kalyani as soon as they have had their meal. Upa, you shall commandeer wagons locally for the foot soldiers. These wagons will later be returned to their owners with compensation for their use. Your battle group will be reinforced later by such elements of the former Kalyani army, loyal to King Ra-hula, as will give up monasticism for the barracks and whatever other soldiers Prince Jaya can muster.'

Hearing murmurs of doubt that arose from his commanders at this last statement, the king told them of his decision regarding Prince Jaya, and his reasons for it, and was eventually rewarded with nods of approval from all except Ujjeni.

'The remaining companies of chariots and two of foot soldiers, forming battle group two under Uraw, will return to Thamba-Panni as soon as they have finished the tasks allotted to them here,' the king continued. 'Battle group three, commanded by Vijit and consisting of the remainder of our forces, shall accompany us to the mountains to fulfil our second intention, to take the Yakka capital of Sita Eli-ja.'

The commanders exclaimed their approval in unison as the king continued. 'Today's victory will be hollow if we do not drive the enemy from his lair. After we have conquered all this side of the island, we shall proceed to bring the Ruhuna kingdom under our sovereignty, either by an alliance of subjugation or by conquest . . .'

'Arey! . . . Arey! . . . Arey!' the commanders gleefully cried.

'Three kingdoms in one operation,' my brother declared. 'Meanwhile, you will each work out detailed plans for your moves, including weapons, supplies and transportation. Ujjeni will prepare them for battle group three. Report these details to us within the hour. Remember, it is imperative that battle groups one and three move out with the utmost speed. We want the capital of Kalyani held by nightfall and we expect to seize Sita Eli-ja with our cavalry elements within the next two days.'

The king was right to press home the strategic advantages of victory, improved morale and the effects of today's battle both on our troops and on the people of the *uda rata* kingdom while its capital lay defenceless. Besides, King Tikka's guerilla warfare option would be greatly diminished without a base.

'Prince Lala shall proceed immediately to Kalyani as its ruler and sub-king, assisted by Prince Jaya,' I heard my brother say. The words stunned me. Was I being banished from his side? It hurt and I looked bewildered. Then I remembered my decision to be my own man and thought of Sundari. Some of the pain dissipated, to be replaced by a sort of wild joy. Perhaps God had responded to my need for her and my desire to be free from fraternal bondage.

By the time we had finished our noonday meal and King Vijaya had gone over the marching plans of the group commanders, a semblance of order had been restored to the area of the battlefield. Our wounded had been looked after by our physicians and evacuated in commandeered wagons. The king and I had our own spear-wounds examined, cleaned and treated with medicinal *patthus*, ointment, and covered by field bandages.

The dead had been placed in orderly rows, our men and the Nagas by great funeral pyres, the Yakkas beside newly-dug graves. It was a sad sight, friend and foe united under the wide and sunlit sky the common bond of death, yet separated even in death by religious beliefs.

When the men were assembled on the plain, I said prayers aloud for the dead, commending their *atman* back to Brahma the Creator, thinking secretly to myself that I was commending their souls to God. Upa had found a Yakka priest among the prisoners, a lean hunchback with white hair and dark skin who looked like a wizard of old. He uttered prayers in a strange, mystical hodge-podge of words and performed the ceremony of fire, earth, air and water over the bodies of the Yakka dead before they were consigned to their flower-strewn graves.

When the earth was shovelled over the graves and the flaming funeral pyres were roaring, blazing and spewing grey smoke, the men had an hour's break before marching again. The king bade me walk with him along the river bank. The pitiless sun had combined with trampling feet and hooves to make the green grass of dawn brittle and sere. Smoke from the pyres drifted in our direction, brought by the winds of the fires' own creation. Before long, the horrible smell of burning flesh intruded.

As I glanced sideways at the king, I knew with sadness that more than a separation of our bodies had occurred today. His tawny eyes were bright in the sunlight, opaque with his own withdrawal. 'You shall rule Kalyani as king, answerable to no one but us,' he stated firmly. 'So you shall rule as we would rule.' A grim note entered his voice. 'You shall follow our policies to the letter. We have no doubt as to your fiscal and administrative capabilities. It is your liberalism that we fear.' He stopped to face me, the black pinpoints of his eyes sharp, but with a hint of tiredness on the sides of his face.

'Sire, I can but give you loyalty despite my views,' I responded gravely. 'If the time ever comes when I feel that my loyalty to you is in fundamental conflict with my ideals and principles, I shall tell you and you can relieve me of my responsibilities.'

'What principles, what ideals?'

'Those that spring from my *atman*.'

'Your *atman* must compel you to give absolute obedience

to your king.'

'In all temporal matters, certainly, Sire. And you know you have it from me. But when we come to the elements of human rights, the basic equality of man, I must follow the dictates of my God.'

He stopped in his tracks and I with him.

'Your God? You mean the One God you have occasionally spoken of? Ahura Mazda?' His low laugh seemed to be one of relief. 'We are glad that you believe in gods at least. We have been concerned lest you share your Buddhist friends' refusal to believe in gods.'

'Sire, I did not speak of gods. Those who believe in gods are indeed, as you once said, relatively harmless. They can produce a new god whenever they need to set aside their principles in order to obey their monarch, or can even turn him into a god if need be. I'm very much afraid that my one God could lead me to a position I would not give up for any living man or woman of whatever rank.'

He drew in his breath sharply. Anger flamed in his eyes. Yet I felt only a great calm, for I was free at last; my mind had escaped from the prison of all the conceptions it had acquired since I was a baby.

'Can you not accept the concept of a god-king who, though subordinate to your one God, still speaks for Him?' My brother seemed to be pleading.

'Sire, how can you ask that of me when you yourself do not believe in gods? Would that not be hypocrisy?'

'You dare defy us?' The question came out in a low growl from deep within.

'Never that, Sire,' My voice sounded as gentle and serene in my own ears as my liberated mind felt. 'I merely wanted to be truthful with you, as always. You will unfailingly have obedience from me in all things temporal, in the ruling of the kingdoms, but you cannot compel me, or any man, to change ideals. Even if we appeared to agree with you, how could you know what lay within the secret recesses of our minds?

So, rather than being defiant, my words are truly the humble submission of a devoted subject, the truth from depths that no man may normally probe. If there seems to be defiance, it is not in my words, or my attitude, Sire, but in your inability to accept them. I beg you to see this.'

He stared at me awhile, then turned to look at the river, glistening in the sunshine, splashing and flowing unconcerned. 'Perhaps you are right,' he declared, but I could sense the formality of the words and beneath it the same heartache and aloneness within him that I was experiencing. At least I had God. He no longer had anyone.

'I do not believe in a God,' he finally stated in a low voice, dropping the royal plural, as if communing with himself. 'Like our grandfather, Sinha, I do not believe in God, or gods, or religion, or worship. In fact, I do not believe in anything except what *is* at any given moment and realities such as I am aware of . . .' he hesitated, 'like the godliness of kings or Arya superiority, which are not so much facts as such entities as sunshine and rain, peace and storm, but nonetheless realities of my present situation. The earth, space, the stars, sun, wind and rain, people and things, merely *are* and will continue to be. There was no creation, therefore there is no Creator. There is superior and there is subordinate, the lion is king of the jungle, the deer trembles at his approach, the jackal feeds off his kill. There is neither time, nor space, not even infinity or eternity, except within the consciousness of man or beast, as they measure it.'

He stared at the ground and I knew he was merely reflecting, not expecting any response from me. 'Since we merely *are* at any one given moment, we must accept the facts of each moment,' he continued gravely. 'For you, among those facts are that, as your king, I have the power of life and death over you, that you value your life and that you must follow my dictates. You may therefore have any ideals you like, but never dare to give them practical expression even in words, while I am your king.'

379

I did not know whether to be appalled at the negative aspects of his thinking, impressed by its profundity or thrilled that he should have bared himself to me at long last – something I knew he had never done before with any man – or angry at his threat. My most dominating reaction, however, was total surprise at finding him such a deep thinker. I had always regarded him as a purely practical man, acting nowadays on the sure instinct of good judgement. Now his philosophy frightened me, for we were both men of principles and our principles were diametrically opposed, the opposite points of the circle of which Uday had warned.

Then realization of the far-reaching nature of his demand gripped me. I suddenly shook with anger at him. Hot words rushed to my lips, but I held them back. I said a silent prayer to God for help and the right words came out almost immediately. 'You have my humble submission, Sire.'

As King Vijaya cantered at the head of the detachment heading for the mountain kingdom, he felt disturbed by the conversation with his brother. Thus far he had been content to allow Lala to play with the toys of idealism. This afternoon, he had run into the strength of the individual for the first time and he felt pre-empted, a jumper who had missed his timing. He knew men with such firm convictions were strong, inflexible, even dangerous. More, he felt let down where he had expected unquestioning love. It never occurred to him that unquestioning obedience was not necessarily love. He tried to forget his concerns by reflecting on his pride in the advance guard that rode with him, on how to get to Sita Eli-ja without delay and occupy it while the main invasion force, consisting mostly of foot-soldiers under Ujjeni, followed in horse-drawn wagons.

The mounted scouts he had sent ahead to patrol the front entered the foothills of the mountains. Soon, when these changed to the lower reaches of dark, wooded mountains, their pace slowed. Flow-sounds reached him above the drumming of hooves and the creaking of leather and his pulses quickened. It was the river. The maps Ra-hula's spies had prepared of the region above eastern Kalyani were accurate.

The muddy river appeared round a deep bend in the trail, a red-brown flood racing towards them, broad, swift-moving, swollen, splashing and frothing between high banks and over great black rocks before veering sharply away. The trail, now running alongside, must have been merely a footpath originally, for it hugged the steep side of the mountain, where it had been widened by the cutting of sharp embankments. The drippy desolation of the place, shrouded by the cloudy evening and the choking smell of rotting vegetation, heightened his sense of unease. Some instinct pin-pricked its warning. He had never liked being locked in. He turned in his saddle. 'Race down to Sena, who commands the main body of our vanguard,' he ordered a young aide. 'Bid him halt at the first available clearing, take up defensive positions there and await word from us by rider to continue his advance. We shall move cautiously from now on, a section at a time.'

The young aide swivelled his horse and began threading his way back along the side of the long lines of the advancing cavalry column. Satisfied but still alert, the king slowed his black to a trot. Soon, however, rubble and small rocks along the winding trail made it safer for him to pull back his mount to a walk.

They passed a looping bend revealing a series of narrow ravines, through which the trail began twisting and turning tortuously. It was cooler here, with a light rain falling, the sun hidden behind grey clouds and the mountain range.

Two of the scouts suddenly appeared, trotting back as fast as the ground would allow, their chestnut horses, mouths flecked by foam, pulling against the bit, hooves slipping on uneven stones. King Vijaya reined in, raised his hand to halt the column. A silence descended on the trail, broken only by the diminishing clippety, clop, clop and slither of the approaching hooves. The two riders brought their steeds to a halt in front of the king and saluted him. They were both clean-shaven, well-built young Arya, with sunburned skins and dark hair, their helmets and uniforms wet, faces dripping.

'Trouble ahead, Sire!' One of them announced. 'The trail round a sharp bend is impassable.'

'How?'

'It's definitely a roadblock of some kind. Trees hewn down and boulders . . .' He paused at the sound of a rumbling behind the column, followed by great crashing sounds and a thunderous roar. The earth trembled like a mansion rattling in a storm. Even before he turned his horse, the king had identified the cause and the knowledge hit him in the pit of the stomach with sickening force. He had under-rated the resolution and cunning of the enemy and had allowed himself to be trapped exactly as in Upa Gama, with a rushing river on one flank, a high embankment with dense jungle on the other, roadblocks ahead and at his rear. Only this time the river was no refuge.

'We are trapped!' Vijit cried, drawing his sword.

Fresh rumblings, thuds and jarring resounded directly above. The king glanced up knowing that boulders were rolling down even before he saw them. Bows twanged from the mountainside and arrows came hissing. A stricken horse neighed and reared, unseating its rider. An Arya cavalryman groaned, sighed and gently slid off his horse, another toppled with an arrow in his chest.

Chapter 28

Seated in the lotus pose, meditating in his cell at the Kalyani palace, Uday heard a knock at the door. The attendant who entered was the ancient *upasakaya*, clad in a white *dhoti* and sash.

'The Arya have won a great battle against King Tikka and Prince Jaya, *ney*,' he mouthed through toothless gums. 'Now they have come and taken over the palace. They are white like you. Only splattered with blood and dust. Apoi! . . . Their leader is a fine-looking man, named Lord Upa. He desires you to attend him immediately in the audience hall, Venerable Sir.'

'Please tell Lord Upa that I shall attend him without delay.'

He acknowledged the attendant's obeisance with a slow nod of his head.

Within minutes, Uday was in the audience hall. He saw a burly man with black hair facing one of the high-grilled windows, gazing at the golden evening sunlight, the green outlines of trees against a blue sky scarred by grey clouds, with an ear cocked towards the sound of children's voices from a nearby playground.

Upa turned swiftly at the quiet swish of Uday's robes. He had broad, florid features, now dust-streaked, and a hawk-like nose poised above a great black moustache.

Upa came directly to the point. 'Greetings from my lord, King Vijaya Sinha-Bahu, who by conquest of the *pata rata* this day is now its king and, being the ruler of two independent kingdoms, is now a *maharajah*, Great King. We won a great battle today over the joint armies of King Tikka and Prince Jaya. King Tikka has fled. Prince Jaya, whom we took prisoner, will return to the palace as Prince Regent, under Prince Lala Sinha-Bahu, whom you know and who is the new sub-king of Kalyani. The Great King has graciously spared Prince Jaya's life and bestowed the new appointment on him as a token that the rights and traditions of the native people of Kalyani will be safeguarded.'

'Why do you tell us this?'

'I would like to say that it is because of the person you are, where you come from, the respect we have for your Noble Order and your eminence as a missionary monk.' Upa paused, his piercing dark eyes sharp on Uday's face.

Uday had already sensed that Upa was a thinking man. Now some instinct told him that he should also inspire the commander's respect. 'That is what you would *like* to say, my dear sir, but what is it that you *do* say?'

He was rewarded by the flicker of interest that shot through Upa's eyes. 'Do you not believe that they are both the same?' The commander demanded.

'We of the Noble Order, who have conquered the passions, neither believe nor disbelieve anything except the Four Precepts.'

'Do you not believe that King Vijaya has the power of life and death over you at this moment?'

'We do not.'

'How can you say that?'

'There are so many fallacies in your statement, child. Firstly, only the *kharmic* cycle causes life and death. And that is no power, merely the chain of causation. For instance, if your Great King decrees that someone shall die, that person could die before the execution of the order, or the king could change his mind, or could himself die before the order is carried out, when someone else could countermand it. And even if the order was indeed carried out, death would be caused by the severing of the prisoner's head, the executioner's sword merely being an instrument, not by the Great King. Who or what then has the power of life and

384

death? The Great King, his executioner, the executioner's sword, circumstances, the laws of life, the inabililty of the prisoner to survive without a head? Wherein lies the power?'

Upa's interest had obviously quickened as he listened to Uday's words and some of the tiredness left his face. 'That is a unique exposition. Please go on.'

'Other men yet would say that the Great King is no more than the executioner of their gods, who wield the real power. What is power, after all? Merely a word that human beings use to describe an authority they ascribe to the elements, kings, landlords, Brahmans, even beggars and their loved ones. It is merely a recognition of the ability to cause physical and mental pain, or a change of circumstances, though all the while everything does keep changing. As for whatever it is that you claim for your king . . .' He allowed a faint smile to touch his features. 'He can hardly exercise this power you have just arrogated to him at this moment, my dear one, can he?'

Upa shook his head, as a shaggy dog that has just escaped the river shakes its body. 'You have given me much to ponder on,' he conceded. 'No wonder Prince Lala is reported to be fascinated by you.' He paused. 'You and he will have ample opportunity for discourse.' His white teeth became bared in a mischievous grin. 'Presumably by virtue of the power the king has to make such an appointment!'

'You must ask yourself again, what in truth is that power?' Uday smiled again. 'We presume our new sub-king will be along shortly.'

Upa clasped his hands behind his back. 'He was to leave about two hours after we did.'

'Doubtless with the rest of the army of occupation.'

'No. The entire army of occupation came ahead with me. The reason why I asked to see you immediately was because the Great King commanded me to do so, in order to request your cooperation in obtaining the support of the local Buddhist population, who are said to hold you in veneration.'

'Words, my child. We but preach the Four Precepts and commend the Noble Eightfold Path to all men, including yourself. We have no power. The power of sight is within each individual's human consciousness. The power of individual change is within each individual's *kharmic* consciousness. But we do admit that many of the Buddhists of Kalyani will follow our lead.' He paused, his gaze benign. 'Your king will undoubtedly deem it to be what it is not, our power!'

Upa acknowledged the thrust with an upraised hand. He rose slightly on his toes and then settled back firmly on both feet. 'Prince Lala will be here before nightfall.'

Trapped on the trail beneath the wooded mountainside, with the raging torrent of the river below and a cascade of rocks, boulders and arrows from above, the trail was mass confusion, horses screaming and neighing, men groaning, hooves clattering. Three men were killed by arrows, two others, dumped by their horses, were crushed by boulders, before King Vijaya directed the squadron to the shelter of the embankment. Within moments, discipline told and men began edging forward on foot along the trail under cover of the bank to explore the possibility of climbing the mountain and closing with the enemy. Others, on horseback, trotted back, seeking a way up the hillside.

Thanking his instinct for having ordered the main body of the vanguard to halt at the clearing, thus avoiding the ambush, the king quietly assessed his situation. The embankment gave protection from the boulders still thundering down the hillside and the hail of stones and arrows. The enemy must be inferior in numbers, otherwise they would have closed in by now as they had done at Upa Gama. Also, having fled the battle only that morning, they would be poorly armed. Quite apart from any possible help from the main body, his conclusion was to go for the enemy.

'Dismount!' His voice rang out above the din. 'Troop

leaders assemble alongside us.' He turned to Vijit, grim-faced beside him. 'Not you, Vijit. You've got to reach Sena and his men.' He nodded towards the rushing torrent. 'That's your route. Lead them up the mountain and attack along its crest.'

Vijit nodded. A man of few words, he waited for a lull in the barrage from above and spurred his bay across the trail. Man and horse slipped down the steep slope, headlong towards the raging, mud-red waters. They were still slithering when they reached the river's edge. King Vijaya stiffened in his saddle, held his breath.

Somehow Vijit's horse found its rear-legs again and shoved into the river, slanted by Vijit to face upstream. Horse and man hit the water with a tremendous splash. Vijit slipped off the saddle, holding firmly to it. The waters soon swept him round the bend.

The king turned to the ten troop-leaders. 'Lalith, you're the senior, aren't you?'

'Yes, Lord.' The reply came from a lean, dare-devil Arya, a thin, black moustache accenting the rakish lines of his face.

'Get back to the men exploring the rear. Leave a few to look after the horses and lead the rest up the mountain. Attack the enemy from the east. Make sure that none of them escape over the other side. We shall lead the rest up the trail and take the enemy from the south, driving them towards Sena's men under Vijit.' A grim note entered his voice. 'That will leave the Yakka with only one alternative.' He nodded downwards. 'The river. The signal to commence your attack will be a long halloo. Let's go.'

Excitement seethed within King Vijaya as he led the long line of his men on foot up the narrow gully, keeping away from a fast-flowing rivulet of muddy water that gushed down over orange and brown stones. Two scouts ahead ensured that the gully did not become a deathtrap. The rain had ceased, but continued to drip off the dark-green branches of the occasional spathodea tree that spotted an otherwise barren hillside. Leaping lightly from stone to stone, clambering on well-sprung joints up the face of a rock, the king was alert for danger.

As he neared the summit of the hill, he saw it lightly covered by a film of low cloud, just below which his two scouts crouched side by side behind a great black rock. One of the scouts gave him the open palm signal for caution. He bent low, raced up to them and threw himself flat beside the men, getting his breath. The scout pointed silently down a slight slope and across the flat plateau beneath.

Mist lay like damp smoke on the plateau. At the edge of a copse to the left the king saw the shadowy figures of the enemy, obviously regrouping. He estimated that there were about thirty of them. King Tikka must be with them. He would face his mortal enemy at last. There was not a moment to lose. He clenched his right fist and moved the hand quickly up and down, giving the fast-run signal to the rest of the men. He waited until the first dozen had joined him, rose to his feet, drew his sword and silently pointed in the direction of the enemy. 'We've got them,' he whispered fiercely to the leading men. 'Follow me in line along the summit, fast and quiet. Attack from the edge of the copse. Drive them west.'

He climbed up the rock and leapt lightly down to the wet grass below. Half-hidden by the mist, he began loping lightly along the plateau, followed by the long line of grim-faced men. Never dreaming that they would be out-manoeuvred, the Yakka were chattering to each other with delight. 'We got the fornicating bastards!' One of them, a stumpy black gorilla of a man, shouted.

He must have sensed the attackers before he saw them, for his eyes suddenly widened and his jaw dropped. King Vijaya leapt forward with a wild cry. His sword flashed out, thrusting. The point sank into the Yakka's stomach like a stake into mud. The man groaned and groped for the sword. But the king had already withdrawn it. The man's trembling hands reached to staunch the dark red blood gouting from the wound. His eyes crossed, he gave an agonized croak and collapsed.

A burly Yakka, long knife drawn, made for the king. Screaming madly, the king swung his bloodied sword in a tremendous sideways slash. The blade sliced through the thick neck. The force of the blow sent the man sprawling, the severed head dangling from his body.

With blood-curdling war-cries, Vijaya's men leapt into the attack. The king went berserk. Roaring like a lion, he charged into the mass of the enemy, slashing, thrusting, shoving, smashing, cutting, chopping. His sword became useless in the crush. The Yakkas quickly recovered from their surprise. Long knives drawn, they closed for in-fighting. The king dropped his sword, kneed a Yakka who charged him and drew his knife. Two Yakka jumped him from both sides. He stumbled and fell, both men on top of him. Desperately using his enormous strength, he turned as he fell. He saw a shock of matted hair, a black-bearded face, white teeth bared in a bestial snarl. The upraised knife pointed straight at his heart.

I left for Kalyani with a cavalry escort of six men about two hours after my brother and his force had crossed the river in rafts. Within minutes, my shoulder wound opened up again and I began bleeding profusely. About two hours later, I began to feel depressed and ascribed it to loss of blood. Yet part of me was buoyed by the hope that I would somehow see Sundari again.

I was barely conscious of anything, except for the pounding hooves behind me, which seemed to go Sundari . . . Sundari, as I rode through the evening in a stupor, mechanically, my mind a blank, and it was with relief that I saw the flare-lights of the palace thrusting through the gloom. By the time we reached the palace, I felt so faint that I could have toppled from my saddle, except for deep-rooted resolve.

I was greeted in the audience hall by Uday and Upa. Though utterly exhausted, I summoned some reserve of strength to check with Upa regarding the disposition of our troops and their welfare. I directed him to summon me if there was an emergency and was led by Uday and followed by attendants to the king's former quarters. These were not the bare, monastic cell he had occupied during the last years of his life, but the old, luxurious rooms he had latterly reserved for visitors. I impatiently dismissed the attendants and turned to Uday. 'How is Sundari?' I began and a great wave of blackness enveloped me. I tried to speak but lost sight of the words. I felt myself sinking, sinking . . .

As always when in mortal danger, the upraised knife made King Vijaya's mind crystal clear, his reflexes sharp. He jerked violently upwards from the hips, wrestler fashion, using all his strength, twisting to the right just as the knife flashed downwards. It sliced through his doublet and embedded itself in the soft soil, leaving his opponent off-balance. The king turned back fully in the same movement, tossed the man from his body and ended on his haunches in a crouch. His left hand slashed sideways with all its power. The edge of his palm smashed into the man's neck. He felt the bones crunch. The stricken Yakka remained poised for a moment. Then his broken neck gave, his head slumped and he toppled over.

The king was already on his feet. The second Yakka, a slim, clean-shaven youth had risen also, Vijaya leapt forward and grabbed him, arms and all, in a bear hug. He started to squeeze. The youth was powerless even to struggle. His mouth opened as he clawed vainly for air. The king tightened his grip. In a haze, he noticed curious red swellings on the youth's neck, just below the ears. Then the dark eyes began to bulge. Croaking noises emerged from the throat and a spray of saliva hit the king's face. The smell was worse than a camel's breath, but the king kept squeezing regard-less. Blood started to ooze from the youth's nostrils, dribbling to his mouth. Suddenly the rib-cage cracked and the body went limp. The king flung it aside as if it were a scarecrow. Disgustedly, he wiped his saliva-strewn face on his sleeve. He grabbed a slim Yakka by the ankles, up-ended him, screaming and struggling. Using him as a club, the king leapt back into the wild struggle. Above the pandemonium of the battle, he suddenly heard the familiar Sinhala war-cry. The rest of the advance guard had arrived.

Knowing they were beaten, the Yakka broke off and fled towards the plateau at the summit of the hill. The king did not notice the dark figures scudding down the wooded slope towards the trail and the river because he was searching frantically for his sword. He saw it lying on the decayed leaves and pounced on it. With a blood-curdling cry, he led his men, screaming madly, in pursuit of the Yakka. As they raced across the green grass, a long row of heads appeared silhouetted on the skyline at the far end of the plateau. The fleeing men came to a shuddering halt. The heads became figures. Vijit had made it downstream and led Sena's group to the attack. What a perfect action, the king thought with elation as he raced forward with a burst of speed.

Totally surrounded, the fifty or so Yakka on the plateau were soon massacred to a man.

The king placed the point of his bloody sword on the ground and paused, panting, to survey the scene. It was good to breathe deeply of the pure mountain air. A flight of birds, winging homewards, speckled the overcast sky. He looked down at the sprawled figures of dead Yakka, some in grotesque poses, bloody wounds gaping like hungry mouths, the guts of one showing white against the open red drain of a stomach wound. The fury of battle had subsided and now all he felt was a tremendous elation. He was a conqueror. He was the invincible Arya. It was his destiny to lead the super-race. Therefore he was more than a superman. A feeling of immense power began surging through him. Though he did not believe in gods, he was a god-king. Standing four-square on that mountain-top, the world at his feet, he gloried in his station and none of his men dared approach him.

Finally, one of them found the courage to intrude. 'Sire, King Tikka and two others escaped down the hillside.'

That very evening the Princess Kuveni was seated on a stool on the verandah opposite the room that fronted the centre courtyard of her house, indulging in her favourite pastime, spinning. Normally, she found the whirr of the wheel soothing, a quiet, domestic sound that brought her tranquillity. This evening, however, it jarred on her, sending the same shivers through her body as when a sharp wooden nail scrapes brick. Not even the golden sunlight, lying quietly on trees, overgrown bushes and neglected flower beds, could erase the feeling of apprehension within her.

Suddenly, she could bear it no longer. She stopped her spinning. 'Rupa, I don't know what it is, but I am just terrified!' She exclaimed.

Rupa, seated on a yellow mat on the flagstone floor beside her, shelling raw cadju-nuts, glanced up sharply, dark eyes full of concern. 'What are you afraid of, my lady?'

'My lord is in grave danger.'

'Why should that worry you, when you have placed a charm to destroy him?'

'Not to destroy him, Rupa. Merely to isolate him from people. Yes . . .' a fierce note entered her voice . . . 'even from Prince Lala. So that I can have him all to myself.'

'Not to mention a slight disability, you requested for my lord, that he should have no more children,' Rupa commented drily.

'Oh, Rupa! You never understand, do you? I did not intend that he should not have any more children from *me*. Of course I want that. In fact, the more children he gives me the greater will be my hold on him.'

'But the charm is absolute, my lady. Besides, how could you wish any of it for someone you love?'

'You have never loved with such passion, never sacrificed so much for love, so you cannot understand. Well, even if the charm does make him completely infertile, I shall still be satisfied, for I shall then have the treasure of the hunt, his only heirs.'

Rupa grew thoughtful.

'Once he is isolated, he will need me, he will turn to me again,' the princess continued. 'I feel it in my blood. Rupa, Rupa, if you only knew how much I love him, how much I desire him, how I yearn for him to be my own. I have described our lovemaking to you, the giant size of his organ, the tenderness of his foreplay, the ferocity of his love. And my response . . . Oh! . . . We are perfectly matched, he and I, the lion and the black panther.'

'I did not know they could be crossed.'

'Any two organs can be crossed when they become erect! Don't you remember how Karuna, the queen's maid, was caught with a dog at her rear and the story of that great hunter, Suda, with his she-goat?' The princess chuckled at the recollection.

Rupa laughed. 'Indeed I do, my lady.' She hesitated . . . 'You have not been yourself in recent weeks,' she finally ventured. 'Today, you are suddenly and completely different. It's almost as if you have twin masks that you can take on and off at will.'

'I'm a *katussa*, chameleon, Rupa.' Kuveni's eyes, her fears forgotten, were dancing with merriment.

'A *katussa* changes its colour to suit its surroundings. You are different.'

'I know, I feel as if I have suddenly been released from a prison. Some power that held me in thrall has let go.' She paused, reflecting. 'Yes, that's it. Returning to our gods gave me that release. Now I can feel again, feel concern for my man, too. A great darkness has been lifted from my mind since our ritual last night. Yet now I know my lord is in danger. If anything happens to him, what will I do? I shall wither and die like the leaves on that pomegranate bush. I don't want to be angry with him or withdrawn from him. Whenever it happens, it comes from a blinding pain within me, pain *he* has caused . . . then . . . then, I'm someone else . . . from way back in the past, perhaps from another birth. I'm a prisoner of that person, with no real will of my own. Words, actions, spring forth from me, regardless . . .' Her voice trailed off.

'If my lord is in danger, we can both *will* him out of it,' Rupa said quietly.

'Of course. Let's put our work aside, fix our minds and do that. I want him back safe!'

Chapter 29

Here we go, into a river again, Hamy thought, as he, King Tikka and Kira struggled against the rushing waters. Only this time, it's colder and muddier than before. Seeing King Tikka making for the opposite bank, where alone safety lay, he dog-paddled, warding off the rocks that seemed to spring at him with his hands, allowing the river-flow to hustle him downstream but making diagonally for his objective.

What a day it had been, beginning with such promise at dawn, crushed by the ignominy of defeat before noon, a see-saw back to the hopes of a typical Yakka ambush in the evening and now a rout before nightfall. What was the cause? Whenever King Tikka gave way to emotion, as distinct from ambition, he rushed in where even the devas would not tread. Hamy could not blame his leader for the decision to give battle to the Arya with such vastly superior numbers and the elephants. Victory would have assured him of all four kingdoms. He had gambled and lost. Soaked to the skin again, Hamy suddenly knew that the Yakka were destined to be a subject people. The Arya were more modern, a superior race. The Yakka had best acknowledge this stark fact, learn to live with it, and attempt to capitalize on it.

The three men finally stood shivering in the gloom beneath the trees on the opposite bank.

What should he do now, Hamy wondered. Desert? The knowledge that he would not lay even colder in him than the water outside, for he recognized that his loyalty to King Tikka was greater than his desire to preserve himself. He would stand beside his king to the end. After that . . . he allowed himself a few moments of dreaming. He would go to Kalyani to learn the Buddha's doctrine. The kind of blessed peace that had allowed King Ra-hula to die with dignity attracted him like a light at the end of a black tunnel.

'Lord, I know a farmer, one of us, who lives a short distance away,' Kira volunteered through chattering teeth. 'Let us make for his place. He will have fresh clothes, food and a warm bed.'

King Tikka was silent. Standing erect, he gazed at the opposite bank. He would have cut a pathetic, forlorn figure were it not for the unquenchable fire that blazed within him. He seemed to be savouring some secret delight. That secret suddenly dawned on Hamy, almost paralysing him with terror. His king's defeats, including the one they had just endured, from which they had been lucky to escape with their lives, had only added dry wood to the obsession with vengeance that consumed the man. Far from seeing the ashes of defeat, King Tikka was now warming his chilled heart with a dream of vengeance so vivid that it suddenly brought a fiendish smile to his lips.

'Very well,' King Tikka agreed, coming out of his trance. 'We shall rest at the house of your friend for tonight.' He sounded perfectly calm and normal, as if discussing a stop in the middle of a hunt. 'The gods obviously do not intend giving us victory of the Arya in open battle.' He paused. 'We shall therefore achieve it by other means. Since the enemy are heading for Sita Eli-ja, it would not be safe for us to go there. Also, it will be difficult to rally our people to what they would now consider a lost cause. Tomorrow we shall make for the Ruhuna kingdom, not to enlist the aid of its decrepit King Deva Raja, but to hide until we can achieve our goal of killing King Vijaya.'

'Lord, how will that help?' Kira enquired timorously.

'Cut off the head and the snake perishes.' Only an edge that crept into King Tikka's voice betrayed his mental condition. He is mad, Hamy decided, then remembered his own dream whilst in the river, of ending his days as a student of the doctrine. Is it insane then to dream at all, or to want to achieve one's dreams, he wondered. If so, all men are mad.

Though eager to regroup his forces and press on, King Vijaya decided that it would be important to obtain as much intelligence as possible from the few prisoners they had taken. Also, the rain had ceased, darkness was approaching and night falls quickly in the hill-country. 'The men shall make camp along the trail,' he commanded Vijit. 'Join us there and have the first prisoner brought to us for questioning.'

By dusk, the troops had rubbed down, watered and fed their horses and had managed to get campfires blazing. King Vijaya now sat back against the embankment, over which a rough canopy had been erected, his feet spread out, feeling very relaxed. His stomach was nicely full from the field ration of warmed up *chupatti* served with mutton barbecued on an improvised spit, which had been brought up by the cook detail from the service wagons. A pleasant sense of comradeship permeated the makeshift encampment. The yellow-red glow of the flames, the crackle and spit of burning wood and the scent of the grey smoke made him feel once again that here was his real home. How different from the palace, with a wife from whom he was estranged and two Yakka children who would end up looking like devils themselves. It made him want to savour everything he had, his birthright from his grandfather, comradeship with other men around a campfire. He felt it an intrusion when Vijit brought the Yakka prisoner to him.

In the flickering firelight, the man was revealed as small but burly, with the Yakka's out-thrust chest and buttocks. He was of middle-age. His black hair was long, curly and matted, his dark face wide with high cheek-bones, a flat nose, wide-flaring nostrils and thick purple lips. His eyes were small and almost black, but sharp and alert. With his long arms and loose-jointed gait, he could have been an ape save for the deerskin cloth and cotton cloak that did not hide a hairy chest. Is that what my heirs will look like, the king wondered.

Yet the man bore himself with an inner dignity and seemed unafraid, even resigned to his fate, as he came to a halt before the king.

'What is your name?' the king demanded.

'Ranna, Lord.' The voice was husky, rusted with lack of use.

'Where is your home?'

'In Sita Eli-ja.'

'Capital of the *uda rata* kingdom. Whom do you serve?'

'King Tikka.'

'Did he lead you today?'

'Yes, Lord.'

'Where will he now make for?'

Ranna's eyes had been on the king. They dropped and he remained silent.

'Speak, fellow.'

Ranna continued looking at the ground.

Vijit started forward, his hand upraised. 'Answer the king!' he commanded angrily.

King Vijaya signalled Vijit to hold back. 'It is obvious that you know but don't wish to speak,' he said pleasantly. 'We commend your loyalty. But you must realize that loyalty has to extend from both sides. Twice today, in battles with us, your king has deserted his men. Why should you be loyal to him?'

The man's eyes lifted to those of the king. 'May I speak freely, Lord?'

'Certainly.'

'You are a king. You know that rulers have higher purposes, often dictated to them by the gods. To that extent, they too are gods. It is not for a subject to question a king's motives or actions.' A tremor of earnestness arose in Ranna's voice. 'Lord, I know my king to be a brave man. We have often hunted together in the jungles. He never once ran away through cowardice. And if he did, Lord, all I can do is give him my loyalty, not my judgement.'

A long and moving speech for one who obviously does not speak much, the king reflected. But I can't let him get away with reticence. 'While we understand and even applaud your loyalty, we must still have the answer to our questions,' he stated. 'We have ways of making you talk, you know. Would your loyalty stand the strain of torture?'

Ranna looked down again, a stoic expression on his face. The king nodded to Vijit, who strode away, while the other four commanders stood around the fire watching some of the men pressing curiously behind, their faces gaunt in the dancing flames. If I don't make this man talk, I'm going to lose caste, the king told himself. Suddenly, discovering King Tikka's whereabouts became secondary to winning the battle of wills against the prisoner.

Vijit returned with a giant of a man who held a long whip in one hand and a flat iron bar in the other. His head and round face were cleanshaven, eyes small and dark, their expression strangely bleak. His massive body, draped only in a *dhoti*, was olive-skinned and gleamed as he made obeisance to the king, his muscles rippling in the firelight.

'This is Indra,' the king told Ranna pleasantly. 'Like our splendid war charger, he too is named after the god we call the Destroyer. This Indra destroys people's willpower, or their bodies. You may select whichever you desire.'

Indra advanced towards Ranna. The smaller man did not flinch, merely continued gazing at the ground. 'Speak, vermin!' Indra grated.

Ranna gave no reply.

Indra stepped up to Ranna and tore off his cloak. He stepped back again and raised his whip. It hissed and whined, then cracked on Ranna's shoulders. The force of the blow nearly toppled the Yakka. A great red weal appeared on his back. He soon recovered his previous stance, however, and merely stared at the ground again.

Six times the whip sang its murderous song. Ranna fell with each stroke, but bore it without a murmur. He seemed to have removed himself from his body, so that it reacted only to physical pressure, not to pain. King Vijaya began to feel a grudging admiration for the man and the first doubts entered him. Supposing Ranna died under torture, without speaking? I've got to make him speak, damn him, the king thought savagely. He could sense the angry mood of the watching men. They had lost comrades to the Yakka that very day. Given the chance, they would tear Ranna to pieces, but who would have won?

'You are a hunter,' Indra said softly. 'Your life depends on your limbs.' He dropped his whip and grasped the iron bar in his right hand. 'And on your senses, but we shall come to those only if necessary.' His thin lips bared themselves in a grin so evil that a loud report from one of the blazing logs passed almost unnoticed. 'I'm going to smash your kneecaps with this bar. You will never walk again.' He stared at Ranna as if willing him to look up, but the Yakka merely stood with slumped shoulders, still staring at the ground. 'Speak, filthy dog,' Indra hissed.

This has become a battle between Indra and Ranna too, the king thought. He looked at both men, one a giant, the other so much smaller. His gaze drifted to his watching commanders and men. So many dozens against one puny Yakka. Worse, if the Yakka did not speak, it would all have been to no purpose. A king is a god, he has to behave like one, without involving himself in personal battles with peasants and hunters. Gods go to war; they do not indulge in petty squabbling or bully the weak.

The king's eyes shot towards the prisoner. Indra had raised the iron bar sideways, but Ranna still remained resigned.

'Stop!' the king commanded.

All eyes were turned to him. He rose slowly to his feet, standing a little taller even than Indra. A force had begun vibrating within him, emanating from him, causing him to dominate the scene. As on the field of battle that morning, he could feel his total power over his men. His right arm raised, the forefinger pointing, he advanced slowly towards the prisoner and stopped a few feet away. Moments of silence passed, heightened by the crackle of wood and the quiet roar of the flames. By sheer willpower, he compelled Ranna to lift his eyes.

I have won, the king thought with savage joy. This is but a man, a puny man. Now I shall consummate my victory. 'We are the Arya, the Noble Ones,' he stated slowly and concisely, his deep voice magnetic. 'We are the most superior race on earth. We are the superior of the Yakka, the Dasa, the Naga, the slant-eyed races, the Pahlava, the Arabi of the desert regions. We are the conquerors. Our Kings are gods. They do not compete with mortals.' He felt a thrill at having given his message not only to this miserable Yakka but also to his men. 'We have taken this entire island of Lanka through valour in battle. We do not require help from traitors.' He dropped his hand. 'Release him!' he commanded Indra. 'Let him return to rot in his jungles or to fight us another day. We ride at dawn and we shall have their kingdom before nightfall.' He strode up to where a red Sinhala banner with a golden lion rampant lay against a tent pole, seized it and brandished it aloft. 'Victory to the Sinhala, the lion race!' he cried.

Noting with satisfaction the astonishment on the Yakka's face, he turned towards his men. The banner, held high in his hand, snapped and fluttered before a sudden breeze. The cheering started softly, then rose to a crescendo that reached for the heavens.

I spent a restless night with thunder crackling outside, rain pounding on the roof. The tightness of a new bandage around my chest told me that Uday had had the palace physicians minister to me during my last deep sleep. Occasionally, I found myself shivering in a bath of sweat from a fevered body. Then I tossed and turned, half-asleep. When I finally awoke, it was morning.

Rain-washed daylight streamed in through the high-grilled, yellow and red lacquer windows. Motes danced in a bright sun-shaft before it hit the floors of white mountain crystal and the black and red Pahlava rug. Weakly, my eyes lifted to the gold and white square mosaics of the ceiling, travelled to a large ebony chest with bronze fittings beside the far wall. A vivid tapestry of a prince and princess in a royal bedchamber, done in orange, white and red, hung there. Then I became fully conscious of my own miserable condition, completely drained. My skin was so dry I could feel the bristles on my chin without touching them. My mouth was parched, the back of my head ached and the stabbing of my wound was almost unbearable. Suddenly light-headed, I let my eyelids droop wearily.

I heard the rustle of garments, but was too exhausted to open my eyes. A soft, cool palm was placed on my forehead, then the back of it felt my neck. A delicate scent, tinged with sandalwood, reached me.

I opened my eyes instantly. And there she was, dark eyes moist with unshed tears, pale cheeks trembling with concern, her thin, fine nostrils dilating. 'You are badly wounded, my Lord!' She exclaimed and a crystal teardrop stole down her cheek. It was Sundari. Had I died and gone to heaven?

I looked at her without speaking, all my weariness gone. I felt myself drawn irresistibly to her, my spirit merging with hers, my eyes melting into her gaze. That one long glance was surely the continuation of a life we had shared before, that only death had interrupted. Within my beating heart was fear that these moments had to end, a tiny miniature of the pain of our former life's ending. All my defences had crumbled before the advance of destiny.

Strangely, the first words I spoke to her were not of my love, but sprang from it. 'What are you doing here, Sundari? An unwed maiden in a man's bedchamber?' The words came out half-whisper, half-croak.

'It is part of my duties in the palace, Lord. I have supervised the attendants, the cleaning, the supplies, the meals, the needs of its residents for several months now, in addition to my studies.' She smiled. 'It's a lot of work, but the Venerable Sri Ra-vindra bade me attend you personally, with a female waiting lady who is outside. Since we had neither a king nor queen in the palace, he suggested that I act as hostess to our new king . . . until the king decides to make other arrangements.'

Seeing my expression change at her last words, she blushed. It was one of the most exquisite sights I had ever beheld. The delicate pink from within her, starting at the neck and swiftly mounting to suffuse her cheeks, causing the black eyes to glisten, reminded me of the slow-mantling of the earth's cheek, the sky, when the soft light of the rising sun touches it.

> 'Oh! I wish that I could paint
> With the lightest feather brush
> The colours deep, yet faint
> Of a beauteous maiden's blush.'

The words came out of me without thought. I was rewarded by the deepening of her blush, but she would not remove her eyes from mine.

I could not believe that this was the young woman who had once held back from me. 'This king will never presume to alter a venerable *bhikku*'s arrangements,' I interjected. Her eyes went moist. 'Never!' I repeated. I was rewarded by an amused crinkling of her eyes. 'You know I would not *wish* to change it either, don't you?' My look was commanding, but in my heart was a plea. I beg you to acknowledge our knowledge of each other at least this time.

'I had so hoped, my Lord,' she whispered.

'I have waited a long time for you, Sundari, long before my eyes met yours along this life's road. There has never been anyone else, nor had I dreamed there would be anyone at all. I thought my life ended when I could not get through to you.'

'Forgive me, Lord, but I hope you will understand.' Her

eyelids fluttered briefly. 'The gap between us seemed so insurmountable. You were an Arya prince . . . And yet, when you asked my father . . .' Her voice broke . . . 'my father to allow you to marry me . . .' She paused, unable to go on.

A vivid flash of memory lit my mind. 'A sob escaped you,' I said, remembering.

'Yes, Lord. But it was too late. I was in honour bound. You must understand what my life was like. We were a peaceful, happy family even after my mother died and I assumed the responsibility for looking after my father and brother. We had prayers every morning. I then cooked our meals, cleaned the house, swept the garden; by then it was time for the pre-noon bath, the noon meal and rest. I did my studies every evening before cooking dinner and we went to the temple once a week. I led a very settled existence, with obedience to my parents . . .'

'Hush, say no more. I respect you for your integrity.'

'I did not love Pattakanu, lord, but had known him almost like a brother since we were children. The marriage was arranged by our parents and I would have tried to be a good wife to him.' Tears started pouring down her cheeks. 'I can't . . . can't forget the night he and my father and my little brother were murdered . . . and Loki . . .' She started sobbing then steadied herself. 'The doctrine has helped me . . . be calm . . . be calm about it.' The words were coming between sobs. 'But there are . . . nights when . . . I awake remembering . . . and the horror of it chokes me.' She broke down again, weeping without restraint, staring at me with tear-filled eyes.

My throat ached, my chest felt tight and my own tears were not far away. I longed to hold her in my arms and comfort her. Instead, I reached out and took her soft hand in mine. The silent minutes of shared sorrow somehow drew us closer.

Presently her sobs subsided and she smiled ruefully at me through her tears. She reached for a linen square that lay on the table, sniffed once, said 'Please forgive me, lord,' and blew her nose. She wiped away her tears, then straightened her slim shoulders. That surprising inner strength I had briefly noticed the first night showed on her face. 'There now,' she said resolutely. 'One bout of weeping is enough. I have not re-entered your life to bring you misery. I only want to serve you, to make you happy. What has happened can never be altered by dwelling on memories. I promise never to refer to those events again. Do I have your promise too, Lord?

Choked with emotion, filled with wonder at the greatness of her spirit, I whispered hoarsely. 'I promise.'

A great weariness suddenly engulfed me. I fell asleep almost immediately with her hand still in mine.

Chapter 30

King Vijaya had decided that the advance party should proceed as fast as possible to Sita Eli-ja while the main body followed at its own pace. Vijit had been able to enlist a lean, silver-haired Yakka villager as a guide to lead them along the shortest route to the *uda rata* capital.

When they resumed their advance, they wound up a seemingly never-ending range until they finally came to a pass, no more than a wide crack in the rocky face of a mountain. Here they paused briefly. Surveying the fissure, the king thought, if this is its only entry-way, no wonder the mountain kingdom has always been impregnable from the west. To their right, the range swept down sheer into a green valley, then rose again to high hills surmounted by a huge circular rock with a strange flat top.

'That must be the dining table of the gods,' Vijit remarked, then turned his mount into the passage through the rock.

'You are now safely in the *kanda uda rata*,' the guide stated once they were through the pass. 'The kingdom upon the hills.'

They proceeded east along fertile green flatlands, small plots of paddy swaying before cool breezes, hazy blue mountains in the distance. After riding a few miles, they veered north towards more ranges. The guide pointed to a blue peak in the distance supported by twin mountains on either side. 'That is Sira Pada,' he stated. 'The Buddha alighted on it from his air-chariot. The mountain beside it is Samanal Kande, butterfly mountain where butterflies go to die.' True enough, great hosts of black and yellow butterflies seemed to be fluttering in that direction.

As they climbed, the air became colder, more invigorating,

rather like the northern parts of the continent in the spring. Each time they passed a village, people rushed to the trailside to stare at them. Most of the population had fair complexions. A snotty-nosed child essayed a toothless smile. All the houses were built of mud bricks on bamboo strip frames, with roofs of yellow paddy thatch.

They paused for their noonday meal in a large glade through which a silver stream meandered over pale sand and coloured pebbles. Across a great valley, waterfalls nestled in green ravines, emerging as sparkling streams below. Brown and black cattle grazed on green mountain pastures. Fern banks and clusters of wild flowers brought sharp scents of marigold and wild grass.

As they rode on, the guide had noticed the king's interest in the cultivated lands. 'We are proud of our ancient cultivation. The fields look really pretty when the young paddy sprouts its brilliant green.'

'You shall have more,' the king responded. 'We shall introduce a system of terracing your paddy fields down the hillsides and using your mountain streams for irrigation, that will bring you great prosperity.'

It was late evening before they finally reached the last of the high mountains and broke through its crest. Beneath him, in what was left of the sunlight, the king saw the spreading blobs of a small township built around a large lake. The entrances of the houses, behind their tall, mud-brick boundary walls plastered with a white *chunam* were already lit by *chulu* lights, but not a soul was in sight. 'People in these parts retire early, to avoid the cold night air,' the guide stated. 'The palace is over there.' He pointed towards an avenue of flaming red torches that split the darkness at the near end of the town, patches of light making a mosaic of yellow and black. 'It is said to be as beautiful as that of Kalyani.'

'We shall build a new palace in Lanka,' the king told Vijit, who was riding beside him. 'People need to be able to look up to their rulers and a palace is one way of establishing the separation of peasant and king. The lifestyle of kings must seem remote, unattainable. There must be no possibility whatever of anything but admiration, reverence, in the minds of the masses who are ruled. Men never think of seizing what belongs to the gods. Only when something seems reachable will envy, greed and the desire to take over arise.'

Vijit pondered his words, made no comment.

The palace proved to be a sprawling, single-storey structure built, Lanka fashion, round a great *meda midula*, centre courtyard, with smaller courtyards within each set of quarters.

Word of their arrival had somehow preceded them, for they entered without being challenged and the kneeling guards and attendants were all unarmed. A log fire blazed in the main hall, crackling merrily, light smoke from it bearing a faint scent of eucalyptus. The king, accompanied by Vijit, strode to a great teakwood table at the centre of the hall. He sat on a wooden settle. A retainer wearing a black tunic coat reaching to his ankles, obviously the chief attendant, had followed them. 'Have our troops suitably fed and quartered,' the king commanded the man, then stretched long legs towards the fire, glad of its warmth. 'Ur . . . u . . . ur . . . that feels good. Come, sit beside us,' he directed Vijit.

They remained seated for a while in comfortable silence, staring at the flames, each lost in his thoughts.

'The beauty of Sita Eli-ja had not been exaggerated,' the king finally remarked.

'No, Sire! Now let's hope their food and lodging are equally good. I'm famished. I'll be ready for dinner as soon as the men have been fed.'

'So shall we. Let us also hope their beds are comfortable. Oh by the way, since we have taken the *uda rata* capital without firing a single arrow, send word to Ujjeni to return with his company to Thamba-Panni, where his presence would be more useful.'

'Yes, Sire. He'll be glad to avoid the cold, Br . . . r . . . r . . .

It's almost freezing.' Vijit leant towards the fire to warm his hands. 'I don't suppose they have snow and ice up here?'

'We think not, but they are known to have hail. Yet this climate is more bracing than our warm Priti.' The king pondered a moment. 'Thamba-Panni's climate is warm, at times debilitating. We shall make Sita Eli-ja our resort for the hottest times of the year, in the months of Vesakha before the rains come.'

'We must first secure the kingdom, Lord.'

'So we shall, never fear. When our first footsoldiers reach the capital will be the real time of our victory.'

Vijit's expression changed. 'Sire, there is no victory without cavalry!'

'Ah! The cavalryman speaks. Indeed you are right, Vijit. We have taken this kingdom because of your cavalry. To strike with the speed, accuracy and strength that only the cavalry possesses was essential, but no victory is complete until the conquering footsoldiers enter the enemy citadel.'

Vijit reflected on this. 'What you say is true, Sire,' he finally conceded. 'We cavalrymen are the tillers preparing the soil so that the foot soldiers may produce crops.'

The chief retainer entered, approached the king and made obeisance to him. Still kneeling, he proffered a small package covered in red silk with both hands. 'Sire, a messenger from the Ruhuna kingdom arrived just before you and desired that this message from his king be delivered to you.'

A puzzled frown crossed King Vijaya's face. 'Did the message arrive here directly from Ruhuna?' he demanded of the attendant.

'Yes, Lord, so he said.'

'This missive is addressed to us here at the palace. How did the Ruhuna king know we would be here?'

'Lord, the king of Ruhuna is also a sage. He comprehends much that is beyond the understanding of ordinary people.'

The king looked at Vijit again, seeking some explanation.

'A ruler with a superior spy system, a knowledge of human

nature and an astute brain can always comprehend much that is beyond the understanding of ordinary people,' the cavalry commander responded drily.

The king nodded. Yet somewhere inside him was a lack of conviction. While he did not believe in magic or in supernatural powers, he did concede that some human beings have the capacity to perform miracles. Had he not, in his own way, done so these past two days? 'Open the package,' he commanded the chief retainer.

Still kneeling, the man undid the string with trembling fingers, then proffered a yellow roll of *ola* to the king. The king rose, Vijit with him, and strode to a lighted taper. He read the *ola* aloud:

'To Vijaya Sinha-Bahu, King of Thamba-Panni, Deva Raja, King of Ruhuna and Guardian of the Sacred Shrine of Katara Gama, sends greetings.

'By the will of the gods, we are the ruler of Ruhuna. Though self-contained because of its rivers, mountains and forests, Ruhuna is but a sub-kingdom. We endorse your intention of making the entire island of Lanka a single state, for so it has been created by Lord Brahma, the Creator. It shall only achieve true greatness through unity.

'When messengers brought word to us of your advance against the Kalyani kingdom, the blessed gift of the inner sight revealed your victory to us. It also gave us a vision of your plans, which had to take you to Sita Eli-ja, the capital of the *uda rata* kingdom, by tonight. For this reason, we send you our message to Sita Eli-ja, where you shall be at the time appointed for your presence.

'A military campaign into Ruhuna would be costly to you and to us, in men and materials, time and energy. We ourselves are old and without progeny. Do you therefore accept, by this missive, our submission to you as Great King of Lanka. Let there henceforth be three kingdoms, not four, in this fair island, all under your divine sovereignty: Raja Rata to the north, north centre and east, where you shall have your court; Malaya Rata embracing the kingdoms of Kalyani and the *uda rata*; and our blessed Ruhuna Rata. Upon our death, you may decree who our successor shall be, so long as such successor shall retain and safeguard our sacred shrines, customs, traditions and institutions.

'We are Arya, like you, O King, so our customs and traditions will not conflict with those you have brought from your native Sinha-Pura.

'We await your pleasure, assuring you, Great King, of our highest esteem,

Deva Raja, King of Ruhuna.'

King Vijaya stared at the scroll for long moments, then silently read it again, his mind awhirl with conflicting thoughts. King Deva Raja was an old man, reported to be dying of the wasting disease. He glanced at Vijit, who was looking at him with shining eyes and his tiredness dropped from him as if it had been a cloak. 'Imagine, in a single day, we have become the Maha Raja, Great King of Lanka, a conqueror with a kingdom larger than that of our father. We Arya did this together. We can finally laugh at those who captured us, shamed us, drove us away from our native land. What a pity our royal father is not alive to learn of this moment of our triumph.' He added under his breath. 'And our royal mother.'

'Supposing this letter is a ruse, Lord, to buy King Deva Raja time?' Vijit enquired, the first flush of his excitement over.

'Not likely from reports we have received. But we can easily check his honesty through our spies.' The king stared thoughtfully at the blazing fire, tapping the *ola* against the palm of his hand. 'We have it. We shall now demand that the Ruhuna king receive an embassy from us immediately. Ambassadors and their staffs make the best spies of all!'

'What a splendid idea!' Vijit beamed.

'You shall lead the embassy to Ruhuna tomorrow, guided by King Deva Raja's messenger. You shall settle the terms of this surrender . . . it is no less . . . with the king. We shall give you full instructions before you leave, but we intend remaining in Sita Eli-ja for fourteen days, to reorganize and establish our government, before departing for Thamba-

411

Panni. You shall return from Ruhuna to Thamba-Panni thirty days hence, by the low-country trail along the eastern base of the mountain region. Somewhere within Thamba-Panni, close to the borders of the two kingdoms, you shall select a site for a mighty fortress, mightier than any we have built heretofore, to serve as a base of operations against Ruhuna, if necessary.' He smiled grimly. 'Or our defence against attack.' He paused. 'It will be an opportunity to show the people of Lanka what a real Arya fort looks like! Once built, the fort shall be named after you, Vijita Pura, city of Vijit. It shall serve as your headquarters, for we hereby appoint you governor of a new province we shall create, stretching eastward from the mountains to the ocean.'

Vijits's dark eyes gleamed and his shoulders automatically straightened. 'My lord, this honour is so unexpected. You are indeed gracious. I shall give my life if need be to justify your trust.'

'You have already devoted your life to us, good comrade and subject.' The king exchanged a glance of understanding with Vijit, then, as always with men of strength who feel the embarrassment of the rare moments that express personal feelings, he abruptly changed the subject. 'Now we come to King Tikka. We can either ask King Deva Raja not to give him sanctuary, to avoid any dealings with him, perhaps even to hunt him down, or we can refrain from raising the subject at all. We have decided on the latter.'

Vijit's eyebrows arched in surprise. 'Why, Sire?'

'It will help ensure that there is no secret collusion between the two kings, for Tikka will certainly make for the Ruhuna kingdom. In this way, we have a better prospect of discovering more about King Tikka's whereabouts and plans. He is too well known, perhaps even too cordially hated now, to remain in the *uda rata* a fallen monarch. The only course open to him is personal vengeance, no longer against the Arya, but against their king.' His smile was careless. 'We would welcome an end to this feud. And that will only occur when one or the other of us is dead.'

I awoke in the evening from a deep and dreamless sleep to find the tapers lit in my bedroom at the Kalyani palace. For the first time in over a year, my first dawn of consciousness was a source of delight that made me glad to awaken. In a flash, I knew what it was, Sundari loved me. For one ghastly moment I wondered whether it had been one of my dreams that always ended in bitter reality.

Then I saw her seated demurely on an ebony settle across the room from my bed, just looking at me. Finding me awake, she rose and came to the bedside with a rustle of her skirt. During a brief instant, seeing her in the golden taper-light reminded me of my first vision of her in the cottage at Priti. Her face had been tense then, the dark eyes filled with terror. Now she was very relaxed and even more beautiful than I had known her in my dreams.

'I hope you slept well, Lord.'

'For the first time in over a year.'

She dimpled with pleasure.

'You were watching me?' I enquired.

This time she blushed and looked down. 'Yes, Lord,' she whispered.

'For how long?'

Blushing more deeply, she hesitated. 'Since you fell asleep in the morning, Lord. I had some food brought in at noon. Pray forgive me if I have done wrong.' Her downcast eyes lifted to mine and I saw they were misty.

'Wrong?' I cried, half-rising and falling back on the cushions from the wrenching pain of my wound. 'You are so beautiful,' I said and held her gaze. 'I could lose myself in your eyes,' I added in a whisper.

The feel of her spirit, gentle, sensitive, the refinement of her manner and something I had never realized before, my yearning for home, seized me at that moment. Sundari was my home and this was life, a man and a woman together in their house. The work of the court, its protocol, the aloneness of the priest, all had their advantages, but not for me. I wanted love, a quiet home in taper-light . . . yes, children, from a complete woman. In that instant, I made up my mind and my eyes went hard with determination.

An expression of alarm crossed her face. 'What is it, Lord.'

I smiled then. 'Perhaps it is something that should indeed cause you alarm. I want you to become betrothed to me. We can be married as soon as I receive the approval of my brother, the king.'

She became terrified. 'My Lord, I am honoured, glad, delighted . . . but . . . oh . . . oh.' She burst into tears.

I stared at her, moved to the depths but puzzled, not knowing how to respond, for I could not do the one thing I wanted more than all the world at that moment, take her into my arms. 'You spend all your time with me crying,' I said lightly. 'You cry when you're sad, you cry when you're happy.'

A crystal tear-drop fell on the back of my hand. I gazed at it in wonder. No one had ever wept on me, for me, before. Feeling the caress of that tear, the tenderness it had emerged from, alive on my skin, 'Oh, *larla*, beloved!' I cried.

She composed herself, sniffed once and smiled wanly through her tears. 'You should not marry me,' she stated firmly. 'Consider our differences of race and estate. It would create too many difficulties for you. Just let me be your concubine, that is all I ask. Marrying you would indeed be wonderful, but that is not why I love you. What I desire to give you and, yes, to receive from you, can be achieved so long as I am wherever you are, go wherever you go and can always be close to you.'

'You could not have said anything that pleases me more,' I replied huskily, my smarting eyes controlled only by years of training as a prince and a man. 'It makes me even more firmly convinced that you and I have been one in past births and should fulfil the love of God within us through the estate man

414

has created, marriage. Yes, there will be enormous difficulties. My brother had a great belief in Arya superiority. He warned me the night I met you that I must only consider marrying one of another race if it helps strengthen the kingdom. Since then, the failure of his own marriage to the Princess Kuveni has made him bitter, convinced him that we Arya men should only marry Arya women and breed Arya children. Besides, my duties as a priest, occasional though they are, create a further impediment. But I don't really care. This is what I want to do and I shall do it.'

'But *I* care, Lord, and I want none of these problems for you on my account.'

'Do you want me to be happy?'

'With all my heart, Lord. I desire nothing else.'

'Then stop being selfish about what *you* want and do what I want.' I crinkled my eyes to rob my words of offence. 'You might as well get used to doing that from now on, so tell me that you will marry me.'

Still she hesitated. 'You are the king of Kalyani,' she volunteered.

'Do you think I care a jot for that position or any position? Kingship is temporary, love is divine, eternal. I would not lie to you and say that I do not care about the opportunity to serve people, to fulfil my duty as a prince, for which God has given me the birth and people have extended to me the training. Had it been in some other kingdom, I might have had to pause, even to sacrifice love for duty. But here in Lanka, in Thamba-Panni and in Kalyani, we have no permanent institutions or traditions. We are creating them and I for one refuse to pander to silly prejudices.'

'My caste will stand in your way even if my race does not, Lord.'

'Did it stand in the way of King Sri Ra-hula when he took you in? Is Kalyani not a Buddhist kingdom? Are you not treated as a respected lady of this court because your qualities command it?'

415

She dimpled again, eyes downcast. 'Yes, Lord.'

'Then I shall be proud to have you for my wife, even though you cannot be consecrated queen.' A sense of urgency to have her in total, immediate accord with me on this one issue seized me. Suddenly it seemed vital, because it was *right*, not because I wanted it. I reached out and grasped her hand. The slender white fingers were soft and full, the skin silken. I held her gaze firmly. 'It is important to me that you say yes right now, Sundari, without further demur. Here I am, the sub-king of Kalyani, pleading with my subject to marry me as if I were some yokel! Have you no sense of propriety . . . and is all romance dead before the needs of practicality?'

An ineffable expression crossed her face. 'Don't be upset, Lord,' she begged. 'I will do as you say.' She raised my hand to her lips. Yes, this most exquisite woman in all the world, kissed my hand, not because I was a king, but because I was her man. Tilting her head, she placed the back of the hand gently against her wet cheek. 'Did anyone tell you that you have the most beautiful green eyes, Lord?' she enquired.

'No,' I replied softly, amazed at the first compliment I had received about my looks in years.

'I noticed them the first night I saw you, even though I was afraid for a moment that you were a third person come to rape me. They have haunted me ever since. And now I find that your hands are strong, so strong.'

'Soon they will hold you, *larla*, beloved.' I laughed lightly to push back my welling emotions. 'But first I must make an honest woman of you, now that you have compromised us both by spending all this time in my bedchamber.' Then the recollection of my oath to Pillai hit me. 'But what about my oath?'

'What oath, Lord?'

'The oath I gave Rasiah that I would leave you in peace.'

'I shall send word to him that you have kept your oath by bringing me peace.'

416

Chapter 31

A gust of wind blew through the open door, bending the yellow taper flames that lit the small hallway as Uraw entered Ujjeni's residence. This was a modest brown daub-on-wattle house with a red tile roof in the north-west corner of the Priti fort. It had once belonged to a Yakka nobleman, a relative of the slain King Kalu Sena. Ujjeni had obviously selected it after the massacre because it was located at the end of a dark alley, adjoined the fortress wall and afforded a greater measure of privacy than any of the other residences.

Uraw was reminded forcefully of this when he saw Ujjeni's face as he emerged through the fitful light and gave him the palms together greeting. The taper-glow wavered again as Uraw closed the door behind himself and Ujjeni slid the door bar into place with a click.

'The others are already here,' Ujjeni stated, taking Uraw's elbow and guiding him down the short passage that led into the hall, a large room, well-lit flares hissing on bright sconces that had been nailed to the bare grey walls.

Ujjeni lived a spare existence, Uraw knew, devoid of luxuries and frills. Since the events at Mada Kalapuwa, his entire life had become centred on his work, his existence completely disciplined. He might as well have taken the vow of *brachmachariya* for all the contact he now had with women, or for that matter young boys. His domestic needs, such as food and a clean house, were looked after by two Yakka soldiers, his financial affairs by his Arya aide, a young supply service captain named Ranjan.

All the commanders, excluding only Vijit, were already seated on settles around a plain brown *nadun*-wood table. Upa, Anu, Sumitta and Pandu had clay goblets and earthenware platters containing skewers of fried mutton in front of them. Some of the palm-wine from a large red clay pitcher, topped with a light froth, had spilled on the table.

Uraw drew up an empty settle, straddled it and reached for a skewer of mutton. 'I'm hungry,' he said and started gnawing at the meat. Ujjeni filled him a goblet of wine.

'Food and drink!' Pudgy-faced Upa observed, wiping his black moustache and clearing his throat. 'As one gets older, food and drink become more and more important, while sleep and sex fade into the background.'

'You speak for yourself,' Pandu bade him and the others laughed, for it was well known that Pandu, though older and grey, had an insatiable sexual appetite and consorted with Yakka women.

Noting Ujjeni's distaste, Uraw remembered his own Arabi mistress and wished he were back in bed with her.

'That's one of the subjects we're going to discuss tonight,' Ujjeni intervened, his voice more hard and grainy than ever. 'Sex, that is . . . uh . . . not sleep. For there can be no heirs without sex.' His purple lips curved over the prominent yellow teeth in a mirthless smile.

'What's on your mind, Minister?' Sumitta, a lean, tough-looking man demanded.

'Our king has two Yakka-looking children, whom he abhors, as his only heirs . . . right?'

'Correct.'

'If he dies, which the devas forbid, Prince Lala, who is not only a Yakka-lover, but, as I understand it, also worships the One God, Jahweh, of that wandering tribe, the Juda, whom all nations rightly persecute, will succeed him . . . right?'

'Right,' Pandu agreed. 'But what is all this about the prince's worship of the Juda God?'

'All in good time, my friend. My information on that score comes from one who has overheard some of the prince's conversations with various people, including the Great King.' Ujjeni glanced at Anu. 'Anu, you know the source to be absolutely reliable, don't you?'

Anu grinned, remembering the woman, Rupa. 'Watertight.'

'So would I! To proceed . . . I have already told you of Prince Lala's treachery with the Dasa girl I coveted. He actually broke the oath he gave our king and yet, being the king's brother, he bears a charmed life. We must help the king in his sad situation, because I'm sure he will eventually agree to Prince Lala's marrying this woman who has bewitched him.'

'Bewitched?' Upa, always a fair man, demanded. 'Come now, Minister, that's a strong word.'

'I use it deliberately,' Ujjeni retorted fiercely. 'After all, I should know because she bewitched me too at one time. Anu and Uraw can testify to that.' He glanced briefly at the two men, then proceeded quickly before either could comment. 'But that's another matter which I shall address later. For the present, my main concern is to ensure that we are never ruled by anyone but an Arya, of the Arya religion.'

'You're right,' Anu declared, rapping his approval on the table! 'Mine too.'

Ujjeni placed his hands on the table for emphasis and glanced at the remaining ministers. 'We all have a stake in this kingdom, haven't we, if for no other reason than because we live here?' He must have realized the error of his admission vis-a-vis the Yakkas and Nagas, because he quickly pulled away from it. 'Those of us who have helped create this kingdom have the right to live in it with decency, self-respect and a sense of long-term security. Isn't that so?' He gazed challengingly around the room.

'Ahey! . . . Ahey! Ahey!' The agreement was unanimous.

'All right then, here is what I propose.'

Ujjeni leaned forward and dropped his voice. He analysed the situation and detailed his plan to them. 'As Uraw knows, I have already discussed the more important aspects with the Great King,' he finally concluded. 'It will probably take some years for the first stage to materialize, but remember, the stakes are high and these things always take time, especially with the distances involved. We must be patient and . . . uh

. . . wise.'

You nearly said 'cunning', Uraw thought and suddenly did not feel so good about participating in this deep-laid plan. After all, he for one had no problem with foreign women. His Arabi was terrific in bed and he would soon have a child of mixed blood. Then he remembered that, having given Ujjeni his Arya word of honour to go along with the group, he was no longer a free agent.

The message from Ujjeni, requesting permission to wait on her immediately after the noon meal as he had news of importance, came ten days after Ujjeni's return to Thamba-Panni and the Princess Kuveni awaited the visit with trepidation. She sat on a red-cushioned settle facing the open door with Rupa standing beside her. It was warm and close here, the courtyard garden so laden with bright sunlight that the few trees and the pomegranate bushes she could see through the open door drooped beneath its weight, while the entire world, except for some buzzing bees, was sunk in noon-day torpor.

Ujjeni's gaunt figure soon filled the entrance. His casual salute and the look in those deep, sunken eyes told her that he resented having to give her even that much respect. Standing there with the sunlight behind him, his white *dhoti* and *kurtha* gave him greater height and accentuated the darkness of his skin. He looks like a skeletal ghost such as I invoke for bringing curses on men, the princess decided. 'Pray be seated,' she bade him aloud, indicating a settle across the room.

Ujjeni stepped forward, hesitated and shook his head. 'What I have to say will take but a few minutes, Princess, and I would not want to detain you with pleasantries.'

'You and I have nothing pleasant between us.' The words were out of her lips, the emphasis on the word 'pleasant' before she could restrain herself.

Hatred sparked in Ujjeni's eyes for a moment. You Yakka bitch, how dare you address me in that manner, he seemed to

420

say. Then his face broke into a smile, the thin lips curving over prominent purple gums to reveal the twin curving yellow combs of his teeth. 'I shall remember that, Princess.'

'Come to the point.'

Again the eyes fired twin sparks of hatred. 'Certainly, my . . . er . . . lady.' He paused, nodding at her, as if assessing her personally for the first time. 'My lord, the king, intended returning from the *uda rata* by now, as I have previously informed you, but he has sent me word by a messenger, who arrived this morning, that he will be indefinitely delayed. Three days before he was due to depart, he was stricken by sickness. The *uda rata* palace physician states that it will be two to three weeks longer at least before he can leave.'

The princess felt a stab of alarm. For all their quarrels and her hurts, she loved the king and did not want ill to happen to him. Besides, if he died, with Prince Lala away in Kalyani, she would be at the mercy of people like Ujjeni. 'What is wrong with my lord?' She enquired, trying to appear composed.

'Oh! Nothing too serious, as far as I can determine. He developed a sore throat, vomiting and a fever that kept rising. About ten days later, he experienced swelling and rawness on either side of his neck, just below the ears. Shortly afterwards, he began to suffer the same inflammation and pain in those parts of his body that hold his seed. The physician assures us that the king will recover within three weeks of the symptoms' appearing. Apparently, this disease, though unknown to us Arya, afflicts the Yakka in epidemic fashion, but its consequences are not fatal. Our king has obviously caught a Yakka curse.'

A thrill of triumph shot through the princess. If King Vijaya was expected to recover about one week from today, he must have become infected the day after she placed the charm on him. She knew the disease. It was common knowledge that when it afflicted a grown man he lost his fertility if his twin sacs became inflamed and would never beget children again. She flashed a knowing glance at Rupa, who avoided her gaze. Ujjeni suddenly became alert, so she wiped all expression from her face. 'You are right!' She assured Ujjeni. 'Our king has indeed been afflicted by a known illness. As the physician has said, it is only temporary. The treatment is also well known to us. We keep the affected parts daubed with a blue ointment made of certain herbs and ingredients rubbed with sandalwood and give the patient a *cassaya*, a mixture, every few hours in order to cleanse his blood. Is that all your news?'

Ujjeni stiffened, hesitated, then seemed to make up his mind. 'All from the *uda rata*,' he stated malevolently. 'But we do have an interesting item from Kalyani. The king's brother plans to marry a low-caste woman.'

'Oh! That is good news, regardless of caste.'

'On the contrary, it could be bad news for Prince Lala. He acts as our priest and is therefore expected to remain celibate.' A malicious gleam entered his eyes. 'Besides, this woman is also not an Arya, but a Dasa. As a matter of fact, you know her because you allowed her a mat in your servant's room one night. Hardly a match for the sub-king of Kalyani, eh?'

Hamy found King Tikka's leisurely pace across the mountains strange, in view of the normal impetuosity of his leader's nature and the speed of his actions prior to the lost battles. Not daring to question the king as to the reasons for his changed attitude, Hamy wondered as the days went by, whether defeat had demoralized the man. He thought not, however, for he could detect, beneath the king's seemingly placid, unhurried exterior, a deadly purpose, more deepseated and implacable than that which had prompted hasty action.

While still in the *uda rata* kingdom, they were unfailingly made welcome, the king with reverence, by the people of the villages they passed. Gifts of gold and silver ornaments and jewels from the chieftains they stayed with compelled them to obtain horses for their journey. These were stocky country chestnuts, with sturdy limbs, capable of negotiating the mountain trails.

They had reached the last major *uda rata* village, closest to the Ruhuna border, before they received news of the birth of the Princess Kuveni's twins and of King Vijaya's illness, from the chief headman in whose mansion they spent one night.

'Serve the bastard right,' King Tikka gritted, his dark eyes malevolent. 'Our gods have smitten him, with infertility and only Yakka heirs. We are now clearly the heir to the four kingdoms.' They had heard of the secession of Ruhuna. 'We take precedence over Kuveni and her children by birth. We were right to decide that time should pass and the Arya be compelled to spread their forces to the utmost before we strike again. Once we kill Vijaya and dispose of his brother, Lala, we shall be the only king of royal blood who can lay claim to the throne of the entire island, unification of which the Arya have accomplished for us.'

'Will the Arya accept you as king, Lord?' Kira enquired timorously.

Surprisingly, King Tikka did not turn on Kira, and Hamy decided that defeat and exile must have mellowed the man. 'Once the lion's head is cut, the body is helpless,' the king responded. 'At the very least, whatever is left will prey on itself, by which I mean that the seven commanders will be at each other's throats. Divided they shall be at our mercy, for the Yakka and Naga will remain united.'

'What of Prince Jaya?' Hamy enquired.

'We shall slit his fat throat,' King Tikka stated pleasantly.

Once across the border, they proceeded along secret jungle paths known only to King Tikka from his hunting days. To the left the triple mountains kept an endless blue vigil: Samanal Kande awaiting its corteges of thousands of multi-coloured butterflies, flitting there to die; Siri Pada in the centre, a sharp-etched peak constantly reminding Hamy of the Buddha's visit to it and his own desire for a monastic life at the end of his days.

They wound downwards through the fetid odours of dense, damp jungle, where wild orchids bloomed white and yellow and purple beneath the chattering of parakeets. Occasionally a waterfall would splash silver in the sunlight of a bare hilltop, but the region was devoid of habitation, so they slept in the open. They finally came to the bright, green grass-covered slopes of the *patana* lands. Here, stunted spathodea of the dark green leaf, the wrung-out red flowers and the withering grey bark grew in the hollows and halfway up the hillsides. Small villages, with homes covered by yellow-brown roofs of paddy-straw, nestled in the low-lying areas, beside the glint of an occasional stream and green patches of paddy. White, brown and black cattle grazed peacefully in meadows and sometimes the laughter of children, the shrill scream of a scolding woman or the hoo . . . oo . . . oo of men calling across valleys reached them, accompanied by smells of woodsmoke and the tang of dry grass. Ruhuna was obviously peaceful, more prosperous and better administered than the *uda rata*.

Though Hamy was on his first visit to the area, he knew they were close to Devun Dara when they breasted a hill that mid-morning and paused to look down its green slope at the ocean beneath them and saw sunlight winking and flashing off the circular copper roof of the temple dedicated to the sun god, E-ra, a thing of beauty and wonder to him, a beacon for ships.

'We have chosen Devun Dara for our refuge,' King Tikka declared. 'It is at the southernmost end of the land from which the ocean stretches to the ends of the earth, where no man lives and only the ocean gods rule. Even Maha Gama, the capital of Ruhuna is many miles away. Devun Dara has a mixed population of Arya, Dasa and Arabi, of locals and foreigners, of peasants, seamen and traders, so that our own arrival as wealthy strangers will not excite undue comment. Besides, we have a trusted Yakka relative here, a former *uda rata* chieftain, named Banda, who fell in love with a maiden of mixed Arabi and Arya blood during a visit some years ago. He settled in the township and is now a prosperous trader and a power in the region. We sent secret word to him and he responded with an enthusiastic invitation to stay with him as long as we pleased.' He paused. 'Of course, knowing cousin

Banda, we rather suspect that he has other motives for his enthusiasm, but time will reveal everything. Let us proceed without delay, for Banda is expecting us.'

As they rode downhill beneath great *mara* branches fissured by sunlight, Hamy wondered at King Tikka's secretiveness, then decided that it showed maturity. He had heard of Banda, a notorious figure, perhaps the right person for King Tikka in his present plight.

They soon came to a *kabook*, orange-red clay, path strewn with rocks and cattle droppings, flanked by the straight grey boles and spreading green fronds of coconut palms. Through open glades they could see houses in green groves. Crows cawed busily overhead and the rich, sweet scent of ripe *jak* clung to the air, wafted by a dank ocean breeze, cooled by the shadows and soothing to the skin. An occasional villager, bare-bodied, but clad in a sarong tucked up at the waist so that it looked like a short skirt, passed them with no more than a curious glance. Travellers from the *uda rata* were obviously not an uncommon feature of these parts.

They clip-clopped past the granite temple, not close enough to make it necessary for them to dismount from respect for the god. Hamy marvelled at the smooth perfection of its domed copper roof. The treeline ended abruptly at the bottom of the hill, giving way to groves of spreading green *manioc* across which the path led straight as a flying spear towards a small village. Somewhere a cockerel began crowing then stopped, as if it had finally realized that this was not the right time of the day for such vocal exercises.

Hamy noticed that the homes had sandy gardens planted with onion beds, green chillies and *brinjal* bushes, banana and payaya trees in the background. Green creepers sprawled over some of the straw-thatched roofs and two yellow melons lay like great, fat eggs on one of them. A withered crone came hobbling up the path, aided by a stick. 'Ah! Wealthy visitors,' she quavered through toothless gums. 'You are always welcome, my masters.' She cackled loudly and hobbled away, as if her task was done.

Two sturdy men, dressed in white *kurthas* and *dhotis*, climbed with agility over the stile of one of the larger homes. They could have been brothers, light-skinned, their long curly, black hair glistening with oil, their eyes pale brown in the sunlight. The taller man greeted them with hands at the chest, palms together. Hamy noted that his eyes and teeth were bright with his smile, but the mouth was hard. 'You must be the visitors our lord Banda is expecting,' the man stated in a curiously even voice, as if repeating a lesson. 'I'm Ranna, one of his bodyguards and this is Suramba, my brother, who also guards our lord.'

'Yes,' King Tikka replied. He dropped his voice. 'But as you know, we do not wish to be identified. We are merely wealthy traders visiting lord Banda.'

Ranna's hands had been moving up to reach his forehead, the greeting reserved for kings, but he held himself in check at the warning. 'Please follow me,' he bade them. Grasping the bridle of King Tikka's mount, he led them along the path that now wound between the shady gardens of larger houses.

Round a bend, they came unexpectedly to a high granite wall, topped by a pink flowering creeper, above which the yellow roof of a dwelling glistened in the sun. Here they paused. 'We have arrived,' Ranna stated. 'This is the lord Banda's mansion.' At a call from Ranna, the great wooden entrance gates creaked open.

Hamy could not restrain a gasp of amazement, for in front of them was more than a mansion, it was a veritable palace, with tough-looking retainers everywhere. The two-storey brick house lay at the far end of a long gravelled driveway, which was threaded by wagon ruts and lined by flower-beds of yellow marigolds and white daisies, with red and white temple flower trees in bloom behind them. Tall coconut palms and shade trees were set well away from the building on green lawns, so that the structure itself was bathed in stark sunlight pouring down from a cloudless blue sky. The scent of the flowers mingling with that of ripe guava and the penetrating odour of new dung, added to the unreality of a scene heightened by a strange silence within the walls of what was almost a fortress.

They dismounted at the front doors. Bare-chested grooms rushed up and led their horses away to the rear of the mansion. At the large, flag-stone entrance foyer of the mansion stood a small, sprightly figure, richly attired in gold silk tunic and pantaloons. His complexion was unusually fair, accentuating a thin black moustache surrounded by laughter lines on each side of a narrow bird-like face. It was the dark, gleaming eyes straddling his beak of a nose that commanded Hamy's attention. They were piercing as a hawk's. This must be Banda, a sharp, tough individual, Hamy decided. In Devun Dara he has acquired wealth such as he could never have achieved if he had remained in the *uda rata*. He is a gambler too, some of his wealth ill-gotten, through smuggling and organized crime, but he is also a great romantic, courageous and strong-willed, for what first drew him to this township was a beautiful woman of a different race and even of mixed blood.

'My home is your home, Sire,' Banda declared. His voice was unusually deep and booming for such a small man.

'We thank you,' King Tikka acknowledged. 'You shall know your reward some day.'

'Not for reward, Sire,' Banda assured him proudly, a faint smile touching his lips. 'And to give you the proof of my allegiance, I seek your leave to break with convention and to present my family to you.'

Obviously taken aback, King Tikka glanced briefly at Hamy and Kira, then nodded his agreement.

Banda called out, 'Rahila!' As if on cue, the inner door opened and three boys entered, followed by two women.

'My entire family, Sire,' Banda said. 'My oldest son, Loku Banda, my second son, Meddumma Banda and my youngest son, Punchi Banda.'

The boys, who were about twelve, ten and eight years old, were all like their father, small and birdlike, with fair, pointed features.

'My wife, Rahila.' The woman who approached and made obeisance was tall, fair and buxom. Just the sort of figure that most small men like, Hamy thought, but what really compelled the breakaway from Banda's past? Destiny? Then he noticed the woman's face. She was an absolute beauty, the high cheekbones topped by masses of rippling black hair, with large green eyes, the lashes black and tipped with *kohl*, long and sweeping, the whole expression one of kindliness. Here was a woman whose radiance came from within.

'And this is my wife's unmarried sister, Razeena.'

One look at the young woman who glided forward and Hamy's breath caught. He saw a sultry-eyed goddess, exuding sexuality from every pore of her magnetic being, from every curve of her sensuous body. She was tall, with wavy reddish-black hair and the surpassingly fair skin that goes with it, but of a silken texture. Her waist was trim, between bulging breasts and full hips. Her face was oval, the large dark eyes of her Arabi blood alluring. Though her bearing was demure, she had only to lift those liquid eyes to reveal the depths of her person. She is the embodiment of every man's desiring, Hamy thought . . . before King Tikka's indrawn breath penetrated his senses.

King Tikka was alert as a hunter. His eyes had locked into those of Razeena. She was looking at him, startled, as if by some vision. The entire room became filled with the unmistakable vibrance of something shattering, far-reaching between these two people.

428

Chapter 32

As they awaited King Vijaya in his study, Uraw wondered for the umpteenth time why Ujjeni had asked him to be present at this meeting, the first since the Great King had returned from Sita Eli-ja three days earlier. He could only think that Ujjeni needed him as an independent witness and supporter.

The brisk sound of sandal-shoes on the flagstone verandah floor preceded the Great King's arrival. When Uraw rose from his obeisance, he was shocked at the Great King's appearance. Though his movements were as decisive as ever when he took his place behind the yellow jakwood desk, his face was grey and drawn. 'Pray resume your seats, gentlemen,' the king directed. 'It's good to see you again. Now please state your business.'

Uraw perched himself on a settle beside Ujjeni.

'Lord, since you have many weighty matters needing your attention, I shall be brief,' Ujjeni declared. He closed his lips over his curving yellow teeth without quite succeeding in hiding them. There was concern in his deep-set eyes. 'We have come on an intensely personal matter, but as your loyal subjects . . .' He paused, obviously to assure himself of the king's total attention. '. . . we have evidence that on the eve of our battle against the combined Yakka and Naga armies, your spouse, the Princess Kuveni, performed a certain devil-worship ceremony at the Yakka graveyard in the high jungle.'

The king banged a fist on his desk. 'We had commanded her not to conduct such rites,' he ground out, his tawny eyes sparking with anger. 'We shall demand an explanation from her immediately. Send for her.'

'Not so, my lord,' Ujjeni begged. 'Please hear me out.'

The king quietened but his fingers drummed a tattoo on the desk. 'All right. Proceed.'

'I do not need to impress on your majesty the stark disloyalty of this action. But note the timing. The event took place on the eve of a battle which could have seen you win or lose, wounded or dead. Such conduct is surely unbecoming in a spouse, so she failed you both as queen and wife.'

The king made no comment, merely waited for Ujjeni to go on.

'What is worse, however, is the nature of the ceremony that your spouse, our queen, conducted. It is called a *hooniyam* and was a Yakka ritual directed to the sole and exclusive purpose of rendering you sterile, infertile, incapable of ever giving your kingdom heirs other than the twins this Yakka b . . . princess has already bred.'

Somehow the news went deeper than Uraw had expected, for the Great King's eyes widened, his great jaw slackened and he stared into space. 'So she created that with which . . .' He began, but stopped abruptly to glance at Ujjeni. 'Tell us more about this ceremony,' he commanded.

'Before I do so, may I also respectfully remind your majesty that it was soon after that you were stricken by a disease which the Yakka claim can deprive a grown man of fertility. All this news is most disturbing to our men.'

'We do not believe in charms, *hooniyams*, gods, or old wives' tales,' the king replied, but somewhere in his voice Uraw detected a lack of conviction and some instinct told him that the Great King was more than angry, he was worried.

'I do not believe in charms either, Sire,' Ujjeni responded. 'But it brings the future sharply to our attention, especially since four kingdoms are involved.'

'You mean the question of an heir?'

'Yes, Lord.' Ujjeni's voice turned fierce. 'We can't bear the thought that some day, which we pray will be far in the future, these kingdoms which we have worked so hard to establish and we ourselves, or our progeny, may be ruled by unworthy persons of inferior race who practise barbaric rites and know nothing of Arya manners and customs. As for Prince Lala, we have some distressing news about his conduct as well.' He turned to Uraw. 'There are some very personal and confidential matters I wish to discuss with the Great King. Would you please excuse us now, Minister Uraw?'

Only when he made obeisance and left did Uraw realize how neatly his dismissal had involved him in what went before.

King Vijaya stormed into the Princess Kuveni's workroom while she was at her loom. She rose to her feet, terrified by his anger. Rupa, standing beside the two bassinets in which the babies were sleeping, cowered back.

'Madam' the king shouted. 'We hear that you have flouted our command and performed rites to your demon gods. Is this true?'

The princess made no reply, her downcast eyes an admission.

'We also know the nature of these rites.' The king calmed down and his tawny eyes narrowed. 'One more such from you and you will be put to death.' The words were spoken quietly, coldly. 'And from now on, you may remain in this palace, but you are our spouse only in name.'

The king turned on his heel and stalked out. Rupa wondered whether her mistress would realize that her demon rites had caused the king to isolate himself even from his spouse.

I had already written to my brother, felicitating him on becoming the Great King of all Lanka, but when I entered his study in Thamba-Panni forty days later I was taken aback by the change in him. His coldness added to my apprehension about his possible reaction to the news of my betrothal to Sundari. Although I had had frequent messages from him while he was in Sita Eli-ja, the weeks of silence since his return home had puzzled and worried me; but, having recovered

431

quickly from my shoulder wound, I had been so totally immersed in affairs of state in Kalyani and my blissful time with Sundari, that the days slipped by without my taking any action. Ruling a kingdom Arya fashion is a hard, gruelling business. The ruler has a fixed routine, commencing with the waking birds and ending long after nightfall. His working hours are divided into watches, which contain specified times for military training, exercise, reviewing troops, receiving reports, religious observances, staff discussions, supervising administration, dispensing justice, meeting embassies or deputations, attending Council sessions and even for bathing and meals. What had made it much more difficult for me was that I had taken over a divided kingdom, governed under different systems and in different styles.

The people were split into three factions: first those who had supported Prince Jaya and King Tikka, now, not entirely unexpectedly, a minority; second, those who had been loyal to the dead King Ra-hula; and finally, an inevitable majority, the neutralists, whom the people defined as '*dinana patthata hoi-ya*'. *Hoi-ya* is the cry that crowds of workers use in unison when pulling heavy weights, so the phrase had to come to mean, literally, 'towards the winning side of weight-pullers'.

Prince Jaya had proved to be extremely valuable. His wit, his charm, the pretence of being childlike when his agile brain was working most furiously, were a delight. He combined these qualities with a surprising knowledge of the kingdom and its affairs and considerable influence, all so remarkable that I could not help concluding that he had been grooming himself a long time for a takeover. My main goal was to introduce the Arya's decentralized form of government, with a system of reporting and accounting to the top that gave the central administration effective control. It would take years to get the people to accept it and my task was not made easier by the schisms between families and by various factions led by princes and nobility, especially the *dissawes*, regional lords and *rate mahal mayas*, chieftains.

During this period Sundari proved to be so loving, kind and understanding that I knew I had made the right decision. I would marry her, with or without my brother's permission, even if it meant giving up all I had and returning to Sinha-Pura. Her eyes would light up each time she saw me or heard my voice, her normally soft tones would become even softer, a caress entering them whenever she spoke to me. Only one unidentified concern nagged in the perfection of my happiness with her, a wistfulness that would enter her eyes at times, a tinge of sadness in her spirit, the cause of which even she could not identify, for she assured me that it did not come from the tragedy that had once smitten her, to which, by our spoken agreement, we never referred.

As I rose from my obeisance to the Great King, I was also shocked at his appearance. He had lost so much weight that his white tunic was loose on his shoulders. His leonine face was drawn, the cheeks grey, the wide jawbones prominent. His red beard, which had once become him, now hung incongruously. Even some of the glitter was gone from the tawny eyes, replaced by a strange hardness. This was a bitter, worried man.

I had expected him to embrace me when I finished making my obeisance, but he merely indicated my usual settle. 'We thank you for attending us so promptly, Prince,' he stated. 'Did you have a comfortable journey?' He might have been talking to a stranger.

'Yes, thank you, Sire,' I almost stammered, with equal formality. My eyes searched his face for some relenting, some sign of love, and found none. My spirit silently cried out its protest. I am your twin, flesh of your flesh, blood of your blood. Why have you become alien to me? How could you tear yourself from me in such a short space of time? Twenty-four years we have been as one, even when our lifestyles differed. Did I pull myself away from you when you led a gang of thieving, murderous princes and noblemen in your attempt to seize power from our royal father?

A moment's anger at his unjust attitude was quickly extinguished by deep hurt. I struggled against the bitterness it engendered, reaching for the source of that hurt, discovering it to be my love for him. From that love, I drew forth its purest essences, understanding and compassion. As waves of that compassion swept through me, I saw him to be a man in the throes of anguish, sick in body and mind, but mostly from a spirit in torment. Sad, I reflected, for you were once so strong you did not need to be tough and now in triumph you are sick.

I searched his face again. He must have felt my love for him, but he shook it off like a wounded lion the spear at its side, though there was just a hint of relaxation at the sides of his eyes. 'Give us your report, Prince,' he commanded.

'First tell me, Sire, are you well?'

'We are very well,' he stated flatly.

'I heard that you had contracted the Yakka's swollen cheek disease,' I persisted. 'It has caused you to lose weight.'

'It was nothing,' he almost growled.

'And your wife, the Princess Kuveni. I trust she is well?'

'She is well . . . your constant concern for her is touching.'

I decided to plunge into my report. 'I have organized the Kalyani sub-kingdom exactly as you have done in Thamba-Panni, Sire,' I began. 'I have divided the kingdom into five administrative districts, each district ruled by a governor, appointed by me on the advice of my Council, which consists of twelve Ministers, including Prince Jaya, representatives of the former king's faction, neutralists, noblemen and the people. I selected the people's representatives after receiving recommendations from their existing town councils and *gan sabhawas*, village societies. All these appointments were made shortly before I received your summons.'

'Having no knowledge of the region or of its people, how did you make your final choices so quickly?'

'That was what took me longest. And I might have experienced further delays had it not been for the guidance I received from Prince Jaya and our grandfather's former follower, Uday, the Venerable *bhikku*, Ra-vindra.'

My brother's jaw tightened and the tawny eyes shot me a glance. His fingers drummed their brief tattoo on the table and I felt a prickle of apprehension. 'Go on,' he directed.

'My twelve Ministers will overlook each of twelve departments I am creating, except for one of those departments, the Armed Forces, over which I shall retain control. The other departments are Education; Religion; Justice; Village Works; Food and Fisheries; Mines; Industries; Transportation; Taxes and Revenue; Foreign Trade and Customs; and Internal Security. Each of the district governors will also have a council of twelve district ministers, with the same division of functions, except that the local Armed Forces Departments will be confined to raising and equipping troops. My own ministers and their secretariats will supervise, coordinate and provide general direction and control to their respective departments in the five districts. Since the Kalyani village societies have traditionally provided people's courts for arbitration of disputes, I shall personally overlook the affairs of the town councils and the *gan-sabhawas*, of which there are over one hundred. Similarly, all criminal cases that come before the chief village headmen, their chieftains and the district governors can also be appealed to me.'

I went on to give current details of our military recruitment, the elephants, horses, chariots and equipment I had rapidly assembled, the revenues collected and spent to date, my plans for roads, schools, hospitals and court-houses, for maintaining the political stability I had rapidly established, the unity I was striving to introduce.

'You were always a superb administrator and once again you have done well.' There was a note of grudging admiration in his voice.

His praise emboldened me to reveal a totally new idea. 'Sire, I have also commenced having my edicts inscribed in stone and placed in public places so that all men may see and know them.'

His shaggy eyebrows lifted. 'Why?' He demanded.

'Sire, the king's laws are announced and his justice administered from wherever he may be – on horseback, in the field, reviewing his troops, in his audience hall, or even in his bedroom. These laws and edicts trickle down to the people only by beat of drum or word of mouth. The people are therefore often ignorant of the laws and can hardly be expected to know what they are, except for such basic ones as the death sentence for murder. Even the king's taxes, levied as a portion of the produce of his people, are collected by his appointees and there is nothing to prevent a tax collector in a distant region from pretending that the king has decreed a higher percentage and secretly keeping a personal share for himself, thus cheating both king and subject and possibly causing resentment against even a fair sovereign.'

I had expected my brother to be pleased at my enlightened act. Instead, his face contorted with anger. 'What are you trying to do?' he exploded. 'Show yourself a better ruler than ourselves?'

This was a man I did not know. 'No, Sire,' I explained patiently. 'I rule in Kalyani under your sovereignty. The people will, as always, surely know that all good flows from you and all ill from me.' I managed a wry smile. 'What I have done in Kalyani could not have been instituted here in Thamba-Panni because the Yakka people are not educated or cultivated like the Nagas. Few of them can read or write. You can, however, introduce the system to Ruhuna and perhaps extend it gradually to the other two kingdoms.'

His expression changed. 'You may be right.' He was still somewhat hesitant.

'All edicts are issued in your name, Sire,' I assured him. 'They make your justice consistent and absolute.'

'What if your edicts do not reflect our views?'

'Surely I know your mind, Sire, and I shall only issue them when I am completely certain. Consistency is essential for the well being of the people.'

He obviously saw the merits of my action, but some perverse devil within him kept gnawing at his mind. 'Consistency is not essential,' he retorted. 'Nothing is essential except the will of the ruler. Any choice between consistency and inconsistency is the king's prerogative.'

I decided that the time had come to take a firm stand. 'Sire,' I responded clearly. 'Over a year ago, on the night you seized this kingdom, you and I stood on the bund of a lake not far from here and you requested me in effect to be the voice of your ideals. Do you remember?'

'Yes,' he growled. 'But we did not give you the right to do more than voice those ideals. The right to accept or reject them was always ours and we can tell you now that the weight we give to your views will always depend on how you live up to your own ideals.'

'Consistency is vital,' I urged. 'Have I not been consistent with you?'

'No.'

'Where have I erred?' I knew, even as I asked the question, but did not even begin to suspect how deeply he thought I had erred.

'Ask yourself, Prince. You cannot be the voice of our conscience until you have looked clearly and honestly at your own.'

'Sire, I have always tried to be honest with myself and since I always regarded myself as a part of you that honesty extended to you. There is only one important aspect of my life that you are unaware of and I awaited a personal meeting to reveal it to you.'

His expression became bitter. 'It was the consistency of his faith in his son that caused our grandfather, Sinha's death at the hands of that son. We hope you do not seek to make our faith in you so consistent that it becomes our own death compulsion.'

'Birth is the first death compulsion,' I stated.

He stared at me, taking my words in, then nodded, his face softening. 'Well said, Prince. Your written edicts may stand. Send us some of your artisans so that we may follow suit in Thamba-Panni, side by side with the education we are slowly extending to the Yakkas through the village schools.' He reflected a few moments and a grim note of warning entered his voice. 'But have a care that your edicts accurately convey our own wishes, else they could become written evidence of defiance or even treason on your part.'

That he should even consider me capable of any act of treason was a wound that shocked me into silence. Treason I was absolutely incapable of. Inevitably the question arose, however, in my mind: What of defiance?

It suddenly struck me that his desire to wound must come from his own deep wounds. Loving him, I had to discover them, whatever the cost, to ease them without judging him. If nothing else, I now had love in my life. What did he have, if I too denied him true love? I half turned to face him, removed all else from my eyes, my expression, save my love-force, which I poured out to him freely. Long tense moments followed. Finally, his face began to lose its hardness. Soon his eyes widened and became moist. He leaned forward, his wrists on the desk, his great shoulders slumping. A half-sigh, half-groan escaped him. 'You do not deserve to find us in this state!' he exclaimed huskily.

'You do not deserve to be in such a state, Sire!' I cried. 'What has happened?'

He passed a hand across his brow. You are the Great King now, I reflected in anguish for him, yet you must stroke your own brow. You do not have a loving woman to tend you. Women are the breezes that caress a fevered body, the rain that gives life to a parched earth, the substance of the soil that brings new birth. The Princess Kuveni is a lost soul too. She has her own soul needs, but you cannot satisfy them, so she will for ever deny you the fulfilment of your own. Yet you are bound to her in honour, because you made a devil's bargain with her and can never have another woman while she lives.

'We have reached the zenith of our ambition, achieved a life's purpose, entered the gateway of success, only to find turmoil, confusion within,' he replied.

'How so, my lord?' I knew the answer even though I asked the question.

'No peace in the home, children whom we cannot even bear to look at, betrayal by you and . . . and . . . no hope of perpetuating what we have begun.' He stared into space.

'How have I betrayed you?' I cried.

'You tell us.'

'Sire, the only area of my life of which you are unaware, is that which I had intended bringing to your notice today,' I replied firmly.

'Is it any the less betrayal when you give us news of it?' His face hardened again and his look was challenging.

'You must be the judge of that, Sire. I told you that I had fallen in love with a young woman, Sundari, the very night it happened, here in this very fort. Remember, Sire?'

'Yes.'

'I met her again in the Kalyani palace the day after our battle against Prince Tikka. She had acquired an honoured place in King Sri Ra-hula's court where the king had given her refuge after her father, brother and betrothed were murdered. She nursed me back to health and now I am betrothed to her.'

'So it's all true.'

I made my mistake then. Instead of asking him what was true, I readily responded. 'Yes, Sire.' He was back in his shell again, remote from me.

'How dare you become betrothed without our permission?' he demanded.

'Sire, under our tradition, the betrothal compact is initially between two agreeing parties. It is its formalization and the marriage that require royal or parental approval.'

'You are right.' His agreement was grudging. 'Are you now

seeking our approval for the betrothal?'

'Yes, Sire. And I also beg your permission to marry the girl.'

'All this time and you hid it from us,' he mused.

'Sire, if I may say so respectfully, up to now my only concern has been you, your thoughts, your feelings, your desires, your aims, your ambitions. I have been your shadow since we were born. Now, for this first time, I am seeking something from you, something I desire with all my heart. Will you deny me?' I looked him straight in the eye.

He trembled slightly then looked away beyond the open doorway through the morning sunlight into some hidden recesses of his mind. Who knows where a man looks at such times? Minutes trickled by and I still kept my eyes on him, my love firm and steady. Finally, he sighed and his eyes flickered to mine. 'At this time, when all seems to be lost though we have gained all, we wish we could at least be sure of you. Don't you know that only your absolute obedience to us would give us the assurance of your love?'

There! It had come out again. He was pursuing my personal subjugation with the same relentless persistence with which he once pursued his quest for a kingdom. He would never give up. And I? What of me? Flesh of his flesh, indeed his twin, I would hold to my principles with like determination. I gazed in horror at the position we were in, for when we were not in opposition we had made a perfect team, complementing each other in every respect. Now that we were opposed, however, I was just as strong in my gentleness, my idealism, as he was in his thirst to be obeyed beyond reason.

He searched my face for my response. Not finding what he desired, his eyes went blank, his expression slowly hardened. He straightened abruptly in his chair. 'So much for that,' he coldly declared. 'The young woman you seek to wed is a Dasa of low caste. While you were dallying with her, a single kingdom has become four and the entire island is united.

440

Since our own progeny are half Yakka, whom we shall never name as heirs, you are next in line for the succession, which has suddenly assumed far greater importance. You now have a greater responsibility than to yourself, Prince. We shall convey our decision to you in due course.'

In spite of my grievous disappointment, I could see he was right about the succession, though I did not agree that his children should not succeed him.

He must have mistaken my silence for resentment for he added, 'we are contemplating certain actions that might help all parties,' speaking soothingly for the first time.

His words bothered me, as did the fact that he no longer felt free to confide his plans to me. I seemed to have gained Sundari only to lose him. Why was he so concerned with absolute obedience? What significance did such obedience have for him? Could he expect it of anyone? I was too young to know that there are always those who could seem to give it, so I made my second mistake of the day. 'Sire, Sundari means more to me than any kingdom,' I declared resolutely.

'Does she mean more to you than your brother, your king?' He grated harshly.

'Never, Sire,' I earnestly assured him. 'She and my brother, my king are one, for they are both the objects of my loving heart.'

'Words! Words!' He shouted. Then his anger broke loose. He rose to his feet, his settle flying back, and I rose with him. He raised clenched fists aloft, his mouth twisting. 'We trusted you to rule the Kalyani kingdom as we would have done, with impartiality and wisdom. You have created a sound administration but have aligned yourself with this Uday and his Buddhist followers who would subvert the fighting spirit of that nation. You have selected a low-caste Dasa for your betrothed and are openly living with her within the palace. The Dasa are not even one of the major races of Lanka. You are a known Yakka lover, fighting against our principle of Arya supremacy. Do you know that it is the curse of the Yakka

441

princess that may have robbed us of our seed?' He paused abruptly, as if he had divulged too much, then took another tack.

'Who are you? What kind of hypocrite have you become? Why are you sacrificing principle for expediency? Do you want to prove yourself better than we are so you can usurp our throne?'

I began to tremble with horror, shock, outrage. He must surely be possessed. Then, pride took over. Showing none of my pain, I drew myself to my full height and looked the Great King squarely in the face. 'Sire, I do not know from what sources you derive your news,' I asserted boldly. 'But, even if your mind does not, your heart will tell you it is totally false. If you still consider me to be all that you accuse me of, please remove me from the position of authority you have given me and inflict on me any punishment you deem fit for whatever crimes I may have committed.'

I returned his insane glare with cold dignity, barren of any love for him. 'As for my love for Sundari,' I added. 'It has prevented me from living with her in the manner you allege and no power on earth, no human agency can kill it, for my rotting bones, my scattered ashes will bear it even after I am dead.'

He was stunned by the intensity of my words, but only for a moment. He blinked once, then gave a bellow of fury and made for me round the table, his hand upraised to smite me. I held my ground, looking him in the eye. He stood there, his face thrust close to mine, shaking with rage, his hand still upraised. We battled each other, eye to eye, his weapon flaming fire, mine sleet.

He turned away first. 'You may leave now, Prince,' he stated over his shoulder. 'We shall consider your request to marry this woman and give you our decision in due course. Meanwhile, you have much to do while you are here.'

He had not even given my love the title of 'lady'.

Chapter 33

That same morning, in the Kalyani palace, Uday, the Venerable Sri Ravindra, received Sundari in his cell. His sole possessions were in the corner of the room, the spare yellow robe, neatly folded, his black begging bowl, an *indikola* fan, the pale, circular palmyra palm umbrella placed against the whitewashed wall. He acknowledged her salutation with a crinkling of his eyes, for he had liked her from the first day he met her. Indeed, she reminded him of his dead mother. The same masses of wavy black hair, framing a small face, the bones exquisite beneath a flawless pink complexion, the same slim body, clad in long bodice and skirt, capable of such grace of movement, mostly the same sensitivity and slenderness of spirit. Noting these characteristics objectively, he was not averse to finding them pleasing, for even his Master, Lord Buddha, had found certain people specially congenial without permitting his pleasure of them to become a source of desiring in any shape or form.

Seated on his beige-coloured mat, in the lotus pose, he noted her glancing around the small room, from the flagstone floor to the high-grilled window through which white-gold sunlight slanted. He gestured to her to sit down. Crossing her ankles, she sank easily into the lotus pose before him, arranging her pale blue skirt around her sandalled feet. The young are always easy and graceful of body, he reflected, the old should make up for it with ease and grace of mind.

He knew she would not speak until he opened the conversation. Such a respectful human being. 'You wished to see us, dear child.'

'Yes, Venerable Sir.' Her voice was low, her head still bowed.

'Speak then.'

'I'm afraid, Venerable Sir.'

'Of what, dear child?'

'I don't really know. At this very moment, however, I fear for my Prince Lala.'

She lifted dark eyes momentarily to Uday's and he saw that they were moist with tears, the fair cheeks trembling. She is only a child, though grown-up in her love, he thought. Knowing something of what lay ahead, he could not restrain a sigh. 'What is it that you fear for him?' he enquired.

'I fear that all is not going well for him at this moment,' she replied hesitantly. 'He is probably with his brother, the Great King, so he should be happy, but since I think of him all the time and respond to his every feeling, even when our bodies are apart, I sense that he is deeply troubled. I believe I lived my entire life just for the moment when he and I met. You know . . . I am so much a part of him that his sorrow immediately becomes my sorrow. I asked you please to see me because I have had strange forebodings since last night.' She smiled wryly. 'I even had a nightmare and my lady attendant said it was from eating burnt jak seeds in the evening, that it is not good to eat indigestible foods at night. But how is it then that she eats them all the time without bad effects?'

'You still have not told us the cause of your fear,' Uday reminded her gently. 'You know what it is, so why not bring it out to the open?'

'The Great King will not approve our betrothal and marriage.'

'He has no cause to oppose it, but kings do not always act with cause, so you may well be right. What do you think Prince Lala will do if the king refuses his consent?'

'The prince loves me. We shall be married regardless.'

'Then there is no problem, is there?'

'But if so, the prince will have to give up everything.'

'What is everything, dear child?'

'His position, this palace, his work, his brother . . .'

'Do you think Prince Lala sets much store by such worldly things?'

'N - n - no, Venerable Sir.'

Uday made up his mind. 'You are part of the prince's *kharma*, just as he is part of yours,' he firmly advised. 'Your love for him is part of what he has earned by his past good lives.' He held up his hand as Sundari lifted her eyes, now eager, to his. 'Not for enjoyment as you conceive it, my child, but as the gateway to his salvation, just as our Lord Buddha wed the Princess Yaso-dara and begat a son so that he could later find enlightenment.'

Her eyes became round as saucers and a hint of real fear entered them. 'You mean Prince Lala will leave me for the doctrine?'

'What is leaving when there is no arriving, child? "Leaving" such as you fear is inevitable, if at no other time, then in death. Fear of being left is merely a part of *thanha*, desire, which we must eliminate.'

'I have not reached that stage, venerable Sir. As you know, I have embraced the doctrine, but since meeting Prince Lala again, I have given up thoughts of becoming a *bhikkshuni*, a female monk. Being young, I want to be with my prince.' She paused. 'Will that harm my future?' Her eyes widened. 'If so, I don't really care, so long as I can be with my prince. I suppose that means I am in a poor state of development.' Her voice grew resolute. 'But I don't care about that either.'

Uday sighed. 'Who is to say that a good love such as yours is a poor stage of *kharmic* development?' He enquired gently. 'Have no fear. Let your heart guide you and all will be well.'

'Do you really mean that?'

'Certainly, my child. Good *kharma* is good *kharma*, whatever form it may take. Even if you cannot commit yourself permanently to *dasa sila*'s ten precepts, you are still in an exalted state.'

'Oh, I'm so relieved to learn that.' She hesitated. 'Now there is one more thing I must confide in you, because I cannot tell Prince Lala without making him worry. There are moments when I feel that death is not far away from me.' She paused. 'Also, my prince is such a good man, there are moments that I know his enemies will want to destroy him.' A piteous expression entered her doe-like eyes, the tears began running down her cheeks. Still in the lotus pose, she lowered her sad head.

Uday directed the force of his compassion towards her, willing his strength into her being, until her sobs subsided into occasional head jerks. 'That is what . . . sob . . . my nightmare is about,' she whispered. 'I see flames. I hear their crackle and roar, I feel their heat, their intensity, I smell the smoke and it chokes me. Suddenly, I see Prince Lala, clad in white. The flames are creeping towards him. I want to run to him, but my feet are heavy, chained to the ground. Each step feels as if I am dragging the weight of the world along. I am powerless to help him.' She lifted her palms to her face and covered her eyes with long slender fingers, through which the teardrops trickled and fell. 'The nightmare always ends suddenly, without result, and I awaken, terrified.'

Uday heard again the roar of flames from Sinha's funeral pyre and looked beyond. His eyes widened.

Hurt and angry at my brother's reaction, feeling fiercely protective of Sundari, I left my brother's study in the Priti palace after our discussion and made my third mistake of the day. Why is it that these things always occur in cycles?

With the wisdom of hindsight, I know that I should have understood my brother's mental state, which had been clearly revealed by the see-sawing of his responses and his unwonted emotionalism, whether it was his outcry or his withdrawal. I should have acted with love and discretion. Instead, I rushed from the study to seek out Ujjeni. I was told that he was by the river, overlooking the arrival of a shipment of timber from the hill country.

I pushed my way through the clamorous crowd of bare-chested Yakka labourers on the *maidan* opposite the fort. The affection with which they greeted me released some of my tension. I found Ujjeni and Uraw on the river bank giving instructions to the *mahouts* of the great, grey elephants that were standing by in a row, drag chains around their necks, chomping on the green leaves of branches spread before them. The timbers, strapped together to make rafts, had been floated downstream, guided by dark-skinned men clad only in span-cloths, and would be dragged out by the elephants.

Ujjeni glanced up at my approach, excused himself and walked up to meet me. He greeted me with a pleasant, 'Good morning, Prince. It's good to see you.'

I returned his greeting. 'I would like a few words with you in private, Minister.'

'Certainly.' He did not seem surprised.

We walked down the river bank beneath the shade of tall trees, sunlight glittering on the grey-green waters splashing and chuckling below. I paused when we were out of earshot of the crowd. 'This won't take long,' I stated, trying to keep my anger, still intense, under control. 'This is man to man. The young lady, Sundari, whom you once attempted to molest is in the Kalyani palace under my protection. I have asked my brother for permission to marry her. I believe you murdered her family. If anything were to happen to her, I would hold you personally accountable and kill you, Minister.'

Ujjeni had been eyeing me superciliously when I started speaking but I felt him quailing for an instant at the quiet ferocity of my last words. 'Are you threatening me, Prince?' he demanded, recovering quickly.

'Yes,' I stated flatly. 'You now have a vested interest in the lady's safety and in mine for that matter, because I have also taken steps to have you brought to account should anything untoward happen to me.' I was bluffing now, but he was not to know it. I smiled with my teeth, not my eyes. 'As Minister for Internal Security you have a duty to ensure our safety. Good day, Minister.'

I turned and stalked away, but not before I detected once more the bitter hatred I had already seen in his sick mind.

Uraw saw Prince Lala returning to the palace and waited for Ujjeni to join him, noting that his colleague was thoughtful.

'That was brief,' Uraw remarked. 'What was it all about?'

Ujjeni silently watched the retreating figure of the man he detested with narrowed eyes. 'Nothing!' He finally responded. 'But I'll tell you this, Minister Uraw. I had sworn to myself that I would forget women and concentrate on my job. As you know, I have kept that resolve and shall continue doing so, but the day will come when I shall break it to wreak vengeance.' He paused, his face tight, suddenly gave his deep, mirthless hee . . . hee . . . hee belly laugh, then added. 'Ujjeni has always waited, years if necessary, for the right time, but in the end, Ujjeni has always got even with those who shamed him.'

Three days later, after endless meetings and conferences, furnishing statistics and reports, planning and receiving orders, I was free to return to Kalyani. During that time, I had hoped that the Great King would at least discuss my request that I be permitted to marry Sundari, but he made no mention of it at all. It was with a bleak feeling therefore that I prepared to leave. Appropriately, it seemed to me, the morning was cloudy, one of those days when the earth did not seem to be able to make up its mind as to what clothes it would wear.

To my surprise, the Great King came to the palace courtyard to see me off. What amazed me, however, was his attire. He had on a gold *kurtha*, red pantaloons and, surprisingly, a turban made of cloth of gold, with a peacock feather at its side. He must have known I would react. 'These clothes arrived from Madura last night,' he explained. 'Ujjeni has established a regular post by ship between our two kingdoms. Ujjeni is a visionary. He feels that a king should at all times be a symbol of grandeur, close to the gods. So, the clothes . . .' He smiled and shrugged. 'And since a god must reside in an appropriate temple, Ujjeni is having plans drawn for a grand new palace on this very site. We shall show the people of Lanka what culture really means.'

His words startled me. The palace protocol and procedures I had established from the commencement of our rule in Thamba-Panni helped to ensure that the king would perform the duties and obligations of an Arya ruler to his subjects. Now it seemed as if plans were afoot to remove the ruler from his people, to make him remote. Sadly, the only way this could be done was through taxing the people more.

Also, why the link-up with distant Madura instead of with Dasa kingdoms closer to Lanka? Was it part of the Arya syndrome? I mistrusted Ujjeni, who was fiendishly clever. By courting such baser whims and fancies of the Great King he was undoubtedly acquiring affection and trust. 'Sire, why is it necessary for you to remove yourself from your subjects?' I enquired. 'Surely it is better to have them love you as a man than to make yourself a remote figurehead?'

'A king is not a man,' King Vijaya snapped back. 'He has to stand aloof, as a symbol of his law. He cannot be a politician either, bending to the wishes of the people. Do you know what happens to the elected representatives of the people? They start off young, starry-eyed visionaries, but are soon consumed by the need to retain the support of the people in order to remain in power. They become practical, covering foresight with the blinkers of expediency, vision with blind lust for position. They buy support with the assets of those who support them. An absolute monarch does not have to curry the favour or love of his people, thus he rules long and effectively. We do not want the love of our people, only their respect.'

I knew I would never convince him, so I fell back on the devious. 'You look simply magnificent in your new clothes, Sire. Though your natural regality needs no more adornment than the lion needs a crown, your attire does not embellish you but rather is embellished by your person.'

He stared at me, taken aback, then the bellow of his laughter echoed through the courtyard, causing a covey of house sparrows to take flight from a neighbouring jacaranda tree, reminding me of happier times with him. 'You always had a glib tongue,' he observed, his shoulders still shaking with laughter, looking more his normal self at last.

'It's called diplomacy, Sire.'

'Well, diplomat and sub-king, we now bid you farewell. Remember your responsibilities.' To my surprise, he opened his arms to me. As I clasped him, however, I knew everything was different and might never be the same again.

The exchange between King Tikka and his sister-in-law, Razeena, had certainly not escaped Banda, for immediately after the ladies and children had withdrawn he shot a knowing glance at King Tikka, his eyes bright. 'We still follow the *charlithraya*, customs, of our *uda rata* within the walls of our humble abode, lord,' he stated. 'You shall have the proof of it in your bedchamber tonight and it will honour my home. Now your bath and fresh clothes are ready, after which we can eat.'

Hamy knew that Banda was referring to the *uda rata* custom whereby a host made available any female member of his household, even his wife, to an honoured guest. In this case, the lovely Razeena would bed with King Tikka tonight. He could not help wondering what the outcome would be, for his king had such an insatiable sexual appetite that he always wore out any woman he took and immediately sought another, as he had done that fateful night of his betrothal to King Kalu Sena's daughter at the Priti palace. Had that been another lifetime, Hamy wondered, as he followed Banda, the king and Kira to the well at the back of the house. To his amazement, water from the well had been made to flow naturally into enclosed bathing pools, set amid green shrubbery of white-flowered jasmine, green *anodha* and red-flowering pentax bushes.

King Tikka, Hamy and Kira stripped beneath linen towels and donned span-cloths, then lay on white sea sand in the largest of the pools, The water was warm and scented with sandalwood. So different from bathing at village wells, using pitchers to draw water. These were the first real moments of peace that Hamy had enjoyed in a long while. A clear day was flung down from a bright, cloudless blue sky. Shiny-winged dragonflies skimmed over the water and the buzzing of bees told of honey in the pentax flowers. Banda dismissed the three bare-bodied male attendants and sat down on a black granite garden seat. Hamy closed his eyes and decided to let any conversation run over him, like the lapping water.

'It is better to talk of private matters out in the open,' Banda observed to King Tikka in quiet tones. 'I trust my men, but not the walls of my house.'

King Tikka merely grunted his agreement.

'I have had news of your reverses, Lord,' Banda went on quietly. 'As you know, our King Deva Raja has ceded the Ruhuna kingdom to the Arya.' A bitter expression flitted across his face, though his naturally booming voice remained even. 'It was a betrayal of all I have built in this region, but the Arya king is too far away for us to bother about him. What are your own plans, Lord?'

'To lie low until Vijaya stops searching for us. We can then put together a really strong, effective guerilla group to resume our attacks on the Arya,' King Tikka answered, his voice fierce. 'It would be impossible to train and field an army that can defeat the Arya in battle. You know the mentality of our people. They are reluctant to bestir themselves in defeat, which is why they were our slaves in the first place. So we shall wear down the Arya as we did before, using Yakka patriots for sabotage activity. This should be easier now that the enemy are dispersed so widely, but the one way in which we shall make the plan finally effective is by assassinating Vijaya, Lala and the seven commanders.'

King Tikka said the words as casually as if he were going to send presents to the Arya leaders and Hamy shivered in the water, especially because he noted that Banda received the words with equal casualness.

'I know people whose profession is murder.' Banda responded. 'Their price depends on the degree of risk. But if I may humbly suggest it, killing the leaders alone may not achieve the object.'

'You obviously have some ideas. What do you propose?'

Eyes downcast, Banda reflected a moment. A crow's caw streaked through the quiet, ending in a grumble that was lost under a clamour of voices arising from the rear of the mansion. 'As you are aware, my wife is part-Arabi,' Banda finally began. 'What few people know is that she comes from a very powerful royal family in the Arabi country close to the continent. Her's is a nation of warriors, traditional enemies of the Pahlava. The Arabi would dominate their region except that they prefer fighting to unity, banditry to farming and cultivation. They are mercenaries by profession, mainly cavalrymen with the finest of horses, whom the great Emperors, Ky-roos and Dhar-roos, used for their campaigns. They would be more than a match for the Arya. The Arabi are already aware of the vast treasure trove that Lanka has become and would love the opportunity to . . . uh . . . visit . . . If you can go to their lands and inspire them with gold, jewels and promises, you could return in a few years with enough men, say a thousand, to rally the Yakka to our cause, overpower the Arya in open battle and gain mastery of the country.'

Hamy gaped at the sheer dimension of Banda's suggestion and he could sense King Tikka's immediate interest.

Then caution set in. 'Bringing in foreign mercenaries could

end in our exchanging one set of masters for another,' King Tikka demurred. 'At least the Arya are a known element, unlike a race of Arabi bandits.'

'We can easily dispose of them after they have helped us achieve our object,' Banda observed soberly. 'Bribe them well enough to return to their homeland or kill them.' Hamy shivered at the callousness of the little man, but King Tikka sat up with a splash. He wiped water from his eyes. 'How will we get there?' he enquired.

'By ship. I shall arrange it all.'

'And the money for mercenaries?'

'That too. I have trading posts and vast sums accumulated abroad, which I can never use and had intended for some . . . uh . . . deserving cause.'

King Tikka's eyes began to shine. 'What a fantastic idea,' he began, then stopped abruptly to shoot a suspicious glance at Banda. 'But why would you do all this, provide ships, regal sums of money, contacts in a strange land?'

'Shall we say, because I am a patriot and abhor Arya rule, which I see as a source of danger to my own commercial empire?'

'You could say it, cousin, but we would not believe you.' King Tikka pondered briefly, then made up his mind. 'What is your price?'

Banda was obviously taken aback by the bluntness of the question, but only for a moment. A gleam of respect entered his eyes and he began to stroke his black moustache, a half grin on his face. 'Do you know the sources of my wealth, Lord?' He enquired softly.

'You're a trader, an importer, an exporter, a shipowner. You own most of the stalls in the Devun Dara fairgrounds and you organize the purchase and distribution of produce as well as manufactured goods in the two kingdoms.'

Banda's sigh was obviously bogus. 'Taxes will kill me,' he stated. 'And they are imposed by the Arya.'

'So?'

'Lord, humble people like us must make a modest living, so I have become a smuggler, a fence for stolen goods, a receiver of produce that has not been declared for government taxes and a protector of the weak.'

'Meaning?'

'Meaning that manufacturers, traders, farmers and ship-owners pay for the use of my small army of guards to protect them from government officials, thieves and robbers, harm to their crops and produce.'

'Then you are virtually the king of crime in this region.'

'Better to be king of something, Lord, than a slave of anyone.'

'You still haven't named your price.'

'When you become king of Lanka, I would like to be your Chief Minister. I realize that this may take years, but I have always proceeded on the basis that it is better to wait and be certain than to rush in and . . . uh . . .' He paused, obviously not wishing to give offence.

You are right, Hamy thought, yet you must desire more than you are saying, for you are obviously a man of tremendous ambition. What if you, as the paymaster of the mercenaries, decide to use them in Lanka and become king yourself? He shrugged and cast the thoughts aside. The issues were becoming too complex for him. One thing at a time. He hoped that he would not have to cross the ocean. He did not care for the sound of crashing waves in the distance.

'Supposing we accept your help and don't keep our share of the bargain?' King Tikka inquired.

'That is a risk I have to take.' Banda's voice hardened momentarily. 'Of course, as you know, I am not entirely defenceless. But why worry about that? I shall make only two conditions to seal our pact.'

'And those?'

Banda glanced towards Hamy and Kira. 'The first is that you go to the Arabi lands alone, without your two companions, whom I could use here.'

'Easy enough.' The king responded and Hamy's anxious heart settled. 'And the next condition?'

'Your marriage to King Kalu Sena's daughter is non-existent. I request that you marry my sister-in-law, Razeena, immediately, so that she will become Queen of Lanka some day. It will certainly add to your credentials with her Arabi cousins.'

'We accept,' King Tikka readily replied. 'But what if we marry the girl and cast her aside once we have all Lanka?'

Banda threw back his head and laughed merrily. 'Now as to that there is no risk, whatever,' he spluttered. 'You shall see tonight.'

Razeena slid into King Tikka's bedchamber that night, a cloaked figure observed only by Hamy, who had slept through the day and kept guard at the entrance. She stole out at dawn, smiling bright-eyed at him, looking as fresh as ever. Hamy peered through the door of the bedchamber. King Tikka lay sprawled on the gold silk sheets and cushions of the canopied bed like a jack-hare Hamy had once accidentally released overnight in a cage of doe-hares, completely exhausted.

One week later, King Tikka, having married Razeena in a simple Yakka ceremony, set sail for the Arabi lands.

The Princess Kuveni sat on a stool beside the two cane bassinets in the courtyard, as she had been wont to do every morning since the twins were two weeks old. It was pleasant and peaceful here, with only bird sounds, the screech of a mynah, the twitter of house sparrows and the cooing of doves to enhance the silence. The sunlight was white-gold, the shadows cool. Rupa, standing as usual beside the bassinets, occasionally waving an *indi-kola* fan over the sleeping babies, now just over three months old, to drive away tiny black eye-flies and the odd mosquito, felt the calm that had finally settled on the spirit of her mistress since she came to accept her physical separation from the Great King.

Rupa was glad not only for her mistress but also for herself, because now she had nothing to report to the hated Ujjeni.

'Do you know, I have begun to enjoy these mornings,' Rupa said involuntarily. 'Only you and I, alone with our babies. Look how their small dark faces pucker in their sleep. It makes them seem so old. People say this is from the dreams that babies have of their past old age. They are so tiny and helpless, I want to shield them from harm. I swear to you on them, my lady, wherever you go, I shall follow you.'

'Why did you say that, Rupa?' The princess demanded. 'Where else would you be, but in your rightful place, in this palace?'

Rupa could do no more than shrug her shoulders.

'You're right, Rupa, it's really peaceful here.' The princess continued in her rich, low voice. 'I'm beginning to realize that though I no longer have a spouse, I have much to be thankful for. I have a pleasant home, food, clothing, attendants to do my bidding, security, these two beautiful babies . . . and always you.' Her smile was so humble and sweet, Rupa felt ashamed of her perfidy. 'I have security, so now I must find peace within myself. This was hard in the past, because I made my Lord everything, worshipped his very breath and desired him solely for myself. Now that I have his children and am certain that no other woman will ever have the precious gift of his seed, I have a part of him exclusively and for ever. That is enough. It gives me fierce joy, satisfies some longing within me and makes it easier to bear the severance from him that still tears at my chest at times, causing it to ache unbearably. I know I'm different from other women. Tell me frankly, Rupa, do you think I'm mad?'

Rupa looked down at the ebony face lifted to her, noting the innocent enquiry in the dark, lustrous eyes, the beauty of the high prominent cheekbones and the wide full mouth. 'No one who is really mad would ask if they were mad, my lady,' she replied. 'I'm as truly thankful for the miracle that has brought you peace of mind as I am for the miracle of motherhood bestowed on you by our gods.' For an instant, Rupa felt the old yearning for the feel of a child in her own womb. 'After all, what is madness, my lady, but that which is unusual within us when we are driven beyond normal conduct by frustration, loneliness or despair? If to be different is to be mad, then all men are mad, for we are all the same and yet we are different. People who show insanity when the moon is full are called mad because they cannot control their actions, yet men and women who cannot control their need to cohabit and over-indulge these desires, or men of insatiable ambition, are not deemed mad though they are crazed by their longings.'

'H'mmm! You think a lot for a village woman. It's all too deep for me.' The princess looked away, staring first at a pomegranate bush without seeming to notice it, then up at the green branches of a shower tree laden with purple blossoms and finally at the pale blue morning sky. 'Since you know so much without learning, tell me, why is it that we do not see our *tharuwa*, our red planet, during the day?'

The apparently irrelevant question startled Rupa. 'Why . . . why . . . it is because, like the other stars, it slowly moves away before dawn, out of respect for the sun, as subjects back away from the presence of their ruler.'

'Do you think it runs away in fear from the sun's stare?'

'Oh no, my lady. The red planet of all the stars is the least likely to be afraid. Remember, it is the planet of war.'

'How do we know?'

'Because our old ones have told us and their old ones told them . . . on and on, since time first began and our tribe was placed upon this earth by the demon gods to create an abode and shrines for them.'

'I want to think about it, but my mind will not let me. It is as if I have a thick layer of mud in my head that such questions cannot penetrate.' The princess passed a dark hand over her forehead and gripped her temples with her thumb and middle finger as if to press out the mud. 'I sometimes think that our demon gods use the sun as a weapon to drive away the dark influences of the planets, of which they too are afraid, so that we mortals may have some freedom from fear at least part of the time. Do you realize that it is easier to be afraid at night than during the day?' She removed her hand from her forehead, gesturing with it towards the clear sunshine.

Rupa shook her head vehemently, suddenly afraid that questioning the wisdom of the ancients, the history of man and god, handed down, like the history of the tribe, by word of mouth from generation to generation, might bring bad luck. 'Oh no, my lady. You must never even think such things.'

'I can and I shall.' There was defiance in the voice of the princess. 'My demon god, Reeri Yakseya alone will give me wisdom and strength. I fear nothing except his intolerance and ruthlessness. I shall continue worshipping him, though I can no longer perform my duties as his priestess. I now believe that my two babies are Reeri Yakseya's. This new peace I have begun to feel can only come from him. He gave me storm as a virgin, but he now gives me calm as the mother of his children. I am certain that he has a final purpose for me, which will be revealed in the fullness of time.'

The baby boy whimpered in his sleep and the princess stood up to hush him, gently patting his side. The whimpering subsided and the princess looked squarely at Rupa, her dark eyes magnetic. 'I believe that our demon god created our two babies to save our race.'

Chapter 34

Six months after I became the sub-ruler of Kalyani, I had still had no word from the Great King on my request for permission to marry Sundari. His silence was the only cloud on our horizon, for I would not hold Sundari in my arms until we were married or she had become my concubine, an estate I was determined not to bestow on her. Yet she and I found so much happiness by just being together that I was prepared to wait, however impatiently.

Then real clouds filled the skies to send down the annual rain that falls only on the south-western parts of Lanka and the mountains, at the end of the months of Vesakha. It poured forth as never before, destroying crops in the Kalyani kingdom and causing terrible earthslips. The river rose, flooding the countryside and destroying homes. Several deaths were reported.

People consider their rulers to be bringers of good luck or misfortune and look to them as a last resort for appeasing the gods of catastrophe. Was I the cause of these happenings? What could I do to halt them?

Prince Jaya had not only proved a tower of strength to me, but had become so close a friend that he visited me in the palace, from his residence next door, at least once each day for a 'nice chat', as he called it, after the pre-noon watch, for by then I had finished the audience I gave the public. The unceasing rain had put a stop to those visits for three days, so I was glad to see his bulky figure enter the audience hall on the fourth morning.

I stepped down from the dais and hastened towards him. 'I am so happy to see you again, Prince,' I declared warmly. 'I had begun to fear that the incessant rain had finally washed you away.'

His pudgy features crinkled into an affectionate smile, the dark eyes vanishing inside the folds. '*Aney*, how can any amount of rain wash away a man mountain, Lord?' He responded. 'I kept away because I knew you would not want me to get wet and develop, a *peenussa*, catarrh, but I came no sooner the rain eased the weeniest bit, because I did not want you to think me a fair-weather friend.'

'So being a foul-weather friend you waited until the rain let up,' I retorted, glancing through the window grille, noting that the air was clear though damp and dark from overhanging clouds. 'I missed you.'

He gave his high-pitched giggle. 'You're a fine one, no? Who told you this is fair weather? Maybe it is fair in the land you came from, but in our fair island of Lanka, this is still foul weather.' He feigned a hacking cough and cleared his throat. 'See! I braved the elements though I'm very sick, just so that the sunshine of your presence could cure me.' He coughed again, drily this time. 'See, you have cured me already, though I was almost at death's door.'

I laughed, warming to him and clapped a hand briefly on his massive shoulder. The dark eyes appeared as slits for an instant. Before they vanished again, they told me that my instinctive gesture had moved him. In that flush of warmth for him, I realized that he was easier to be with than my brother.

Prince Jaya grew suddenly serious, looking like an overgrown child. 'This rain is the worst we have had since I can remember,' he observed soberly. 'Already people are saying the gods have sent it to avenge King Sri Ra-hula's death.' He raised a deprecating hand. 'Tchickay! You know I never wanted it. That fellow Tikka. No class, no? My plan was to keep the king alive and use him for the good of the kingdom.' He shrugged beefy shoulders. 'Now even the river has risen against me. Did you see, Lord?'

'I had no time to look this morning.'

'The town is getting flooded, a few people killed. One of my

461

sp . . . retainers brought word today that many are homeless all along the river banks. Houses washed away, crops destroyed. And do you know the worst?'

'No.'

'Aiyo! Why should I have to be the one to bring you the bad news? All the paddy and other seed for re-planting has been destroyed too. What are we going to do next season? We will require a whole year to recover. Meanwhile the people will starve.'

'Not if I can help it,' I ground out, staring boldly at him in spite of the fear that swirled around my stomach at the awesome responsibility of looking after the thousands of people hit by the disaster.

'One thing I have to say,' the prince continued. 'I hated the guts of these Buddhist people until I saw how . . . how . . .' his voice faltered. 'King Ra-hula died. Such a noble person. I wish I had his . . .' he paused, grinned wryly, 'guts . . . These past few days, I have also heard that the Buddhists are helping those who have suffered. They call it *dana*, alms-giving, which they claim enables them to acquire merit.' That mischievous smile creased his features. '*Apoi!* How to agree that this can happen? People cannot barter with the gods, like selling dry-fish for gold. But what these people are doing is good for others, that I can't deny. So I'm beginning to like the Buddhists.'

'You should study Buddhism seriously, Prince. I believe you were made for it.'

'Too fat and lazy to get into any religion.' I knew he lied, that he had taken to studying the doctrine immediately after he returned from the big battle. 'I want you to come outside and look at the river.'

'I thought you came to talk to me and be cured by my radiance.'

He gaped at me for a split second, then rode on the wings of that high-pitched giggle, the great shoulders shaking this time, the flabby pectorals beneath his white tunic jittering like *dodol*, jelly. 'You are too quick for me, Prince,' he gasped. And I knew he lied again. 'Seriously though, your palace and my mansion are safe because we are on a hillock overlooking the river bank, but the town is in grave danger.'

'In that case, let us hurry,' I rejoined. 'Meanwhile, here's our relief plan. The refugees shall build temporary camps for themselves with timber from our warehouses and all the thatch we can commandeer. Then we shall provide them with food and clothing. All necessary payments shall be made from the king's Treasury, wherever private contributions fall short. You, Prince, shall be responsible for coordinating arrangements between the government and private charity. Use the Buddhist clergy. Camps can even be established in their temples. Luckily, Thamba-Panni is spared the rains of this season, so we can look to the Great King to give us paddy and seed for replanting. Now spread the word quickly to give people hope for the future. Convince them that these rains came for their good, to destroy the past, so that we can organize farming communities as in Thamba-Panni and bring prosperity to Kalyani.'

His eyes glistened. 'You are a good person, Prince,' he stated huskily. 'I pray that those who oppose you in high places will not pounce on your generosity to do you harm.' He sighed, shaking his head at my surprise. 'I make it my business to know what is going on. Be assured, however, that here in Kalyani you have no enemies, only friends, whom you have made through your unfailing kindness and humanity.' He smiled, embarrassed by his own sincerity. 'But we are wasting time, no? Let us hurry and inspect our present enemy, the river, before our late enemy, the rain, attacks once more.'

Surprised and moved by his words, I led the way to the rear of the palace. I had merely been myself, little dreaming that I was earning the loyalty and gratitude of the people. As we passed Uday's cell, the *bhikku* emerged. He acknowledged our greeting with a gracious nod. 'We see you are in haste,' he observed. 'Perhaps we have the same mission in mind?'

'We are going to inspect the river,' I replied. 'Prince Jaya says it has risen alarmingly during the night.'

'So we fear. May we join you?'

'Of course.' I was puzzled by Uday's interest in what was after all a worldly matter, but made no comment.

Walking more slowly now to accommodate Uday's sedate pace, we proceeded along the courtyard verandah then entered a narrow corridor before emerging outside into the great back garden of the palace. The roar of the river, interwoven by the occasional thunder of logs crashing against one another, became almost frightening. Soon the ground rose sharply and we squelched over muddy grass to the rear boundary wall of the palace. Though the rain still held back, it threatened more heavily from grey clouds that seemed to be lowering themselves on to the green treetops and squeezing water-drip from them. We passed through a small wicket gate and climbed a knoll to stand on the dank dead leaves at the edge of a grove of jak trees.

The river was revealed in awesome splendour, an enormous wide spread of muddy brown, racing past us faster than the stars that drop from their sockets in the heavens at night. It forged towards our left, where the township lay, a great spread of homes with tiled or thatched roofs beyond a black outcrop of rocks, then veered right to disappear abruptly round a bend. With horror, I saw on that grotesque brown bosom the proof of the river's marriage with death and destruction, reminding me of the obscene revelries of its parent, the ocean. Great logs swirled and twisted like mad dervishes in the maelstrom. The black corpses of cattle, branches and debris, even the remains of a home that slowly disintegrated before our eyes, were swept past us at incredible speed. As we watched spellbound, a small, dark island, with a solitary trunk upraised like a coconut palm whose branches had been destroyed by lightning, sped by.

'By the devas, an elephant!' Prince Jaya cried. He pointed. 'Look! What a fantastic sight. The creature has its trunk raised to be able to breathe and is battling the currents, slowly heading for the bank. Oh! What a magnificent struggle of life against the elements. The elephant is going to win.'

'Not so,' Uday rejoined somewhat sadly. 'The animal's fate is already ordained by *kharma/vipaka*; it had to be placed in these circumstances at this particular time.'

The raging waters carried the elephant along, the great, grey hulk quickly diminishing in size. My stomach clenched with the knowledge of what would happen. Fighting against the bend of the waters, the elephant was borne headlong towards the rocky outcrop. I could almost hear the great thud as it crashed into the rocks. The upraised trunk wavered and collapsed, the vast hulk rolled over and vanished, submerged by its own lifeless weight. If it had not sought to escape death, it might have been carried to the ocean and lived. My stomach became queasy, I fought down the urge to be sick.

'The waters are rising fast,' Uday stated urgently. 'Soon they will not be able to take the bend and will smash through the town. We must rush there immediately and order evacuation.'

'Too late,' Prince Jaya broke in. 'We'll never get there in time.' He grinned. 'But have no worry. The town has already been evacuated on my orders.'

I heaved a sigh of relief, the knot within me dissolving. 'Good man!' I exclaimed. 'But let's go there anyway to organize relief.'

The river bank was steep at this point. I led the way along a path that skirted it to the edge of the palace gardens. Here the grove of jak trees ended at the boathouse and the ground, now dotted with scrubby cinnamon bushes, sloped downwards to the river's bend. Before our very eyes, the raging river waters slowly crept upwards and began to cover the grass. As one, we paused to look. The muddy line became a creeping sheet, spreading, ever fanning out to swallow up the earth. Within minutes, the sheet had risen and was lapping greedily against the first row of houses. Soon the sheet became its own lake, rising and spreading through the abandoned dwellings that had yesterday teemed with life, but now looked like a ghost town, Mohenjo Daro after it was abandoned by the Hari Appa, the righteous forefathers. This would have been a grand sight if human life, death and destruction had not been involved, for the main flow of the river continued round the bend, while the waters that could not take its swift turn were now crashing over the bank, leaving a great wedge of land in between with vacant homes untouched upon it. Before our very eyes, this wedge of land became an island as the waters that rose in the township swirled around it and hastened to rejoin their parent river.

'Dear devas, look!' Prince Jaya pointed a shaking finger at one of the homes. A woman and three small children had emerged from its entrance, bearing boxes on their heads.

'They returned for some of their possessions,' I exclaimed.

'They must have eluded the guards I posted to prevent it,' Prince Jaya interjected. 'Oh, the stupid, stupid people. Now they are trapped. They have no hope of escape.'

'Oh yes, they have,' I cried. 'Quick, to the boathouse. Help me launch one of the boats before it's too late.'

We raced back to the boathouse. Inside, under cover, three long canoes and a larger boat, covered with a roof, lay on blocks. These boats had once been used for the king's pleasure, but neither the late King Ra-hula, nor I had used them. By the time we released the wedges and dragged one of the canoes down to the water's edge, I had cause to be surprised at the speed and agility which the obese Prince Jaya could generate in an emergency, his great limbs pumping away, and at Uday's physical strength and resolution.

Both men held the boat while I leapt into it and seized a paddle. 'Now give me a shove!' I shouted, raising the paddle.

'In a moment,' Prince Jaya puffed.

Stunned, I felt the canoe keel over with his weight. It righted itself after he wedged himself on to the seat. 'Hey! It's dangerous,' I began.

'A foul-weather friend, remember,' he grinned and seized a

paddle. 'You'll need another elephant to battle the waters.'

I did not even bother to ask Uday to give us a shove, because I knew his mission. He had already tucked up his yellow robe and swung curiously white limbs into the canoe. 'I shall guide the boat,' he quietly stated. 'The two of you can paddle.' He sounded so completely calm that it had a steadying effect on my thudding heart.

'Trust a *bhikku* to do the least strenuous work,' Prince Jaya giggled and dipped his paddle in the water.

We skirted along the edge of the still rising flood-waters, then turned and headed through the town. Waves splashed against the side of the canoe as we turned right to push through the township. So swiftly had the waters risen that they were half-way up to the barricaded entrance doors of most of the shops that lined the central street. The waters here had become a fast-moving stream, on which we had to use our paddles to break our speed and avoid being whirled to destruction. Uday was doing a superb job of steering us on our mad trip between houses and beneath tall *mara* trees, amid the clamour of floodwater and the fetid stench of flood-mud.

So intent were we on keeping control of the boat that at first I barely heard the shouting. When it finally penetrated, I glanced at its direction. A great crowd thronged the high open ground above the township. There must have been hundreds of them. What were they doing there?

Prince Jaya must have sensed the question in my mind. 'They were evacuated to the safety of the hill, where the Buddhist school buildings can house them,' he explained between puffs and deft movements of his paddle. 'They must have stood there to watch their homes being flooded.'

'Surely they must have seen the plight of that woman and her children,' I cried.

Prince Jaya's comment was unspoken, except for a snort.

'Remember, unlike us, they have no boats,' Uday gently reminded and I felt ashamed at his implied rebuke.

We had reached the end of the township now and edged our way along it, heading on an oblique course for the island.

'There they are!' Uday exclaimed. 'They have seen us. Row as fast as you can.'

We bent to our task. I could literally feel Prince Jaya's enormous strength with the paddle and I strove to keep time with his strokes.

I saw the wave before it hit us, but so sudden was the thrust that there was nothing I could do except shout a warning to Uday, who had his back to it. We were swept along at giddy speed, our paddles flailing empty air. I knew that we could soon crash into the artificial island. Even if we survived, the flood waters would engulf us. For an instant, I remembered the day our three ships were borne through the reef to land on Lanka's shores. Briefly, I said a prayer to God, not for myself, but for those three small children trapped out there.

Then a cross-tide charged into us. Caught between two currents, the canoe teetered. 'Row for your life!' Prince Jaya roared.

Before I could get my paddle into the water, the canoe careened to one side. Desperately I leaned to the opposite side, to steady it, plunging my paddle into the raging waters. In vain. The boat keeled over, then capsized. We were flung overboard.

I held my breath. My feet touched soft ground and I kicked away. Thank God, the wave had subsided and the water was no more than about three cubits deep there. Prince Jaya and Uday were already on their feet, the prince gasping and spitting. We were wet as dogs in a pond. The capsized canoe slapped against me.

'Grab the boat!' I cried, holding on to one end.

The canoe suddenly seemed to have a life of its own. Its slippery sides kept eluding my grasp, bucking, twisting, turning. We finally held it firm in the churning water, but it was Prince Jaya's enormous strength that enabled us to right it. Rather than attempt to climb aboard, we dragged it slowly to the island.

The refugees proved to be a lean middle-aged woman, her

black hair liberally strewn with silver, and three girls, perhaps seven, eight and nine years of age. They were dressed alike in shabby red cloths and jackets. Uniformly lean and gaunt, the same haunted look in their staring eyes was a pitiful sight. 'Thank the devas you have come!' The woman cried, recognizing us and making obeisance. 'We returned for our possessions, but were caught by the sudden flooding.'

'Why did you sneak back?' Prince Jaya demanded roughly. 'You had no right to endanger the lives of these three children against my orders.'

'*Apoi*, lord! What meaning does life have for the four of us after the children's father, my husband, died last year? We are so poor, if we did not rescue my jewellery and our few possessions, we would have become beggars or starved to death.'

'Let's not waste time,' I intervened. 'We may all die anyhow. Get in the boat, all four of you. Leave your goods behind. You shall have better and more from now on.'

The woman fell on her knees before me, but I raised her up and found that she was trembling.

The waters were rising at an alarming rate and the island would soon be swamped. We held the boat steady while they boarded it. Uday selected a point that we could make for, across the floodwater area. 'Going back will be easier,' he stated. 'We can land anywhere.'

And so it proved, though we had a couple of close calls, the first when the boat rammed a jacaranda tree, the second when we were caught in a whirlpool. As we drew close to dry ground, I heard the sound of cheering above the roar and lash of the waters and glanced up to see the hill packed with even more people, over a thousand of them. Only then did it dawn on me that a defeated prince of Kalyani, a victorious Arya prince and a prince of the doctrine had united in a simple act of mercy that none of us could have performed individually and, by endangering our lives for the humblest of our people, we had enriched our respective rules.

Later that afternoon, having bathed and changed into dry clothes, I was seated in the audience hall with Prince Jaya beside me, receiving reports of flood damage, when I was told that a deputation of women relief workers waited outside requesting an audience. Since there was a lull in the flow of visitors, I directed that the delegation be shown in immediately.

'The ladies have discovered a strong new leader,' Prince Jaya remarked, with a mischievous smile.

'Who is it?' I enquired, then glanced towards the door as the group entered and made obeisance.

For a moment, I could not take in what I saw, then my jaw dropped. It was Sundari, my beautiful Sundari, clad in white, who led the group. I looked sideways at Prince Jaya. His eyes had vanished beneath their folds, but his cheeks were crinkled and the flabby pectorals shook with his laughter. 'You have a formidable leader to deal with, Prince,' he declared.

'I'll get you for this,' I whispered to him.

The group consisted of twelve ladies, all dressed in white. It would not have been proper for them to wear bright colours at a time of national disaster. Sundari stood below the platform and presented them to me. They were all of royal blood, except for Sundari herself and three ladies well known for their Buddhist piety. I wondered how in the world Sundari had managed to become involved with a group of the haughtiest, most birth-proud women in the sub-kingdom, especially as their leader.

'Please sit down, ladies,' I commanded.

They took their seats in a single row facing the throne.

'Who will speak for you?' I enquired.

Princess Thaiyal, a tall, handsome woman, of olive complexion, impeccably groomed as always, rose to her feet. She was the wife of Prince Jega Nathan. 'It is my privilege to introduce the Lady Sundari, whom we have elected leader of our group, due to her piety, goodness and compassion,' she declared.

Sundari stood up and looked at me with those dark, luminous eyes that caused my heart to melt. I barely noticed the Princess Thaiyal resuming her seat.

'Lord Prince, I am honoured to lead this delegation of eminent ladies,' Sundari stated. 'Our presence here reveals the truth of Lord Buddha's words . . . not by birth is a Brahman made' . . . for these ladies are more than noble, they are Brahmans.' She paused, a hand gesturing gracefully at her colleagues. 'We of this delegation believe that all people are one in tragedy. We also believe in self-help and are here to place our services and those of all women in the sub-kingdom of Kalyani whom we can reach at your disposal for relief work.'

I was deeply moved. At that moment, my love for Sundari suddenly went deeper than ever before. 'Do you have anything specific in mind?' I enquired, thinking the delegation might be planning merely to raise donations of various kinds.

'Yes, lord,' Sundari replied firmly. 'We believe that the royal palace, being the centre of government, should also be the focal point of succour to people in distress. For years now, the ladies' quarters of the palace have been used mainly by women of Buddhist piety and ladies-in-waiting. We propose that they should become the collection and distribution centre for food and clothing and for placing children orphaned by the floods in new homes, or establishing nurseries. By removing the burden of what we call the distaff side of relief from your administration, we believe we can release you for other pressing duties. We also humbly request your permission to organize committees of women throughout the kingdom – we have already drawn up a list of areas and centres – to decentralize our work.'

Sundari's gaze was respectful, enquiring and I felt so proud of her I thought my heart would burst. 'I certainly approve,' I declared smiling. 'You ladies are to be commended for your patriotism and compassion. But pray tell me, who conceived

471

this idea, who took the initiative?'

Sundari blushed. The other ladies rose as one, looking at her, applauding. 'The Lady Sundari,' Princess Thaiyal stated, giving my love the title by attainment that she never had by birth. I remembered her father, that scholarly, dignified man, and thanked God for him. I glanced at Prince Jaya. He studiously avoided my gaze.

It took no less than an hour to settle the details of the operation, because the ladies had it all worked out and I had merely to repeat 'Approved . . . Approved' . . . and shake my head in agreement. Yet, why should I have been surprised? It is women who run households, even finding food for their families when they are poor, managing somehow, with a kind of biological ingenuity. Why should they not show themselves superior beings in such a dire emergency?

Two weeks later, the floods completely subsided, leaving in their wake echoes of the horrible slurp of waters receding from mud, collapsed homes, destroyed property, the dank stench of stale ooze and slime and bereaved families. Having retreated to its normal course, the river now smiled greeny-brown in the sunshine, denying any participation in the terrible destruction it had wrought. Who me? it seemed to say.

On the plus side, we had successfully housed, clothed and fed all flood victims throughout the sub-kingdom, Prince Jaya and Uday organizing the men and Sundari leading the women in our relief efforts. I had also finalized plans for the future of the victims, for creating a new Kalyani township, located on high ground away from the river's reach, and for the establishment of advanced rural communities. Most important, however, disaster had brought out the best, the most charitable, in everyone, and the people had learned that they could depend on their rulers for support in times of emergency while the sharing of dire problems had established a closer bond throughout the entire sub-kingdom.

All the work of relief had been a drain on the resources of

the sub-kingdom and the Great King's Kalyani Treasury, but we had coped. Now the tasks of reconstruction required outside assistance and this could only come from the Great King, whose Thamba-Panni Treasury was full and who had surpluses from the other sub-kingdoms and accumulated wealth from the entire island of Lanka at his disposal. I therefore supplemented the reports of the disaster I had sent him by messenger from time to time with a special report and details of the measures and aid necessary to overcome it. I was pleased when he replied promptly, bidding me wait on him, without delay, at the Thamba-Panni palace.

I left on my journey, accompanied only by a cavalry escort, the day after I received his summons. I had all the facts and figures of our requirements at my fingertips and reckoned that I did not need Prince Jaya, or my ministers or a delegation, for the Great King to provide assistance to one of his territories.

We proceeded east along the south bank of the river to make an easier crossing. Unfortunately, we were delayed by damaged ferry boats, so it was the third evening before we drew close to Thamba-Panni. I decided to press on and reach the palace the same night, however late it might be.

Cantering easily at the head of my small column, I was tired from the ride and a little saddle-sore, but soothed by the drumming of hooves, the creak of leather and the occasional snorting of a horse. A mixture of scents from dark groves and the constant odour of the sweaty flanks of our mounts hung on the air. The night was clear, the heavens so cloudless that their thousand glittering stars hung low and seemed to travel with us. The quiet villages, the long stretches of open paddy, betokened a peace and prosperity sharply in contrast with all we had known in Kalyani the past two weeks, so I rode with a sense of exhilaration in my heart, confident that I would return with my mission accomplished, since the donor to be was my brother.

It was an hour to midnight before we reached the last bend in the new highway at the environs of the palace. I was surprised to see flare-lights dancing in the distance between the dark boles of the trees, and to hear thuds, rattles and sharp clinks above the sound of our hooves. Alarmed, I urged my horse to a gallop, my escort thundering behind me. As I rounded the bend, I saw that the entire area between the moat and the village, including all the village homes, had been cleared. Hundreds of men were at work, digging long trenches in the ground under the watchful eyes of supervisors. I slowed my mount and drew rein before the nearest group of labourers, who had placed the points of their *alavangoes*, digging tools, and pickaxes on the earth to stare at us.

A tubby Arya, with a square face, thin moustache and prominent nose, detached himself from a small group of supervisors and came forward to greet us.

'Anu!' I exclaimed, allowing my shoulders to relax, 'What goes on here?'

'Greetings, Prince!' Anu saluted me, but even in the uncertain light I could see that his smile did not extend to his eyes. 'As you can probably guess, we are excavating the foundations of our new palace.'

'So huge? I knew the Great King had plans to extend the palace, but what is to happen to the old buildings? I mean, are you going to construct a new moat and . . .' my voice trailed off as I surveyed the scene more closely.

'The old fort will be totally renovated and will form the citadel,' I heard Anu reply. A note of malice crept into his voice. 'Minister Ujjeni arranged for architects from Madura to draw up the plans. They have designed a worthy residence for the Great King of Lanka, who rules four kingdoms, so we all enthusiastically support Ujjeni in this very necessary enterprise. As you can see, we are working night and day to make it a success. To answer your question, Prince, there will be no new moat. The fortifications of the citadel will be improved behind the old moat. We are presently working on residences and government offices. When these are completed, the palace will be moved here temporarily until the citadel is completed.' He pointed in the direction of great, dark piles along the outer edge of the excavation. 'We have assembled all the necessary material, much of it imported, but the Yakka have benefited from local production of brick, tile and mortar.'

Slave labour, I thought and was immediately ashamed of myself, for the thought had emerged from a tinge of bitterness because my brother had not revealed these plans to me. Also, while the people of Kalyani were short of food, shelter and an assured future, here was a luxurious palace being built for their king. 'What sort of material have you imported?' I enquired, more to be polite than because I cared at this stage.

'The finest,' he replied proudly. 'Butter-clay from the great Ganga region in the north of the continent, silver, copper, iron, arsenic, sweet-scented marumba and mountain crystal from the Himalaya. Minister Ujjeni also has on order beautiful beds, couches and chairs, carpets and coverlets, tapestries and ornaments, dinnerware and utensils, jewellery and fine raiment. Our palace will be a source of pride and joy to the entire kingdom.'

And a drain on its wealth, I knew, this time without shame. ' I am really delighted,' I said, lying. 'Well, Minister Anu, we have ridden far and hard. The Great King will doubtless want to show me the work tomorrow, as for now I wish to proceed to my quarters.'

'Oh yes, indeed.' Something told me Anu was put out. 'Pray forgive me my lack of hospitality, Prince, but we did not expect you so late at night. The Great King has commanded that your old quarters be assigned to you. He will see you in his study tomorrow when the pre-noon watch is over. You are to have the noon meal with him . . . er . . . as in former times.' An ironic smile crossed his chubby cheeks but was quickly erased. 'You will find that nothing has changed in the palace itself. Here, let me summon your former chief attendant, who has been detailed to look after you. Your escort can sleep in my company's barracks. Meanwhile, please follow me through the construction site.'

At his sharp command, one of his aides came forward and received his instructions to race ahead and alert the palace attendants of my arrival.

Anu turned towards the palace. 'One moment, please, Minister,' I called. He stopped and turned back. I gestured towards the site of the village. 'What happened to the people and their homes?'

'Oh!' He suddenly sounded abrupt. 'The people of the village are helping with construction. Their homes have been razed to the ground, so they are presently being housed in temporary shelters. When the work is completed, they will be given land and a home in one of our rural communities, as a reward.'

Just perfect, I told myself, no longer ashamed of the bitter sentiment. The people of one sub-kingdom are displaced by the gods on a flood rampage and have to be housed in temporary sheds, while the people of the neighbouring sub-kingdom are displaced and housed in sheds by their god-king's flood of vanity.

Chapter 35

Worn out from my ride, I slept late the next morning. The sun was well risen, with the promise of a warm, clear day, by the time I performed my ablutions, changed into formal white pantaloons and tunic and broke my fast in my room. I remained seated at the dining table after it had been cleared to go over my notes, preparing for my conference with the Great King. All the while, I heard unusual bustle in the verandah. The old, leisurely pace was undoubtedly gone. Ujjeni, who now controlled the palace routine, must be responsible for the change.

When I was finally satisfied with my knowledge of the facts, there was still time left before my conference with the Great King. I could tell too, from the constant passage of people along the verandah, that his audience watch would be fully extended. Why not make use of the time at my disposal to pay a brief call on the Princess Kuveni? Even as I rose from behind my desk, however, some inner sense intruded a warning note, so I resumed my seat and spent the rest of the time in meditation.

As soon as I was announced by my chief attendant, the Great King came forward to meet me at the entrance door to his study. This time, he looked fit and well, and this time I was not surprised by the grandeur of his attire. He looked every inch a king, tall, commanding. His gold tunic sat well on his brawny shoulders, the dark blue pantaloons closely fitted his muscular limbs. His red hair and beard were well trimmed, the hollows of his cheeks had filled out and the leonine features were noble again.

'It's so good to see you!' he exclaimed after I made obeisance to him. Yet when he embraced me, the feel of his *atman* was still different. Some inner warmth towards me was lacking, making his gesture more a concession to form than the spontaneous act of a loving man. Only when he released me and turned to go back to his seat at the head of the yellow jakwood desk, did I notice the figure standing at the left of the desk. Ujjeni at least never changed. His gaunt, skeletal figure, hunched shoulders, humped back, sunken eyes, the death's head face with the prominent yellow teeth barely concealed by dark purple lips, still gave him a sinister aura. He saluted me with his usual grin, which, like Anu's of last night, never reached his eyes, in his case probably because it escaped inwards through his open mouth down his throat, choking him for having to seem friendly!

The Great King indicated my usual place on a settle at the right of his seat. 'We hope you had a pleasant journey,' he said.

'Yes, Sire, except that we were held up at the ferry crossing.'

'Oh! What happened?'

'Flash floods had damaged the ferry boats.'

'They are repaired now?'

'Yes, Sire.'

'And you slept soundly last night in your former room?'

'Like a ruined city.'

His shaggy red eyebrows lifted and the tawny eyes sparkled. 'A nice turn of speech. We have missed it. You are right, Prince. Mohenjo Daro for instance, sleeps soundly in death. We for our part are building a new city, alive, vibrant.' His eyes sparkled. 'But tell us, before the noon meal is brought in, what can we do for you? Your reports of flood damage and the toll of the rains on our people have been most exhaustive. Minister Ujjeni too has studied them and we both compliment you. You seem to have relief work well in hand, what else do you need?'

I glanced at Ujjeni. Was he to be present at a discussion

between a Great King and his sub-king, between brother and brother?

The Great King noticed my glance and his lips compressed firmly. 'Minister Ujjeni will be present during our discussion, because he will have to appraise your needs in his dual capacities of Minister of Finance and our chief aide.'

Noticing Ujjeni's look of triumph, I remembered a time, commencing on the second morning of our arrival in Lanka, on the road from the Princess Kuveni's house to the fort, when Ujjeni had wanted me excluded from his discussions with the Great King and the Great King had refused. The sand has indeed run out; the clock had now been reversed.

'Sire, I have used the resources of the sub-kingdom I govern in your name to give food, clothing and shelter to all those of your subjects who have been stricken by the floods.' I was choosing my words with care. 'With the help of a great many people who have rallied round the helpless, I can safely say that no one is presently in want.' I looked towards the Great King for approval, but his gaze was noncommittal. He was merely listening at this point.

'You say that you have used the resources of the sub-kingdom for this purpose, Prince Lala,' Ujjeni interposed quietly. 'What resources precisely do you mean?'

'I mean the paddy, flour and spices in our king's barns, the clothing which we obtained and stored by way of tithes, timber and thatch from the king's warehouses for temporary shelters.'

'How will these be replaced? Ujjeni demanded. 'Remember, we are going to need some of the material to build our new palace . . . uh, the new capital city.'

'Why should they be replaced?' I demanded indignantly. 'They were the Great King's property, to be used for the good of the people.' I turned to King Vijaya expecting support, but his look remained noncommittal.

'Wrong, Prince,' Ujjeni retorted. His eyes were flat and cold. 'The Great King's property is not to be distributed to the people. He alone determines how it should be used for the welfare of the kingdom. I repeat, he needs it for his own purposes.'

'That portion of the Great King's property that represents his personal share of taxes is certainly his own and sacrosanct. I have not used any of it. But should not the share that is meant for public works be directed towards the good of the people who contributed it in the first place? Has that not been the Great King's policy since we first instituted the *raja kariya* system?'

Ujjeni's eyes flicked towards the Great King and I realized from their exchanged glance that they had discussed the situation earlier and were presenting me with a common front. The room suddenly felt unbearably warm and the sound of digging in the courtyard garden outside could have come from the graveyard of my hopes.

I faced King Vijaya squarely, challenging him. 'Sire, pray forgive me if I have erred, but I have always considered it to be your directive that one-fifth of our tithes is to be held for the good of the kingdom. Has that policy changed?'

'No, it has not,' he replied clearly and succinctly. 'But what we are questioning is the use to which you have put that property. Our directive has been that it should be used for development purposes such as new roads, new communities, schools and hospitals.'

'Ah, hospitals, Sire. Are they not for people in need?'

'Certainly.'

'I directed the assets to other needs of the people.'

'You were in error to do so, Prince.' The Great King's voice was hard, its tone final. 'We alone can make that determination.'

I was appalled, but my mind worked furiously. Pride for myself and for my gallant people intruded. 'I am sorry to have erred, Sire, and I beg your pardon. All that was taken

480

from the State shall be replaced.'

'How?'

'By using what remains of my private treasury and appealing to the people for more donations.'

'Appealing to the people? What kind of rulership is that?'

'The best of all, Sire, as I have discovered, when people follow the sharing philosophy, *shrama dharma*.'

'Ah! The new liberalism. A very dangerous concept.'

'How so, Sire?' A note of passion had entered my voice.

'The people always expect something back for extending such favours and are never content to take it back in like kind. They will extract their reward from you through the abrogation of some of your rights to rule. Moreover, it tends to make them independent of their rulers.'

I was stunned. The Great King's philosophy was diametrically opposed to mine. 'Do you then forbid me the course of action I propose, Sire?' I demanded.

He pondered that awhile. 'No . . . no,' he replied hesitantly. 'We need the return of what you have expended for the pursuance of our own policies, so you may proceed accordingly. But we shall watch its repercussions closely.'

I knew, with a sinking heart, that he needed the resources principally in order to build his fine new palace and live in the style of a god-king. Some of it, I had to concede, was for building the mighty fortress of Vijitapura and a new township between it and Thamba-Panni to be called Anu, after the minister who was in charge of creating that community. Those were perhaps laudable objectives, but Thambi-Panni's palace and city were only the products of my brother's vanity.

'You must understand, Prince,' the Great King continued, probably sensing my thoughts, that the building of a beautiful new palace is far more essential for the welfare of the entire island of Lanka than mere development works. A palace creates the mood of the kingdom, instils a proper spirit of subservience in the people, which is the only way they can be contented and accept their *dharma*, their station in life. It impresses foreign governments, with which we are dealing on an ever-increasing scale for the benefit of the country. We must set aside parochial ideas, suspicions of vanity and extravagance, and look to the ultimate good, the deep and ultimate good of all concerned, including posterity.'

I eyed him levelly, ignored Ujjeni. 'Sire, there was a time when you looked to me to remind you of idealism. Has that time ended then?'

His face immediately hardened. 'Every single one of our subjects has the right to speak to us of ideals, so long as they are not traitorous or heretical,' he stated, his voice cold as granite. 'As we told you before, you are free to voice your ideals, but remember that, once we have rejected any recommendation, there can be no criticism of our course of action.'

'Once again, I beg your pardon, Sire,' I replied. Somehow this interview was taking a far different course from that which I had intended or anticipated. I had a shrewd suspicion that Ujjeni had deliberately set it off at a tangent with his first comment. I must put it back on course again. 'I would never question your commands. I did not realize that the statement you just made was a firm decision.'

'Very well, Prince,' he replied. 'We expect you to replace whatever has been removed from our general treasury. What else do you need?'

How could I tell him? What use would it be? A great hopelessness seized me and I fell silent.

Help came from an unexpected quarter. 'Your report indicates that you also have medium-term and long-term needs.' Ujjeni prompted. 'Please state them and let the Great King know what assistance you expect from him.'

I was amazed. For a few moments, I actually warmed towards Ujjeni. Had I misjudged the man? Had he merely been trying to do his duty by his own lights? Then I looked into his sunken eyes and saw the craftiness lurking beneath the surfaces of the lower lids, I sensed the devilish cunning of his mind and knew that I had to fear him most when he seemed kindest and most cooperative. Yet I had come to Thambi-Panni to obtain my people's requirements, so I sorted through my *olas* and silently proffered my lists to the Great King. Seed paddy, chillis, onions, manioc, *kurakkan* for replanting programmes; timber, tiles and brick for rebuilding; food, clothing, labour wages and a host of items besides, all of which had been carefully worked out, based upon the time frame and the needs of each village. With Ujjeni watching him intently, the Great King looked over the lists carefully, while my heart beat out the silent seconds that stretched out interminably to long minutes.

The Great King finally laid down the *olas*, glanced at Ujjeni and pushed them towards him. 'All this comes within your province now, Minister,' he observed. 'Can we afford all this? Why don't you study them?'

My heart sank.

'Certainly, Sire.' Ujjeni kept his voice even, but I knew he was enjoying his victory. 'It seems a long list,' he ventured. 'Before I study it, may I say that, with a good harvest this year and prosperity through trade, Thamba-Panni should be able to meet any reasonable requirement of the Kalyani sub-kingdom.'

'Good!' I exclaimed involuntarily.

'The question that we should settle now is how and when we can expect repayment and what profit we get on our investment.'

I could not believe my ears. 'Repayment? Investment? Profit?' I cried, half rising in my seat. 'What are you running, Minister? A country or a dry fish store?'

'Sit down, Prince!' My brother commanded and I subsided with a muttered apology.

'Well you might apologize,' the Great King continued, a harsh note in his voice, a scowl on his face. 'Surely you did not expect to obtain any of this aid free.'

'Sire, indeed I did. I am here as the humble petitioner of thousands of your subjects for the assistance of the Great King in their plight, their dire need. Whom else can they turn to?'

'They have certainly come to the only source, their Great King and, as Minister Ujjeni has just stated, the Great King will accommodate them. What we must settle is the terms of such aid. We do not intend any part of this nation to become beggars. Else, it will be a national disaster today, laziness tomorrow. Our feudal duties to our subjects do not extend to handouts. Any self-respecting peasantry will surely want to repay what it has borrowed, will it not?'

Remembering the work of Sundari and her women's organization, I felt sick at the injustice of his statements. Yet, I could also see the force of his argument.

Noting my hesitation, the Great King continued. 'Answer a few questions, Prince.' He sounded like a prosecutor at a trial. 'Did we cause these disasters?'

'No.'

'Are either the Great King, or his sub-king, or his ministers or his administration responsible for them?'

'No, my Lord.'

'Who caused them?'

'Nature, the elements, perhaps the gods.'

'Or the One God in whom you believe.' It was Ujjeni, sneering.

The Great King swept away the unseemly interruption with an impatient wave of his hand. Irrelevantly, I noticed the fine red hairs on the backs of his large fingers. 'Since we are not responsible for the disaster, why should we be responsible for any long term solutions?'

I immediately had the answer to that one. 'Because you are the Great King, a god in the eyes of your people, a good god who rescues them from misery inflicted on them by evil gods. Because you are a human being and a god of compassion and mercy, firm but full of the charity of which

484

only the truly strong are capable. Because you are the father of your people and must look after them.'

I did not need the flashing of his tawny eyes to know that I had used the wrong metaphor. 'Father!' he exclaimed incredulously. 'Did you say "father"? Why, Prince, have you forgotten how our father treated us?' He glowered at me, breathing hard, then slowly regained control of himself. 'There is no need to prolong this discussion,' he stated quietly. 'Please understand that we do not intend to create a welfare state. The people of Lanka will work for what they need. To each according to his contribution, we say. Only the halt, the infirm, the maimed, the aged shall receive charity. You shall have the aid you request. How soon will you repay it with a return on our investment? Remember, we are committing our resources on trust in the people's ability to work.'

I thought desperately, then made another mistake. 'If repayment is required, may I study the figures again, Sire, to pare down our requirements?'

I caught Ujjeni's devilish glee without ever looking at him. The Great King smiled slowly. 'You see, Prince Lala, how the length of the play changes when you have to pay the actors?'

A feeling of shame swept over me. 'You are right, Sire. I erred in compiling those lists! I included therein our requirements for reconstruction of many communities of the sub-kingdom, which will bring you, the Great King, a handsome return in due course through your share of vastly increased production and of course a contented people.' I did not dare add that I had also erred in estimating his generosity towards his afflicted subjects. 'If the people are not taxed on their produce, I believe we can repay modified requirements – which I shall confine to recovery from the disaster and which I shall submit to you tomorrow – within the space of a single harvest for the produce you advance and one year later for the remainder. I would donate my

485

personal one-fifth share to the cause and the producers will agree to giving up one-half of their own share.'

'You guarantee this with your personal fortune?'

A knot burned in the pit of my stomach, yet it was a dull fire. 'Most of my personal fortune has gone towards flood relief already, Sire.'

'Commendable, but hardly prudent,' he remarked drily. 'And what profit do we get on this investment?'

'What do you suggest, Sire?'

He turned to Ujjeni. 'The hypothecation of the entire harvest following the end of that first year,' Ujjeni replied.

'But that is almost a one hundred per cent return,' I protested.

'For one hundred per cent of the risk, Prince,' Ujjeni retorted.

I turned to the Great king for relief but the hard expression in his eyes and the set of the leonine features told me that I looked in vain. My breath caught and my throat began to ache. I felt utterly beaten.

'My people need help desperately,' I said. 'I have no alternative but to accept your terms.' Then the words came out and I could not help them. 'God forbid that there should be frequent recurrences of disaster in Kalyani, or we shall be mortgaged for our entire lives.'

What finally drove the roots of bitterness firmly into my spirit was that my brother, the Great King, insisted on showing me the plans for the new palace, the citadel, the township, after we had partaken of our noon meal, and then gave me a personal tour of the work in progress.

All the old residential buildings in the fort were to be demolished to make way for a magnificent new structure of brick and tile, cement and marble, ebony and teak, satin and *nadun* wood, rising from the moat behind fortified rampart walls of granite that would be complete with battlements and sentry towers. There were to be separate quarters for the Great King, his queen, his consorts and the royal family, all fronted by a great new centre courtyard and overlooking the river on two sides. The palace would include quarters for the Great King's advisers and his immediate staff. Outside the moat, an area extending far beyond the demolished village was already laid out as a typical Arya city. Broad streets divided it into four sectors, each sector being respectively for priests, temples and schools; princes and noblemen; tradesmen; and workers.

The contrast between his extravagance and the abject poverty of the Kalyani refugees and also the plight of the Thamba-Panni Yakkas made my gorge rise. I viewed all I was shown, however, with apparent enthusiasm, making appropriate sounds of approval and admiration. I wished that I could generate the pride my brother obviously felt in the temple in which he would be enshrined.

PART III
Cause and Effect

Chapter 36

The Great King's harsh terms created bitterness in the minds of the people of Kalyani, especially Prince Jaya and the other princes and noblemen. Yet these terms challenged our pride and we worked together 'to teach the bloody bastards that we're not beggars', as I overheard one of Prince Jaya's cousins say when he thought I was out of earshot.

The months extended to years and I was proved wrong on two counts. The first was my hope that I would receive the Great King's permission to marry Sundari. It was a miserable period for me in this respect, for I was torn between the desire to remind him, even to beg for his approval, and my pride. Finally, it was not pride for myself, but for Sundari that won. Thus time went by until both Sundari and I gave up all hope of being married. Nevertheless, we were content to love each other without physical contact, as the code demanded, and to find joy in the blessings of our love and our living beneath the same palace roof.

The second count on which I was proved wrong was my estimate of the time required to repay the debt to the Great King. I had not only underestimated the requirements of my people in attempting to pare them down, but had also overestimated our productive capacity. Actually, it took three full years for us to repay the debt and give the Great King his profit.

Fortunately, the three years that followed brought prosperity, so by the seventh year, we were sufficiently well recovered to commence executing plans for the development of advanced rural communities such as now flourished in

Thamba-Panni.

In the seventh year, we were hit by a drought! With a sinking heart, I realized that we would have to mortgage ourselves once again to the Great King.

Prince Jaya and I discussed the situation while taking a stroll along the bank of the Kalyani river for our pre-noon chat that day. It had been extremely warm inside the palace buildings. Here at least a light breeze that rustled the branches overhead was cool and soothing to the skin.

'Perhaps the Great King, your brother, was right after all,' Prince Jaya observed. He had lost none of his fat, so he was sweating profusely, his chubby cheeks almost oily. 'If he had given us charity, we might have become emasculated and we certainly could not have looked to him for more at this time unless we had proved ourselves reliable debtors.' His grin was mirthless.

I glanced sideways at him with affection. 'What the Great King compelled us to achieve was indeed for our good,' I conceded. 'We retained our pride and self-respect, our initiative and enterprise. We worked harder than ever.'

'All that may be true, Prince.' His voice was low. 'But the Great King's racial policies degrade us.' It was the first time he had really broached the subject. He stopped, the dark slits of his eyes peeping from their folds were hard as onyx. 'Our well of bitterness increases with each passing day. We Nagas, the Yakka, the Arabi, are all looked down upon. We have become second-class citizens.' He paused, his eyes softening. 'We know that you and the lady you love have also suffered from this attitude and that, although you never mention it out of loyalty to your brother, you have fought for the cause of racial equality. Believe me, we are all grateful, Prince, and some day the people of Kalyani will demonstrate their gratitude. They adore you, but I would have you know that many of us feel rebellious.'

'I understand, only restrict your rebellion to feeling!'

He nodded and, as we resumed our walk, I warmed

towards him, partly out of sympathy. 'As for me, I have but one lack,' I volunteered.

'What is that?'

'The man I probably love most does not adore me as the people of Kalyani do.'

He stopped again, a strange look crossing his face. 'Your brother? Well . . .'

'No, not my brother. My friend, Prince Jaya.'

The slits of eyes peeped forth again, this time with a look of incredulity. 'Who? . . . Me?' I had caught the normally urbane man completely off guard. He gestured helplessly with his hands, then that grin creased his face. 'Aney, Prince, how wrong for you to tease me like this.'

I looked squarely at him. 'I'm deadly serious,' I assured him.

The fat cheeks seemed to crumple and I knew he was fighting back the tears. He turned away. 'Me too, Prince,' he muttered. 'Me too . . .' and gazed across the river. A crow cawed furiously overhead, while the water beneath us seemed to quicken its pace.

Ashamed at my sudden, unexpected display of emotion, I coughed slightly. 'Well, enough of that . . . it's sentiment enough for an entire lifetime,' I stated. 'Since we have already decided that I will undertake a debtor's mission to the . . . er . . . source of wealth . . .' I nearly said 'money-lenders'. 'Shall we resume our walk? I now have a philosophical question for you.'

'Ah! That is more in my line than sentimentality,' he declared, turning to resume our stroll. And I knew that he was lying again!

'Tell me, Prince Jaya, is it the stars that create periods of major events in our lives? We in Kalyani have had our share of natural disasters, but I am not referring to collective *kharma/vipaka* that nations seem to have. What I am asking about is the periods of upheaval in our personal lives.'

'Why do you ask?'

'Because I woke this morning with the strangest feeling that the period of calm in my personal life has ended.'

'You have forebodings, premonitions?' There was concern in his voice.

'Of a sort.'

'The early morning vision of one born under the watersign.'

'Perhaps. But what it has done is to make me wonder whether life is really peace interspersed by periods of storm, or whether in reality all of it is storm, with peace merely an illusion in between, like the ocean which consists of wild demons of tempest bearing the illusion of a placid breast. Is there ever real peace? Or is the state of 'is' one of chaos from a Universe perpetually in motion?'

'My, my, Prince! No wonder you feel gloomy today, for you are sunk in the deep, deep depths of your own introspection.' He kicked aside a fallen branch with a fat leg. 'But why is it important for you to find the answer to this question? Why can't you just live, like the rest of us? Why do you constantly probe?'

'The sailor scouting the seas,' I responded, more jauntily. Prince Jaya and I had been this route before. 'Another trait of one born under the water-sign. Also, I leave again for Thamba-Panni next week on another begging mission, seven years after the first.'

His smile was impish. 'Your periodic visits to Thamba-Panni make you as tense as some women in their periodic blood-letting,' he declared. 'But it goes beyond that, I'm sure. Do you sense an inner chaos there, with the demon incarnate, Ujjeni, creating it, ruling over it?'

'Something like that. My relations with the Great King remain cordial, but formal.'

'Ever since King Deva Raja died in the year following his sucession of the Ruhuna sub-kingdom, the Great King has ruled it directly from Thamba-Panni,' Prince Jaya stated. 'He visits it frequently, but along the Vijita-pura route. Is it to avoid contact with you? As for Minister Ujjeni, he must detest you more than ever since the people of Kalyani foiled his plan to bring us into a lifetime of economic subjugation. Yet he has become the power behind the throne of Lanka. We have heard nothing of King Tikka these seven years and more, so presume he is dead. The Great King is estranged from his spouse but has had no heirs from his consorts, so perhaps the Yakka disease dried up his seed. Somehow, things are not normal in the capital.'

'I suppose your analysis is correct.'

'Gods don't have offspring,' Prince Jaya proceeded quietly. 'Do you know why?'

'Tell me.'

'Because gods are the products of the imaginings of human beings, who first render them impotent in order to deify them, then invest them with the miracle of procreation whenever they desire to create new gods.'

My laugh went echoing across the river. A Yakka, clad in a span-cloth, his dark body glistening in the sunlight, poling a raft down the grey water, looked up briefly at the sound.

'I'm sorry for your brother,' Prince Jaya observed soberly. 'He is a lonely man in his splendid isolation. Like that boatman,' he nodded towards the raft, 'he believes he is heading towards the ocean. Perhaps he is right. But what awaits him at journey's end?'

'*Kharma/vipaka*,' I answered. 'His past and his present. What he was, what he is, what he does, says, thinks, feels at any given moment, all these await him.'

'Your life and your brother's have parallel lines,' Prince Jaya observed soberly. 'You are the living proof of Lord Buddha's exposition of *kharma/vipaka*. You both became rulers at the same time. You have both been busy working for the good of your people and have both achieved much. You have both known the extremes of love life without total fulfilment – yours warm and tender, his cold and lonely. You both seek far-reaching goals with the same assiduity. His objective is to remain the god-king, yours is subjective, to seek the godhead.' He sighed heavily, the flabby pectorals jiggling. 'Yes, indeed. Your brother and you have shown that you have a single *kharma*, separated only by physical circumstances when some accident split a single seed in your royal mother's womb into two.'

I left on my visit to Thamba-Panni two days later, having also received a summons from the Great King. I had been away from the capital for almost one year. Although I was to be gone less than seven days, I hated the thought of leaving Sundari and as always this had weighed increasingly on my spirit until the last night before my departure, when it reached its climax, culminating in a bleak awakening on the day I had to leave. Frankly, I did not relish a repetition of my beggar role either.

During the past seven years Sundari had grown in beauty, kindliness and goodness. She never lost her slim, girlish figure, or her youthful appeal and she proved herself a lady of rare compassion and sensitivity. She would not intentionally kill an insect, or trample a plant. She never once uttered a harsh word to me, or gave me an angry look. A remarkable human being.

Accompanied by my usual cavalry escort, I reached Thamba-Panni in the evening three days later.

I found that construction of the palace had just been completed, but work on the township was still proceeding, so labourers thronged the area in front of the moat. We were formally challenged by uniformed guards at the entrance to the fort and permitted to ride through the great new wooden gates, ribbed with metal, up the broad sanded centre street that led to the palace.

My grey-haired chief attendant greeted me with a smile that now emerged from toothless gums, but his wrinkled body trembled with pleasure at seeing me. 'The blessings of the gods be on you, Prince,' he quavered. 'It is such a joy to see you again. The Great King has gone hunting and is not expected back until nightfall, so let me conduct you to your quarters.'

I followed him to the suite reserved for visiting dignitaries, who had started to arrive at the capital in increasing numbers. These were generally heads of embassies, mainly from the southern kingdoms of the continent, but they had even included missions from Pahlava country and the slant-eyed race, whose emperor audaciously demanded annual tribute but had to be satisfied with costly presents of gold, silver and rubies from the Great King. The fame of the new Lanka, prosperous and peaceful, the land known from earliest times as resplendent because of its beauty, had now spread far and wide.

The tapers and flares of my chambers had been lit for the evening. It was my first visit to the interior of the new palace, and certainly everyone concerned had done a magnificent job. Regal elegance was evident from the white mountain crystal floors to the black and white mosaic ceiling, from the Pahlava carpets to the colourful tapestries and the heavily carved yellow and dark brown tamarind wood furniture. There is enough wealth here to look after the drought-stricken people of Kalyani, I thought, even if it has to be done through the same old method of mortgaging our future. At least my begging mission would produce results.

The chief attendant supervised the installation of my baggage, made obeisance and withdrew to the entrance foyer. 'You have only to call me if you desire anything, Lord, and I shall see to it,' were his final words.

Hearing the splash and gurgle of water against rocks, I peered through the red and yellow lacquered grilles of my bedroom window overlooking the river. A magical, restful time, late evening, when the earth is hushed at the approach of its own dark death. Nostalgia filled me and I longed for Sundari to be with me.

A loud knocking on the door disturbed my reflections. I heard the rumble of the king's voice through the passageway leading from the entrance foyer to my reception room and my chief attendant's reply, 'Yes, Lord. The prince is in the bedroom.'

The king bustled in before I had taken five paces towards the entrance.

Rising from my obeisance, I found a new man before me, vibrant as a war-horse before battle, his massive body eager, his tawny eyes a-sparkle, the red beard almost bristling.

'Ah, there you are!' He exclaimed. 'Welcome to Thamba-Panni. What do you think of your new quarters?' He looked around him with satisfaction and indeed he had a right to be pleased. 'Far superior to Sinha-Pura, eh?' He questioned, rubbing his hands together in satisfaction.

'Indeed and such elegance besides,' I remarked, though I could not help some surprise at this revelation of an additional driving force. Clearly competition with our father had secretly motivated my brother.

'Good. Good. You have timed your arrival to perfection. The great fleet from Madura approaches our port of Mantota.' Noting my concern, he laughed merrily in reassurance. 'No, it's not a war fleet but an embassy. With fair winds, it has arrived earlier than expected, so we must hasten to Mantota through the night to receive it tomorrow morning. Our ministers and most of our comrades are already on their way. This is the greatest single event that has happened to us since we conquered Thamba-Panni.'

It seemed odd that no information regarding the mission had been passed on to me. Come to think of it, none of the ministers and very few of the Arya had been in the capital when I arrived. Surprise gave way to momentary annoyance because missions from other countries do not manifest themselves from thin air and the least my brother could have done was to notify me of something he had obviously been aware of for months. 'May I enquire what the purpose of the mission is, Sire?' I enquired. 'Remember, I'm not privy to anything that goes on in Thamba-Panni.'

His bushy eyebrows lifted. 'You mean that your spies did not report it to you?'

I looked at him. puzzled. 'I do not have spies anywhere, Sire,' I assured him, somewhat primly.

His great jaw dropped a fraction, then a loud guffaw exploded from him and he pointed a shaking finger at me. 'You know, we believe you.' He shook his head. 'Amazing . . . but true . . . that's our brother, Prince Lala! Well, let us enlighten you. This mission from the King of Madura is perhaps the greatest ever assembled in the world's history. It consists of a huge fleet of ships escorted by war galleys and will arrive at Mantota shortly after dawn tomorrow. We ride out tonight, with every available Arya as escort, to receive our visitors at the port. You shall accompany us, but since you know nothing about it, first your oath that you shall ask no questions until tomorrow morning.'

I gave him my oath, wondering why the secrecy, but consoling myself with the thought that this event had changed him. He seemed suddenly to have freed himself from a dark curse that had lain on him for eight years. His bubbling enthusiasm even reminded me of my brother of the old days. Yet I decided that my request for aid had best await a more auspicious moment.

The port of Mantota lies in a curving bay on the western seaboard of Lanka, far enough north for the lush lands to have ended and sandy wastes with dark scattered shrub, salty swamps and groves of palmyra palm to dominate the landscape. It is merely a sheltered arc of land, not a great port, but has provided ready access throughout centuries for sailing ships and even row boats, principally from the south of the continent, wafted on regular ocean tides and currents through gaps in the great reef to sanctuary. In much the same way, Devun Dara in the south serves as a destination point for Arabi ships sailing across thousands of miles of that ocean.

The Great King and I left the palace that evening, after a quick dinner. It took us and our cavalry escort five hours of steady riding through bright moonlight to reach Mantota.

My first impression of the port at night was of a host of yellow flares across the swampy flats through which our highway ran, a damp breeze and the unmistakable tang of ocean air. As we drew closer, rows of dark wharves appeared, jutting into the moonlit sea, at the base of which were go-downs for the storage of cargo. The largest building was the customs house the Great King had established close to the principal wharf for the levy of taxes on all imported and exported goods. The township sprawled along the waterfront, with shops and eating houses on either side of the highway in the areas closest to the wharves and houses elsewhere, all served by dirt roads. The houses we passed were generally wattle and daub structures, covered with dried palmyra palms, but I also noticed larger ones of lime-plastered brick with red tile roofs. I already knew that a distinctive feature of the town was a street containing row upon row of houses fronting the shore. All these houses had common walls and roofs of dried palmyra palm and had been constructed in such a manner that smugglers and smuggled goods could be moved rapidly and secretly away from one house to the next and finally to safety whenever our customs inspectors made a raid. Though the hour was late, the streets were full of people, mainly our comrades, but also some men who were obviously foreigners and a few local beggars. I wondered how they put up with the combined smell of dank seaweed and dry-fish, though some of the men were well insulated against it, shouting and singing, more

500

than a little drunk on the local palmyra wine.

We were received in the well-lit centre of the town by Ujjeni, the other ministers and local dignitaries. Accompanied by them, we trotted to the lodgings allotted to the king and me. This proved to be an ornate mansion, built in the Dasa style, belonging to the district headman, at the township's northernmost end. Opposite the mansion was a patch of open ground with a fringe of palmyra palms, through which the ocean glimmered in the moonlight. A few hundred yards away from the shore were the light-pricked silhouettes of a great fleet of ships, riding easily at anchor.

Our lodgings were not luxurious, but comfortable. Being tired, I slept well that night on the white cushions of a great, canopied bed. True to my word, I had asked no questions about the event, and no one volunteered information, probably assuming that I knew all the facts.

As planned, we were up early. At dawn the king and I, preceded by our cavalry escort, trotted our horses towards a reception area that had been cordoned off at the base of the principal wharf. The king, riding his magnificent steed, black Indra, looked like a god. He was dressed in a cloth of gold tunic and white silk pantaloons. A broad gold belt studded with the nine lucky gems and a jewelled turban with a white plume made him seem to glitter. I wore white satin and rode a bay. The ministers and our Arya troops, clad in their finest, followed us in close-packed array.

The entire port area had been cleared of all except groups of bare-chested labourers – their skins burnt near-black from the fierce dry sun of those regions – under their *kankanam*, overseers. Armed guards, clad in red pantaloons and white tunics, drawn swords at the rest position, lined the streets and guarded the reception area, where we finally sat our horses in our allotted positions facing the ocean. Daylight had begun to cast silver rays on the water. I could now count twenty large trading ships and twenty great war galleys from which figures were disembarking into row boats.

At first I did not identify the figures, then something jolted me. No, it had to be a trick of the light. I blinked my eyes and looked again. Women! All the figures were those of women. What had women arrived for? Bewildered, I glanced questioningly at the Great King. His half-smile was defensive, yet his eyes twinkled with a mixture of amusement, happiness and triumph. He anticipated my words. 'You are wondering about the ladies?' He enquired, then laughed lightly, white teeth showing. 'That was our big secret.' He grew serious and Indra jerked his head restively against the reins. 'We commanded your presence in Thamba-Panni because we desired you to accompany us here to greet the ladies from Madura. It was only fitting that you, our brother, should be present on this historic occasion.' He paused, tawny eyes sharply enquiring. 'Tell us, what do you consider to be the greatest need for the development of the economy and culture of Lanka?'

I did not need more than a moment's reflection. 'Artisans, Sire.'

He smiled his triumph and pleasure, his eyes crinkling at the sides. 'You have them!' He nodded towards the ships. At that moment the sun must have cleared some low-lying eastern clouds for it slanted seven great rays from behind us on to the ocean. 'Look! Look! An omen indeed!' One of the men cried, 'Seven blessings from the sun. Lucky seven!'

'Craftsmen of eighteen guilds, the best in Madura and the northern continent, are also on those ships,' the king continued. 'They have brought tools, machines and equipment. All thanks to our good friend and commander here, whose foresight and wisdom alone made it possible.' He turned slightly in his saddle to nod his head towards Ujjeni, who had been listening intently to our conversation.

I swung round and bowed to Ujjeni. 'A fantastic achievement,' I stated warmly. 'You have done more for the progress of Lanka by this single move, Minister, than all of us, save our king, have achieved in over eight years of steady endeavour.'

I do not know what he expected of me, but my sincerity obviously displeased Ujjeni. Perhaps he would have preferred me to offer some contradiction, or to damn him and therefore myself, with faint praise. How could I be otherwise than pleased, when I had wanted so much to break my sub-kingdom free of the constraints of Naga and Dasa culture, literally to have the right tools with which to do the job of bringing progress to the people from their small-holding and cottage-industry mentality? The vistas for such progress now seemed endless to my excited mind, yet a still, small voice whispered its question: Yes, but is such progress happiness?

Ujjeni bowed his tight-lipped thanks to me, but the other ministers, especially Vijit, smiled back their appreciation of my attitude.

I turned to my brother. 'But the ladies, Sire? Surely they are not artisans?'

His guffaw brought us curious glances. 'Certainly not! And we are glad you refer to them as ladies, for they are all indeed of royal or noble blood.' He nodded towards the ships. His voice dropped, as if he were talking to himself. 'Six hundred ladies. Wives for those of our original seven hundred who still remain alive. We cannot have a true Arya kingdom here without Arya families, Arya manners and customs, Arya traditions, Arya bloodlines. These ladies can also assure us of true Arya progeny, a proper succession, a pure Arya heritage.'

I was dumbfounded. The whole concept was too much for me to grasp. My brother mistook the reason for my silence. 'Do not worry,' he said. 'We are not providing a bride for you. Now listen carefully. Our plan goes to the heart of the future of Lanka as a nation. We shall never have real security without an Arya majority. All around us are men of other races, the Dasa, especially those of Chola origin who have settled to the north and east of our kingdom, the Yakkas, the Nagas, the Arabi. We cannot hope to ensure an

503

Arya majority in our lifetime, but by the devas, we can now hand it down to posterity. Twenty-five years from now, our small band of Arya will have expanded to three thousand, twenty-five years later to fifteen thousand and to over two hundred thousand by the end of a century. No more betrayal by the Yakkas or Nagas. No more fear of support for Dasa raiders. We shall have achieved what no living man has achieved. We shall for ever be remembered as having literally given birth to a nation, as being not merely a part of history but its founder.'

I was appalled. What my brother contemplated was brilliant, now inevitable, but nonetheless genocide. Some reserves of wisdom, perhaps of self-preservation, enabled me to maintain a calm, approving exterior, but my head started to spin before a deed which inside I regarded as monstrous. Then I realized that under no circumstances would Ujjeni or the Great King spare me the time on this visit to listen to the woes of subjects in a distant sub-kingdom. My people and I would have to work out our own salvation. I could have wept, for I would gladly have sacrificed this grand, extravagant farce for a single measure of rice.

Chapter 37

I went through the initial stages of that reception in a state of shock. I had never seen a more remarkable sight than the wave after wave of ladies arriving at the wharf. They were of all shapes, sizes and shades, but were uniformly dressed in the most gorgeous silken *kurthas*, pantaloons, and scarves of reds, blues, greens, purples and gold. Their jewelled gold necklaces, earrings, bracelets and head ornaments glittered in the early sunlight. The scents they wore were wafted above the stench of decaying fish with every breeze. The wharf soon became a vast, moving garden of peacocks – or, rather peahens!

I soon discovered that the Great King had omitted to mention one small detail. A slim girl of about sixteen, with a very white complexion, was the first to disembark and be presented to him. She was dressed in a pale blue skirt, bodice and shawl, bordered heavily with gold thread. She wore a gold necklace studded with large dark blue sapphires, matching ear-drops and bracelets. Her gold headcomb framed tawny hair drawn back from her forehead and hanging down to below her trim waist, giving piquancy to a small oval face of exquisite proportions. Her merry brown eyes sparkled behind their long black lashes, two tiny laughter lines crinkling on each side of her rosebud mouth. Something about the set of the pointed chin, however, warned of inner strength. She was escorted by an elderly grey man, with saturnine features, dressed in a silver tunic and pantaloons, who introduced himself as Prince Raja Gopal, brother of the Madura king. 'This is the Princess Anula, daughter of our Great King,' he declaimed, no less, in high formal tones. 'Your newly betrothed and the future queen of Lanka.'

My heart sank with dread and a rare anguish.

'Madam, the reports of your beauty did not err,' I heard my brother say gallantly. 'Except that they fell far short of the truth.'

Giving him the hands together at the forehead salutation, the princess dimpled a smile at him, obviously impressed by his magnificent appearance and charm. I could not help but notice how the courtliness of this princess brought out the innate courtier in the Great King, something which the Princess Kuveni sadly was unable to evoke.

It took two hours for all six hundred ladies to disembark and be presented. All this time, my churning mind allowed me to be only half-conscious of the creak of oars, the banging of boats against the wharf, the calls of the bare-chested rowers, the slap and wash of the waves. The smell of rotten fish, persisting above the high scents worn by the ladies, was somehow symbolic of something rotten in the historic event.

My mind kept working furiously during that hot day of pomp and ceremonial. Six hundred Arya brides for our six hundred Arya noblemen, the daughter of an Arya king for our Arya king. Notably absent, a bride for me, for which I was fervently thankful. What was to happen to the Princess Kuveni? Did my brother regard his marriage to her as annulled? If so, were his two children bastards? What did he intend for the three of them? Was there to be a cosy foursome in the women's quarters? That determined little chin of Princess Anula's – whom I had liked on the instant – told me she would not stand for it. What impact would all this have on the other races, especially on the Nagas, including Prince Jaya, who made up the nation? For eight years the Arya had treated them as second-class citizens while paying lip-service to equality. Today the sham was over. The master race had finally revealed the truth. Not since the Arya crashed into the north of the continent, many centuries before, had such a blatant act of racial arrogance been carried out. Worst of all, I could feel Ujjeni's gloating and my brother's smug self-satisfaction. For the first time I had to fight hatred of them both.

Dear God, help me, was my cry. In a lull between two boatloads of visitors, my eyes had sought God in the cloudless blue heavens.

You have learned where to find me in your peaceful moments, he answered, but not all the years have taught you where to look when you are desperate. And I was ashamed at having looked for God where people in their ignorance and despair search for devas, supernatural beings that are but a part of God in the human spirit. So I looked within me and at all things instead and discovered the truth of Him for that particular moment.

This is cause and effect, inevitable. Just as your own destiny is inevitable, so is that of Lanka and the people who dwell in it. The cause of what you consider to be such a dire event was not the arrival of you Arya upon these shores, for that event was but an effect of other causes, going back through the Arya invasions of the continent and the beginning of what you call creation to the original cause that is not an effect but a creator of effects, Myself. I am the only state of 'is'. Within Me, the teeming effects that are all things, including man, take place. I alone am eternal, unchanging, yet containing the causes and effects. If you understand this, you will cease to regard the new invasion of Arya taking place before your eyes as appalling; from this travail, can be the birth of a noble nation. Do not question, therefore, but let all things be revealed to you, accepting what you cannot change with good grace.

The crowded day passed quickly and I must confess that I continued to be amazed at the way in which Ujjeni had organized everything. In accordance with our customs, every princess and noblewoman had been spoken for and betrothed to a specific Arya before she even set sail from Madura, and each had arrived with her attendant and even her dowry of jewels and gold, clothes, furniture, household

507

utensils and horses. The artisans had not merely brought the stuff of their trades but even certain types of plants and saplings, carefully packed.

The dinner feast that night was served on trestle tables set up in the grassy *maidan* fronting the district headman's home where the king and I were lodged. As was the custom for these occasions, the ladies were served separately in groups at their various lodgings. Our own meal consisted of boiled fish, mutton, chicken, rice, vegetables and fruit. A superb entertainment of singing, dancing and mime, principally in the Dasa tradition, followed.

When the feast was over, the Great King invited me to stroll with him along the seashore. By unspoken consent, we headed north into the darkness to avoid people, leaving behind a scatter of flaming torches, a babble of voices streaked by shouts, laughter and an occasional song. As we walked along, the odours of food were gradually blown away by a sea-breeze rustling through the circular palmyra palms. Soon the crowds thronging the *maidan* became mere shadows in the distance and the deserted white beach was an oasis of soughing breezes, the sweep of moonlit waves, their splash and hiss upon the shore bringing a strange raw odour, as of a man's emission, from some decaying sea-plant.

The king broke our silence. 'Ujjeni conceived this plan over seven years ago,' he explained.

'A remarkable man,' I observed, holding back any further comment.

'Absolutely.' My brother's face shone with enthusiasm. 'He has proved himself to be the perfect vehicle for our ideals.' He paused in his stride and laid a hand on my arm, making me halt to face him. 'And that is one of the matters we wish to discuss with you. As you know, the bride chosen for Ujjeni, with our consent, is a daughter of the brother of the Great King of Madura and therefore a first cousin of the Princess Anula.'

I had observed the Princess Padma that afternoon, a

508

rather plain, matronly woman of over thirty, with broad features, a slight double chin and shiny black hair. She looked placid and about as intelligent as a cow and I was not surprised that her father had agreed to her marrying a man who was a noble but not of royal blood, for it is easy to be generous even with regal possessions when they have become a liability. At least the princess seemed the kind of lady who would remain docile and obedient, ever grateful that someone had wed her.

'This will make Ujjeni our kin by marriage,' the king continued. 'It confers on him the one attribute of a ruler that he lacks, royalty. You will admit that he certainly has leadership, initiative, patience, tremendous organizational powers, dedication and, above all, loyalty to his king and his king's cause.'

My heart cried out that kings need more than attributes, they need quality and ideals, honour, compassion, concern for the people, a sense of justice and fair play, openness, but this was not the time to speak up and it would have been futile in any case, so I merely nodded my agreement, guessing at what was about to come.

'So we have decided,' my brother ended, 'that Ujjeni shall, as a wedding gift from us, be granted the title of *raja* sub-king, of Thamba-Panni. He shall hereafter be known as Prince Ujjeni and shall function as you do in Kalyani.' He looked searchingly at me. Receiving no reaction other than polite attention, he proceeded, choosing his words with care. 'One of our deepest concerns is the perpetuation of our policies after we die. Your views on many of these policies are opposed to ours, as are some of your personal beliefs.' He looked at me for comment.

'As I have already told you, I really have no interest in becoming the Great King of Lanka, Sire,' I assured him. 'Should I survive you, my intention is to enter the Noble Order of Bhikkus of the Buddha's Doctrine.'

He scowled. 'A godless religion.'

'But one that poses no threat to anyone as far as I am concerned.'

'Hr . . . r . . . mph!' He cleared his throat. For a moment his face hardened as if he were caught in some reflex from the past, then suddenly it cleared and he looked almost amiable. 'The question of succession need not concern us, for like our father, we shall give the Princess Anula many sturdy children, especially males.'

It hit me immediately. My brother had envied our father his twenty children all these years. 'Of course, Sire,' I readily responded. 'You will be blessed with many children. You have earned that reward.'

He laughed lightly. 'In that expectation and because we want you to share in today's joyous event, we have decided that it is no longer important to the united kindom of Lanka that you have pure Arya children. So you have our permission to marry this woman, Sundari.'

I was struck almost dumb with joy and gratitude. 'Sire . . . Sire, this is most . . .' I found myself stammering. Tears filled my eyes as I stared at him through the gloom. In moments, I got a firm hold of myself. 'Sire, Sundari and I will be eternally grateful to you. Please be assured of our complete devotion.'

'She will not be consecrated queen of course, and we expect you to make your wedding simple and private, but we feel, that you have both earned this reward through your exemplary fidelity and devotion to each other,' he added gruffly. 'We also appreciate the way in which you have performed your duties these many years, Prince, without displaying bitterness. Now we can only hope that our marriage to the Princess Annula will be full of such love as you and Sundari have shown for each other.'

Uday, the Venerable Sri Ravindra, had conducted the taking of *dasa-sila* at the Kalyani temple all night. Although over sixty now, the observance had left him feeling more refreshed than tired. He paused at the entrance door, ready to leave the temple premises which adjoined the palace. How often he had crossed the sandy compound, shaded by coconut palms, and walked towards the wicket gate in the side wall of the palace with King Sri Ra-hula, who had ordered the gate to be constructed for their mutual convenience. The years of added mental discipline since the death of King Sri Ra-hula had not made Uday forget how the king had died.

Hearing footsteps, he turned to find Sundari, clad in the white of the devotee, approaching him. She made obeisance. 'Venerable Sir, may I have a little of your time to discuss something important to me?' she enquired.

'Certainly, my dear.' He noted that Sundari looked drawn and detected an undercurrent of worry.

They walked across the sandy temple compound, through the open wicket gate to the little verandah that connected with Uday's cell, which was lit by a single taper because daylight had yet to stream in through the high-grilled windows. Once in the cell, they sat, as usual, on the beige mats, in the lotus pose.

Eyes downcast, Sundari was silent for long moments, gathering her thoughts. When she finally lifted her eyes to his, Uday enquired encouragingly, 'What ails you, my dear?'

Her reply was direct. 'I have developed pains in the centre of my chest and at times a burning sensation in my arms, just at the shoulders.' She crossed her arms and touched her shoulder bones at their top joints with the shoulders. 'I have also found myself short of breath at times. I'm not concerned about myself so much as being in perfect health to serve my prince.'

Not all Uday's self-control prevented the little tremor of apprehension within him. 'Have you seen the physician?' he enquired.

'No, Venerable Sir. I have been in perfect health all my

life and had not thought to do so.'

'We suggest that you go directly from here and have him examine you.' Cause and effect, Uday thought, suddenly full of compassion for the girl and her prince. What effect would this possibly dreadful cause have on their lives?

'Meanwhile, do not over-exert yourself, especially in your drought relief work which we know you have tackled with your usual dedication.'

She smiled then. 'I can reduce all that, but never my dedication to my prince.'

Uday was touched. 'Prince Lala would not want anything bad for you,' he remonstrated.

'If something is really wrong with me, I shall not tell him. I would want to give him all I can, while I can.'

Uday pondered this and could not escape its simple beauty, indeed its truth, even its wisdom.

'Are you afraid, my dear?' he enquired, changing course. Noting the unspoken answer, he added. 'What frightens you?'

'I don't know. Death, pain, being alone, leaving the prince alone, suffering . . . I don't know.'

'You will remain afraid if you do not identify the source of your fear.' Uday deliberately gentled his voice. 'Fear has many faces. The first is death because it is an unknown entity. But it is all around us and we do indeed know it. It may even be the only beautiful, the ultimate truth of life. Every living thing dies, so it is a gateway to *kharmic* fulfilment, as much a part of nature, of life, as your heartbeat. Only those living things that have the power of observation see it for what it is not, a radical change, instead of merely the effect of that cause, life. Viewed from the other side, the side to which death is not an effect but a cause, it is no more than a leaf that withers and falls from a tree to enrich the soil, to bring forth new life, a state you need not fear. Being of the doctrine, you must realize that death is merely a change in *kharmic* forces. Being devout in the doctrine, you need have no fear of whatever may lie for you beyond.'

Her eyes turned sad, causing Uday to reflect that neither words, nor their logic, not philosophy, nor its accuracy, not even the truth, can comfort the human heart in its travail. Only after the baby is born does the pain die. Then joy in the new birth can commence, or new pain at its mutilation, its suffering or its death.

'I'm also afraid of leaving my prince bereft and of being somewhere without him,' Sundari advised quietly.

'That is the second fear, the sorrow of those we love and leave behind. Though you and your prince are bound by love in this life, remember each of you carries that love with you into the next birth, so in this birth your love can rise above desiring, above clinging for the happiness of your loved one. Especially you must remove craving for them or for yourself from this love. Take it, know it, find joy in it without craving. Knowing the truth about *kharma/vipaka* and accepting that you cannot change the laws of cause and effect for yourself or for your dear prince will help you. Rejoice in what you are presently experiencing with him and reject all desire to perpetuate it in any other form than *kharma/vipaka* will permit.'

'I see that, but it is so hard.' Her deep, dark eyes were brimming with tears. 'I beg you, help me not to be afraid.'

'Indeed it is hard, my dear, but that is part of the price you pay for such love. I can help you with my words, the deeds must be yours. Some day, your love will become more objective and you will experience its more divine elements without fear.' He nearly added, if you live long enough, but decided not to say the words.

'I also fear the physical pain. It is unbearable at times.'

'That is the third face of fear. Remember that the body only takes as much pain as it can endure, after which unconsciousness sets in. When the pain comes, do not fight it, rather ride on its wings, as our wonderful King Ra-hula did with a sword at his breast.'

As they talked on, compassion from his lesser, lower senses broke loose once more within Uday, so that he deliberately set aside his own *kharmic* needs and gave full rein to his desire to comfort the young woman, not yet twenty-four.

The Great King and I returned alone with our escort to the Thamba-Panni palace two days later, days during which I simply longed to return to Sundari with my joyous news. Indeed, I would have sent word to her through a messenger had it not been for my selfish desire to break the news to her myself and to watch the dawn light up her face after our long, long night.

As soon as we entered his quarters, the king, still silent as to his intentions, sent word to the Princess Kuveni advising her that he desired to see her alone and would be calling on her shortly. Having bathed and changed, the king and I ate our noon meal together, each preoccupied with our thoughts.

When we had finished, we walked along the *meda midula* verandahs, past shady trees, grassy lawns, bubbling fountains and multi-coloured flowerbeds to the new rooms of the Princess Kuveni. These were separately located within the ladies' quarters, around their own small courtyard. When the new palace was being built, I had wondered why the ladies' quarters were being made so extensive and elegant, when the Princess Kuveni had only a few female attendants, under Rupa, who catered to her simple needs. Now I realized that they had been created for a sophisticated Arya princess with her ladies-in-waiting. Ujjeni had thought of everything. Now, his own bride-to-be, the Princess Padma, would also live in the palace with her own ladies and there would be new palace appointees to fill the female wing.

The Princess Kuveni, dressed in a skirt and bodice of blue, her favourite colour, was seated alone on an ebony settle in a small room fronting the courtyard, the inevitable loom beside her, clumsy on those beautiful floors of white mountain crystal. Fresh bathed and combed, she had obviously dressed up to receive the king and exuded the faint scent of sandalwood. But when she rose from making her obeisance, the apprehension in her glance told me that she must have received reports of the new arrivals.

My brother remained standing, towering over her, seeming to crowd the room. 'Madam, we have come to see you on a matter of enormous importance,' he announced without preliminaries. 'This kingdom, this united kingdom of Lanka, needs and deserves an Arya succession, which you are unable to give us. When we accepted your assistance in seizing Thamba-Panni, we agreed that you should be its queen.' He paused, his tawny eyes fixed piercingly on her. She avoided his gaze, merely stood still, with downcast eyes, reminding me of a condemned person awaiting the executioner's axe.

'We kept the promise,' the king proceeded. 'We made you queen. But you, being incapable of functioning as a queen or a worthy spouse during these past eight years and more, you broke your side of the contract.'

My spirit groaned within me. My brother, my king, why must you mutilate the body before destroying it? Why the hypocrisy? Why specious arguments to justify your decision? Why logic that a poor, ignorant woman could never understand? Can it be that you do indeed have a conscience, somewhere beneath your ruthless exterior?

'We have therefore invited a princess of the most royal blood, daughter of a Great King, trained in the ways of the cultured courts, to come here and be the queen of Lanka.' Now he had added poor taste to indiscretion. 'She arrived in Lanka yesterday and will be here, in the palace, tomorrow. It is therefore necessary that you, your children and your attendants vacate these quarters immediately.' He surveyed the room and his lip curled. 'Undoubtedly the rooms will require cleaning before the princess and her retinue arrive.'

Only years of training kept me from bursting out in

fury. Only the knowledge that I could perhaps serve the poor Princess Kuveni best by remaining silent prevented me from erupting in outrage. Ujjeni was responsible for this tragic situation, the foul fiend.

The princess raised sad, dark eyes to the king. She seemed to be taking in every single feature, the massive head, the red hair and beard, the leonine cast of countenance, finally the tawny eyes with their black pinpoints. It was not a look of reproach, but a farewell to something she had once loved. Her glance paused at his eyes, searching, yes, searching for some sign of relenting. She must have found none, for she sighed heavily and looked down. A single tear-drop gathered to form a clear crystal on her dark cheek. 'When you and your comrades were alone and friendless, cast by the gods upon our alien shore, I took you in.' Her normally golden voice was hoarse with emotion. 'I gave you food, lodging and comfort when you needed it. I gave myself to you and delivered you a kingdom. I destroyed my people, my father. I lost favour with my gods. Is what you are now doing to me an example of the Arya honour of which you are so proud?' She paused, her eyes lowered, awaiting his reply.

It came, harsh and brutal. 'Madam, you were already the outcast of your father and of your people when you made your contract with us. As for your gods, we do not believe in gods. Your motives were selfish. You used us as an instrument of vengeance. You have had over eight good years as a reward. That must suffice.'

She raised her eyes to him again. This time, she fearlessly held his glance. 'Did you say *good* years, Sire? Surely you can't be serious, for these have been years of banishment, years in which I and my children have been more outcasts than I was during my father's lifetime.'

'Then you should be glad they are over.'

She shook her head in disbelief. 'You are so hard, Sire. How can anyone be so hard? Well, perhaps I can accept your being hard on me, but what about your children, your own flesh and blood? Can you cut them out as you would some infected part of your body?'

'Have a care, madam.' That warning growl had entered the king's voice. What can this poor woman do to you that you should warn her, I asked myself, or is it the truth you are growling against? 'We did not come here to argue with you, or to listen to your whining.'

She straightened up with a curious new dignity. 'I am not a dog to whine, Sire. You have delivered your command. Pray tell me, where can I go?'

'Wherever you wish in our kingdom of Lanka. You shall have gold, jewels and coins enough to look after yourself and the children for the rest of your lives. You shall have property, both low cultivated land and high pasture land as well as cattle, wherever you desire, as much as you need. Our only condition is that it cannot be in Thamba-Panni.' He glanced sideways at me and added, obviously as an afterthought. 'Or in the Kalyani kingdom.'

'Sire, as you know, my own people in the *uda rata* still hate me for my act of treachery. They would kill me on sight. At least let me remain somewhere in Thamba-Panni, where I would be safer.'

'You cannot remain in Thamba-Panni. That would be offensive to its new queen.'

'Can I not go to Kalyani at least with Prince Lala?'

'She would certainly be most welcome, Sire,' I intervened.

I was stunned at the look of fierce anger the Great King shot at me. 'Do you want her with you as a focal point for Yakka support, so that you can rally them to whatever cause you desire?' His voice was low and ominous.

For a moment, I was struck dumb with hurt, then the words burst forth from me. 'What cause can I have, Sire, other than serving you and your kingdom?'

He simmered down suddenly, looking away, head bent, as if in retreat to some secret lair. 'No cause, Prince,' he said quietly, then inclined his head towards the princess. 'You may not go to Kalyani, madam,' he stated. 'You may stay three nights at your home in the village, but you must be gone by the fourth morning. With enough money and property, your future is assured.'

'Will you not give me some guards at least, Sire?'

'We cannot spare Arya guards.' A cutting note had entered his voice, his defence against his conscience. 'If you so desire it, you can have Yakka guards.'

'Who would slit my throat.'

'That is absurd, madam. They are all our soldiers. Now let us have no more debate. You have heard our command. Prince Lala will arrange with our secretariat to supply you with the necessary treasure. Come, Prince.'

He turned on his heel and stalked out of the room. The pity in my heart must have shown on my face, for the princess glanced at me and a piteous sob escaped her, just a single sob like that which jerks out of a heartbroken child. I made deep obeisance to her and left the room.

Chapter 38

The seven-year construction plan Ujjeni had instituted in Thamba-Panni included houses for all the Arya, so there were no moving-in problems for the ladies. Yet the entire operation had everyone so fully occupied and even pre-occupied that I simply did not find the opportunity to present the needs of Kalyani to the Great King and Ujjeni. I therefore dispatched a brief *ola* to Prince Jaya through one of my cavalrymen, telling him that aid would not be forthcoming and that we must look to our own resources.

Since the Princess Kuveni's village continued to house the palace menials, I had to make a special time in my schedule to meet her. News of her banishment had already spread among the Yakka and it was with a heavy heart that I finally made my way to her house. I had decided to suggest that she take up residence on the *uda rata* border with Kalyani, so that I might be able to afford her some protection.

The more quiet sunlight that heralds the approach of dusk lay upon her compound, shaded by the tiny-leaved green branches of the giant tamarind tree under which she had erected her pavilion for my brother on the night of our arrival in Lanka. Even that old hint of jasmine lay on the air. I sighed at the memories and at seeing the warehouses, long empty, in which my comrades and I had slept that night.

I walked through the open gateway of the residence and headed along the familiar path to the front door. Before I reached it, a flash of colour behind the former shrine at the rear of the compound attracted my attention. The princess and Rupa were walking into the jungle.

'Wait!' I called. They did not hear me, so I raced after them.

I was not far behind when I noticed that they were both carrying sacks. Some instinct made me drop back and follow silently along the narrow footpath, treading warily, making no sound through the rustle of the wind overhead, the creak of branches, the whistle of a mynah and the screech of a parakeet. Soon thorny undergrowth began pushing inwards and the air became so warm and close that I began to sweat profusely. The stench of rotting animal flesh, rising above the smell of hot, close earth and decayed leaves, suddenly made me wonder what in the world I was doing there, a sub-king trailing a banished princess and her attendant through an alien jungle, but some instinct urged me on.

The couple came to a large clearing and hurried across it, casting anxious backward glances. I remained in the shadows until they were in the jungle again, before continuing my pursuit, but I was becoming more and more disenchanted with each step and had almost decided to turn back when they reached a second clearing. Through the screen of trees, I saw the dark mounds of the graves, the fresh ones covered with soil strewn with flower petals. I knew with a sick heart that we had reached journey's end.

The princess began her invocation to the single beat of Rupa's drum. I listened in horror to the words, but remained only long enough to identify the ritual as one of hatred and vengeance. Seven years after she first placed a curse on my brother, she was beseeching the demon god once more to confirm his infertility and his *tani-cama*, total isolation from people, from all affection. Today, she also sought his destruction as a human being.

I stumbled away blindly. What was that flash of white ahead of me? A shadowy figure? Impossible. Who would want to follow a woman who had just been exiled, and on such a grisly mission?

Darkness had fallen when the ritual in the clearing ended. In the light of a flaming torch held by Rupa, both women started to gather up their containers and replace them in the sacks. When they finally finished this task, they straightened up and stared at each other. The face of the princess was dark and brooding in that fitful light. 'I repeated the words, Rupa, but I fear my gods have left me,' she stated tonelessly. 'I no longer have the power. I am accursed, deserted by god and man.' In the light of the flare, the broad, full face of the Princess Kuveni somehow seemed gaunt, her whole body was bathed in sweat, her cheeks quivered and her eyes were distraught.

'You have me, my lady,' Rupa assured her in a low tone, her voice breaking on the words. She had decided to accept banishment with the princess and the two children, whom she had come to love as her own, for at long last, her time of treachery and betrayal had ended. No longer would she have to give reports about her mistress to that horrible Ujjeni and the bland Anu, or submit to their questioning.

'Rupa, I am grateful for your loyalty,' the princess said. 'The gods will reward you. I have given careful thought to where we should live. Our safest refuge would be in the Ruhuna kingdom for few Yakkas of consequence live there. Once we get to Ruhuna, we can obtain money from the Great King, which he promised me, to buy a house and some land and settle down.' She paused. 'So let's slip away early tomorrow morning.'

'How wise, my lady. At least the Great King has given us the means to continue living.'

The princess stared at Rupa with eyes suddenly gone wild. 'Given us what, Rupa? The means to die afraid?' Suddenly, all she had been holding back broke loose. She tore her hair and grovelled in the dirt, screaming like a wounded animal. Then she knelt and raised her hands to the dark heavens, shrieking, 'I curse him . . . I curse him . . . I curse him.'

The words resounded through the clearing, hit the dark wall of trees and were absorbed by the branches but small echoes of sound kept circling . . . 'I curse him . . . I curse him.'

*   *   *

That same night, as he had done for years, Ujjeni waited on King Vijaya in the sumptuous new chambers that had replaced the king's former study, this time accompanied by Uraw, who never failed to observe the splendour of the rooms. The floors of white mountain crystal had been brought in from the abode of the gods, the Himalaya. The cream-coloured walls were hung with silken Pahlava tapestries of blue and gold, interspersed by black ebony pedestals that supported carvings of pink marble. The Great King sat on his high-backed chair at the far end of the room, before a heavily carved ebony table with settles around it. Above him, high windows with red, green and yellow lacquered grilles, faced the river gurgling below. 'You have rejuvenated us, good friend Ujjeni!' the king exclaimed, as they took their seats. 'We have new hope for which to thank you.'

'My lord, I live but to serve you,' Ujjeni responded. 'I am but my lord's shadow.'

Ujjeni gave his deep hee . . . hee . . . hee laugh, then came directly to the point. 'My lord, this should really be a carefree time for you, but Uraw here has some distressing news which we felt we should give you immediately.' He must have seen the king's changed expression, for he hastened with reassurance. 'No, it is not a matter of State, but of people, those close to you who should strive to serve you, instead of . . . instead of . . .' He left the sentence unfinished.

Having watched Ujjeni in action during the past years, Uraw knew that he manipulated words, even silences, to compel the king to draw graver conclusions than he himself could have portrayed. 'Uraw here is witness to the events which I shall now describe.' Ujjeni paused for effect. 'This evening, your former spouse, the Princess Kuveni, whom you so generously permitted an extended stay in her village home before she left on the banishment she so richly deserves, went to a Yakka graveyard in the heart of the jungle, once again to carry out obscene rites intended to destroy you.'

'Another *hooniyam*, charm?'

'Worse, Sire. This time she has cursed you.'

The Great King did not seem dismayed. 'Is your source of information the same, her attendant woman, Rupa?'

'She told me yesterday of her mistress's intentions, but today I also have Uraw to bear witness.'

Uraw was about to protest that it was not he, but one of his men, who had secretly followed the princess and witnessed the events, but fear of Ujjeni's wrath made him remain silent. What was the difference anyhow?

Ujjeni went on to give details of the ritual in the jungle. When he had finished, the king's face grew red with anger, his fingers began their tell-tale drumming on his desk. 'So Kuveni seeks to destroy everything we have, even hope,' he observed softly. Then his anger exploded. 'Have her arrested immediately,' he shouted. 'We do not believe in demon gods or charms, but this is an affront to our person. We shall try her summarily as a witch and decree her execution.'

'Not so, Lord, I beg you,' Ujjeni pleaded and once again Uraw saw the devilish craftiness of this man who seemed able to manipulate events like a juggler with a swirlstick and coloured balls. 'Execution will not negate the effects of such charms if they were effective.' Ujjeni paused. 'Your decision to send Kuveni away will prove punishment enough for her, Lord. Let her execution be at the hands of her own people. Also, as the Great King, a god, you cannot have your former spouse, the mother of your children, executed.'

The king simmered down. 'True . . . true.'

'There is, however, another matter, of much graver importance. Uraw and I both debated as to whether we should bring this to your notice, and we finally decided to do so, because our loyalty to you transcends all else. I beg you to hear it with calm.'

'What is it?'

Ujjeni gazed at the king, his sunken eyes almost tearful. 'You have been betrayed once more by your own brother,

Sire.' The words came out half between a croak and a sob. He looked down and fell silent.

The king was alert in the instant, but suspicious. 'How so?' he demanded, his tone warning that Ujjeni had best have proof of anything he stated.

'Prince Lala accompanied Kuveni and Rupa on their mission tonight.'

'Prince Lala has been in the palace all . . . no . . . he was gone for almost three hours before dinner. We tried to find him.' The king's jaw tightened. 'You mean he went to visit the Yakka bitch at that time?' He looked towards Uraw.

'Regretfully, on my oath, he did, Sire.' Uraw stated.

'He always had some link with her, some hold over her,' Ujjeni interposed. 'Certainly it is not a sexual liaison.'

The king grew thoughtful. His chair scraped over the mountain crystal floor as he pushed it back. He stared into space. A little tic began on his right cheek. 'Are you saying that Prince Lala participated in a demon's ceremony with the Princess Kuveni and her attendant . . . wha. . her name? . . . Rupa, in the jungle tonight, a ritual that seeks to destroy our fertility and happiness?'

'Sadly, yes, Sire.'

'What evidence do you have?'

Ujjeni looked at Uraw, commanding his acquiescence in the deliberate lie. 'Uraw here searched for Prince Lala when you desired his presence this evening, lord. He was told that the prince had left the palace and walked in the direction of the Yakka village. He saw Prince Lala in Kuveni's house, from where he proceeded with the two women to the Yakka burial ground in the heart of the jungle, where they performed their evil rites.'

Noting the tragedy in the king's eyes, Uraw's heart went out to his leader. He wanted to cry out the truth, that he had personally seen nothing, that his trooper, who had been assigned to follow the two women after Rupa told Ujjeni of the Princess Kuveni's intention, had not reported the three as being together, only that Prince Lala had also followed the women. Some instinct of ambition, of self-preservation, held Uraw back, then the moment was gone and it was too late.

'Why would Prince Lala, my own brother, my twin, want to do such a thing? Especially after we gave him permission only two nights ago to pursue his own personal happiness.' The Great King was obviously stricken by the news.

'Sire!' Ujjeni's voice was low and sympathetic. 'Children grow up together in the same family with love and harmony. They are united under a common roof. They compete with each other only for the love of their parents. Once they grow up, they have to make their own way. Prince Lala seemed to sacrifice his whole life when he accepted exile with you. But did he really? Or was he more clever than the rest of us who followed you blindly? Did he hitch his aims to your star, which he knew would one day be in the ascendant? Consider what has happened in recent years, I beg you. You have seen Prince Lala's unwillingness to sacrifice his views to yours. He has sought to make himself a popular hero with the people of Kalyani. Do any of us, your commanders, act in this manner, Lord?' Tears began streaming down Ujjeni's face and Uraw looked on them with wonder, for this man never wept.

The Great King pulled himself together. 'If what you say is true, Prince Lala should be arrested, faced with his accusers and receive a fair trial.'

'My lord, this is but a solitary incident,' Ujjeni reasoned smoothly. 'Let Prince Lala be for the present. As with Kuveni, life will find him out. Uraw and I brought this to your notice merely to forewarn you. After all, Prince Lala is your brother. Pray forgive him his ambitions.'

'You are generous, Minister, but Prince Lala's disloyalty could amount to treason.'

'Be patient, Lord. Let Prince Lala return to Kalyani. I shall have him watched day and night.'

*　　*　　*

My final mistake of this unfortunate visit to Thamba-Panni was not to tell my brother of the Princess Kuveni's ritual in the jungle. I felt the poor lady had suffered enough, and she had left by the time I called on her to bid her farewell the next morning, probably assuming that I too had abandoned her.

Three days later, after the mass marriages, which revolted me, I departed for Kalyani. My main mission, to obtain help for my starving people, had only been briefly discussed and I had been told that the Thamba-Panni coffers were too drained by the historic event for any aid to be considered at the moment. No wonder the wedding festivities sickened me, the rich food stuck in my throat. Somehow we shall survive, I had decided with grim determination, we poor of Kalyani, helping one another as before while the master race feasts and makes merry. Yet I was sick at heart.

Darkness had fallen by the time I finally reached the Kalyani palace two days later, my spirit heavy with the failure of my mission, but a part of it expectant with the joy of being able to ask Sundari to marry me, a scene I had rehearsed a score of times. In one of those remarkable coincidences of life that would seem unbelievable from the lips of the wandering minstrel, Uday happened to enter the palace at the same time. One look at my face and he knew that my mission had failed.

'I'm afraid the news is bad,' I began, pausing in the anteroom and dismissing the attendants so that I could talk to him.

'It was no more than all of us expected when we learned of the . . . er . . . festivities at Mantota and Thamba-Panni,' he observed.

He listened in complete silence while I told him all. 'What a sad time it must have been for you,' he finally remarked.

'There is one bright feature for me personally though,' I stated. 'The Great King has given me permission to marry Sundari.'

I had expected him to display calm joy at the news, but he immediately seemed so troubled that alarm bells began ringing in my brain. 'What is it, Venerable Sire?' I demanded, half-reaching for his arm. 'Has anything happened to Sundari?'

'Oh, no,' he responded. He drew his yellow robe closer around him, then, unusual for a *bhikku*, he groaned. 'It is best to give you the news and give it to you straight, Prince. Your Sundari cannot consummate a marriage.'

The world started to spin before me. 'What . . . what . . . what do you mean? Is she ill? I must go to her.'

His smile was reassuring. 'She is perfectly well so there's no need for you to rush to her . . . at least not on that account.' His deliberate tones calmed me. 'Besides, what I tell you must be in the strictest confidence.' He went on to give me details of what Sundari had revealed to him and the view of the palace physician, that she had a very serious heart condition which could cause death instantly. 'We do not know how this condition develops,' he added. 'It may be a kind of birth defect, manifesting itself later in life, but it is undoubtedly aggravated by physical and emotional stress. The arrival of the Arya had many evil effects on the lives of thousands of people. Save for that, Sundari might have lived longer as the humble wife of a goldsmith, with a placid existence.' His voice grew more firm. 'It is doubly your obligation therefore to safeguard her, without letting her know that you are aware of her danger. She certainly does not want you to know of it.'

My throat had begun to ache and my eyes to burn. I had been one of the causes of Sundari's condition, an evil cause from my desiring, pure though it might have been. 'Does this mean that she will die soon?' The words came out in a whisper almost.

'She will die when her *kharmic* forces are exhausted, in the fullness of time, not because of her condition, but possibly from it. She will live long if she avoids undue excitement and

527

physical or emotional strain of any kind.'

During all the years of our celibacy, I had sometimes wondered what it would be like to make love to Sundari. We had seldom talked about it, but both of us had known the times when desire was very close to the surface. We had reached a stage, however, when we knew how to sublimate that desire by simple expedients, such as taking a quiet walk in the courtyard when our feelings mounted, but more, we constantly avoided any situation that could evoke passion. 'If Sundari does not want me to know, does it mean . . .?' I hesitated.

Uday understood immediately. 'She told me that she would never deny you anything, whatever the cost to her, so she would give you her all regardless.'

I was torn between wonder at Sundari's love and outrage. 'Whatever the cost?' I cried. 'Dear devas, her death would be my highest cost.'

'All can be well since you acknowledge that,' he soothed me. 'Her condition is a fact. Your love must enable you to live happily, harmoniously with that fact.'

My face twisted with grief. 'But I can now marry her,' I began, then stopped abruptly before the look in Uday's eyes.

'Let love be your guide,' he quietly urged.

'I must think this out,' I responded. 'My head is whirling. All these years of waiting and the moment I am able to marry her . . . this.'

'What?'

The single word jolted me. What indeed? It was up to me not to diminish the happiness of this time. Desperately my heart sought the answers. 'You are right, Venerable Sir,' I finally responded more calmly. 'Nothing is important except our love. No part of it can be greater than the whole. Please forgive me, but I need to be alone now to sort out the hideous confusion in my mind.'

'And to commune with your God,' he suggested.

Amazed at his sensitivity, I made obeisance to him and

walked through the audience hall, across the verandah, into the *meda midulla*, perfunctorily acknowledging the obeisances of the attendants. The mood of the earth matched mine, for the night was dark and oppressive, not a breath of wind stirred the black branches. The sky was overcast with glowing white clouds. As I paced the walkway, my desires gusted through me. Oh God, why did you do this to me, my heart cried in bitter anguish. Why did you hold the cup to my thirsty lips, only to snatch it away?

You wanted marriage, now you have it, God replied smoothly.

Why are you so smug in your righteous perfection, God? Why? Why? Why did you do this?

It is you who find me smug or perfect. As for Me, I am what I am. The forces within Me are unchangeable.

But I love this woman. I want so much to mate with her and have her bear my children.

I am not stopping you. Go ahead and mate with her. She is perfectly capable of bearing children.

And dying in the process?

That is for you to determine.

At that very moment, as if God had guided my footsteps, I stood beneath the second-floor balcony verandah on which I had seen Sundari that first time in the Kalyani palace. It was now lit by a single flare. Sundari had seemed so unattainable in the semi-gloom then. How often I had thanked God through the years for giving me the knowledge of her love.

A cool breeze sprang up, riffling through the leaves. I looked above the palace roofline and saw a patch of blue sky within the cloud layer, a single star in its centre. You are right, God, please forgive me my resentment. Tonight, I have even more than I have given you thanks for in the past.

Then I knew what I had to do and God smiled. My eyes flickered down from the sky towards the verandah again, like twin homing pigeons. Sundari emerged into the yellow half-light. She must have known instinctively that I stood beneath. 'Prince,' she said softly, with gladness in her voice, but no

529

surprise.

'Come down, Sundari,' I bade her. 'I have some important news for you.'

I waited for her with a beating heart, for nothing mattered except our love. I held her life more precious than any selfish desiring and I would safeguard her. God had given me the gift of this unique human being, at a time when I had decided on a life of celibacy. He had found her a celibate prince to protect her.

There she stood, slim and erect before me, in her white skirt and bodice, looking more beautiful than the night. 'I'm so happy you are back, Lord,' she whispered.

Our eyes locked in sweet communion. All my resentment and bitterness melted away, leaving only fear for her life.

I cannot bring myself to speak of what followed when I gave her my news. It is too sweet and private to be shared, but I held her in my arms for the first time in over eight years of knowing her. The joy bells were ringing in my mind, their clamour strangely stilling my body. God even cleared the clouds from the sky and sent us the fragrance of night jasmine borne on his winds.

King Vijaya had led a celibate existence since his departure for the big battle against the forces of King Tikka and Prince Jaya. It had been easier than his men, who knew about it, imagined because he seemed to have been robbed of all sexual desire since he was laid low by the Yakka sickness in Sita Elija. The principle that he was committed to having only Arya heirs, and no bastard children, became his refuge and his Arya admired him for it. In the privacy of his secret thoughts and fears, however, he had wondered whether he was impotent.

Tonight, the wedding festivities were over and he was faced with the moment of truth. He had a young woman for a bride, in a marriage that had been arranged so that he could impregnate her with his seed. As he stood at the entrance door

530

of the nuptial bedroom in the Thamba-Panni palace, he wondered how he would fare. Anula was a virgin. Tomorrow morning, the laundry women would knock on the door of the bedroom to carry away the silken bedsheet that must bear the bloodstains of proof. How could he penetrate the veil if he could not become stiff and hard? Once capable of a tremendous erection without physical stimulation, he groaned inwardly at his present flaccidity. For the hundredth time, he wondered whether Anula would, in that event, cooperate with him in artificially making the tiny cut, a device which non-virgins used to proclaim a non-existent virginity. He felt ashamed at the thought, but it had been so many years since . . .

Clad in a pale green robe, he barely noticed the gold cushions on the creamy satinwood furniture, the blue-canopied bed with its white silk linen, as his eyes sought those of his bride across the bright taper-light. She stood beside the bed, clad only in a gauzy white nightdress, a small virginal figure, exquisite as fine porcelain. Her skin glowed pink, the mounds of her breasts pushed through her dress revealing the tiny thrust of erect nipples. Her glistening eyes were tremulous. He was struck by the sheer beauty of her. The delicate scent of jasmine perfume reached his nostrils, stimulating all his senses. Here was a woman to be adored. He thought of the pink lips that divided her cleft and knew that they would be delicate, beautifully formed, not gross, beneath the thin, fine down of her pubis. He felt the need to kiss them and his eyes drifted downwards to that darker patch on the soft pink of her skin.

When his eyes moved back to hers, he detected her carefully concealed apprehension, the slim shoulders held a little stiffly, and his heart went out to her. For all our poise, we are two scared people, he thought. A wave of tenderness such as he had never experienced before swept through him, an overwhelming desire to protect. 'Do not be afraid, my queen,' he said gently. 'This is new for both of us and we will explore it together. We do not wish to hurt you in any way, only to give you understanding and delight.'

She saw the tenderness in his eyes and her shoulders relaxed, her eyes glistened with unshed tears. 'Such kindness, Sire,' she whispered. 'I have been told that men are mostly rough and brutal, especially those who are big and strong.' Her gaze wandered to his massive chest and limbs, then back to his eyes. It drew him towards her now, like a magnet.

He crossed the room slowly, his eyes soft on her, his being deliberately gentled. He stood beside her and saw her chest rise and fall, the fine nostrils quivering with each breath. 'Such beauty!' he exclaimed. 'A shrine of beauty to be worshipped.'

The words released something within him. His penis stirred, but still would not rise. He felt the vibrance of her body, sending thrills through his own. Suddenly he knew that he could speak to her. 'It's been so long,' he said quietly. 'We are going to need your help as you need ours.'

Young as she was, she understood. Her nostrils dilated and she nodded. 'We shall be patient with each other,' she said. 'And it will be perfect, I promise you, my lord.'

He reached for her . . . and joy of joys, he felt himself harden. It was a half-mast, not the old proud erection, but with the help of this beautiful human being that too would happen.

Sundari and I had talked in my quarters each night, before we finally retired, with an attendant lady out of earshot as a chaperone. So, later that evening, after I had bathed, changed and eaten, Sundari already awaited me. We sat on our usual settles in my study and I told her all that had transpired since I left Kalyani. She knew the facts. 'It is common knowledge in the palace,' she stated. 'I hear that Prince Jaya and all the princes, nobles and chiefs are simply furious. It would have been a tough enough situation for you by itself, my poor prince, but now that you have also come back empty-handed, terrible problems will surely arise.'

'Nothing need be that terrible,' I reassured her, feigning a confidence I did not feel. 'Once the Great King's policy is explained to the people and it is known that the marriages are no more than the hankering of men for their own kind, the Yakkas and Nagas will be appeased. But I must confess that I dread my meeting with Prince Jaya tomorrow.'

She looked at me directly then, with her usual innocence and sincerity. 'Do you think that what your brother has do e is right?'

The simple question staggered me. Thus far, I had avoided making any moral judgement as to the Great King's actions save for condemning his banishment of the Princess Kuveni, and my natural reactions to the importation of the Arya brides. Now this childlike woman had compelled me to face up to it. I could only respond with the honesty I had always given her. 'No, I do not think it is right. Lord Buddha said 'Not by birth is the Brahman made.' This is an *akusala kharma* of great magnitude and it will have evil consequences.'

'What happened to change the Great King, your brother? I remember your telling me how he once wanted you to be the voice of his conscience.'

I had always avoided discussing anything personal about my brother, even with Sundari. Tonight, however, I felt that I had to speak frankly to prepare her for whatever might lie ahead. 'My brother is an unhappy man, the victim of forces within himself that are both hereditary and imposed from outside. He regarded his seizure of this country not only as a mission, but as an opportunity to reform himself. He genuinely wants to be a good king. But he took this country by an act of treachery and betrayal even worse than his former acts of brigandage in Sinha-Pura. On the other hand, he is also a great romantic, and the Princess Kuveni not only failed to give him what he needed, but her rituals and certain aspects of her temperament even filled him with repulsion. For instance, he is so terribly sensitive that he has never got over

533

the sight and smell of cockerel blood on Kuveni's breast all those years ago. Because he was unhappy and unfulfilled in his personal life, he directed his all to his ambitions, telling himself that achievement is more important than happiness, respect more vital than love. Hence his thirst for power and his desire to be a god-king. The repeated betrayals by the Yakka confirmed his belief in Arya supremacy, while victory bred in him the illusion of being that god-king. Now he has developed a compulsive urge to be all of history instead of merely creating it.'

'Is it because you will not subscribe to these designs and motivations that he has become estranged from you?'

'We were close until circumstances created a parting of the ways that was inevitable because of our differing ideals. When this happened, since he has always needed a crutch, despite his strength – you know, it was our mother first, then me – he found another when he thought I had failed him.'

'Ujjeni?'

'Yes. Ujjeni is an evil, conniving, treacherous man, *larla*, a spiritual pander. From the time I saw my brother gradually coming under his influence, I grew more and more afraid. He made things easy for my brother by catering to his every secret ambition, seeming to be the 'other him' of my brother as both man and king. He has been extremely clever in diagnosing my brother's fundamental needs, but there are three things he has forgotten.'

'And those?'

'First, the innate goodness in my brother, which only awaits deep causes to emerge. Second, his love for me, literally his flesh and blood, and, finally, his wisdom, even cunning.'

'I can understand the first two, but the third? Forgive me, Lord, but I see nothing except blind ambition, ruthlessness and cruelty in your brother's actions. And of late, again please forgive me for saying so, I have begun to lose my respect for him, because he seems to have become a mere puppet, manipulated by Ujjeni.'

'I don't blame you for thinking so, beloved, but I realized during my conversation with him on the shores of Mantota, that my brother is really a man of great wisdom and strength. Many of his actions are based on the conviction that this country does need Arya domination and Arya succession, if it is not to be over-run by the Dasa in the future.'

'The Dasa?'

'Yes, the Dasa, your people. We have not discussed it, but I'm sure that my brother perceives your people to be his real source of danger. Now that our country is rich and prosperous, the Dasa who live in the barren southlands of the continent will surely invade Lanka some day. When that happens, their compatriots in Lanka will support them. Only a strong Arya majority can save the country for all its people. When I failed to give my brother support in these aims, he turned to Ujjeni. I am, however, convinced that the Great King is using Ujjeni and not the other way round. Strong men, such as he, care nothing about appearances so long as their objectives are achieved. Look at the hold he has established over the whole of Lanka, his achievement alone. He has consistently used the strengths and weaknesses of all its people, including the Yakkas and Nagas. The only difference between him and me is not in our analysis of the situation, but in our methods, for he considers the end to justify the means.'

'Where will it all end?'

'I don't know. I have premonitions, but I believe that where there is essential good, it will always come out in the end. I pray that it will be so with my brother.'

Her eyes melted into mine. 'You are such a good man,' she said, her voice low. 'I am so fortunate to have found you. It makes me think of poor Princess Kuveni, so alone, and feel even more sorry for her. I wonder where she is at this moment. Probably wandering around the countryside in fear for her life and the lives of her two children . . . those abandoned babies.'

'I love you so much.' The words jerked out of me.

'I love you, my prince.'

I was so weary from my journey that I fell asleep, leaning back against my seat, while talking to Sundari. I suddenly awoke to find the tapers still lit and Sundari dozing with her head on a table. My mind was white-bright on the instant. By a simple, childlike question, Sundari had opened my mind to right and wrong. It was not merely the possibility of Naga displeasure with my brother's policies that I faced, but the question of my own moral stance, an issue I had been avoiding for years. My thoughts inevitably turned to God. Placing myself within His body, I tried to comprehend the true state of cause and effect over the years of disagreement with my brother's views. God sent me his answer in an unexpected manner, for Sundari stirred and suddenly sat up, wide awake. 'You are not sleeping. Is anything wrong, beloved?' She enquired in a slumber-misted voice.

'I've been thinking, but I do not wish to disturb your rest.'

She placed a finger on my lip. 'Hush! You sometimes speak great foolishness. Tell me what you have been thinking.'

I was grateful to be able to share my thoughts with her. 'I have just realized that I have been afraid, or at least very reluctant, to oppose my brother. I have allowed loyalty and the habit of devotion to him to blind me to my obligations to truth and to the people of Kalyani. I have given him obedience even when I disagreed completely with his policies and actions. I have been the slave of my entire past, since birth, always making the excuse that the king's policies should consistently be supported, or at least condoned. Tonight, you opened my eyes to my most important duty of all, dedication to what I believe to be right. I love you the more for it, but I am ashamed of my past emotional cowardice.'

Sundari replied quietly in the darkness, but she must have been inspired by God, for her voice had the force of heavenly bells. 'You have been but the coward of your love for your brother, as you are the coward of your love for me, as I am the

536

coward of my love for you. You are no physical coward. Your daily *yoga* training during many years makes you capable of enduring any kind of physical suffering, at a level now that can even compare with the late King Ra-hula. And you are certainly not a coward in spirit. It was just necessary for you to realize the truth.'

'And you helped me come to that realization.'

'You know what is right and wrong. If you knowingly do what is wrong, it will have evil consequences for you and for all those close to you. Worst of all, it will develop in you reflexes of wrongdoing, making it easier and easier for you to do what is wrong and gradually diminishing your strength to combat evil actions.'

'I am tempted to make some grand, glorious gesture to courage,' I responded. 'But that would be merely a natural swing back from my past acquiescence, an immature deed of bravado to appease myself. I must act with wisdom and a due sense of responsibility towards everyone concerned.' I paused, reflecting. 'I have taken my first action tonight, by accepting my guilt. My second must be the decision to sever myself from policies I can no longer support. I have no option but to request my brother to relieve me of my appointment as sub-king of Kalyani, which throws the greatest burden of conflict upon me. I have given away most of my wealth to help the people, but your needs and mine are modest and I have enough to enable us to lead a good life.'

'I do not mind being poor. My father gave up opportunities for wealth in order to pursue the doctrine. If you retire from public life, I will have more of your time. Perhaps some day you and I can join the Noble Order.'

The eagerness in her voice thrilled me, our oneness of purpose gave me peace at last. 'Thank you for your support,' I responded. 'I shall commit my views to *ola* as a missive to King Vijaya first thing in the morning, stating my objections to his policies, setting forth my fears, my concern for the Yakka and Naga peoples. I shall also outline my beliefs, both temporal

537

and spiritual, and inform him as to what I propose doing with the remainder of my life, craving his approval and understanding. At last he will know where I stand on every issue. I shall read you what I have written, then show it to Uday and place the *ola* in my strong box for delivery to the Great King when the timing is right. The timing is most important.'

Sundari and her attendant left for their quarters shortly afterwards.

I awoke in the morning to the sound of cocks crowing at the false dawn, slipped out of bed and lit a flare.I sat at my desk and wrote out my missive to the king. When I had finished, I completed my ablutions, dressed in white pantaloons and tunic, picked up my *ola* and left my quarters to call on Uday in his cell, sending word to Sundari to join us there. While waiting for her to arrive, I told Uday of my decisions. He listened gravely to all I had to say. By the time I was ready to start reading, Sundari arrived.

Both Uday and Sundari expressed pleasure at what I had written.

'You are taking a very noble stand,' Uday observed. And I glowed, for I treasured his opinion. 'But is there not something lacking there?'

'What, Venerable Sir?'

'Your views differ from those of the Great King, yet you have not told him what *you* would do in his place, if you had the responsibility for ensuring the equality and wellbeing of all races in Lanka, including the Arya, for promoting prosperity and high living standards, for safeguarding the realm today, tomorrow and perhaps throughout history.'

'I had not thought about it.'

'Think now, my dear.'

Sundari's head had been turning towards each of us as we spoke, as if she were a spectator in a game. Uday's question was indeed a tough one, but the answer came to me suddenly. 'That is not my problem, Venerable Sir. I neither desire, nor seek, the high estate of Great King, nor any of his responsibilities.' I tapped the *ola* on my knee. 'This missive makes my position clear. I want to divest myself of any responsibility for governing anything but my senses, so I do not have to offer solutions to someone else's problems.'

'If you do not have solutions to the problems, what right do you have to an opinion on your brother's solutions?' His deep voice was gentle but firm, his black eyes, with that strange, hypnotic shine, commanding.

I was taken aback, as much by the unexpectedness of his question as by its logic. I heard the distant bray of a palace donkey and thought, how symbolic of my own!

Uday drove home his points, but still gently. 'How can you judge your brother wrong, if you do not know what is right? Is not your reluctance to discover what you consider to be right a form of intellectual cowardice?'

The truth of his words hit me with the force of a battering ram. 'You are right, Venerable Sir, and I am most grateful to you for opening my mind to it. Pray let me think awhile.'

He nodded. Assessing the factors involved, I proceeded slowly. 'My most important concern is to determine what is right.'

He nodded, smiling. A glint of sunshine slanted through the grilled window and caused his shaven head to shine.

I warmed to my task. 'Human events have an ecology of their own, if we do not interfere with them, especially in a drastic fashion. Levelling mountains and denuding forests, for instance, can create havoc with Nature. So it can be with people. The human race, including our Arya ancestors, have long lived nomadic lives of mass migrations, but these have all resulted from the vicissitudes of Nature and the demands of extraneous circumstances. When we Arya came to Lanka, in enforced migration, we should have allowed ourselves to absorb and be absorbed by the local people. The importation of Arya ladies and Arya artisans on a large scale interferes with the orderly progress of human events. It levels Nature's population mountain and substitutes a man-made one. It cannot do the present or the future real good. Rather than guaranteeing against Dasa invasions, it might even aggravate them.' My eyes were alight with the excitement of discovery.

'Should you not include that eloquent statement in your message to the Great King?'

'I certainly shall.' Then I had an exciting afterthought. 'I shall do more. I shall state that I feel so strongly on this issue that I would not blame the Yakka and Nagas if they took up arms to defend their rights.'

Uday's expression became grave. 'That would not be wise,' he stated.

'There are rare occasions when wisdom must give way to the courage of one's convictions,' I declared pompously, my heart beating faster, wanting to show off to Sundari.

When I left the cell, I proceeded to my quarters, added to the *ola* and placed it in the metal strongbox underneath my bed, to await the day when I could deliver the message to my brother, the Great King.

Chapter 39

I had barely completed my morning meal of sarsaparilla root crushed in goat's milk, soft rice, vegetable curry and fruit when my chief attendant informed me that Prince Jaya awaited my pleasure. A Prince Regent would intrude on a ruler's schedule only in the event of some emergency. Having a shrewd suspicion as to where the emergency lay, I hastened to the audience chamber.

When Prince Jaya rose to give me salutation, I recognized that he was not his normal, easy-going self. His massive jaw was set, the black eyes peeping through their slits were devoid of merriment, the whole of his great physical bulk tense and hard as granite.

We had acquired the habit of being informal with each other, so we sat side by side on the dais, I on the golden throne on which King Ra-hula had been murdered and he on the ornate chair once reserved for the queen on state occasions. Sunlight had begun to glance in from the high-grilled windows, through which a patch of clear blue sky was etched by the green branches of a cassia tree. I heard the faint chanting of children's voices in the distance and that donkey's bray again. Peace on the earth and conflict within me. I sighed and took a deep breath, inhaling Prince Jaya's sandalwood scent.

'You desired audience with me, Prince?' I opened the conversation formally.

'Yes, Lord.' His normally high voice was couched deliberately low, the small puckering red lips closing on the words like a trap. 'As you probably guess, it is on a matter of gravest importance.' He paused, the slits of his eyes now boring into me. 'You have returned from your mission empty-handed and I know the reason why. While our miserable people starve, the rich Arya reside in magnificent dwellings and fill their bellies with food and wine, their senses with music and dancing. For seven years, the Yakkas and Nagas have endured the ignominy of being subject people. While this situation was one of the Arya way of life rather than of outright discrimination, we could tolerate it. Now it has surfaced in a most outrageous and humiliating fashion. Worse, we have been refused even the crumbs that pi-dogs receive from a master's table.'

I was about to protest but remained silent in order to hear all he had to say.

Prince Jaya's eyes closed and he breathed deeply, obviously trying to hold back an outburst. He finally spoke with deadly quiet. 'When I swore an oath of allegiance to the Great King eight years ago, I offered him two choices, my life, which he could have taken anyway, or my service on a condition. He chose the latter. I expected that he would honour his word by ruling Kalyani wisely, well and with justice to our people. You, Prince, as the ruler of this sub-kingdom made my task easy during the years that followed, for you have looked after my people and given us all justice and prosperity.'

'With your constant help and support.'

He inclined his head, though slightly because his great triple chins got in the way. His plump cheeks quivered. 'Now you too have turned against us.' His voice broke and he paused, then resumed slowly and with great dignity. 'The Great King cares not one mustard grain for us, but intends that Yakka and Naga, prince and noblemen, chieftain and peasant, should all be second-class citizens, subordinate to the Arya in every respect, even excluded from Arya festivities.'

'Do you realize, Prince, that I too was not invited to these festivities, which were a purely private affair at which there were no guests?' I cried.

'Strange that your visit to Thamba-Panni, after one year, should have coincided with the event,' he countered bitterly.

542

Caught in one of those situations that occasionally beset rulers, I ignored the implication of his charge. As a man, I agreed with all he had said and felt just as outraged as him. After all, Sundari was a Dasa. In fact, I had but a few hours earlier set my position down in writing to the Great King. I had already decided that I would soon ask to be relieved of my responsibilities. But I was the sub-king until I did resign and, as such, had to do everything in my power to maintain order, peace and harmony in my realm. 'Some of your facts and all your conclusions are wrong,' I told Prince Jaya flatly.

'You cannot help but say that in order to excuse your own involvement. You were even in the receiving line at the port.' The words were out before he realized it.

'Have a care, Prince,' I warned quietly, but with ice in my voice. 'You should know me better than that. I do not blame you or the other princes and nobles for feeling outraged.' This last was a bow-shot in the dark but I struck home and was rewarded by the merest slackening of his face. He knew I had no spies anywhere and must be wondering how I came by my knowledge of his talks with others. 'First, you have my word that I was totally unaware of the Great King's plans until the morning the Arya party landed. As a matter of fact, I accompanied the Great King to Mantota at his request without knowing the truth.' I outlined the course of events to him. 'So you are making an impassable mountain out of an ant-hill.'

I should have said a termite-hill, I thought to myself. 'What the Great King and his Arya comrades have done is to exercise the right of every single Naga, Yakka and Dasa in this land. Do you not all marry your own kind? Would you yourself have dreamed of marrying anyone but a Naga? Did you not refuse to allow your own daughter to marry outside her race and rank?' This last was a cruel but necessary reference to a young Arabi who had desired to marry Prince Jaya's only child and had been refused. The girl had eloped with her suitor and now lived in distant Ruhuna, disowned by

543

Prince Jaya and his family. 'Why then do you deny the Arya rights you arrogate to yourselves? Are they second-class citizens in your eyes?'

He was taken aback. 'The artisans?' He began.

'Are meant to give the Arya homes a familiar culture such as every other race on this blessed island enjoys and, mark my words well, Prince, enjoys under the protection of the Great King.'

My lips were uttering impassioned words that did not come from that true source of passion, the heart, yet I knew I was right to speak as I did, pinning my faith in the ultimate goodness of the Great King. I also knew I was rationalizing again, playing for time.

'Why the secrecy then?' Prince Jaya demanded.

'Would you have the Great King publish it to the beat of trumpets that six hundred, no six hundred and one, sex-starved Arya were soon to be provided with soil for their seed?'

He smiled naturally at that, his eyes crinkling and disappearing beneath their fleshy folds. 'Few of them were sex-starved, *aney*.' I noted with relief that he was reverting to his normal mode of speech. 'They have cast their seed all over the four kingdoms and we now have the beginning of mixed races. *Tchickay*! That is not good. Must keep the blood-lines pure, no?'

'Precisely . . . So what are you all complaining about?'

'All of us feel . . .' He began, then blinked as the impact of my words hit him. 'You are very cunning, no? You trapped me. *Tchickay*, Prince!'

I decided to bluff him in the interests of peace. 'Look, I am aware that there have been discussions among you about raising the standard of revolt.' I was again rewarded, this time by the tiniest wobble of his neck, where his larynx would have shown save for the fat. 'But it's no good. Take my advice and do not rush hot-headed into actions that you will all regret. You will never win against the Arya in battle. You know that.

So even if the Great King intends what you say he does, work with his policies and try to gain equality by proving your worth, as you have done these many years. Remember, we are all slaves and equality is only a state of mind.' My voice became earnest. 'Even a slave can be the equal of his master if his mind does not acknowledge the subordination of his true self, but only of his body and part of his conduct, so that any man can lift bales with dignity, or any woman can be raped without loss of chastity. Consider the Venerable Uday. He is the lowliest-seeming among us, with no position in the four kingdoms, depending on others even for his food, yet is he not the greatest among us all? Do we not all acknowledge him as our Chief Monk and deem him the Great King of our morality and wisdom?'

'You were always wise.' He pondered me for a while, his eyes wide open. 'I shall counsel my colleagues to wait and see.' Then the words burst forth from him. 'But you, Prince. How can we trust you? Even if you did not know of the king's plans, you joined in the revels. You made yourself a part of it, instead of running away, screaming for justice.'

'I will never sit in moral judgement on others,' I responded. 'Knowing me, knowing my love for our people, can you imagine how I suffered at having to do my duty with a cheerful face?' My voice rose passionately. 'How the food stuck in my throat? Yet I have been trained to behave as an Arya prince, with dignity and decorum. to practise *dharma*, the duty of my station.' I suddenly felt haughty. 'We princes do not run away screaming from unpleasant duties. Your suggestion is more than absurd, it is preposterous, something I doubt that you would have done had you been in my place.'

Prince Jaya looked at me with admiration. He clapped his hands in mock applause but I could feel him warming towards me again.

'Remember, Prince,' I advised firmly. 'While I hold my office, I support the Great King unreservedly in all actions. Any discussions you have had with your fellow princes, the nobles and especially with the Naga commanders of the armed forces that even hint of revolt is treason. For that crime, I shall ruthlessly and without hesitation exact the supreme penalty from any guilty person, regardless of rank.'

He pushed his bulk up suddenly and towered over me, vibrating with a strange mixture of dignity, power and, yes, love-force. 'Your threats mean nothing to me, Prince,' he declared solemnly. 'Your affection means more to me than your position and I am more afraid of . . . of . . . my love for you as a person . . .' the difficult words came out in a rush . . . 'than of your power as the sub-king.' His eyes opened wide, glistening, then he shut the lids tight to force back his tears. 'But I will sacrifice anything, everything for my people and my country.'

I rose to my feet and eyed him levelly. 'You know how I feel about you, Prince,' I replied. 'I believe that I love you even more than I love my brother, and like you, I love my people and my country. The difference between you and me is that I will sacrifice anything, everything even my people and my country, for what is right.'

He stared at me, wide-eyed. I then administered the clinching blow. 'The Great King, whom you accused of being a chauvinistic Arya has granted me permission to marry a Dasa of low caste, Sundari. I would be honoured if you would attend our nuptials tomorrow night. Only you and Uday are being asked.'

The following night, Sundari, clad in white silken skirt and bodice and I, in white tunic and pantaloons, were married in a simple Buddhist ceremony at the Kalyani palace. The entire night before had been dedicated to the chanting of a *pirith*, by Uday and twenty Buddhist monks, followed by our taking *dasa-sila*, the Ten Precepts. It was the *pirith-nool*, thread, made pure by the chanting of the holy words, over and over again, in unbroken cadence, while it was passed through the fingers of the monks during the hours of the chanting, that was used to bind Sundari's hand to mine in token of our wedlock.

More than any previous event, these Buddhist rites confirmed me as a follower of the doctrine. Though my belief in God grew by the day, I had decided to keep this completely to myself, because my relationship with God was intensely personal and I simply could not share it with the rest of the world, not even with Sundari, who had to find her own God. God can never be proved. The knowledge of Him must come from within to each person separately, from experience and not from logic or persuasion.

So Sundari, who had reigned over my heart even before I met her in this birth, became my wife and queen. As I awaited her in our bedchamber, I confronted a more haunting question than that which every husband must face on his wedding night. How could I make love to Sundari without draining her? Suddenly, I was afraid.

Then she was inside the bedchamber and I barely heard the door click shut as I rose from my settle. The long room was lit by tapers placed in bronze sconces on the walls. In their light, I no longer saw the floors of mountain crystal, the hung tapestries, the ebony chests, the mosaic ceiling or the great canopied bed. I only saw my love standing at the far end of the room and she glowed so wondrous fair that my heart beat high with ecstasy. She had taken her gleaming hair up above her ears, revealing a slender swan-like neck, setting the delicate bones of her face in exquisite relief. Her face gleamed pink-gold as the *ran thambili* in the gentle light. She wore a white silken gown that revealed pale, rounded shoulders and the first hint of the rise of her small breasts. Her waist was tiny, but the hips flared in beautiful contours beneath them, above the fullness of her limbs. I gazed at her in awe, for she literally shimmered within and without, radiant, a goddess.

I sought her eyes. They glistened, dark and intense, fixed on me with an overflow of melting love and a trembling expectancy such as I had never dreamed possible. Our glances locked and the air before me started to vibrate, my breathing became hushed, time ceased to exist.

A single deep breath that was almost a sigh, then, in a trance, without even realizing that I had done so, I started moving slowly towards her. I simply could not take my eyes from hers, for our gaze was a single eternal, unbreakable thread drawing me to her like a boat on a ferry-rope, the waters beneath the gentle rise and fall of her breasts. Then I stood before her, but not yet against her body. I could feel the magnetism from every pore of our beings linking us as surely as if we had been locked in each other's arms.

I took in her beauty with reverence, the gentle curve of her translucent cheeks, the flare of her fine nostrils, the small red bow of her mouth. With joy I noted the tiny, brown freckles behind her shoulder, sheer beauty on an otherwise flawless skin.

We stood thus apart, but merging, for long moments. Dear God, the full consummation of two such bodies would be more exquisite than a warm death.

She sighed, her nostrils flaring slightly. That evidence of life, of breath, of passion maddened me, but yet I had to hold back, slowly reaching out instead with both hands, to touch her fair cheeks, my fingers quivering. She trembled and blushed, reminding me of the poem I had made at her first blush.

This is a new heaven and a new earth, opening before me. I cannot believe that I stand upon its threshold. It is enough to do so without entering it. My love for her makes that possible.

She moved to me and my body blazed with excitement. Thrills hitherto unknown shot through me, yet I kept my manhood under control. With a gentle moan, her soft body came against mine. Flesh of my flesh, yet it was the flesh of her flesh that made it so wondrous sweet, the feel of her body sheer magic.

I knew as I bent down to kiss her lips that I desired fervently to first worship at her shrine of beauty before entering it, to offer her flowers blossoming from my imagination in order to earn our final ecstasy. True love can only exist between a virgin man and a virgin woman. With such love as Sundari's and mine, a man and a woman would be for ever virgin to each other, because virginity does not depend upon the piercing of a veil. I already knew what I had to do. I let her think that I did not have the virility, the life, to fulfil her, so that I could save her life.

What sweet, gentle understanding she gave me for my pretended inability, but God, how it hurt.

Chapter 40

Four months after his wedding, King Vijaya found that he had been spending more and more time with Anula, the beautiful child-bride he had consecrated his queen. He watched her now, seated straight-backed on a settle beside his sofa, hands crossed over her lap in the prim fashion of princesses, and his heart went out to her for her youth, her beauty, her refinement. They were seated in her elegant reception chamber at the Thamba-Panni palace. The hour was late, the mantle of deep night's silence had fallen around the buildings.

Queen Anula had arranged for an entertainment dinner and he was feeling very relaxed. 'We thank you for the concert, Anula,' he told her. 'The strains of flute and pipe, the beat of cymbal and drum will soothe us even after we fall asleep tonight and the *natya*, dances, of Madura, will remain a haunting experience.'

Her cheeks dimpled her pleasure. 'My Lord, you have been so good to me, it was so little to do in return. Besides, it is part of my duty as your wife.'

'Ah, duty! It is good to have a queen who understands the duties of her rank and station.' He sighed. 'We feel we now know you well enough to share our thoughts with you.'

'I want to share everything with you, my Lord, not merely your bed.' She blushed. 'Do you wish to tell me something now?'

He looked at her searchingly. Finding genuine love in her eyes, he decided to proceed. 'The past months have brought us ever-increasing concern about having sent Kuveni and our two children away. It was easier to do at the time than to live with today . . . uh . . . Please be assured that we have no regrets whatever over the act itself, which was something we had to do as the Great King. Personal concern, sympathies, can have no place in government and a ruler must abide inflexibly by the rules of *dharma*, the duty of his station. We also want to assure you that, even if we had had any feelings for her – which we did not! – we would have had to take this step regardless because of our responsibility towards our men, the country and history.' His tawny eyes searched her face again. He found only approval and concern on it, she seemed like a child displaying a grown-up's interest.

'That is as we have been taught in our Arya courts, my Lord,' she responded.

'Good. The arrival of your ladies has brought much needed elegance to our court. It heralds the creation of a new race, a master race, of which you, our wife, are a symbol and will soon be the fount.' His whole being distended with pride at the thought, then grew flaccid before a thrust of fear as to his fertility, the fear which had haunted him through the years since the day in Sita Eli-ja when the *uda rata* physicians had broken the news to him that the Yakka disease might have destroyed his seed for ever. Anxiously his eyes sought his wife's abdomen between her white silken skirt and bodice for some sign of swelling but found it as trim and flat as ever. With an effort, he cast aside his concern. Time enough. 'This evening's dinner, just the two of us, enjoying the delicacies prepared by the Arya cooks you brought here and the entertainment, have been a revelation to us, further proof that Arya culture is the best of all. We also find new strength in the union of the kingdom which your royal father rules with Lanka. His fleet of fifty ships, including war galleys, still at Mantota for cleaning and greasing of their keels, is a tangible symbol of the strength we derive from such unity. And yet,' he paused, his gaze tender upon her. 'We want you to know that the dearest, truest symbol of unity in our heart is you, our lady.'

He was rewarded by seeing tears of joy glisten in her limpid brown eyes. He reached out and took her hand. 'Do you remember how scared you were our first night together?'

Her eyes became round as saucers and a mischievous glint entered them. 'But you were so bee . . . eg, my Lord!'

He smiled and squeezed her soft fingers. 'We had been celibate for years and wondered whether we could ever get bee . . . eg again. But you, Princess, performed the miracle.'

Long moments passed while they simply looked at each other, their love flooding out. Finally she inquired. 'Can you not see how much I love you?'

'Yes and it is wonderful. We . . . I . . . love you, Anula.' He paused.

More long moments of silent communion passed before he could bring himself to change the subject. 'Now for an official topic,' he finally said. 'Do you believe that our ministers, especially, Prince Ujjeni, are manipulating us?'

She straightened up, head to one side, her face very serious. 'My Lord, I believe you are too strong to be manipulated, but you sometimes give the impression that Prince Ujjeni has a great deal of influence over you and is therefore too powerful.'

'Thank you for speaking so frankly. The truth, however, is that we use our ministers for the good of the four kingdoms. For instance, by avoiding male heirs from the Naga, Dasa and Arya concubines of the early years, and also by refusing to be consecrated without an Arya queen, we subtly exerted pressure on them to find us a suitable queen. For about one year, we were greatly influenced by the ideals of our brother, Prince Lala, but as our responsibilities expanded, he expressed differing views so we had to sever the connection and Prince Ujjeni took his place. Prince Ujjeni shall therefore continue wielding power while he conducts himself as an extension of our self. Our personal happiness, however, now depends solely on you, for you have made us realize how much we need family.'

'My Lord, I am honoured,' Anula responded huskily. 'I shall try night and day to be a good wife to you and a worthy queen. I shall also do my duty as I have been taught, without wavering and as my heart now dictates.'

'We know you will. You are always so clean, so fragrant, it is easy to love you with . . . yes, a poet's love. A king's life is lonely, for he must remain aloof, remote from all, even his ministers and especially his people, if he is to be completely objective. His closest advisers and most trusted aides should never exercise independent judgement, but must make his government so efficient that it runs smoothly under the guidance of his invisible hand. We are well aware that Prince Ujjeni cooperates with us not through love but from sheer personal ambition, but we have been using his brains and abilities for the welfare of the kingdom. As for trust . . . ,' he laughed shortly. 'We trust only you.'

'What can I say, my Lord, except that I would give my life to be worthy of your love and trust?' She responded.

'You must not imagine that we are totally without conscience,' he declared, suddenly needing to unburden himself. 'We frequently wonder about Kuveni and the two children. Where are they? What are they doing? Are they safe and happy? Yet even when we have such thoughts, it is always objectively, as if they were strangers.'

Noting Queen Anula's anxious glance, he relaxed and smiled. 'We need some diversion,' he said, glancing down at the lute lying on the floor beside Anula's settle. 'Will you sing for us, please?'

'Certainly, Lord.' She picked up the lute and began plucking the strings with small, slender fingers, sending tendrils of sound tinkling through the air. Soon her voice rose softly in a love song. She sang effortlessly, on the surface of the music, which now became a quiet lake, her voice a bird skimming over its waters, her brown eyes sparkling in the taper-light.

His thoughts drifted idly on the wings of her song, but returned inevitably to his major preoccupation. He had injected her with his seed on their first night together and nightly thereafter. Why had she not conceived as yet? Was she barren? What would he do if she did not bear him an heir? Already he was becoming dependent on her, had fallen in love with her.

He realized that his wife had suddenly stopped singing and was staring at the door, her fingers poised above the lute. So engrossed had he been in his thoughts, he had not heard the knocking.

'Enter!' the queen commanded.

The door opened and the chief female attendant, Nona, a grey-haired woman clad in her customary green *kurtha* and pantaloons, made obeisance. 'Pray forgive this intrusion, Sire,' she said. 'But my lord Ujjeni seeks an immediate audience with you in your audience chamber.'

King Vijaya exchanged a glance with his wife. This had never happened before. It must be a crisis situation.

The princess pouted in a most delightful, coquettish way. He kissed her lightly on the cheek, excused himself and hastened down the flare-lit corridors of the women's quarters to its entrance, where his two bodyguards fell in step behind him. He walked briskly through the main courtyard, past armed sentries, whose greeting he returned. The night was unusually black, with dark clouds for a canopy. The loud whirring of crickets, rising above the splash of silver water from the courtyard cascades, seemed to protest the silence.

Ujjeni's death's-head face was more gaunt and bleak than ever when he rose from making obeisance. The king took his place behind his new ebony desk, bidding Ujjeni be seated on a settle across from him.

'Pray forgive me the intrusion, my lord,' Ujjeni commanded. 'But I have serious news that demands your immediate attention. A fleet of some twenty ships from the Arabi lands has been spotted about three days' journey away, heading for Devun Dara. It would appear that several of these ships have been damaged by a storm, so they are effecting repairs at sea while limping towards their goal.'

The king felt a moment's relief. 'Why is the news so critical?

These ships come over at least once a year for the annual Fair.'

'But the Fair is several months away, lord and the fleet is reported to be crammed with armed men, estimated at over a thousand, and even war-horses.'

The king jerked to attention. 'How was this discovered?'

'By chance, my lord, through the intervention of our Arya gods, I swear. One of our small trading ships out of Mantota, on its way to Sopara in the continent, sailed past the fleet and noted that it had problems. The captain slowed down to ask if he could be of any assistance and was given a surly refusal. Realizing that he was exposed to danger, he veered off in another direction until he was out of sight, then doubled back to make Mantota, instead of proceeding to Sopara.'

'Is he here?'

'Yes, lord. He hastened to the palace and awaits your pleasure in the ante-chamber.'

'Good. He shall be rewarded after we have questioned him. Meanwhile, what do you make of this?'

'Armed men and horses can only mean an invasion. Remember, you have turned Lanka into a paradise. The Arabi believe in paradise.' Ujjeni grinned cynically. 'Perhaps they are hoping to find it on earth. And where safer to land than at Devun Dara bay in the far south?'

'You are right.' As always in a crisis, the Great King was at his best, his mind ice-cold. Calmly, but with lightning rapidity, he considered relative strengths, factors, alternatives open to him. Suddenly the ideal solution flashed through his mind and he almost laughed aloud.

Three nights later, Hamy stood silently with Kira in a large open glade that had been cleared by Banda some years earlier at the bottom of the hill that housed the temple to the sun god, to serve as a receiving station for the caravans. Burnished white clouds from an overcast sky obscured the stars and pressed on the earth, cloaking the copper roof of the temple and even the highway leading from the mountains in a blackness which provided the ideal conditions for the event.

The highway between the *uda rata* and Devun Dara had been built three years earlier by the Great King, to form a ready link between the two sub-kingdoms, and Banda exploited it for his own illegal purposes. While awaiting the arrival of the convoy from the *uda rata*, Hamy found time to ponder on the news they had received the previous evening. His thoughts were interspersed by absent-minded slapping at mosquitoes that whined around him and the occasional scratch of an itch in his groin from the warm weather.

The fateful meeting with Razeena years ago had changed King Tikka even before he left for the Arabi lands. While becoming much more relaxed, however, he had developed a fierce possessiveness of his new wife. Razeena represented a challenge to his manhood, took all he could give and demanded more, so he was too drained to look elsewhere and he certainly did not want her looking. Depleted of the life and energy to wander from the marital bed, he spent every possible moment of his time with Razeena. To this day, Hamy could not suppress a smile each time he remembered the way in which life had neatly turned the tables on the king. Somewhere the best of us always meet our superior, he reflected, and finally there are the gods.

The past years had been uneventful ones for Hamy. He had been content with a room in Banda's house, though Kira had found himself a wealthy Arabi widow of buxom proportions, with three children, who made him welcome in her home, cooked exotic meals for him and made him fatter than ever. Hamy, on the other hand, spent most of his free evenings in a small *avasa*, priests' abode, that had been taken by two followers of the Buddha, who lived as *bhikkus* and were available for discourses on the doctrine at any time, except when they were in meditation or observing *sil*.

As if echoing his thoughts, Kira posed the question that had been triggered by the news they had received that evening.

'Have you really become converted to the doctrine?' he enquired, his voice low.

'Yes,' Hamy replied.

'Is it not wrong, according to your doctrine, for you to earn a livelihood by unrighteous conduct, helping Banda as the tally clerk for goods brought from the *uda rata* without tax payments?'

'I hope to make a change some day. It is part of my *kharma* in this birth, to know, to believe, but not to change my mode of living for the present.'

Kira relapsed into his habitual silence and Hamy shrugged mentally. Tonight, the regular convoy was due from the *uda rata*, along the route that he, King Tikka and Kira had once taken almost eight years ago, and he had a strange feeling that it would be the last he would superintend.

'You know, Kira,' he ventured. 'Ever since we had the news, three months ago from the captain of that trading ship that King Tikka was leaving immediately for Lanka with a fleet carrying an army of Arabi mercenaries, I felt that eight years of comparative calm were over. This was confirmed tonight, when that deep-sea fishing boat reported a fleet of at least twenty crowded ships lying off our coast, awaiting daybreak to make the port. King Tikka has finally arrived, so we go to war again. I wish I could generate some enthusiasm.'

Kira sighed. 'Me too,' he rejoined whole-heartedly. 'I guess the years of easy routine and comfortable living are hard to give up, even though our Banda's activities have been exposed to more and more danger as the Great King tightens his grip on the country.'

'In my case, the doctrine has had a gentling effect,' Hamy stated. 'All this killing and maiming is evil *kharma*. Besides, having neither wife nor children, nor concubines, I am content to live the life of an *upasakaya*. Playing for power never really works. Look what happened to that poor, misguided Kuveni.'

'Banda is of course overjoyed at the news.' Kira remarked.

'He plays for power and this is the moment he has been waiting for. Well, I guess he will be Chief Minister of Lanka soon, perhaps even the Great King some day.'

'Yesterday nothing, tonight the convoy, tomorrow the fleet; that is how life works,' Hamy declared.

At that moment, the first dislodging and rolling of stones, followed by the creak and rattle of waggons along the rocky slope, reached his ears and he came alert. The convoy was approaching and he could sense the men who waited silently on the fringes of the glade becoming alert.

The clatter and bump was soon punctuated by the clip-clop of horses' hooves and the sharp ring of metal on rocks. The only missing sound was the jingling of the bells that normally adorn the necks of the bullocks. Presently the black outlines of unlighted, open wagons loomed through the darkness like great, grey elephants. One after the other, they turned into the glade and made for the far end, each wagon taking its allotted position in an orderly row. Having gone through this routine a dozen times each year, the wagoners performed it with the precision of an army. When the last wagon, accompanied by a few figures on horseback, finally came to a halt, silence enveloped the glade, except for the stamp of a bullock's feet, the whinny of a horse and that contented sizzle-creak that underlies the bodies of vehicles that have finally come to rest after a trying journey.

Hamy tensed. This was the moment of danger, when the Great King's men would strike if they had secretly followed the convoy. Long moments went by before he heard the harsh scrape of tinder. The first flare hissed into flame at the entrance to the glade, illuminating the faces of the two brothers, Ranna and Suramba. Other flares burst forth, like fireworks, on sockets throughout the glade and in the wagons. Some of the drivers dismounted and began stretching. Hamy relaxed as quiet voices issued orders and Banda's labourers swarmed towards the wagons. Men called 'hoi!' to lift weights in unison, goods thumped as they were unloaded and laid out in the glade for checking by Hamy and Kira before being broken up into lots and carted away in Banda's personal vehicles to barns and warehouses scattered throughout the district.

'Come, Hamy,' Kira urged. 'Time to help me take tally. Have you got the *olas*?'

'Yes.' Hamy held up the roll of parchment, ink and stylus.

'Wait!' Kira paused, placing a hand on Hamy's arm. He stared in the direction of the wagon closest to the entrance to the glade.

Hamy's eyes followed Kira's gaze. Four figures had dismounted from the wagon. They stood briefly in the light of its flare, revealing themselves as two women and two children. People from the *uda rata* sometimes paid a wagoner for a ride to Ruhuna on pilgrimage or to visit relatives, but during his years of servicing this route Hamy had never seen women and children alone. Then his heart thumped and he tried to distract Kira's attention.

Rupa had sent word ahead to Gona, a Yakka relative in Devun Dara, asking whether she, a lady whose service she had entered, recently widowed and desirous of buying a farm in the area, and two children could visit him for a few days as paying guests. Rupa knew Gona to be a shrewd, successful petty trader who dealt in hides. With a wife and six children, he could do with the money. As she had anticipated, Gona readily consented to the arrangement. Since he regularly bought the hides of cattle illicitly killed in the *uda rata* from Banda, he was able to arrange for the four visitors to travel in Banda's caravan.

When Rupa led the princess and the two children, all carrying their bundles, into the pathway, she was not surprised therefore to have the tall, portly Gona greet them. She gave him the palms together salutation. '*Aney*, cousin Gona, how good of you to have come in person!' she exclaimed softly.

'I have business with the caravan.' Gona had a squeaky voice as if emerging from a sore throat, which contrasted strangely with his large figure and important manner. 'I recognised you in the flare-light, cousin Rupa, but it was best not to greet you in the open.' Gona's eyes sought the princess. 'And this is your mistress?'

'Yes. This is my lady Leela,' Rupa responded, pausing for the princess to give Gona salutation. 'And her twin children, Gamba and Gambini.' Fondly she watched the sleepy-eyed children greet Gona as they had been trained to do in the palace.

'You are all welcome,' Gona assured them. 'And what a pleasure to meet people of obvious refinement.' His eyes sought the face of the princess, hidden by her hood and the darkness. 'Now you must not remain in this cold damp air. Its humours are bad for the lungs. I have a cart waiting for you. I have business to finish here, but my servant will conduct you to my house. I shall be lucky to finish before daybreak.' He shrugged massive shoulders. 'Such is the life of a poor trader.'

Gona's house was in a rural area about a mile away. It was built of red *kabook*, the local brick carved from stony earth, with a yellow tile roof. Set in a grove of *jak* and mango trees, coconut and areca palms, it showed large and square in the semi-darkness. The servant dropped them off at the door and drove the buggy back for Gona. They were greeted in the dim taper-light of the entrance hall by a tall, scraggy woman with prematurely grey hair, aquiline features and furrowed cheeks, who introduced herself as Bindu, Gona's wife. She wore a pink skirt and jacket and a harassed air. 'The children are already in bed,' she stated. 'You can meet them tomorrow. And your own children are drooping on their feet. You must all be exhausted, so to bed, I say, but first, would you like some food?'

'No, we ate on the move in the caravan,' the princess responded, tears springing to her eyes at Bindu's kindliness. 'We thank you all the same. You are so good to give a poor widow sanctuary. May the gods reward you.'

Bindu nodded and turned away to hide her own emotion. 'Follow me,' she said.

Seizing a taper, she led the way through a long reception room to the verandah of the *meda midulla*, turned right, walked down to the end of the verandah then proceeded left along it to the farthest end of the house. The teakwood door of the room creaked as she opened it. Holding the taper aloft, she gestured to them to enter. 'This is small and you will all have to share it,' she explained apologetically. 'But we are a large family, as you know, and we moved two of the children from this room. You will find everything you need here. I have the adjoining room. Call me if there is anything you need. Sleep well.' She left, closing the door behind her.

Rupa and the princess placed their packages on the flagstone floor and surveyed the room. In the light of the two tapers on brass sconces on each of the bare side walls were two wooden beds with yellow mats on them and faded cushions. Spare mats were rolled up in the far corner of the room. 'The babies can occupy one of the beds and you the other, my lady,' Rupa suggested. 'It's the floor for me, as usual.'

The children were so worn out that Rupa put them to sleep without even changing their clothes. The princess lay down on her bed and Rupa spread a mat for herself in the centre of the room with a cushion for her head. Her bones ached from the long ride and she stretched herself, hearing her joints crack and thinking, I'm growing old.

The princess broke the silence. 'I feel peace at last,' she said. Her golden voice, soft and mellow, was slightly grained with sleepiness. 'It's as if a far longer journey than we have just completed is over and I have come to my final resting place. Since we left Thamba-Panni, even my demon gods seem far away. Perhaps other gods rule here, such as the god of Kataragama or the god E-ra of the copper-domed temple. Rupa, I decided during the journey that I would not look back but only to the future. No more men for me though. You can never trust them. You're lucky to have escaped love and marriage.' She locked her hands behind her head and stared up at the roof tiles.

Rupa knew her mistress so well, she could almost hear the thoughts rolling in her mind, like oiled cart-wheels. 'I have no regrets,' she responded quietly. 'These two babies and you now make up my entire life. So long as we are together, I shall be satisfied.'

'I've come to realize that being satisfied with what we have is the greatest blessing we can bestow on ourselves, Rupa. I tried grasping for what I wanted, not even knowing all I really wanted, but the more I grabbed the more it slipped away from me. Love, marriage, sex, all of it finally comes to nothing. I think I can find peace in Devun Dara.'

'You could not have found a more peaceful place, my lady. Here you can enjoy the blessing of your children as well, watching them grow.' She did not want to add that she too felt peace at last from the constant spying on her mistress, the regular reports to the hated Ujjeni and the terrible burden of betrayal that had lain on her mind for years.

'These two children have a great destiny in store for them, Rupa.' A snore escaped Gamba and Gambini moaned in her sleep. 'I don't know any longer what form it will take, but it will come to them.' The voice of the princess was solemn and prophetic.

A jackal's howl slashed through the night and a goat went um-baa . . . aa . . . as threads of gloom laced through Rupa's mind. She suddenly felt the room warm and close. 'When you lease a farm, it will be the ideal place for our babies to be trained for their destiny.'

'Yes. They can feel the wide open spaces, the stretches of green paddy, instead of being confined in a palace. They can see the earth bring forth tender shoots, bright flowers, sweet fruit in their own cycles instead of under the hands of men. They can listen to the sounds of wild animals and of birds rather than those in cages. They can walk barefooted, smell fresh-cut grass and the beautiful stench of raw dung. They can learn to hunt, to sow, to reap, to become human beings who inherit plain and mountain, forest and meadow. And when they have learned all this, they will be invited by the Arya some day to rule Lanka, which will be left without an heir. Rupa, I even feel that they may wed each other, as my . . . as King Vijaya's parents did.'

'Why, my lady, you sound like a *kavi*-master, a poet,' Rupa declared, wonderingly.

'The words came to me without thought, Rupa.' The princess hesitated. 'Yet I know that we ourselves must not expect anything from the children either. They will grow up and go away. Each of us must learn to be sufficient unto our own selves.'

'You are so right, my lady. Yet life makes us dependent on one another too. As human beings need food and water for sustenance, so they need one another for support.'

'True. But you know what's strange? Since I've had to fend for myself, I have become better able to do it. I do not even feel bitter towards King Vijaya. He did what he had to do. I have seen where I failed and I don't want to brood on it.'

'We should be safer and safer here as the Great King increases his hold over the region. Remember what the wagoner told us?'

'Yes. I couldn't help wondering where my . . . the Great King is tonight. It's hard at times, Rupa.'

Chapter 41

With sacrifices on the part of everyone, we somehow coped with the drought, but this time the old wonderful feeling of a people uniting with their rulers in common adversity had been absent. A mood of intense bitterness prevailed throughout the sub-kingdom, especially among the princes and nobles. For my part, having witnessed the daily suffering of a drought-stricken people, with gaunt faces, emaciated bodies and desolate eyes, did not make me proud to be one of the Arya. In contrast, my life with Sundari was blissfully happy. Though we had no sexual intercourse, after our wedding I discovered the profound joy of sleeping with the woman one loves.

I felt strangely weighed down by a premonition of doom the day the first rains came, almost four months after my visit to Thamba-Panni. It eased towards evening to drip from the branches upon a steaming earth, but the sky remained overcast, the air was cool and damp and the harsh cawing of crows seemed muted.

Darkness began to shroud the palace by the third watch after the noon hour, at which time I was scheduled to meet my Council of Ministers. Bare-chested attendants bustled about, lighting the flares on brass sconces along the *meda-midula* verandahs and the tapers inside the chamber adjoining my personal quarters, a small room opening to the verandah, with flagstone floors and furnished with creamy satinwood furniture, which I used for meetings of the council. On its white walls I had hung a large red, yellow, green and black tapestry depicting the Buddha in the lotus pose, attaining Enlightenment under the *bodhi*-tree.

To my surprise, Prince Jaya was seated alone on a settle at

the opposite end of the long table when I entered. He lumbered to his feet and gave me salutation. I did not have to look at his face to know that something was very wrong, but I calmly bade him be seated and took my place at the head of the table.

It was most improper for Ministers to keep the ruler waiting. 'Where are the others?' I asked pleasantly, not wanting to show any signs of disquiet.

'They are not coming,' he responded abruptly. 'I might as well tell you outright, Prince, that we Nagas have seized power in Kalyani today.'

I was aghast, hard put to it not to betray my reactions. 'What do you mean "seized power"?' I demanded. Though I still sounded quiet, my heart had begun to thud against my ribs.

'Exactly what I said, Prince.' He shifted on his settle and the slits of his eyes peeped out, fierce with determination. 'A council of princes and noblemen, representative of the entire kingdom and headed by me, has finally decided that we are tired of being insulted and treated as an inferior race. We may never again be blessed with a time such as this, with an all-Naga army – provided so conveniently by the Great King withdrawing the Arya commanders for their nuptials – leaderless and ripe for action. We have therefore used the army to take over the palace, the Treasury, the fort, the go-downs and warehouses, the military barracks and the armaments throughout the kingdom. Also, there is another important event, which will be revealed to you later, that makes the timing just right.'

'You will still have to reckon with the Arya.'

'We may never have a more opportune moment in which to face that challenge.'

'Your opportunity is only as far away as a forced march.'

'Do not be so sure of the Great King's whereabouts,' he replied mysteriously. 'Meanwhile we are sending him a mission, consisting of six princes and nobles, to propose a new plan for a separate Kalyani kingdom under his suzerainty.'

'You should know him by now. He will never accept it. He will regard your act as treason. You have rebelled and will have to pay the price.'

'We are prepared to do so.' He was very quiet now, his huge jowls quivering with pride. 'The Great King has driven us to the wall. We shall die there for freedom if need be, rather than live as slaves. Besides . . .' Again that mysterious smile. 'One never knows about fate.'

I was tempted to ask him how he could have done all this behind my back, how he came to betray me, his friend and the benefactor of his people, who had sacrificed much for the principle of their equality, but I held back. I did what I did for my principles, not expecting or deserving gratitude. I had to extend to this man the generosity of believing that he had been driven by that most selfish motive of all, adherence to his own principles. I therefore decided to take another tack. 'I am sure you know what you are doing, Prince, and I shall accord you the honour of believing that you are moved solely by patriotism, but I am the sub-king of Kalyani, duly appointed by the Great King. What do you expect of me?'

He shrugged his heavy shoulders. 'Nothing.'

'Nothing? Who now rules Kalyani?'

'I am its ruler.'

'Do I address you as "Sire" then?' I regretted the question as soon as it had been asked, and I got what I deserved.

'You can call me anything you like, so long as you are respectful, Prince, for you are not a subject of mine but of the Great King.'

'Will I then be permitted to return with my wife to Thamba-Panni?'

'Not for the present. And we will ensure that you do not leave, except at our command, because we need you here to assist us with those affairs of State, the details of which are known to you alone.'

'Ah! A reversal of roles.' I was in a tight situation. What would the Great King expect me to do? Fight to the death? Attempt to escape? Try as I might, I could not think clearly. Vaguely through the fog in my brain, however, I glimpsed the possibility that I might be accused of collaborating with the enemy if I gave Prince Jaya's new revolutionary council any help at all.

On the one hand, the peace and stability of the kingdom should be maintained until my brother recaptured it, on the other, as the sub-king, I should attempt to put down the revolt. But with what? And where did my sympathies lie as a man, an individual? Undoubtedly with the rebels.

The knowledge illuminated my brain with a great white light. I felt a surge of spiritual relief and my stomach began to settle. The question suddenly crashed in: Can you support what they are doing merely because their cause is righteous? 'And if I refuse?' I heard myself asking aloud.

He smiled without amusement, the slits of his eyes vanishing beneath their folds. He leaned forward on his settle and said, very pleasantly, 'Always remember you are our hostage.'

When he left the chamber, I remained seated alone, staring into space. In a few minutes, the entire course of my life had been changed and I had had no control whatsoever over the events that caused that change. Or had I? Was I too not one of the causes of these events by my actions or my inactions, by my ideals and principles? If I had been of the same Arya mould as my brother, I would have ruled Kalyani with an iron hand and this rebellion might never have occurred. Had I let my brother down? Had I let my subject people down? After all, the duty of a king is to rule, regardless of personal views or inclinations. Conflicting thoughts, fears and doubts prevented me from finding any answers, yet an unexpected spurt of guilt chilled my heart. My brother! My brother, who had trusted me to rule as he would have done, now faced the consequences of my independent judgements, independence to which I had no right. Who was I to have sat in judgement over him? We were now brothers in adversity, twin flesh and blood. A tremendous revulsion of feeling swept back my love for him and it burst forth to flood my being.

The *ola* I had written and put away in my strongbox for safekeeping! It was a symbol of my revolt against my brother. How priggish and pretentious it now seemed. At least I could destroy it immediately as a symbol of my love for him.

I rose to my feet and rushed towards my bedchamber, barely acknowledging the salutes of the Naga guards on the flare-lit verandahs of the *meda-midula*. The burning tapers cast golden light and dark shadows within the ante-room. I dismissed the attendants and locked the teak door behind me. I walked to the great canopied bed, bent down and reached for the handle of the metal strong box. I drew the box out into the open, fumbled with the bunch of keys hanging in my waist belt, selected the right one and unlocked the box. I lifted the hasp and raised the lid.

My souvenirs lay as they had for years, some old *olas*, a scarf my brother had given me, my collection of *yantara* and *mantara*. My own *ola* was missing.

Early next morning, Hamy, Banda and Kira stood side by side in the semi-darkness of a sandy beach just south of the rock-strewn Devun Dara headland, waiting for the dawn. Hamy lifted his face to the cold breezes, listened to the rumble of white-laced breakers, but their restlessness only aggravated the conflict within him. He and Kira were dressed in new blue linen *kurthas* and pantaloons. Banda, as usual, wore cloth of gold with jewelled ornaments, but unusually for him, he showed suppressed excitement. And well he should, Hamy decided, for he has years of labour and planning plus a mint of money behind today's event.

Ranged behind them were Banda's guards, over one

hundred men, bare-chested, swords at their sides, long knives stuck into their white uniform *dhotis*. They were a tough, vicious bunch, like a small, guerrilla army, mostly tall men, brown-skinned, lean-hipped, wide-shouldered, many sprouting black hair on their bodies. Ashok, standing to Hamy's right, was, however, a fair, local Arya, barrel-chested, stout, huge-muscled. His florid face was adorned by a white scar that ran down its side, giving a grim twist to otherwise placid features. Immediately next to Ashok was a slim, slight, golden-skinned boy, almost feminine in appearance. Hamy knew him to be Gehan, one of the deadliest of Banda's hit men.

Since they were standing where the island ended its north-south journey to veer east, the rising sun appeared in the horizon to their left, the slit of a large red-rimmed eye, up, down and up again, three times, before clearing the ocean bed and casting its rays beyond the reef on to the anchored ships, their masts lowered, sails down for the night, riding easily in line one behind the other. Now that it was daylight, passengers could be rowed through the opening in the reef to the wharves in open boats. Banda's men had cleared the waterfront of the regular port workers, but Hamy knew that the curious eyes of townsfolk watched from the houses that fringed the coastline and were scattered on the palm-covered hillocks close to the beach.

'There they are!' Banda exclaimed, forefinger pointing. His slim sprightly figure had come alert, a white smile showed beneath the trim black moustache. 'That must be King Tikka, coming ahead of the others.'

Hamy observed the rowing boat leaving the side of the first ship and gliding swiftly towards land. What would King Tikka look like? Had he changed? Was his wife Razeena with him? Hamy strained to identify the dark blobs silhouetted in the boat. Before long he made out four rowers, two on either side, bending forward, leaning back, graceful as dancers, the blades of their oars entering the water smoothly with hardly a ripple, re-emerging with the barest splash of silver. A fifth sailor was at the helm, his hand on the tiller. In front of him, seated on the thwarts, were six figures. Hamy soon identified them as King Tikka, his wife – Hamy had never been able to think of the shapely Razeena as queen – possibly the leader of the Arabi warriors, a deputy and two attendants.

'Let's go!' Banda commanded. Gold-sandalled feet crunching over the sea-sand, he began making his way towards the nearest of the wharves, within the lee of the headland.

By the time they stood on the wooden pier, the sun was casting bright rays on the ocean, whitening the breakers and causing a mirror-sheen on the clear water slapping beneath them. As the boat drew closer, Hamy could distinguish its occupants. King Tikka sat very erect in the stern, facing land. His black hair had acquired a brown gloss to it and seemed shot with silver. He was grandly dressed in a long red tunic of the cut affected by the Arabi and a wide *dhoti*, held in place by a broad studded belt with a curving sword attached to it. He wore a gold necklace and a large jewelled pendant. His beard and moustache were neatly trimmed. He held himself with a new dignity and his wave to them across the intervening space, when he recognized Banda, was regal.

Razeena, seated beside her husband, looked more glamorous than ever, in a lacy tunic and pantaloons of pale blue. Rosy make-up on her lips and cheeks made her face glow in contrast with the dark *kohl* on her eyelashes and brows. Her red hair was adorned with a carved gold pin and she wore a necklace, earrings and bracelets of some blue stones which Hamy recognized from his inventory-taking of Banda's imports as lapis lazuli.

The boat scraped against the side of the wharf. King Tikka did not wait for the attendants to hold it, but leapt ashore lightly, then turned gracefully to help Razeena disembark. This is indeed a new man, Hamy thought. His newly acquired gallantry must spring from loving his wife, not from the Arabi, who are even less courteous towards their women than the Yakka.

While Banda, Kira and Hamy made obeisance to the king, the Arabi leader leapt ashore, causing the boat to rock. He was a giant of a man, clad in a brown leather tunic and loose *dhoti*, with the curious white head-dress affected by certain Arabi clans as a protection against the terrible sun of their desert lands. Red hair, fierce moustache and beard framed a broad, tanned face with a great hooked nose stuck between gleaming black eyes. Introduced as Khan, he looked every inch a warrior. His deputy, Salim, was lean, tall and grim-faced.

'We are back at last,' the king observed. 'And so very grateful to you, dear cousin, for having made it all possible, after seven years of toil and untold amounts of money. But you shall be more than repaid, we assure you.

'We trust you have made arrangements for accommodating all our men,' the king continued. A note of pride entered his voice. 'We have one thousand of them, the best warriors in the world, with the finest Arabi horses, chariots and support systems.' His voice spoke the normally mellifluous Yakka dialect with the hint of an accent. 'We shall massacre the Ayra.'

'Yes, lord,' Banda responded. 'Everything is ready, thanks to the able assistance of your faithful servants, Hamy and Kira.'

'And what about the local resistance elements?'

'We can muster about seven thousand men from our Yakka people, but we must move rapidly to attack the Arya before they become aware of our presence. We can talk while your troops are landing. We have another fortunate circumstance in that the princes and nobles of Kalyani will also be in rebellion.' There was a note of exhilaration in Banda's voice. 'That could mean reinforcement by a Naga army of five thousand fully trained and disciplined men if our initial thrust is successful.'

'How so?'

Banda briefly explained the course of events resulting from the arrival of the Arya brides and artisans, the contact he had made with Prince Jaya upon learning that King Tikka was due to return in three months and the timing of the Kalyani revolution, based upon a system of fire signals that had been pre-established and sent through the night as soon as Banda had learned of the arrival of King Tikka's ships. An early link-up with Prince Jaya was therefore vital.

King Tikka's eyes glowed. 'Simply fantastic!' he exclaimed. 'So the Arya have played into our hands! You have done a remarkable job and shall indeed be our Chief Minister. Now to action.'

And action burst forth.

'Look! Look!' One of the sentries on the wharf screamed.

'Look! Look! Look!' The cry from the ranks of Banda's men on the shore came rolling over.

Hamy turned to stare south across the ocean in the direction of the pointing fingers. Two long lines of great galleys had appeared from the west and were speeding under full sail towards King Tikkas's convoy.

At first, Hamy thought that they were a delayed part of the Arabi fleet, then he noticed the stationary vessels feverishly attempting to hoist sail.

Breathless minutes passed. The visitor ships headed relentlessly towards the anchored fleet without diminishing their speed. Hamy wondered why, until he noticed the great pointing battering rams on their prows, just above the water line, obscene, like huge erect penises pointing at the Arabi ships.

'By the gods, what's this?' Khan roared, adding as an afterthought, 'My men no can swim.'

Speechless, rooted, they watched the attacking war galleys plunge headlong into the Arabi ships, in gigantic copulative thrusts that caused the Arabi vessels to reel backwards. Moments later the thunder of the collisions, followed by the screech and crackle of stricken timbers, rolled across the ocean. Oars flailed rhythmically in the attacking galleys, the battering rams were slowly withdrawn as the attackers backed away and veered off. Tiny figures, their cries reaching faintly over the water, leapt from the flooding vessels. A second line of attacking galleys now sped forward, their own battering rams proudly pointed.

The hail of arrows caught them totally unawares. Men screamed in agony. Hamy turned towards the land and saw lines of men, in the Great King's red and white uniforms, charging from three directions towards Banda's army.

Some of the guards on the wharf began leaping into the water. With a curse, Khan and his deputy raced for the boat.

'We have been betrayed.' King Tikka seized Banda by the throat and shook him as if he were but a hare.

'No, Sire!' Banda croaked. 'It's I who have been . . .' The words were stifled, ending in a groan.

A woman's shriek rent the air, followed by a gurgle. Flinging Banda aside, King Tikka spun towards his wife. Her mouth open, gasping for breath, she was clawing at an arrow in her chest. Heart pounding, Hamy rushed forward to help her, but King Tikka smashed him aside with a single blow, then held and supported his wounded wife. 'No one shall touch her,' he screamed, his voice anguished. 'Oh, beloved . . .'

Agonized eyes wide open, tears smudging black kohl on to her cheeks, Razeena stared at her husband for one long moment. Then her eyes clouded and she started to collapse. Blood from her wound trickled bright red in the sunlight, hideous against the blue lace and the fair, unblemished skin.

King Tikka felt her heart. 'Oh gods! She is dead.' Torn with grief, he began roaring and screaming like a wounded animal. He turned towards the shore. 'Murderers! Assassins! You shall pay for this!' Somewhere Hamy recalled having heard the words before, but his heart was pounding with fear and the source eluded him.

Heedless of the arrows falling around him, and of the advancing soldiers cutting through Banda's army on the beach, King Tikka lifted his dead wife in his arms and staggered to the boat. While the giant Khan held the craft steady for him, the king dropped into it and dragged the body inside. The arrow became dislodged and clattered on to the wharf. Blood spilled from the woman's torn breast. Heedless, the king sat on a thwart and cradled Razeena's head on his lap, her red hair spread like a storm moon's halo.

Hamy instinctively leapt into the boat and seized an oar. Kira followed. Two of the oarsmen had taken the first arrows and the others had plunged into the water for safety. Kira and Salim heaved the dead men overboard. Khan grabbed the tiller. Disregarding the din of battle from the shore, the clash of metal, the screams and curses of men, the shrieks of the mortally wounded, they began pulling away from the wharf.

Arrows continued to fall around them, but, moving faster now, they were soon out of bow-shot. As the boat turned, Hamy saw the ships of the great Arabi convoy slowly sinking in the distance. More by instinct than by judgement, having first steered south towards the open sea, Khan had veered west, to keep parallel with the land. 'Make for the jungle,' Hamy requested, pointing, glad that he had learned the Arabi language from the local traders. 'I shall guide you.'

King Tikka seemed oblivious of all else but the bloodied corpse he was holding. Weeping unashamedly, he crooned to it, stroking the red hair, kissing the cold cheeks. Only respect for the dead and for his king gave Hamy the strength not to vomit. He looked towards the shore. The fighting had ended. The red and white figures of the Great King's men dotted the waterfront, some racing up the wharf, others spread along the beach to cut down any survivors from the ships who reached safety.

What a mighty action, Hamy reflected with grudging admiration, once he recovered from his first terror and his heart had stopped pounding. I always knew the Great King Vijaya and his Arya to be invincible in battle, but where did they obtain the war galleys? Suddenly he knew the answer. These must be the ships that protected the fleet in which the Arya ladies had arrived. Dear devas, what a master stroke of destiny that, after seven years, King Tikka should have arrived at the very time when the galleys were at King Vijaya's disposal. Whatever gods there were intended the Great King to rule. Tears began streaming down Hamy's cheeks. He did not know why he was crying, but in a single day, in less than an hour, seven years of peace, security and hope had ended, two empires had crumbled, Banda's established empire and King Tikka's which was to have been.

Recalling the doctrine, Hamy wondered whether it had all really happened in a single day?

Uraw watched the Great King seated firmly astride his black charger, Indra, gazing down at the inert figure lying face down on a wharf now stained with blood and strewn with the dead and wounded. It brought to mind a similar morning years earlier, on the Kalyani riverbank, when King Vijaya had sat Indra after the battle against King Tikka's forces, to look down on the fallen Prince Jaya.

The Great King sheathed his bloody sword and raised his voice to be heard above the pounding of the surf and the groans of wounded men. 'Look upon Banda,' he commanded. 'Yesterday king of his domain, today abject in defeat. What was *he* doing on this wharf? How was he connected with the Arabi invaders?'

'See if he is alive, Minister,' Ujjeni, sitting on a tall bay beside the king, bade Uraw. 'He can tell us.'

Uraw dismounted, walked towards Banda, stooped and rolled the body face up. The chest pumped at once, in a heaving breath, against the cloth of gold tunic. 'He is alive,' Uraw declared. He squatted to examine the figure more closely. 'He has bruises around his neck where someone has tried to strangle him . . . and . . . uh a contusion on the left temple.'

'Bring him round and get the truth out of him,' King Vijaya ordered grimly. He removed a white linen cloth from his saddlebag and wiped the sweat from his brow. 'A good action, don't you think, Prince Ujjeni?'

The gaunt Ujjeni, clad in a black leather tunic, gave his mirthless hee . . . hee . . . hee belly laugh revealing the yellow teeth and purple gums. 'A successful action, Sire, thanks to your brilliance. To have used the Madura war galleys was a stroke of genius.' There was genuine admiration in his grainy voice. 'Combining it with a land attack by columns that by-passed Kalyani, one through the mountains the other from the east, to converge and destroy Arabi survivors on the beaches, was the inspiration of a great general. As for using the action to clean up Banda's illegal empire at the same time . . . that was a political master-stroke that leaves me speechless.' True to his statement, he relapsed into silence, shaking his head in awe.

'And it was your superb planning and administration that enabled us to conclude the entire operation within a three-day period,' the Great King conceded. 'You are a genius in your own sphere, Prince Ujjeni, and we make a good team. Dozens of enemy bodies are being washed ashore, no loss. Pity about the horses though, for those we were able to save are fine Arabis and should prove extremely useful for our cavalry.' The king looked down at Uraw, still squatting beside Banda. 'Have the man revived.'

Uraw nodded a command to one of his men. In less th n a minute, the contents of a clay pitcher of sea-water were being dashed on the unconscious man's face. Banda jerked with the shock. He shook his head once, spluttered, gurgled and sat up suddenly, droplets on his black moustache, his lean face reddening as he coughed violently to clear the water from his lungs. Uraw reached out and slapped his back. Banda retched; his eyes slowly opened, then widened as the reality of his situation hit him. 'The Great King!' he gasped, and resumed his coughing.

Tawny eyes merciless, King Vijaya stared down at Banda without comment. Uraw rose to a half-crouch, grasped Banda by the arm and yanked him into a semi-upright position. 'On your knees before the Great King,' he commanded.

The sprightly little man, looking very nervous now, made obeisance and lay there, prostrate. Men started converging curiously around the little group.

King Vijaya clicked his fingers and gestured to Banda to rise.

Banda scrambled groggily to his feet. In his soiled and stained finery, he looked more pathetic than a clown. He stared around him, surveying the entire scene, blinked once then seemed to make up his mind. 'May I speak, Lord?' he enquired.

King Vijaya merely nodded, still silent, his expression sombre.

Banda looked the Great King in the eye. 'I am Banda, as you know, Sire, a member of the royal Yakka family of the *uda rata* kingdom, a chieftain in my own right and . . . er . . . king of an enterprise I built up over the years.' He blinked again, this time against the bright sunlight and lifted his eyes to the pitiless blue skies, as if seeking inspiration, before directing an even gaze at the king once more. 'I am prepared to tell you all I know, Sire, and to bestow on you my great wealth, here and abroad, in exchange for a boon.'

'You're in no position to bargain for anything,' Ujjeni interjected fiercely.

The Great King surveyed Banda appraisingly for long moments then nodded his agreement.

'The boon I seek is that my wife and three young boys be spared any indignity,' Banda declared.

'Too late!' Ujjeni broke in brutally. 'They took up weapons in your mansion against our men and paid the price. All four of them are dead.'

A gasp escaped Banda. His shoulders sagged and tears glistened in his eyes. Then his head lifted. 'Better they died with dignity than lived in shame,' he declared. He swallowed once, his prominent larynx wobbling on the scrawny neck. 'There is nothing left, not even hope, so I might as well tell you everything without any conditions,' he quietly stated. He began speaking in level tones and a strange hush settled on the crowd. Even the groans of the wounded seemed to become stifled as he recounted all, the early days of his struggle to establish an empire, the astonishing wealth from his trade stored throughout the world and his bargain with King Tikka. If the Great King was stunned to learn that King Tikka was still alive and behind the attempted invasion, he did not show it, for he listened quietly to Banda's entire recital before speaking.

'Where is Tikka?'

'After he tried to kill me, he escaped in the row boat, Sire, carrying his wife's dead body. Khan and Salim, the Arabi leaders and King Tikka's two devoted Yakka followers, Hamy and Kira, were with him. I was hit shortly after they took off and lost consciousness.' Banda gingerly felt his forehead.

'We shall find him and hang him,' the Great King promised soberly.

'Which brings me to the question of my own punishment, Sire.' Banda's chin went up. 'I have done grievous wrong throughout the years. I have broken every written and unwritten law of your kingdom and I did so with full knowledge of the consequences, if I were caught. I enjoyed success hugely. Now I must pay the price of failure. I deserve no mercy, only death. I beg you permit me to be beheaded as a nobleman, with the red hibiscus at the nape of my neck.'

A slim, slight figure standing alone among his towering enemies, Banda was not pleading, merely making a dignified request. What a man, Uraw thought. No wonder he built an empire.

'You have nothing left to live for, except mourning and regret, so death would be but a reward to you,' the Great King responded pleasantly. 'That is not how we punish crimes of such magnitude in our kingdoms, especially when committed by well-born persons such as you.'

Banda blinked once. 'I understand, Lord. You wish to humiliate me first. That is your privilege and the price you may command.'

'No. You shall live to be shamed by your own past conduct and to atone for it. You are too valuable a man to lose. We shall spare your life on condition that you make restitution by serving the people to the fullest extent of your talents, without rewards. One-third of your local wealth shall be distributed to the families of those who have suffered through your protection service, one-third shall be used to develop this region and the remaining one-third, together with all your foreign assets, shall accrue to our Treasury. Throughout your life, however, you shall suffer from the knowledge that you caused the deaths of those you loved most.'

Chapter 42

Since their only hope of escaping the Great King's men was to vanish into the jungle, Hamy directed the boat along the shoreline. Once they rounded the headland, proceeding north, the dense expanse of tangled growth appeared and each stroke took them closer to safety. But what about the two Arabis, Hamy wondered. Could desert people survive in the jungle? And how would they ever get back home now that Banda's empire was smashed and every port would be watched by the king's officials? Also, what would happen to the rebellious Nagas of Kalyani? Hamy felt so much pity for them all that he forgot his own plight.

His reverie was interrupted by Khan's voice, raised above the splash of oars. 'Why your king no help us row?'

'Our kings don't work,' Hamy replied.

'He no longer king.' Khan spat into the water gurgling past the boat. 'No money, no king.' A thought obviously struck him. 'No money, how I get home?'

Salim grunted acknowledgement from his seat at one of the oars.

'Hey, amir!' Khan shouted to King Tikka above the sough and crash of a wave. 'You take other oar, right?'

Though King Tikka sat directly in front of the giant, he seemed not to have heard the words.

The boat rocked as Khan stood up with a curse. Hamy steadied it with his oar, but Kira and Salim stopped rowing.

The giant began making his way aft. King Tikka stopped his crooning. He looked up, heaved a great sigh and gently laid Razeena's dead body at the bottom of the boat.

The giant stood above the king, arms akimbo. 'Hey amir, bad luck for have woman's dead body when trying escape, huh? Why you no dump her in water for fish and help with oar?'

King Tikka nodded slowly. He must know Khan's superstitious belief from his seven years in the Arabi region, Hamy concluded, but what about our own Yakka customs? We bury our dead with honour and sprinkle blossoms on the heaped earth of the grave so that the dead person may walk on flowers to the new life. He was surprised to find the normally quick-tempered king so calm and compliant.

King Tikka rose slowly to his feet. As Hamy bent down to the oar, holding the boat steady, he heard a soggy thud followed by a gasp and a groan. The boat rocked violently. Hamy looked up. Khan's giant figure was taut, like a bowstring. Then the arms sagged, the huge body bent slightly forward. A swift movement from the king was followed by another thud. Khan went 'ur . . . ur . . . urph,' his figure stiffening again. This time the great arms stretched out in a desperate attempt to get at his assailant. Too late. The king withdrew his knife again and stepped to one side. With a deft push, he sent the giant overboard with a great splash. Hamy struggled desperately to prevent the boat from capsizing. As he brought it under control, he noticed the king's eyes, fiery, almost red, with rage.

'Row!' the king commanded. 'The son of a bitch is dead. Let him sink.'

Hamy heard a roar of rage and saw Salim rising to his feet. Bloody knife glinting in his hand, the king half crouched, facing the man. Hamy quietly slipped the handle of his oar from the rowlock, lifted the oar sideways and slammed it against Salim with all his power. Arms flailing madly, Salim tried to steady himself. As he teetered, Hamy drew back the oar and lashed out again, smashing the Arabi over the side into the frothing waters. As one, Hamy and Kira rowed madly away.

Salim rose to the surface, water streaming from his face, eyes wide with terror. 'Help!' he screamed. 'No can . . .' He thrashed desperately, swallowed water and went under once more.

'Faster!' the king commanded. He walked over to the tiller, grasped it and sat down.

The boat kept heading north, until the king guided it towards the shore. Soon it slid over foaming breakers and was wafted towards the unending line of green jungle trees. A slow wave carried it up the sloping white sand beach and grounded it. King Tikka lifted his wife's body from the boat. Hamy and Kira followed him through the jungle until they came to a small glade. Here King Tikka laid the corpse on the green grass. 'We dig the grave here,' he directed.

Using their weapons and stakes from broken branches, they began digging a deep grave at the edge of the glade. It was almost noon by the time they finished. King Tikka picked up the body of the queen who never became queen and laid it inside. They gathered flowers – wild red hibiscus, white jungle jasmine and orange *lantana*. Tears now streaming down his dark cheeks, the king began heaping brown soil on the once beautiful body. When it was done, he scattered the mound with flowers. Hamy said the final invocations for the dead, commending Razeena's spirit to the Yakka gods of the trees and the jungle.

King Tikka stood over the grave, his head bowed. What thoughts go through his mind, Hamy wondered, what memories haunt him? King Tikka, Kira and I, always together, have mostly known defeat. He recalled the first day they had seen the beautiful Razeena, and his own eyes became wet with tears.

King Tikka straightened, wiped his tears with the palms of his hands. 'Now she is gone,' he quietly asserted. 'Only vengeance remains, man to man.'

'Lord, I believe we can start right here in Devun Dara,' the normally taciturn Kira volunteered.

Hamy's heart sank.

As he listened to Kira's story, King Tikka's expression gradually changed from grief to fiendish pleasure. He finally clapped a hand to his thigh and exclaimed, 'The gods are merciful after all. The best time to return to Devun Dara is when we are least expected, which is right now!' His mad laughter echoed through the tall *dimbul*, wood-apple trees, causing a flight of parakeets to take off with shrill cries of alarm.

'Lord, the town is about eight miles from here,' Kira volunteered. 'I have a sort of cousin who has a *chena* on the fringes of the jungle about five miles from the town. He is close-mouthed, would ask no questions and would give us a meal. Would you like to go first to his place?'

'Good idea,' the king agreed.

They left the glade, King Tikka with never a backward glance, and proceeded south. As he followed the tall, erect figure of the king along the green shrub-crowded jungle path, Hamy could not help wondering what his leader's thoughts were. He sensed a cold raging purpose, but what about regrets? A single sob, quickly strangled, told him.

The sun was beginning to move westward by the time they skirted a muddy jungle pond, stinking of rotting vegetation, beyond which they saw the cleared *chena* with a coconut thatch house around which *manioc*, yams and *kurakkan* had been planted. The jungle poised around the *chena* somehow seemed to threaten it.

'The jungle god is awesome,' Kira commented. 'Men who dwell in his realm strive pitifully to hold back his remorseless might that seeks to overpower *chena* and home. The men die or move away, their endeavours crumble, but the god lives on, pulsating, growing all the time, ruthlessly pushing aside anything that stands in his way. He has the power even to crush townships and ancient cities.'

'Quiet!' King Tikka commanded.

The cultivator was at home, lying on a mat on the dung floor of his small, shady verandah. Hearing their approach, he sprang to his feet, a dwarf of a man with dark, wrinkled skin weathered by the elements. Curly grey hair, framing the heavy-set Yakka face, tumbled untidily over bony shoulders. He had the bulbous stomach and protruding buttocks of his people, yet as he stepped into the sunlight, Hamy could sense the inner strength and alertness of the Yakka hunter in his sharp eyes.

'That is Joti, the cultivator,' Kira murmured.

Joti recognized Kira immediately. 'Ah, friend, how?' He enquired in a high, rusty voice, giving the traditional greeting.

'Just being,' Kira replied, equally formally.

Joti nodded, then looked at King Tikka, who stood towering before him. 'This one seems to be an important personage,' he observed.

'He is our King Tikka,' Kira responded.

Joti made obeisance. Hamy could not help but admire his natural courtliness. No alarm, no questions, no comments on their bedraggled appearance. The king was here and had to be greeted as such, regardless of the circumstances.

Having acknowledged the obeisance, the king took command. 'We would appreciate the hospitality of your home for about two hours,' he said. 'And some food.'

'My home is your home, though my fare is poor.' Joti glanced over his shoulder and shouted into the house. 'Menika!'

A lean young woman emerged from the shadows of the hut's interior, tying her black hair in a knot at the nape of her scrawny neck.

'This is my woman,' Joti announced proudly. 'Menika, this is our king. He needs food.'

Two hours later, a meal of roasted wild pork, *kurakkan* balls tipped with chilli and buffalo curd tight in his stomach, Hamy followed King Tikka, Kira still leading, along the path that led to the township. One of the jewels that had adorned King Tikka's person had gone to Joti as a reward. The rest were in a pouch at the king's waist. A combination of their own clothes and the loincloths Joti had given them provided effective disguises. They looked like peasants now, so people in the huts they passed gazed incuriously after them, then returned to droop in their noonday torpor, like the occasional pi-dog that merely raised a sleepy head only to lower it again.

They walked about three miles before the jungle began to thin, revealing green paddies in golden sunlight. Homes of wattle and brown mud-daub topped by roofs of yellowing straw appeared. Peasants worked their fields or vegetable patches, a group of half-naked children shouted, screamed and splashed in a narrow irrigation channel.

The path now became a roadway, rutted by cart and wagon tracks which had dried hard in the fierce sunlight. Only the reeking cattle dung, knit with flies, that strewed the road was fresh.

King Tikka suddenly stopped and laid a hand on Kira's arm. 'If that whore arrived last night with her children, she might be at . . .' he raised thumb to chin. 'Lead us to the fairgrounds.'

'It is very close to the beach where we were attacked this morning, Lord,' Kira warned.

'No matter, lead us there,' the king commanded.

The first evidence of the fair was a distant rumbling of voices, which resolved itself into the shouts of vendors and the occasional tinkling of the bells they used to attract attention. Hamy had frequented the place through the years, on Banda's business or simply to mingle with the people. Their bright coloured clothes of blue, green and yellow now appeared through the trees, with a sprinkling of the red and white uniforms of the Great King's men, crowding the rows of open-sided wooden stands roofed with coconut thatch. One could buy anything here, each product in a separate little 'street' of sheds. Once a year, traders came from other lands to the Great Fair, which lasted thirty days.

Led by King Tikka, they began pushing their way through the din of voices towards the vegetable stalls, but in an apparently incurious, casual way. They passed the streets of bright coloured clothes, of brass lamps, of bronze flares, of shiny trinkets, each with its own distinctive smell, the old metal of brass, the pungency of oil, the fragrance of spices. The sheds containing farm produce bore the reek of onions.

A fat, bald townsman, obviously a trader, clad in a blue silk *dhoti* and a tight, white *kurtha*, beneath which his stomach bulged, bargained loudly, in a shrill, commanding voice, at one of the stalls, while his pretty young wife and five small children gazed at him, awe-struck by his toughness. Hamy wondered what it would be like to have such a doting family, but it was not for him. He was a loner, a follower not a leader.

Still very casual, they paused at a vegetable stall, heaped with bunches of green *gotu-kola* leaves, sliced yellow watermelon with pink pulp and black seeds, purple brinjals and red-gold mangoes. The vendor was a shrivelled little man, furrow-cheeked and alert-eyed. Sensing a prospect, he jerked his grey beard upwards. 'My wares are fresh from my own vegetable garden,' he announced. 'And what can I give you worthy people this evening?'

The king's glance directed Hamy to pause, while he himself drifted through the crowds, searching, searching.

'How much for these *brinjals*?' Hamy picked one up and twisted it slightly, testing for over-maturity.

'Two coppers each,' the old man responded without batting an eye-lid. 'And cheap at the price.'

The price was very high. Hamy sensed a foe worthy of his blade in a bargaining bout. 'Two pieces for this tiny vegetable? Why, it must be made of gold.'

'*Apoi*, yes, child. To us poor people, our vegetables are gold, *ney.*'

'Then you must take it to the government treasury and they will give you much for this gold. Of course you will first have to prove to them that purple is gold, no?'

A flicker of appreciation shot through the rheumy eyes. 'This shed is my treasury, child. And the people are my appraisers. Can you eat gold?'

'Not at your price. Come now, why not stop teasing a poor man?'

'I'm the poor man. How can I reduce the price when I have a starving wife, ten grown children and many grandchildren to feed?'

'Feed them the *brinjals*.'

'You are a hard man. All right then, how about one piece?'

'Four *brinjals* for one piece.'

'You are trying to ruin me. I might as well give it away.'

'I'll take it.'

The weathered cheeks broke into laughter lines. 'You are a sweet child. For you, three *brinjals* for one piece.'

Hamy would have liked to remain and conclude the peaceful bargaining session, which he and the old man had enjoyed, but King Tikka appeared and tugged at his sleeve, so he bought six of the *brinjals* and handed over two coppers to the vendor. The old man carefully selected seven of the best, 'A special price for you, child,' he said, as he put them into a sack.

As Hamy turned to follow the king, his heart stood still. Dressed in a blue skirt and blouse, she was standing in front of a vegetable stall. A blue shawl, covering her head and shoulders, partly hid her face, but there was no mistaking that figure, with the large breasts, tiny waist and flaring buttocks.

King Tikka had stopped too and was staring in her direction. Through the welter of sound swirling about them, Hamy could physically feel the hatred, the bitter pent-up hatred of the years, within his king, then a gloating that spewed forth like some horrible creature of the marshes. Finally a strange calm, for the king had reached a journey's end.

587

The woman turned, drawn irresistibly towards the source of interest in her. She looked at King Tikka blankly. No wonder, Hamy thought, no one would recognize the bearded king, in his disguise, for the clean-shaven prince of over eight years ago.

Recognition came by instinct, rather than knowledge. The eyes of the Princess Kuveni widened, her face tightened.

Sundari and I had dinner early that evening in my quarters. When the attendants had cleared the table and finally left us alone, we remained seated at the dining table, free at last to discuss the events of the day, of which I had been able to apprise her only briefly.

'As you can see, I am the victim of tremendous conflicts, both outside and within,' I concluded, smiling wryly at Sundari. 'Much as I love my brother and feel I have done wrong to everyone concerned by not supporting his Arya policies while I was ruler of Kalyani, I cannot help other thoughts. This revolt has placed Prince Jaya, the Nagas and the entire kingdom in serious danger. I believe in the justice of their cause. What I find wrong is the method they have used to ventilate their grievances, without ever bringing them to the notice of the Great King. Have I failed them in this as well, by not representing their cause adequately? Prince Jaya discussed these problems with me from time to time during the years, but I never suspected how deeply feelings ran. I wanted to believe that, minor irritations apart, my just rule in Kalyani kept everyone happy.'

'You must stop blaming yourself, *larla*,' Sundari begged me. 'You are merely one of the forces of cause and effect.'

'I know, I know, my beloved, but it hurts to be that. And *kharma* does not absolve me of blame.'

After we retired for the night, the princess and I lay side by side on the great canopied bed in my chamber. In the golden taper-light, I could see her large, dark eyes brimming with concern as we began to talk.

'They had no right to do it without first attempting to obtain redress from the Great King!' I stated, perhaps for the twentieth time that evening.

'What redress could they have hoped for, *larla*? She enquired, perhaps for the twentieth time. 'The Great King was set on a course of action he had planned for years. You know him. He never deviates from his purposes, least of all when he is convinced of their wisdom and desirability.'

I groaned. 'Two magnificent elephants in the jungle, speeding towards each other on a collision course – and I knew nothing about it.'

'Cause and effect. *Kharma/vipaka*, beloved.'

'You are right. We are in the grip of terrible *kharmic* forces. The knowledge fills me with dread.'

She reached over and drew me to her. 'That is only natural, since you fear the ill effects of Prince Jaya's actions.'

'No! My fears run deeper than that. They are personal to you and me.'

She hesitated. 'The Great King will retaliate ruthlessly, will he not?'

'I'm sure of that. What also bothers me about the seizure of power is its timing. Prince Jaya hinted at something more than their own revolt. I thought I knew him pretty well but in this context he is an enigma to me. Could there be some link-up with other subversive elements in the kingdom?'

'So that they can confront your brother in another great battle?'

'I doubt that. They must know that our chariots will rout them as before.' I paused, reflecting. 'No, Prince Jaya obviously contemplates obtaining a compromise from the Great King through some position of strength greater than appears to us on the surface. I wish I could fathom what it is.' I shook my head in frustration.

'The Great King will never accept a compromise, will he?'

'Definitely not. Prince Jaya does not know my brother, whom he probably sees only as the victor who gave him back his life after the last great battle.'

'Will the prince be prepared to give up his luxurious life and take to the jungles as a last resort? If nothing else, he is too fat to be a guerilla!'

'Beneath the levity and charm, Prince Jaya is at heart a patriot. Yes, he would indeed shed his comfort and his blood, not to mention his fat, for Kalyani. Of that I'm certain.'

'You are worried for yourself too.'

'Of course. At the very least I stand to be accused of incompetence and negligence for not having suspected what was about to take place.'

'And at the worst?' she looked at me steadily. I could sense the fear mounting within her, but she also exuded a strength that made me think that she could stand the truth.

'Because of my liberal views and my sympathy for the Nagas and Buddhists, my enemies could accuse me of complicity and therefore of treason.' I deliberately omitted mentioning the lost *ola*.

Her breathing fluttered. She released me and sat up, hand to chest, gasping for air. I jerked upright in alarm. 'What is it, my beloved?'

She broke into a cold sweat. 'It's nothing,' she whispered, trying to smile, but one pale hand was still clutching her chest.

'Does your chest hurt?' My heart was beating faster and my throat was dry with alarm, for these were the symptoms of her condition.

'A little.' She was recovering now.

'I'm sorry . . . I'm sorry,' I said. How thoughtless I had been to tell her of my fears. I opened my arms to her instinctively, but held back, not wanting to make her feel smothered.

Her breathing eased and she smiled faintly at me. Dire warnings were, however, thudding inside my head. I watched anxiously until her breathing returned to normal.

'It's nothing to worry about, really,' she assured me.

'Probably something I ate for dinner ... those burnt jak seeds perhaps.' She smiled mischievously and lay back more easily on the white satin cushions, but her face was pale, her fine nostrils distending with each breath, and she seemed very tired.

I reached out and gently stroked her damp forehead, smoothing back the dark, wavy masses of hair.

'I love you so much,' she said softly and the words tore into my heart, for strangely they sounded like a farewell.

And then it happened. Terror such as I had never known before suddenly swept over me, sent my mind reeling. I heard the roar and splash of waves. My fists clenched, an unknown horror gripped me. I stared dumbly into space.

The golden taper-light fast began receding into a blackness, in which I was alone with some unknown evil, an evil mushrooming from things I had wrought in the past. An icy wind sprang up and eddied before me. I not only felt its blast, but somehow could actually see it ... this dread wind ... and its noise was a drumming of thunder, its stench the reek of decaying corpses. A mangled face appeared in its swirling centre, emerging from the darkness with a fierce white ray of light focused upon it, a demon face, strangely familiar, with matted black hair, one smashed eye, torn and pulped flesh, broken teeth. Pity and horror swiftly mingled with the terror within me. I felt myself choking. The blackness began penetrating my brain, the death-stench was from my own body, the thunder was the beating of my heart. A sharp, blinding pain suddenly smote the back of my head, stars cascaded before my eyes. Everything went black.

Chapter 43

The milling crowds on the fairgrounds, the chatter of voices, the cries of vendors, receded for Hamy, leaving a darkness lit only around the Princess Kuveni and King Tikka. Hamy noted with mounting horror that, though the princess could not have recognized King Tikka's features, some instinct warned her of mortal danger, and her gaze was fixed on the king like a hare's on a cobra. When the truth finally hit her, stark terror flooded her eyes. Her face loosened, the jaw dropped, but she stood rooted, unable even to move her eyes. It was as if she had lived this moment before and had always known she could not avoid it.

Long moments passed while King Tikka held her in his hypnotic grip. Then he slowly began advancing towards her, shouldering his way through the crowds, never once taking his eyes off her. Hamy glanced fearfully in all directions. Not one red and white uniform was in sight. He wanted to intervene somehow, to appeal to the crowds perhaps, but he knew he did not have the moral strength. His very weakness increased his pity and horror. Instinctively he began following the king.

Then the two were close to each other, their bodies almost touching. Hamy moved sideways to face them both and it seemed to him that for them no one else existed in the world. This is an ancient battle, another scene, Hamy thought and the blood-smell was in his nostrils. The feel of drama became so high that it vibrated in the air, so that people nearby sensed it and paused to gaze curiously at the couple.

The princess continued staring at her opponent, unable to take her eyes off him. She knows whom she faces, Hamy thought. What thoughts are going through her mind?

Remorse at what she did so long ago? Regret at having decided to come to Devun Dara? Fear for her children, terror for her own safety? Does she wish to plead with her enemy for forgiveness? Or is she beseeching her gods for help?

A piteous expression swept across the face of the princess, her features crumpled. King Tikka's pebble eyes grew more hard and merciless, red sparks of madness glowing in them. Suddenly, he removed his gaze from her and looked at the curious onlookers crowding around him. 'All patriots of Lanka bear me witness!' He cried. A hush fell on the crowd. He pointed an accusing finger at the princess. 'This woman is Kuveni, who eight years ago betrayed us all, even her own father, to the Arya. She caused the spilling of the finest Yakka blood and then consorted with the foreign leader. She is a harlot who sold her people for bed and her ambitions.'

The crowd began backing fearfully away, leaving the couple a cleared space, with only Hamy standing beside them. Tears sprang to the eyes of the princess, her mouth worked, crystal drops, growing heavy, slowly coursed down her dark cheeks. She seemed to want to say something, but the words did not come.

'Do you deny it, bitch?' King Tikka demanded.

The princess slowly shook her head from side to side. How could she deny it?

At this first sign of animation from her, something broke loose in King Tikka. 'Harlot! Harlot! Foul harlot!' He screamed. 'You murdered my wife!' Fist clenched, he drew back his shoulder. The fist shot forward like a bolt. It caught the princess full in the face. She screamed in pain, rocked back, sprawled to the ground. Blood gushed from her broken nose. She sat up, covering her face with her hands. 'Save me, Reeri Yakseya!' She implored and spat out a bloody tooth. King Tikka raised both hands aloft, fists clenched and brought them down with shattering force on her head. She fell back with a groan.

All the pent up rage of the years, the frustrations and disappointments, the torment of that day, found their expression in a single great cry, the cry of a maddened animal. King Tikka leapt on the fallen princess and started stamping on her, smashing her face and body as if to obliterate his agony. He kept on trampling her savagely, even after she finally lay still. No one dared interfere.

The chill of death fell on Hamy's spirit. In a daze, he saw the first flare being lit in one of the booths to light the approaching darkness.

Uraw stood on the wharf where Banda had been captured that morning and gazed along the Devun Dara beach, darkening with the first shadows of night. The Great King's tent, erected at the base of the wharf, was a large blob immediately on his left, while the army campfires, at which the evening meal of *chupatti* and fried mutton was being cooked, stretched along the beach into the distance, a border of flame for the silver grey ocean on one side and the dark quilt of coconut palms on the other. The laughter and singing of men happy in victory rose above the ceaseless thrust of white breakers sweeping towards the shore.

Surveying the scene and recalling the highlights of the action, Uraw felt a warm sense of pride in himself and his comrades. Not only had they warded off the grave threat of an invasion in a single operation that morning, but they had also demolished Banda's illegal empire, taken over his wealth and collected over three hundred fine Arabi horses and much booty from those of the stricken ships that had drifted on to the reef.

A few soldiers seated on the wharf, their legs dangling above the incoming tide, talked to one another in quiet tones, threw an occasional scrap of food to the fish in the phosphorescent water below. A horse whinnied from a dark coconut grove. Uraw looked up at the sparkling stars dotting the dark blue centre of the heavens, then south to their great cross that guided travellers. Whither will you lead me, he suddenly wondered for the first time in his life . . . and felt a hand touch his elbow. He spun round to find that Ujjeni had materialized from the gloom, silently as usual, looking, again as usual, like a skeletal ghost.

'You are contemplative tonight when you should be rejoicing,' Ujjeni observed, his normally dry voice somehow moistened by the damp air. 'Will you share your thoughts?'

'Certainly, Prince,' Uraw responded, ready to lie. 'I was offering thanks to the star gods for giving us leaders such as our Great King and yourself.'

Ujjeni gazed searchingly at Uraw. 'Yet I have the impression that you are thinking of more than you have admitted, my friend. No matter. All we have that is secret, even from the gods, are our thoughts.'

Uraw decided to change the subject. 'I was also wondering whether we should not move immediately to smash the Kalyani uprising. They timed it so neatly,' he grinned. 'Now they're in for a rude shock. *Adey*, we'd have been in real trouble if they had joined forces with the Arabis and Yakkas.'

'True, but I knew what was happening all along.' Ujjeni gave his hee . . . hee . . . hee belly laugh. 'Prince Jaya and Banda have been in touch with each other for several months. My spies kept me informed, so we'd have out-manoeuvred and smashed them in any case. Their real problems would have arisen if they succeeded!'

'Why d'you say that?'

'Can you see the fat Naga and the lean Yakka ever working together?'

'H'mmm. You're right.'

'As for any move against Kalyani, timing is vital, but what I want you for now, Uraw, is a more immediate matter.' He flourished a scroll of *ola* he had been holding in his hand. 'I have here an extraordinarily revealing document. You can use it in the historical records you are keeping. Come, let's find the Great King.'

In the fairgrounds, unaware of what had befallen her mistress, Rupa walked through the milling crowds, shepherding the two children. Gamba was already testing the bow and arrow she had bought him and Gambini was clamouring for a bead necklace. They paused at one of the trinket stalls. Eyes round as the beads themselves, Gambini gazed at the coloured necklaces, bangles and bracelets on their metal rods, shining silver and gold, purple and blue, green and red in the flare-light.

The vendor, a plump jolly-looking man, offered her a blue bead necklace. 'Here, try this on,' he bade her. Giggling, Gambini donned the necklace. 'That's beautiful!' Rupa exclaimed. Hearing a commotion, she turned it its direction. The crowd was pushing towards one of the other streets. Gamba plucked at her hand. 'Something's happening over there,' he said, pointing excitedly. 'Let's go over and see.'

A strange man stood in Rupa's way. He was agitated, his voice an undertone. 'You are the attendant of the princess?'

For a moment, Rupa was about to deny it, but something about the man, his intensity, compelled the truth. 'Yes,' she replied, terror stirring within her.

'Something terrible has happened. Pretend you are my wife and come with me.' Aloud, he said, 'I've run out of money. No use trying to spend it.'

'Come, children it's time to go home,' Rupa said firmly. She undid the necklace and handed it back to the vendor. 'I want it,' Gambini wailed, but Rupa grabbed her hand and started walking away, following the stranger.

The vendor spat his disgust. 'Some day I'll levy a charge on people who simply come and fondle my wares.' he exclaimed.

The stranger hurriedly led Rupa and the children away from the fairgrounds. Shaken by fear, Rupa could barely keep up with him as he strode along. 'Who are you? Where are you taking us? What has happened to my mistress?'

The man paused and glanced fearfully backwards. There were tears in his eyes. 'My name is Hamy,' he said quietly. 'I am King Tikka's aide. The king did not die, as was generally believed, but married and departed for the Arabi lands to muster an army of mercenaries. It was he who headed the Arabi invasion force which the Great King destroyed this morning. You must have heard about it. King Tikka's wife was killed during the action, but he escaped and has just murdered your mistress by buffeting and trampling her to death. Oh god, it was awful.' He shook his head sadly. 'I couldn't stand it and I came to help you escape.'

The earth spun before Rupa. She reached out and clutched Hamy's arm. 'How did the king find us?'

'My colleague, Kira, and I spotted you in the caravan last night. Unfortunately, Kira blabbed and King Tikka decided that you would be here this evening.'

'Does he know where we are staying?'

'Not yet, but he'll soon find out. You must be gone by tomorrow morning.'

'Where can I go?' Rupa wailed. Then suddenly she remembered the words of her mistress. 'If anything happens to me . . .' She steadied herself. All she could give her dead mistress now were courage and resolution.

Uraw and Ujjeni found the Great King seated on the white beach sand by the campfire farthest from the wharf. Clad in brown leather pantaloons, his red-haired chest bare, the king relaxed with the men lounging around the campfire, firelight dancing in his tawny eyes changing their colour to gold. Vijit sat next to him, telling a story. 'So the Nepalese swung with his *kukri*, right through the giant Pahlava's neck,' Vijit said. 'And nothing happened. "You missed that time!" the Pahlava exclaimed. "Wait till you sneeze!" the Nepalese retorted.'

Ujjeni held back until the guffaws had subsided before

entering the warm glow of the firelight. The Great King glanced up. 'What is it, Prince?' he enquired. The murmurs of the men around the fire became hushed.

Ujjeni bent forward and whispered in the king's ear, then proffered the scroll to the king, fingers of the left hand to the right elbow in the proper manner. The king looked down at the document, opened it, raised it to the firelight in order to read. Now only the crackle of wood, an occasional sputter and the soft roaring of the flames disturbed the stillness.

When the king had finished reading, his eyes remained on the document for a few moments. He then re-read it, more slowly this time. When he was done, he rolled it up and thoughtfully tapped his bearded chin with it. He gazed into the fire, his expression inscrutable. Finally, he seemed to make up his mind. Placing the scroll on the sand, he levered himself to his feet. All the men around the fire rose with him. He glanced at his palms, then mechanically dusted off the sand, stooped and picked up the scroll. 'Come to our tent,' he commanded Ujjeni. He turned to the fire, 'Excuse us, men.' He nodded to Vijit, turned and plodded in the direction of the wharf.

As they followed the king, Uraw wondered again what the scroll could possibly have contained.

The Great King paused at the entrance to the tent. Uraw slipped ahead of him and undid the tent flap, raised it and threw it on to the roof. A strange high odour smote his nostrils. The Great King stooped to enter the oblong of light. Uraw stood respectfully aside, while Ujjeni followed the king. A breeze caused the yellow flames from the tapers on the table in the centre of the tent to waver and smoulder.

Uraw stooped and walked in. A great gasp made him straighten quickly. The Great King stood in shock at the centre of the tent. Ujjeni, immediately behind him, had become tight as a drum. As Uraw stepped well into the tent, the sickly odour became more revolting. He glanced again at the Great King, his stomach churning with unidentified

598

fear. The giant figure, carved into immobility, seemed to have stopped breathing. The nostrils were distended, the red hair almost bristling, the tawny eyes were fixed at the far end of the tent.

Uraw followed the Great King's gaze and his heart almost stopped beating.

Dangling from the central tent pole of the roof was a hempen rope holding an open receptacle. Placed on the receptacle was a devil's head. Long matted black hair fell around what seemed to be a crude face, one eye smashed in, the black cheeks a bloody pulp, the gaping mouth a grinning crater of broken teeth.

It was a demon. Uraw turned to run. Then the *ola* fell from the Great King's nerveless hands and an anguished cry choked out of him. 'Kuveni!'

Then Uraw recognized the face. His stomach heaved and he turned aside to vomit. Vaguely he saw Ujjeni hurtle towards the object, naked sword in hand. At the same time, a dark figure leapt from beneath a rough table by the entrance to the tent.

Uraw jerked upright with a warning cry. Too late. The upraised bludgeon smote the back of the Great King's head with a sickening thud. The king staggered forward under the impact, clutched his head and collapsed sideways. The assassin flung away the bludgeon, spun round and fled from the tent.

Uraw drew his sword. Uncertain whether to seize the assassin or go to the Great King's aid, he cried out to Ujjeni, 'Look after the Great King!' He leapt for the entrance and charged outside, his eyes frantically searching the darkness. There was not a sign of the intruder. He advanced cautiously, some instinct quelling the urge to raise an alarm. He checked the base of the wharf, the beach, the dark treeline. No one. The men at one of the campfires started singing a bawdy song.

* * *

Hamy returned to the scene of the Princess Kuveni's murder as soon as he had arranged to meet Rupa again. Miraculously, none of the Great King's men had been in the immediate vicinity, so Yakka loyalists formed a cordon around King Tikka, Hamy and Kira and swept them away, along with the corpse, in a vegetable cart. They went to the house of Ratana, another fierce loyalist, who lived close to the oceanfront about quarter of a mile north of the wharves.

It was Ratana's brother, Gamma, a young hunter, who revealed to King Tikka how he could get to the Great King's tent and escape unobserved. Gamma had done this frequently in order to steal goods from the wharf. The body of the princess was severed at the neck and dumped into the ocean, a terrible fate for a dead Yakka.

Razeena's death had driven King Tikka into a world all his own, so Hamy was not surprised when the King returned dripping wet but still uncommunicative from his assassination mission.

'We killed the son of bitch!' he declared triumphantly, then relapsed into a moody silence.

Ratana's wife served them a late dinner of curried fish and rice, followed by fruit, on the verandah of the two-bedroomed cottage. Afterwards King Tikka remained seated on his settle at the side of the verandah while Hamy and Kira sat on the front steps. The king had remained silent during dinner, but now he began mumbling incoherently. He chuckled quietly once and his face twitched. Hamy and Kira exchanged glances, but neither of them dared to speak to the king, still less to question him. Hamy was so concerned at King Tikka's mental state that he preferred to listen to the squeaking of mice from the dark grove of *jambu* and breadfruit trees in front of him. From where he sat, he could catch glimpses of the starlit sky through the dark mosaic of overhanging branches. A sickly odour of crushed green-bugs warned of the deadly cobra, reminding him that his *polonga*, snake, king could still strike. In contrast, within the house, a single oil-lamp cast its golden glow and there was the murmur of children's voices, punctuated by an occasional giggle. A happy home and I am an outcast, Hamy reflected without bitterness.

'We accomplished alone what entire armies failed to do in battle,' King Tikka suddenly cried into the night. 'Our two enemies killed in a single day by our own hand. The tent site was beautifully selected for protection from the land. But what of the sea? Ha! ha! ha! They forgot the sea. So that's where we attacked from.' His laughter shattered the stillness outside, hushed the voices within the cottage. 'The sea was so calm, we were able to get the bitch's head there in the container, hardly wetting it. We swam under the wharf and entered the tent with ease.' He was musing now. 'We expected Vijaya to be alone, but these men appeared, permitting us to strike but a single blow with the bludgeon. But we got him all right.' He bared fierce white teeth. 'Oh, if only we could have remained and pounded his head to pulp.' A fleck of spittle appeared on the side of his mouth.

Hearing no comment from either of his aides, the king proceeded. 'You should have seen their terror and consternation at the demon face,' he chuckled. 'At first they were puzzled. Then the bastard whispered "Kuveni!" We wanted him to identify that face before we struck. That was when I leapt at him. One of the other two pigs came after us. He searched everywhere except in the water!' He shook his head in disbelief. 'Stupid bulls! Stupid bulls!' His voice rose, demented. 'We Yakkas can outsmart them every time.'

Two children came to the door to investigate, but were shooed away by their father.

King Tikka's murder of the Princess Kuveni had left an indelible impression on Hamy. Whether this was caused by its sheer brutality, or his helplessness to intervene, or both, Hamy did not know, but it had finally decided him. It was as if this ultimate act of bestiality simply erased his loyalty and devotion to the man with whom he had never had a real

601

home and whom he now saw as having destroyed his whole life. Where could a follower such as himself find a new leader? Buddha beckoned. He recalled his most dramatic experience of the power of the doctrine, on the morning King Tikka slew the Kalyani king, Sri Ra-hula. That Arya monk who had continued the *Dasa-sila*, the ten precepts, while the king was dying, what was his name? . . . Sri Ra-something or other – Uday, he had been called – was the one remaining link with that event. By helping Rupa and those two helpless children earlier that evening, he had literally been shown the way.

'The people are still with us,' King Tikka now stated flatly, his voice under control. 'Did you see how they supported us at the fair? And after we decapitated that Yakka bitch with our sword, did you see the head . . . the head . . . ?' His voice rose again. 'The battered head . . . what a beautiful sight! . . .' His laughter tore through the night once more, then suddenly broke off.

'Now we have killed Kuveni and assassinated the Great King, only that attendant, Rupa, and the two bastard brats remain. Never fear, we shall get them all.' The tone, now gentle, gave King Tikka's words greater menace. 'The Yakka people will rally to us as they did this evening. They will give us their best for the final battles. We shall then become the Great King of Lanka.' His voice broke and a sob escaped him. 'Oh, Razeena, why are you not here to share my glory?'

That finally decided Hamy. He glanced at Kira, sitting silently by the verandah steps. Sensing his mood, the portly man nodded. Something unspoken passed between them through the semi-darkness and Hamy knew that Kira too was ready to abandon their crazed leader.

Hamy rose to his feet with a grunt. He cautiously felt in his waistband to reassure himself that his little stock of coins was intact. He walked into the compound, as if to find a bush. When he was sure that the darkness hid him from the king, he headed for the street, making for Gona's house.

By the time Uraw returned to the tent from his vain chase of the assassin, Ujjeni had slashed the hempen rope that had held the Princess Kuveni's head and hurled the grisly object into the ocean, as was appropriate with the relics of witches and demons. He now bent anxiously over the fallen King Vijaya. 'Did you get him?' Ujjeni demanded, half-turning, his eyes blazing.

Uraw shook his head. 'It may have been a demon, for he simply vanished.'

'Bullshit!' Ujjeni retorted, with unwanted crudeness. He straightened up. 'Run for the physician,' he directed. 'The Great King is alive, but unconscious. Say nothing of what has happened to anyone. Not to anyone at all. We don't want the men to become alarmed. Remember the news we had from the fairground earlier this evening? I'm sure the assassin was King Tikka. Only a Yakka can act with such stealth. But we shall get him.' Did Ujjeni sound half-hearted? Would he not like King Tikka to finish this handiwork some day, so that he himself could assume power? 'Merely say that the Great King injured himself in a fall, striking the back of his head against the edge of the table.'

When Srihan, the Court physician, a wisp of a man with a large, bald head arrived, Ujjeni swore him to secrecy. He remained in the tent while Srihan conducted his examination.

'The Great King is suffering from concussion,' Srihan finally concluded. 'There's nothing I can do until he recovers consciousness.'

'Will he?' Ujjeni demanded.

'Oh yes, but it may be minutes or hours. Meanwhile, absolutely no visitors.'

'Good. He'll have no visitors even after he regains consciousness. Not till he's fully himself again. I want these to be your orders.'

Srihan stared at Ujjeni, then shrugged. 'Very well then. It will certainly be for the Great King's good.'

'This is not an unusual phenomenon for such a serious

head injury,' Srihan continued. 'With leeching, purging and total rest, some of the blood in his brain caused by the blow will be drained away. He may recover his memory in stages over a week or two.'

The Great King lay passive the whole of that day and night. Early the next morning, he was still inert on his pallet when his breakfast was brought in. The soldiers left the fried chicken, ripe yellow bananas, white curd and golden honey on the rough table and departed, leaving Ujjeni and Uraw alone with the King. For the umpteenth time, Uraw berated himself. Why did I not look under the table? He glanced at the Great King's face. It seemed serene, the massive frame, clad in white *kurtha* and *dhoti*, lying totally relaxed on the yellow cushions. The red hair and beard were neatly trimmed, the face was well scrubbed but the eyes were still curiously blank. Uraw's heart went out to his king. He glanced up at Ujjeni. The sunken eyes were watching him speculatively. What goes on in that fiendish mind, Uraw wondered, taken aback by his own realization that Ujjeni's mind was indeed fiendish.

Once again, Ujjeni read his thoughts. 'You must not blame yourself,' he said abruptly, then looked out through the open tent flap, his attention drawn by the trample of feet. Uraw followed his gaze. Dawn had just broken in the east and was casting the sun's red-gold rays across the land.

A tall, stalwart figure, clad in red tunic and white pantaloons, became outlined at the entrance of the tent. Uraw recognized the guard commander, a fair, broad-faced young Arya. 'One of your agents from Kalyani demands to see you immediately, Prince,' the commander explained. 'He says he rode night and day to get here with urgent news.'

'What's his name?'

'Vaman, he says.'

Ujjeni sprang to his feet. 'Have the entire area around the tent cleared so that no one can come within earshot,' he commanded curtly. 'Look to it yourself. Then send the man in.'

Vaman was soon ushered into the tent, a dust-streaked figure, drooping with fatigue. Yet his general appearance was so ordinary that he could easily have passed unnoticed anywhere.

'Speak!' Ujjeni commanded. Vaman's eyes shifted to Uraw. 'You can speak freely in front of Lord Uraw,' Ujjeni assured him. Vaman's gaze flickered to the pallet on which the Great King lay reclining. Recognizing his ruler, Vaman dropped to his knees in obeisance. Uraw realized that Vaman had been trained to observe everything.

'The Great King is unwell,' Ujjeni intervened swiftly. 'Give me your report.'

'There is serious trouble in Kalyani, Prince.' Vaman had a curiously flat voice that matched his ordinary appearance perfectly. 'Prince Jaya and all the other princes and noblemen have revolted. They have taken over the Naga elements of the army and seized the armouries, the Treasury and the granaries. I estimate they have the use of about five thousand men. They demand to be an independent sub-kingdom again, with Prince Jaya as ruler, subordinate only to the Great King himself.'

'Tell us something we do not know already,' Ujjeni interrupted brusquely.

'I beg my lord's pardon. Does he also know that a mission of six princes and noblemen with their retinue is on its way here?'

'Now *that* is news,' Ujjeni pondered awhile. 'And what of Prince Lala? Did he have knowledge of the revolt? Is he a participant in it?'

Vaman hesitated. 'Prince Lala is alive and well, Lord. He appears to have accepted the seizure of power and has been forced to cooperate with the traitors.'

'Good!' The word, fiercely uttered, escaped Ujjeni before he could control himself. A fleeting glimpse of how deeply

Ujjeni hated Prince Lala made Uraw's guts go weak.

Thereafter Ujjeni listened in silence to Vaman's report. Only when the spy had finished did he question the man in the greatest detail, eliciting all he needed to know. Uraw was astonished at the nature of some of the questions, but sickened by his comprehension of their purpose.

'Have all the commanders report to me immediately,' Ujjeni finally directed Uraw. He turned to Vaman again. 'When will the mission from Kalyani arrive?'

'Late tomorrow evening, Lord.'

Uraw had risen to his feet and was adjusting his sword. 'Just one moment, Minister,' Ujjeni bade him, then glanced at the Great King, who appeared to have fallen asleep. 'We must not disturb our ruler. I know how we should handle this. Please tell the commanders and the captain of the fleet that we shall met in Vijit's tent.' His grin, baring the purple gums and prominent yellow teeth, was evil. 'We shall break the back of this shameful rebellion which the Nagas dignify by calling a war of independence.'

Chapter 44

Administration of the Kalyani kingdom by the rebels went on so smoothly that it made me wonder whether government as we understand it is so necessary, because the people carry on living regardless. I learned to keep calm during this time, except for the occasional nagging caused by my nightmare vision.

On the third night of the rebellion, I had just finished dinner with Sundari when a messenger came from Uday requesting my presence. Uday and I had made it a point not to discuss the event, so as I hastened to his cell I wondered what he could want of me at such a late hour.

The flare-lit verandahs had become strangely deserted since the day of the takeover, because the centre of power had shifted to Prince Jaya's residence. How ephemeral is authority, I reflected as I followed the yellow-robed figure of my messenger past the few saluting guards on duty. Even the splash of fountains, the hiss of the flares and the whine of a mosquito suddenly seemed unreal to me. And why not, when reality is but our perception of each single moment and, having perceived places in their context, under regular circumstances, we tend to identify reality with those conditions.

I found Uday seated in the lotus pose as usual, on his beige-coloured mat at the far end of his small cell. The messenger monk announced me and left, closing the door behind him. To my surprise, Uday had a visitor in the cell. The man had risen from his mat on my entry and now saluted me. I first made obeisance to Uday, then returned the visitor's greeting before looking closely at him. He was a lean, cleanshaven Yakka, a little older than my thirty-two years. Unusually for a Yakka, he had a fair complexion, his face was gaunt and the cheekbones narrow. His dark eyes were kindly and gentle, his long, black hair in disarray. He had obviously travelled a long way, fast, for his dark pantaloons were dusty, the white *kurtha* soaked in sweat.

Uday was very direct. 'This man's name is Hamy and until three days ago he was one of King Tikka's two closest aides.'

I was stunned. I had indeed heard of the two aides, Hamy and Kira, and had wondered what had happened to them. Uday's dark eyes travelled slowly back towards the man. 'Hamy is a believer in the true doctrine. Our talk with him reveals that he has already acquired knowledge of it.' His gaze returned to me solemnly. 'Please be seated, both of you.' He waited until we had assumed the lotus pose in front of him, then continued. 'Hamy is here with a woman you know, the attendant of the Princess Kuveni, Rupa by name. They fled together from Devun Dara to escape King Tikka's wrath . . . But let Hamy tell you the story in his own words. Rupa's will follow. She is outside. Since it will take a great deal of time, we have advised your wife so that she will not become alarmed. Listen therefore with patience and compassion.'

My head was in a whirl. Where had King Tikka been? And where was he now? And what was I, the duly appointed ruler of the sub-kingdom, unseated by a rebellious prince, doing here with the closest associate of the Great King's arch enemy? What a bizarre situation! Highly dangerous to me, too. Why would Uday want to expose me to such peril? I looked at his calm impassive face, the shaven head shining, the dark eyes deep in the taper-light and realized that to him, right was right and had to be done, regardless of the consequences.

As the spy, Vaman, had forecast, the Naga mission, with six leaders, arrived in Devun Dara that same night. In accordance with Ujjeni's instructions, the mission was received with courtesy by Arya captains and given dinner before the leaders were conducted to the Great King's tent.

Uraw could not help but notice that, by demanding his constant attendance at the Great King's tent, Ujjeni was giving the impression that King Vijaya was in fact issuing the orders himself. Uraw was becoming more and more certain that he was being enmeshed by Ujjeni in some deep plot.

The open ground at the entrance to the Great King's tent had been prepared for the meeting, the entrance flap deliberately left open so that people could see the ruler reclining and assume that he was able to overhear all that transpired. The entire area was brightly lit by flares, smoking in the damp air from an earlier rainshower. Armed guards lined the three sides of a square opposite the wharf and the Great King's tent, before which a guard-of-honour, in red and white uniforms, was drawn. Ujjeni and Uraw took their places beside each other on settles, their backs to the wharf, with Vijit, Anu, Pandu, Sumitta and Upa seated immediately behind them.

Negotiations with diplomatic missions never took place at night, still less in the open air, so the splash of wavelets and the soughing of a steady ocean breeze lent strangeness to the entire scene. Yet, conditions could have been worse, Uraw reflected, for the passing rainshower had swept even the skies clean leaving blue heavens spangled with stars, echoed on dark treetops by countless fireflies. The fires of the men blazed along the beach, but their songs were hushed.

As the mission approached, the honour guard commander called his troops to attention and they raised their spears to the present position. Uraw took stock of the Nagas as they approached the site. At their head was a giant, very fair, broad of shoulder and obviously tough of sinew. He was a middle-aged man with florid features, a sensual nose and fine dark eyes. He carried himself with pride, even when he paused and saluted Ujjeni. 'I am Jega Nathan, Prince of

Kalyani, leader of the mission from Prince Jaya, our ruler,' he introduced himself. He turned towards his companions, indicating each in turn with a graceful wave of a heavily ringed right hand. 'This is Prince Muttu Samy.' A lean young man with curly black hair, thin moustache and a haughty expression on his cleancut face stepped foward and saluted. 'Prince Wetta Muni.' This was a small, round, jolly-looking prince, with a bald head, chubby cheeks and a puckish smile. The others followed in turn, Prince Soma Pala, a gaunt hunchback with dark saturnine features, Prince Palitha, a squat, moon-faced dwarf, and Chief Minister Ratnes Waram, a tall silver-haired nobleman. The bearing of each man was dignified, even courtly.

'I am Prince Ujjeni, sub-king of Thamba-Panni,' Ujjeni responded, his voice cold and hard as a fire-grate. 'I have just heard you refer to a Prince Jaya, who sent you on this mission, as the ruler of Kalyani. As far as I am aware the Great King has made no change in the appointment of his brother, Prince Lala, as sub-king.'

Prince Nathan flushed. 'Four days ago, the great King's edict was altered by the will of the Kalyani people,' he declared curtly. 'Prince Lala is our hostage and we are here to negotiate a treaty of independence with the Great King, whereunder he will still retain complete suzerainty over the sub-kingdom.'

'You act first and then come to treat with the Great King?' Ujjeni's voice held an ominous note. 'That is hardly proper, still less loyal.'

'We are here to discuss those very matters with the Great King and crave leave to see him. We assume that he is in his quarters and will now grant us audience.' Prince Nathan nodded towards the tent. 'Meanwhile, we thank you for your hospitality – the dinner was excellent – and for the honour guard, all of which does you honour in turn.' A supercilious note entered his voice. 'We trust your courtesy will extend to inviting your guests to be seated.'

'You may not be seated.' Ujjeni's tone was harsh and rude. 'Nor will the Great King see you.' He pushed back his settle. ' How dare you arrive without invitation, a rebellious faction, and demand an audience with the Great King? You are nothing but a bunch of dirty rebels.'

'You are mistaken, Sir,' Prince Nathan replied coldly. His voice had dropped a tone and had lost its earlier suaveness. 'We are here as the representatives of a free people demanding audience with their sovereign.'

'Demanding?'

'Yes, demanding. No less. We earnestly desire a peaceful resolution of our problems and are here to attempt it.'

'You rebel against the Great King. You subvert his army, seize his armouries, Treasury and granaries and still talk of a peaceful resolution. Why, Sir, you must be dreaming. The Great King will not see you and I have extended to you the only honours you will receive from his court.' Ujjeni rose to his feet, gaunt, menacing, his sunken eyes flaming, his death's head face bleak as a dark tombstone. He pointed a long, bony finger at each of the six men in turn. 'You . . . you . . . you . . . you . . . you . . . you . . . are all traitors and shall be given the punishment you deserve.'

'We are not traitors, Sir, but patriots.' It was the haughty Prince Muttu Samy who stepped forward to protest, his head lifted proudly, his voice ringing clear. 'Since we may neither see our sovereign nor treat with him, we demand the traditional safe-conduct accorded to peace missions by your own Arya code, so that we can return to Kalyani.'

Ujjeni turned a sneering face at the prince. 'The Arya code for peace missions applies only to those of sovereign people,' he stated with deadly calm. 'You are rebels and secessionists. The Arya code does indeed have provisions for such as you.' He dropped his arm and half-turned towards the honour guard commander. 'Seize them!' He roared.

The guard commander barked an order. His men pointed their spears at the mission.

'We have walked into a trap of our own making,' Prince Nathan advised his comrades, his voice quiet as if he were making some pleasantry. 'I for one shall never be taken alive to be sentenced like some pitiful peasant.' In one swift movement his long sword gleamed in his hand.

'Nor I,' Prince Muttu Samy declared, his own weapon already drawn.

The swords of the other four men were out as one and all six formed a box for defence. The guards, spears at the ready, converged silently on them, step by slow step. Prince Nathan looked bright-eyed at Ujjeni. 'Why did you extend your hospitality to us if this was your intention?' He shouted the question to be heard above the slow tramp of the men's feet on the wooden wharf.

Ujjeni's grin was fiendish. 'You will observe that you were not assigned quarters,' he shouted back. 'The meal was meant to be your last, which is a privilege accorded to any condemned man. As for the honour guard, it performed your last rites.'

'We thank you for your courtesy,' Prince Nathan retorted and came on-guard.

'Now!' Ujjeni roared. Men appeared from behind the guards. A swishing noise cut through the air. A great fishing net swirled and settled on the six men, then another and another. Vainly they tried to cut themselves loose. The nets were slowly, inexorably drawn around the struggling men. Finally they were all trapped inside, like some monstrous catch of sea-creatures.

'They are traitors,' Ujjeni spat the words at the guard commander. 'By order of the Great King, I command you to take them and behead them as an example to all rebels throughout the realm. Place their heads on spikes and post them high in the town square. Fling their bodies into the ocean to feed the fishes.' He turned to his companions, eager eyes blazing, 'Now for the next stage of our plan.'

*　　*　　*

I listened to Hamy's story in fascination. When he came to the murder of the Princess Kuveni, however, my heart was torn by compassion. What a dreadful end to a sad life. *Kharma/vipaka*, cause and effect, could not lessen its terrible impact on me. Sensing my anguish, Hamy fell silent, allowing me to recover. As I relived the terror, the hope, the final resignation of the princess, bitter bile rose in my aching throat, tears stung my eyes. At least she is now free of the sorrows of this life, I finally reflected, and bade Hamy proceed.

He commenced telling of King Tikka's plan to swim to the Great King's tent and my stomach knotted. I recalled my nightmare experience, call it what you will, of that murderous night and the apprehension I had felt began to mount to certainty. Even before Hamy reached the part where King Tikka attacked my brother, fear made my chest tight and I wanted to scream at him to spare me the details and tell me the worst. Then he did, leaving me in a sudden vacuum, numb, devoid of all feeling, yet enveloped by horror. Was my brother dead? I could not take it. Suddenly, all my pent-up love for him was released. Panic seized me. Dear God, I cannot live without him, for I would be nothing, one-half living, one-half dead, indeed nothing. Remorse came charging in like some dread horseman of the graveyards. What had I done? Had my brother died estranged from me, believing that I had betrayed him as a person and as my king? If so, I could never set it right. How hideous are the things we do without sufficient thought, how selfish a stand for principles can be. Oh God, I would sacrifice all, all, all, if you only spare my brother's life.

A sudden wild urge to ride to Devun Dara seized me, then helplessness, for even that would be denied me by my captors. Why not escape, sneak out somehow? And place Sundari in jeopardy? I was caught, trapped, like a man sunk in a bog. And at that moment, I realized with ghastly clarity that this was not God's doing but the inevitable effect of causes I had created.

Some instinct for survival produced hope, and hope generated strength. With a tremendous effort, I steadied myself. 'Is the Great King dead?' I enquired.

'I don't know, Prince.' Hamy must have read my grief, for compassion touched his dark eyes. 'I for one doubt that a man as big and strong as the Great King can be killed by a single, wild bludgeon blow. He was probably stunned. King Tikka did not remain to check or to finish the job.'

I thought, bless you for your reassurance, Hamy, then searched Uday's face. His gaze was firm, the eyes compelling. He was trying to remind me of the princely code, my duty to remain calm.

'You and your brother were always as one,' Uday reminded me. 'If he were dead you would surely have known.'

Some of my dread eased. 'Please go on,' I bade Hamy.

'There is not much more to tell, Lord,' he replied, then went on to give the news of his escape from King Tikka's thrall. He had proceeded directly to Gona's house, collected Rupa and the children and fled through the night in a wagon belonging to one of Banda's former contacts. He had left the two children at the home of another of Rupa's relations in the high country, since it would be safer for two grown-ups to travel alone, and made directly for Kalyani. King Tikka was still on the loose, alone perhaps, for Kira too would surely have left him.

It was almost midnight by the time Hamy ended his narrative. He then left the cell briefly to return with Rupa. The gaunt woman fell on her knees and broke into uncontrollable sobs when she saw me. 'My mistress told me, the night before she was foully murdered, to seek you out, Prince, if anything ever happened to her,' she said, her voice breaking. 'That is why we poor destitute ones have come to you.'

'You did right to come,' I assured her, though I did not

know how I could be of any help to anyone in my own desperate situation. 'Please sit down and tell us your own story.'

Rupa told all, in the minutest detail, from the first day she took service in the palace right up to the present, freely admitting her role as Ujjeni's spy.

The pre-dawn watch had commenced by the time she finished speaking, leaving us lost in thought. So many memories, so many regrets, such terrible grief. If I had my life to lead again . . .

'We can do no more, say no more, think no more at any time than we have done,' Uday interposed gently. 'All is *kharma/vipaka*, cause and effect. We must fight the battle of the senses, free ourselves of all desires, even those that spring from worldly love, if we are to avoid suffering.'

I nodded. 'You are right, Venerable Sir.' Looking into those depthless eyes, I suddenly realized that Uday had much more in mind when he summoned me than to present Sinhala history to its future chronicler. 'But I must assume that you required me to attend you tonight for other reasons than to favour me with the facts of history.'

He smiled gently. 'Ever the precocious one, my dear,' he observed. He nodded briefly towards Hamy. 'This child desires to be pardoned of his sins and to join the Noble Order of Monks so that he may hasten the journey he has already commenced towards enlightenment by his interest in the true doctrine.'

'With all due respect, what has that to do with me? I am no longer the ruler of Kalyani.'

Uday's eyes twinkled. 'The present rulers of Kalyani, whom some may call usurpers, have nothing against our brother Hamy. So, as far as they are concerned, he can remain here without let or hindrance. It is the Great King's wrath, the Great King's justice, the Great King's vengeance that are Hamy's sources of danger, possibly even Rupa's for having come to Kalyani against the Great King's orders. Only

615

the Great King can remove you from the office he bestowed on you, or take away the powers you exercise in his name. You therefore still hold the absolute right of pardon in this kingdom. If you will execute it on *ola*, for these two unfortunates, under the Great King's seal, all will be well.'

'But where will they go?' I protested weakly.

'We have, as you know, established many cloisters in this realm. Our brother, Hamy, will vanish into the yellow robes and none will ever learn that he took them or where he may be. Our sister, Rupa, will have the two orphan children of the Princess Kuveni join her in a village close to Hamy's cloister, so that she can render services to our monks' abode there and the children can be brought up in the doctrine.' A strange look crossed his face. 'We fear, however, that these poor children may have another destiny.'

With Uday as my example, for he was exposing himself to terrible danger, I plucked at the handle of my courage and its blade was resolve. 'I shall do it,' I firmly stated. I turned to Hamy. 'Never will the Great King's pardon have been exercised in a better cause.'

I executed the pardon documents immediately and returned to my quarters. Sundari had stayed up for me. 'I simply could not sleep,' she said with a sweet smile. I told her all I had learned. Her gentle reassurances that my brother must be well steadied me, but my mind remained fine-honed, unwilling to be blunted by sleep. So I excused myself from Sundari, fished out some *olas* and started writing all that Rupa and Hamy had told me. It helped me forget my fears.

Moved by some inexplicable force, I worked feverishly most of that day and night, the following day and night and well into the third day until I was done. Each passing hour without news that the Great King had died had given me added hope of his safety.

Prince Jaya visited me only once during this period. Like everyone else in Kalyani, he was eagerly awaiting the return

616

of the diplomatic mission from Devun Dara. He took advantage of this visit to beg my forgiveness for having placed me in a position of danger. I assured him that I did not blame him for what he had done, that I respected his stand. But the mischievous crinkle at the sides of his eyes, the deliberately naïve turn of speech were gone. The puckish child had grown into a deadly serious man, strong yet fearful. I could not bring myself to tell him that I loved my brother so much that I wished with all my heart that I had subordinated my principles to love.

I completed the *olas* shortly after dinner on the third day. Sundari had been reading them as I wrote and her praise of the finished work made it all worthwhile. Moved by some impulse, I decided to entrust the *olas* to Uday for safekeeping. The memory of my stolen letter to the Great King was fresh in my mind, I suppose, and I did not want my precious record of history to fall into unfriendly or destructive hands.

Having delivered the *olas* to Uday, I returned to my quarters, content of mind from a feeling of accomplishment and, yes, from having played my part in destiny. Yet now that my preoccupation with the writing was over, I faced reality once more and it lay grim on my spirit with a terrible sense of foreboding.

Sundari and I lay in bed touching and caressing each other, murmuring endearments, as we had done before falling asleep every single night since our marriage, though our love had never been sexually consummated. We were both very tired, however, so that within minutes we drowsed off to slowly diminishing caresses. My last conscious thought was that I should extinguish the tapers, but my body was heavier than my mind's command and I was soon fast asleep.

At first it sounded like the distant drumming of horses' hooves, then of thunderous rain upon the roof. Finally it resolved itself into the pounding of my heart. And I was awake on the instant, staring at the gold canopy above me, sideways at the outlines of commodes and settles.

Someone was hammering insistently at the door to my quarters.

'Who could it be?' Sundari enquired, sitting up.

She had her answer. Faintly through the great teak-wood door, across my entrance foyer and outer chamber, came the authoritative shout. 'Open, in the Great King's name!'

My first reaction was one of relief. 'My brother is alive and well!' I exclaimed, reaching for my robe.

Sundari stretched her arms towards me, held on to me. 'Don't go,' she pleaded. 'I'm afraid.'

Her fear re-sparked my own and I had to pretend an ease I did not feel. 'It is the Great King's men, beloved,' I assured her. 'They have arrived. Now all will be well.'

I held her soft body to me once, stroked her soft hair and felt the pounding of her heart. Some desperate urge within me never wanted to let her go, but I released her.

'Hold me,' she begged, and I enfolded her in my arms again. She clung desperately to me.

I finally swung out of bed and donned my robe, sped to the door and waited for the bout of hammering to end. 'Who is it?' I enquired.

'Open up!' The voice was deep, unfamiliar.

'Has the Great King arrived?'

A moment's hesitation that I barely recognized. 'Yes.'

'All right. Just give me a few minutes to get dressed.'

I hastened back to the bedchamber and changed into black pantaloons and a white tunic. The night was humid and I broke into a light sweat. Sundari had risen and donned her blue robe by the time I slipped into my thonged sandals. She looked so frail, so delicate, standing by the great bed on which we had known such ecstasy, such peace, the finest hours of sharing. Her dark eyes were tremulous in the flare-light, the tears not far away. I took in her pale delicate features, the slender nostrils, the pomegranate lips, the masses of dark, wavy hair that I had caressed so often. She came into my arms, trembling. I held her close to me, her body soft and supple merging into mine, so that I lost contact with that part of my body that was against hers and she and I were physically one. I wished that we could die thus.

'If only I could die in your arms,' she whispered. Her voice broke, but she held back the tears.

I kissed her cheeks, her lips. She clung to me as if she would never release me. 'Go now,' she finally said. 'I love you.'

Letting go of her was like an abandonment of my final and only tangible security. I believe I cut my heart out at the moment I replied, 'I love you.' I turned and went towards the door. I slid the heavy wooden bar and placed it against the wall. I unlocked the latch and opened the door.

Six Arya men stood before me in rows of two. The first two were guard captains in the red and white uniforms of the Great King. I recognized them. On the left was Pali, a stalwart infantry commander, with a broad face, sweeping black moustaches and brown-blue eyes. On the right was a tall, slightly hunched man with a cleanshaven hatchet face down which a brown scar ran from the right eye almost to the mouth, giving it a perpetually grisly appearance. I could not recall his name, but knew him to be one of Ujjeni's troop commanders. Behind these two men were lean, bare-chested army attendants wearing white *dhotis* and holding up flares. Behind the attendants, naked, bloody swords in hand, were Uraw and gaunt Ujjeni. One look at Ujjeni's eyes and I knew the worst. For in that brief instant, they blazed their hatred and malignant triumph at me from sunken sockets. Then he closed purple lips over his protruding yellow teeth, his expression merely stolid, but the face still like a death's head. 'Prince Lala,' he said quietly. 'We are here in the name of the Great King to arrest you for treason. You had best come quietly.'

I heard a gasp, quietly stifled, from the bedroom. Sundari

619

must have heard Ujjeni's voice and identified it. What would it do to her after all these years? As for me, I had expected to give some accounting, followed by serious censure, for my unwitting failures in Kalyani, but never this. Ujjeni had heard the gasp, for his eyes slid through the open door. Sundari must have moved to the bedroom entrance, for Ujjeni immediately saw her. An expression of such devilish satisfaction as I had never before seen flashed across his face. Remembering the past, my guts turned to water, yet I drew myself to my full height. 'I am here in Kalyani as the sub-king, duly appointed by the Great King,' I responded steadily. 'That appointment can only be revoked by the Great King himself and he must do so either in person, or under his seal before I can be arrested. Do you have such a mandate, Prince Ujjeni?'

The two guard captains had glanced at each other. Sensing their uncertainty, I pushed home my advantage. 'Remember too that I happen to be the Great King's brother. He well knows that I need not be arrested to compel my attendance on him. I shall willingly answer his summons.'

The two commanders turned to Ujjeni for orders. His eyes blazed anger, venom, hatred at me. 'You are a traitor!' He shouted. 'Neither the Great King's seal nor his express command are needed to punish traitors. It is the right of every true citizen of the realm to cut down treason on the instant.'

I turned away. 'Return when you are legally equipped, Prince,' I stated over my shoulder. 'Till then, pray do not intrude on my privacy.'

I had barely reached for the door when I heard Ujjeni's scream. 'Seize him! I command you, seize him! Seize him!' The hysterical tones went echoing and re-echoing down the corridors, 'Seize him . . . seize him! . . . seize him . . .' and then I heard the ghastly words, 'Seize that Dasa bitch too as an accomplice.'

I started to run for my sword, but the door was pushed violently open. I was grabbed from both sides. A manacle was fixed to my right wrist while rough hands grabbed for my left. Two men rushed across the room towards Sundari. A roar of fury escaped me. I struggled to free myself, but in vain. Blinded by tears of rage, I heard Sundari's sob, her strangled gasp, her desperate reaching for breath. My piteous gaze revealed my beloved slowly crumpling to the floor of the bedroom. My heart thudded against my ribs. I broke loose from my captors with fiendish strength. They leapt on me and brought me to the ground. Struggling impotently, scarcely able to breath, I heard the grim words. 'She's dead.' Oh God, why did it have to be alien, male hands that touched her virgin body for the last time?

A bitter cry escaped Ujjeni and I knew then that God had saved Sundari from a horrible fate.

The life force of my beloved was always delicate as gossamer. Now it has been wafted away and the chill loneliness of that tomb, death, has entered my spirit. I too am dead.

And in the dying, something new is always reborn. Sundari and I are finally released from the dreadful manacles of fear that fettered our spirits for so long. Her body will lie on a bier and be cremated, so only its ashes remain, but all of her became a part of me and always will be, for our perfect love is a part of eternal God and will endure for ever. Sundari and I will find each other in each successive birth, never identifying the one before, but always loving each other.

A great calm had settled within me by the time we reached the audience hall. From that calm flowed courage. Since I only had myself to fear for now, I feared nothing. I was finally ready to acknowledge God to all men.

Chapter 45

To my surprise, all the ministers, apart from Ujjeni, were assembled in the audience hall. Dressed in the white and red uniform of the Great King, they were seated in a single row around a table that had been placed on the platform which normally accommodated the golden throne and the queen's chair, both of which had been pushed to one side. Though sweaty, dusty and tired, the men looked solemn as judges in the golden flare-light. I was glad to see Vijit, for he at least would remain on the side of justice.

I was escorted to the base of the platform and made to stand there, looking up at my judges. They all avoided my gaze, but I did not care any longer. Reaction to the knowledge that Sundari was dead had begun to set in, so that all I could do was to stare vacantly into space, indelibly imprinting into my brain my last glimpse of the face and form, the total physical image of my beloved and the feel of our last embrace.

Vijit cleared his throat and addressed me. 'Prince Lala, you will, I'm sure, be glad to know that although the Great King is not with us tonight, he is safe and well. He suffered a head injury from a fall while we were in Devun Dara and has been advised complete rest by the court physician.'

My brother was alive, thank God, but this story did not tally with what I had learned from Hamy. Some devil's work was afoot, yet I could not tell what I knew without betraying Hamy, even myself. 'Have you seen the Great King since he received the injury?' I enquired, feigning ignorance.

'No,' Vijit replied, confirming my fears. 'But we are assured of his safety by Prince Ujjeni.'

This was indeed the worst. 'I thank you for giving me the

news,' I replied. 'I was seriously concerned.' Then for want of something to say. 'Would you also do me the courtesy of enlightening me as to how you managed to retake Kalyani so quickly?'

Vijit grinned, his teeth very white beneath the black moustache, the chiselled features relaxing somewhat. 'Prince Ujjeni evolved a brilliant plan, based on previous information in his possession as to who the leaders of the rebellion were, where they were located, their guards, the sentries in the barracks room, armouries and sentry posts. The prince organized a timed attack for tonight. When we left Devun Dara, each of our companies had been detailed an objective, with instructions as to how to get there. One detachment left by sea and came ashore from war galleys. The rest of us came along the coast. Everything went very smoothly. With the element of surprise totally in our favour, the rebels hardly put up any resistance.

'What of the Naga mission to the Great King?'

'Prince Ujjeni had them arrested and summarily executed.'

The members of a diplomatic mission summarily executed! What a callous deed. Their faces swam before me, alive, vibrant, men I had known and dealt with almost daily, the florid-faced Prince Nathan, who always carried himself with such pride, the haughty-eyed young Prince Mutta Samy, jolly Prince Wetta Muni, the saturnine hunchback, Prince Soma Pala, the moon-faced dwarf, Prince Palitha, the silver-haired Chief Minister, Ratnes Waram. Then the faces became still, turned into six death masks. 'I thank you for giving me the news,' I stated. 'I'm glad the kingdom is secure.'

'Why should you be glad?' Anu broke in rudely. 'We have evidence that you wanted the Great King to die without heirs, so that you could succeed to the throne and look after your Yakka, Naga and Buddhist friends. We also have evidence of your complicity in this rebellion that has taken so many lives.'

Perhaps it was the knowledge of how Sundari would have expected me to comport myself that made me set aside my grief. 'You do not know me, any of you,' I stated quietly, holding Anu's glance not with anger but with the great compassionate love of God that had begun to flood my being. 'Most of you are men of ambition, capable of sacrificing honour for personal gain. As for you, Anu, I know you for what you are. Was it not you who so terrified and terrorized a helpless attendant woman eight years ago that she became your spy?'

I did not mean the words in anger or reproof, merely as the truth laid bare. Anu's head jerked upwards, as if I had physically hit him on the chin. The other commanders looked sharply at him, then glanced away, seeing his guilt. I had a moment's inspiration. 'All you gentlemen gathered here in Council, are you certain you are doing the Great King's bidding?' Knowing that I must get some of them on my side before Ujjeni joined them, I shook my manacles so they clanked behind my back. 'Is this how the Great King would have treated his brother? Would he not at least have afforded his sub-king the dignity of taking his own life as punishment, without shame? Have a care, gentlemen, for you are all accountable to the Great King.'

'I and I alone shall be accountable to the Great King.' Ujjeni's grainy voice rang through the hall. He had entered silently. 'I shall deliver justice to the Great King so that he need not know the embarrassment of showing pity or compassion to a proven traitor who happens to be his brother by an accident of Nature. The Great King will always endorse my actions, for I think with his mind and act with his spirit ever since I gave up being myself to become him.'

I turned my head and saw Ujjeni's death's head face glowering at me, the flare-light flickering in his eyes. He advanced into the room before I could respond, shooting words at me. 'In this Arya kingdom of Lanka, by the Great

624

King's decree, justice is no respecter of persons. A crime is a crime, whether it be committed by a beggar or a prince. The higher a man's estate, the more he shall be held accountable, especially when the crime is high treason.' He stopped in front of me, so close that I could smell his foul breath. 'We, the Great King's Council of Ministers, are assembled here tonight to deliver the Great King's justice swiftly and surely to the guilty.'

'You will doubtless separate the innocent from the guilty by using those well-known elements of Arya justice, evidence and proof?' I questioned.

'We have ample evidence of your guilt,' he retorted. 'When we have given you the proof, we shall expect a full confession from you.' He paused, eyeing me evilly. 'We may then perhaps consider mercy.'

'I had just told these gentlemen, before you arrived, that they do not know me. Now, at the risk of committing the more unpardonable crime of repetition, I shall tell you the same thing. You do not know me.' Somehow I could feel only hatred for this man, so I deliberately decided to salt his deep wounds. 'My brother, the Great King and you can never be one. It is he and I that are one, born of the same womb. I would no more commit treason against him, or harm one hair of his head, than I would wilfully hurt myself. As for ambition, I am at the moment his heir, but all I have wanted from life is to renounce worldly aims, to conquer the senses and to become a Buddhist monk some day.'

'A married man who has desired to be a monk?' There was a hint of mockery in Ujjeni's tone.

'Yes, just like our Lord Buddha, who once was Prince Siddharta, with a wife and baby, but left them a few years later to become the Buddha, the Enlightened One.'

'Ah! You're a good Buddhist?' He was sneering openly now.

'Yes.'

'And yet you are also a stinking Juda. You believe in one

God.' He spat the words. 'What hyprocrisy is that?'

'Not hypocrisy, but knowledge. My One God is of my own, intimate personal knowledge.'

'Do you then deny that you are a Juda, a Jaweh-loving heretic who would destroy the gods of others as graven images, like that lost tribe of the desert lands whose priests are burned at the stake for practising witchcraft and rejecting our gods?'

Now he had touched those depths of me that he himself had finally made unchanging by murdering my wife, completing my total belief in One God, fixing my unflinching determination to declare that belief, to hold fast to it before all the world, making no excuse, offering no proof, but never denying my God. 'If my belief in One God makes me a Juda in your eyes then I am proud of it. I tell you most sincerely that I would rather be a Juda today than standing in your shoes.'

He gave his deep, mirthless hee ... hee ... hee ... laugh. 'So you are a self-confessed heretic.'

'I believe in God.'

'Heresy too is hereby added to the list of charges against you.'

'If that is to be a charge, I demand that it be held singly against me, without the taint of other, more temporal counts.'

'So it shall, prince and heretic. So it shall.' Ujjeni turned at a commotion by the entrance doors. The guard commander came up and whispered to him. He looked sharply at me, nodded and dismissed the man, then faced me again, his fiendish glee hidden from the others behind a carefully-veiled lack of expression, but directed at me alone from his sunken eyes. 'I'm sorry to announce that your wife is indeed dead,' he said in clear tones.

'I know.'

His eyes widened. 'How could you know? Surely you must practise witchcraft.'

'Yes I do. The witchcraft of a love that you would never understand because there is so much hatred in your heart. Do you think that hatred can conquer anything, Prince Ujjeni? It is self-defeating. It consumes you, so there is nothing left within to enjoy what you crave for, plot for, strive so cleverly to attain.' My words banished the hatred, released God's love for him, yes, even him, within me and it gushed forth. 'You will never conquer love with any other force than greater love. My God is a god of love, not of destruction, and His love shall prevail. I offer it to you with all my being. I have nothing but love for you.'

In the stunned silence that followed I heard his whispered question. 'Do you say that your God will prevail over our pantheon of gods?'

'Yes. Your gods are but a part of my God's body – and so are we all, even you. My God embodies and enfolds all people, all things, all gods, all beliefs, creates them, changes their form. My God is infinite, eternal, unchanging. It is only His component parts, men and mountains, gods and beliefs, that know change, *kharma/vipaka*, cause and effect. Our aim in this life should be to become godlike.'

'So you believe yourself to be a god?'

'No, I am but a human part of God, striving to be godlike, as you are trying to be an inhuman, ungodly part of him.' The words came out from a sudden flash of anger, which I instantly regretted. The anger snapped, gave way again before God's love, and I felt only an infinite compassion for him. 'You are a man blessed with unusual brains, enormous strength of purpose and remarkable ability. You have been made a prince. I beg you, in God's name, from the love I bear for you as a fellow human being, to replace your hatred with love. Study the four precepts . . .'

'You, a blasphemer and heretic, dare attempt in public to convert a true believer to your heresy?' He interrupted me, a note of incredulity in his voice. 'By your own words are you judged. For this impertinence, for this blatant violation of all we Arya believe in, you deserve to die. Else our gods will surely punish us.' In the deathly silence of the audience chamber, I could feel his eyes telling me: mostly you deserve to die for daring to offer me, your mortal enemy, love.

At last I knew what Ujjeni really wanted. From the depths of all my suffering, my misery, my lifetime of doubts and fears and from the heights of my love he had my reply. 'You will never succeed in destroying what is good within me, Prince Ujjeni, for the love of God that passeth all understanding is in my spirit. It extends even to those who seek my death, even to you. It has reached out and touched your heart, though you do not know it. So when my body is gone, my love, which is God's love, will be with you. I bless you.'

'And I curse you . . . I curse you to hell, you foul blasphemer,' he screamed.

'Why don't we stop this foolish exchange and get on with our hearing.' It was Vijit's deep voice, a curt edge to it. 'We have travelled continuously for two days and a night and achieved a near bloodless victory over the rebels through your plan, a brilliant one, Prince Ujjeni. Let us hear the charges against Prince Lala tonight and get some rest. We will be fresh then to hear evidence tomorrow. We owe that to the Great King.'

Ujjeni turned on him fiercely. 'No! I say we try this heretic traitor, sentence him tonight and execute him tomorrow.'

'You have already decided to execute him?' Vijit's eyebrows were raised incredulously.

'I have all the evidence I need. I am satisfied as to his guilt. I can easily convince you of it too.'

Vijit looked to his right and left, bending forward to poll those commanders sitting farthest from him with his glance. 'Is this your desire, fellow ministers? I say we take a poll. In the absence of the Great King, Prince Ujjeni presides over our Council without a vote, so he needs four of us to accept his demand.'

'Right!' Ujjeni leered at Vijit. He was very sure of his votes. 'Anu!'

'I'm with you.'

'Sumitta?'

'Me too.'

'Pandu?'

'I say we get on with it.'

'Upa?'

'No. The prince must have a fair trial.'

'Uraw?'

For all my conquest of fear, my stomach blanched. Uraw was Ujjeni's boon companion. He would surely vote yes and seal my fate. I would be dead by this time tomorrow.

'I'm sorry, Prince Ujjeni, but I must part company from you on this issue. The prince must have a fair trial.'

For a moment, Ujjeni's jaw dropped. If looks could kill, Uraw would have died on the spot from the venom Ujjeni shot at him.

'I too vote for a fair trial,' I heard Vijit say quietly, and I blessed him for it and for his intervention. 'Meanwhile, we have been more than churlish, we have been inhuman not to allow the prince what even a criminal should be afforded in any decent society – the right to private grief for a wife who has just died, the right to arrange for her cremation. There is no need for indecent haste. The trial can take place in a few days, perhaps even after the Great King recovers.'

Ujjeni knew when he was beaten. He was too clever to extend his spite against me farther. 'Agreed,' he said pleasantly. 'Meanwhile, we might even seek and obtain further evidence.' He looked strangely at me and I suddenly remembered his talk of a confession.

Having accepted the decision of the ministers with apparent grace, Ujjeni now slowly mounted the steps of the platform. Something in his bearing made us all pause. He reached the centre of the table. His chair scraped on the wooden platform as he drew it back. He sat down and eased the chair forward, rested his arms on the table, fingers interlocked, and stared stonily at me. 'My fellow ministers, I regret that these proceedings cannot be terminated until we have proceeded with our next order of business,' he asserted. 'I realize that Prince Lala must be under a strain because of his wife's death, but in matters involving the security of the realm, justice must be swift, ruthless and retributive. A certain Prince Jaya has been arrested and has not only confessed his guilt but even boasts of it. He will be brought here now to face sentencing for high treason. Formal sentencing is a courtesy we shall afford him alone, as the leader of the rebellion. Everyone else involved will be summarily executed tonight, without trial, like the members of that so-called diplomatic mission.'

My stomach felt queasy. Was this the Great King's justice? Was this Arya law? For men to be executed without a fair trial was an abomination to me and to give Prince Jaya the honour, however dubious, of being convicted and sentenced while his co-conspirators were summarily executed, was to contradict Ujjeni's very statement that Arya law was no respecter of persons. No sooner had I thought this than I realized why the distinction was being made. Ujjeni wanted to humiliate Prince Jaya in public, not only as the leader of the rebellion but also because he was my friend and had been my aide for years.

A commotion arose at the entrance of the audience hall. The doors were thrown wide open and Prince Jaya stood framed in the flare-light. His dark hair was dishevelled, the plump face bathed in sweat. Bloodstains from a shoulder wound streaked his white silken tunic, the black pantaloons were creased, but the great bulk of him was tall, erect, dignified, fearless. He was pushed unceremoniously forward from behind and nearly stumbled. As he started to walk towards us, flanked and followed by guards in close array, I noticed with surprise that he was not manacled.

'Guard captain, have your guards stand by and let the traitor come forward alone,' Ujjeni commanded.

The entire group stopped. The guard captain rapped out an order. The guards faced about and walked away. The great entrance doors closed behind them.

'Come forward, traitor,' Ujjeni commanded fiercely.

Prince Jaya looked at him, as if searching. He fixed his gaze on Ujjeni through those slits of eyes and shrugged his brawny shoulders. 'The traitor must have left with the guards,' he suggested with his customary urbanity.

Ujjeni was nonplussed. 'Who?' He enquired.

'The traitor you addressed.'

A hiss of indrawn breath escaped Ujjeni. The rest of the Ministers looked grim, except for Vijit, who could not restrain a smile, and Uraw, who had open admiration in his glance.

'You traitor, you dare fool with us when your life is in our hands?' Ujjeni demanded.

'I would dare anything at any time, as you well know,' Prince Jaya responded, pitching his normally high voice low. 'As for my life, it has always been and always will be in the hands of my gods.' He lifted his great head slightly higher. 'You call me a traitor. I suggest that you ask yourself, a traitor to what? To foreign domination? To rule by a usurper? To racial bias? To injustice? To fraud? To discrimination? To hypocrisy? To genocide? Yes, I am indeed a traitor to all these and have gladly risked my life in the attempt to end them.'

'You are not here to level charges,' Ujjeni spat out, an edge to his grainy voice. 'You are here to receive charges and to be sentenced to execution like any common criminal.'

'Come now, presiding official, for I cannot dignify you by any other title, a criminal I may be in your eyes, but hardly a common one. In the first place, most criminals are lean and hungry.' He gestured at himself with hands pointing

631

inwards at his bulk. 'As you can see, I'm uncommonly fat and well-fed. Secondly, my crime is not a common one, although it would be in this kingdom of Lanka if the mass of its people had but the courage. Thirdly, I am of uncommon birth, a prince by descent, of higher rank than, shall we say, a prince by appointment.'

Gone were the '*aney*-s', the '*apoi*-s', the '*tchickay*-s.' Here was a prince indeed, by birth, by breeding, by deportment, by valour. My heart was so full of pride that it rose above my concern for Prince Jaya. But, I asked myself, why is he talking thus? Is it one grand gesture before his sentence, a fitting epitaph? Is he goading Ujjeni to some precipitate action?

'I did indeed rebel against the rule imposed on my country by your Great King,' Prince Jaya said in clear tones, slowly advancing as he spoke. 'I did not rebel against him, but against some of his laws and actions. It is fitting that you have summarily executed every patriot leader of the Kalyani kingdom, for these are the very attitudes against which we rebelled. You have during the past three days cut off some of the Naga's heads, but you must know that the Naga is a multi-headed snake. You can never destroy it, any more than you can eradicate the desire of a people to be free and equal.'

So fervent were Prince Jaya's tones, so commanding his presence, that we all listened in silence. Then he was standing beside me. He glanced sideways and noticed my manacles. He turned to face me, the dark slits of eyes peeping through their heavy lids. 'Ah, Prince,' he exclaimed sadly. 'I never thought I would bring you to this sorry pass. How dreadful that we should have to destroy our own in the process of rebirth.'

I felt rather than saw Ujjeni stir and realized that these last words could be my death knell. Yet I smiled at Prince Jaya. 'I could not choose better company in which to be destroyed,' I assured him – and meant it.

'Your words establish Prince Lala's guilt.' Ujjeni's voice was soft and evil.

Prince Jaya turned on him in the instant, with a speed remarkable for a man of his size. 'On the contrary, I am here to state that Prince Lala is entirely guiltless of any complicity in our attempt at freedom. He was totally amazed when I told him that we had assumed power. He begged me not to rebel against the Great King.'

'He begged you?' Ujjeni laughed scornfully.

'What else could he do when he had no troops, because you withdrew those who would have supported him for their nuptials, leaving your Arya rule ineffective?' A note of contempt had entered Prince Jaya's voice. 'I forced him to remain in the kingdom, under armed guard night and day.'

'The Great King would have expected him to draw his sword and die fighting all odds, rather than to submit and beg. We are rulers, not beggars.'

'Even a ruler is a beggar, as you will discover,' Prince Jaya retorted. 'He begs of his gods, he begs of himself, he begs of his ministers, his people, at least to be allowed to rule. Yes, even your summary executions are acts of beggary, for they are but an expression of the beggars you have become of your personal ambitions, beggars facing the poverty of honour of which you are bereft. This prince is innocent, I tell you.' His dark eyes opened wide as they swept the faces around the table on the platform.

'And you, Prince, shall soon beg for death,' Ujjeni promised. 'You shall be a prince of beggars.'

There was open contempt in the smile that flashed across Prince Jaya's face. 'It would not be a new role for me,' he stated evenly. 'But I promise you one thing – I shall never beg for my life, or my death. I shall command it.'

Strange words, I thought, as Prince Jaya turned to me again. 'I heard the news about your wife's death as I came down the corridors just now,' he said softly. 'I'm so sorry. How I wish . . .' A piteous expression crossed his face. 'But it

633

is too late now. The hour is indeed late, my king, my prince, my true friend, my brother. I shall take the memory of you beyond the grave, for . . . for . . .' His voice became slightly hoarse and the words came out with an effort. 'I shall always love you.'

My eyes were wet with tears that would not fall, but my love-force merged with his and he knew it. Always so hard for me to say the words, I had only once before uttered them to him. Yet I owed him one final public tribute and I made the only gesture I could in my helpless state. 'You are a king, my brother,' I declared softly. 'I love you.'

'How touching!' Ujjeni sneered, but I did not heed the words.

Prince Jaya nodded to me, smiled and began walking forward. The men at the table stared at him in surprise as he slowly ascended the steps. Ujjeni clapped his hands to his sword and rose to his feet. His chair crashed to the ground as he shoved it back. Then the naked sword gleamed in his hand. 'Back,' he shouted and came on-guard.

Ignoring him, Prince Jaya walked past the table. Slowly, ponderously, he made for the golden throne. He faced it, dropped to his knees and made obeisance to it. He rose, turned round and slowly sank to the seat. Left hand along its arm, right hand on the half-bent right knee, he sat in the pose of kings. His eyes locked with mine, his gaze calm and serene. Then I knew what he intended. Atonement, for King Ra-hula's death, a Naga on the Naga throne of Kalyani once more.

With a cry of rage, Ujjeni dashed forward, screaming. 'Foul upstart!' He lunged with his sword. A tremendous thrust, impelled by his rage, it pierced the great mass of flesh that was Prince Jaya's stomach. The other ministers sprang to their feet.

Apart from a first involuntary gasp, Prince Jaya made no move. He merely sat in the position of kings, smiled at me, giving me a message. Blood trickled around the sword and began staining the white tunic. Prince Jaya merely sat there, the sword sticking out of him, still smiling.

Beside himself with rage, Ujjeni withdrew the sword and struck again. Another gasp from Prince Jaya, another smile at me. 'A worthy successor to the throne, Prince, don't you think?' he whispered. Still he would not reveal his mortal agony. Then he reached for breath, the fleshy nostrils dilating fiercely, the mouth opening. His face began to crumple. Slowly he relaxed on the throne, Ujjeni's sword sticking out of his belly as King Tikka's had once protruded from King Ra-hula's.

On that very throne, on that very platform, in this very audience hall, Prince Jaya had triumphed in death. He had indeed proved himself a worthy successor of the Naga kings.

Uniformed guards and bare-chested attendants removed Prince Jaya's massive body from the audience hall. Not even the crumpled, sagging remains could diminish the dignity of his manner of dying. A prince in life had, within a few moments of time, become a hero in death. The contemplative silence that fell upon the audience hall when the door closed behind the group was the final tribute to his end.

His face inscrutable, Ujjeni had stood watching while the platform was cleared of the huge corpse. He then sheathed his bloody sword, resumed his seat and broke the silence. 'We cracked the back of the rebellion earlier tonight. What has just transpired is the severance of the head from an already lifeless body. All sources of danger to the Great King's rule from Naga elements have been removed.'

What need was there to decapitate a lifeless body, I sadly asked myself. Why did you murder the prince? For defying you? For daring to display incomparable dignity though he was an enemy? The truth hit me in a flash of light. Deep inside him, Ujjeni feared noble qualities. They were his real enemy, the true source of danger to him. I knew then, without conceit, that Ujjeni loathed me too, for whatever qualities of strength, nobility and courage I possessed. He would test them in me and do his best to destroy them.

'Minister Vijit, you were right,' I heard Ujjeni say. 'I recommend that we have Prince Lala's manacles removed immediately and that he remain under house arrest while he makes arrangements for his wife's funeral.'

All the ministers said 'Ahey!' in unison and Vijit flashed me a smile of congratulation.

Within minutes my manacles were removed. I rubbed my sore wrists as I walked away to seek out my living and my dead.

I went directly back to my quarters, followed by two guards. The rich, sickly scent of the unguents used to preserve dead bodies smote me as I opened the entrance door. I recalled my Sundari's delicate sandalwood scent. The living had indeed been replaced by the dead. I stood before the entrance door, remembering the times when I had opened it with such trembling expectancy. Now those times were for ever ended. When tragedy suddenly befalls us, we are numb at first. It is as if the mind refuses to acknowledge the enormity of the event immediately, in order to preserve its sanity. Then it permits us slow glimpses of the awful consequences, increasing only within our capacity to cope. As I stood in front of that door, my mind permitted me one of its first such glimpses, and my imagination caught it and sent my mind reeling back with the thunderous force of comprehension. Never again . . . never again. So many things . . . never again. How could I endure any part of it? How could I bear it all? Anguish wracked my entire being so that I had to hold on to the door for support, wishing I were insane for madness would shield me from the truth.

Then I remembered the simple courage of the woman, the loss of whom I mourned. Those moments when she was breathless, when she knew that death was not far away. Yet she had tried to spare me the knowledge, enduring it by herself, always presenting a cheerful mien. Had she been frightened, terrified, my gentle, timid Sundari? Had she felt unbearable anguish in the deep, dark loneliness of the night? I would never know. She had borne it all alone, with nobility and self-sacrifice. Now it was my turn and I knew what she would expect of me.

I resolutely closed my mind to all its images, squared my shoulders and instructed the two guards behind me to remain outside. I opened the doors and paused at the entryway.

The rooms were crowded with palace attendants, some openly weeping. My wife had been loved as gentle people are by those who have true feeling. A hush fell when I entered. The men and women prostrated themselves, without exception, in obeisance they need not have offered an ex-ruler who was under arrest. As their love and compassion flowed towards me, I responded silently with the hands together greeting, tears in my eyes. When one is grieving, nothing can unleash emotion, even in those trained to hide it, like the love-force of others, even when it is motivated by its offspring, pity. My throat began to ache. I felt I could not speak, that no sound would emerge and I would break down with my first words.

But this was not a time for weakness. 'Rise,' I commanded hoarsely, moved to the depths. As they started to get up, Sila, my wife's chief attendant, pushed her way through them. She was a plump, motherly Naga of middle-age, who had never been married and had virtually adopted Sundari in the Kalyani palace. Sila's broad features were twisted with grief, the black hair torn and dishevelled from earlier lamentation, the large eyes swollen and red-rimmed with weeping. 'Aiyo, our golden Sundari, beloved, is no more,' she cried. 'What is to become of us all? What is to become of my prince?' She placed both hands together on her lips and wafted them towards me.

Once again I became speechless. Then I realized that the only way in which I could regain control over myself was by

637

being alone. People, with their beautiful love, their sorrow, their expressions of grief, would bombard my tortured spirit in the days ahead. I simply had to prepare for the ordeal, strengthen myself for it. 'We shall make all necessary arrangements for the funeral,' I assured Sila softly, then I raised my voice for all to hear. 'I thank you, on my own behalf and on behalf of . . .' I had to pause to steady my voice . . . 'the lady whom we all loved, for your presence. Now, if you please, I would like to be alone with her one last time and I crave your understanding of it.'

They made obeisance, murmuring their sympathy, and began moving away, leaving behind their love and their tears as tangibly as if they themselves had remained. I stood in silence until the entrance door closed behind the last of them and only the hiss of flares and the residual vibrance of the mass of bodies remained. I then forced myself to walk slowly and deliberately to the bedchamber, stark dread mingling with a morbid expectancy within me.

Sundari had been clothed in a white bodice and skirt and laid out on the great canopied bed. She seemed to be sleeping with her hands clasped over her chest. In the golden taper-light, her beautiful, oval face looked exactly as it had in life, except for an unnatural grey pallor and a tightness around her mouth which must have been closed by the undertakers after her death. I paused by the bedside, looking down at her.

I wished that she would open her eyes just once so that I could see expression in them. I begged God for this single last miracle. It did not come. My throat was raw and a gush of grief flushed behind my upper lip, reaching for the tear-founts of my eyes.

I stretched out a slow, trembling hand and touched her cheek. It was deathly cold. I wished that it would give forth her warmth just once, so that I could cup it in my palm. I begged God for this single last miracle. It did not come. My throat became more raw and that gush of grief flushed behind my upper lip, reaching for the tear-founts of my eyes.

I bent down and kissed her lips. They were stiff, leathery. I wished they would give forth just one tiny breath again, so that I could take in its fragrance, feel the soft tremble of them beneath mine, know her response. I begged God for this single last miracle. It did not come.

Instead I breathed the horrible sickly-sweet smell of those unguents, meant to simulate life but which would for ever be my reminder of death.

I broke down and fell beside her, sobbing uncontrollably, my head on her cold breasts.

Long moments later, I realized why God had not given me the miracles for which I had begged. In his mercy, He knew that I could not have endured them.

Chapter 46

Enough of my grief. It is my private thing. It has no part in the history of the Sinhala nation and I will not share it either with those who find excitement or solace in the grief of others, or even with those in whom it stirs pity, compassion, memories of their own anguish.

Sundari was cremated in the palace grounds two days later. Uday presided over the Buddhist rites and preached the sermon. When it was over, I was more alone than I had ever been in my life.

My two guards remained outside when I entered Uday's cell for a visit the following morning. He returned my obeisance with his gentle smile. We then sat in the lotus pose, facing each other. He had been given new beige-coloured mats, I noticed, doubtless by a devotee. A shaft of white-gold sunlight slid through the grilled window, causing his shaven head to gleam, heightening the yellow of his robe.

I told him all that had transpired since I last met him, much of which he already knew, for news travels fast in a palace. 'Now that Sundari is gone,' I concluded, 'I am torn between my need to reside in my quarters, where her presence still remains in a very real way, and my fear of all its associations. Each piece of furniture, the linen, the statues, the tapestries, the very air of the rooms is a reminder of her absence which hits me with torturous force. Here, I held her to me, here her eyes caressed me, here her voice rippled over me like cool air on a hot day. Having lost her, I know more certainly than ever the miracle of her. She was too fine, too slender, too fragile for this world and in my heart I always knew it. The tenderest buds are most easily trampled by that heedless visitor, death.'

I paused, pondering, remembering, reluctant to bare myself further.

'Your Sundari was indeed a remarkable human being,' Uday responded. 'Sad though the occasion is, I have a secret of hers which I can now divulge to you, since I have her permission to do so if she died before you did.' He paused, drew a deep breath. 'She was aware of your loving deception as to your virility and your reason for it. She loved you all the more for your love of her.'

His words penetrated my senses with the force of a thunderclap, leaving me stunned. Tears sprang to my eyes, the pain of losing her streaked raw within me. When I finally composed myself, I decided that I owed it to Sundari to pay a last tribute to her ideal qualities as my wife. 'Sundari gave me uncompromising loyalty while she lived,' I stated, my voice breaking. 'She was unfailingly and punctiliously as obedient to me as I was to her. I could always depend on her word. She would rather die than break it, once given to me. She never discussed me disparagingly with anyone and she shunned those whom she knew to have spoken ill of me, though she always treated them with courtesy if she had to meet them. I was enough for her. She preferred to be alone with me, she said, even when I was physically absent, needing neither friends nor acquaintances to fill a gap whenever I had to be away from Kalyani, because there was no gap. An unhealthy life, some may say, but how she blossomed, how our love grew in peace and harmony, unaffected by others.' I looked squarely at Uday. 'Is it better to tend a whole garden inadequately, or to produce and nurture a single, perfect plant?'

'The answer is not important,' he responded. 'What you chose made both of you happy and in consequence you were both able to enrich the lives of others. Now you know equal anguish. Abide by your ideals and let your anguish enrich others in like manner.' A faraway look entered his eyes, surprising me. 'Remember, we too once felt such a love, though we were denied its fulfilment.' His normally gentle voice held an incredible tenderness. I recalled his love for my mother.

'You were one of the most fortunate men in the world to have had the love of a lady like Sundari,' he continued. 'Now you must pay an equal price. But your suffering does not spring from love, or from what you experienced with your beloved, so much as from desire for it, from fierce clinging to what is no more. Remember always that what you have known can never die, nor can its beauty be dimmed. It all happened. It sprang from your *kharma* and became a part of it. It is natural for you to desire what was, but you will be better able to absorb your pain if you slowly abandon desiring what you cannot have, finding joy instead in what remains of your beautiful experiences. Words, philosophy, even religion cannot ease your wounds, yet you must always keep in the forefront of your mind that your pain is caused by clinging, begotten of desire. You alone, not life, are the master of your desire. Whenever you are smitten by the devils of longing inside you, by the need to share with your Sundari as of old, by the desire to touch her hand, to look into her eyes, to hear the melody of her voice, experience it in your mind, where alone it really existed. Tell yourself firmly that all is ended in the form in which you desire it, but will never cease in the form you knew it. Assure yourself of the things that will never end, whence your love came, the memories of your life and whither all these will lead you. Your wife was a good woman. She will have a good rebirth. So will you, because you are a good man. But you must firmly set yesterday aside, to the extent that it creates clinging, in order to take command of your suffering today and tomorrow.'

'But I simply cannot avoid clinging to all that was good, Sundari's goodness, my memories, her tangible presence, the desire to see her. My yearning for that fulfilment often becomes a raw, white fire that sears the sides of my brain, streaking towards madness.'

'You will continue torturing yourself while you cling to what is transient, my dear.' He lifted his eyes to the shaft of sunlight. 'See how beautiful are the sun's rays. They seem even more tangible because of the motes dancing in them.' His gaze dropped to meet mine. 'Yet that shaft of light is as transient as the shadows it seems to pierce, while its source, the sun, remains, to endure even after its own phenomenal power is extinguished because of all it has wrought, the life it has created, or destroyed in order to recreate. What is the truth, what is reality? The sun, the shaft, or the shadow it pierces? Can you grasp any of them? Yet they are all beautiful. When evening comes, they will blend into yellow taper-light and, when the tapers are extinguished, darkness will absorb everything. Yet even total darkness is not an absolute reality. You must therefore enjoy the beauty of the sunlight, the taper-light, the darkness, without clinging to any of them, if you are to know peace. So too with your memories, the feel of your wife's tangible presence in your rooms. They are like scent on fine linen, which, if not renewed, will grow fainter with each passing day, until hardly a hint of the fragrance remains. Then you can only breathe it and clothe your senses with it through the strength of your imagining and the power of your recall, for what created the beauty for you was there all the time and did not need the scent on the linen in the first place. Give back joyously of your pain to the beauty you have known, but do not add to it, or spoil it with the misery of yearnings that can never be fulfilled. If you deliberately recall the doctrine during your worst moments of longing, you will slowly become strengthened by the only true reality, the only enduring reality, the doctrine itself, until you are freed of the suffering.'

I nodded my assent. 'What you say is true, venerable Sir, but it is so difficult to achieve. Now I must confess to you that I have discovered a more ready source of comfort and aid. I have turned to my God in my despair.'

He did not seem surprised, or shocked. 'We have been aware of your belief in One God,' he asserted, to my amazement.

'Who told you?'

His smile was inscrutable. 'You of all people must know that we do not need to be told.' He reflected a moment. 'Lord Buddha did not say there is no God, so tell us of your God. Is He Ahura Mazda, the Creator of Life, the Source of light and power, whom Zarathustra discovered?'

'No.'

'Is He then the One God, the jealous God of the Juda, Who appeared to the prophet Moh-zur in a burning bush?'

'No, venerable Sir.'

'Who is He then?'

'Infinity in terms of space, eternity in time, the Being Who encompasses everything, contains even the *kharmic* law that Lord Buddha discovered. He is the enlightenment that Lord Buddha attained.'

Uday's dark eyes widened slightly. 'You mean that all creation, all time and space, where we came from, whither we are going, are within His body?'

'Creation, a beginning, an end, a body, a corpse, are all human concepts, venerable Sir. We create everything, even the doctrine, even God, from our very limited powers of observation, comprehension and deduction. God is an eternal moment, infinite within our limited comprehension, inside that moment in which we live and move and have our being. Yet even we, as we see ourselves, are not real, but consist of millions of parts, the *paramanu*, atoms, the *paramattas*, components of each atom, of which our Lord Buddha spoke, all of which have their separate realities. So our realities, our concepts, our minds, are circumscribed by the fact that we are not really a complete entity, by our component parts and by entities of which we too are components. We cannot discern eternal truths, only create philosophies. This is why we make God in our own image, as a person, a He, a Him. We can only know the real truth and speak with the tongues of men and of angels when we can see ourselves through God. Then alone can we comprehend that God is the Father, we are the Son and that that comprehension is the blessing of the Holy Ghost. Do we not know more about the truths of the component parts of our bodies than those parts do of themselves? Can they ever begin to comprehend who or what we are? Do they not merely clamour to us for help, the stomach saying, feed me, the skin saying, scratch me?'

He closed his eyes. I noticed the fine line of each of the lids beneath the long, dark lashes. 'You were ever the precocious child,' he murmured, then shook his head slowly from side to side. In the extended silence, I became aware of the scent of incense from a brazier-stand beneath the window and the soughing of a breeze trickling through the green branches outside. 'You say you find comfort in your God?' He finally enquired.

'Yes, by prayer and the knowledge of His love-force that binds us all as one.'

'Thunder, lightning, earthquakes, shooting stars?'

'They are all eruptions within His body, just as wind in a man's stomach, blemishes on his skin, are part of the human body. Do we care any the less for our bodies because of these apparent frailties? There is nothing wrong with any of them. Even seeming conflict is a part of the love that binds us. Fear of it is only in our minds.'

'So enemies are no different from a blemish on the skin? Thunder and lightning are a part of what *is*?'

'Precisely. And when we love them, the pain they inflict on us ceases to be effective, becomes pain in the essence, without the terrible preface of terror, the hideous aftermaths of hatred, bitterness, resentment, the desire for vengeance. A mother does not love the product of her body any the less because it is born blind or crippled. So the love of God

645

extends alike to the good and the bad as we see them. The laws of *kharma/vipaka*, cause and effect, that exist within God's infinite body are not intended as punishment or reward, which are human concepts, products of the limited human mind. God has no intentions, no purposes. He merely *is*. But His love is available to us, so is His succour, provided we seek it in the form in which He has it to give. His laws *are* – and that is the finest truth of Lord Buddha's enlightenment. The nature of the entity will always feel good or bad according to those eternal laws.'

Long moments passed while Uday remained deep in thought. He finally opened his eyes and stared beyond me, as if I were not present. 'Your belief in God and your faith in prayer will strengthen you,' he said, in a calm voice. 'Your doctrine of love, even towards your enemies, will assure you a good *kharma*. Do not cling to these beliefs, however, or seek to derive benefit from them. Rather let them flow from you.' His eyes slowly moved to mine. 'You should continue living in your quarters until they have ceased to overcome you. Then you may want to retire to a cell.' His gaze became blank, as if shutting out things of which he did not wish to speak.

For my part, I was fiercely glad to have expressed my belief in God freely to him at last. For the first time in my life, the spirit of God was so truly within me from the depths of my anguish and loss that I was ready to begin my ministry for Him, even in an alien, hostile world. I realized with deep joy that Uday and I were in closer communion than ever before. It was as if the love of God to which I had opened his consciousness – yes, I say this without conceit – bound us closer together as a part of Him, the heart and the lungs, the pulse and the breath, teacher and pupil, the scion of Sinha and Sinha's aide, the man who could have been the father and the product of another man, the son.

A knocking on the door interrupted our communion. I rose to my feet but Uday remained seated as the door slowly opened. Vijit stood framed at the entrance. I was struck once again by the similarity of his features with Uday's. Apart from Vijit's moustache and black hair, they had the same fair skin, fine, dark eyes and chiselled features.

Ever courteous, Vijit made salutation to Uday and me, in turn. 'I'm sorry to intrude,' he said. 'But I did not wish to leave Kalyani without saying farewell to Prince Lala.'

My heart sank. 'You're going?' I enquired.

'Yes. My presence is urgently required at Vijitapura, due to a drought that is beginning to cause food shortages. I leave before noon.'

'I had hoped to call on you to thank you for your kind intervention the night my wife died. You brought human dignity to the proceedings and I shall never forget that you alone made it possible for me to grieve for my princess in solitude. Unfortunately, I was somewhat incommoded by being under house arrest, so I could not contact you.'

He flushed and cleared his throat to hide his embarrassment. 'It's nothing,' He declared. That devil-may-care smile flashed across his face. 'Till we meet again, courage, Prince. The Great King will be fully recovered soon and all will be well with you.'

'Will the other ministers remain here?'

'No. They return to their respective areas this morning.'

My heart lifted. Ujjeni would be gone too, so my fears were groundless. Being under house arrest meant nothing to me. Once the Great King recovered, I would indeed be safe.

'Since Prince Jaya is dead and you, Prince Lala, are, as you say, somewhat incommoded, Prince Ujjeni and Uraw alone will remain in Kalyani to govern the sub-kingdom.'

I spent the rest of the morning in my quarters. Clad in a loose white *kurtha* and *dhoti*, I sat in meditation trying to conquer my mind by putting into practice all that Uday, whom I believed to be God's messenger for this occasion, had told me and to find peace with my dead wife through prayer and God's love. When the attendants brought in the noon meal of *chupatti* and chicken, I asked them to leave it and retire. The smell of crushed coriander and spices only sickened me. I had been hard put to it to eat since Sundari died and I wondered how I could force some of the food down my throat.

A few minutes later, a thunderous knocking on my entrance door disturbed my reflections. I opened the door to find Ujjeni confronting me. He was accompanied by a somewhat shamefaced Uraw and half a dozen stolid-faced guards, all his own select troops, I noted. I should have been afraid, but strangely I was not. No suffering Ujjeni might inflict on me could be greater than that which I was already experiencing.

I greeted Ujjeni politely. 'Ah, Prince, I am glad to see you.' I half-turned and gestured towards my rooms. 'Do come in. I have not eaten as yet. Would you care to partake of the noonday meal with me?'

He was momentarily taken aback. 'We are not here to visit you,' he declared brusquely. 'You are under formal arrest once again.'

'On what charges, pray?'

'As before, treason and heresy.'

I lifted my eyebrows. 'I thought your colleagues in the Council of Ministers had already decided that investigation of these charges could await the Great King's return.' My gaze shifted to Uraw, who dropped his eyes. 'You, Minister Uraw, were a party to that decision, were you not?'

'You are in no position to question my decision,' Ujjeni broke in roughly. 'I owe you no explanation as to my conduct. I'm the sub-king of Kalyani as of this moment and indeed, as Prince Regent, I rule all Lanka, under the Great King's mandate in his absence.'

'Surely you can, in that capacity, act only in accordance with the Great King's laws and as he would have dictated.'

A sneering cackle escaped Ujjeni. 'You of all people say

that? Is that the code you have followed all these years?'

Sadly I realized that he but spoke the truth. For eight years I had enforced the Great King's laws, but interpreting them in accordance with my own ideals and principles whenever possible, following my own dictates. 'You are right,' I granted.

The simple admission seemed to infuriate Ujjeni more than any denial or argument. He jerked his head over his shoulder. 'Guards, seize the traitor,' he commanded. 'Manacle him.'

'There is no need . . .' I began, but stopped as the men swept forward. Iron manacles gleamed in the hands of one. They grabbed me roughly and chained my wrists behind my back.

'Move!' Ujjeni grated, standing aside to let us pass.

I was shoved forward so brutally that I nearly stumbled. Recovering, I came erect. I resolved not to lose my dignity at any cost. Head held high, circled by guards, I strode down the corridor without a single glance at Ujjeni or Uraw, knowing they would follow. To my surprise, we turned right at the verandah and walked towards the rear of the palace. A warm breeze blowing from the *meda midula* brought the smell of baked earth and made me glance towards its source. The green-leaved jasmine bushes were stiff and crackly in the fierce noonday sunlight, the splash of the water cascade seemed but a fruitless attempt to penetrate the heat. I began to sweat and smelled an acid odour from one of the guards. A mynah fluttered its wings, shrilled and grumbled then settled back on its perch. A crow cawed sadly from the branches of the *banyan* tree under which Uday and I had sat so often to partake of his *dana*, pre-noon meal. My eyes went instinctively to the balcony verandah of the second floor on which I had first seen Sundari and my heart caught, my throat tightened and ached. No matter, I told myself resolutely. She entered my life through that verandah and is within me now.

We entered a shadowy corridor and paused before a great wooden door. Then I knew where Ujjeni was taking me. In the days before King Ra-hula succeeded to the Kalyani throne, a fierce Naga king had built dungeons into which he cast his enemies. I had visited them once, out of curiosity. They consisted of dank, humid cells that had not been used for years. The air was foul, the smell noisome. I had intended closing them up for ever but never got round to it.

I turned round slowly and deliberately, ignoring Ujjeni, Uraw and the guards behind me, to look just once more at God's sunlight, to see His visible presence and find its link with the darkness that awaited me.

When we reached the bottom of the steps, the four flaming torches stuck in bronze sconces, two at each side of the trap-door that led to the dungeons, told me that the way had been prepared for me. One of the guards, a short stocky fellow, his red tunic wet with the sweat from his armpits, seized one of the torches. His companion flung open the trap-door. A gust of fetid air reached greedily for me. Two other guards also picked up torches.

Preceded by the stocky guard holding his torch aloft, I walked down another flight of steps followed by my captors. For an instant I wondered whether I should not fling myself upon the guard and attempt to escape, but I knew that would be futile.

When I reached the bottom, I heard the rattle of the trap-door closing above, shutting out all possibility of escape. The air was suddenly so thick and black that the hissing of the torches sounded impotent as their golden flames tried to pierce the gloom. We walked down a short corridor lined by narrow cells with heavy metal-studded doors, which had traps at the bottom through which food could be passed to the wretched prisoners. I was bathed in sweat now, but felt a cold chill run through my body as we tramped towards what I knew to be the torture chamber. In my mind's eyes, I saw that hideous room with the rusted rack, chains hanging from the roof, the furnace and bellows with metal spikes for putting eyes out, the sharp needle-pointed tapers to be inserted beneath the fingernails and lighted. We went past the door of this chamber before I could conjure up the other horrors of a past barbaric rule and I sighed with relief.

We paused before the wooden door at the far end of the corridor which I knew opened to a long narrow room. Instead of entering this however, the guard opened the door of the last cell to our right. He stood aside, faced me and jerked his head to his left, bidding me enter. I had no option but to walk in. He placed his torch on a sconce just inside the cell. Only Ujjeni and Uraw followed me. The door closed behind us with a muffled thud.

I took stock of my cramped surroundings. The kings of old did not believe in pampering their prisoners. The roof was but a few inches above my six-foot height, the cell itself about eight feet long and four feet wide. The small wooden table and two settles, all heavily coated with dust, were a luxury! A mat spread on the grey, pressed-earth floor and a metal bucket, rusty with age, at the far end, completed the furnishings. The bucket had not been needed for years, but the aftermath of its use remained, the stench of a well-aged mixture of urine, faeces and vomit. The silence was absolute until I heard the vibrations of the room, the groans of men in mortal agony, smelt ancient blood, sensed the hopelessness and despair and identified the scurrying of a rat.

'Sit down, Prince,' Ujjeni bade me harshly, taking one of the settles. His voice bounced off the walls and resounded within the narrow confines of the cell, making my skin jitter.

'You'll have to talk a little more softly if we're not to be flattened by sound alone,' I remarked lightly, sitting opposite him. 'I'm sorry the limited accommodation does not permit me to offer you the hospitality of a seat, Minister,' I told Uraw.

My attitude had the desired effect. Ujjeni's face became contorted with rage and the glint of mad hatred sparked

651

from his eyes, but he controlled himself. 'There'll be more than mere sound before we're through with you, Prince,' he snarled.

'I see the fury is already present. What else is there?'

'You'll see.' His voice was evil. 'You'll see.' He paused, staring at me. I returned his gaze with such gentleness that I was able to stare him down. I wondered how Uraw was reacting to our play, then suddenly realized that it was more ancient than the hills, no different from the struggle between rushing water and the quiet earth, the creeping of jungle on man, the clash of what we call good and evil within the body of God.

Ujjeni looked away, then spoke reflectively. 'You are in my power now, Prince Lala,' he declared quietly. 'I give you one of two choices. Write out a full confession of your guilt and you shall go free, though your punishment will be exile. You could, however, become a Buddhist monk, be anything you like outside Lanka.'

He wanted the confession to justify his actions, and the temptation to give it was there, I'll not deny, for I was weary of conflict and afraid of the dungeon. Getting away, being alone with my grief and my memories, my enemy was indeed offering a gift. 'To what am I supposed to confess?'

'I've already told you, treason against the Great King and heresy against our Arya gods.'

The temptation was still there, like some insidious bait to hook an unsuspecting fish. 'What evidence do you have against me?' I demanded.

He raised a long, clawlike index finger. 'First, treason.' He grinned. 'I have the letter you wrote to the Great King, attacking his policies and threatening to side with the rebellious Nagas.'

'That was never meant . . .' I began, then stopped, realizing the futility of protestations. 'Has the Great King read that letter?' I enquired instead.

'Yes. He believes that you sent it to him.'

This was no more than I suspected. 'And the Great King is convinced of my guilt on a single piece of evidence?'

'It sets the seal on your conduct through the years. Two,' he raised his middle finger, 'I have acquired other evidence of your disloyalty and disobedience.' He scratched the side of his mouth and gave his hee . . . hee . . . hee . . . laugh, only this time it was as malignant as the gust of foul breath that smote me. 'You flagrantly disobeyed the Great King's instructions that neither the Princess Kuveni, nor her children, nor any of her retinue were to be permitted within the sub-kingdom. The woman Rupa, with whom you recently met, and the two misbegotten children have vanished, but we shall find them.' His voice dropped a couple of tones. 'We shall indeed find them.'

A chill hand laid its fingers on my heart. This man knew everything. I prayed silently to God for the safety of Rupa and the children.

'A far more serious crime, however, is the pardon you gave the man Hamy, who was chief aide to King Tikka. How could you do such a thing, Prince Lala?' He was genuine in his righteous rage now. 'To give aid, comfort and protection to such a man, knowing that only a few days before his master sought to assassinate our Great King?'

'I have reasons which I shall explain to the Great King, with the certainty of his understanding.' I was too proud to tell Ujjeni that having Hamy on our side would help us track down King Tikka some day, for Hamy knew his master's whims and fancies, his motivation, the way he would act, his secret abodes.

'I must judge you on the evidence I have, Prince Lala,' Ujjeni rejoined quietly. 'Protestations and explanations cannot contradict the evidence.'

The evidence could be made to look overwhelming. The prospect of torture, discomfort, darkness, solitude suddenly smote me, made me panic. 'If I sign a confession what assurance have I that you will keep your side of the bargain?'

'None.'

My eyes flickered to Uraw. 'Would you be my witness to the bargain, Minister?'

Uraw hesitated, his pudgy features, bathed in sweat, were strained. 'I shall be your witness, Prince,' he responded. 'I cannot guarantee you a safe exile, but I shall at least endeavour to end your imprisonment.'

'With what? Surely even death would end it.'

'Death would be cleaner. You were our comrade once.' Uraw obviously had no stomach for what lay in store for me if I refused. Nor did I.

I looked down, considering my options. None of them were attractive. In fact, they were all singularly repugnant to me. The stench of the cell had begun to sear my nostrils, mingling with the resin from the steadily burning torch that added to the heat. Now I also heard the squeak of rats and saw two cockroaches scurry away from that bucket, which suddenly became a symbol of all I wanted to escape from. To justify my craven desires, I told myself that the principle of right and wrong would remain, regardless of whether I signed a bogus confession or not, nor could Ujjeni destroy the truth of my innocence.

I lifted my eyes to Ujjeni. 'I'll sign the confession,' I heard myself say and marvelled that the voice did not seem to come from me but from that stinking bucket.

He grinned his triumph, placed his elbows on the desk, leaned forward and gave his mirthless hee . . . hee . . . hee . . . laugh again, his foul breath smiting me once more. 'And you will admit your heretical beliefs, confess that you are a filthy Juda who believes in Jahweh, that you abstain from eating the flesh of pigs and believe in circumcision, so that your foreskin can be severed with granite and offered to your God?'

He could say whatever he pleased, for his words were just words to me, no more. I let them flow over me while I clung to the sweet, white knowledge of my objective, the hope of

654

my freedom, the end of conflict and anguish, the beginning of a time when I could mourn for my dead love in peace and work towards achieving enlightenment. Nothing this beast, Ujjeni, got me to say could strip me of my inner dignity. 'Yes,' I replied firmly.

'And you will recant? You will admit that you have been mistaken, that your God is a false God, that only the Arya gods exist and have all power over living things, over trees, rivers and oceans, mountains and valleys, the wind and the rain, over life itself? You will reject your heretical One God and swear allegiance to the pantheon of our gods?'

I was about to say 'Yes,' because nothing I said or wrote could destroy the truth of my beliefs, when the torch suddenly spurted a higher flame and a lizard chirped its ill omen. Unaccountably, the stench of the cell was suddenly tinged with the scent of sandalwood. The fetid cell, the evil man, Ujjeni, slowly receded from my gaze. A great white light shone before me, bathing me in its radiance. My body felt hot, but my skin was cool. Figures began to float before me. Sinha, my grandmother, the Princess Suppa-devi, my father, Sinha-Bahu, my mother, Sinha-Seevali, the dusky Princess Kuveni, the six men of the Kalyani mission to Devun Dara, Prince Jaya. Each pointed a finger at me, saying, 'Learn from our experience. *You* can just as easily destroy the truth, by not acknowledging it, or by denying it.' Then my beloved Sundari appeared, lying on her bier, clad in white. She rose to a sitting position, gazed at me, her beautiful dark eyes wet with tears and whispered, 'I gave you my love, my trust, my faith. You never once lied to me. You were always the soul of honour. Would you deny me now?' She was wafted away on unseen wings.

The white light faded, leaving a stinking blackness, the dark that lay ahead for me. As it filled the cell, God's voice thundered through the firmament: 'I am the Way, the Truth, the Light. You have denied me twice tonight. Will you deny me a third time, knowing that lies and untruths blemish my body?'

'Never!' I cried out in a loud voice. The word thudded off the walls and bounced back at me. 'Never! . . . Never! . . . Never! . . .' Ujjeni swam back in focus. The cell was hot, the torchlight golden, the stench unbearable. With great gladness in my heart, with the shining, white light of my freedom from fear illuminating my mind, with the love of God in my spirit, I looked levelly at Ujjeni and repeated the word. 'Never!' I shook my head, smiling at him, the love of God within me reaching for him. 'The One God is the true God. He is Jahweh, Ahura Mazda and my very own God. He is all things that men of vision have comprehended and believed in. Your pantheon of gods is a part of Him but only because you believe in these gods and what is in your mind is a part of God's body. You may do with me as you will, Prince Ujjeni, but nothing you do can match God's power within me, or erase the truth, or take away His love, which I extend to all things, all men, including you. I forgive you for whatever you have done, for whatever you may do to me. If I must die, I shall go to my death loving you.'

Ujjeni's eyes flamed with a diabolical hatred such as I had never before seen, even in him. His dark, tight-drawn skin sagged. He gibbered his hatred at me and foam appeared at the sides of his mouth. You are indeed the devil, I thought. You represent all the forces of evil that naturally oppose whatever is good. But you know with certainty the one enemy against whom you cannot prevail, because it is the absence of that enemy in your life that created you evil. It is the power of love. 'The love of God that emanates from me shall always be with your spirit, Prince Ujjeni,' I said softly to him.

He rose to his feet, shaking and trembling, hands raised as if to ward off an attack. He sent the table crashing to a side and reeled towards the door, gasping with rage. He opened the door. Its movement and his passage caused the torchlight to waver. He left behind the ghastly odour of rotting flesh in the cell.

Uraw and I were left alone, gazing at each other in a blank communion.

Chapter 47

We righted the table, linked by some common bond that had arisen between us. Uraw sat on the settle Ujjeni had vacated. Long moments of silence passed.

'I have suspected of late that Prince Ujjeni is mad,' Uraw finally ventured, low-voiced, so that no one could hear from outside the cell. 'Now I am certain.'

'What are you going to do about it?' I enquired, also in hushed tones.

'Nothing. I'm a follower, not a leader. Apart from Ujjeni, only Vijit and Anu among us ministers are real leaders. They have both left Kalyani, as you know, and Anu is, in any case, a staunch ally of Ujjeni. No one would believe me if I told them Ujjeni is mad, for they only see his genius. And now they can also see his power.'

'I understand. What hope is there that the Great King will recover soon?'

'I have every hope. The day we left Devun Dara, he remembered his name. Not much more, not even who he was, but it was certainly a beginning. The physician said it could all come back to him suddenly.'

'Let us pray for all our sakes that the Great King will recover.' I paused, reflecting, debating whether to broach the subject, then decided that I had nothing to lose. 'You said that you believe Prince Ujjeni is mad. Is that all you believe?'

He stared at me with a defensive blankness in his eyes. Barely conscious of the sweltering heat, the sweat pouring down my body and the hideous stench of the cell, I directed my love-force towards him, until the barrier of his reticence dissolved. "I now believe that Ujjeni is an embodiment of evil,' he stated.

I was glad that I had Uraw's independent judgement. 'What does he intend with me?' I asked.

'He seeks those full confessions from you, so that he can discredit and damn you in the eyes of all men, especially your brother, thus vindicating his actions through the years. He also wants to eliminate you in any contest for succession to the Great King's throne. During the past few days, with the Great King removed from the scene, he has tested the power for which he has always yearned and striven. He is determined to perpetuate it.'

'Will the other ministers permit this?'

'Prince Ujjeni holds the reins of power from Thamba-Panni. There is no one to compete with him. I believe his plan would be to rule through the Council of Ministers, wielding the real power himself.'

'What about Vijit?'

'Vijit may well establish a sub-kingdom of his own, using his mighty fortress as a base. But he is an honest, simple, loyal man and a confirmed bachelor, so Prince Ujjeni will probably be able to manipulate him.' Uraw paused, then looked me straight in the eye. 'But I have a much more important matter to discuss with you.' His eyes searched my face intently as if trying to probe my spirit. 'Can I trust you?'

I wondered what he wanted. 'To the hilt,' I readily assured him.

'You proved yourself worthy of trust just now,' he quietly rejoined. 'By standing behind your principles.'

I warmed to Uraw, a little regretful that I had not had more communion with him during the past years.

'I have written extensively on *olas* my side of our story since we landed in Lanka,' he continued. 'I shall entrust them and anything I may add in the future to your friend, Uday, the Venerable Sri Ra-vindra, for safekeeping. They contain too much of the truth for my own safety!' He grinned wryly. 'Prince Ujjeni desires me to record our history, but I know he wants it to perpetuate his glory. This I shall do separately and he will find joy in reading the legend I shall create! I know that you have written your own official version of the tale. You did well to hide it. I shall arrange for Uday to visit you with my *olas* and for you to have the time, material and opportunity to complete your history, even if you remain in this cell.'

I was swept by a feeling of exhilaration. Uraw's version was all I needed to complete the story. 'Why would you do this?' I demanded.

'I'm neither a soldier nor an administrator.' He shrugged. 'Oh, I'm adequate in both capacities, I know, but I prefer writing to fighting, which is what administration too is about, when all is said and done. I believe in truth. The only sense of mission I have is to hand the truth down to posterity. Of all the Great King's comrades, I alone sense that one of the reasons why you accompanied us into exile is because you felt that it was your destiny to record it. So you and I have affinities in this sense. If I am wrong, please do not tell me. I would rather go on believing the illusion.'

I was amazed at Uraw's sensitivity. 'You are right indeed,' I hastened to assure him. 'What I find incredible is your sensitivity and perception.' I paused. 'And yet, why not? These are the qualities of the writer.'

He smiled, albeit sadly. 'Then we are one in truth and in our mission.'

'Yes, but please tell me how we can accomplish it, for I fear the sands in my clock are running out.'

He did not attempt to ease me with falsehood. 'They could well be running out for you, Prince, but only Prince Ujjeni knows what he intends – and I sometimes wonder whether even he does.' He gathered his thoughts. 'What I know is that he will return shortly to place you in solitary confinement. You will remain in darkness, not knowing the passage of time, under the threat of being executed at dawn. You will be weakened by being given very little food, dry *chupatti* and a little water once a day, yet the corridor outside will contain highly spiced dishes to tantalize you with their odours. This will go on until you break. If you do not, more will follow, I am sure, but I do not know what.' Tears filled his eyes and his voice broke. 'This is the price we must pay for inspired leadership at times. I'm sorry to be a part of it, but I don't have your courage.'

I reached over instinctively and placed a clammy hand over his, noticing the fine black hairs along the lower joints of his fingers and at his wrist. 'You must not worry,' I declared. 'You have done more than most people would dare.'

His face broke up. He drew a deep breath and a sob escaped him, then he steadied himself. 'I had best be going now,' he said hastily. 'But first, know this. Prince Ujjeni will be away from the palace on official errands from time to time. I arrange the guard rosters, so I shall ensure that only my own trusted men are on guard duty over you during these times. You will then have more food, water, a light, your *ola* materials and, when possible, Uday's company. This can be done when Ujjeni is away for the night, as he will have to be on a couple of occasions. It could be for as many as four days whenever he visits Thamba-Panni, but destroying you in slow degrees will now be his prime goal.'

'I have nothing I can give you for your kindness. I shall, however, faithfully document our mission, as you call it. In this and in adherence to the truth, I shall not fail you. Your real reward will, however, be in what your thoughts, words and deeds have made you. *Kharma/vipaka*, cause and effect. I feel you are receptive to this knowledge, so I shall ask Uday to give it to you. Your discussions with him can do you no harm for, after all, the doctrine is called the *Noble* Eightfold Path.' Uraw left immediately afterwards. Ujjeni did not return, but guards entered soon, freed me of my manacles and removed the flaming torch from the cell. I was left in total darkness.

Fighting down the first feelings of panic, I took stock of my situation, calmly deciding to examine each aspect of it separately.

Firstly, the darkness, so intense that there was no hope that the eyes would become accustomed to it. Frankly, it held no terror for me. As a matter of fact, I had always loved total blackness at night. It is so restful to the eyes and soothing to the spirits, if we do not allow primordial fears to beset us. Too long a period of confinement would of course affect my eyesight, but that was the least of my worries and, after all, Uraw had assured me of relief from time to time.

I must confess that I had some qualms about the rats, cockroaches and other crawling bugs, but I reasoned that these were living things, more afraid of me than I was of them. They would only approach me when there was food around or when I slept. They were welcome to nuzzle me, if they so desired. Did the floor and the roof, over which they constantly crawled, fear them? No, distaste for them could only exist in my mind, of which I had to be the complete master.

The awful stench. How could I possibly ignore the stench, which would undoubtedly grow worse after I started using the bucket? I wondered how often the sweepers would remove it, or whether they would ever remove it, just so that I could be punished the more. Strangely, the recollection of my bodily functions helped. I reasoned that whatever I released was already within me, the stench in my system, a poison simmering there in its potential. The process of elimination could of course make it worse as my faecal matter and urine rotted, but there would be no real stench, nor unbearable heat for that matter, if I did not recoil from them. The ill effects on my lungs and system I could do nothing about, but at least there were no flies here and I would regulate my breathing, *yogi* fashion, by which I was able even to simulate death. I would take only tiny breaths of air through the mouth, instead of the nose, to avoid smells.

My starvation diet and lack of activity would thus be a help rather than a hindrance, because they would create lesser demands within my body and reduce my levels of elimination.

I needed exercise, to keep my blood flowing, though gently, enough to prevent my body and mind from atrophy. I would exercise whenever my body told me of its need. I fiercely commanded my brain to compel my motive self to this end, regardless of how feeble I felt, or how much I lacked the energy through heat prostration – the heat was already intense and sweat was pouring down my body – and exhaustion from my inadequate diet. One can indeed command the brain so that it will act in reflex motion. It is no different from setting a sand clock to a certain time in one's mind when one wants to awaken at an unusual hour.

How to exercise the mind? I decided to go over every part of my life, from my first conscious moments up to the present time, over and over again, if necessary, but slowly and in orderly progression, re-living each thought, word and the sequence of deeds as they occurred. This would not only keep my brain active, but would also teach me mind control, help pass the time and enable me to relive my life with my beloved Sundari.

I could think of only one final problem, that of being able to know time. In what manner could I tell the passage of time? As I pondered this question with no solution, I wondered how much time had elapsed since I was consigned to total darkness. Why is that so important, a voice within me enquired. And I repeated this new question aloud to myself. Why is time important? Hearing my own voice made me realize that I should exercise the faculty of speech as well. I would recite Buddhist stanzas aloud. Ah! The blessed words of those stanzas would also help eliminate the oppressive atmosphere of past misery that lay so heavily within my abode.

But time . . . what is time but a unit of measure based

upon the movements of the sun? God is eternal, and since we are part of His body, time does not exist for Him, but was devised for human beings so that they can measure periods of sleeping and waking, look from meal to meal, task to task, process to process. Other living creatures do not consciously measure time, as far as I am aware, but use day and night, dawn, afternoon and dusk, for their eating, resting and wandering habits. Birds find refuge in their nests at night, apparently to avoid its dangers, yet the snake, the cat can crawl silently to devour them while they sleep and they are perhaps safer while awake and alert. Time as a unit of measure no longer need exist for me, I decided, especially if I lived each moment, each facet of the existence to which I had been condemned, to the fullest, without hoping for the moments of relief or fearing the times of torture.

Pain from torture, I did fear, but terror was a product of my mind and I had learned to separate the body's anguish from the messages it sent my brain. This was what King Rahula had done through his power of mind control and what Prince Jaya had accomplished through another form of mind control, pride, determination and an unflinching adherence to a goal. I would try to meet torture in the same way.

I too had my goal, the glorifying of God and the establishment of God in man. All my *yoga* training, my inheritance from Sinha and my parents, my breeding as a prince, were *kharma*, causes, that could produce my desired *vipaka*, the effects. It was God's will made manifest, not through some pre-ordained timetable or destiny, but merely because His laws of cause produce His inevitable effects.

I can never convey the discomfort, fatigue and terror I fought in my filthy dungeon cell, in spite of my grand rationalizing and my resolves, the number of times my gorge rose, fear emerged screaming silently from my throat and panic seized my whole being. This I will say, however, that each time I fought down these impulses I was left trembling and shaking, but the stronger for the next bout. Perhaps the greatest degree of self-control I had to exercise was not to respond to the tiny scittering-scattering noises in the dark, not to panic each time invisible creatures crawled over me and I instinctively recoiled against the contact, my skin juddering, nausea welling up within me. I finally decided that I would sleep sitting up, with my back against the wall, so that I would not feel so helpless. The time for sleep should have been some hours away, but heat, thirst and tension soon made me feel drowsy. I knew that this too was a battle I had to fight. Excessive sleep would be easy, but it would be bad for me physically, slowing down the processes of my body and my brain, rendering me torpid, affecting me mentally, by undermining my disciplines. I thanked God for the temperate existence I had always led, which had better prepared my body and mind for this ordeal.

My ever reachable source of comfort and strength was God.

Uraw had given me a clue as to how I could keep a rough measure of time when he said that I would be fed once a day. I reckoned that it must be dusk when I heard footsteps in the corridor. The trap on the cell door clicked open, revealing a square of pale light, which I greedily gazed at before it was partially blocked by the platter that was pushed through it, scraping the floor in its passage. I was thankful for the sound, human sound, and resolved that I would enjoy it at least once a day. I picked up the cold *chupatti*, forcing myself to eat slowly despite the clamour of my hunger, prolonging my enjoyment of it, killing time with the act of eating. When I had finished, I curbed the desire to drink every drop of the mug of water and took but a sip of it.

Time moves so slowly here, on fettered feet, dragging great iron balls attached to them. The darkness is total and complete. It creates revolving circles beneath my closed lids. The smell of my own sweat has begun to creep through that dreadful stench of aged excretions and I am hard pressed not to be revolted by my own uncleanliness.

Tiny feet are crawling up my bare hand. Panic-stricken desires to slap at the creature, to jerk away, to move to safety almost overwhelm me. I fight them down, giddy with the effort. Scurrying noises and tiny squeaks urge my skin to judder at the threat of sharp rat's teeth. I tell myself that others have endured this wretchedness and survived. Others yet have killed themselves and triumphed. Death. That would be sweet relief, a closer link to re-birth with my Sundari. I have nothing with which to kill myself. Oh God, why have you inflicted this misery on me? No, no, this is something I brought on myself. It is not Your will, God, but only a manifestation of Your law.

I fought the panic impulses for hours, until I triumphed and then fell into a stertorous sleep, exhausted, my nose raw, unmindful of my resolve to regulate the texture of my sleeping. My mind found its release in sweet dreams of cool, green hills and pleasant meadows carpeted with yellow and pink daisies. I walked with Sundari beside a winding, silver stream that chuckled and babbled over white sand and black and red stones.

Where then does the stench of blood and vomit, urine and faeces emerge from? Why is my body fevered though my skin is cool before a gentle breeze?

On the fourth evening, Ujjeni returned. I knew it was the fourth day because I had been served three meals. It must be evening because I gauged that it was about time for my next meal. He had timed his visit for what in a normal man would have been the breaking point, the period when the body and mind are at their weakest because they have not adjusted to the starvation diet, memories of freedom are still fresh and despair has not yet hardened to unbreakable resolve.

I had taken to improving my hearing by counting the footfalls of the guards who brought in my meal. The first night I could count only six sets of steps, today I actually counted nine. Any change, however slight, relieved the terrible monotony. The creaking of the cell door as it opened was music to my ears, a new sound, like a brief melody arising above the drumbeat of footfalls, this time of four persons. The torchlight, however, hurt my eyes, causing me to blink back the stinging tears.

Once again Ujjeni was accompanied by Uraw. Though weak on my feet, I gave them both a graceful salutation, causing the savage satisfaction on Ujjeni's face to be replaced by anger. I noticed compassion in Uraw's eyes as he took in my gaunt, bristly cheeks, stringy hair, and the black hollows around my eyes. I courteously bade them both be seated.

'You no longer give us orders, Prince Lala,' Ujjeni interjected rudely. 'Sit down.'

'But this is my abode,' I protested mildly, wishing that my voice had sounded stronger. 'Surely I can extend courtesies to my guests.'

I had prepared for this moment, focussing my love-force within my upper chest so that it could be poured out to him readily. As I released it, he felt its impact and recoiled. 'You are a traitor, a homeless vagrant,' he snarled. 'I said, sit down.'

I sat down obediently, smiling at him. He remained standing, towering over me now. 'You have had a taste of what lies ahead for you. It is the fate of criminals to be punished but you have an easy way out.'

The sweetness of my smile must have told him of his defeat. 'Prince Ujjeni, my love-force, which comes from God, is unquenchable. It grows daily, for you as well.' I paused in order to cause the full force of my love to flow towards him, absorbing his gaunt frame, his hunched back, his death's-head face, the sunken eyes and sublimating all the evil within him. Some inner reserves of resolve made my voice sound stronger. 'I not only believe in the doctrine of the Buddha, but also that it is God's word. The Doctrine bids us practise *maitriya*, loving kindness and *ahimsa*, forbearance, even towards those who harm us.'

I paused again, then continued in low tones. 'I had a vision last night. Some may say it was a hallucination caused by my weakened physical condition, but I saw an event that will take place in a desert land some five hundred years from now. My God was made manifest in perfect form as the son of man, as the true example of God's love. He was a Juda and his name was Ya-soof. He was God, yet he was only the best that all men can attain physically, mentally, spiritually. He performed miracles, but only such as any man could perform through the development of *iddhi* powers. He was the embodiment of God's love, which he revealed when he was crucified by his enemies, between two common criminals, on a bare hill. People mocked and reviled him. I even saw a spear at his side, red blood dripping from the torn, white flesh. Yet he offered nothing but love for those who tortured him. He died, rose again from the dead through his *iddhi* powers, then vanished from the ken of man, his ministry accomplished, and returned to God. Prince Ujjeni, it is his love that I offer you, his power that you vainly seek to confront.' I felt a gush of compassion for Ujjeni at his defeated purpose. 'You kept me here too long,' I added very, very gently. 'The spirit of God has grown in me and will only continue to grow with each passing day.'

He had been forced by the power of my words to listen to them. Now he stood stock still, staring his hatred at me, but under perfect control. He too had obviously prepared for this event. 'You are indeed the victim of hallucinations,' he stated firmly. 'Those who believe in Ahura Mazda, the One God, reach him through the drug, *youma*. You have done so without the drug, but we do intend administering it to you, so that this God may indeed become perfect in your wandering mind.' His voice dropped a shade. 'Men say it is a truth drug,' he added, almost absently. 'Perhaps it will force the truth from you, or drive you completely insane. Either way, my . . . the ends of justice will be achieved.'

'You know I will never take alcohol, or drugs.'

'Or eat pig's flesh.'

'I am a vegetarian.'

'You have no choice. You will be force-fed the drug.'

'How will you do that?'

He stared down at me reflectively. 'You have just inspired me as to the method.' His voice was quiet, but ominous. 'You are not worthy of being the twin brother of our Great King. Somewhere, somehow, the bad seed reposed in your half of your lady mother's womb, perhaps from her own mother. You shall be the twin of this criminal yet to come, who you claim will be the son of your God. Let us see whether your God will save you, when, by your own word, he is doomed to fail his son, made manifest in man.'

'How little you understand, Prince Ujjeni. Torture, mockery, reviling, betrayal and death are as transient as our bodies, our lives. Hatred too must pass away. Only love endures for ever. The love of the son of God will reach all men's hearts through the centuries and alter the history of the world. If my own love can have some effect on the lives of others, even yours, it will endure long after my suffering, my anguish and I are forgotten.'

That is how I came to be tied to a cross and force-fed with the horrible sticky white liquid *youma* in the long narrow room at the end of the corridor, by the yellow light of a single flare. That is where my vision of the son of God, crucified because of the sins of man, returned to strengthen me. That is when my boundless love triumphed over the mere confines of torture and the drug, before I lost consciousness.

Chapter 48

First, the hallucinations . . .

I am being pounded on the head by a sledgehammer. Thud, thud . . . thud, thud . . . only the pounding is from the inside. My brain is on fire. The flames are singeing my hair. My ears are ready to burst. My lips are so dry, my throat so parched that my tongue cleaves to the roof of my mouth. My chest feels tight, each breath is agony. My stomach is churning. I am lying in my own faeces. I want to vomit, but I have nothing save nauseous gases to bring out.

Who am I?

I don't know, except that I am love. All this terrible agony, these tortured organs, are a part of love. Only through travail is birth possible. And the love of a mother is inflexible, constant, unchanging. I am the mother. I am the earth in travail. I am the womb of love.

My aching eyelids are closed. If I can just open them, I might release some of the fire in my brain, the smoke clouds that fuddle my reasoning. But my eyes are chained to my cheeks, so that I become desperate with the need, my face trembling. As I strive to open my eyelids, tears pour from my eyes in my struggle for vision. But my tears are fruitless, for they will not moisten the manacles that bind my eyelids.

I feel a gentle touch on my cheek. Ah! I have felt such a touch before. Who touched me then? Who was I then? What is the link? What indeed?

I have it. This touch is tenderness. And tenderness springs from love. Has my love-force returned, like the echo of a voice, to touch me? Or is my Sundari back from the dead? This I must witness.

With one final, valiant effort, I lift my eyelids. A white

mist blurs my vision. I blink my eyes, striving to penetrate that mist, for beyond it love must lie.

A face slowly takes shape in the centre of that mist. First, red hair, then a red beard, then heavy leonine features, finally tawny eyes, focussing down to black pinpoints. Only, the pinpoints are not hard as I once knew them to be. They are wellsprings of the tenderness I felt, the founts of love.

Who can this be? Surely it must be the image of me, myself, or my twin.

My twin? My twin? My twin? My tortured brain contains the answer, I know, so I torture it for the answer.

Like the bursting of a great flame, with the impact of a thunderbolt, knowledge comes to me. This is the Great King, Vijaya Sinha-Bahu. Then I must be his twin, Prince Lala Sinha-Bahu.

It all comes back in a flash and I know I must have died and been reborn. I certainly do not wish to go back to those last days of my life.

'You are awake at last.' The words sound muffled, but I know that voice so well. Only it is a little tired, though it could never be as tired as I feel.

'Where are we?' I barely hear myself speak, so how could he, unless he reads my lips or my mind. Why not my mind, since he is my twin?

'In your quarters in the Kalyani palace.'

It took me long moments to comprehend what he was saying, but when realization finally dawned some of my torpor vanished and I rolled my burning eyes upwards and saw that I was indeed lying propped up on the gold cushions of the great canopied bed, then, glancing sideways, I noted the coloured tapestries and the high lacquer-grilled window. Sounds reached me faintly and the pungent odour of incense began to penetrate the nauseous sensations in my nostrils, pharynx and throat. Yes, I now remembered everything. The terrible drug, *youma*, administered to me in hideous quantities had permeated every part of my being.

I remembered the dungeon cell and my torture with a kind of listlessness. What was it I had tried to conquer? Ah yes, it was time. A concept of man, so unimportant in truth. 'What time is it?' I enquired.

'It is mid-day. We arrived this morning from Devun Dara.' He reached over to the table beside the bed, seized a bowl, picked up a linen wick soaked in water and allowed the precious drops to fall on my lips. Oh, the joy of that moistening, water on parched earth, the hushing of screaming wounds.

When he had finished my tongue was loosened again and my mouth and throat came to life; even the fire in my brain had somewhat abated, though only slightly. 'Has my hair turned to ashes?' I enquired.

He smiled. 'No. Perhaps it feels like that.' I had never heard his voice so gentle, there was almost a tear in it.

'Are you well? Have you recovered?'

'Fully, as you can see,' he replied.

'Good.'

'We arrived in time, though we wish it had been earlier.'

'I want you to know that when Prince Jaya seized the sub-kingdom, I realized how wrong I had been not to support you through thick and thin, regardless of my personal views.' I smiled weakly. 'It is a family trait, I guess, to be hard-headed! When all is said and done, the blood tie counts most. I want you to forgive me for having failed you.' I told him in weak tones of my horror, revulsion, remorse when I had heard of the attack on him and thought that he had died.

I reached out impulsively and grasped his hand. 'I'm very tired now and would like to sleep. Please do not go away.'

'You are the younger twin. We shall never leave you. Remember that if you have lost a family, you have regained one.'

'I need you more than ever now.'

'You must not talk any more,' he gently commanded.

'Sleep and all will be well. For the present, remember this. On the same day, at the same time that your love for me triumphed over all else, I learned of what had happened to you from a Naga who had ridden at the risk of his life to enlist my aid on your behalf. I had the same experience as you did, bitterly regretting that I had allowed my policies to triumph over my love for you.'

It took all of one week for me to recover from the effects of the drug. The Great King was constantly by my side, having dispatched Ujjeni to look after Thamba-Panni. By tacit agreement, my brother and I never discussed what had transpired during the period before he arrived, or any controversial subject for that matter, except when he mentioned that he had caused a beautiful tombstone to be erected to commemorate Prince Jaya.

There would be time enough for discussions. What we needed at this time was to enjoy each other, talk about the past. I came to a better understanding of all that he had suffered, his fears, all he stood for and what he had hoped to achieve. It made me feel inadequate all over again, because my love for him and my understanding had failed. Rather than going back and altering my *olas* on the basis of this new knowledge, however, I decided to interpolate important actions of my brother's viewpoints. So when my physical strength and my clarity of mind improved, I brought the *olas* up to date. Surprisingly, I still found myself filled by a restless urge to complete the task.

Although I sorely missed Sundari, I found life in the Kalyani court pleasant enough because my brother and I lived as we had done before and Uday saw me frequently. The Great King was always very relaxed and affectionate to me in private, making no excuse for not returning to his wife in Thamba-Panni.

On the eighth night after his arrival, King Vijaya and I had our first dinner together in my dining room. Until then, I had, on the advice of the Court physician, eaten in my bedroom, with the king sharing the meal at a separate table set up beside my bed. It was a warm, still night. The golden taper-flames, with their blue centres, were erect and poised, a perfect shape. The odour of spiced vegetables was tantalizing. It had taken privation and torture for me to realize the value of food. Through the open door, across the verandah, I could see moonlight bathing the courtyard and hear the splash of the fountains and the cascade.

'The heat and stillness brings out the little devils,' the Great King said, slapping at a mosquito that had alighted on his upper arm. He flicked the little corpse away with his forefinger and I sadly remembered the Princess Kuveni and blood streaks on the silken bedsheets in the tent she had erected for the man who was to become her lover and her executioner.

'I find that if one does not kill them, others will not attack,' I informed him.

'Really?'

'Yes, I imagine the splattered blood from the dead mosquito attracts others.'

'Some insects, some animals, some people are attracted by blood,' he declared abruptly. 'We must leave for Thamba-Panni tomorrow. We only stayed after arriving from Devun Dara to look after you.'

'Thank you. I know you have your duty to perform, but I hate to see you go.'

His face softened and his gaze became tender as he looked at me. 'It has been like old times. We have missed you these years. We hate to go, but we must.' He actually sighed.

This was a warm, soft brother that I never knew existed. 'I thank God for my tribulations,' I declared impulsively. 'For they brought us together again.'

His expression changed. 'Please do not ever refer to your God,' he directed me. 'Heresy is one of the charges against you. As the Great King, we cannot condone it, still less participate in it. You must understand that this kingdom of

674

Lanka must be ruled under our tenets, both religious and lay. Unbounded freedom, even of expression, cannot be permitted, because it leads to lawlessness. We cannot allow you, dearly as we love you, to question our institutions. You may have private beliefs, now that you are no longer a ruler, but you must not express them in public.'

His words told me that I was no longer sub-king of Kalyani, but they only filled me with enormous relief. I looked him squarely in the face. 'I apologize for my error and I beg your pardon for it. But my thankfulness still remains.'

My smile at the Great King was clear and open. He responded with a nod. He drummed on the table with his fingers. 'We think it is time you knew our intentions,' he stated thoughtfully, his eyes lowered. 'You stand accused of treason and heresy. Those are crimes against the king and against the gods, the most serious in my state. We cannot merely overlook them or nonchalantly pardon you for them. That would destroy the fabric of our system of our justice.' He shot a glance at me.

'Sire,' I automatically adopted the formal mode of address. 'I fully understand that you will have to try me for these crimes and punish me if I am found guilty. But do you personally believe that I could ever be guilty of treason against you?'

'No,' he replied unhesitatingly and my heart leapt with joy, not with the hope of being judged innocent of crime, but because of the affirmation of his trust in me.

'That is all I need, Sire,' I responded. 'As for the other charge, what more is heresy than truth discovered that shakes the security of a society's past beliefs?'

'The security of the state must include those established beliefs of its people in which they have found security.'

'Granted, Sire. But my personal beliefs, unpropagated, can be a threat to no one. I do not promise to keep these beliefs to myself, but so far they have been expressed to few people and only in defence of my actions. I now pray that I be judged by my peers.'

He grinned at that. 'You are either wise or cunning, or both,' he asserted. 'Since we come the closest to being your peer in this realm, it means that we shall have to try you ourself.'

'Precisely. And I expect only justice from you in that capacity, not mercy.'

'You shall have that. Now, as our brother, tell us all that has transpired from your viewpoint.'

I stared intently at him, probing his spirit to see how much of the truth he could sustain. I found him steady and strong as a granite monolith. There was a new dimension to him which I could not define. 'It took a bludgeon to knock some sense inside your thick skull, Sire,' I said, laughing. 'You have changed. Now you are a truly great Great King.'

His jaw dropped slightly in surprise and I was glad to find that he was human. I immediately launched into my story, careful to be just and fair, separating fact from opinion.

He listened without comment for the hours it took me to finish the tale. By then the tapers had half burnt out and the moonlight was shadowed by clouds. 'It is not as Prince Ujjeni told us the story,' he finally commented. 'But we believe you because you have nothing to gain from telling lies.'

'Would I not gain my life, Sire?'

'You do not value that.'

'Then what about the thing I treasure most today from any living man, your trust in my veracity? Surely I stand to gain that?'

'Not if you lied and knew it yourself.'

I was charmed. 'Will you personally try me then, Sire?'

'Yes.'

'When will that be?'

'When we return from Thamba-Panni, which should be in about two weeks, all going well. Meanwhile, we shall give you complete freedom to prepare your defence.'

'There is not much to prepare, Sire. Merely the evidence of a few people. Will you honour the pardon I gave Hamy for this purpose?'

'Certainly.'

'And allow Uday and the woman, Rupa, to testify with total immunity?'

'Of course.'

'And if I am found innocent.'

His brow darkened and the massive jaw tightened. 'Someone will have to pay for crimes against the innocent,' he growled and my heart leapt. He would protect me if he could, I knew. Then I had a crying need also to know the worst. 'What if you judge me guilty of treason?' I enquired.

'The punishment is death by execution, but we might instead consider removal of your rank, forfeiture of all your possessions and loss of your civil rights.'

'What if you find me guilty of heresy? That is not a normal crime in our state.'

He became tight-lipped. 'Our punishment is death by fire, so that the heresy may be burnt to ashes which will be flung into the ocean. There is no clemency.'

I blanched, because I knew what I stood for. 'What if the guilty person removes himself to another region.'

'Heresy is heresy, a heretic is a heretic and must be pursued to the ends of the earth. You may have wondered why we do not regard the Buddhist doctrine as heresy. It is because Buddhism does not set up new gods. Your belief in One God is what offends the tenets of our society.' He hesitated and his jaw loosened. 'If the heresy is not of a serious nature, if it is personal belief and has not openly affronted the pride and dignity of the gods of our society, we might indeed consider exile.' He looked searchingly at me, his eyes crinkled into a smile. 'Have no fear, little brother, we shall look after you,' he assured me. 'We shall of course explain the laws to our Council of Ministers, exhorting them to comply, regardless of personal ties, even if we ourselves are removed by death or incapacity.' He paused and grinned again. 'But we have no intention of allowing such contingencies to arise. As a matter of fact, we shall prepare written instructions that you are under no circumstances to be subjected to torture or placed in solitary confinement again. You are to have suitable quarters at all times.' He looked at me impishly. 'Especially if you are due for execution!'

I smiled back happily, not knowing why his words had laid a cold hand secretly on my heart. 'I have two boons to ask, Sire.'

'Anything for you, Prince Lala Sinha-Bahu. We know you will never make an unreasonable request.'

'Could you have a copy of your written instructions delivered to all the ministers, commanding them to comply? And could you also please include in these instructions orders that Uday, the Venerable Sri Ra-vindra, is to have free access to me at all times, up to the executioner's block, or the stake, if need be.'

Seeing pain flash across his eyes, I remembered his earlier possessiveness and hastened to explain. 'I only need Uday to ensure that one of the missions that brought me to Lanka with you is fulfilled. I have recorded the story of your coming in writing so that your great destiny may be handed down to posterity. Uday is one person to whom I can entrust the *olas* should anything happen to you and me.'

He smiled then and once again I was filled with a great gladness to find him so relaxed, happy, free of the driving forces of ambition, even delusions of grandeur, that had once possessed him. King Tikka seemed to have done him a favour or was it my suffering that had caused the change?

'When do we see the *olas*?' he demanded.

'At the end of your reign, Sire, or after I die, whichever comes first.'

Ujjeni was going over some documents so Uraw had time for reflection as the two of them waited in the study at the Thamba-Panni palace for the Great King to come to a meeting he had summoned three days after his arrival from Kalyani.

Excitement at the Great King's return had subsided and the palace was back to normal. Even security had relapsed to its usual, relaxed state, so that people could freely come and go within the fort, except to the private quarters.

The sun must have been fairly low in the east, for the centre courtyard was still in shadow, deserted except for a bare-bodied gardener bent over a *kapuru* flowerbed adjoining the verandah. Uraw found himself awaiting the Great King's arrival with special interest, since he had received his copy of the king's directives regarding Prince Lala. He had not failed to notice the change in the Great King even during the brief period they had been together in Kalyani. He had not been present at the meeting between the Great King and Ujjeni in a private room of the Kalyani palace at which the Naga revolt and the treatment accorded Prince Lala had obviously been discussed. All he knew was that Ujjeni and he had been ordered back to Thamba-Panni immediately. Since Ujjeni had been totally uncommunicative, Uraw reasoned that, while there could have been nothing but praise for Ujjeni's handling of the affairs of State while the ruler had been incapacitated, he must have been taken to task for overreaching himself where Prince Lala was concerned. If nothing else, a commoner should never lay hands on royalty in the way Ujjeni had done. Having acquired some perception of Ujjeni's thoughts and feelings, Uraw had sensed a carefully hidden, bitter anger simmering within the man, this time against the Great King.

The Great King's written directive to the ministers, a copy of which he had received on the day of the ruler's arrival in Thamba-Panni, confirmed Uraw's suspicions as to Ujjeni's true feelings. Gazing at the skeletal face poring over the documents spread out on the yellow jakwood table, Uraw idly wondered what form Ujjeni's enmity against the Great King would take, if it was ever aroused. Certainly Ujjeni had ceased to be the sychophantic commander and minister. The former unctuousness, whch had seemed natural to him, was now produced only with a conscious effort, very much against the man's inclinations. How people change, Uraw reflected. The Great King and Ujjeni have been like two characters doing a peacock dance at sunset, forward and back, back and forward, but integrated by a single rhythm – which reminded Uraw that he had been sitting since dawn and his limbs were cramped. He rose to his feet and stretched.

Ujjeni glanced sharply at him. 'Where are you going?' he demanded.

'Just stretching my limbs. Why?'

'Nothing . . . uh . . . I thought you were going to the privy. We must not keep the Great King waiting.'

Odd, Uraw thought as he walked to the doorway, Ujjeni seems almost jumpy. Uraw stood at the entrance to the study. The Great King was halfway down the open verandah already, striding along unaccompanied. He never waits for guards, Uraw told himself. He's had one bad experience. He should be more cautious.

Uraw half turned to re-enter the study, so that he could receive the Great King with proper obeisance, instead of doing so from the doorway and blocking the king's way. 'The Great King is coming,' he informed Ujjeni.

Ujjeni leapt to his feet with unwonted haste and adjusted his sword.

Uraw heard a soggy thump and a groan from the verandah. Startled, he swung back swiftly. The Great King had staggered forward and stumbled. A lean, dark, bare-chested man was on his back. The Great King flung his assailant off him as a wounded lion might a hyena. The man went sprawling on the ground, a long, bloody knife gripped in his hand. The Great King whipped round. Horror-stricken, Uraw saw the red bloodstain on the back of his white tunic. The assailant recovered, crouched, reversed his hold to grip the knife by its point. He flung it straight and true for the Great King's heart. His dark bearded face and straggly black hair were somehow familiar. The knife embedded itself in the mighty chest with a great thwack. The king juddered to a stop. Then he extended his arms, fingers stretched, and slowly made for the assassin.

Breaking loose from his stupefaction, Uraw shouted, he knew not what, and darted forward, but he was shoved aside by Ujjeni, gleaming sword in hand, plunging to the rescue. Recovering his balance, Uraw ran towards the group. The bloody knife was on the flagstone floor. The Great King had somehow reached his assailant, seized him in a bear hug and was crushing the man to death by sheer physical strength. Uraw stopped, wide-eyed, his heart beating wildly, his lungs pumping with excitement. Ujjeni too had paused to gaze at the incredible scene.

The dark, bearded face, revealed above the king's massive left shoulder, began to turn purple, the eyes wide, popping out of their sockets, the white teeth bared in a bestial snarl of agony. The open mouth vainly clawed for air. Still the king squeezed relentlessly, relentlessly, until the head suddenly sagged. He then reached up with his right hand, grabbed his opponent by the hair, shifted the grip behind the man's neck. He bent down and lifted the man with his left hand. He bent his knee, placed the man's body across it and broke the body as if it were a stick. Uraw's stomach turned at the horrible cracking and crunching of bones.

The king dropped the body and staggered upright, swaying. Ujjeni sprang forward with a cry. One mighty sweep of his long sword and the assailant's head was severed from the body, which fell to the ground like some great rag doll. The shorn neck, its flesh pink, the bone and gristle white, began turning crimson with blood.

Ujjeni's sword clattered to the ground as he turned to support the Great King. The huge body was too heavy for him. It slowly collapsed sideways, turning over as it fell, to lie upwards, the lungs pumping in great gasps, the spreadeagled limbs like felled tree-trunks, strangely askew. A trickle of blood appeared from the wide nostrils and the mouth, to flow down the red beard, while a great patch of crimson spread on the white tunic.

'Ho there, guards!' Ujjeni shouted. He knelt beside the Great King. 'Summon the physician,' he urgently bade Uraw. 'King Tikka has assassinated him.'

Ujjeni had slipped. In the flash of a moment, Uraw spotted the flaw. How had Ujjeni known the assailant was King Tikka? And why had he severed the neck of a man who was probably dead already?

Uraw glanced once at the still figure of the Great King, then ran down the verandah, past the alarmed guards who had begun pouring in, shouting for the physician.

That same morning I sat with Uday in his cell in the Kalyani palace. Sunlight filtering through the grilled window cast a pale light on his chiselled features, now showing their first tiny wrinkles. He was over sixty-three years old. I remembered that Lord Buddha was said to have retained his beautiful tight skin until the time of his death at the age of eighty. The Buddhist life, with its disciplines of body and mind, could perform miracles.

Inevitably, Uday picked up my thoughts. 'I saw our Lord Buddha shortly before his death,' he stated. 'His skin was smooth as a ripe olive, with the same texture and sheen, but of a pale golden colour.

'I wish I had met him.'

'I recall the first day I saw him.'

'Yes, you told me. I well remember the incident.'

'Have you brought all your *olas* up to date now, my dear one?'

'Yes, Venerable Sir. Here they are.' I picked up the wooden box I had placed beside me on my beige mat and offered it to him, both hands extended, head bowed.

He accepted the box, glanced at it and placed it to one side. 'I may read the *olas*?'

'Certainly.'

'Good. But you have more to write, so why do you give me this instalment?'

Having no answer, I fumbled with words. 'I somehow feel . . . uh . . . that most of what I can do is there.' I nodded towards the box. 'There is more to be written . . .' I hesitated, because the words were now beginning to come out involuntarily, 'but not much more . . . though what little there is left will be important . . . most important of all.' Why was I so incoherent?

I felt a sharp, deep pain in my back and gasped, my head slumping forward. I raised it with an effort and stared at Uday. For once, he appeared to be startled. I was short of breath now and remembered the way Sundari had clawed for the precious breath of her life. What was happening to me? A searing pain ran through my chest, streaking for the heart. Swiftly remembering my *yoga*, I steadied my agonized breathing, eased it past the apparent obstructions, nostrils dilating till I was normal again.

'What is wrong?' Uday enquired solicitously. 'Are you sick?'

'No, I'm all right now.'

'What happened?'

As I began to tell him, a great loneliness slowly emerged within me. It started as the isolated dot of a chill in my heart and expanded outwards, ever outwards, so that I shivered with it though the air in the cell was warm. Try as I might, I could not stop shaking. 'My brother, the Great King, is either dying,' I said between chattering teeth, 'Or has just died.'

*   *   *

The cold chill that gripped me then remained.

Four days later I had just finished my noon meal in my quarters in the Kalyani palace and was seated at the dining table, sipping some red melon juice mixed with honey and a dash of lime. The attendants began clearing away my empty platter and the food bowls. Their bare chests were prickled with sweat, for it was a warm day.

Among the dreadful times in life are those when those of us who have imagination and perception know that harm has befallen a loved one but are impotent to do anything about it. The seconds flap by on wounded wings while we wait for news to reach us. In recent days, I had acquired some ability to fight torture, but the anxiety created by my fears for my brother was new to me, my only previous experience of it being when he was attacked by King Tikka while he was in Devun Dara.

My silver-haired chief attendant hastened to answer the knock on the door. I had a moment of intuitive apprehension even before he returned to announce Ujjeni. At least the Prince Regent was not hammering his way in, as he did the last time, I reassured myself. I asked the chief attendant to show the visitor into the reception chamber. When I joined them there, I was relieved to find Uraw with Ujjeni.

They both rose to give me salutation. I bade them be seated and took a chair facing them.

Ujjeni came straight to the point. 'The Great King was mortally wounded by King Tikka in the Thamba-Panni palace four days ago.' His calm, even tones contrasted sharply with the surge of anxiety within me, which I strove to hide. 'He was still alive but unconscious when I left Thamba-Panni the day before yesterday.' He stopped speaking and looked at me with faint mockery in his sunken eyes.

I knew he was playing with me, but I did not care about petty victories or dignity in the face of his news. 'Are you sure he is dying?' I cried. 'What do the Court physicians say?

What happened?'

Seeing Ujjeni stony faced, I turned my gaze to Uraw. The minister's eye flickered to Ujjeni, seeking guidance. Receiving none, he seemed to make up his mind. 'Prince Ujjeni and I were in the Great King's study four mornings ago, awaiting a conference with him,' he replied. 'I saw a solitary Yakka gardener tending a flowerbed in the centre courtyard. The Great King walked alone down the verandah towards us. What followed is a bit of a jumble. I heard a soggy thud and found the gardener had attacked the Great King, obviously stabbing him in the back.' A bitter note entered his voice. 'Back-stabbing and treachery are no more than we expect from the Yakka. The Great King spun around with miraculous speed and flung the assailant off. As he moved forward to close in, however, the man, now crouching, threw his knife. We have since discovered that it just missed the Great King's heart but punctured the left lung. With remarkable strength and tenacity, the Great King closed in, grabbed the assailant and literally squeezed him till he was unconscious. He then broke the man's body across his knee.'

Uraw paused, his eyes wet with tears, and I remembered Uday's description of the death of Sinha, the lion. Thus do all lions go, I thought with great sadness – magnificently.

'Ujjeni rushed forward and decapitated the dead assailant with his sword, knowing immediately who it was.' I had a flash thought that Uraw was trying to tell me something, but it slipped by me in the great flood of sorrow, pity and compassion that overwhelmed me. So many thoughts. The Great King, my brother, had fought his last fight completely alone, against a madman. He had to be stabbed in the back, there was no other way any living man could have killed him, any more than my father could have killed Sinha in fair combat. Effect and cause. Cause and effect. Thus had King Tikka too ended his quest for vengeance at last. But how had he got inside the palace? What were Uraw's words? . . . Ujjeni rushed forward and decapitated . . . the assailant . . .

knowing who it was . . . *those* had been his words. Why would Ujjeni do that, how had he known who it was, unless he . . . yes, that was it . . . Ujjeni wanted to make sure that the assailant was dead. It would not have been difficult for Ujjeni, with his superb spy system, to get through to King Tikka. Also, since Ujjeni was responsible for the administration of the Thamba-Panni palace, he could easily have arranged for King Tikka to be in the garden at the appropriate time. Ujjeni had the power, the opportunity and the motives, principally hatred and the lust for power.

This foul fiend, who had even turned against his benefactor, now sat calmly before me. I should hate him, but all I felt was hopelessness, even despair, and a slow-surging determination not to allow my spirit to be infused with evil.

Then inspiration flamed. I would give Ujjeni love instead of hate, the love of God that passes all understanding. My hopelessness and despair vanished before a great calm. Yet I must confess to delight in the knowledge that giving Ujjeni love instead of hatred would be his greatest punishment.

Ujjeni must have felt my mood for he was swift to strike. 'As you know, the Great King issued written instructions to the effect that you should be brought to speedy trial and that this should be before the ruler alone.' Ujjeni's grin was more evil than I had ever known it. 'I am in duty bound to honour the dying monarch's last written wish. So I have come here post haste, as the ruler in his absence, to fulfil that command. I shall try you myself in the audience chamber at the commencement of the pre-noon watch. In deference to the Great King's dictates, you may remain in your quarters without a guard, but on your word of honour that you will not escape. Do I have your word, Prince?'

My mind raced furiously over the instructions my brother had issued. He had indeed referred to my trial by 'the ruler', meaning himself, but I was trapped by his words. Ujjeni knew it, for this time his hee . . . hee . . . hee . . . belly laugh was not only mirthless but triumphant.

686

All that remained for me was my dignity as a man and my deportment as a prince. 'You have my word,' I replied, head held high.

'You may summon any witnesses you desire, exactly as the Great King directed,' Ujjeni continued.

I saw the craftiness deep down in his heart and thought swiftly. I would certainly not betray Rupa, and thus Princess Kuveni's children, or Hamy, or Uday, Prince Jaya's family or any of the remaining Kalyani princes by having them give evidence on my behalf. My trial would be a farce in any event, the verdict a foregone conclusion. I could expect neither justice nor mercy from this man, so why should I dishonour myself by pleading a case? I was a prince, by birth and breeding. No man would see me plead a case or grovel. But my heart was suddenly heavy for Lanka. Oh my poor country, my poor people, what awaits you? The finger of God must have pointed the answer, for I suddenly knew that any country could be as good as the noblest of its noble men and women. All I could do was to set an example.

'Who are your witnesses?' Ujjeni demanded.

'I have none. You will be placing God on trial tomorrow and I shall be his witness and his proxy for the execution of your sentence.'

On the following morning, the sun and the rain made a mockery of each other. I was reminded of my first visit to Kalyani and the couplet:

> The sun and the rain in unison,
> It's the jackal's wedding.

My trial was conducted in the great audience hall. Prince Ujjeni was dressed like me in white silk tunic and pantaloons, which contrasted with his dark complexion. He sat on the golden throne, which had been restored to its rightful place on the wooden platform. Uraw was the only other person present. He sat in the body of the hall. I stood just beneath the platform, on which King Ra-hula and Prince Jaya had died with dignity, nobility and gallantry. They were my inspiration. They spoke to me from the throne on which an imposter now sat, they whispered to me from the sunlight that streamed in through the open windows, despite the flurries of rain and from the shadows beyond. Courage, courage, courage . . . dignity and honour, they insisted.

Sunshafts and shadows. I recalled Uday's words. None of it was reality. Yet philosophy could not diminish my sadness that it would all be over for me soon. Would I ever see sunlight again after I died? Would I meet Sundari in the next life? These questions were symptoms of weakness. I thrust them firmly aside, to find refuge in God.

'Prince Lala, you are charged with acts of treason, of which you are already aware, against the Great King and the sovereign state of Lanka.' Ujjeni's tone was lofty; he would not even look at me. 'Are you guilty or not guilty.'

I held my head high. 'Prince Ujjeni, you are not a properly constituted court as the Great King intended for me. I will not dignify you with a plea.'

'Guilty as charged,' Ujjeni intoned. He looked down at me then, with malevolent triumph. I merely felt sorry for his mortal *kharma*.

'Prince Lala, you are also charged with committing acts of heresy, of which you are already aware, against the gods and beliefs of the Arya, the Yakka and the Naga who inhabit the kingdom. Are you guilty or not guilty?'

'Prince Ujjeni, you are not a properly constituted court as the Great King intended for me. I will not dignify you with a plea.'

'Guilty as charged.'

In the moments of silence that followed, I could sense Ujjeni savouring the delight of what was to come. He had waited long years for these moments, years of hatred, envy, resentment and bitterness. The sound of children's voices singing a *kavi*, poem, in unison drifted through the windows of the hall. Ujjeni obviously did not hear it. Nothing has changed, I thought. Innocence and guilt, the innocence of children and the guilt of adults, as we human beings understand them will go on for ever.

'Prince Lala, this court has adjudged you guilty of charges of treason and heresy.' Ujjeni was positively drooling with anticipation. 'It now remains for the court to pass sentence on you.' He paused for effect, seeking out my reactions with fiendish delight. All he received was love. He blanched, then plunged fiercely on. 'The sentence for treason is death by execution. As a prince born, though your conduct has been that of a treacherous betrayer of your family, your friends, your comrades and your compatriots, you will be entitled to have the red hibiscus placed upon your neck before the executioner's sword. Since you also have the sentence for committing heresy awaiting you, however, we shall not pass sentence of death upon you on that count, but hereby decree that you be stripped of your princely rank, that all your lands and property be confiscated and accrued to the Great King's treasury and that you be deprived of all your civic rights.'

I remained motionless, erect, head held high, generating my love-force towards him. Though I had been expecting something like this, his words still appalled me. However strong a man may be, he cannot hear such a sentence without it hitting him in the pit of his stomach, sending chills through his body.

'Now for the sentence of the court for your crime of heresy.' He paused again. This time a dribble of saliva appeared on the side of his mouth and he ran a dark tongue over his purple lips then bared the yellow combs of his teeth. 'You are hereby sentenced to death at dawn, four days from now, at the stake.' Finding me apparently unmoved, he added fiercely. 'Death by fire, death by burning, death from the flames.'

I still remained unmoved. 'Don't you understand?' He screamed, half-rising from his throne. 'You will be burnt to death. Your ashes will be flung into the ocean so that no single hint of you, you foul heretic, filthy Juda, sacrilegious pig, will ever again defile this sacred earth of the pantheon of our gods.'

I was beyond fear now. I smiled at him, love emanating from my being.

Ujjeni's voice rose to a screech. 'May your *atman* rot in hell, Prince Lala.'

'Now that last, Prince Ujjeni, is a sentence you can never impose,' I answered calmly. 'Only God has that power and my God has denied it even to Himself, because He is a God of love.'

It is the third evening after the trial. I sit at the desk facing the open window of my room, having just completed my *olas*. Sunlight lies golden on the air. Mynahs screech in green branches and crows wing lazily across a clear blue sky. The scent of jasmine tinges the air. A perfect ending of the day and for the evening of my life, because I die at dawn tomorrow. Ujjeni had me moved from my quarters to a room facing the palace grounds. He thus kept faith with the Great King's directive that I should not be moved from the palace, but he placed me where I could hear the sounds of digging and see the stake being planted and the faggots piled around it in the open green glade surrounded by tall flamboyant trees.

What kind of sadistic cruelty tears Ujjeni apart? Only terrible hurt, agonizing hopelessness can beget it. I feel such grief for all he must have endured to reach this state, such remorse that I should, consciously or unconsciously, have given him cause to focus his anguished spirit on any human being. Will he derive enough balm from my death to heal his wounds? If not, where will he look next for an outlet to his desperation?

Uraw bade me a quick, abrupt farewell in my quarters, immediately on my return to them from my trial. The tears in his eyes spoke more than words, or any lingering. They moved me deeply. He handed me the last of his *olas*, remarking on Ujjeni's preoccupation with fire as the source of cleansing and retribution. He himself was returning immediately to Thamba-Panni.

The past three days have been strange ones for me. I had always imagined that there would be much to do, setting one's affairs in order, when one anticipates death. Having been stripped of all my property and rights, however, I was in a vacuum, with nothing to do, so I lived in a state of suspended animation, relieved only by Uday's frequent visits. He became God's apostle to comfort and strengthen me. He even agreed to write the epilogue to my story, which now must end.

Having neither property nor heirs, I bequeath my *olas* as my legacy to the millions who will read *The Founts of Sinhala*.

I am not afraid to die. I am not afraid of being burnt to death.

What Prince Jaya told me, centuries ago, on the banks of the Kalyani River, is true. Life is precious to us human beings because we view it with our minds and centre all our endeavours on the act of living. We measure success, failure, happiness, sorrow within life's confines. Birth is merely the death form of another existence, taking more time or less according to the individual's *kharma*. Death, as we see it, is the true reality, the real birth. I do not fear it, but embrace it with hope and love.

Epilogue

You know me from the tale which Prince Lala Sinha-Bahu has told. My name is Uday; my titles are of no significance. On the evening before he was due to be burned at the stake for the alleged crime of heresy, Prince Lala requested me to write the Epilogue to his story. I believe that the prince also intended me to complete the history of his twin brother, the Great King Vijaya Sinha-Bahu, and the creation of the Sinhala nation.

I am neither a scholar nor a writer, merely a follower of truth. I have not the power nor the desire to embellish my words. Apart from the Four Precepts and the Noble Eightfold Path, I know of no absolute truths, not even the sermons of Lord Buddha. For I have discovered that the real truth is that man will always search for truths and will discover only whatever he can believe to be true. He approaches his quest in one of two ways. He either postulates a thesis, such as there is a God, and searches for every possible piece of evidence to prove himself correct to his own satisfaction, or he accumulates evidence sufficient for himself from which to draw a conclusion.

The weakness in either case lies in man's limited ability to search, to observe, to deduce, to conclude, for man is always circumscribed by man. I have been trying to follow the Noble Eightfold Path in the belief that it is the truth. The real truth is that I am trying to act a truth as I have found that truth. Whether my state of mind is a mirage or a reality, the inescapable truth is that I have found peace in it.

Prince Lala spent the entire day before his execution observing *Dasa-sila*, the Ten Precepts. I was with him through the night. Prince Ujjeni had decreed that the execution should take place in public, as an example to all men, so the palace grounds began filling with people during the last watch before dawn. The news had spread quickly, far and wide. The crowds had begun assembling outside the palace gates from as early as the previous evening. I knew that these were not curious onlookers, but devoted admirers of Prince Lala. The people of Kalyani loved him deeply and came to offer him homage, to learn from the example they expected him to offer, not from the punishment decreed.

Shortly before dawn, these crowds densely packed the area set aside for spectators on two sides of the open glade in the gardens at the rear of the palace, where the stake and faggots awaited their beloved prince. Every one of the people was dressed in white, the colour of mourning. Alert guards from Prince Ujjeni's companies, clad in red pantaloons and white tunics, swords drawn, spears at the ready, were stationed at close intervals in front of the gathering. Archers manned the walls behind the spectators. The third side of the glade soon began filling with Naga princes and noblemen, chieftains and officials. They too were all dressed in white. The fourth side had been reserved for Prince Ujjeni, now for all practical purposes, the Great King of Lanka, an office he would, without a doubt secure for himself even if he had to do away with the Great King once he disposed of Prince Lala, the only rival claimant to the throne.

Prince Lala had been completely calm since the day of his sentencing. I knew he had reached a state of being that was neither acceptance nor resignation but of living out his days in the high mental state of *is*. His incredible, unshakeable power of love for all beings and things, even those whom men would have called his enemies, had developed, since the crisis, eternally and infinitely, in the character of his God. The peace he had found proved to me that there are many paths to Enlightenment. Prince Lala had discovered his path through the God of his beliefs, whether imagined or real.

King Sri Ra-hula and Prince Jaya acted out their gallant roles during minutes when death faced them suddenly. Prince Lala's gallantry extended over a period of many days. It has made me wonder whether there may not be a God after all, because such power is not human. It may well be divine, though I grant that what is not of man does not necessarily have to be of the gods.

Shortly before the time appointed for the execution, Prince Ujjeni emerged from the palace and took his stand, a lone figure dressed in white, facing the stake. Groans, growls and hoots broke out from the crowd, quickly hushed by threatening guards.

Four men carrying flaming torches moved slowly out of the palace and took their places on the four sides of the pile of faggots.

An authoritative knock sounded on the door of our room. Prince Lala, dressed in white tunic and pantaloons, made obeisance to me, rose to his feet, moved to the door and opened it. A burly, bearded guard commander and six stalwart guards stood outside. Prince Lala walked out and the guards, in their red and white uniforms, formed up around him. It was as if they had swallowed him up for ever and I remembered that morning, thirty-seven years earlier, when Prince Lala's grandfather, Sinha, and I stood at the edge of the Lala forest watching the king's guards swallow up the deserters, Princess Suppa-Devi with Sinha-Bahu and my love Sinha-Seevali with her, in the sunlit fields beyond.

At a command from their leader, the group started marching forward. I followed them closely. When we reached the park, a great cheer rose from the crowd. Guards tried to hush them with threats and even buffets, but they would not be stilled or deprived of their final tribute to one who had given them his wealth, shared their deprivation and always championed their rights, especially liberty, equality and the pursuit of happiness. Prince Ujjeni was shaking with anger, but he was powerless to still the voice of an entire people. Prince Lala silently acknowledged the cheers with raised hands.

The cheering continued while Prince Lala was led through a gap in the faggots to the stake and bound to it. Only when the gap was closed with more faggots did the deafening noise slowly subside. I noticed that the faggots were not piled high in that part of the gap, which was directly in front of Prince Ujjeni, and had to conclude that he desired to watch his enemy suffer and die. From my position to one side of Ujjeni and behind him, the last glimpse I caught of Prince Lala was a smile on his beautiful face.

The torch bearers moved forward and set fire to the shavings and tinders heaped around the faggots, which soon took fire. As a trickle of grey smoke started rising, a great silence filled the crowd and the entire earth seemed hushed.

Not all my training and discipline prevented the great cry that broke within me: God of Prince Lala, if you truly exist, give me a miracle. My only answer was the crackling of flames that began to soar upwards. I thought of Prince Lala's mortal agony and sent him all the strength of my being. Now the fire had really taken and was licking towards the stake.

'Stop!' A great cry broke from a palace entrance facing the glade. I recognized the voice. It was Vijit's. He burst through the door, sword drawn, followed by Uraw. 'Stop in the Great King's name!' he commanded.

Ujjeni turned fiercely round. I shall never forget the look of disbelief, hatred and crazed determination on his face. He drew his sword. He turned to his men. 'Guards, seize these rebels,' he bellowed, his voice cracking. 'I am the Great King.'

'No, you are not!' Vijit cried. 'You are a criminal and an imposter. Here is the Great King himself.'

A stretcher carried by four men had emerged through the doorway. A huge figure slowly rose from it. Supported by Vijit and Uraw, the Great King finally stood erect. His chest and shoulders were swathed in white bandages and he seemed to have some difficulty breathing. Then through yet another miracle, one of heredity, willpower, magnificent strength, incredible love, the Great King shook off Vijit and Uraw to stand erect. He reached for Vijit's sword and grasped it firmly in his hand. He advanced on Ujjeni, who remained rooted, gaping, transfixed. Step by slow step, the Great King moved forward, through the hush of the crowd and the roar of flames.

Now the Great King was within a few feet of Ujjeni. Through what power, human or divine, he found his voice from his punctured lungs, I shall never know. 'Prince Ujjeni, you have been guilty of the foulest of crimes against your king and the kingdom of Lanka,' he cried, in those clear tones that could carry above the din of battle. 'You even arranged to have us assassinated. You are judged guilty and are sentenced to the will of the people here assembled.'

The Great King raised his arms towards the crowds. 'You alone can save the innocent Prince Lala now,' he cried.

The crowds broke loose, with great cries, stampeding past the bewildered guards, scattering them, trampling on them. With branches snatched from trees and bushes, with clothes removed from their persons, they attacked the fire, some flinging aside flaming faggots with their bare hands. They cleared a passage to the prisoner. I caught a glimpse of a burning body slumped against the stake. A towering figure tore through the crowds to embrace the body and put out its flames. The Great King was holding his twin again, as within their mother's womb.

Something broke loose within me. I turned towards Ujjeni. He had started to run towards the palace. Vijit and Uraw blocked his path. 'You shall await execution by the people!' Vijit thundered.

I walked swiftly towards them. 'We are the people,' I said.

Uraw's eyes widened in disbelief. Ujjeni turned towards me. He came on guard. 'Keep away!' he screamed.

Slowly and deliberately, I walked towards him, unfolding the flap of my robe. He lunged. I swiftly leapt aside. I had been a bandit once. I flung my yellow robe over his sword. He drew it back. I released the robe, his sword enmeshed in it. I stood there my white body naked as the truth and unashamed in the slow gathering light.

'The Doctrine is more powerful than the sword, just as Prince Lala's love was stronger than the *akusala*, evil, in you,' I declared. 'You shall live out the effects of your evil causes.'

'Never!' Ujjeni screamed. Dropping his sword, he turned and raced, demented, towards the still roaring fire. Men paused to watch him in amazement. He broke through the faggots, screaming. He flung himself into the flames. And no man lifted a finger to stop him.

Did Ujjeni cleanse himself by the fire he had used to cleanse the one he hated?

I recorded that event the day after it occurred. Yes, it was Uraw who had ridden night and day in his attempt to save Prince Lala. By chance, Vijit and one of his cavalry companies had been at the Thamba-Panni palace at the time, seeking drought-relief from the Great King as Prince Lala had once done.

Prince Lala lingered between life and death for weeks, tended by the Court physicians. He was so badly burned that he had lost the use of his fingers, so that he would never write again. Hot smoke had partially destroyed his voice, so that he would never speak normally again. His beautiful dark hair had been burned to ashes. By some miracle, he retained his sight. Never once did he complain, though it was months before he began to lead even the semblance of a regular life. But this time, the Great King, who had collapsed immediately after he had saved his brother, was in good health once more.

But King Vijaya was a changed man.

He made every effort to find his two children by Kuveni, but they had fled to the jungle in fear of Ujjeni. Time would bear out their mother's prophecy for them in a strange way. They would wed each other and found a new dynasty, but the blessed gift of inner sight told me that it would be an aboriginal race, enduring for centuries.

The Great King fell back on the request he had made of Prince Lala the day they had first landed on the shores of Lanka, beside the lake that served the Princess Kuveni's village. Prince Lala became his adviser on the ideals of the kingdom. Though the prince himself soon became a *bhikku*, he continued to reside in a cell at the Thamba-Panni palace. Queen Anula proved to be a devoted wife to King Vijaya, but they never had any children.

The people of Lanka came to know equality at last and the kingdom grew and prospered. As Lord Buddha said: 'In a *janapada*, a people's state, when the ruler is righteous, his ministers are righteous. When the ministers are righteous the people become righteous.'

Thirty-five years have gone by since I wrote the Epilogue to Prince Lala's story. The Great King died fourteen months ago, of an infection in his weakened lungs. Prince Lala succumbed to a heart attack a few hours later. He died with a smile of recognition on his face and the words 'Sundari, beloved,' on his lips. Perhaps she was waiting for him on the other side. The twin brothers were cremated together on twin pyres in the great *maidan* opposite the

698

Thamba-Panni fort, where it had all begun. Queen Anula immolated herself on her husband's funeral pyre in the manner of Hindu wives. She had loved him truly, and had made him very happy throughout his life.

After their separation from each other ended, the lives of the twin brothers were basically identical. King Vijaya found peace in his married life and yet was harrowed by the knowledge of what he had lost, his seed, which meant that his line would end with him. Prince Lala had the serenity of the *bhikku* and yet the memory of what he had lost and could never have again must have consumed him. I should know! Love finally united them and all else fell into place until they died. The two arcs of the circle had separated only to become one again. And finally in death they undoubtedly joined their loved ones in a new birth.

Since his own two children by the Princess Kuveni refused to leave their jungle sanctuary, King Vijaya grew deeply concerned over the succession as he became aware of approaching death. He knew that the remaining ministers, especially Anu and Pandu, would attempt to take over the kingdom after he died. He therefore sent a secret letter to his younger brother, Sumitta, who still ruled Sinha-Pura:

I am old and there lives no son of mine. The kingdom of Lanka, peopled with such difficulty, may come to naught after my death. Therefore fain would I have you Sumitta, my brother, come here, so that I may give the government of this blessed island into your hands.

King Sumitta was, however, too preoccupied with the government of his own kingdom to accept the invitation. But he had three sons by the daughter of the Magadha king, whom he addressed thus:

'I am old, dear ones. Therefore, one of you must depart for the greatly favoured and beauteous kingdom of Lanka, belonging to my brother, to assume the sovereignty of that fair kingdom after his death.'

The youngest son, Prince Pandu Vasu Deva, volunteered, after first sending a secret mission to Lanka to assure himself of the success of his journey. He embarked for Lanka, taking with him thirty-two sons of ministers from his father's government. Since the Great King and Prince Lala had both died by then and, as King Vijaya had feared, the rule in Lanka had become divided, the party landed at the mouth of a river north of Mantota, disguised as mendicant monks.

Meanwhile, a soothsayer had prophesied their arrival:

Seven days from now the prince, sprung from the house of the founder, shall come to Lanka. From the line of that prince will emerge a monarch who will establish the Buddha's doctrine in Lanka, where it will be perpetuated for ever in its pristine purity.

The prince contacted Vijit, who had remained a fierce monarchist and maintained an independent sub-kingdom in Vijitapura and Ruhuna, obtained his support and re-established the line of Sinha, the lion, to rule the Sinhala, the Lion Race.

I am now almost one hundred years old. My eyesight is failing and my hand is shaky.

By the grace of my *kharma*, or the divine grace of the God in Whom Prince Lala believed, I have witnessed the return of Lanka to just rule such as the founder would have desired. The blessed gift of the inner sight tells me that my own end is near, through the exhaustion of the *kharmic* substances that created me. So my *kharma*, causes, will soon have their *vipaka*, effects, in some other form. May you who read these words find joy in your own realities, tranquillity through the cessation of desiring, peace through the peace of your minds.

My last gift to you is that which Prince Lala would have

most desired, the assurance of his eternal love and mine for you who follow. Our love has already touched your hearts through the words you have read, now let that love open up the wellsprings of your own love for your fellow men so that you may know peace and joy. Hatred, selfishness, bitterness can only bring self-destruction, such as befell Ujjeni. Love can triumph over all.

My final truth is a question:

Was it God who granted me, an unbeliever, the miracle for which I prayed that morning when Prince Lala was being burned at the stake? If so, may His greatest miracle of life, freedom from the bonds of your own human convictions, reach you across 2,500 years of time.